D1642348

MAN'S BOOK

MAN'S BOOK

THE FREEBOOTERS
Elleston Trevor

★

BROUGHT IN DEAD
Harry Patterson

★

A DEADLY SHADE
OF GOLD
John D. MacDonald

ODHAMS BOOKS
LONDON

MADE AND PRINTED IN GREAT BRITAIN
BY ODHAMS (WATFORD) LTD.
S.568.SAPQ

CONTENTS

CONTENTS

THE FREEBOOTERS

Elleston Trevor

'The Freebooters' is published by
William Heinemann Ltd.

The Author

Elleston Trevor, born in 1920, is the author of such successful novels as *The Big Pick-up* (filmed as *Dunkirk*), *Squadron Airborne, The Killing-Ground, Gale Force, The Flight of the Phoenix, The Shoot* (the three last appeared in earlier volumes of MAN'S BOOK) and many others. He has sold short stories to the BBC and to radio stations throughout the world in large numbers. He is particularly interested in motor-racing, has a Rolls-Royce, and lives in the South of France.

With love to
JONNI

CHAPTER ONE

It was gone midnight but only a few of the men were asleep; they were the kind who could sleep whatever had happened to them during the day, even if they had suffered pain, grief or—as on this day—horror.

The rest of them lay wakeful in the heat, listening unwillingly to the silence outside the hut, to the hum of the mosquitoes, the scuttering of the lizards across the roof, and the sounds that Chignall was making as his head jerked on the pillow and his hands fretted with the sheet. Sometimes they could pick out actual words in the fluttering and hissing of his breath, and although they didn't want to hear what he was saying they found themselves straining their ears in case they missed something that mattered. But they knew that nothing he said would matter now.

Chignall was only a boy and so the older men, the Regulars, had more patience with him than they might; but it wasn't easy having to lie in the heat and the dark listening to him carrying on like that, because they knew what was troubling him and they didn't want to be reminded. There was a limit, of course, and at last someone called out:

'Christ sake pack it in, kid, can't you?'

Everyone felt better with a spokesman for their misery but it didn't stop Chignall. He probably hadn't even heard, probably didn't even realize he was making any fuss at all. He was isolated from them, as much a captive of his waking nightmare as if his wrists were roped. A few of them couldn't see it that way; they were sure he was just trying to work his ticket, because that was the only reason they could think of for anyone doing almost anything. They didn't tell him to shut up: the best of bloody luck to him if he could do it. These last few weeks the whole unit had had about enough, and anyone who could work a home posting would be well out of it all.

The first man to leave his bed was Rickman; he didn't need a torch because the kid was keeping it up without a break now and you could find his bed by sound alone. Rickman sat on the edge of the bed and waited, but there was no pause in the shivering of Chignall's breath; the bed itself was shaking, and

Rickman could smell the kid's sweat, a definably young smell. Rickman was only six or seven years older in terms of the calendar—twenty-six, twenty-seven—but he'd had to make his own luck all the way along with no one to help him, and sitting in the dark on this trembling bed he felt the compassion of a father.

'What's up, Chiggy?' His tone was flat, stone-hard; it was the only way he ever spoke. If you told him he was capable of feeling the compassion of a father, or any human emotion at all, he wouldn't bother to answer but you'd get a look that dismissed you for a stupid sentimental sod, take it or leave it. He said: 'Bloody Getcliffe been chasing you all bloody day has he? That it?'

Sergeant Getcliffe hadn't let the kid alone since breakfast-time —saluting-drill, fatigues, orderly runner, till he could hardly keep on his feet. It wasn't that, of course, but it might make him think about something else, give him a decent excuse for this bloody caper.

Chignall didn't answer, didn't hear him.

At the far end of the hut Corporal Bruce added another dog-end to the heap in the tin and leaned on one elbow, listening. Someone was talking to the kid; it sounded like Rickman. Others were stirring, sitting up, and a flame flickered against a face as a man lit a fag. Jamie Cleaver said into the dark: 'Ours is a nice house, ours is!' The change of mood swept right through the hut within seconds: nobody pretended any longer that they had any hope of getting to sleep. The reason why they hadn't turned on young Chignall in a body and *made* him pack it in was that they probably wouldn't have got much sleep anyway, even if the hut were quiet.

It had been difficult for some weeks now, catching enough kip, because of the heat and the silence outside the camp, the silence of hundreds and thousands of miles of African night. You'd lie awake listening for the sudden knocking of rapid fire and the chorus of unearthly screams, and if it came you couldn't sleep because of it, and if it didn't you couldn't sleep because it hadn't come.

This was no different from other nights, a bit worse, that was all. Ask Chiggy.

Corporal Bruce could hear Rickman talking to the kid and could hear it was doing no good, so he slid out of bed and went down there.

'You'll just have to forget it,' Rickman was saying, 'forget it, kid.'

The corporal spoke to the boy, first softly, then sharply, and at last got some sense out of him. 'I'm trying not to think'—each word a shiver—'I'm trying not to. But I can't.' That much came out quietly enough but suddenly he sat up and plunged his head between his raised knees and began moaning, on and on, until someone threw a boot, the anger mounting so fast that speech couldn't express it, only violence. The boot hit a dixie and it rang like a bell and then the whole hut was in an uproar and Cpl Bruce was shouting—

'All right, all right, turn it in, will you now? *I said turn it in!*'

When it was a bit quieter he told Chignall: 'Get dressed, then, just your slacks an' sweater'll do, and find your small-kit.' He peered at the man sitting on the bed. 'That you, Rickman? Give him a hand, then. I'm taking him to the M.O.'

Chignall must have heard because he said on a long shuddering breath: 'Outside? You taking me outside?'

'It's only across the way an' I'm coming with you.'

'I'm not afraid.'

Corporal Bruce went back to his bed-space and got into his drill tunic because this was kind of official and he'd need to see the orderly officer first. Then he picked up his torch and put it down again, remembering the blackout orders. A week ago the camp had become dark by night and there'd been an issue of hand-lamps for those who didn't have one, with free batteries for those who did. Two nights later one of the men in No. 6 hut, crossing over to the lats, had been killed by a poisoned arrow, and it was realized that a man carrying a torch was just as good a target as when the main camp lights were on. The issue was withdrawn and the new order went up: no hand-lamps to be used outside the huts, even if privately owned. In addition it was forbidden for more than two men to walk together by night—the bigger the group the bigger the target—and any two men walking together must keep five paces apart. The next night a group of men from 'B' Company walked out of the NAAFI hut and forgot to split up; the orderly sergeant saw them and slapped them on a charge, and the morning afterwards the M.O. stood on an ammo-box and lectured the whole unit:

'Some of you may feel contemptuous of bows and arrows in this day and age, even though you've recently seen what they can do. They're none too accurate, especially in the dark, but when one of those arrows does hit a man it's more deadly than a bite from a black mamba, because of the poisoned tip. I'm going to tell you something about the poison these Vendettu are fond of

using. Their witch-doctors are pretty good chemists. They may
not know the clinical names of the stuff they concoct—ptomaines,
saponins, eserines, strychnines, strophanthins—but they know
from hundreds of years of experience handed down through the
tribe that if you extract the essences of putrefied reptilian remains
—snakes, lizards, toads and so on—you can stop a human being
dead in his tracks more effectively than with a bullet, because
you've only got to hit his little finger or the lobe of his ear and
the poison does the rest. A bullet doesn't travel around the body
after it strikes, but this poison does, and it's wickedly fast. It's
also wickedly potent: dilute one drop of the saponin group in
a tumblerful of pure water and you can *still* dissolve the blood-
cells in a human body to a lethal degree. Just think that over,
please. If anyone gets hit by one of these arrows he'll be lucky
if he can get as far as my office to tell me about it, and even if
he does there's not much I can do to help. The only way to help
yourselves is to obey the orders about not using torches and not
walking in groups. If you do get hit by a lucky shot it's up to
you to pull out the arrow within five seconds. So don't underrate
these things. Once you're hit you've got five seconds to live, and
if you can pull out the barb in that time, walk to the sick-quarters.
Don't run, but walk, otherwise you'll speed up the circulation
and help the poison round. Now please remember what I've told
you. I'm not an alarmist—I'm just trying to make sure that none
of you goes the way of poor Corporal Radford. We're more intelligent than a bunch of witch-doctors so let's try to prove it.'

It had shaken them up a bit. There was something almost
healthy about a bullet: it played the game. Getting a dose of
putrefied toad in your bloodstream made you sick just to think
about it. There were no more groups of men seen about the
camp at night.

Leaving No. 2 hut with young Chignall, Cpl Bruce felt the
darkness about him and his flesh crept, as it always did for the
first few seconds. You'd never hear an arrow coming, or a spear
for that matter; you could never even be sure that one of those
bastards hadn't got past the guards and wasn't waiting for you
with his knife. They were so quiet, the Vend'u. Quiet as black
snakes. You never saw them either. They'd come in by dark and
find some poor sod outside the huts on his own, catch him before
he had chance to call out; and that was his lot. They'd take him
away and they'd do what they'd done to—

'Come on, Chignall,' he said brusquely, 'we've got to split up,
keep five paces apart. Then we'll be safe, see.'

'I'm not afraid.'

That was true, thought Cpl Bruce as he stepped out and set the pace. It wasn't fear that had got the kid into this state; it was the weirdness; he still couldn't believe what he'd seen this morning, couldn't get his young mind round to such a thing.

It was not quite dark in the camp; there were stars and the few lights of Lisolaville making a glow three miles away. Since the first trouble in the town they'd kept some of the streets lit all night, and sometimes there'd come the sound of shooting and voices. But there was no light anywhere in the camp itself; the huts were black humps against the skyline and the glow from the town, and Cpl Bruce had to get his bearings as best he could: there was white-washed gravel outside the C.O.'s quarters and the big metal plaque beside the door of the NAAFI hut. If you got lost you had to go for the flagpost and begin again from there.

He felt sudden anger when he thought of the flagpost, hoisting the Jack every morning, Rule Britannia and all that, flag-lowering every evening with the C.O. at the salute as if it was something sacred, as if you'd done a good day's work. But you hadn't. Kit inspections, bullshit and rifle drill till you could swear you were back at training-camp if it wasn't for the heat and the flies and the glare, Getcliffe barking behind you wherever you went; and all the time the news coming in, rumours mostly but you knew they were true—another farm raided in the night, an Englishman's farm, white-skinned fair-haired women and blue-eyed kids with the Vend'u coming at them out of the dark, worse than a pack of wolves and less than an hour's ride from here in a truck across the bush. But you'd got no orders to go and help them. What odds, so long as you kept your hair cut and polished the bottoms of your boots? You'll be all right now, mates, the Army's here, that ought to give you courage. It won't give you anything else.

'All right, Chignall?'

'Yes, Corp.'

It was so quiet that they'd needed only to whisper. Despite the orders and despite his common sense the corporal closed in a bit, because every time the kid disturbed a stone his flesh crept again and his hand flew to his bayonet. It was all they were allowed, the junior N.C.O.s, since the night when someone had let off at a shadow with his rifle and put one clean through the wall of No. 3 hut a foot from a man's bed. All you had now was a bayonet as side-arm, fat lot of good.

The Vend'u were big. They could see you in the dark. They

could smell you from a distance. They were a hunting tribe and
they took you for what you were, whether you admitted it or not.
An animal. The only cheerful bit of news in the past week was
that the C.O. had sent an urgent signal for dannert coils to be
trucked in from the coastal supply base so that the whole camp
could be fenced in with barbed wire. Roll on the day.

He heard Chignall's unsteady breathing, too close. Instinct
had brought them together in the dark. Bruce didn't say anything;
it was only a few yards now and they'd passed through the worst
of the open spaces. He thought of telling the kid to brace himself
up a bit before they saw the orderly officer but decided against it.
If Chignall didn't seem in too bad a state when they reported,
the corporal would have to take the can for making a fuss over
nothing.

He said only: 'Unless Mr Keene puts a direct question, I'll
do the talking.'

All material was scarce at the camp; even the ration-truck from
Lisolaville came only twice a week. In one of his morale-building
orders of the day Colonel Gray had called it 'an excellent opportunity for the exercise of improvisation'. Be that as it might,
there was nothing in the camp from which to make blackout
recesses, and since anyone passing through a lighted doorway
was a first-class target the orders were to knock and wait, regard-
less of rank or purpose of visit.

'Password?'

'Whitechapel. Corporal Bruce, sir!'

A slit of light at the edge of the door went out.

'You can come in.'

Lieutenant Keene put his revolver back into the holster before
switching on the light again. 'Well, Corporal?'

'Sorry to disturb you, sir—'

'There is no question of disturbing an orderly officer. He is at
the disposal of anyone with a report to make.'

Lieutenant Keene felt the Colonel would have approved of
that. The whole structure of discipline and inter-ranks relationship was based on the observance of such nuances; the men had
to know where they stood and it was the officers' duty to tell them.
The 'Sorry to disturb you, sir' approach was slack and familiar,
and if this N.C.O. was made of the right stuff he would turn the
rebuff to advantage and do better next time.

Chignall stood with his head down, his eyes half-closed against
the brightness of the light.

Lieutenant Keene glanced at him and looked back at the corporal. 'Who is this man?'

'Private Chignall, sir.'

'And why have you brought him to me improperly dressed?'

'He's sick, sir.'

'I see.' He looked again at Chignall.

Corporal Bruce had kept his gaze the required two inches above the orderly officer's head; now he could glance down and watch his face, because Lt Keene was looking at Chignall. Lt Keene had the face of a typical Sandhurst product, youthful, well bred, well fed, imprinted with an arrogance capable of full concealment in the presence of superiors and of full exhibition before inferiors. It was his good fortune also to be handsome. The corporal watched his face for any sign of reaction and saw none. But the voice wasn't unkindly:

'Get your head up, Chignall. That's it. At ease, Corporal.'

Quietly the corporal passed on the order, doing what he could to see that they both moved together. His face itched with sweat but he knew that it wouldn't do to lift a hand. Perhaps it didn't matter much, all this. They'd both crossed the camp in the dark without fetching a poisoned arrow; that had to be enough.

'What are your symptoms, Chignall?'

Time went on and Cpl Bruce thought there wasn't going to be any answer; then the kid just said: 'I don't know, sir.'

Lieutenant Keene studied him. Face rather pale—probably the brightness of the lamp—and covered in sweat. Sweat was normal enough in this heat. Very slack attitude, eyes trying to close again. Seemed to be shivering—well, anyone could turn *that* on. Could be a clear case of lead-swinging; it was almost an epidemic recently.

'You don't know what your symptoms are?'

This time the silence drew out until Cpl Bruce couldn't stand it. 'Answer the officer, Chignall.'

The boy had begun swaying; his head was drooping lower by small degrees and his eyes were shut now and squeezed tight against the light. Sweat ran from his smooth cheek and formed a rivulet at the side of his neck; his mouth had fallen open and his breath gusted in and out unevenly. There was a ruler on Lt Keene's desk and he took it by one end, bringing it down flat with some force, his eyes raised unblinkingly to note the result. The boy jerked like a marionette and his breath exploded as if to a blow in the stomach and Cpl Bruce heard himself saying, 'The man's sick, sir. Sick.'

'That is for me to judge—'

'I know, sir, but—'

The ruler hit the desk again. Conversationally Lt Keene said: 'If you want to avoid a charge of blatant insubordination, Corporal, you'll do well to wait for my express permission to speak.' He put the ruler aside and composed his hands on the desk. 'I think we have a malingerer here and I will tell you what I propose to do. I am going to telephone the Medical Officer'—with a studied movement of the wrist—'and we note that it is now one o'clock in the morning—and tell him that we are bringing him a man for urgent examination. Since I am of the opinion that it's a case of malingering and you claim that it's a genuine case of sickness, the responsibility will be yours, Corporal, if you are proved to be wrong. We should bear in mind that the Medical Officer will hardly thank us for disturbing him without good cause. Now think it over. Am I to use the telephone?'

'As long as we get him there, sir, quick as we can.'

'You accept the responsibility?'

'Just let's get him there, sir.'

Corporal Bruce closed his eyes wearily for a moment as Lt Keene lifted the receiver. Perhaps it hadn't taken as long as it had seemed; it didn't do to exaggerate this kind of thing, and it wasn't this young feller's fault when you weighed it up; he was fresh out of college and full of himself, never seen action; you couldn't expect much more. He'd grow, and if others had to share in his growing-pains, well, that was the Army.

The M.O. had told them to go straight to his own room and he'd put on a pair of shorts. He was using a fly-swat on the mosquitoes and dropped it on the bed and asked Chignall to move nearer the light. Without giving him more than a glance he said: 'This chap's suffering from shock—why wasn't he sent along before now?'

Lieutenant Keene said: 'He's only just reported to me, sir. Otherwise I would have seen to it much earlier, of course.'

CHAPTER TWO

THE morning patrol left camp as usual, thirty minutes after sun-up. Today it was the turn of No. 2 Platoon, 'B' Company, and the officer in charge was Lieutenant Millburn; with him in the truck were Sergeant Proctor, Lance-Corporal Rivers and ten men. Already the cloud of dust lay a mile long between the truck and the camp; already the sun's heat had driven most living things into the shade of umbrella-topped thorn.

After this first mile the patrol was happy enough. The truck took the same route every day and the Vendettu knew it, and would leave any memento a short distance from the camp and in the middle of the track where it was sure to be found. It had happened only three times since the unit had moved in but the morning patrol always set out with a queasy stomach. Private Chignall had been one of the men in yesterday's party.

Lieutenant Millburn sat beside the driver watching the track through the bush. It was for the most part wide and ill defined but sometimes it passed through close-grained scrub and thorn, and in these places the patrol officer watched with particular care because there was a snake called the five-stepper and it had rated a mention in special orders. There had been cases reported in Lisolaville of such snakes having been flicked into moving vehicles by the snapping of twigs as the front wheels passed over them. The name of the snake derived from the fact that a man on foot, bitten by it, took five more steps and fell dead.

Along the wider stretches Lt Millburn was able to watch the vastness of the land. This vastness was a special thing. Composed of colours—the ochres, greens and yellows of earth, bush and parched grass, and the blue of distance—it was more than mere landscape; it was vastness. One did not look *at* it: one was *in* it, absorbed by it, robbed of one's identity, lost, a fish in an ocean. Millburn had sometimes tried consciously to express this special feeling he had about the vastness, but the best he had done so far was this: you could see two hundred miles from horizon to horizon and were therefore lost, being so small; yet if you drove on for two hundred miles nothing would change; the vastness would still be there and so would you; therefore you could never be lost, because wherever you were you were 'here'. The only 'place' was 'you'.

It was his answer, anyway, to agoraphobia. The mild intellectual exercise also helped to keep him sane in this world of animal values, because he sometimes wondered what he was doing here and the question was unnerving. Less than a year ago he had broken off his studies at Sussex University so abruptly that his parents believed it to have been a whim. It was in fact a calculated decision. At twenty-four he had been ready to begin a career in applied logistics and it had suddenly occurred to him that despite his brilliant promise as a logistician he had serious limitations as a person. Since adolescence his life had been sheltered, cloistered physically by ancient stones. He had mixed very little with humankind and had given himself neither time nor chance to rid his spirit of original aggression. He had never known rage, drunkenness, shame, carnality, humility or pride. What he had instead acquired—apart from a masterly talent for logistics—were a pair of glasses and a stoop.

His mistake in entering Mons Officer Cadet School for a short-service commission of three years derived from the very lack of knowledge of affairs that he wanted to overcome. Seeking adventure for a limited period he had chosen the Army as its precinct, not realizing he would exchange the disciplines of the academic milieu for those of service life; the rituals and traditions were different but just as confining. Certainly he had mixed with men and learned their divers ways, but he could have done that by taking on factory work or a job as a tourist guide.

The idea of serving his country had not entered his head; that could better be done by a study of international diplomacy than by picking up a gun. The killing of one man by another was the expression of the inarticulate: thoughtless and speechless, one had recourse only to murder, and there seemed small value in convincing somebody of one's point of view by an act that denied his sharing it. Today's fashionable argument—whether the citizen was more important than the State or vice versa—was not reasonably to be resolved in terms of nuclear physics: the cries of the dying made poor debate.

He had been stupid, then, to invite the Trust and Confidence of Elizabeth the Second in his Loyalty, Courage and Good Conduct as an Officer of her Land Forces when his sole aim was to rough it a bit before taking up a rather more serious career. Stupid, untrustworthy and disloyal.

In the 4th Royals he had met officers—like Jones—who were 'in it for the uniform and the gin, old boy', but that made his own case no better. He was becoming increasingly sensitive about this and had lately given it some serious thought; only rarely did he suspect that this was a trick to keep his mind off the other thing—yesterday morning, for instance—the thing that wouldn't go away.

The patrol reached the hill. It was a freak upthrust of volcanic rock dominating the plain to the north of Lisolaville, and was known, because of its shape, as the Tit. Farther north still was a second hill, much higher, but the first was good enough for the object of the exercise, which was to survey the surrounding terrain and report any sign of the Vendettu.

Millburn walked from the truck and climbed the hill slowly, sometimes pulling off his glasses to wipe the sweat from his eyebrows. Sgt. Proctor deployed the men around the base of the hill and left them in charge of the corporal. They were to keep watch for any approaching trouble; in the event of its coming they were gallantly to defend the life of their officer even at the cost of their own. Sgt. Proctor, climbing unhurriedly to join Millburn, had decided long ago what action he would in fact take if the patrol were approached by a Vendettu group of any size. He would bundle his officer into the truck and drive like hell for the horizon. The men were no problem: they'd be in the truck before he was.

It was the C.O. who had formulated this ritual of the morning patrol; it was therefore a small gem of military imagination. The truck would proceed defiantly across the open bush and reach its objective against—if necessary—all odds. The officer would climb the hill and stand proudly at its top, symbol of far-flung dominion. He would raise his field-glasses and observe the land below, bravely exposing himself to whatever enemy lurked there. In due course he would return with his report, and a signal would be sent to Battalion H.Q.

Sergeant Proctor was quite at a loss to understand why Lt-Col Gray had not included the planting of the Regimental Flag at the hilltop, with bugle accompaniment.

He found his officer sitting on his haunches mopping at sweat, and sat down beside him, elbows on his knees.

Millburn wiped his glasses and put them on again. 'I've told you before, there's no need for both of us to come up.'

'It's in orders, sir.' Proctor's eyes ranged over the landscape.

'Well you know I wouldn't say anything.'

'It'd be on my conscience, sir.'

Millburn looked at the long bony face. He didn't see all that much of Proctor, even though he was his platoon sergeant, and his judgement of men was still unmatured. Would any N.C.O.— even a hidebound Regular—sweat all the way up this hill for the sake of 'orders' when there was absolutely no need? It irked him not to know, not to be able to deduce it. They sat with their elbows inches apart; how far from mind to mind?

'You must find your conscience rather demanding.'

'Yes, sir.'

Millburn licked the salt from his lips. 'And you can drop the "sir" while we're here. We get too much of it in camp as it is.'

'Right.' The corners of the sergeant's long mouth were turned up slightly but Millburn knew it was just the set of his features. The man seemed to spend his life savouring a private and cynical joke.

In a minute or two Millburn stood up and took the field-glasses from their case, observing the terrain full-circle. In the blue haze the shadows of the thorn-trees and low grey scrub were darker than the bush itself, and it was deep in these shadows that he caught the movement of hyenas milling about a carcass a mile away, a leopard stalking at the fringe of a sansevieria clump where its prey sought moisture, an eland herd flowing slowly westwards, warned by the leopard's scent. The earth itself quivered in the heat; waves of light and colour rolled across the land, disturbed in the far distance by a dust-devil whose top spilled saffron as the sun's light caught it. Everything moved, as the ocean moves, and in the same silence.

Millburn lowered the field-glasses. There was nothing to report. He said: 'We've never seen the Vend'u in daylight, have we?'

'Never.'

'We know where they go, when they clear off from the camp. To the caves in the escarpment south of Lisolaville.'

'Correct.'

'This hill's north of there and there's nothing but open bush —no shelter, no water, nothing to attract them into this area. Can you think of any reason why they should come here?'

'I can't.'

Millburn put the field-glasses back into their case and shouldered the sling. They went down the hill together, the younger man sliding sometimes over the shale, a slight figure with thin arms burned sore by the sun, his legs unconfident and his hands flying out to keep his balance, the older man moving more slowly yet as fast, leaning forward so that he never slipped, his eyes looking straight ahead and narrowed to slits against the glare, his shadow taller than the other's, and steadier.

'Can you think of any reason, then, why we should be sent out here on a daily observation mission?'

'It's orders.'

Millburn's blood was pulsing behind the eyes from the effort of the climb and the descent, and one ankle throbbed painfully. The heat from his skin had misted his glasses again. 'For God's sake, what kind of reason is that?'

'The only kind I know.'

Private Chignall was taken before the C.O. in the company of a medical orderly. Colonel Gray spoke to him for a moment to get some idea of the man's condition; the answers came readily enough so he sent the escort and medical orderly outside and told Chignall to sit down.

The Medical Officer's report was before him on the desk. A very full examination had been made and the subject had been observed without his knowledge while in the sick bay. Clinical report attached. Recommendation: home posting for psychiatric treatment.

Colonel Gray had sent for the conduct sheet and had questioned both the Company Sergeant-Major and Sergeant Getcliffe. The sergeant had more to do with the boy than the C.S.M. and his remarks were the more valuable: 'He's a cheerful enough lad, sir, normally, and I've never had trouble with him. On the sensitive side, being still young. I'd hoped to shake him out of it by giving him no time to dwell on it—chased him up and down all day till he was that tired he should have slept right off —but it only postponed it, seems like. Of course, Mackenzie was a mate of his, always about together. That's why he's taken it so bad, I reckon.'

Others had been called in. Sgt Proctor and Cpl Bruce confirmed the man's general good behaviour. Lt Keene had remarked that it was a pity he hadn't seen Chignall earlier, because he would certainly have sent him straight to the M.O.; but he was careful to stress that he blamed nobody for this delay, since Cpl Bruce (in charge of No. 2 hut, 'B' Company) could not be expected to judge the extent of a man's psychological malaise and would tend to suspect malingering, there having been so many cases of it recently. Colonel Gray had been impressed by Keene's grasp of the situation and his fairness to the junior N.C.O. This young officer seemed to be shaping into first-class material; his understanding for the lower ranks was especially admirable, and the Colonel decided to watch him more closely in future. Good officers were scarce and at a time like this, when morale was under pressure, they were the more to be cherished.

'Well now, Chignall,' he began encouragingly, 'we're going to pack you off home for a while. What do you think of that?'

The boy sat stiffly on the hard chair, his eyes flickering as if he found the light too bright.

'Yes, sir.'

'I wanted to talk to you before you left us, because it might be easy for you to think that you've let the side down, or that you've buckled under where your comrades have shown more

fortitude in the face of all these disagreeable things that have
been happening to us lately. But *we* don't think you've let us
down, so you mustn't add any self-blame to your—to your present
feelings of unhappiness. There is no question, no question at all,
of your having done anything wrong.'

He looked uneasily at the flickering eyes.

'Yes, sir.'

As before, the answer was dutiful, no more. The Colonel
glanced away. He had wanted to say a great deal to the boy, talk
to him carefully, search him out and perhaps inspirit him—
perhaps even repair the damage and return his courage to him
so that he could remain here among his friends instead of being
committed to the hands of some heartless quack in London.
Surely a commanding officer could achieve no higher thing. But
Chignall was remote from him and unapproachable, perhaps
unstable to the point of real dementia. The M.O. had not sent
one of his own orderlies along for nothing.

'I wanted also to ask a favour of you, Chignall.'

It brought no response. The boy seemed unaware that it was
unusual for a C.O. to ask a favour of one of his men. No matter.
'When you reach home, you'll be eager to talk to your family and
your friends about the life out here—Africa is a very exciting
place—and about our resolute defiance of a strange and difficult
enemy. By all means remind England that her sons remain
devoted to the safeguarding of her interests, however far from
home.'

He was aware that this poor boy could hardly appreciate
such sentiments in his present state, but he had spoken them
without thinking, as they were always in his mind. 'But I am
going to ask you not to talk about Mackenzie.'

He was startled to see a spasm shake the boy, but it passed so
quickly that he wondered if he had imagined it. His instinct,
refined by his long experience in the handling of men, told him
in any case that he must deal with this point as briefly as he could.
'Mackenzie lost his life while under attack from hostile forces,
however disorganized those forces and however haphazard their
method of attack. He thus merits the posthumous distinction of
having been killed on active service and that is what you must
tell people, Chignall, when you reach home. You see, it doesn't
matter *how* he died; a man's soul is quite untouched by whatever
circumstances God has chosen for its release. It matters *why* he
died. He died because he was a soldier committed to the defence
of his country's interests. This will offer boundless consolation to

those bereaved, and you will only give them pain if you tell them that when you last saw him he was—'

'Kennie . . .'

The sound had been jerked from the boy's throat and his eyes were wide open, staring at the Colonel.

'What did you say?'

'Yes, sir.'

The Colonel watched him nervously. He would have liked to say nothing more but it was his duty to ensure that the family of the deceased should suffer no more brief than was necessary. It was his duty towards Mackenzie himself.

'This is most important, Chignall, and you must try to understand what I'm saying. If it is unavoidable you must deny any knowledge of Mackenzie's death, or should I say the *manner* of it. All you know is that he died on active service. Is that clear?'

He noticed that his own hands were shaking a little, and felt an impulse to summon the escort and have the boy taken away, out of his sight; there was something indecent about the slack mouth and flinching eyes; it was sickening to witness the desertion of all courage in a man.

'Sit up straight, Chignall.'

'Yes, sir.'

There was obviously a fundamental weakness here that didn't show up on the conduct sheet. There had been nine other men on the morning patrol when Mackenzie was found and only this one was affected. Certainly the patrol officer's report had been unpleasant to read: *At 0640 hours the progress of the truck was stopped by a wooden post in the middle of the road. On it was the head of a man recognized as '683 Private Mackenzie. Half an hour's search failed to locate the body, so the patrol returned to base in order to report.* But if nine other men could recover from the shock within a few hours, surely their example should have rallied this one.

'I am sorry to have to dwell on the subject, Chignall, but I need your assurance that you understand how important it is, for the sake of Mackenzie's family—'

'*Kennie!*' It was hissed out and the boy lurched up from the chair, sending it over and stumbling against it and nearly falling. '*I said to him Kennie what's happened, what's happened, what's happened*—' His voice became shrill and the Colonel shouted above it for the escort. The door banged against the overturned chair as they came in, pinning the boy's arms—

'All right, mate, it's all right—'

'Take him away—'

'Yes, sir.'

The Colonel remained at his desk and his hands drummed on it uncontrollably; his clerk had come in and went quickly to shut the door after the others, turning sharply as he heard the unsteadiness in the voice of the C.O.

'Poor boy . . . I took such great care. . . . Poor boy.'

CHAPTER THREE

THEN there was the night of the drums.

Most of the personnel were in their huts soon after the evening meal. Following Cpl Radford's death and the M.O.'s warning, there hadn't been much falling off in attendance at the two messes and the canteen; everyone seemed quite ready for a hero's end. But this phase passed quickly: a dead hero was no better off than a dead duck and in their hearts they knew it. There was also the unnerving atmosphere created by the no-grouping order. Not long ago the camp had been lively in the evenings, a sociable place, and friends had joined up and walked across for a drink and a game of darts, talking together on their way under the lights; now the camp was dark and they were allowed only one companion five paces distant, so they lost their way and lost their friends and finally chucked it and kept to their huts.

This voluntary form of curfew was irksome enough, and fights broke out for small reason, but it was better than wandering like blind untouchables, the nerves feverish and the flesh exposed to the chance bite of an arrow at every step. *Walk to the sick-quarters—don't run.* Sod it—stay in the hut.

But even in the safety of the huts the evenings weren't very lively or sociable; there was only one place to sit and that was on your bed so you might just as well lie down and catch up on some kip. With half the hut turned in the others hadn't much heart for darts or talking, and anyway you didn't have to talk for long before you'd got into a pointless argument that led to bad feeling or a fight. It wouldn't have happened back home but it flared up quick as you like out here where you were plagued by the heat and the flies and the blood-sucking ticks and Sergeant-sodding-Getcliffe.

Some of the men in No. 2 hut had managed to drop off early on this particular evening and the rest kept more or less quiet, polishing kit or writing home or just lying thinking about the whores in Lisolaville.

The drums began soon after nine o'clock and for a time nobody heard them, they were so soft at first. Then a man looked up.

'What's that?'

'I can't hear anything.'

'Listen, then.'

'It's only old Brucey snoring. Give him a bloody pillow and he'll go into his number like a—'

'Shuddup an' listen, can't you?'

The heat pressed down from the roof of the hut, pressed in through the insect screens at the windows, pressed up from the floor.

'Thunder.'

'Balls, there won't be a storm for weeks.'

Rickman was wandering about, head cocked on his stocky neck. 'It's drums.'

'The voodoo!' someone said, trying to make it sound blood-curdling to get a laugh—'The voo-doo . . .' Nobody laughed.

Rickman went to a window and listened. They could all hear it now, except those who still slept. The drums weren't loud but there was rhythm to them, very slow; their sound came in waves, rising between long intervals of silence or near-silence in which you still seemed to hear them or perhaps did hear them, but rarely. It was this that made the men listen.

Suddenly Rickman pulled the blackout aside and stared through the insect screen at the night; at the far end of the hut Cpl Bruce jumped for the switches and the lights went out—

'Rickman, you're askin' for trouble, I'm warning you!'

No one protested at the sudden darkness; all they wanted to do was listen to the drums.

'They're gettin' louder.'

'They're not.'

'They bloody are.'

'Shuddup an' listen.'

'Who the hell are you, telling me to shut up—'

'Oh for Christ sake—'

'Pack it in, there! I'm not tellin' you again!'

'All right, Corp, but just tell Rickman to stop chucking his weight about, will you?'

It would have gone on like that; it had gone on like that before in the heat of the hut and there'd often been blows at the finish; but it stopped now because of the drums. Their rhythm was faster—still slow but faster than before—and they were loudening, there was no mistaking it.

Jamie Cleaver got off his bed and stood beside Rickman looking out, looking out at nothing, at the darkness. Out there beyond the insect screen and the camp fence and the wall of night where no one went after sundown, the land and the sky pulsed to the drums. Their pace had quickened to the rhythm of a heartbeat and a fancy took Cleaver—now this sound would never become weak or die; it was the heart of the Vend'u beating.

He heard Rickman keeping time with it softly: 'Bastards—bastards—bastards . . .'

You wouldn't say, thought Cleaver, that Rick would let this kind of thing bother him; it was only a noise after all.

'They'd do well in a jazz group,' he said. 'Go over big in the Gorbals.'

'Bastards.'

Close to their faces they heard a lizard scuttle across the screen, the faint snap of its jaws as it took an insect; its body made a dark trickle against the stars and then it was gone. The drums became louder.

Others had come to the window, unable not to listen. There was nothing to see but they gathered there as if to watch a storm in which there was only thunder. Cpl Bruce left his bed-space, uneasy, sensing the mood of the hut; there were twenty men in here and he was already on the peg for failing to keep good order and discipline a couple of nights ago when a fight had broken out.

None of them were any longer asleep.

'What's on, then?'

'Only some drums.'

'What drums?'

'The Vend'u.'

'Fuck 'em.'

Cleaver turned away from the window: 'That's it, mates, don't take any notice of them.' The sound was so loud now that he had to call above it as if there were rain on the roof 'Can anyone hear anything? Bust if I can!' He went across to his bed-space and others left the window—

'To hell with 'em—'

'They can break their bloody arms at it for all I care—'

'Jamie, you got a fag for me, you mean old bugger?'

They drifted back to their beds, all except Rickman.

Lighters flickered and smoke began scenting the dark. They

lay leaning against the wall or on one elbow watching the glow of their cigarettes and the black shape of Rickman as their eyes grew used to the faint glimmer of the stars framed by the screen; they lay pretending not to listen, not to mind, then listening and saying nothing, doing nothing, accepting it as the minutes passed until the time came when the drums were bigger than they were, their sound rolling across the ground and into the camp and through the windows, through the walls of the hut and into their bodies, into their heads, drumming inside their heads while they lay like men drowning below black water, a hand moving, a mouth opening to speak without sound. They lay helpless under the tumult.

Rickman's fist smashed through the screen and his fingers clawed the stuff away and he shouted, thrusting his shoulders through the gap and shouting at the night, at the drums, no words but just a throat full of animal sound, any sound so long as it was louder than the big one; then the other men came to life and yelled at him to stop, throwing things at him until a Brasso tin hit the back of his head and he spun round ready to fight.

'Pack it in!' bawled Cpl Bruce, but someone had snatched up a dixie and was beating on it with a fork and the rest caught on, finding in the gloom whatever they could to make a noise with, one man setting a rhythm and the others following, suddenly comrades—bash-bash-*bang*—a little army with a little plan, to fight the noise with a noise of their own—bash-bash-*bang*—until the drums were no more than a vibration under the hellish din of their own proud making as they kept in time and kept it going—bash-bash-*bang*—watching one another and laughing fit to bust because they couldn't hear the drums any more, they'd beaten the bloody Vendettu.

The orderly sergeant of the night stood in the shadow of the guard hut, alone and thinking. It was hardly shadow, just an absence of starlight; the three-quarter moon wouldn't be up for an hour and there was no other light in the camp.

He had been thinking on and off about his platoon commander, a man he couldn't sum up. Only in his twenties still, but with his own ideas: 'I've told you before, there's no need for us both to come up.' And 'You can drop the "sir" while we're here—we get too much of it in camp as it is'. Yet Millburn wasn't a Commy or a snob, the sort of snob who'd show matey just to prove you were equals—and slap you down the minute you

overstepped the mark. No strength in him, came down that hill
like a tipsy scarecrow, but there was a hardness in him that you
could sense now and then, maybe only impatience, bloody-
mindedness, you could tell the Army wasn't for him, got no time
for it; no, he'd set his mind on other things, special things. Put
it this way: Millburn saw more through those specs of his than
what he looked at.

When the drums began Sgt Proctor lifted his head and listened,
an image forming in his mind—black faces and black bodies, the
whites of eyes in the dark and the shine of oily skin, knees each
side of the drum and the hands just touching, flying down and
away and down again like birds in a cage. When the drums grew
louder he stopped thinking about them and found his mind on
Sgt Getcliffe, drunk tonight in the mess, the first time he'd ever
seen him like it, not toppling drunk but angry and unsure of
things: 'Look at the officers, look at the N.C.O.s, look at the
men . . . can see it in their faces, the way they go on. . . . You can
smell it in the air, it stinks, it bloody stinks!'

Proctor had left him, going on duty. Getcliffe had talked a lot
of piss and wind, being drunk and not used to it, but there was
sense at the back of it—this week had gone badly, just as he said.
Mackenzie's head stuck on a post like a freak in a fairground,
his eyes still open and the sweat still on his face, so that you'd
almost say, 'What's wrong with you, Mackenzie?' but for the
blood black on the post and the buzz of flies. You could see now
what was wrong with Mackenzie. No wonder the Chignall boy
couldn't stand it—they'd lived in each other's pockets; not that
it mattered, except to Chignall, sent home with his mind marked
for life; he'd be replaced and the unit would be up to strength
again.

The real damage was in the other nine men still here in
camp, because they'd been as shocked but hadn't shown it, not
in the same way. Three of them had since been slapped on a
charge for first-time offences and were down for punishment drill;
two more had started a fight in No. 2 hut and Cpl Bruce was on
another one for not keeping order.

There was sense all right in what Getcliffe had gone on about:
Lance-jack Simmons stripped of his tapes by the C.O. for
inefficiency—a name for a lot of sins and some not sins at all if
you took the trouble to look at them and bear the conditions in
mind—and Corporal Hewitt cutting up rough over a mere flea-
bite. 'Aren't you one of the men,' Mr Keene had asked him, 'who
were on morning patrol when—' And Hewitt had cut him short

quick enough: 'I'm an N.C.O., sir.' Charge: insubordination. And fifteen more requests for posting, true enough, among them Rickman and Cleaver, two men you'd say would weather anything. And all the time, bullshit and drill, bullshit and drill. . . . 'We have to understand the importance,' the C.O. had said, 'of keeping these men occupied mentally and physically. Otherwise the morale is going to slip and I won't tolerate that.'

Iron rations were no help. Thursday, the supply truck didn't turn up and there was not much in reserve because nothing would keep in the heat. Daily Orders had tried to make a joke of it: *Belts in all ranks will now be tightened for a few days, so let each of us console himself that he will shortly present a better figure of a man.* But biscuits and bloody chemicals weren't any laugh.

There was no wind but the air wasn't still; it vibrated because of the drums. Proctor listened to them consciously for a while and wondered how far off they were; he could see nothing beyond the vague shapes of the huts. They weren't far or they wouldn't sound so loud as this; every time he breathed in he could feel the vibration in his rib-cage.

He moved off. It was no good standing there any longer. He'd hoped to hear one of the Vend'u creeping about inside camp bounds as they sometimes did, and catch him with his bare hands, break his neck. Nobody armed with a revolver was allowed to use it except 'in extreme circumstances of immediate danger to life', but Proctor wouldn't use it anyway because you didn't need a gun when your hands were itching and you remembered Mackenzie. There'd be no such luck tonight: you wouldn't even hear a bloody elephant in the camp.

He was passing the ammunition hut when a man's cry came in the distance—man or animal, he wasn't sure—and a bell began ringing, a bell or something metal being hit. He stood with his head turned, one ear to the source of the sound. The shouting was taken up now and people were banging on tins, so he started off again, working his way through the huts and knocking into a fire-box and cursing and going on. Near him a door opened and he called: 'Blackout, there!'

Someone shouted from the lighted doorway asking what was happening; it sounded like Mr Keene. He didn't trouble to answer but loped on as fast as he could towards the hut where the shindy was. The whole camp was showing cracks of light and he could hear sharp voices. He reached the open parade-ground and began running.

It was dark in No. 2 hut and they didn't see him come in; it was no use shouting because Cpl Bruce was already doing that and no one wanted to hear him; in this uproar you couldn't even hear the drums. He found the light-switches and squinted in the glare; even then they didn't stop. He looked along the hut. It wasn't disorderly; they were just sitting on their beds beating away at whatever they had in their hands—dixies, tin mugs, water-bottles and emptied fire-buckets—grinning at one another and keeping time.

Sergeant Proctor walked slowly down the hut, looking a man in the face, tapping a man on the shoulder, halting in the middle and putting his hands on his hips until little by little the noise fell away, sliding to silence like something gigantic and physical slowly collapsing. They sat with their hands still for a moment and then without any one man leading them into it they raised a cheer, getting to their feet and giving it all their force while Proctor stood patiently, knowing why they did it and knowing they had to get it over with.

For weeks these men had suffered something that came hardest of all to a soldier: they'd been forbidden to fight. Since the day when the town patrols had been withdrawn they'd been confined to camp, and from then on they'd had to take the baiting of the Vend'u every night, losing their sleep and losing their tempers and finally losing their pride. Afraid, after Radford's death, of meeting the same dirty end in the dark, they'd confined them-selves to the hut, bent in on themselves with nothing to think about but the day's business—bullshit and drill, drill and bullshit —and all the time knowing more and more bitterly what they'd become: so many badgers in a barrel. Forbidden to fight back— and for reasons they didn't understand—they'd grabbed at the first chance to show what they felt, bashing and banging their anger out for everyone to hear. It must have been heard in Lizville . . . Now they were done, and as Proctor looked at their sweaty sublime faces he knew that he could now do anything he liked with them, order them naked into hellfire if he chose. They were men again, and they were his.

It was very quiet in the hut. At the far end a man murmured: 'They've stopped. The drums.'

Another said: 'And I should bloody 'ope so.'

Sergeant Proctor heard voices outside; people had followed him to see what was going on.

'You. Fix that blackout and look sharp.'

Rickman tugged at the curtain. The others began putting away

THE FREEBOOTERS

their dixies, straightening their beds. Proctor made his way back to the door and came abruptly to attention.

The C.O. was fully dressed, stick tucked under his arm.

'Who is in charge here?'

'Sir! Orderly Sergeant.'

Colonel Gray looked along the bed-spaces and Proctor turned and drew the company to attention.

'Where is the corporal in charge of this hut?'

Bruce stepped up to him.

Sergeant Proctor heard someone coming in noisily from the group outside. 'What the hell was all that bloody—'

'All right, Mr Keene.'

'Oh. Yes, sir. Orderly Officer.'

Colonel Gray waited a moment and then said: 'Corporal Bruce, I think you are at present on a charge for failing to maintain good order and discipline in this hut.'

'Yes, sir.'

'Very well. I am going to ask you a question, and you will be required at a later date to confirm whatever answer you will give. Is that clear?'

'Sir.'

'This is my question. When this commotion began tonight, what steps did you take to stop it?'

Proctor stood facing down the hut, the position he'd finished up in when he'd brought the men to attention. They couldn't see him; each faced the bed-space opposite; they couldn't see Cpl Bruce or the C.O. or anyone up this end. But they could hear. A single mosquito that had got in through the broken screen was the loudest noise in the hut.

He could hear Cpl Bruce, just behind him, swallowing.

'I told them to give over, sir.'

'You ordered them to stop the noise?'

'Yes, sir.' It wasn't much more than a whisper.

Proctor thought: They won't blame him. They know those things on a corporal's sleeve aren't chevrons—they're a cleft stick. A corporal gets the kicks from above and he gets no thanks from below. Go on then, Bruce, they won't blame you. There's a bastard in this hut tonight but it isn't you.

'And they heard and understood your order?'

'They might not have, sir. It was just a bit of high spirits and—'

'That's enough, Corporal, I'm quite satisfied with your answer. For your information I may tell you that there will be no further charge made against you in connection with this affair.'

Proctor heard the C.O. swing round. 'Mr Keene, you will take the names of all other ranks present in this hut at the time when the commotion began, and place them on open arrest on a charge of convening a mutinous assembly.'

CHAPTER FOUR

AT 1800 hours the men got into their kit, not talking, not looking at one another as they buckled their webbing with deliberate fingers. Their faces were hard and there was a straightness to their backs that was unconscious, self-imposed. They had the look of men going into battle and against an enemy they despised and had no fear of; but they were only going as far as the parade-ground.

Three men watched them, glancing away as they met someone's eye; they were Cleaver, Tewson and Cpl Bruce. They were not going. Cleaver had foot-sores and was on medicine and light duties; not his fault—he'd as lief go with the others if he could. Bruce, as an N.C.O., could not be awarded punishment drill and was in any case not on the mutiny charge. No one quite knew how Tewson had got off.

The men started out of the hut and Cleaver asked one of them: 'Who's takin' you?'

'Getcliffe.'

Cleaver winced. 'Why did ye have to pick that bastard?'

'They're all bastards, aren't they?'

'He'll grind you into the ground, mates.'

Suddenly another man was standing over Cleaver. 'All right, he'll grind us into the fuckin' ground—you got any more free information?'

Cleaver watched them going down the hut, humping their packs. You couldn't say a word to anyone these days, that was a fact. He got up and stood at the window. They marched towards the square, their long shadows beside them. 'By God,' he said, 'it'll be like an oven out there.'

'Of course it'll be like a bloody oven!' said Cpl Bruce sharply, and Cleaver looked across at him. It wasn't like Brucey to show temper.

'What've I said now, for God's sake?'

The corporal had turned his back to him. Tewson was finishing a letter. Cleaver heard Sgt Getcliffe shouting at them on the square and looked from the window again. The sun was low beyond the near horizon of huts; it would be down soon but the heat would stay. He wished he were out there with them.

The flag was limp on the post; its shadow reached half across the square, almost to the place where they'd found Cpl Radford and put him on the stretcher.

'Hell,' he said, 'they're comin' back.'

Tewson folded his letter and sealed the edges, glancing up at Cleaver. Bruce was by the door when the first of the men came in. 'What happened?'

They began swinging their packs off, helping one another.

'Getcliffe's gone soft.'

'He's what?'

'Well, he told us no packs. We didn't object.' They were sweating but their eyes were calmer, and their voices.

Tewson asked: 'Who told you to wear packs?'

'Keene.' They were straightening up, free of their loads.

Cleaver said: 'And Getcliffe told you to take them off?'

'That's it.'

When they had gone again, walking more freely, the corporal came over to Tewson. 'All right, you tell me.' There was never much that Tewson didn't know.

'Why me?'

You always had to dig it out of him. 'Because you've read the book. I sometimes think you wrote it. Come on.'

Tewson lit a cigarette, his movements precise. 'I'd say it was just one of those little mistakes. Keene hasn't been in all that long and he's eager as hell, but Getcliffe knows his Queen's Regs. Full marching order for punishment drill doesn't include packs. Of course, I could be wrong.' He gave Bruce one of his quick disarming smiles.

'You know you're not.' The corporal resented Tewson, his air of confidence, his education, his easy acceptance or rejection of things, his ability to make a quick decision when others would flounder. Bruce resented him more than ever just now because he believed that Tewson, a private of less than two years' service, could have stopped that outbreak on the night of the drums just by saying the right thing to all of them.

A pair of stripes were no use to you unless you'd got whatever it was that Tewson had, and then you didn't need them. Bruce knew it was his own fault that those men were out there on the square sweating like pigs; worse, they didn't blame him. But he wanted their obedience, not their charity. A week or two ago he wouldn't have worried so much: he'd tried to keep order and they hadn't taken any notice and they were stewing in their own juice, maybe learning a lesson. But these days he couldn't seem to throw things off so easy.

'How did you dodge this punishment drill anyway, Tewson?' He hadn't meant to ask; it wasn't his business; but he wanted to know how this feller could do things that the others couldn't.

'I didn't exactly dodge it, Corporal.'

There it was again. None of them ever called him that except on parade or in front of an officer. 'Corp' was as much as he got, here in the hut, and it was all he wanted. This wasn't the Glass-house. But Tewson hadn't said it out of respect; it was a reprimand.

'Well it's not my business.' He turned away, angry with himself.

'You've every right to know—you're in charge here.'

True enough. He was in charge here. That was why they were out there on the square. It was what Tewson didn't put into words that riled him.

'It was just that I didn't happen to be party to the offence,' said Tewson. 'I was too interested. I wanted to see what happened—after all we were taking on the Vendettu, weren't we? That hadn't happened before.'

Bruce didn't want to talk about it but now it was too late—he'd asked the question and he was going to get his answer. He felt his gorge rising and knew he ought to get control of himself and knew that he couldn't—

'Like you wouldn't pick up a gun with the rest of us if it came to a fight with them—you'd be too interested?'

Tewson smiled amiably. 'Self-preservation's a different matter. Anyway the point is that I denied the charge and the C.O. quite correctly dismissed me.'

'I see.' Cpl Bruce was taller than Tewson by a couple of inches but he didn't feel it. It wouldn't have been so bad if Cleaver weren't listening. 'Bit of luck, then, I mean the C.O. being so correct. Or you'd've found yourself out there on the square, wouldn't you?'

'No.' He turned to tap his cigarette-ash into the tray. 'I would have asked for a court martial. The C.O. knew I could do that —we all could have—and he wasn't taking the risk. The whole thing would have looked a bit odd if he'd let it go any higher, because he'd made enough mistakes already. I mean you can't charge a group of men with mutiny and then let them off with a spot of punishment drill; it doesn't add up. Mutiny's a damned serious charge, isn't it? He couldn't have made it stick.'

'Oh? Then what did he start it for?' Bruce had his arms folded, trying to look relaxed, but his body felt stiff; he'd tried to make the question sound casual but it hadn't, because there was temper in his throat. He wanted to trip this feller somehow, prove he wasn't as smart as he made out, no cleverer than the rest. It wasn't so easy because the rest were out on the square.

'He probably got a bit upset,' Tewson said. 'It can happen to the best of us. There was a hell of a din going on and we're all feeling the strain.' He hesitated, studying the corporal's face. 'You mind if I speak personally? The corporal in charge of a hut has to live with the men, swop fags with them and share their troubles—practically speaking he's one of them. How can anyone expect him to crack down on them the minute they get out of hand, particularly when they're living on the edge of their nerves and ready to blow off steam at the slightest provocation? It doesn't make sense.'

Bruce had him. 'You're forgetting something. The C.O. didn't blame me. He blamed them.'

'Exactly. So why should you go on blaming yourself? That's what I'm really talking about.' He smiled pleasantly. 'Of course, I could be wrong.'

They had been punished for three days and on the fourth day the Colonel went alone into No. 2 hut and spoke to them, in the hour before the evening meal.

Lieutenant Millburn had been to see him in the morning, confessing himself to be worried about the increasing strain on the men. He had offered his opinion that while the officers understood the reason for the unit's inability to combat the nuisance tactics of the Vendettu by armed action, the other ranks were suffering frustration based partly upon ignorance. It was quite right of Millburn to bring this point to the attention of his commanding officer: the Colonel placed the well-being of the men second only to the interests of the Country; they were, after all, her sons. But it had already been in his mind to deal with this matter, not least because he was so charged by Army Orders: 'A Commanding Officer is responsible to the Queen for the maintenance of discipline in the unit under his care. He will, by advice and timely intervention, endeavour to promote good understanding and to prevent disputes.'

Entering the hut he found the men standing at ease by their bed-spaces. Cpl Bruce was present and Sgt Proctor in charge.

'Company . . . attention!'

The Colonel noted the pleasing smell of polish and the absence of cigarette-ends on top of the sand in the fire-buckets. He had told the sergeant that he would be making an informal visit and that no special measures should be taken to welcome him, but as he looked along the two rows of beds—not one with even a paperback or a writing-pad spoiling its neatness—he silently appreciated these small signs of respect.

'Thank you, Sergeant.'

'Sir.'

'Now we're just going to have a friendly chat, so we'll have to carry on as best we can without you. We don't want any important persons hanging about to make us uneasy.' He brought himself to attention while the sergeant retired, to point the pleasantry. The hut remained quiet.

He dropped his cap on to the nearest bed. 'At ease, then, gentlemen. Gather round this end so that we can all see each other and so that I don't have to shout—I sadly lack certain powers which we have noted in the good Sergeant Getcliffe.' He paused, but the silence was broken only by Cpl Bruce telling them to take off their caps. When they were settled, sitting rather stiffly along the edges of the nearest beds, he sat down with his hands clasped round one knee. 'If anyone wants to smoke that's perfectly all right.' He disliked the habit but knew that it was one of the prime needs of the modern soldier. 'Now I shan't keep you long. I am as aware as you are of a certain aroma issuing from the cook-house.'

A metallic sound was heard as Bruce balanced himself gingerly on his kit-bag, disturbing a tin there.

'First a word on a disagreeable subject: punishment. For the past three days at this hour you have been doing punishment drill and I'm going to repeat what I very often tell people at a time such as this, when the punishment is over. You must never for one moment believe that any officer or any N.C.O. derives pleasure from the awarding of punishment. It is awarded partly as a deterrent, to show that the law must be respected, but mostly as an opportunity for the miscreant to purge himself of his guilt. That may come as a surprise to you, but the mechanics of sin and expiation are very simple. If we sin we lose some of our self-respect, and only by our willing submission to a just punishment can we rid ourselves of the feeling that we have let the side down, that we have dishonoured ourselves and also our comrades, that we have spoiled by however little the good name of the Regiment. You have now been freed of this wretched burden and can hold up your heads again. That is why I felt myself able to come to you and to talk with you, man to man and with respect on both sides.'

He surveyed his audience. Some were watching him and now looked away; some had not looked at him since they had settled on the beds. He noticed that despite his invitation nobody was smoking.

'Secondly I want you all to understand why we can't hit back at these Vendettu people who are making themselves such a nuisance. Let me put it in a nutshell for you. President Makarik has led his countrymen to independence from British colonial rule, and has now asked our help in averting a serious revolution and the risk of a coup d'état by the Vendettu leader, General Kiutsho. Now, politics being as complicated as they are, the situation is difficult. It's felt in London that if General Kiutsho *can* displace President Makarik, he'll make a far more enlightened statesman once he's in power. Our loyalty is therefore to Makarik, but our real hopes are for Kiutsho, and it will be difficult—if he wins the day—for Great Britain to welcome him as the new leader of the Tamalese Republic if the British Army has been busy killing off those most active in his support—the Vendettu tribe. Our Prime Minister, through the War Office and the G.O.C. East Africa Command and our excellent Sergeant Giles over there in the signals hut, has given us his official message: "The 4th Royals will defend their camp by every means short of active retaliation." What he really says is this: "We hope General Kiutsho will win his own battle in Lisolaville, so please grin and bear it and give him time, and don't throw a spanner in the works." That is our position, you see. We've patrolled the town and maintained order for President Makarik; we've now withdrawn our forces to save embarrassment to both sides in a changing situation; and we must remain entrenched.'

It was at this point that Colonel Gray felt he should invite questions, but decided against it. In these faces around him there was visible a certain lack of response; there was no question that they weren't giving him their closest attention—they could hardly be insensible of the chance he was giving them to understand their situation, to feel personally the part they were playing in the drama of emergent Africa. But from his long experience in handling men he could judge their mood; it would indeed be better for them to raise their questions among themselves after he had left them, so that the more intelligent could help the others along.

Cramp was starting in his knee and he lowered it, to clasp his hands round the other. 'You may ask why we must remain here at all, if we can't show any fight. I will tell you. We must remain here to persuade both the civil power in Tamala and the revolutionary leaders that sober parleying will avail them better than violent acts, because if they start a really serious fire it will be up to us to put it out, and we can't guarantee not to hurt anyone in the process. We are here not as a threat but as a presence, a symbol of strength, a steadying influence in times when the soil of Africa is shifting as if to an earthquake. You may ask why the Vendettu are attacking the white settlers and ourselves when their leader, General Kiutsho, has the as yet unwritten support of Great Britain. It is because he is not powerful enough to call off his terrorist forces, in case they should turn against him before he can bring the Tamalese Army to his side and enforce peace. The Vendettu are hunters—' and suddenly he was on his feet, his gestures automatic as he spoke of the people he knew so well— 'they are hunters and warriors with their roots deep in this ancient land. During seventy years of British rule they've been forbidden to hunt game and to raid other tribes; now they've been told that they're soldiers of the Tamalese Democratic Front —and this gives them an outlet for their hunting and their warring instincts. They're playing a game with us; they know we must have orders to shoot only over their heads, but they still fear our guns and they know that if they tried to raid our camp en masse—and there are thousands of them—we would *have* to repel them with all our force.'

He realized now that he was no longer sitting down; it was easier, walking about, to tell them what the Vendettu meant to him, what Africa meant. 'And that would be a terrible thing, if we had to turn our guns on them. Because they're children. Children. That's why they play with us, just as they'd play with an injured snake—oh, I've seen them do it—teasing it with a stick and darting off when it tries to strike, laughing and screaming half in fun and half in fright. Children. And if we can understand that, we'll put up with their naughtiness more easily, and we shall also become better men because of it—more tolerant, more generous and more strong. Haven't we a supreme example to follow? "Forgive them . . . they know not what they do." Then let's follow it. Let's look on these few months as a time of trial and emerge from it all the stronger—better soldiers and better men.'

He picked up his cap and put it on, lifting a hand as Cpl Bruce

stood up. 'Now I don't want you to move, any of you. I want you
to remember that this chap who's taking his leave of you is not
only your commanding officer. He is also your friend.'

His footsteps were the only sound, crossing the polished boards
and crunching over the gravel outside the hut. They sat listening
until there was nothing more of him to be heard.

The heat flowed in from the doorway; they felt it on their faces
and against their eyes. The camp was quiet; the parade-ground
was empty and the air was still. In the distance a truck's engine
started up and then died away; a faint tinkling came, like goat-
bells, hardly disturbing the silence, as men began queueing outside the cook-house with their mugs and irons. Very far away a
hyena cackled in the bush.

Then a man lit up and Rickman said:

'Permission to move, Corp?' He remained sitting stiffly,
speaking from the corner of his mouth. 'I don't want to let the
side down, you know. Don't want to do anything sinful again,
now I've had me purge.'

Bruce bounced the kit-bag to straighten the top, not troubling
to answer. His legs ached from only half-sitting on the thing,
trying not to crush some biscuits he had in there.

They began moving, not with any purpose but just separating
because of the heat. One or two of them found their own beds
and lay down with their hands behind their heads, gazing at the
ceiling through half-closed eyes. Someone fished a book out
of his kit-bag and opened it but didn't read more than a few
lines.

'It's quite right,' said a man named Spragge. 'That's all they
are—children. A bunch of kids. I didn't realize it before. Mind
you, I'm not so sharp—I need telling things that are obvious to
other people. What you say, Jamie?'

'I think you're daft,' Cleaver told him. He began polishing his
knife, stabbing it into a sand-bucket.

'Wouldn't say daft, exactly, but not so sharp either.' Spragge
squinted through the smoke he was making, as if striving to
discern eternal truths. 'That's why it did me good, listening to
the C.O. You can't say he doesn't know what he's talking about.
Once we begin to look on the Vend'u as a lot of children we'll
be better off, like he said. They're only playing a game, see? Take
Mackenzie, now, what they did with him, remember?'

'Shuddup,' said Rickman.

'We thought they'd done something awful, see? But it wasn't
like that at all—I can see it now plain as anything. They were

just havin' a little game with him.' He broke off, seeing Rickman standing over him. 'They were just bein' naughty, but of course he didn't know that, because no one had told him. He wouldn't have minded, if he'd known it was only in fun.' His eyes had gone very narrow and he drew smoke into his lungs and blew it upwards into Rickman's face. 'When we were out that morning and found Kennie's head stuck on that post, we didn't realize it was just one of their toys they'd been playin' with, or we'd have—'

Rickman was on him. There was no question of telling him to get on his feet and make it a fair fight—Rickman was at his throat and they were both across the bed. Because it wasn't a fight, though it looked like one. Rickman had warned Spragge —they'd all agreed in this hut never to talk about Mackenzie again, because it only made them feel worse about not being allowed to pick up a gun and shoot down the first Vendettu they set eyes on—but this struggle wasn't the outcome of his warning; he'd gone beyond that. All Rickman knew was that there was something alive under his hands and that he wanted to kill it. He wanted to break bone, rip flesh away and feel something alive become dead. He was only half aware of what he was doing but he could hear himself shouting something over and over again about 'killing children'. Before the corporal could get near them Spragge had freed one arm and knocked him out cold.

No one had let the news get out to the rest of the camp about Spragge and Rickman; it was their own business. But Sgt Proctor came along later to find out why the whole of No. 2 hut had failed to turn up at the cook-house for the evening meal. All he could get out of them was that they didn't like the 'aroma'.

CHAPTER FIVE

IT was worse because Timms was well liked. Most of the men in No. 7 hut were his friends and he was popular among the whole of 'B' Company. He wasn't gifted in any way—couldn't talk well, couldn't sing a true note or draw a straight line or throw a good dart, wasn't an expert on anything, didn't even go for women. He was just one of those people you'd find yourself thinking about when you'd got so browned off that you didn't know what to do; then you'd search him out.

That may have explained his popularity: everyone was permanently browned off so he was much in demand. He wouldn't do anything for you, wouldn't know how; you just felt better for seeing him. Nothing worried him, so five minutes in his company left you wondering what you'd been so bloody depressed about. When things were all right you'd forget he existed but when you lost your girl or caught the clap or your Mum died you'd go and find Timmy and tell him. But you'd never find him again now.

The Vendettu had left him propped against the wall of the wash-house behind No. 7 hut with his throat cut and his eyes out and his privates hacked off and stuffed into his mouth. The M.O. said he'd been dead since midnight or thereabouts; someone must have disturbed them because this was the kind of memento they usually took away with them and left on the track outside the camp for the morning patrol to find. Luckily enough it was Sgt Getcliffe who found him, coming off guard at first light; he'd seen a lot worse than that in twenty years' campaigning and he threw something over it and fetched a stretcher-party without any fuss.

It could have been made light of—'545 Private Timms could simply have been reported as killed—but everyone knew enough about the Vendettu to put the worst rumours about; and they were no worse than the truth.

The day went badly of course. The M.O., Major Ward, could judge the reaction of the whole unit by simply looking out of his window and counting the men on sick-parade. There were very few this morning. Firstly, no one wanted to come near the place because they knew Timms was there. Secondly, a man with a boil starting on his neck was ready to forget it and to count himself lucky. Thirdly, the men were angry, and damned if they were going to ask anyone's help with a foot sore. Let it fester.

Major Ward was angry too. It was time Colonel Gray realized that his detachment of the 4th Royals was up against more than a pack of savages. The Vendettu had leaders expert in psychological warfare who knew that horror outvalued pain, that fear of the unknown was more effective than fear of the known and that loss of sleep could knock out an army more efficiently than poison gas—you could put on a gas-mask and stay on your feet but there wasn't such a thing as a sleep-mask, soldiers for the use of.

As an example of the horror-technique the trick they'd pulled with Mackenzie's head was a classic: because they had taken away the body. He had never been seen again, in his wholeness.

Those who had been on patrol that morning no longer remembered Mackenzie as a man, even a dead man, but only as a *head*. (Ward himself had passed a nasty moment when he'd supervised the boxing up of the remains: should they put the head at one end of the coffin where it ought to be, or in the middle because it was all there was? And how to stop the damned thing rolling around inside?)

Fear of the unknown was easily induced. The Vendettu came only by dark and two or three of them flitting about could fill the camp with phantoms. Loss of sleep was the easiest of all. The Vendettu slept in the daytime in the caves south of the town, so that their energy was greatest when the unit most needed rest. These were the tools of professional interrogators and secret police agents, designed to break a captive's will; here they were extended for use against a massed body of men, virtually captives, whose will to resist must be broken so that they would pack up and go home. And apart from the odd exceptions like Mackenzie and Timms, General Kiutsho would be able to say that his forces had never attacked those of Great Britain during his struggle for leadership.

Ward looked from his window again. 'Foster!'

'Sir?'

'Get that queue out of the direct sun and send the first man in—what's the hold-up this morning?'

'We were waiting for you sir.'

'Look, you do the organizing, I stick the needle in. Shan't tell you again.'

He was particularly angry because nothing was being done to combat these nuisance-attacks by the Vendettu. Shooting at them wasn't permitted—unless of course you caught one inside bounds, then you'd drill the bugger and plead 'immediate danger to life'. They knew you'd do it given the chance; that was why you never saw or heard them this side of the boundary fence ; you wouldn't know they'd been here last night if it weren't for that thing under the sheet. No, this was psychological warfare and there were suitable defences, but none were being organized. Those chaps in No. 2 hut had demonstrated this by sheer instinct and without even understanding how the mind of the Vend'u worked: that wasn't just a shindy they'd kicked up; it was white magic, louder and more powerful than even the drums. If the drums could work such mighty voodoo, what dread gods could those metal bells not summon? The Vend'u had packed it in, not knowing that the first dread god to be summoned was Sgt Proctor.

'Right—Wilson, how's it going?'

'Settling down, sir, I think. I can eat almost anything now.'

'You're lucky. The rest of us are still on iron rations. Corp'ral Foster—specimen. All right Wilson, go and pee in that bottle. If it's hard going, run the tap for a bit.'

It would have done the whole unit a lot of good, that little success by No. 2 hut, if the C.O. hadn't gone and cocked it up. He should have organized that shindy himself, got the whole camp at it, wakened the dead. Gray knew these Vendettu better than anyone; he'd passed half his career in East Africa. But just go and suggest a thing like that. 'This Regiment, Major Ward, has been granted no fewer than thirty-seven Battle Honours during its proud history. I am happy to say that none was gained by beating upon mess-tins.'

'What's your trouble, Rawlings?'

'It's hard to say, sir.'

Ward nearly told him to get out, but stopped in time. This was another one. The eyes jumpy, skin reactions, the speech dull.

'Have a try, Rawlings.'

'Lay awake most of the night, sir, even when it's quiet. Don't want any food, can't stomach it. Can't get interested in anything.' An attempted smile. 'Sounds like I'm swingin' the lead, doesn't it?'

'It does, but you wouldn't say it if you were.' They were always the worst trouble because you couldn't do anything but talk to them, and the value of that depended on the listener; once they were in this state they were convinced you were only trying to fool them. The best thing would be to give them a stick and a mess-tin but if he did that he'd be sent home to London for treatment himself. Not that that would be any bloody hardship. 'On the other hand, Rawlings, there's nothing wrong with you that we can't fix. Report back here at 1200 hours for a complete examination.' That was a must; they had to know they were being helped. 'In the meantime we're going to start you on a course of Salvelitone H. You heard of that?'

'No, sir.'

'It's the latest thing out of America and we get it flown in to H.Q. at the coast in refrigerated packs. It's therefore scarce at present and it has to be kept cold, so you'll need to come here three times a day to be given it. Corp'ral Foster, will you organize that?'

'Yes, sir.' Even Foster was looking impressed.

Ward made out the chit. *Medicine, light duties and visits as prescribed.* The chilled glucose-water would refresh him and give him some useful energy at least. The rest was up to the voodoo.

Rickman had been last into the truck because he wanted to sit at the back and watch the trail of dust and the camp getting smaller. It wasn't easy to be last in because they were all trying the same trick and for the same reason; they all wanted the back seat, where the view was. Sometimes the sergeant in charge had to yell at them before the first man would swing himself up—

'Don't you want to go, you stupid bunch o' gits?'

'You kiddin', Sarge?'

But the M.T. drivers soon got it to rights: put her in gear and throttle up and before the truck had moved a yard it was full of desperate soldiers. Each man got his turn on the roster only once in two weeks and the Tit Patrol was as good as ten days' leave: it lasted no more than a few hours but it meant that much time away from the camp, free of the huts and the square and the drill and the bullshit and everything and everyone they loathed the living guts of.

Rickman was last into the truck this morning but it had been a near thing; the moment a vehicle was on the move it sent up dust and they didn't know he was still running after it trying to catch up until he found the breath to holler out. It was about the only time in his life he'd ever panicked: it didn't bear thinking of, being left in that camp and watching the truck get smaller out there till even the dust had gone.

Now it was the camp that was small; he could see it only when a bend in the track made a curve in the mile-long yellow-red wake, but he looked for it again whenever the truck heaved over on its springs, wanting to see how small it would get before the blue of the heat-haze blotted it out. Then he drew a deep breath and felt as if he'd just had a woman.

Someone up front began singing. *'We'll be comin' roun' the mountain when we come . . . We'll be comin' roun' the mountain when we come . . .'*

Then they were all at it and Captain Jones heard them from the cab and lit a cigarette for the driver, settling back to watch the road as they plunged through close-grained bush. Even though he was Acting 'B' Company Commander he had decided to take the patrol out himself and he would have been as happy as the men if only the truck were bound for Lizville instead of a bloody slaghead in the wilds. He hadn't been out of camp officially for three weeks since the troops had been ordered off street-patrol, withdrawn from the town and the whole unit confined to camp. He doubted if he'd ever see Cinthie again; for a couple of nights she'd brought the car along the road to the disused airstrip and waited for him within half a mile of the camp, but with the Vend'u around it got too risky. If they caught her he'd never forgive himself and if they caught him he'd never be any use to her again with the damned thing stuffed in his mouth. The best thing to believe was that her old man was back from the coast by now, in which case there'd be nothing doing anyway.

He knew he wasn't the only one. If ever the unit got out of that camp, even the goats wouldn't be safe.

'*She'll be wearin' silk pyjamas when she comes, when she comes . . . She'll be wearin' silk pyjamas when she comes . . .*'

In an hour the truck reached the hill. Capt. Jones decided to take Cpl Bruce to the summit while the men waited below under L.-Cpl Judd, who had the sense to group them on the west side in the shade.

'All right, you can rest your rifles.'

'I'd clean forgotten I'd got one, it's so long since I fired the fucker.'

'That's enough.' He fished up a fag from his shirt pocket and they took the hint, finding their own.

'You want to be up there with the captain—you'd get some action then.'

'Up at the top of the Tit? There's no bloody—'

'Not him. Captain Carey.'

'Oh-ah.'

Rickman asked in his toneless voice: 'Something new?'

'On the squawk this morning—Radio Liz. They wiped out a Vend'u mob not far from here, at it all yesterday, two hundred dead, no wounded—you know what Carey is.'

They gathered round.

'Where, then, for Christ sake? Everywhere's far from here!'

'Two 'undred of the Colonel's children? Poor little sods, I call that cruel, don't you?'

Some of them laughed but Rickman didn't. 'Not far from here, was it? Where, then?'

'Somewhere up the Road.'

Rickman asked nothing more. Radio Liz was always putting out reports like that to give General Kiutsho the guts-ache. But Carey was known to be in the area—if you could call half a million square miles an area; there weren't many landmarks: Lizville, the coast, the mission station up north. Even the Road didn't have a name. It ran for three hundred miles through the range of mountains that reached from the rain-forests south of Lisolaville to the north-west limits of the Republic. There was water to be had in the foothills, though the river had long since dried up; and there was shade, morning and evening. Everyone in the unit knew the Road, because they'd been flown in to the airfield at Battalion H.Q. and put into trucks for the last leg of the journey. The Road was fifty-odd miles from the camp and their convoy had left it east of the town, taking the track that led to the abandoned airstrip. In the last three weeks they had often thought of the Road, where there was shade and water. It was the way home.

They never thought of Captain Carey except when Radio Lisolaville issued a communiqué. As professional soldiers they looked down on the rag-tag-and-bobtail mercenary force that Carey had scraped together and offered for hire. President Makarik was said to pay them good money and from all reports they weren't short of guns; but the worth of a soldier wasn't in his pay or you'd never see a Victoria Cross in a pawnshop.

The corporal put out his dog-end. 'Good luck to him, I say, so long as he keeps on knocking the Vend'u.'

'So long as he does, but we're not to know, are we? It's nine parts propaganda, Radio Liz. Two hundred killed? Call it twenty an' you'd be nearer the mark.'

'Well twenty's a start, isn' it? You're only jealous because we can't shoot the bastards ourselves.'

There was a short silence because everyone knew it was true.

'Anyway, that mob's not for me—you've heard their reputation. March into a town and before they've killed off the opposition they're looting the bank and raping the women and collaring all the beer.'

'Disgustin', ain't it? Where can I sign on?'

Corporal Judd cut the laughter short as he saw their patrol officer coming down the hill. 'Right—fags out and pick up your rifles.'

Corporal Bruce reached them first, wiping the sweat from his face and neck. 'No noise, now. Dead quiet.'

'What's up?' asked Judd.

'Don't know. His orders.'

Captain Jones came up, the field-glasses slung at the shoulder. 'Who's the best shot in the platoon, Corporal Judd?'

'Shot, sir? Coleman, I'd say. Him or Marriott.' He looked at Bruce.

'Marriott,' said Cpl Bruce. 'Bisley medal.'

'Fetch him up. No noise, mind.'

Captain Jones took the man aside and gave him the field-glasses, pointing to the cloud of thorn he'd been observing from the summit of the hill. 'You on?'

'Yes, sir. Have a try?'

'Have a try nothing. We're taking it back with us.'

Marriott found a boulder and got down on to one knee, settling his rifle and then raising his head to study the target. It was a big eland buck and the range was less than three hundred yards but there was heat-haze already flowing over the ground, so that he seemed to see the animal through water.

Jones didn't move except to refocus the field-glasses. He would need to know, if the shot didn't kill, whether it was a clean miss or a wounding, because they would have to get over there and finish it off if necessary. He would give Marriott a smart kick up the orifice if they had to do that; it could lead to an hour's chase through thorn, and the hill had been quite sufficient for this morning.

Marriott watched the delicate head turning, lifting, listening. The eland must have left the fringe of the herd, no longer afraid of the sounds made by the patrol arriving; now it was worried for some reason. Any second it might decide there was a risk and take to flight and Marriott saw this and brought his head down, sighting and pulling off without any fancy preliminaries.

Captain Jones put the glasses away and signalled the driver to start up. The whole party climbed aboard and as the truck bounced across the volcanic scree towards the thorn he called to the corporal through the window-flap, 'Any of your chaps been a butcher in civvy street?'

One of them said he could do the job; he'd spent two seasons in the bush with a Dutch South African. The rest of them piled out to watch him as he went to work on the buck, asking someone to hold the horns and someone else to hone a bayonet on a stone while he used his knife on the legs, slitting the hide from knee-joint to stomach, slashing the belly and pulling out the intestines, his arm red to the elbow. He got the skin peeled off inside five minutes, panting and sweating, then took the sharpened bayonet and hacked off the slender legs.

When he braced himself foot-sure above the beast's head and severed the neck at the fifth stroke one of the men turned away and threw up, because this had been done to Mackenzie. The others began moving back to the truck; they came from Dover and Surbiton and Dorking and one of them took his wife to feed the deer at Richmond every leave; they understood the bus-routes and what to do about greenfly; they didn't understand—or want to understand—what this bloke was doing with something almost still alive, and doing it without any hate.

There was no singing on the way back to camp; no one wanted to sit at the tailboard because all you could see was the hill getting smaller; it'd be worse in the cab for Capt. Jones and Sarge and the driver—all they'd see was the camp getting bigger.

Some slept or half-slept and were jogged awake into minor nightmares. *Left a book on the bed again—Getcliffe'll fix me for that, he's warned me twice. Fatigues, soon as we report in—be the fucking lats again. Dexterity-drill, 1,000 hours on the square with the C.O. watching from his window like he did before, so I'm bound to drop the sodding rifle—like I did before.*

These were not thoughts, but images: a book and the sergeant's face, a latrine brush and the scum, a rifle on the ground and the blank square of a window; and there were countless other images with no association, yet they were as hateful: whitewashed stones, the split in the base of the flagpost, a bicycle, the roughness of wooden walls, the glare of a bulb—and the images of smells: boot-polish, creosote, sweat—and of sounds: marching, voices, doors.

They were not hated severally for what they were, but together for what they made: the camp.

Captain Jones told his driver to drop the men and take the truck round past the cook-house. The A.C.C. sergeant didn't believe it.

'That's not in from Battalion Stores, sir. That's meat, that is, not got-up knuckle an' scrag. Make Christmas dinner for fifty men, an' 'ere it is July.' He stroked the carcass, looked for the liver, didn't find it and said nothing; you didn't want to look a gift-horse in the mouth. 'Which fifty men, sir?'

'Alphabetical order, my Company, other ranks only.' Jones sent the truck away, telling the driver to get the floorboards scrubbed before anyone looked inside.

'I'll see to the list,' said the Cook sergeant. 'Fifty lucky lads, an' God knows they've earned it.' He cocked a look at the captain. 'Been a change in orders, then, has there?'

'Not exactly, no. So keep it as quiet as you can.'

But by nightfall the rumour had got round and was well out of hand: the supply-truck had come in at last from Lizville and there'd been double meat-rations ordered for the whole unit to help morale.

Just before 1800 hours a utility vehicle left the camp and dropped its load a few hundred yards outside, coming back empty.

At 1800 hours the first of the night-guard was mounted and in the fading light of the sundown the two sentries at the gates watched the hyenas loping in from the bush, scenting carrion. Within minutes there was a pack of them milling around the meat, and in the onset of darkness the two men listened to the snapping of their jaws as they devoured it.

'Go on, you buggers, stuff it down.'

'What 'appened, then?'

'Morning patrol brought back an eland today.' He was one of the Adjutant's clerks, well informed and independent of rumour. 'Captain Jones gave it to the cook-house.'

'It wasn't the ration-truck come through, then?'

'No. It was private enterprise. Not enough for the whole unit, but fifty men were on the list for a decent meal. What's your name?'

'Brewer.'

'You'd have got a tuck-in, then. So would I. But in the law-abiding Republic of Tamala there's a little thing called a game-licence and without it you can't shoot game. I overheard the C.O. telling Jones about it—I'm an authority now myself. It also happens to appear in orders. Jones said something about Nelson turning a blind eye in special circumstances, but it didn't go down all that well. He's on a charge.' He listened again to the sounds of the feasting. 'Go on, you hungry buggers, stuff it down.'

CHAPTER SIX

THE eyes of Brevet-Major Sir Philip Westerby Gray, V.C., looked out from the silver frame with the absence of expression peculiar to his times. Men, in 1885, were men, and vanity was a vice; it was thus held seemly to pretend that the *camera obscura* did not exist, if one found oneself in its presence; but since it was not easy to ignore totally a vast glass Cyclopian eye perched upon three legs and funereally enshrouded, the sitter chose to believe himself inopportunely closeted with a dead fish, and the tenets of

nursery, Public School, Club and Regiment dictated that nothing
in the face should hint of suffering.

But there had once been a man of flesh and blood in this faded
sepia uniform of the 7th African Mounted Rifles. As often with
heroes, he had died young, struck down by an assagai flung from
the remnant of Chief Moabanta's defeated forces as they fled
from what history remembers as the Repulse at Ashton's Drift.
History was but little changed by that valiant affray; the stoic
stand of the 4th Royals against the Vendettu tribesmen, eighty-
odd years later, would leave as slight a mark; but a soldier asks
small motive for what he does; otherwise war would be impossible. Given his motive—which can be as meaningless as a political
slogan he does not even understand—he is ready to kill and to die.

Thus Major Sir Philip Gray, commanding the central column
of cavalry on that July day in 1885, hurled his forces at the enemy
in a last attempt to hold the redoubt, leaving in his wake the
thousandfold dead of a decimated army amid a wasteland of
slaughtered oxen, mules and men. It was a caprice of the gods
that he should emerge unscathed from the main assault, only
to receive the assagai thrown at random from a dying hand as
the rout entered its final stage. Wheeling his horse, so the records
had it, to survey the scene of his endeavours, he was vouchsafed
the sweetness of his victory before he fell. Near him was found the
silver snuff-box that now reposed in a drawer of the desk on which
stood the photograph in its silver frame.

His grandson, Lieutenant-Colonel Sir Philip Cosford Gray,
D.S.O., M.C., glanced at the photograph on entering the room,
his homage as perfunctory as that of a good Catholic who crosses
himself while thinking of other things, but whose faith in his
God is such that he belittles outward show. Gray too revered
God; his grandfather was the subject of his idolatry.

It was by comparison with this image that he judged his fellow
men, and it was not surprising that most were found wanting. He
understood their weakness and his tolerance was inexhaustible,
but he wished ardently that there were more signs of strength
among his unit and less call for his patience. It needed only a
few native drums to disrupt the discipline of a whole platoon,
only a few days on short rations to drive an officer to flagrant
disobedience. These men were not in the mould of those who
had carried the Repulse at Ashton's Drift. Couldn't one ask of
the modern soldier the qualities so manifest in his forbears?

Certainly the present struggle was of a different kind; it was
irksome to turn the other cheek when training had instilled more

active virtues, and he had tried yet again to bring home to them
the facts of their situation, taking as his opportunity the memorial
service for Private Timms:

'We have lost a comrade, but with his passing there has passed
also another day and for us another victory. Because that is our
bounden task: to wait, to stand firm, to hold ourselves prepared
for great events in whose furtherance our armed strength may be
sorely needed. But most of all it is our task to hold our heads
high in the eyes of these people whose country finds itself in
torment—these young people of an ancient race who in all
ignorance make their mischief against us, yet perceive in us those
qualities that one day they will come to emulate, proud citizens
of a new-born State. You notice my repetition of one certain word.
That word is "hold". And you know why that word is constantly
in my mind. It is the motto of our Regiment: "Hold". Aptly,
that is our present task. In remembering our fallen comrade, then,
we should think of him as our exemplar. Proud, strong, impervious to the frustrations that inaction brings, he held on even
to the death. Therefore should we honour him and praise him
for what he did, and may God grant that in his going he left his
strength with us, as a warrior who, in falling, hands his sword
to those who must fight on.'

He had already composed a letter to Private Timms's parents,
using the same theme. They would not be expected to read
between the lines, but it was to be hoped that the company
assembled at this morning's service would take his meaning. This
unfortunate boy had made the supreme sacrifice, compared with
which the inconvenience of short rations and confinement to
camp could surely be deemed supportable.

He found himself looking at the photograph again. How would
that great man have handled the situation with which his grandson was faced? How would he have countered these growing
dangers to discipline that could no longer be ignored? He had
been known and praised for his resolute faith in God, so that
the way would be amply clear to him. He would attack with all
his force, choosing as his weapons the godly attributes of tolerance,
wisdom, justice, mercy and wrath.

So must his successor strive to do.

When his corporal clerk came in he asked for the charge-sheet,
reference Capt. Jones, and checked it through. He must deal with
it this evening, the earliest opportunity following the offence.

*... in that he did contravene Standing Order A.O.17/S/1/1967
in which it is expressly commanded that no wild animal in the*

territory of the Tamalese Republic may be killed either for sport or for use as sustenance, and caused thereby the expenditure of one B.A.P. Mark II bullet (Price One Shilling and Tenpence) in pursuance of the said unauthorized act.

'Corporal!'

'Sir?'

'This has to be rewritten. The matter contained in parentheses should read first in figures, then in words.'

'Excuse me, sir?' His clerk edged nearer the desk.

'Look.' Colonel Gray used his pen. 'Open parenthesis, *Price is. 10d.*, open second parenthesis, *One Shilling and Tenpence*, close both parentheses.' He replaced the top on his pen. 'Small details are important, and no one knows that better than a commanding officer.'

'Be another lesson for me, sir.'

'I'm sure you'll profit from it. Now see to it straight away.'

They rushed screaming to the barbed wire, rushed in hundreds from the bush and danced at the barbed wire, screaming. Somewhere a rifle banged and the shot was hardly heard; the guard commander shouted to his men to hold their fire but only those near him heard him and another shot cracked faintly, then a third. The searchlight came on and began revolving and where there had been blackness there was the shine of oiled skins and the white of teeth and eyes flashing and leaping at the wire. As the light turned full-circle it was seen that the camp was ringed entirely; their bodies washed in dark waves at the wire and above them drifted a red-yellow spume of dust sent up by their stamping feet. The screaming did not stop.

Someone had got to the loudspeaker control. '*Hold your fire. We are in no danger. Hold your fire.*'

The searchlight spun slowly; either its beam gave exaggerated effect to the scene as it swept over the massed figures, or those caught for a moment in its glare were made the more frantic, leaping higher as if to greet it, their hands raising phantom shapes against the dust-clouds.

'*Hold your fire. . . .*'

There were no further shots but here and there a soldier ran through the underglow as the beam passed over him; from the guardhouse a reserve party of men was making its way to the wire at the double, rifles at low port and bayonets fixed. Lights showed everywhere among the huts and voices called below the screaming, faint as the cries of sailors overwhelmed by storm.

The screaming did not stop. Perhaps it could not stop: the sound was no longer voluntary but had passed beyond control to become the voice of frenzy instead of the will; they were changelings; once creatures, they were now mere vessels, the source of terrible sound.

Men ran about the camp. An officer waved his arm, trying to signal someone. There was movement around the three machine-gun posts. A sergeant was shouting to a guard but could not be heard.

This was worse than the drums. The Vendettu were not hidden by the dark and the distance, subtly casting their voodoo across the air with disciplined hands—they were here, close, visible, evil, alive; they were an inundation.

They had come because of the wire. It had not been here yesterday. This morning five trucks had moved in along the by-pass road to the airstrip bringing reels of dannert coils, dumping them at intervals round the camp perimeter, their crews spinning them out expertly like giant spiders, heavily gloved and armed with pincers. By evening the camp was webbed into a steel-grey barbed cocoon two miles in circumference, and when the R.E. crews climbed back into their trucks the 4th Royals had cheered them away.

Among the advantages of barbed wire, as listed in the field manuals, was its high morale effect on troops who knew that it was proof even against wheeled vehicles and light tanks, since it chocked up the axles. But it was not proof against sound. The Vendettu leaders, already shown to be versed in the tactics of psychological warfare, were making an immediate answer to this attempt by the British unit to protect itself. Their message was plain: *even behind your wall of iron barbs you are not safe from us.*

Just as they had extended the methods of secret police interrogation to weaken the morale of men in number, they now extended the technique of the Karate yell, whose function is to discomfort the adversary and inspire fear in him. Success had been immediate: three sentries had fired their guns from sheer terror; there was not a man in the whole camp who was not, for these first few minutes, mortally afraid.

The screaming did not stop.

The orderly officer and the guard commander had between them mustered the reserves and deployed them immediately behind the wire; the officer was now trying to locate the C.O. in case there should be special emergency orders. In the constantly shifting beam of light it was difficult to find one's way among the huts; their distorted shadows swung across the ground and night shapes became hallucinatory.

Sergeant Proctor was leaving his quarters in search of his platoon commander, Lt Millburn. He wasn't on duty but must hold himself available to interpret whatever orders were issued; he didn't expect there would be any, as yet. This was the kind of situation where action could be explosive; whatever you did would be dangerous. He was still shaking with fear disguised as anger; he had been dozing off in his bed when the screaming had begun; shocked awake he had found himself standing with his back to the hut wall and his hands spread flat against it, not knowing how he had got there. It was as if the camp had been a ship moving at full speed through a calm sea, with all in order, and had suddenly hit a rock, its timbers screaming and glass smashing and the night turned bedlam.

He hadn't minded the drums; they'd begun quietly and there'd been time to reason; he could put up with a certain amount of noise so long as he knew what it was. But this collision of sound against the senses had withered him and left him shaking and he had run from the hut into the fullness of it because his fear expressed itself as anger and anger must attack. When the search-light came on he saw the Vendettu and stood still, watching the beam ripple across their frenzied movement as they danced in the orange dust, their feet stamping and their arms flailing and their hands fluttering like mad birds held captive, their heads thrown back with the scream coming out of them, the awful scream that was worse than the drums because it was alive; and as the beam swept round he saw that the camp was encircled; he could see no gaps anywhere; wherever the light fell they were there, the Vend'u—not men any more but a thing, a monster from a nightmare; and the thought flashed into his mind: *it's eating us alive*.

It came to him that he wasn't thinking straight, and he moved on, aware that he must find the lieutenant or Captain Jones; but he had reached the main guard-post before he knew where he was going, because here was the nearest machine-gun and he wanted it in his hands; it was the only thing that would stop the screaming and he wanted to see them going down like reaped corn and lie there quiet.

The voice came over the loudspeaker again and two officers met below the light-beam, one of them pointing. Lt Keene was shouting for the guard commander. The orders were filtering through and those men who could hear the loudspeaker were coming away from the barbed wire and re-forming near the guard-post. Torches were flashing as platoon leaders tried to muster their groups at strategic points: the C.O.'s orders were that it should be assumed that a physical assault would follow the war-chant, and the perimeter sentries and reserve guard were being called back from the wire so that if the machine-guns opened up there would be a clear field.

An N.C.O. looked at his watch as the beam swept overhead. It was seven minutes since the screaming had started. He was already incapable of remembering the time, eight minutes ago, when there had been silence.

One of the men who had fired in panic as the Vendettu had rushed the wire was standing alone against a hut wall with his head rocking in his hands because noise is a special thing that attacks the nerves, and its penetration is most acute in the higher register.

Someone was raising his rifle and a man near him knocked the barrel down, shouting to him. The dust enveloped them, drifting from the camp boundary, and turned yellow above them as the searchlight beam swung through it.

The screaming did not stop.

At No. 3 machine-gun post a figure emerged from the dust-cloud and pushed the guard away and a new sound came into the night as the gun opened up and followed the swinging beam, and where the shot went stitching through the wire the screaming became suddenly more shrill and then died away as the dark dancers began falling.

CHAPTER SEVEN

THE camp was quiet. The searchlight had been turned off but there were torches on the move and some of the main lamps were burning.

Minutes ago the last sounds had become faint as the Vendettu had streamed from the wire in a crescent wave, joining and running south into the thickest part of the bush; they had flown chattering like starlings disturbed from a tree. The bright dust was settling, thinning under the lamps. The air was as still as after the passing of a storm.

No one wanted to break the new silence; they wanted only to listen to it. Even the loudspeaker was subdued.

' "A" Company to stand by and keep to their present positions. "B" Company retire to quarters with as little noise as possible. Blackout orders are again in force and will be strictly observed—repeat—strictly observed. Medical parties report immediately to the main gates.'

The last of the lights began going out in groups and a man called: 'Taffy, where are you?'

As 'B' Company fell out and made their way to the huts there was the sound of engines from the vehicle park. Two ambulances moved up to the main gates and halted for the medical crews to board them. An armoured car led them through the gates and another followed; both turned and stood off as the ambulances kept close along the wire and pulled up in the sector where the machine-gun had been fired.

A voice called from somewhere near the centre of the camp: 'Blackout, there!'

Men coughed as they blundered towards the 'B' Company huts, the dust in their throats.

'Taffy, where are you, mate?'

Someone laughed softly.

Outside the wire the M.O. directed the stretcher-parties, using his torch to distinguish the dead from the wounded. There was no moaning from among the prone bodies though he could see that some were in great pain; the tribal African had not learned the idea of sympathy, even for his brother, and made no sounds to evoke it. The unscathed had fled without a thought for the fallen: there was the sun and there was the moon; there was life and there was death; one had a brother, then one had no brother; it was the way of the lion and of the hyena, and here it was also the way of man. Major Ward, shining his torch into dead eyes and into eyes that still had recognition, knew that few if any of these people would be alive by morning; even those with only a flesh-wound would die, even though he would take out the bullet and show it to them, telling them it had no more power over them—look, he would throw it into the rubbish-vessel, so worthless was it; but in the morning they would be dead, their wound still clean and uninfected. They would die because they believed they would die, having been hit by a bullet; to save them you would need a *mundumugu* in a monkey-skin cloak with his red and black beans and his cowrie shells, the eye of a goat and the heart of a ram and the dried blood of an oryx; these things could exorcise the *thahu* of the bullet and they would live. Send for a panel of the world's most brilliant surgeons—fly them from

Rome and Paris, London and Geneva and ask them to do a job that any good student could do with his eyes shut—and the patient would die. Then make an autopsy and you'd find nothing wrong, because the spirit left no scars.

He stooped over them, looking into their eyes.

'Foster! Here's another one.'

'Right, sir. *Stretcher!*'

Occasionally the M.O. straightened up and listened, watching the black horizon of the bush against the stars. There'd been several hundred of these chaps and if they came back at a rush he'd rather be inside the wire again. If they came at all it wouldn't be to pick up their dead—these bodies here were already forgotten, as a dead kitten is forgotten by its mother; there was simply no understanding that anything was different. Then how the hell could you expect them to feel it was wrong to creep into the camp and kill a man in the dark and hack off his genitals and cut out his heart? (The heart of Private Timms had been taken from the body: they would eat it as a ritual so that the power of the white warrior would pass into their own body and give them strength.)

The ambulances started up and turned, going slowly back to the gates on dipped lights.

He heard a man say: 'Only one on each stretcher, George.' They had begun shifting the dead.

'What's the difference? They're only fucking cattle.'

And how the hell could you expect the white warriors to respect an enemy who had left Mackenzie's head stuck on a post and Timms with his eyes cut out? How many proud British soldiers of the 4th Royals would do the same to a Vendettu in their anger if they could catch one in the camp? Not many; but some would; there would be some. If asked, he could list their names. And would they be right or wrong? Wrong, of course. The white civilizations shouldn't do such things. Dresden and Coventry and Hiroshima were different, as everyone knew.

'All right, Foster, that's the lot.'

He was sweating hard and could feel the dust caked along his eyelids.

'Is that Mr Keene over there?'

'I think so, sir.'

Major Ward went across to him. 'There's only the dead left. Why not pile them on your two cars and save my ambulances coming back? If those buggers decide to make another rush we'll be better off in camp.'

'We can deal with any attack, sir, providing we're unencumbered.'

The M.O. grunted and left him. Master Keene didn't want any nasty dirty bodies in his nice clean armoured cars even if it was the obvious thing to be done. Couldn't say anything—the men were listening. He told Foster to look after the business and began walking to the main gates because there was a lot to do and he'd need a shower to start with. (*But if they're going to die anyway it won't matter if the dirt infects their wounds.* Quite true, but wash before work, must always observe the ritual.)

He had counted nineteen wounded and fifteen dead; No. 3 M.G. post had a fixed vector of 50 degrees, otherwise casualties would have been heavier. It was long before midnight yet but it would take him till dawn to deal with the wounded and he'd be wasting his time; it wouldn't matter how careful he was, how clean.

The guard gave him the salute as he walked through the gates. The ambulances were coming back over the rough ground, their lights sending his shadow leaping and jigging against the wall of the guard-post.

Then why not fetch down the flag and put it round his shoulders, send to the cook-house for some chicken claws and giblets, recite a bit of Kipling while he made some magic for them? *It would work, it would bloody well work.* He'd save most of them that way. He was meant to be a healer, wasn't he? Then why the hell not? Because he was a civilized white man and it wouldn't do. Teach the backward nations how to run machines and finally how to make an anti-anti-anti-missile missile, but don't stoop to their own primitive standards or you'd revert to a savage. Let them die of their own faiths if they won't have yours. Right or wrong? It was hard to make up your mind a thousand miles from anywhere in the dark of the African bush; better not to think too much; better to surround yourself with a barbed-wire hedge and sit with your back to it.

The ambulances passed him and he squinted against the dust. Cpl Foster would have things organized by the time he'd taken a shower. There was no hurry.

Better not to think; but that was difficult. There was going to be a lot of thinking done because of what had happened tonight—but it wouldn't be his job to do it, thank God. That was for others, the official thinkers. But unofficially, what was the real answer? That bloody-minded idiot—whoever he was— who had grabbed that gun and let it rip because he couldn't stand any more of it: was he right or wrong? Wrong, because he'd done it against orders. Fair enough—he was for the chopper. And if, a few weeks ago, orders had been received to wipe out the Vendettu terror groups to a man—and such orders might well be received a few weeks from now—then that bloody-minded idiot wouldn't be doing wrong. He'd be doing right, because it was orders. And those orders . . . would *they* be right or wrong?

Leave that one to the official thinkers; they'd produce an answer even if it looked like a double rupture. It wasn't his job, thank God, to think. His job was to succour nineteen men in pain, beginning now: wash off the dirt and disinfect the hands, choose the correct scalpels and make the correct incisions and extract the foreign bodies according to the established techniques while the thing that was left inside them, out of reach of his knife, went on quietly killing them off.

Dobbs asked: 'Where the hell's Taffy, then?'

They had found their way back to the hut through the new darkness and Cpl Bruce stayed at the door so that no one put the lights on till they were all in. They were most of them quiet, even Jamie Cleaver. Rickman, who said things only when he had to, gave Spragge a light. 'That did me good. Christ, that did me good.'

They stood together facing each other, the light of the small flame on their faces; then Rickman lit his own cigarette and they moved apart but not far. The bruise on Rickman's jaw-line had almost gone but he still felt it when he shaved. Since the day it had happened he often found himself near Spragge, or Spragge near him, when there was talk on; but they never said much to each other.

Cleaver groped for his bed-space and sat down. He wished it had never happened. They were a lot of heathen bastards and they'd done for Kennie and Timms and others besides and they'd do it again if you didn't watch out. This'd teach them to plague the life out of good men, come hammering their bloody drums and yelling at the wire—by God, they'd asked for this. But he wished it had never happened.

He heard the corporal at the doorway. 'Come on, Tewson, don't hang about.' Bruce was always getting at Tewson of late.

Spragge leaned against the wall in the dark; he couldn't think properly sitting down, not now anyway. By a bit of luck he'd seen the whole show and he wouldn't have missed it for a fortune, the way the sound of it had gone cracking into the noise they

were making—*chuk-chuk-chuk-chuk*—he'd never forget it, all
the colours too, their faces daubed with white and the palms of
their hands pink in the light of the long bright beam as it swung
across them, the shine on the black of their bodies—there'd been
the flick of silver flying into the beam and keeping pace with it
as it turned, and the wire coils had quivered when some of the
bullets had hit them—he'd seen everything, every little detail,
maybe because the shock of the gun had brought all his senses
jumping alive—the colours had been so bright, almost artificial,
and the red had come springing through the wound in one
whitened face, it was like an egg breaking, he remembered
thinking it. And the sounds of the gun and their voices. When
the sound of the gun had hit the sound of their voices, the
screaming had risen suddenly like an engine freed of the load
and revving out of control and breaking up. And the rich hot
smell of the gun: there was no mistaking that smell because
when it got into the air you knew that things were real, that
there was life and death about. He'd not seen the gun or the
gunner because he couldn't look away from the swinging light
and the colours. Someone said it was one of the blokes off his
rocker.

Standing, thinking, half-listening to Bruce getting the others
in, he knew it hadn't been the Vend'u he'd hated so much;
they were cattle, animals, a murderous bunch who'd have your
balls off as soon as look at you; they'd died on the wire like
flies on a fly-paper, not even knowing much about it—the wogs
were like that. No, it was that stupid sod of a C.O. he'd been
thinking about when the bullets were going in, and that's why
he'd enjoyed it. Children, were they? Then you want to look
after them better, mate, wipe their arses for them and keep them
out of harm's way. You've us to reckon with now.

He could see the silhouette of Rickman's head in profile
against the open doorway. 'Rick.' The head turned. 'Who was
it on the gun?'

'I never saw.'

Rickman had been one of the last out of the hut; he took his
time these days when he could. The gun had been sounding
off before he'd found the No. 2 Platoon assembly point and
all he'd seen was the Vend'u swarming away, still screaming but
only in fright now, more like birds twittering. It hadn't been
orders, he knew that—you mustn't harm a hair of their heads.
The boy on the gun must have started firing before he knew
what he was doing, just got trigger-happy. He'd get no gong for

that. He'd shown what you could do if you wanted to, just with one M.G. There must have been three-hundred-odd Vend'u round the wire and most of them had got away; it didn't make sense. No need to ask what Captain Carey would have done if he'd been in charge of this unit; you wouldn't see a black arse for miles after tonight. All right, you fuckers, there's three hundred of you cooled off for a start—any more for tomorrow? You wouldn't need two miles of wire round the place—truck it back to H.Q. and send in the rations instead. But there was no one in charge here with any sense. The only one to show any sense was the boy on the gun and he'd get no medal for it.

But it had been good while it lasted. He felt now as he did when he was at the back of the truck on the Tit Patrol and the camp got small in the distance: as if he'd just had a woman.

The corporal said: 'Come on, Taffy,' and shut the door, putting the lights on.

Every man was in his own bed-space; they had found their way in the dark through the hut, knowing where they were by the feel of an obstacle—a kit-bag, sand-bucket, pair of boots. Their own bed-space was the only home they had, the only place where their existence was real because of the biscuits Mum had sent and the fag-tin with the bent lid and the letter from Betty; everywhere else they were a number. The bed-space was very personal to them, but now they came into the aisle that ran the length of the hut and gathered towards the end where the door was, and where Cpl Bruce had his space.

'Taffy, where the hell did you get to?'

Dobbs was always worrying about him; they lived almost next door to each other in Bristol and their families met at the whist-drives, and Mrs. Williams had asked Mrs Dobbs if Nobby could kind of look after her boy a bit, like, since they'd be together and Dylan was easily led. Nobby was older, nearly twenty-one, and took his responsibility seriously. The trouble was that Taff was far from being easily led—you could never damned well find him.

'I saw them take him away.' His eyes were deep with the drama of it and he looked from one to another of them.

Dobbs asked: 'Take who away?'

'Sergeant Proctor. It was him who fired the gun, didn't you know?'

Corporal Bruce turned from checking the blackouts and came over. 'You sure about that?'

Taffy swept off his cap as if taking the oath. 'I was there, Corp!'

Bruce looked at the others. 'Who else knew it was the sergeant?'

Some of them had known, had seen it happen; now they wished they'd spoken up, first with the news; they believed everyone had known.

Tewson said quietly, 'Good God.'

Rickman said: '*Proctor?*'

There fell a silence and in the silence Taffy said: 'Awful, it was.' He didn't mean the shooting; there'd been something natural in that. There were ten of those guns set up round the camp and they were manned every night by the guard in case of trouble; tonight there'd been trouble enough with hundreds of savages rushing at the place screaming—another minute and they'd have got through the wire, and then what? No, it was what happened after the shooting that he couldn't get out of his mind: Mr Keene running up and shouting at the guard to hold the sergeant. A lot more people were milling about asking questions and no one seemed to know what to do. And there was Sgt Proctor getting up from the gun and standing and looking at nobody, very tall in the dust and the flickering light, taller than any of them and the only one not excited.

'*Take that N.C.O.!*' Mr Keene had shouted. (Why hadn't he used his proper name? Everyone knew Sgt Proctor.) '*Take him to the guardroom!*' And when two of them got him by the arms he shook them off, saying not to touch him, and although he spoke quiet it sounded louder than Mr Keene's shouting. Awful, it was, because Sergeant Proctor was a different person in that minute. *Mark . . . time! One two—one two—keep your dressing, that man! Le-eft right, le-eft right—come along then heads up chins tucked in—one two—one two—squad . . . halt! Still, now! Stand-at—ease! No talking, now. Williams, fall out and do up your boot-lace!* That was Sgt Proctor, put you through it but never swore at you, never made you a laughing-stock whatever you did, just told you not to do it again and that was that. He was a drill sergeant. Ask anyone what Proctor was and they'd tell you he was a drill sergeant. Now all that was gone and he was a man in trouble. '*Take that N.C.O.!*' And Taffy had almost cried out: 'But that's Sergeant Proctor!'

Then of a sudden he was moving away from the machine-gun, going with them, and Mr Keene and the others yapping around him like dogs and not daring so much as to snap at his heels. They weren't taking him to the guardroom. He was taking them.

Taffy had stood for a long time, his mind hushed by it. The

others were going back to their huts but he stayed where he was; he didn't want their company. The lights were nearly all out now, and when the last one went off it was like a big coloured picture going dark, a picture of Sgt Proctor with his chevrons and medal ribbons, tall on the parade-ground, tall as the flagpost and as straight and hard and unknowable. Now it was dark and over there through the dust went a man only just come alive, a man in trouble whom Taffy wished, until his eyes stung, that he could help.

CHAPTER EIGHT

'WHAT exactly happened?' asked Millburn.

The M.O. didn't answer for a minute. Everyone was asking him what had happened, because he was expected to know; but he didn't.

'I don't know,' he said.

Captain Jones stared into his glass. There was another fly in his drink and he wondered whether the damned thing had shat in it yet because if it hadn't he could fish it out and carry on. If he fished it out and carried on and it *had* shat in it he'd spend all next week in the bog again with dysentery. Better not take the chance; there'd be more to do next week in this place than sit in the bog. He said to the steward, 'Chuck it down the drain and give me another. Bloody aeroplane.'

There were only the three of them in the mess bar. It was too hot for lunch, too hot to breathe; every time you moved you broke out in sweat. Jones wondered how the flies managed to get about; it made you sweat just to watch their energy.

'But you've talked to him,' Millburn persisted.

Major Ward nodded. 'I've talked to him, but he hasn't talked to me. Not to any effect.' The C.O. had asked him to go across to the guardroom first thing this morning and he'd spent half an hour trying to get into Proctor's mind. Proctor's mind was shut, like his face.

'I'm not sure,' Ward had told him carefully, 'what the general procedure is going to be; the C.O. hasn't set it out for me, and frankly it might be because he doesn't know either. On the face of it you've disobeyed orders and knocked off a few wogs; there were plenty of witnesses and I don't suppose you're going to deny it.'

He paused in the hope that Proctor would have something

to say, but he said nothing, standing punctiliously at ease and looking into the middle distance. 'Look, I wish you'd sit down as I ask. The door's shut and we can behave like two grown men with a problem to sort out.'

The sergeant sat on the end of the metal bed but still couldn't relax. Ward didn't think it was anything to do with his being in the presence of an officer; Proctor didn't seem to feel he was in conflict with him, except inasmuch as he was in conflict with everything and everybody.

'The first thing I've got to ask you officially is whether you'll submit to a physical examination.'

'I'm fit, sir.'

That was probably true. Proctor's eyes were bloodshot and his face more hollow than ever but that would be from lack of sleep. Ward looked like that himself just now, after a night at the operating-table.

'I've got to put it on the line, Sergeant. Do you refuse an examination?'

'I'm the fittest man in this unit.' Then he seemed to appreciate the question. 'I refuse, sir.'

'Very well. Second thing is, how were you feeling last night at the time when you had the urge to fire the gun?'

Proctor was a long while answering and the M.O. couldn't decide whether he was thinking about his situation or trying to work things out as he went along.

'Normal, sir.'

So that was it. Ward wasn't surprised. It fitted what he knew of the man's character: he was going to face what he had to face without any dodging, without making it easy for himself. The nuisance of it was that he'd be making things difficult for everyone else as well.

'Since the unit was sent out to this Godforsaken hole,' Ward told him, 'I've had quite a few people come to me with every sign of going troppo. I don't just mean browned-off—we're all of us that. We've had a hell of a lot to put up with apart from the heat——'

'I've not weakened. I'm fit, normal and——'

'It's not a question of weakening, you see. It's a question of becoming disorientated, losing our sense of place and direction and especially our sense of purpose.' He got up and leaned with his hands flat against the cool wall, one of the few concrete walls in the camp. The chair was going to collapse the next time someone sat on it anyway; it was like the rest of the furniture in this place. 'I'm not talking about you, but about all of us. This unit's all right. Given a decent chance of a battle on open ground it wouldn't weaken sooner than any other unit. But we're bottled up. We've got an enemy but we're not allowed to take a crack at him. We thought it would be all right when the dannert coils arrived—at least the buggers couldn't creep in and murder us one by one if we were surrounded with barbed wire. But it's worse, isn't it? The stuff wasn't there five minutes before we realized that. You particularly, Proctor. That wire isn't keeping them out—it's keeping us in. We're not just confined to camp now—we're in a cage.'

He stood away from the wall and took a pace or two, not meeting the man's eyes, cursing himself, blaming it on fatigue. It had been a stupid slip to make; Proctor was in the smallest cage of the lot.

'And it's hit our pride whether we realize it consciously or not. It doesn't matter how often we're told that we're instrumenting political policy and taking our part in African affairs; we know what we are—rats in a trap. And there's nothing we can do now except hope to God we get the orders through to hit back at these bastards who——'

He broke off but it was too late again. Proctor's tone was quiet: 'Maybe we'll all feel a bit better now.'

Ward looked at him. Was that the suspicion of a smile on the man's face? No, it was the habitual set of his mouth, he knew that. But Proctor was smiling, inside where it didn't show. There wasn't a man in this unit who wouldn't have given a month's pay to get behind that gun last night and let them have it where it hurt, and when Proctor had done it he'd done it for all of them. That wouldn't have been his reason but it made no difference. That had been his act.

'I suppose there's nothing,' asked Ward, 'that you'd like to tell me before I go?'

'No, sir.'

'You may wish later that you'd given yourself a break. Just one break. The C.O. may be able to keep this incident quiet to some extent; he values a senior N.C.O. with twenty-seven years' service and a record like yours. But if the Vendettu leaders decide to make a political issue of it Colonel Gray won't be able to do much, and if it comes to a court martial your defending counsel's going to have a bigger chance of helping you if you've prepared the ground for him.' He was suddenly impatient—'Damn it, I'm not asking you to lie! Just admit it was the heat and the strain of having to control men who were ready to break out in the same way. Say it was the screaming you couldn't stand—that's natural enough, isn't it?'

He saw Proctor's eyes flicker; or he imagined it.

'I shan't need any help,' he said quietly, 'at my court martial.'

Ward had put on his cap and left the cell, angry with himself for having bungled it. He'd spent all night pulling twenty-six bullets out of nineteen wogs who'd made up their minds to die anyway, and if he hadn't been so bloody tired this morning he might have handled the interview more intelligently and saved one decent English sergeant from the high jump.

He'd gone to bed for a couple of hours but hadn't slept; his room was near the square, which was hardly ever empty of men being drilled.

'But you must have some idea what made him do it,' Millburn said. '*Some* idea.'

Ward looked into his rather earnest face. The brown eyes, magnified by the glasses, were troubled. 'Why don't you go and see him yourself?'

'I doubt if the C.O. would let me. I'm only his platoon commander and anyway the C.O.'s just chewed me up.'

'Oh?'

'I suggested we set up some butts for rifle practice so that at least the men could blast off at something. He said that if the Vendettu made an attack we'd have no supply-route, so we've got to conserve ammunition. Reasonable enough, but I persisted, so he gave me a rocket——'

'Oh Christ,' said Jones with a squeaky laugh, 'that's three of us now. I've just fetched a severe rep for shooting up the livestock, Keene's on a charge for losing safe custody of a certain machine-gun, and now you've got your arse in a sling.' He looked at the M.O. 'If I were you, Doc, I'd quietly bugger off back to bed. We've got to have someone left in the good books of the all-highest.'

Ward looked into his drink. The steward on this shift was Thompson and there was nothing they couldn't say in front of him. But in principle it was dangerous to imply that the rot was spreading upwards from the lower ranks.

'*You* could see Proctor,' Millburn suddenly told Jones. 'You're his company commander.'

Jones seemed surprised. 'What good would that do?'

'You could get him to talk about it. He respects you, and if——'

'He doesn't, old boy. As far as he's concerned I'm a rather dangerous buccaneer, and he only tolerates me because I look after the troops.'

'Oh, nonsense,' Ward broke in.

'Not altogether. Anyway it's no good my going to see him because it'd only be to tell him that in my opinion he deserves a bloody medal, and I don't think that'd go down frightfully well at the court martial if he quoted me. I've got my living to earn.' He said to Ward: 'I suppose there will be a court martial?'

'We can't make any guesses at this stage. Anything can happen.' He had talked to the Colonel an hour ago.

Jones finished his drink. 'Then let's hope it won't.'

'What does "anything" mean?' asked Millburn and the M.O. looked at him quickly. Proctor's act seemed to have affected him personally, though as far as he knew there was no particular rapport between the sergeant and his platoon commander. Proctor was twice this boy's age, apart from the difference in rank.

'It means anything from summary jurisdiction by the C.O. if he can keep the lid on things, to repercussions at government level if the lid comes off.'

'I'm all for that,' said Jones.

'For what?'

'Putting a bomb in the Commons.' He nodded to the steward for another gin. 'It's the bloody politico's fault in the first place. The Army's subordinate to civilian authority, fair enough, but we're not just a bunch of lackeys. Whitehall sends us out here to shoot the place up and then tells us to put our guns away and not to be nasty. Christ, you send for the Army when you want some action, don't you? Either let them withdraw the unit and leave Kiutsho and Makarik to fight it out for themselves, or send us orders to make a punitive raid against the Vendettu to cool them off. But all they've done is to leave us frying alive in a chicken-run till one poor bloody sergeant "loses his nerve"— or that's what they'll say. In fact he's only done what he should have been ordered to do: he's made his own personal one-man punitive raid and because someone forgot to give him the correct order he's got to take the can back himself.' He looked at Millburn. 'So what's the good of my seeing him? To tell him that? He knows it.'

'Wouldn't it comfort him,' said Millburn deliberately, 'to be told that he isn't alone in his opinion?'

Jones stared at him. 'Are you off your nut? The hole unit's with him to a man and he knows that too.'

'And will we all be with him to a man when he's put on trial?' His tone had become vibrant and Major Ward noticed it. Inside this thin and awkward-looking boy there was something growing, and if it went on growing it would become bigger than himself— and there'd be another man in the guardroom. 'Or will we conveniently forget, in the meantime, that he once spoke out for us all?'

Two lines had deepened in Jones's forehead and he was no longer looking at Millburn. 'I'm not sure I follow.'

'You said just now that you wouldn't want your true opinion quoted at a court martial, because you've got your "living to earn". I can understand that. A company commander isn't expected to support an act of grave disobedience on the part of an N.C.O., whatever his private feelings. But the fact remains: you'll be no help to him when the time comes.'

The M.O. moved his eyes, studying Jones obliquely and seeing the frown deepen again. It wasn't, he thought, because Jones resented being criticised by a junior officer, or that it was being done in the hearing of the private soldier behind the bar. Any other captain would have stopped him short and chewed him up for it later; but Jones didn't worry about that kind of thing. It might have been simply because young Millburn had exposed a nerve to which Jones was sensitive.

'Please go on,' Jones said carefully.

'I'm trying to say that we're all limited by self-interest, and that's why Proctor won't get much help from anyone if it comes to a trial. The time to help him is now, while the whole unit is—as you put it—with him to a man.'

Jones swung his head and looked at him. 'The C.O. has ordered a special inquiry, so that we can find out just what happened last night. Until we've done that, I don't see what anyone can do to "help" Sergeant Proctor.' He waited patiently.

Millburn was looking at him in disbelief, as if he couldn't accept that Jones was unable to see the obvious. The M.O., watching him from over his raised glass, saw this clearly. Millburn felt he was talking to a man who stood a thousand miles away, and he didn't know how to bridge the gap.

Softly and hopelessly he said: 'But we don't need an inquiry. We know what happened last night. He killed fifteen men with a machine-gun. Now he's under close arrest, alone in a cell. If you don't think that man needs help, I can't hope to explain it.'

Jones put his drink on the bar without looking away. 'What kind of help do you suggest?'

Suddenly Millburn gave in. 'I don't know. You're his acting company commander, and you're mine. That's why I'm appealing to you. You're so much more experienced than I am. I hoped you might know something we could do for him—now, before it's too late, before we all forget.'

Jones nodded. 'I see.' Then he said what the M.O. had been wanting to say, but hadn't dared to. 'You know, Millburn, it might one day be you yourself who'll need the help, because I rather think you're stuck with something that could lead you into a lot of trouble. I believe the trick-cyclists call it "association with martyrdom".'

That morning everything looked much the same about the camp. On the parade-ground they were a sergeant short but Cpl Bruce took over and the men's precision was no worse, no better. There was even an attempt made, particularly by the officers and senior N.C.O.s, to conceal the fact that a change had come about in the fortunes of the 4th Royals.

It was in any case a change hard to define. It would be harder still for anyone to predict its long-term effects. The difference between yesterday and today was marked only in men's minds, not in their actions. Their actions remained habitual.

'Le-eft—*wheel!* Come on, swing those arms, keep 'em up, keep 'em up! Shorten the pace in front! Le-eft right—le-eft right— arms up, now, head up and chest out—you can do better than that! One two—one two—squad—*hult!*'

A carpenter was mending the split in the flagpost.

Those changes that were apparent were small. The orderly-room runner was busier on his bicycle; Capt. Jones was called away from the kit inspection in 'B' Company just before the middle-day meal and Lt Millburn took over. And there was a special order sent round for pinning on the notice-boards:

All ranks are informed that mail will be censored as from 1200 hours of this day until further orders. It may be pointed out that if no reference to events solely the concern of this unit is made in correspondence, the task of censorship will be greatly eased and letters will suffer no defacement.

'Not a bad sign,' said Tewson.

Spragge edged his way from the group round the No. 2 hut notice-board. 'You like the Adj reading your private letters?'

'If it makes life easier for Proctor it's a consolation.'

And here was the biggest change apparent in the camp: whenever men talked it was of Proctor.

'You mind spelling it out?' said Spragge. 'I'm not so sharp, remember?'

Tewson gave him a token grin. Spragge was big-bodied and slow-moving, but any lack of sharpness was an affectation. 'It just looks as if the C.O.'s decided that the glorious 4th Royals should do their dirty washing inside camp bounds, at least for the moment. Smoke?'

Spragge's hand moved and then stopped. Tewson's cigarette-case was always open and it didn't do to take advantage. 'Have one of mine.'

They passed Dobbs's bed-space. Nobby was full-length, his transistor on his stomach. They could hear the woman announcer on Radio Liz. The hut was noisier now, filling with men coming in from blister-inspection after the morning's drill.

'How's that going to help Proctor?' Spragge asked. It seemed an obvious question but he knew Tewson wouldn't mind that. Just because of his accent a lot of people—Bruce was one—thought he was talking down to you.

'It'll keep the public out of it for a start. This is a red-hot scoop for the gutter-press—*Mad Sergeant Runs Amok: Mass Slaughter of Africans in Lost British Outpost.*' He lowered his voice. 'It's worth fifty quid for anyone to send a short letter to Fleet Street just at the moment. You could ruin Proctor with a spot of prejudice in the wrong quarters. The African's coming of age at last and we're all falling over backwards to forget he ever picked our cotton for us at the end of a whip—that's why the C.O.'s hog-tied by Whitehall at the moment. So anyone shooting him down wholesale with a machine-gun won't be too popular back home.'

Spragge's face had become hard. 'I suppose they know back home that the wogs are doing their own share? Didn't the Morgan Farm massacre get into the papers last month? Christ, the way you talk—'

'Don't get me wrong, Spraggey.' Tewson gave him a very straight look. 'If I had the guts I'd clear out of here and join up with Captain Carey. I don't like the news on Radio Liz any more than you do.'

'It's not,' Spragge said, 'that you haven't got the guts. Is it?'

'Why shouldn't it be?' He disliked talking about himself; in a hut full of men, personal intimacies were public coinage in a matter of hours. But he trusted Spragge more than most.

'You just don't strike me as gutless, that's all. And what could you lose? Your career's not in this mob, I know that much.'

Tewson looked along the hut, watching the last of the men coming in, their side-arms banging against the walls and their boots coming off even before they'd reached their bed-space. He could feel the wave of heat they brought in with them; it flowed through the bottleneck between the corporal's cubicle and the store-room, and reached his skin. With the heat came the noise and the final stifling loss of privacy. There probably wasn't a man in here he didn't like, and wouldn't miss when he left the service; but he feared crowds; they threatened his self-identity.

'I want you to give it a spell,' his father had said. They were the last words of a long and fruitless argument. 'Two years and I'll buy you out. I want you to serve as a private in the ranks, and volunteer for overseas duty. Then we'll talk about putting you into the business.' There wasn't much choice. A key position in Tewson Productions was worth two years' frustration and this was the only way in.

Without knowing it Spragge was right: so long as he was roughing it somewhere his father wouldn't care whether it was in the 4th Royals or Carey's rag-bag mercenary force. It wasn't his own point of view.

'No,' he said, 'my career's not in this mob, and it's not in Captain Carey's. I don't like the sound of his outfit; I just meant I'd like to do something more useful than forming fours all day inside a barbed-wire birdcage.' He dropped some ash into the tin. 'What about you?'

The question was casual and Spragge wasn't ready for it.

'What about me?'

'You're sharper than that, Spraggey.'

'You talking about Carey's mob?'

'Yes.'

They were suddenly talking about something serious and neither had meant to start it. Tewson would have let him off the hook, but he was interested in whether Spragge was going to lie or not.

'You mean,' asked Spragge, 'would I sign up with him if I had the chance?'

'Yes.'

'We don't know what we'd do if we got the chance of doing it. No good talking, is it? It's the chance that makes us think different.' He looked at Tewson woodenly. 'That what you wanted to know?'

'I didn't want to know anything.'

Dobbs was still listening to his transistor when the orderly-room runner came with a list.

Corporal Bruce walked down the hut. 'These men report to the main gates 1400 hours, overalls and hats. Brewer, Cleaver, Dobbs, Nairsworth, Rickman, Smithers. All right?' He went back to his cubicle, pinning the list on the board.

'Issue of shovels,' someone said.

'What the bloody 'ell for?'

'Grave-digging.'

Cleaver came over to Dobbs. Rickman said: 'Are you serious?'

'Who's kicked it, then?'

'That lot last night. Or don't you remember?'

There was a silence; the only voice was on Dobbs's little radio, a Lisolaville police-chief calling the safaris.

Then a man said: 'I saw the shovels there when we was comin' off the square. Must have been fifty of 'em. Sod your luck, mates.'

Tewson was perched on Dobbs's bed trying to listen to the broadcasts, but the sight of Rickman's face drew his attention away.

'Bury their dead for them? Those fuckers?'

'What else can we do? They won't come back for them.'

Dobbs was getting off the bed, looking at Cleaver. 'Right. I'm refusing.' He was glad Taffy wasn't on the list; he'd promised to keep Taffy out of trouble.

Cleaver put his head back and eyed Dobbs along his nose. 'Refuse, can we? On what grounds?'

Rickman said: 'I'll bury 'em. Like they buried Mackenzie. Like they buried Timms. I'll want a knife, not a shovel.'

They heard the rage in his throat and Tewson knew it wasn't so much against the Vend'u; it was against the order. The insult.

Brewer looked at the others. 'Have we got a right to refuse?'

Tewson said: 'It's a fatigue, like any other. What can we do with fifteen bodies—'

'They say there's more—'

'All right, what can we do with them? Leave them to rot in the sun? We'd never sleep tonight because of the hyenas.'

'Why pick on this hut?' asked someone.

'They'll be picking them from every hut; it'll need fifty men.'

Rickman was putting his boots on. 'There's one they'll not fucking get.'

'Where are you going?' They gathered towards him.

'Reporting sick.'

'What with?'

'Wherever I look I see red. Maybe the M.O. can tell me why.' He broke a lace and began pulling the longer half through. 'If not I can tell him.'

Dobbs said: 'That's it. Report sick.' He noticed Cleaver watching him. 'You on, Jamie?'

'Ay. I'm on.' He went to find his boots.

In the end they left the hut in a group, every man on the list. Tewson stayed on Dobbs' bed, watching them go. Even Nairsworth had been moved to insurrection. You wouldn't have seen this kind of thing happen a bit earlier when even close friends had been falling out; the mood had changed and the ranks were closing and it wasn't on anyone's order. You wouldn't have seen this kind of thing happen even yesterday. The sound of these boots going down the hut was the echo of a machine-gun.

A man asked: 'What price they'll fetch themselves a malingering charge?'

No one answered. The hut had gone quiet. Until the six men came back the others wouldn't be easy in their minds.

A reconnaissance patrol of the Tamalese Army rounded up a group of forty-two terrorists of the Vendettu tribe in the Wahikima'o Reserve area this morning and held them for questioning.

'For Christ sake find some music, can't you, Tewey? Everyone's doing something except us.'

Nine Vendettu tribesmen were hanged at Lisolaville Prison yesterday. All had been sentenced for the illegal possession of firearms. Three other—

Tewson changed the wavelength. Fraser was right: there was a price to pay for listening in to the outside world; it reminded you of your own uselessness.

. . . than yesterday. Please remember that we have no means of defending ourselves and that there are seven young women working here on the medical staff.

Fraser gave a wolf-call. 'What's the address?'

Tewson cut the switch and got off the bed and Fraser saw his face and said: 'What's up, then?'

'It's the mission station again. I know a girl there, that's all.'

CHAPTER NINE

THE Regimental Sergeant-Major took the prisoner and escort into Colonel Gray's office when duty was resumed after the middle-day meal at 1400 hours, and since they were three senior N.C.O.s the words of command and the banging of boots was heard right across the camp.

'I'll see the prisoner alone, Sar'nt-major.'

'Sir! Escort, a-bout—*turn!* For-ward—*march!*'

The C.O. was standing at the window and when the door was closed he said: 'Come and stand here, Sergeant Proctor.'

The windows were open and they heard the orders from the main gates as the working-party of forty men was drawn up and moved away. The blades of the shovels glinted in the sunshine until the dust began clouding up from their feet.

'They are going to dig graves.' The Colonel didn't turn his head to look at the sergeant; he looked out at the marching column. 'I would like to know how you feel about that.'

In the distance a spade touched another and the bell-like note rang clearly above the rough rhythm of boots.

'Dead men have got to be buried, sir.' There was no compromise in Proctor's tone.

Colonel Gray turned to him now. 'It means nothing to you beyond that?'

'No, sir.' He'd been given no order to move so he remained looking through the window. Although he stood with his shoulder turned to the C.O. he was aware of the Colonel's scrutiny. The silence lasted only a few seconds but he felt the resentment rising quickly and knew that if the silence went on much longer he'd speak up and break it and wouldn't watch what he said. It felt like a fever suddenly racing through his body and up into his head; it had felt like this last night when he'd gone close to the gun.

'I'll tell you what it means to me,' the Colonel said at last. 'This evening we shall bury some dead men. We shall bury also our last chance of acquitting ourselves well in a difficult campaign.' He left the window. 'Stand easy, Sergeant.' In a moment he said: 'You appear surprised at the use of the word "campaign". Yet that word is used advisedly. Our detachment of the 4th Royals was sent here to campaign against the spread of violence, to show the world that a force of three hundred and fifty soldiers fully armed with modern weapons is capable of standing its ground, impervious to the most ugly provocation, immune to the most calculated acts of intimidation and steadfast in its resolve to carry out its allotted task until those in authority can release it from its long travail.'

As he sat behind his desk the sergeant was able to look at him fully, and saw how worn he had become in the last twenty-four hours. He'd never seen the C.O. like this, and it struck him that the Colonel was older than he'd thought.

'Take that chair, Sar'nt Proctor.'

Through the open windows drifted the far sound of the shovels breaking earth.

Proctor sat down and folded his arms, watching the older man moving the silver snuff-box an inch aside and clasping his hands on the desk.

'Do you really believe,' asked Gray, 'that I am not prepared to order this unit to open fire against a thousand unarmed men, to slaughter them where they stand until not one remains, if it will profit, in the eyes of God, the safety of England? Do you believe that what happened to Radford and Mackenzie and Timms left me indifferent, that there was no sorrow in me, no anger, no pain for them? They were Englishmen!' His hands moved once, and Proctor saw how tightly they were held together. 'And they were in my care.' He paused to stare at the sergeant and then spoke more quickly. 'And what would you have me do? Avenge those Englishmen by killing an equal number of Vendettu tribesmen, one for Radford, one for Mackenzie, one for Timms? But which ones? Those that murdered them? Which ones were they? Or should we have simply shot a dozen, or a score, or fifty, in reprisal, as the Nazis did when there was murder done among them? I think that is what you would have had me do, since that is what you did yourself.'

He got up and paced from the desk to the windows and back. 'Since your act of last night there has been an unceasing exchange of signals between this unit, Brigade Headquarters and the War Office. The Foreign Office has been informed and the Prime Minister is being kept in touch with events. Those events are political. General Kiutsho knows of course that the British Army in Tamala has opened fire upon a group of unarmed Africans loyal to his party. No one can say what he may do. It has been his policy, so far, to sanction the efforts of the Vendettu forces to undermine our morale and persuade us to leave Tamala. It may now become his policy to oust us by force, using for his

excuse the unwarranted attack made on those tribesmen last night
—an attack, Sergeant Proctor, of which you were the sole author.'

Proctor lifted his head a little but didn't look up at the C.O.
Outside the building the heat of the afternoon lay over the camp;
for the next two hours there was no drill period and the square
was empty. All they could hear was the digging.

'The Vendettu tribe numbers four thousand warriors. Four
thousand. We number about three hundred in this camp. Supposing that our barbed wire and machine-guns and rifles gave us
superiority enough to repel the first wave of a massed attack by
night and we killed a thousand of them—suppose we killed
double that number, treble that number. The odds against us
would still be more than three to one, even if they inflicted not
a single casualty. Do I need to go on? You're an experienced
soldier and you know what the outcome would be. Within a
matter of hours this detachment of the 4th Royals would cease
to exist.'

He stood over the sergeant, allowing the silence to go on.
Proctor sat listening to the sounds from outside, to the tick of
the silver clock on the desk, to the Colonel's breathing and to
his own. Then he got to his feet.

'Permission to leave, sir?'

Gray's face went blank.

'To leave?'

'Yes, sir.'

The Colonel's voice was hushed. 'Before I give you permission
to leave here I would suffer you to make an answer.'

Sergeant Proctor stood correctly at ease but he looked Gray
directly in the eyes instead of two inches above his head. 'There
wasn't a question, sir, was there?'

The C.O. showed little in his face; he simply looked tired of
the struggle to explain the enormity of what this N.C.O. had
done. Certainly there was no anger in his eyes. Proctor had never
seen him roused to anger.

'If what I have said to you, Sergeant, leaves you without any
wish to answer, I shall call the escort. Is that what you want?'

'Yes, sir.'

On a sudden thought Gray said: 'The escort was dismissed
when you came in here so that you could speak freely to me.
Perhaps I should remind you of that.'

'I appreciate it, sir, but there's nothing I want to say. We've
all heard about the situation out here and what we're meant to
do; you've told us often enough. The politicians've got a job on,

running with one bunch o' wogs while they make out they're running with the other; it's not easy for them, I can quite see that, but it's not easy for us either, because there's one thing they didn't allow for when they told us to grin and bear it—the poor bloody infantry's made up of human beings and we've got human instincts. You say you want my answer, but I'm not good at talking and there's nothing I want to add to what I said last night.'

'Last night?'

'When I took over the gun. That was my answer, and it still is.'

There was one other thing that nobody had allowed for, and Proctor thought about it again when he was back in the guard-room. He didn't blame anyone; nobody could allow for something they didn't know existed. It was nothing concrete; it was a situation—his own. He hadn't known about it himself, consciously, until he'd fired the gun; but afterwards he had wondered if that was something to do with it—with his firing the gun.

The situation in which Sergeant James Norman Proctor found himself at the age of forty-seven could be put into one short phrase: he had nothing to lose.

When this can be said of a man it means either that he never had anything or that whatever he had he has lost. With Proctor it was both. The biggest thing he had ever had was a family, and he had lost it piecemeal over the last six years. It was six years ago, almost to the day, when his daughter had got married; he had seen her only twice since then because it was painful for all of them to meet and they settled for that. He wasn't the first father who'd made up his mind that his only daughter had made a disastrous marriage. Three years ago his son had gone out to Canada and was still there and still wrote regularly and sent pictures of his wife, who was very pretty. He had come to London only once. The last time Proctor had seen his son and his daughter was at the funeral of his wife.

That was just over two years ago. He had been happy with Olive for what had then been exactly half his lifetime and that was something he could never lose; but it was nothing he could do anything with; it could never be lost but it was finished.

It had been the biggest thing, and the only thing. The rest wasn't a possession but a background, and a background doesn't belong to a man: he belongs to it. It is not anything that can be lost, but only changed. For twenty-seven years Proctor's background had been the Army; now that was going to change.

In the later hours of last night he had thought about this and
had wondered whether he would have fired that gun if he'd had
anything to lose by it; because it had been an irresponsible action.
And he had worked it out, right or wrong, that you can be
irresponsible only when you know—without having to think
about it—that there's nobody dependent on you.

Colonel Gray would say that in the Army an entire regiment
depended on the loyalty and conduct of any one private soldier
who belonged to it; but Gray said a lot of things like that and
certainly believed in them because he wanted them to be true. It
might be a good thing if they were true; the fact was that they
weren't.

There would already have been a signal sent: one sergeant no
longer available for duty, please replace.

All he had to think about now was his own future. It was going
to be different from his past: he was not proud of his past. Any
man still a sergeant after a quarter of a century wasn't in it for
a career. When he'd joined up there'd been barrage balloons
over Hampstead Common and everyone was enjoying the novelty,
till Dunkirk. Six years later he'd meant to put on his civvies but
there was no job he knew how to do, except soldiering. So he'd
soldiered on, and twenty-one years after that he was sitting in a
guardroom with stripes on his arm and a thought in his head:
I've got nothing to lose.

And certainly nothing to gain. They were going to give him
a fair chance, a full court martial with all the trimmings, and
Colonel Gray would say what an exceptional N.C.O. he'd been
and the Doc would say that when three or four hundred savages
screamed their heads off at a man it was liable to affect his nerves
so much that he didn't know what he was doing—by God, he
wouldn't have that!

He stood up suddenly so he could feel tall again.

No thank you, he'd give his own answers.

*Despite the confusion at the time, Sergeant Proctor, you may
have had some definite reason for doing what you did. Can you
tell us what was in your mind? Or was it—as Major Ward has
suggested—wholly the result of the assault on your nerves—'*

'*It got my blood up, sir. Nothing to do with nerves.'*

'*Yes, quite. But apart from your emotions, was there any clear
thought in your mind, any definite reason—'*

'*There's reason in anger, to my way of thinking. If we'd shown
a bit more anger earlier on when they first started on us the way
they did—'*

'*Sergeant Proctor, I am not asking you to judge the handling of the situation by your superiors—*'

'*I'm doing it just the same. If they'd handled things differently there'd never have been any reason for me to fire that gun, and that's what we're talking about, isn't it? That's what I'm here for —to tell you why I did it. And there's my answer: because nobody else would.*'

Maybe they wouldn't let him go on as he pleased. He'd marched enough men in on a charge to know that the best thing was to say you were sorry, and hope to get off light. But whether they gave him a fair chance or no, he was going to get it where the chicken got the chopper.

The Glasshouse, it'd be. Five years? Ten? It'd make no odds. In twenty-odd years you got to know a bit about the Glasshouse; you met men who'd been there. The public never heard about that place, didn't know it existed—there was always plenty in the papers about the civvy prisons, yes, but never the Glasshouse.

Not for Jim Proctor. He'd take his own way out.

It was quiet in the camp, when you listened: two M.P.s talking in the main guardroom, very low; a bin being scraped out in the cook-house, some way off; and the noise of the shovels.

He went to the barred window. Through the dust-haze he could see some of the working-party on the far side of the wire.

Dig one for me, mates. Dig one for me.

CHAPTER TEN

THEY had met in a filthy teashop near the native quarter a week before the patrols had been withdrawn from the town. Coming off duty he had wanted to quench his thirst; the bars would be crowded at this hour so he had come to this place, propping his submachine-gun in a corner where a cockroach ran. He preferred it to the company of men, even of those men he liked well enough; he shared a hut with them most of his days and all his nights and he didn't want to stand jammed together with them trying to get a beer when there were places like this, even places like this.

There was no one but the Indian proprietor and a huge African with ritual burns on his arms and a dozen cheap fountain-pens stuffed like medals in the pocket of his bush-shirt; he grinned enormously at his beloved brother the British soldier, who sat within immediate reach of the submachine-gun; given the least chance the African would catapult across the room and try to beat him to it. The Vend'u were desperate for guns.

Then she came in and it obviously wasn't by mistake; she just asked for a long mint fizz and sat down, saying something in Swahili to the African, who grinned absent-mindedly and stared at the gun again. The Indian came over with her drink and slapped the table-top with his hippo-tail to send the flies away, and when she lifted her glass Tewson took up his own and said: 'Cheers.'

Her smile was quick and she talked so easily that he could soon ask: 'Do you often come into this kind of place?'

'More often than the other kind. I like people but not by the thousand.' Seeing his smile she asked: 'Is that funny?'

'No. Rare.'

While they talked he wondered if she were pretty; sometimes she was, he thought, but it was nothing to do with her face; it was the changing light in her eyes; they expressed everything, spoken and unspoken. She'd be dull on a telephone; you'd only catch half her meaning.

Someone passed the doorway, someone the African knew; he went out with a big white beautiful grin. Tewson finished his drink, freezing his throat, and said: 'I've got to be going.'

'Good-bye, then.'

If it hadn't been for the way she expressed everything with her eyes he would have gone. What she had said without saying it was: Do I smell or something?

'There's a bit of trouble coming,' he told her.

'I didn't ask.'

'I know.'

One African couldn't do anything against a submachine-gun but he'd caught sight of a tribal brother and gone out to tell him to bring reinforcements. Even a dozen of them couldn't do anything against a submachine-gun without some getting killed, but that wouldn't worry them: the survivors would have the gun. It often happened, especially with the Tamalese troops, who were careless.

'What sort of trouble?' she asked him. 'Are you going to make it or just invite it?'

He shouldered the sling of the gun. 'Avoid it.'

She deliberately drained her glass. 'Don't I need your protection?'

He nearly said she'd be all right if she stayed here, because it was true. She was making the running and he didn't like that; he always preferred to make it himself. Then suddenly—because of her eyes again—he saw that she had meant it. Behind the casual attitude, the indifferent set of the head, the calm mouth, she was afraid; she really thought she needed his protection.

He said: 'Of course you do.'

They went out together into the narrow street and he told her to walk in front of him where he could see her; there was no risk now because he could pick out the shoulder-flashes everywhere —this street was fully patrolled at all hours until curfew; but if she felt better for his 'protection' it was a small enough concession.

They reached one of the main avenues and talked for a while under one of the scraggy water-starved trees, and he asked where she was staying. It was a hostel near the Lisolaville Medical Institute, and three days later he was passing it on patrol and remembered her, and decided not to try seeing her again because she wasn't his type, and went to the hostel as soon as he came off duty because if she still felt frightened he might be able to reassure her in some way.

They talked in the garden: a square made of board fence with a few bushes. He didn't remember, the next day, what they had talked about. There had been orders on the notice-board in No. 2 hut that evening: all street-patrols were to be withdrawn from the town and off-duty evening passes were to be discontinued, reference all ranks. In short the unit was henceforth confined to camp. It was known (as everything immediately became known) that Capt. Jones had asked the C.O. whether people could not go into the town in their civilian clothes and unarmed, as the unit was under no 'alert' or even 'readiness' orders. The suggestion was rejected on the grounds that most members of the unit were recognizable in the town by their faces alone, and since the 4th Royals were in Tamala partly to 'show the flag' they must not be seen in public divested of the authority inherent in their uniform.

There were three trucks going into Liz the next day to collect and bring back mobile barricade-sections that were the property of the Crown, and Tewson wangled a place among the work crews simply as a private gesture against the curtailment of freedom. Just the same, there was a chance of passing the hostel on foot, and he had the luck to find her there.

'We're pulling out of the town,' he said.

'You'll miss the life here.'

'Yes.'

She said: 'I'm leaving, too, in a few days.'

He knew she was here on short leave from the White Cross
Mission station in the north province.

His truck was coming past the entrance of the hostel, the
driver dabbing the throttle to clear a path through the merchants
and Tamalese troops—the local army was here in force now that
the British had gone, and the place felt nervous.

'Good-bye, Edna.'

The smell of the Diesel gas blew past them.

'Good-bye, Bob.'

Taffy Williams had curly red hair so that even in his quieter
moments there was an air of excitement about him; when he
decided to have intense feelings about something new his whole
head appeared to be on fire.

'They've shifted him!'

The hut didn't collapse at this announcement and he stared
wildly around with his bright china-blue eyes, wondering why not.

Most of them had just got in from the square and all they
wanted to do was sprawl on their beds for a bit. Three of them
were worried—Dobbs, Cleaver and Rickman—and some of the
others were worried on their behalf; Spragge felt Rickman's anger
and it sparked off his own in sympathy.

'They've shifted him to the spare hut!' Taffy told everyone.
'I saw him going in there with Sergeant Gosse, both marching it
out like clockwork.' He jerked his head about like an auctioneer
desperate for a bid.

Nobody asked him who he was talking about; nobody had
talked about anything all day except Proctor.

'There's no point in keeping him in the guardroom, Taff. He
was only whipped in there till the panic died down.'

'Besides,' said Jamie Cleaver, 'they'll need more room in there
now for us three.' When he'd stopped laughing at his own joke
Spragge said:

'You've got a wonderful sense of humour, you have. The
trouble is it's going to fetch you a tap on the trumpet one of
these days.' He wouldn't have said it if he hadn't been worried
over Rickman.

Brewer, Nairsworth and Smithers hadn't come in yet; they
were still out with the digging-party. Either the M.O. had been
specially fly this afternoon or the six on the list hadn't taken
enough trouble in making out they were sick enough for light
duties. It must have looked suspicious for six men of one platoon
to turn up on the afternoon parade anyway. The M.O. had told

them that he'd slap them straight on a malingering charge if they
didn't clear out, and that was being generous. He knew what was
on, all right, because he'd added a few words to Brewer: 'If you're
too proud to pick up a shovel you can always refuse the order,
if you can think up a more acceptable reason.'

Brewer, last out, had told the others and gone off to the main
gates with Nairsworth and Smithers to join the digging-party
twenty minutes late with a foolproof excuse: they'd been on sick-
parade. Dobbs was hesitating when Rickman said: 'I've got an
acceptable reason. The Vend'u can bury their own bloody dead.'
It was all Dobbs had needed, and Cleaver went along with them
because he'd throw in his lot with anyone who either had trouble
or was going to ask for it.

They reported to their platoon commander, Lt Millburn, and
in case Rickman couldn't keep his temper Dobbs spoke for them,
saying that after the treatment received by men of this unit at
the hands of the Vendettu they had no respect for them as an
enemy and refused on moral grounds to help bury their dead.

Mr Millburn had sat thinking about it for some good few
minutes before he said: 'I see.' He seemed to be taking it very
calmly but very seriously. 'And you're quite honest about this?
The idea isn't simply to dodge this fatigue because it's a hot
day?'

Rickman said: 'I'd've done it for Mackenzie or Timms, sir.
But not for those bastards.'

Their platoon commander nodded. 'All right. This will have
to go through to the Adjutant and you'll be hearing from the
orderly room. You're all from No. 2 hut, aren't you?'

They knew why he asked that. No. 2 hut was beginning to earn
a fair reputation for bloody-mindedness.

Mr Millburn told them to report to Cpl Bruce for normal
duties and by 1800 hours the orderly-room runner still hadn't
been round; so now they'd begun worrying, because of the
waiting, and Taffy was no help.

'He can get away now, whenever he wants! Only one N.C.O.
guardin' him an' that's Gosse—Proctor could eat him, eat him
an' go!'

'Oh for Chri' sake, Taffy—go where?'

'Well I don' know, quite. But he could escape, couldn't he?'

Nobby felt it was up to him to quieten the kid down. 'What
the hell for? He'd only get as far as the wire, wouldn't he? They'd
let him have the run o' the camp if it wasn't to save him embarrassment, don't you know that?'

'Embarrassment?' Taffy was thinking more in terms of a do-or-die attempt by Proctor to seize an armoured car and ram the wire with it.

'He's on a serious charge, isn't he? Up for court martial. You think he wants to be gawped at wherever he goes?'

Arguing with Taff was like putting your thumb on a drop of quicksilver. 'Serious charge, knockin' off twenty wogs? Captain Carey did for two hundred, man! You heard what they said on the wireless, di'n'you? An' you won't find *him* in the spare hut, you'll find him up the Road lookin' for more!'

It was bound to happen. Within a minute half the hut was talking about Carey, and the three men who had been subconsciously listening for the thump of the orderly-room runner's handlebars against the wall outside joined in and forgot their worry.

Tewson sat listening as usual, not taking part, sitting on his pillow with his back to the wall, one leg crooked and his elbow across his knee, a cigarette loose between his fingers. Sometimes he looked across at the transistor on Dobbs's bed, thinking that it was almost callous of them not to switch it on and at least listen to the appeals for help even if they could do nothing about it. At this hour the calls would be mostly from farms big enough to need their own transmitting-post; a farm like Morgan's had upwards of two thousand native labourers and valuable herds, and if the water-supply failed or a lion got in or someone had a bad accident with machinery they could call up the emergency services; but everyone was busy now and even the white hunters had been drawn in from the safaris to support the Tamalese army and police against the Vendettu, and the last call that had gone out from Morgan's Farm had been too late: there just wasn't the help available. There had been thirty whites there, seven of them children.

There were calls going out now, Tewson knew; you'd only to switch on that damned little black-and-chrome box to hear them.

There was a tiny scar just below her right ear, he remembered; he'd never seen it consciously but he remembered it now, and other things that hadn't impressed him when they'd met: walking behind her through the jammed street, to 'protect' her, he had watched the little rippling of her vertebrae under the skin of her neck, and only now realized how fragile her body was; standing with her under the scraggy tree he had seen her smile suddenly at a wolf-whistle from one of the Royals who was passing, and he'd never thought—as he thought now—that it had been friendly of her, and natural, when most girls hid their pleasure behind a wooden stare.

There were other things he could remember and didn't want to remember, because the mission radio had said, *'Please remember that we have no means of defending ourselves. . . .'*

Taffy had lost his hold on the argument and had calmed down, content with having started it. Spragge was saying—

'Supposing he *could* get through the wire or past the sentries at the gates, you think a man like Proctor'd be seen dead in a mob like Carey's?'

'What's wrong with it? They're having a better go at the Vend'u than we are, aren't they?'

'That's not our fault! The thing is they're bloody immoral—they only fight for the money and they'll fight for anyone that pays them.'

'Well, they're mercenaries, aren't they?'

'Don't we get paid?' asked Rickman in flat tones. 'Would you be in this mob if it weren't for the pay?'

'None of us would, but we're fighting for our own country, aren't we?'

Rickman said, 'Is that what we're doing? I thought we were sitting on our arses.'

Spragge was losing his temper, and Tewson, watching him, knew that it wasn't with Rickman or the others. He'd got himself into a corner and Tewson knew why, and decided to talk to him about it, alone.

'All right, we're sitting on our arses—but we're talking about Carey—'

'I'm talking about us,' said Rickman. 'Three hundred troops with machine-guns and armoured cars stuck here in a fuckin' rat-trap while all you hear on the radio are distress-calls from people out there in the bush with only a few shot-guns between 'em to keep off a pack of savages—three more farms burned down last week an' you know what happened to the people in them.' He had moved to stand close to Spragge. 'And the women and kids were lucky if they only got burned alive. English people—'

'Think I don't *know*?'

'English people. I'll tell you something, Spragge. The Army can keep my pay. All I want is orders to march out.'

'You think you're the only one?'

Rickman said: 'I know I'm not.'

'P'r'aps we'll get them,' someone said and Rickman wheeled on him—

'Orders to fight? With that bloody old woman in charge of us? He's shit-scared, didn't you know that?'

Dobbs said quietly: 'Watch it, Rick.'

Tewson looked past the group and saw Cpl Bruce in the doorway, standing with his back to them looking out. The sun was going down and everything was turning rose-gold for a minute or two before the horizon cast its shadow. Perhaps Bruce just wanted to look at that.

Rickman had turned because of what Dobbs had said. Now he swung back and he didn't trouble to lower his voice. 'He's a good bloke, our commanding officer. One of the best. Got a handle to his name an' decorations after it. He's the perfect C.O. for us lot, I'd say, except he's on the side of the fuckin' Vendettu.'

Dobbs closed his eyes in resignation; he should have known better than to warn a bloke like Rickman. Maybe it didn't matter; the Corp had been acting a bit tricky since the time when the Colonel had slapped them all on the peg but his heart was in the right place and he was just as browned off as the next man at not being allowed to fight. Only a bastard would pass on what was said inside this hut, and Brucey wasn't a bastard.

But nobody spoke again for a while, and the group began breaking up. The corporal turned back from the doorway.

'All right—blackouts!'

In five minutes it was full night and as soon as the screens were up Bruce turned on the lights. Tewson's bed-space was next to Spragge's, so he didn't have to find an excuse for talking to him.

Dobbs had switched on his transistor as he always did at this time. Jamie was getting out his button-polish, the next bed along. Taffy had begun sorting his kit out, making a lot of noise to show he didn't care if no one would listen to him about Sgt Proctor. Fraser was brushing his boots.

Tewson said: 'Smoke?'

'Try one of mine,' Spragge said.

'That's what you always say. These made of cow-shit or something?'

Spragge took one and as Tewson held his lighter for him he saw that the flame wasn't perfectly steady; he didn't think Spragge had noticed.

Even with the transistor on and the noise Taffy was making it wasn't going to be easy to talk without being overheard, and he didn't want to lower his voice because it had to be done casually. He'd chosen Spragge because he felt he knew him better than Rickman—and Rickman was too explosive, too outspoken, too full of himself to listen carefully to someone else's point of view before bursting out with his own.

Now it was worse because Taffy had quietened down, finding a letter among his kit and reading it over—then suddenly it was better because Brewer was coming into the hut with Nairsworth and Smithers—

'Know what we had to clean the shovels with? Bloody emery-paper! Christ, you'd think this was the Guards!'

'They pushin' up the daisies now, are they?' a man asked.

'Pushing up the spuds, anyway—we were clean out of coffins so we had to put 'em in sacks, shame, wasn' it?'

They were making much of it, feeling they should have refused the order like Rickman and the others; they ought to be slinking into the hut, so they shouted the louder.

'You should've 'eard the Padre! You got to bury the enemy in 'is own language, see, so that's what 'e done!'

'What did he say, then?'

''Ow the 'ell should I know? I'm from Commercial Road, fer Chri' sake! Yer know what I hope 'e was sayin', don't yer? "That'll learn yer to come an' swing on our gate, yer bloody lot o' black-arsed bastards, 'ail Mary an' Amen." '

The three of them had found their bed-spaces and were looking for fags, and their boots were coming off as some of the others went over to hear the details.

The hut was as noisy now as it would ever be, and Tewson made himself wait until Spragge had lost interest in the digging-party and was facing him again; and as he began speaking to him it seemed that a sudden quiet had come over the hut and that every man in it was listening; but that was only because he knew that what he was going to say was so dreadfully important.

CHAPTER ELEVEN

'ALL right now. . . . Aiming-position—*move!*'

The sun was nearing the roof-line of the NAAFI canteen and they were faced away from it. Sgt Getcliffe's eyes were narrowed to slits against the glare.

'Butt circling downward . . . forward . . . upward—rest on the shoulder—Hopkins, watch that grip! Right—reverse movement! One—er—two—er—three. . . . Hold steady now!'

They were doing it automatically but the sweat was a nuisance and they had to grip the stock harder than usual; their hands had begun throbbing painfully.

'Right. Starting position! Left hand grip releasing—one—er—two—come on, Fraser, what's your trouble?'

The S.L. rifle hit the next man's arm and clattered down.

'Sprained my thumb, Sergeant.' He hugged his hand to his stomach.

'Pick up your rifle an' fall out. Double over here! Rest of you —reverse movement!'

When they were back to the aiming-position he said to Fraser: 'Sick-quarters. Leave your rifle here.' He didn't look at the thumb; if Fraser said he'd sprained it, he'd sprained it; you couldn't trust many like that.

'Williams, face the front! What the hell are you gawpin' at?'

'Nothing, Sarge—'

'*Sergeant*, that's my rank!' He knew what the Welsh kid was gawping at. They should never have put Jim in the spare hut, for his own sake; there were too many windows. Not that the guardroom was any place for him either, by God.

'Right—arms stretching forward, don't forget the left hand undergrasp. *Move!*'

In moments of rest they looked at the shadow of the flagpost; it had reached the corner of the square by the stores hut, marking off the last of the hour for them.

Taffy was facing his front but his eyes were turned to watch the face in the window, farther on. He'd like to do something for Sgt Proctor, something that would let him know they were all thinking of him, but he didn't know what he could do.

'All right—shoulder . . . *arms!*'

The orderly-room runner was waiting for Sgt Getcliffe as he marched them off the parade-ground.

'Le-ef'—right, le-ef'—right, squad—*hult!* Coleman, fall out an' take this rifle back to the hut for Fraser. You're in charge of it, mind, till he claims it.' He looked again at the slip of paper. 'Cleaver—Dobbs—Rickman, report to the Adjutant 1815 hours —got that?'

The runner's bicycle went swerving away and Cleaver thought how free it looked, like a bird.

'Squad . . . di-iss—*miss!*'

The message was differently worded that evening.

Our urgent medical supplies are now cut off, since there is an independent Vendettu group camped between the Road and

*Mukongo'go village. Our rations will last another ten days at the
most, and we cannot shoot meat because we have to conserve our
small stock of ammunition. We do not ask help for ourselves, but
on account of our nursing staff and five hospitalized patients.*

Tewson got off the bed and went back to his own space.

'P'raps Captain Carey'll get there first, Tewey.'

Deliberately he said: 'Where?'

'The Mission. You've got a girl there, haven't you?'

'Who told you that?'

'I dunno,' Marriott said. 'Isn' it right?'

'No.'

Marriott looked at him for a couple of seconds longer and
turned away. 'That's good, then.' He tried to find Radio Liz on
the transistor but he didn't know where it was on the dial.
Nobby was away, seeing the Adj.

Tewson got a cigarette and sat on the bed, drawing his knees
up and doing his best to look relaxed. That was the danger now
—a word spoken unthinkingly to one man was common knowledge the next day. Fraser was the only one he'd mentioned it
to, and he was no gossip, but it had still got around. It was only
a small point, but he didn't want Spragge or any of the others
to think he was interested in the Mission just because he'd got a
girl there.

Anyway it wasn't true. He'd told Fraser he 'knew' a girl there,
that was all. Damn it, he'd only seen her three times.

She was a part of it, maybe, but only a small part. The whole
thing had come together in a matter of minutes yesterday, fusing
in his mind—the distress calls, Proctor, the machine-gun, Edna
perhaps, and that stupid argument about Capt. Carey. And
Rickman saying that all he wanted was orders to march out.
And Spragge's bit of self-deception—perhaps that had been the
finishing touch, to see a man as big as Spragge standing there
helpless with his great arms hanging by his sides and his hands
empty and his rifle cold in the rack while he tried to convince
himself that Carey's mob was 'immoral' and that the British
Army was out here ready at least to fight for its own Queen and
its own country.

Yet Spragge wasn't simple-minded. He could see the sense of
a mercenary force pitting itself against savagery because there was
no one else to do it, earning its pay no matter who paid it. Carey
might be a half-crazy lecherous drunken Irish or whatever else
they said he was but you'd never find gold enough to bring him
over to the Vend'u against his own kind. Spragge would admit

that, if he weren't so desperate to get out there and fight with
Carey; it was a case of sour grapes.

There hadn't been time last night to soften the approach. Time
was running out, and when the whole thing had taken its shape
so suddenly in Tewson's mind he'd felt a kind of panic because
he'd left it so late.

'Spraggey,' he'd said, 'it's not the answer, you know.'

'What isn't?'

'Joining up with Carey.'

'Who's talking about doing that?'

'I am.'

'That bunch of bastards?'

'They're saving lives out there. That's what you can't stand.
You can't go out and help them do it.'

'I wouldn't join up with that—'

'Yes, you would. It's just that you can't. None of us can. We
can't break out of here in daylight because we'd be seen doing
it. We wouldn't get past the guard at the gates and we can't go
through the wire. And if we tried breaking out at night we'd
risk walking straight into the Vend'u.'

He noticed that Spragge was looking past him at the bed-spaces
near them, his head turning casually and his eyes idle. He said
nothing, but dragged more frequently at his cigarette.

Tewson felt steadier, less nervy. He'd been right to start with
Spragge. He wouldn't have got this reaction from Rickman—it
would have been like lighting a fuse.

'You've worked it out for yourself,' he went on quietly. 'Quite
a lot of us have, I expect. But it's not so simple even if we did
manage to get out of this bloody lobster-pot. We don't know
where Carey is, do we? Somewhere "up the Road", that's all we
ever know. The Road's a thousand miles long. If we found him,
would he take us on? It's doubtful; he's doing very well without
us. If he took us on we'd be burning quite a few boats; it's one
thing to break camp and go absent without leave and another
thing to commit a breach of loyalty and offer our services to a
force not established by the Crown—one's desertion, the other's
treason.'

He was doing the same as Spragge, watching for anyone to
come too near, especially Cpl Bruce. Whether Bruce would report
anything seditious he overheard, Tewson didn't know; he just
wanted to make sure the corporal wouldn't have to face such
a problem.

Spragge spoke for the first time.

'I don't know how you can sit there looking so bloody cool.'

Tewson wanted to laugh but didn't. It was good that nothing showed. He said: 'It's the only way to play it, Spraggey. Otherwise we'll come unstuck.'

Then Spragge put on his act, looking particularly dim. Perhaps it was habit, or he wanted to avoid the direct question. 'Any case it's only talk, isn't it? You've said yourself there's no way of getting out of this bleeding lobster-pot.'

'Suppose there were. Would you be on?'

The sweat was gathering on Spragge's face and he wiped it away. Tewson could see that he wanted to talk, to burst out with his thoughts. He said only:

'I'd want to know more about it.'

'Would you?'

Spragge flicked him a glance. 'No.'

'So for the record, you'd be on.'

'I would.'

Tewson hadn't said any more last night because he wanted Spragge to get his breath. Tonight he would give him most of the details. Spragge was the key man at this stage: the others would trust him and trust in his stolid good sense.

As he smoked his cigarette, knees drawn up and hands relaxed, he looked along the bed-spaces. In some cases there were doubts and he eliminated those men from his mental list; even a small doubt disqualified them. Those remaining didn't have to be courageous or extra intelligent; they had to have two things: the ability to keep their mouths shut and a genuine need to break out of this place and help people who were going to die if they didn't.

That was how they would have to see things. It wasn't complicated. There were major reasons for staying on and sticking it out, every one of them sound and understandable. Fraser, Coleman, Smithers—he knew what some of them would say:

Suppose we got copped?

What about pay? The wife depends on me, you know.

'Andful of us against the Vend'u? Not fuckin' likely!

Amounts to desertion, doesn't it? I'd never face my old man.

You'd never get past the guards. Forget it, mate.

We got orders to stay, haven't we? Then we got to stay.

You've got the wrong address, chum. I'm no hero an' never will be.

They were all good reasons but he was looking for the people whose wives depended on them and who respected orders and

who were scared of getting killed—and who would *still* take
the chance for the one single reason he could offer them: that
somewhere out there in the bush there were people alive today—
on this evening, at this minute—who would not be alive a dozen
days from now unless they got help.

The list was critically short.

Spragge.

Rickman.

Cleaver.

Dobbs.

And even some of them might turn it down.

It was quiet in the hut tonight. They were waiting for the
three of them to come back: Dobbs, Cleaver and Rickman.
They knew it could be serious with them. Another thing was
that last night there hadn't been a sign of the Vendettu near
the camp and it was a worry. Nobody thought the Vend'u would
leave twenty-odd dead and do nothing about it. No. 2 hut was one
of the nearest to the wire fence and it was dark out there, and
they could come in hundreds if they wanted to, each one with
a spear heavy enough and sharp enough to pierce the weather-
board at fifty yards.

People sat near the foot of their beds, away from the wall.

Spragge had seemed quiet all day. Soon after blackout he said:
'Let's have some details.'

'Not yet,' Tewson told him.

Taff Williams was on about Sgt Proctor and Marriott was trying
to make him shut up. There was nothing they could do about
Proctor.

Rickman was first into the hut and Tewson noted this: it was
Rickman who led Dobbs and Cleaver in.

Fraser was the first to ask.

'How d'you get on with the Adj?'

It was Cleaver who answered and Tewson noted this too.
Rickman and Dobbs had shut faces and walked to their beds
with the deliberateness of anger.

'Slapped us on the peg, mates. C.O.'s Orders at 1200 hours
tomorrow.' His cheerfulness was genuine. Jamie Cleaver's only
concern was to join up with people in trouble; the trouble itself
never bothered him. 'It'll be nice to see him again—I've almost
forgotten what he looks like.' His boots hit the floor with a
flourish.

'P'r'aps I can remind you,' called Brewer. ' 'E's got a face like the shit-end of an ostrich an' when 'e talks 'e produces the same fuckin' substance.'

They moved towards Cleaver, letting Dobbs and Rickman alone.

'Why isn't Jones taking the charge?'

'C.O. wants to do it personally, the Adj said.'

'What'll you tell him, Jamie?'

'I'll have to think o' something.'

'I'll think o' somethin' for you, cock,' said Brewer.

'Christ, I'm in enough trouble as it is.'

Marriott said: 'Nobby, how d'you find Radio Liz on this bloody set?'

Dobbs said without turning his head, 'Those batteries don't last forever, you know.'

'Okay, Nob.'

Marriott turned off the transistor and went back to his own bed-space.

'What's the exact charge, Jamie?'

'Refusin' to obey an order. That's what we did, isn't it?'

'Or were you just stickin' your neck out, you stupid Glaswegian?'

It was Smithers, one of the men who'd reported sick and then lost courage. Rickman moved so fast that Smithers took a step back without being touched. 'That's it,' Rickman said—'we were just stickin' our necks out because we don't like bein' pushed around by an incompetent prick of a commanding officer, all right with you, Smithers? If there'd been more of us we'd've had a better chance of makin' a case but there were only us three. Not that I'm objecting—we can do without the help of a gutless bastard like you.'

The whole hut was looking on and Smithers knew he had to do something even if it was going to get him hurt, but Spragge had moved and was closing in on them——

'Rick——'

Corporal Bruce was out of his cubicle. 'Cut that out, will you now? Cut it out!'

Smithers dropped his guard, willing enough, and Spragge put a big arm around Rickman's shoulders and led him away. He was making a token attempt to free himself—'When I want you to interfere I'll ask you, Spragge.'

'You were leavin' it a bit late,' Spragge said with a grin—and Tewson noted this too. Spragge was the only man here with any control over Rickman; that could be valuable; one day soon it could be vital.

The hut fell quiet and the corporal went back into his room. Someone got his irons out and others did the same; nobody felt like talking. Tewson didn't look at Spragge when he came back to the bed-space alongside; there was no hope of telling him anything without being overheard.

Corporal Bruce had noticed the rattling of irons and although it still wanted fifteen minutes he called: 'First two for the cook-house!'

They had to leave the hut in pairs and at intervals because of the recent orders, and Bruce turned off all the lights except one; the blackout curtain at the doorway was only a bit of camouflage scrim and not even black.

Tewson knew that several men would stay behind because of the heat; whatever you reported sick with, the M.O. was liable to put you on a light diet. He didn't have to say anything to Spragge: they left the hut together.

In the cook-house it was possible to talk.

'I can't give you all the details yet. You'll have to rely on me to see that the operation works and you can take it from me that it will.' He'd managed to use a typewriter during the lunch-hour in the welfare hut; there was only one more thing to do until the day itself. He didn't think about the final few minutes because they'd need some luck and might not get it. He looked at the beef on his plate and thought it strange that only a couple of days ago he would have been able to eat it. He said to Spragge: 'You ask the questions.' He didn't want to volunteer anything, and he wanted to know which questions were the most important to him.

'When do we go?'

'Thursday.'

'Jesus . . .' In three days. 'What time?'

'First light.'

'How many of us?'

'We need ten men but I don't think we'll get them. Less than five and it's not on.'

'What sort of weapons?'

'Our own S.L. rifles, one machine-gun and some grenades.'

'Where do we go?'

'To wherever help's needed most. That's probably the White Cross Mission.'

CHAPTER TWELVE

Dobbs woke to a day worse than he had ever known. His last two-hour shift had ended at 0200 hours and the day-guard came on at dawn, so that he was awakened by the shouting of the guard commander as the parties were changed.

It had happened soon after midnight when he was out there manning the wire, first sentry along from the main gates. There was no moon and the lamps weren't burning in the town so there was no horizon: the bush had been black. No one had seen them coming because their skin was black too and they came naked. The sound had been eerie and it had frightened him—it had been like a gust of sudden wind, a rushing in the air near where he stood; then they'd begun laughing as they turned and ran— it was a screaming kind of laugh that had drawn his scalp tight—and the searchlight came on at once. They were running together and in the brightness they looked like the flowing of dark oil across the ground until the dust hid them.

He had heard orders being called as the light came on, and the gun crews were alerted, but there was no firing.

They had come and gone, all within a minute, and no one had seen them properly; but it was known there had been twenty of them because there were twenty arrows in the body of the sentry at the main gate. He hadn't cried out; they had struck him in a flock, their combined force knocking him down and spitting him to the ground. No one had heard anything but the strange rushing in the air until the laughter had broken out.

It was this that Dobbs couldn't forget: the way they had done it. When the night-guard was relieved he made up his bed and went across to No. 2 hut, sitting there alone and wanting badly to talk about it, yet knowing that if anyone had been there he wouldn't have said anything: his tongue felt too thick in his mouth.

The way Sergeant Proctor had done it was bearable to think about; if they had brought up a machine-gun and lit the target there would have been time to fire back and people would have ducked and thrown themselves flat and it would have been a little war, a thing you were expected to manage, something you could understand. But they'd done it in silence except for the faint rushing in the dark (that was now so terrible as he sat listening to it again in his mind and knowing what it was), and they'd run off laughing like kids who'd knocked on somebody's door.

The arrows had been sticking up out of the man on the ground, and he couldn't think what they were when he ran over to the gates; they looked like railings. Why so many for one man? Sgt Proctor had killed twenty of them, so they killed one man twenty times, was that it? The Vend'u were like that; he'd heard Tewson talking about their symbolism, which probably meant this sort of thing.

They were terrible people, the things they did. He'd only heard about Kennie and Timms and the others, but this he had seen. There were reports on the wireless, too, about farms and isolated places; and he'd never realized what it could be like. This was an armed camp with barbed wire and machine-guns and if the Vend'u ever made a proper attack they'd just get mown down. But what was it like on a farm without any fence at all, only the darkness outside, and your wife and children there, soft and young—and you heard them coming, running up to the doors. . . .

Suddenly he was thinking of home, of Bristol, the shape and the smell and the sound of its streets, great stones and buses and a policeman at the corner, *Frying Tonight*; and he thought with love of his people there, Mum with her white gloves and the cards in her bag, asking Dad if he'd got the keys. (Have I ever forgotten them? No, but you might do one day, mightn't you?) And his sister Gladys, in tears the last time he'd seen her, because Cliff had slapped her face at the bus-stop for taking up with Dave.

Slapped her face. You'll be all right, Glad, if you get no worse than that.

They didn't know, and he loved them all the more because they didn't have to.

Someone was coming and he got off the bed, finding his boots and starting to dust them. He could sleep till 1000 hours if he wanted to, having been on guard, but he'd never drop off if he tried.

Corporal Bruce saw him and came down the hut. He'd come in to check on tidiness, and shifted a fire-bucket an inch with his foot as he asked: 'You all right, Dobbs?'

'Yes, Corp.'

'Look at these bloody biscuits—that's your chum Williams again.'

'I'll put 'em right, Corp.'

'I never saw anything.' He came back past Dobbs and gave him a slow glance. 'Not much of a night for guard, was it? Never mind, it could've been you, that's what you want to remember.' He straightened a kit-bag and went into his room.

Dobbs hadn't thought about that. Just the rush of air, that was all he would have heard; he would have died thinking, *That's funny, there's a bit of a wind rising.* And they would have got a telegram in Bridge Street; no whist-drives for a bit and Gladys in tears again—she cried easily. Then they'd know. They'd have to know.

What was your poor Nobby doing there then, Mrs Dobbs?
He was sent out there with his Regiment.

Yes, but what was he doing, for such a dreadful thing to happen? Was there some fighting?

I suppose there must have been, though we're never told much. I don't rightly know what he was doing.

Dobbs stopped on his way across to Taffy's bed-space to see to the biscuits, and stood still with the sweat breaking out on him. It could have been *him,* the Corp had said, and by Christ he was right! And he would have been doing *nothing,* just standing there like a bloody lemon, doing *nothing*—nothing for himself or for anyone else, just standing there waiting for it and bloody getting it and not even knowing what had happened. He would have been doing what the whole lot of them had been doing for weeks on end. *Nothing.*

All except Sergeant Proctor.

He stood still and couldn't move and the sweat ran down him.

Christ, he could see now what had got into Proctor. No wonder Taff couldn't talk about anything else—he'd got imagination, that kid; he'd seen there was only one man in the whole of this useless bloody camp with any sense. That was why they'd got him under close arrest. You didn't get paid for having sense in this unit: all they wanted you for was a fucking lemon.

By Tuesday evening the most difficult bit of the ground-work had been dealt with and Tewson was going through a phase he'd fully expected. He was frightened of what he'd started. This reaction was just as unnerving as if he hadn't been prepared for it; perhaps it was worse, because your defences went up faster against a fear that was sudden; another thing was that fear was an emotion and therefore difficult to overcome mentally.

Those nearest him in the hut noticed that he was in an odd mood and left him alone, thinking he was worried about his

girl up at the Mission, because from what they heard on the radio
the Vendettu were rampaging in that area and last night there'd
been a massacre at the sheep-station not far away in the same
province.

No one was too cheerful this evening anyhow. The poor
bastard's name was Lumsden and you could add him to the list
with Mackenzie and Timms and Cpl Radford. A lot of them
had got their blood up about it—you couldn't go near Rickman;
not that you'd ever feel inclined. And Nobby hadn't said a word
since they'd come in from punishment drill, the three of them.
Nob had been on guard last night, so it was worse for him.

Even Jamie was quiet. When they'd asked him how it had gone
he'd just blown a feeble raspberry. 'He told us it was for him to
decide whether we had to bury the bleeders, not us. If we
questioned every order he gave us, where would we all be? In
bloody clover, I told him.'

'You told him that?'

'Maybe I didn't, come to think of it—slipped my mind, it
must have.'

Only Spragge had spoken to Rickman.

'What was the prize?'

'Ten days field punishment.' He said it through his teeth.

'Didn't he ask you for a reason?'

'Yes. I told him I didn't think the Vend'u would dig many
graves for us if they caught us outside the camp. He said we're
here to show an example to those less privileged. Christ, I don't
know why I didn't smash his face in. All he can think about is
our gentlemanly fucking manners while Lumsden's there waiting
for his funeral, stuck like a pig.' His flat tone cracked and he
stared at Spragge with bright eyes. 'Doesn't he *know* what they
did to Lumsden last night? Is that man *blind* as well as stupid?'

Spragge had tried to calm him down but for the first time
it wouldn't work. Rick had murder in him.

This evening Tewson had asked Spragge if he'd talked to him
yet and Spragge had said: 'No. He wouldn't be able to take it in.
I'm going to have a try later tonight.'

'You'll have to. We've got thirty-six hours left.'

It had been agreed between them that Tewson would sound
out Dobbs and Cleaver, and Spragge would see Rickman: 'You
know him better than I do, Spraggey. You're the only one who
can handle him.'

Cleaver would be the easiest and Tewson was going to leave
him till tomorrow. He wasn't sure of Dobbs, partly because of

last night: he'd been shown at first hand what the Vend'u could do. Once they'd left camp they'd be in Vend'u territory, the open bush, and this was the worst time to ask him if he'd be going out there with them. But he had to be asked. There was no one else. Tewson had shortened the list to these four men and then gone over all the others again in his mind because the ideal number was ten. He'd even begun talking to Coleman, who was a crack shot and had a useful temper, but there'd been a cable for him a week ago through Signals: it was a boy, eight pounds two ounces. And Tewson had baulked it before reaching the point because Coleman had to see his son and he'd be more certain of doing that if he stayed in camp. It wasn't safe here but it was safer than outside.

He nailed Dobbs in the cook-house at the evening meal; it was dangerous to talk in the hut now that time was so short; it all had to click into place and a bit of carelessness could blow it apart.

Dobbs was toying with a scrap of bread and cheese; he had no stomach for meat. When Tewson put it to him straight he just sat thinking, not looking at him, and Tewson had to wait, sweating it out, knowing that if Dobbs could be had with a little persuasion he couldn't persuade him, not with one word, because of the responsibility. It had to be yes or no because it was going to be their lives they were taking out there. He must keep it to the one short question: I'm going—are you?

He'd warned Spragge about that when he'd asked him to see Rickman. No persuasion, however badly they wanted to make up the number.

Spragge had said: 'You think he'll need persuading?'

But he might. You could slaughter the whole of the Vendettu tribe single-handed, inside the hut, inside the barbed wire with two hundred armed troops around you. Out there they'd be on their own. Five.

If Dobbs said yes.

The clatter of the cook-house was getting on his nerves and he wanted to clear out and go back to the quiet of the hut and think again, tell himself again that what he'd started was basically good and basically right: some people were in bad need of help and this was the only way to give it to them. Politics, racial considerations, flags, orders, discipline and regimental traditions —they all had their blinding arguments but this time, on this one small occasion, somebody had to do something humane, not as a duty but an instinct.

When Dobbs spoke Tewson knew that he must have thought out his answer and gone on thinking beyond it, because he didn't say yes or no; he said: 'Why didn't we think of this before?'

Rickman had been two years on the trucks in New South Wales because when his old man had got killed he had to go somewhere far off for a while; he shouldn't have left the old lady but there were his sisters, and the women could look after themselves at a time like that.

His father had died young and left nothing but a pickaxe and some old clothes, and while he was out trucking half across the world Rickman had time to think about him; maybe that's what he'd gone there for; you never had much time to think about people when they were alive. And he had decided that the old man had been too easy with the world, giving too much and taking too little, never questioning the terms he was expected to live by. That was why he'd died with a pick in his hand and a hundred tons of rock on top of him.

Rickman had been there when they'd got him out. They'd worked for three days as if he was valuable, his mates all there helping. He didn't remember much except seeing his old man's helmet and thinking: If that's what his helmet's like what's his head like? Then his stomach had gone freezing cold and he'd doubled up, sitting on his haunches on the bright wet slag and feeling the rain on his neck.

The only other thing he remembered was when he led his old lady away; there was a young feller with his car, one of the directors, holding the door open for his old lady and saying he'd take her home. She'd tried to refuse, saying he was being too kind, and he'd said quietly, 'It's the least I can do, Mrs Rickman.' She had got in, the clay on her shoes streaking the carpet—it was a Bentley, with carpets—and the young feller had waited for Rickman to get in too, but he said: 'I'll walk.'

He didn't hate anyone or anything that day, even the blue carpets or the camel's-hair coat or the pigskin gloves; the young feller was damn near tears, he could see that, when his mother got in the car. But he wanted to walk home over the slag in the rain, because that's what his old man would have done. And he wanted to get something to rights in his mind: this was the last time he'd do anything his old man had done, because it was wrong to spend your life shovelling coal down there in the ground when there were people living like that young feller.

No, he didn't want a Bentley. But he wasn't going to buy one for anybody else.

He'd been due to sign on at the pit in a month's time and when he chucked it in they said of course it was understandable, with his old man getting killed like that. They thought he was scared; he didn't mind; he would only have minded if he had been scared.

In Australia he worked for seven different trucking companies, walking out of one job after another because they tried to drive him too hard. He'd hit one of the bosses and there was a case about it. He'd told another one: 'You can buy your own fucking Bentley,' and didn't trouble to explain what he meant.

Then he joined up because the life looked easy and he wasn't interested in money, and he found that half the blokes were like his old man, accepting whatever terms the officers thought out for them. It was his own bloody fault, he knew that, but he couldn't keep patience with them. He should have known what the Army was like before he joined, and he couldn't keep patience with himself either. But there was one thing about the Army: they could send you out to a tick-infested hole like this till you sweated more than you pissed but the officers came with you and lived as you did, and if any of them had a Bentley they'd got to leave it at home. They were still the bosses but you weren't expected to earn their living for them; they had to do that for themselves.

For the present the Army was good enough for him, otherwise he'd have cleared out before now, back to Australia. He might even learn to find a bit of patience with himself and everyone else, given time; but that wouldn't happen yet, and for one good reason: the 4th Royals were being run by the biggest prick in Christendom—Lieutenant Colonel Lord Fucking Fauntleroy, B.O., N.B.G.

Maybe they'd all have more patience in No. 2 hut if it weren't for that. Not that he gave them much thought; they were the same as you'd find in the pits or the trucks, take 'em or leave 'em. There was only one bloke he'd got any time for, and that was Spragge, and the only bloke he couldn't stick the sight of was Tewson.

That was why, when Spragge told him what was on and told him who was running it, Rickman said no.

CHAPTER THIRTEEN

'Okay, Rick. That's your answer.'

'It is.'

'You've got your reasons.'

'Want to know them?'

'No.'

They'd rinsed their irons in the communal basin and now they were standing together in the corner by the door. Men were going past but it was all right to talk because of the clatter at the tables.

'If you were running it you could count me in, Spragge. But not if he is.'

Spragge was turning away. 'I don't want to know your reasons.' He felt physically sick; the food he'd just eaten had turned in his stomach at Rickman's answer because there had to be five—that was the minimum, Tewson had said. 'Less than five and it's not on.' They'd felt sure of Jamie Cleaver and with luck they'd get Dobbs. The last man he'd expcted to say no was Rick, and that was why it was so much worse.

'Get him out of it,' Rickman said, 'and I'm in.'

Spragge moved back to him, the sick feeling turning to anger. 'He's running it, you bloody fool!'

'That wet?'

'He *thought* of it. It's his own idea.'

'Then it won't work.'

Spragge stared at him. 'What've you got against Tewson?' Rick had never mentioned the bloke in his hearing; the two of them had never had a ding-dong, never spoken a word to each other in the hut.

'He knows it all.' Yet he felt uncertain of what he was saying even as he spoke, and had to explain to himself as well as Spragge. 'He's too bloody smooth for my liking. See the rest of us out there bashing on the square but you don't see Tewson—'

'He's out there with us all day!'

'I mean punishment drill—you ever see him on that?'

'But he's never on a charge, for God's sake!'

'That's what I mean.'

'But half the blokes in the hut are never on a charge!'

'The whole lot of us were once, remember? And there was only

Cleaver not with us on the square because of his blisters. Him an' Tewson, of course, it goes without saying.'

Spragge left him. It was the only thing to do. He went out of the cook-house into the dark and blundered his way to the hut, more bewildered now than angry. He'd thought he'd known Rick; he'd said to Tewson, 'You think he'll need persuading?' But Tewson hadn't been certain of him. Tewson knew the blokes in No. 2 hut better than a bloody fortune-teller. And Rick had called him a wet.

He stumbled into a fire-bucket and said, *'Shit!'*

'Who goes there?'

'Oh, Christ . . .'

'You're too near the wire. Keep nearer the huts.'

'Sod your luck, mate, I'd rather be me than you.'

He got his bearings and found the hut. Tewson was back from the cook-house and he lit a fag with a shaky hand and blew out smoke and said: 'The answer's no.'

Tewson's face didn't alter but it was a minute before he asked: 'Did he say why?'

'I wasn't interested. All we wanted was a straight answer, wasn't it? No persuasion. Okay. So it's not on, is it?'

'I don't think so, Spraggey.'

Rickman hadn't looked at them once since he'd come back from the cook-house. His movements were over-casual as he cleaned his gear and then sat with a cigarette, looking at nothing. If it weren't for the thudding of his heart in his ears and the quickness of his breathing he might have convinced himself that there was nothing on his mind.

Spragge must have thought he was daft, going on about Tewson like that. What *had* he got against Tewson? Too bloody smooth. He knew it all. He was one of the men but he talked like a bloody officer—so polite to Cpl Bruce that it made you puke to listen to him, because you could tell what he thought of Bruce: he was just an ignorant swede-basher with stripes on his arm. If Tewson was too good for the ranks why didn't he get himself a commission and done with it?

But it wasn't that. Tewson was one of those clever blokes who'd think up a dodge and then drop you in the shit when it went wrong, and you'd be on the bloody square while he took it easy in the hut, smoking a 'cigarette'. Why couldn't he call the fucking things fags? You couldn't even talk the bloke's own language.

It wasn't that either. Then what was it? He was too bloody good-looking, too frightfully elegant for words, old boy, stuck there on his bed with his arm across his knee and his hand dangling with a 'cigarette' in it as if he'd not got enough strength to lift it. A right one for the girls, that was a cert, so long as they didn't mind helping him on, because he was so awfully tired, you know.

Rickman sat and sweated it out, hating the sod and dragging in every rotten thought he could think about him whether it were true or not, justified or not, till the hate turned hot in his stomach and burned up and went out, leaving him quiet. And in the quietness he thought: All I've got against Tewson is that his face puts me in mind of that young feller in the Bentley.

Most of the blokes had been out to the lats and the wash-house and were coming back. There wasn't much talk; they just wanted to turn in and wait for Lights Out and try to sleep before the heat got worse towards midnight and kept them awake, lying in the dark thinking about the sentries out there by the wire where Lumsden had been last night.

The hut was too quiet for talking, if what you had to say was private, so Rickman waited until Tewson had gone out, gave him five minutes and then followed him.

The place was like a cow-shed, stone partitions and zinc troughs. There was a date cut into the concrete somewhere on the outside wall: 1927. The lats backed on to the wash-house and there was the mixed smell of toothpaste and disinfectant. He couldn't see Tewson at first because there were only two bulbs in the whole place and they'd been painted blue when the blackout orders were issued. When he found him he said:

'Spragge told me about it.'

'I know,' said Tewson. He put his toothbrush and sponge into a striped bag, not troubling to look at Ricklman after the first glance.

'He tell you why I turned it down?'

'No.'

A tap dripped somewhere.

'I might not've given him the real reason—it was sprung on me, see. I didn't have much time to think. The thing is, I don't think you can do it. He didn't give me much to go on, but it strikes me that anyone tryin' to break out of camp in broad daylight's going to get shot up an' no argument.'

The shape of Tewson's head moved in the gloom and he listened for a moment before saying quietly: 'It's not going to be easy. There'll be a bit of confusion at the last minute if anything goes wrong, and they'll try to stop us getting out, in which case we'll go straight into the guardroom. If we do manage to break out of the camp it's going to be tougher still trying to reach the White Cross Mission.' He slung his towel across one shoulder. 'We were looking for people who'd take the chance. We thought it might be worth it.'

Rickman said: 'You don't think I've got the guts?'

'It didn't occur to me, but since you mention it——'

'You don't get me that way.'

'I'm not trying to "get" you. I think it was you who followed me out here, wasn't it?'

'I came to clean me teeth, same as you.'

'Then I'll leave you in privacy.'

He made for the door but Rickman stopped him and they talked for another minute or two and when Tewson got back to his bed-space he murmured to Spragge: 'Rickman's coming with us, so it's on.'

The night had passed without incident. Trip-flares had been set up soon after dark so that if the Vendettu came the guard could see them and scare them off with a few rounds above their heads. They didn't come.

The M.O. said he believed they were now using a new trick in the war of nerves, keeping away on certain nights so that the unit would never know which night they were coming. Captain Jones asked the C.O. a question: If the Vend'u came *en masse*, halted beyond the ring of trip-flares and sent several hundred poisoned arrows at random into the camp, would it constitute an organized attack, enabling the guns to open up? Colonel Gray said that in such eventuality he would give immediate and suitable orders. When Major Shaw, commanding 'A' Company, asked Jones what the C.O. had said, Jones told him: 'He said that officers are reminded that there is only one man here with the right to open his mouth, and that is Lieutenant-Colonel Sir Jesus Christ himself.'

The camp woke more noisily this morning; everyone had slept better for the night's having been quiet. Taffy Williams was first out of No. 2 hut before it was light, hoping to see Sgt Proctor; he was taken for exercise in the hour before dawn and Taffy thought there might be a chance of seeing him on his way back to the spare hut as the sun came up; he'd give him a wave, maybe, to show they were all still thinking of him. But he didn't see him.

Spragge made a point of being at the next basin to Rickman when they went into the wash-house to shave.

'I hear you changed your mind.'

'You can call it that.' His tone was as flat as ever but there was blood among the lather with every stroke.

'What happened?'

'Came to me senses.'

'What about Tewson?'

'What about him?'

'We've got to get on, all of us. That's vital, so you'd best make your mind up here and now.'

Rickman drew some more blood and said: 'He's all right. If he can do what he says he can do I'll kiss his arse—that convince you?'

Spragge saw Tewson only for a minute, to talk to.

'All okay?'

'Of course.' Tewson looked drawn and there was a pallor turning his sunburn muddy; that was why Spragge had asked.

'We'll have no trouble with Rick, after this.'

'That's fine.' He wouldn't even meet Spragge's eyes.

The sun cleared the roof of the next hut along.

They stood in a double rank, their shadows reaching the edge of the parade-ground.

'Andrews?'

'Corp!'

'I'll have a correct answer.'

'Corporal!'

Inside every corporal, thought Andrews, there was a sergeant hollering to get out.

'Brewer?'

'Corp'ral!'

Across the parade-ground the doors of the cook-house were being opened and bolted back; there was the clink of irons.

'Rickman?'

'Corporal!'

The last time. This was the last morning roll. This time tomorrow they'd be gone and the corporal could yell his head off for him and there'd be no answer, correct or otherwise. He wanted to laugh, shout, bash somebody. What was all that about Tewson last night when Spragge had first told him? A brainstorm. It could happen to anyone.

'Spragge?'

'Corporal!'

There hadn't been a chance to talk to Tewson but maybe it didn't matter. He'd said Rick was coming with them and Rick had confirmed it this morning. The only thing that made him anxious was that Tewson looked so nervous now that it was all plain sailing.

'Tewson?'

'Corporal!'

'Williams?'

'Corporal!'

'Right. Lance-Corporal Rivers, you'll be in charge for a while when you leave the cook-house. Get the platoon on parade and start with saluting-drill, all right?'

'Yes, Corporal.'

'Tewson, stand fast. Rest of you fall out.'

There was still a chance. It had happened but there was no need for panic. He'd got all the arguments ready; he'd been presenting his case most of the night because sleep hadn't been possible. Getting into bed after leaving Rickman in the wash-house he'd lain thinking for ten minutes; then Rickman had come in; then, after an interval, someone else. He had known it was Cpl Bruce because the door of his room had a sound different from the other two, a lighter sound. Bruce hadn't been in the wash-house. He must have been in the lats adjoining.

The rest of them were falling out, going into the hut to fetch their irons. The corporal came up to him and said: 'Report to me after breakfast outside the platoon office. I'm taking you in to see Mr Millburn.'

So now there was no chance.

CHAPTER FOURTEEN

'Now don't forget—long way up, short way down. To the right . . . *Salute!*'

The cooks were banging the bins. The sick-parade was mustered in the shade of the medical hut.

'To the left . . . *Salute!*'

The shadow of the flagpost was shortening but still too long, three and a half bloody hours too long.

'Come on, Williams, that the best you can do? Fingers together, head still, left arm straight, thumb down the seam. That's more like it. Squad . . . *halt!*'

Rivers hadn't got the makings, thought Cpl Bruce. He'd got the terms of address but not the tone. You'd got to have the tone of authority.

He hadn't spoken to Tewson. There was nothing to say to him. Let him stand there and sweat it out. He'd learn now, p'r'aps, what authority was. It wasn't a lot of airs and graces and a condescending manner; it wasn't something magical you were born with. It was a pair of stripes on your arm that you'd worked for and earned the right to wear. And the right to use.

The orderly-room runner propped his bicycle outside the hut and took some papers in.

When Tewson had reported to the platoon office his manner had been punctiliously correct but he had said: 'I was wondering if you might give me an opportunity of talking to you, Corporal, before we—'

'By this door, Tewson. Stand at ease. Eyes front.'

Since then they had stood in silence side by side.

The runner came out and cycled away.

Lieutenant Millburn arrived soon afterwards and the corporal took Tewson in.

'I've a report to make, sir.'

'Go ahead, Corporal.' He settled his glasses higher, one thin finger prodding the bridge. The sun was above the nearest hut and the sweat was already on.

'I've reason to believe that Private Tewson intends breaking out of camp, sir, with a party of other men.'

Millburn studied them while they gazed at the wall behind his desk. Bruce, tall, blocky-figured, his hands large and roughened, his face honest and at this moment in a strange way exalted. Tewson, an inch shorter, a leaner man, his face more sensitive and at this moment expressionless.

The lieutenant wondered what was going on between them. It was an extraordinary thing for this N.C.O. to come and tell him immediately after breakfast, without a written report.

'You have "reason to believe", Corporal. What reason?'

'I overheard some conversation, sir.'

'In what circumstances?'

'This man was talkin' to someone in the ablutions last night, sir.'

'And where were you?'

'In the latrine, sir.'

'M'mm. Tewson, what have you got to say about this?'

'Nothing, sir.'

'You mean you deny any intention to break out of camp?'

'I don't need to, sir. With respect, I'd like to wait and see if the corporal has anything of substance to report.'

'Of substance?'

'Evidence based solely on an overheard conversation has no value, sir.'

Millburn took up a pencil, stood it on end, slid his fingers down it, reversed it and began again. His head had started to ache as it did every day at this hour. The Doc said it was frustration. But it was worse this morning; during the last few minutes it had begun hammering, and he knew it was more than frustration. He was aware that something important was happening and it was a feeling he couldn't possibly have analysed.

'Wait outside, Tewson.'

'Sir.'

Millburn said when the door was shut: 'I'm not going to ask you for any further evidence outside this man's hearing, Corporal. I just want to remind you that you'll have to make a full written report and that unless you've any factual evidence to support what you've already said, such a report isn't worth writing. Have you any factual evidence? I'm not asking you what it is, but only if there is any.'

He noticed the corporal's large hands were clenched.

'I thought that'd be enough, sir.'

'I'm afraid it isn't.'

'I thought I was doin' my duty in coming to you, sir.'

'Certainly you are.' Looking up at the honest yeoman face he knew that he could tell Cpl Bruce only those things he could understand easily. 'And of course I shall treat this report very seriously. But you see how careful we have to be about this business of overhearing conversation. It's never enough for us to go on, because anyone can report something he "overhears", just because he wants to get a man into trouble. I'm sure this isn't the case with you, Corporal—there's no question of your wanting to harm this man Tewson, is there?'

Bruce could feel the heat of his own face.

'No, sir.'

He'd heard what had been said in the ablutions and it had been by accident and he knew one of them was Tewson because of the way he spoke. But Mr Millburn wouldn't have it. It wasn't enough to wear stripes on your sleeve; it didn't give you the authority to say, *This man means to break out of camp and that's a serious thing and I want something done about it.*

Tewson had got something he hadn't got, something he'd never have. And it was something he'd never want. He'd rather be himself with a pair of useless stripes on his arm than a man like Tewson.

'If you think you should make a written report,' Millburn told him carefully, 'then I'll see that it's dealt with in the usual—'

'No.' The big hands had suddenly come unclenched. 'No, sir.'

'I think you're wise.' He laid the pencil flat. 'Please send Tewson back to see me on your way out, Corporal. If anything useful comes of my talking to him I shall of course let you know.'

Outside in the passage Cpl Bruce had a mind to bring the man to attention and march him in as he'd done a few minutes ago, but it wouldn't look right now, it'd be like play-acting. He didn't have the authority.

'Mr Millburn wants to see you.'

'Yes, Corporal.'

Bruce wanted to hit him and say, *Don't call me that!* But he did nothing and said nothing and walked into the heat of the morning with the habitual parade-ground step of a junior N.C.O.

The phone was ringing when Tewson went into the platoon commander's office and he shut the door and came to attention and waited, his eyes fixed on a knot in the timber of the wall behind the lieutenant's chair. It was the Padre on the line and there was a long conversation about the arrangements for Private Lumsden's funeral.

Tewson looked down at Millburn now and then when his head was turned away and tried to get an inkling as to what kind of person he was; he'd only seen him on the square and at P.T. before and had never thought about him. He wasn't the type of man to impress himself on the ranks; most of them referred to him as Milly but not from any kind of affection; if he had any popularity at all it was because he left people alone.

It was dangerous anyway to try forming any sort of judgement about him from his profile. He wouldn't let Bruce's report go any further; there was no question of a charge. But Bruce would be watching him relentlessly from now on and Millburn would certainly alert the M.P. warrant-officer without mentioning any names.

The operation was off and he had to accept it and somehow muster the guts to tell Spragge and Rickman and Dobbs and then forget it and try not to blame Rickman's stupidity and his own stupidity, try not to blame anyone or anything. Get through the day and this evening ask Dobbs to leave that radio switched off, leave it silent, leave it dead.

The whole thing was pretty uncertain but if they could have pulled it off and got up there in time to do anything useful she could have gone on dispensing bismuth or whatever the hell she did up there, and gone on smiling at wolf-whistles in the street. Anyway if they . . . went there and she was out of luck—say it, the Vend'u, say it—if the Vend'u went there and she was out of luck—she'd never know it was the . . . fault of a good honest-bone-headed Sussex ploughboy who wouldn't hurt a fly or that someone called Bob who said he'd protect . . . protect her if there was trouble . . .

'Of course, Padre. I'll get the orders. . . .'

Do you often come into this sort of place? It didn't matter, they . . . probably couldn't have done anything useful. . . .

'All ranks formal dress . . .'

Good-bye Edna, good-bye Bob, fly away Peter. . . .

'. . . Padre . . .'

Don't hate Bruce.

A bell tinkled and a hand was on him. 'You'd better sit down.' It had never happened to him before and there was something euphoric about it. The coming back was worse than the going under, though, you didn't want to come back; that was what it was probably for—just a way of forcing you to forget.

'All right now?'

'Yes.' He was surprised it had had such an effect on him; having not to show anything, that was the trouble. Old Doc Bickersteth—God, that was a long time ago—had said, 'If only he'd yell his head off and tear his hair out a bit when something worries him, he wouldn't have these nightmares.' He still had nightmares.

Millburn had gone back behind the desk again and was watching him with interest. 'Take off your cap, Tewson, and relax. Cigarette?'

'No thanks.' He dropped his cap on the floor beside the chair. 'It was keeping to attention so long—like the Guards. And the heat. Sorry.'

Millburn lit a cigarette and noticed Tewson leaning forward slightly as the blue smoke clouded into the air; he pushed the packet across and Tewson took one and Millburn reached over and lit it for him.

'D'you feel up to talking?'

Tewson smiled wryly. 'It depends what about.'

'Look,' Millburn said, 'it's quite clear that Corporal Bruce was telling the truth, because even if he wanted to get you into trouble he'd never think up a story as weird as that one. However Kiplingesque it may sound, we're cut off from civilization and surrounded by hostile savages and our best way of surviving is to stay dug in behind our guns and our barbed wire until the wogs have settled with each other. This camp is the safest place in a million square miles and you want to break *out* of it. Why?'

Tewson felt his head becoming very clear, and he thought it was partly due to Millburn's attitude. It was so unexpected that it was as if he'd stumbled on a piece of crystal among an endless pattern of khaki-coloured bricks. Millburn wasn't interested in trapping a man into a confession and marching him to the guard-room; he was interested in the idea of a man wanting to do something illogical.

'It's really for private reasons,' Tewson told him. 'I'm in the Army for another year and whether it's been good for me or not I don't know. But I don't want to look back and realize it was a waste of time. This Tamalese thing's going to resolve itself before long and people I respect are going to say, "You remember those awful massacres last year? You were out there, weren't you?" And they're going to ask me what it was like. So what'll I tell them? "Well it was all right for me because I was comfortably dug in behind guns and barbed wire—not a scratch, thank God." ' He looked at Millburn with hard eyes. 'Even if I didn't have to say it I'd have to think it.'

After a moment Millburn said: 'I see. But had you got some kind of objective in mind?'

For the first time Tewson hesitated, not from mistrust but from a reluctance to talk about something that was in an odd way sacred. Then he remembered that it would only become sacred if she died. 'Yes,' he said, 'there's a medical mission not far off, a couple of hundred miles north—'

'The White Cross?'

'Yes. They keep asking for help; we sometimes get on to their wavelength.'

Millburn nodded. 'I've heard the Padre talking about it. That area's full of Vendettu.' Suddenly he asked: 'Why don't you think the whole unit could go?'

Tewson answered before he considered the question. 'I think it could, but the C.O. won't let it. We've had enough provocation —our chaps have been killed, haven't they? But he's obsessed with keeping the peace.' He paused and added: 'I suppose that's seditious, but you did ask.'

Millburn said: 'That's all right, but you'd better keep your voice down—or won't you ever learn?' He flicked his cigarette and pushed the ashtray towards Tewson. 'What gave you the idea of doing this extraordinary thing?'

'Nothing particular. It just began incubating. If anything definite started it off I'd say it was probably the machine-gun.'

Millburn's eyes became intent. He said:

'Machine-gun?'

'Sergeant Proctor's little effort. Maybe it was just what I'd been waiting for.' He had said it casually, looking down and away, but Millburn was silent for so long that he looked up again and saw that his face had become strained; he had pushed up his glasses and was kneading the bridge of his nose, his eyes shut tightly. It looked like a headache, a bad one.

'Tewson,' he said wearily as if he had fought something and lost, 'when did you intend doing this?'

When there was no answer he took his hand away and opened his eyes and said: 'I've freely invited confidences from you, Tewson, without any attempt to warn you that you should take care of what you say to me. Do you now think I'm going to revoke an implicit privilege and let you hang yourself on your own words?'

There was no hint of rhetoric in the question; he wanted an answer. Tewson looked into the young academic face and saw no guile there.

'No,' he said.

The window of the small room was on the other side of the hut from the parade-ground but the sound from out there was audible in the quietness, echoing from the near buildings. Cpl Bruce had taken over from L.-Cpl Rivers; his commands were louder and more authoritative. Neither Millburn nor Tewson was aware of this. Perhaps Millburn alone was aware of any sound at all; perhaps he knew without conscious thought that it had a certain significance for him at this moment, because it was the sound of an army, of a large group of men committed to mutual ideals and bound together by abstract values and considerations: loyalty, obedience, comradeship. In terms of physical action these abstracts had become and would again become steel, shot, flame, blood, a medal, a wreath, a ribbon, a black band on a sleeve, music, tears. They had made and would make again the difference between freedom and slavery for whole

nations. The voice of an army was distinct and manifold; its
spirit was expressed no better by massed bands than by the cry
of a single corporal on the square.

It was as if this particular corporal were reminding Millburn
of what he was and where he was, of what he must do and not
do. This made it very difficult for him, and his head throbbed
so painfully that even speaking was an effort.

'Then I'll ask you again. When did you plan leaving the camp?'

'Tomorrow.'

'*Tomorrow?*' He looked at the regimental calendar on the desk.
In a moment he said: 'You'll report back on duty.'

'Yes, sir.' Tewson stubbed out his cigarette and picked up
his cap.

'If Corporal Bruce happens to ask you about your personal
situation as it stands at present, you can tell him that I'm pur-
suing the matter. And I want you back here at 1400 hours—is
that fully understood?'

'Yes, sir.'

'Bear it well in mind, because in the meantime I don't want
you to do anything stupid.'

CHAPTER FIFTEEN

THAT evening towards sundown the camp fell quiet. In the
minute following 1800 hours, when the last men left the square,
you would have said the silence was quite unbroken. Now that
the duties of the day were over, people were free to look up at
the sky, blue-green and fragile as an eggshell, and remember how
large it was and how small they were; as if by common accord
no one disturbed the quietness for this little time; it seemed
that the slam of a door might shiver the balance of air and earth,
light and dark, and send a crack across the universe.

Soon the guard turned out and Colonel Gray came on to the
parade-ground. The small company was brought to attention
and a man put his hands at the lanyard, then the first notes lifted
from the bugles, pure and melancholy, as the flag of the Regiment
was lowered.

In charge of those representing 'B' Company this evening was
Lt Millburn. Standing impeccably to attention as his commanding officer inspected the Retreat, he recalled to mind certain
phrases of the document in which his Queen had bound him to
her service.

*You are therefore carefully and diligently to discharge your
Duty . . . and are prescribed by Us to exercise and well discipline
such officers and men as may be placed under your orders from
time to time . . .*

The man at the flagpost alone moved; in the last rays of the
sun the shadows of his hands flew across and across the dusty
ground. As the flag came down the air took it and lifted a corner
and once almost unfurled it to reveal the crossed swords and
pimpernel of its device.

*. . . and to use your best endeavours to keep them in good order
and discipline. . . .*

The flag came into the man's hands and the last notes of the
bugles, infinitely fine, died all away.

In the morning Rickman was already in the wash-house before
reveille. It was still dark but others followed him; they were
mostly those who had slept well and were refreshed, or those who
had lain awake these last hours and were bored with their
thoughts.

The smell of toothpaste became gradually stronger; a door
banged shut along the line of latrines; in the dim blue light their
faces peered closely into propped mirrors, ghost-white with
shaving-cream.

'Wonder who copped it last night, Fred?'

'P'r'aps nobody copped it.'

'Not us, any'ow.'

'Pull up the ladder, Jack.'

A china shaving-mug slipped and hit the floor and didn't break.

'Christ, you can't beat bloody Woolworth's!'

Tewson came in and found Spragge and Rickman at the two
basins on the left by the door as arranged.

'About now,' he said as he passed them.

Cleaver came in. '*Je-sus wants me . . . fo-o-o-or a sunbeam* . . .'

'You'll wake the bloody camp!'

'I *am* the bloody camp!'

The long galvanized pipes banged to an air-lock.

Tewson was back at his bed-space ten minutes before first light.
Dobbs was opposite, stuffing his transistor into his pack, clumsy
in the dark, sweat on his hands.

Spragge and Rickman came back from the wash-house and
stowed their gear, doing it quickly. Jamie Cleaver was groping
his way along to his bed-space; his knee struck a bed and a man
said: 'God strafe that fuckin' somnambulist!'

'Time you were up, mate. Stop floggin' it, you'll only wear the poor wee thing out.'

Someone crossed the width of the hut and whispered: 'Rick?'

'I'm here.'

They went out by the door at the back end, passing the wash-house and making straight between the dark humps of the huts; there was faint starlight but they didn't need it; the spare hut was three down and one along; it was the corner one, the most remote. It was still dark when they reached it and stood listening. Then they went in.

The footsteps passed the hut three times at something like one-minute intervals; then they approached. In the darkness there was no means of knowing who had come in first, so nothing happened until the door was closed and the M.P. sergeant switched the light on. Spragge was nearer him and judged it dead right, getting an arm-lock round his neck before he could shout. Rickman jabbed the flat of his foot into the back of the sergeant's knees and he went down with Spragge now in full command of him.

Proctor's hands had moved instinctively to the guard position and his eyes were glazed with shock for a second or two. Rickman said:

"There's five of us getting out of camp an' taking a machine-gun with us.' Tewson had told him to give a pause there so that Proctor could take it in. 'We're going to the mission up north, they want to help there.' Pause. 'You want to come with us?'

Proctor's eyes had lost their glaze and his hands were slowly coming down. 'Well, you bloody *fools* .'

'There's room for you if you want to come.'

'You're for the Glasshouse, know that?'

The M.P. sergeant was beginning to choke and Spragge loosened the lock on his neck a bit.

Proctor looked tall, taller than ever. He stared down at Rickman.

'You've got one minute, Sarge. Then we got to go.'

Proctor said wildly, 'Clear out of here! He didn't get a chance to recognize you, nor did I. *Get out!*'

Rickman bent quickly. 'He conscious?'

'Yes,' Spragge said.

Rickman hissed into the M.P. sergeant's ear: 'Spragge an' Rickman, got it? That's us, an' fuckin' proud of it!'

He straightened and looked into Proctor's eyes and said: 'You want to come? We're pushed for time.'

The breath came out of Proctor and his voice was hollow. 'I'll have to come, you bloody fools—someone's got to look after you out there.'

Spragge said: 'Sheets, Rick.'

'Okay.'

They did the job just as they'd rehearsed it and when Proctor tried to help them with the gag Rickman knocked his arm away. 'Don't you touch him.'

They switched off the light and waited for their eyes to accommodate; thirty seconds, Tewson had told them. All they could hear was their own shaky breathing. Proctor didn't say a word; he'd tried and he knew it was no good trying again.

Light was along the horizon when they left the hut and there were men moving about, some of them in a group ready for roll-call.

Three men came away from No. 2 hut and fell in with them: Tewson, Cleaver and Dobbs. Rickman had told Proctor to leave the tapes on his arm and march them as a squad. If they took a line between the outermost huts and the barbed wire they wouldn't be seen clearly in this light.

Only one man had been watching the spare hut and he was Taffy Williams, hoping to see Sgt Proctor as he came back from exercise, give him a wave, like.

They were marching at a brisk light-infantry pace and for the sake of appearances Proctor was telling them, 'Le-eft, right—le-eft, right—come on, pick it up, pick it up!'

They heard someone trotting beside them but didn't know who it was until he called in disbelief: 'Nobby!'

'Le-eft, right—le-eft, right!'

'Nobby!'

'*Fuck* off!'

'Where's he takin' you, man?' Taff was nearly sobbing, so moved was he by the miracle. Wandering in the witching half-light he had come upon the Lord God Himself complete with a cohort of angels, some of whom he even knew by name.

'Jamie! Where's he takin' you? Where are you takin' him?' He trotted to keep the pace, tripping on stones. With five in the squad there was only one man in the rear—Dobbs—and when Taff tried to ease him over and fall in with them Dobbs shoved him hard enough to send him pitching down and wondered what Mrs Williams would say. The others were quiet; it was recognized in No. 2 hut that Dobbs was responsible for Taff Williams, though Taff himself never seemed to know this.

He got to his feet and was after them again, this time appealing directly to the godhead. 'Sarge! Sarge, I'm comin'! Where are you goin'?'

Dobbs was sweating badly and could hardly get any words out. 'Taff, this is very serious—you've just *got* to *fuck* off!' He took a quick swipe but Taff was on his other side.

Tewson said: 'Let him fall in.'

'But I said I'd look after him!'

'Then look after him.'

'How the hell can I?'

'Either let him fall in or you fall out and keep him behind.' Tewson threatened nothing; his tone was enough.

'I'm comin', I told you!'

'Le-eft, right! Le-eft, right! Pick up that step, then!' It was all Proctor could do, try to cover their talking. They were rounding the parade-ground and heading for the pick-up point below the main gates. The light was strengthening quickly now.

Dobbs's vision was blurred by tears of frustration.

'Taffy, you can't come with us!'

'I wish you'd bloody shut up,' Taffy said.

Tewson turned his head again. 'Dobbs, fall out and take him with you.'

'I'm not staying behind!'

'Then he'll have to come.'

'I'm comin',' Taffy said to everyone in general, 'whether he stays behind or not.'

'There's your answer, Dobbs—there's nothing you can do.'

Dobbs settled for it. 'Taff, I'm no longer responsible for you, d'you understand that?'

'God, the years it's taken for you to realize!'

'Le-eft—le-eft—le-eft . . . You'll have to do better than this!'

Tewson said: 'Williams, no more talking, right?'

'Who the hell are you to—'

'No talking!' Proctor told him.

Taffy shut up.

Spragge, nearest Proctor, said: 'Halt us by the fire-post, Sarge.'

The cool air of the morning took on the taint of Diesel gas. A truck had stopped near the armoury.

'Squa-ad—*hult!* Stan-dat—*haice!*'

Proctor had seen the truck and he knew the time. There was no one nearer to them than the gate guard so he said quietly:

'This is your last chance, you know that?' They heard by his tone that he was angry with them.

Rickman said: 'Drop out if you want, Sarge. We're on our way.'

'Then God help you.' He looked across the heads of his squad and saw the weapons and ammunition going into the truck.

Spragge had begun shaking and couldn't stop it. The way Tewson had told them it had sounded foolproof except for bad luck—an officer going past, something like that. Now they were stood here in the open, six of them with the sergeant. Only six. 'We're too bloody *soon*,' he said.

A pinkness came into the light as the rim of the sun showed.

'Don't worry,' said Tewson. It had to work. The whole operation had been planned on that assumption; it was the only way to plan anything. He had also told them as few details as possible so that they wouldn't become vulnerable to doubts. But they could see what was on now and they knew there should be ten men standing here, not six. They were halted facing the nearest building, the guard-room; that was all right; nobody there, looking at the column, could tell if there were six men or sixty. But there were other huts on their right, several between here and the armoury; and the camp was well awake now, with people on the move.

No one would have to notice. If they noticed they must think, That looks a short column this morning, and believe they were deceived, believe there must be ten because there had always been ten.

'Sarn't Proctor . . . If you could come round this side . . . between us and the huts . . .'

Proctor moved slowly, casually, looking up at the sky, turning a glance on the armoury, inspecting his boots, until he was standing to the right of the squad. His question was only just audible. 'This lark your idea, then, Tewson?'

'We all thought of it,' Spragge said. 'All of us.'

And if they didn't get through those gates they'd all share in taking the can back, all of them. Except for the job on the M.P. sergeant; that was for him and Rick.

The third ammunition-box banged into the truck.

The sweat was cold on Rickman and he stood thinking of what would happen when the first officer happened to walk past. Proctor would have to get the squad to attention and order the eyes-right; he would have to salute and the officer would have to return it and find he was looking straight at a senior N.C.O. who was meant to be under close arrest. They'd take him to the guardroom and someone would ask how he could have got away from the spare hut and someone would go back and look for the M.P. sergeant. The sweat was cold on Rickman and he cursed Spragge and Tewson and himself, marvelling at his own idiocy.

He heard Tewson say quietly: 'Dobbs.'

'Yes?'

'Tell Williams.'

The door of a hut opened suddenly and Rickman's breath hissed in.

'Don't turn your heads,' Tewson told them. There was the creep of gooseflesh over his whole body. 'Another minute and the truck'll be here, then we're all right.'

Men walked from the hut, talking together, their voices dying away. In a moment Dobbs said in a quick rush: 'Listen, Taffy, we're leaving camp and going on our own up north to see if we can help them at the Mission. It's long odds we'll ever get there because of the Vend'u. *Now* do you understand?'

'We'll have the sergeant with us, won't we?'

'Look, Taff, we can end up dead, the lot of us.'

'How else can anyone end up?'

'Oh for Christ sake, Taff—'

'I think you're a crummy lot, not telling me this before—'

'Taffy, it's not too late!'

'It's on'y by luck I'm here at all, no thanks to you crummy lot. Now shut up, Dobbs, you get on my tits.'

Jamie Cleaver had started to wheeze and Rickman realized it was trapped laughter so he jabbed an elbow into his ribs hard enough to make his eyes water.

Sergeant Proctor was watching the truck down by the armoury and he still couldn't work it out. The officer—it should be Millburn and looked like him from here—would be getting into the truck as soon as he'd signed for the weapons, and the truck would move up here to the pick-up point. As soon as the men were on board the sergeant in charge would climb into the cab and sit between the officer and the driver. But that wasn't possible today. His pride had stopped him asking a direct question up to now but this was a situation where a slip would mean the Glasshouse for these men.

By rights he should have marched them straight on to the guardroom five minutes ago, not from duty but from mercy: they'd survive the Glasshouse; it wasn't a killing-ground like the Vendettu-ridden bush. But they'd risked a longer stretch by thinking of him and coming to him with a chance of freedom of a kind; even to talk to him they'd first had to assault an M.P. sergeant. They hadn't known what he would decide to do—stay or go with them; but they'd given him the choice. The one thing they'd known for sure was that if he chose to stay he'd do nothing to stop them going; without that much trust in him they couldn't have come to him at all.

He should still do it, by rights. March them into the guard-room, where they wouldn't be hacked to pieces and their young bones left for the buzzards to pick. There was evidence enough and an M.P. ready to give it. That was the one thing he should do, and the one thing he couldn't.

A door of the truck's cab slammed and the engine was started.

He said to Tewson: 'What do I do when we have to get in?'

'Normal routine but don't let the driver see you. As soon as the officer calls you, get into the cab with him. He knows about you.'

Proctor heard the truck coming. Softly he said:

'Millburn?'

'Yes.' The gooseflesh had become rhythmic and he had begun feeling light-headed; he wondered if he ought to tell the others what to do if he flaked out: keep him upright and bundle him into the truck.

The sun was warm now on their faces and necks; the glare had come into the sky.

A body of men marched past them, the day-guard on their way to relieve. Sergeant Proctor had his back to them.

An officer came out of the guardoom and Tewson saw him. It was Mr Keene. He returned the salute of the day-guard and came on towards Sgt Proctor's squad. He would pass them fairly close: the path was some ten paces from where they were halted.

In the front rank Spragge whispered: 'Tewson.'

'Don't worry.' But there was nothing they could do. The truck was nearing them now but Lt Keene had the edge; he would be abreast of them first. He would pass them on the other side from where Proctor was now standing, but Proctor couldn't stay where he was. Any officer or N.C.O. in charge of a halted party was expected to acknowledge passers-by of superior officer rank; the C.O. himself might chance to be one of them and he would never pass a squad of men remaining at ease without putting the officer or N.C.O. on a charge simply for not seeing him.

All this was automatic routine; Spragge and Tewson, together in the front rank, were by force of habit lifting their heads a little and dressing their stance. If Rickman had been in the

front rank he would have said nothing; Spragge had to express
what he felt and then he could steady up, relieved of some of
his tension. He murmured:

'That's it, then.'

Tewson took a full breath and was able to say: 'Don't panic.'
The threat of his flaking out was over; it had been the waiting,
the strain of not knowing, that had brought him near fainting.
Now there was an actual emergency and his head was clear;
images and sounds were sharp again. But he couldn't see any
way out.

Keene was closing on them. If Sgt Proctor ignored him he
would stop, call him over for the purpose of charging him outside the hearing of the men, and recognize him. If Proctor
followed routine procedure and saluted, Keene would look
directly at him while acknowledging, and at ten paces recognition
was again inevitable. There was only one hope: Proctor had
already noticed Mr Keene; an N.C.O. of long service knew at all
times when an officer was anywhere near him inside camp
bounds. He would see the danger and might try to avoid it by
taking a pace towards the truck as it neared him, making ready
to present himself to the officer in charge of his party, Millburn.
It was a matter of timing.

Tewson couldn't judge precisely from the sound of the truck.
It hadn't begun slowing yet and until it did there was no chance
for Proctor to try the only way out. Mr Keene had not slackened
his pace and was now close enough to expect recognition.

As he heard Proctor move, Tewson knew that they had missed
their only chance by a matter of seconds.

'Squa-ad . . . Atten—*shun!*'

Proctor took seven smart paces to the other side of the standing
party and banged his boots together.

'Eyes . . . *right!*'

His salute was exemplary. Looking past him, those on the right
flank of the column saw Lt Keene's arm swing up and then falter.

The truck was slowing. Dust from its wheels drifted across
the boots of the squad.

Keene had stopped and was coming towards Proctor.

As the truck pulled up the cab door opened and Lt Millburn
swung down.

Sergeant Proctor's immediate responsibility was now to the
officer in charge of his party, Lt Millburn; and since he had
correctly acknowledged Lt Keene's presence he came down from
the salute.

'Eyes . . . *front!*'

As Proctor moved smartly past the head of the squad to present himself to Lt Millburn, Lt Keene called to him by name, but the rattle of the idling Diesel was fairly loud and he seemed not to have heard.

He again came to the salute, three paces from Lt Millburn.

'All present and correct, sir!'

Millburn had noticed Mr Keene and nodded to Proctor.

'All right, Sergeant, get the men on board.'

'Sir!' He swung round. 'Break ranks! Into the truck, smartly now!'

Keene was calling something but nobody seemed to hear as the squad broke for the truck at the double and Proctor hit the bolts free and swung the tailboard down.

'Come on, then, look sharp!'

Cleaver missed his footing on the metal step and bruised his knee, half falling. Spragge steadied him and gave him a bunk up. Rickman followed. They went aboard as rehearsed, Cleaver and Spragge going forward to obscure the canvas window; Rickman, Tewson and Dobbs grouping near the tailboard so that when they drove through the main gates the guard would see a full complement. Proctor swung up the board and they helped him. He took his time with the bolts.

Keene was talking to Millburn.

'What the devil's Sergeant Proctor doing here?'

Millburn was turning the sheets on his exercise-board, only half attending. 'He's been released for selected duties, didn't you know?'

'I'm damned if I did! Whose orders?'

'Colonel Gray's.' He straightened the bulldog clip and looked at Keene, lowering his voice. 'Frankly I think it was a wise move; the morale's bad enough without keeping our No. 1 hero under close arrest with the whole camp sorry for him.' He opened the door of the cab.

'Well my God, you'll have to keep a damned sharp eye on him out there.'

'Are you serious? Where could he run to? Only back to the camp. The C.O. knows his onions, take it from me.' He called to the rear of the truck. 'Right, Sarn't?'

'All in, sir!'

As Proctor came round to the cab Lt Keene turned and walked off; he was quite aware that people like Jones and Shaw would have said a word to Sergeant Proctor out of charity, but it was his opinion that after such an act of flagrant indiscipline he should never have been released from the guardroom, let alone the spare hut. Millburn was worse than anyone, referring to him as a 'hero'.

The driver was dabbing the throttle to keep the cylinders clear.

Millburn's hands had lost their steadiness and he gripped the exercise-board harder, blocking Proctor and looking up at the driver. 'Is your name Saunders?'

'Yes sir!'

Millburn checked the top sheet on the board again.

'I've just seen the runner. You're wanted at the orderly room, 0800 hours. We shan't be back till well after that time so we'll have to leave you here.'

Saunders turned off the engine and got down. 'I'll fetch a reserve driver, sir.'

Millburn looked at his watch.

'We're late starting as it is.' He said to Sgt Proctor: 'Call Rickman. He's driven trucks all over Australia.'

'Right, sir.' He turned and slapped the canvas. 'Rickman! Out of there—you've got your old job back!'

Saunders was standing uneasily. With any other officer he wouldn't have spoken up, but Millburn was a short-termer and the rule was strict: only M.T. personnel were allowed to drive service vehicles.

'Should fetch an M.T. driver, shouldn't I, sir?'

Millburn jerked his head up. 'I happen to know the rules and it's my responsibility. You're dismissed from present duty.'

'Sir!' Smart salute, two paces backward, right turn and quick march, and let the bloody fool try and explain it to the C.O. when he got back to camp, because that's where the M.T. Officer would take him, quick as you like.

Millburn stood back from the door. 'Right, in you go, Sarn't!' Rickman had climbed in on the other side and started the engine. Millburn followed Proctor and slammed the door shut. Rickman put the gears in and gunned up. The main guard saw them coming and swung open the gates; knowing there was an officer on board they presented arms as the truck went through. A face showed at the window of the guardroom and the brief report was made on the observation-sheet.

Morning Patrol, departure-time 0705 hours.

CHAPTER SIXTEEN

THIS was arid land. Mountains stood on rock hard as themselves; valleys had sharp brinks and were still dark at mid-morning, the only places where there was cold. The rest of the land burned.

It was a land not much different from what it had been a million years before. Sculpted by the cataclysm of the earth's making it had been changed only by the heat and the winds and changed only a little. A thousand miles west of the coast were escarpments ranged in echelons, their faces a mile high and vertical, their flanks broken and falling away to the white glare of pumice beds, a petrified flood of lava never to move again. The land rose here and there eastwards only to fall again, its mass too heavy to support itself. Outcrops of blue rock held clouds aloft and made a haunt for eagles.

Between the great escarpments and the ocean lay the plains and the wastes of bush; a hundred thousand square miles of scrub, prairie and thorn was scarred by low rifts, red in the morning and yellow by noon; between them ran game-trails, crossing and joining and sometimes vanishing where the wind had torn dust into the air and cast it in meaningless directions. The few rivers were sluggish, oozing between banks of red mud a mile wide; trees clung to them at angles, their leaves dipping to touch the spiked tops of reeds whose stems were hidden in thick red water.

Lion and leopard were here, never going far from where water was more than a day's journey away. Hyenas were wider-ranging, and everywhere were vultures because carrion was not scarce. The heat killed, and thirst killed, and beast killed beast.

This morning a dust-storm had lifted from the plains a few hundred miles from the south Tamalese frontier and some villages were destroyed by its haphazard passage; from the town of Lisolaville the storm could be seen far to the west, a long smudge of black that was the shadow of the higher layers of dust that flowed yellow under the sun. From the height of an eagle's flight, eastwards of there, the storm made a wash of dark, low across the scrubland, and the capital of the Tamalese Republic was a white pebble cracked across with streets. The British camp was too small to leave any mark on the land.

There was only a faint puff of colour lengthening across the plain and moving northwards by indiscernible degrees. It was the dust of the truck.

They had thought they would raise a cheer, once clear of the camp, but they didn't. There was no singing even, as there usually was on the morning patrol. But Cleaver and Spragge had lurched to the rear of the truck and crouched at the tailboard with the others so that they could watch the camp getting smaller. Nobody said anything for the first mile or two.

They had thought they would watch the receding clutter of huts with feelings of elation or triumph; but they felt only a kind of surprise that what they had planned so desperately was now achieved so easily.

Cleaver's knee throbbed from the bruising and he kept a hand over it in case the movement pitched him against the machine-gun.

The yellow-red dust billowed in their wake and it was all they could see for minutes; then a curve in the track showed them the camp again, much smaller each time. But they'd seen this before; nothing was different today except a thought in their minds: the morning patrol had set out as usual but this time it wasn't going back.

Tewson shut his eyes sometimes against the glare that was coming off the dust. He looked tired but his face was relaxed; his hands hung slackly, jogged by the movement of the truck.

Then another curve came and they all lifted their heads again; and as the dust-curtain was drawn aside they could see only the flat horizon. Cleaver slowly raised his hand, jerking two fingers, and the others nodded.

Just before 0900 hours they reached the Tit, the smaller of the two hills, and Rickman kept his foot down, sending the truck through the scattering of loose shale that had been sliding down ever since the hill's cone had been raised. The wheels slipped and the shale flew up to rattle under the mudguards and Lt Millburn said to Rickman:

'Watch it.'

'Yes, sir.'

Sergeant Proctor remembered the time he'd climbed the hill and talked with Millburn. That seemed years ago. He asked:

'You bring all we need, sir? Maps, compass an' that?'

'Yes.' Millburn turned his head and tried to see how Proctor was feeling. There was only the faint set smile. 'I'm glad you're with us, Proctor.'

'I just hope I can be useful.'

'We'll be all right.'

'It's these lads I'm thinkin' of. Bloody mudlarks.' He looked suddenly at Millburn. 'What made you join our little army, then?'

Millburn looked through the windscreen again. 'D'you really want to know?'

'I didn't count on an officer bein' with us.'

After a while Millburn said: 'The reason's not very interesting. I joined the Army—not ours, the big one—to get myself an education. The real thing. Adventure, knowledge of men. It was all right for a time but then I began to see that it was pretty selfish; I was just using an organization for my own ends, taking a free ride. A lot of people have done the same, but it didn't make my case any better. In the end I found myself sitting on my backside doing nothing at all while a whole lot of English people were getting carved up by the blacks all around me.' He fell silent as the truck slowed through a patch of close-grained bush where there might be an odd five-stepper. 'That didn't worry me as much as it should have because I thought there was nothing we could do. Our hands were tied. Then you showed us that all we needed was a bit of honest anger. Even then this chap Tewson had to give me the final push. The trouble with me, Proctor, is that I lack initiative.'

The truck gave a bad lurch and the fringe of a thorn-bush whipped past the canvas, tearing it.

'Look, Rickman, you'll have to watch out. This is the only home we've got.'

They could still catch a glimpse of the Tit sometimes above the dust-trail, and a new feeling was coming into them. They'd never been here before, this side of the hill. It was new country.

'I'd never have come, without him,' Taff Williams said. His aureole of red hair was flying about in the draught from the torn canvas.

'Him?'

'Sergeant Proctor.'

'Nor would we,' Spragge said.

Tewson opened his cigarette-case. Cleaver took a fag but Taffy shook his head. 'They'll smell the smoke up front.'

'Forgetting something, aren't you?' Dobbs was trying to find a match.

'What am I forgettin'?'

'We're on our own now.'

Taff's deep blue eyes were clouded with the struggle to under-stand. 'I know, but what difference does that make? Mr Millburn's an officer, isn't he? An' Sergeant Proctor's an N.C.O.'

Spragge held Dobbs's wrist for a light and blew out smoke and said to Taff Williams: 'Listen, mate. This isn't just a light-ning raid on the Vend'u with the C.O. back at the camp turning a blind eye. Nob tried to explain it to you but you wouldn't have it. We're going to try reaching the Mission two hundred miles north, and if we're set on by too many Vend'u on the way we won't make it, see? If we reach the Mission we might do some good or it might be too late or we might find the Vend'u stronger than us. But if we stay on our feet, Taff, an' we can get the Mission people somewhere safe, we'll look for some more trouble—plenty need help in this area. An' when the ammo runs out we'll hole up till we can get to safety ourselves.' He put his big hand on Taffy's arm. 'But it won't be back to the camp, see?'

Taff's pupils had become large with wonder.

'It won't?'

'I'd better tell you what we are, Taff. Deserters.'

'Us?'

'Deserters. If Mr Millburn goes back he'll be put up for court martial and cashiered. Sergeant Proctor's already for the chopper an' they'll strip his tapes off anyway. For us lot it's the Glasshouse.'

Dobbs said bitterly, 'You *would* bloody well come, Taff. Didn't I try to warn you?'

'Oh, shut up. They'll never get me in the Glasshouse! There's ships in Bristol wantin' hands, aren't there?'

Dobbs held his tongue. He knew what Taff was picturing: Captain Williams, renegade from justice, braced at the helm of a rum-running merchantman with a cut-throat crew bound for hell or Buenos Aires, whichever the gods decreed. Mrs. Williams didn't know what she'd been asking; half a million sheep-dogs would never manage her boy.

'So we're just a bunch o' blokes,' Spragge finished, 'all equal in the eyes of the Lord. An' may He think fit to smile on us.'

Taffy slid forward on his ammo-box, stuck his hands into his pockets and stretched his legs out.

'If you lot hadn't brought me I'd've put a Welsh curse on you worse than a witch's giblets, so you wouldn't have got far. Count yourselves lucky, that's all.'

Jamie Cleaver gave him a fag and lit it for him.

The last of them to feel the new mood—the sense of being free and together and glad of it—was Tewson. It was still only a few hours since he'd stood in the front rank of the squad watching Lt Keene coming and knowing that their desperate little show was over.

It had been worse for him because of yesterday's alarms and the shock of Millburn's decision. Until yesterday the thing had gone without a hitch; the trickiest part had been dealt with early: having told the orderly-room clerk he'd accidentally left a private letter among the returns he'd brought in from No. 2 Platoon, he had hung about while the clerk had searched for it. The printed forms he'd needed were within reach and the clerk had twice turned his back. The typewriter in the welfare hut was for the use of the men and always available. That evening, appointing himself duty runner for a few minutes, he had posted up the new orders in Nos. 2 and 7 huts. They were to the effect that the five men in No. 7 hut already warned for morning patrol on Thursday were to be replaced by the undermentioned personnel: Cleaver, Dobbs, Spragge, Rickman and Tewson. Changes in the roster weren't unusual: it was affected by men going sick, being put on light duties and warned for night-guards at short notice.

Except for a message to be left in safe hands at the last moment it was all he had needed to do. The five men already on the roster from No. 3 hut remained on it; they made up the full complement of ten for the patrol. Until the time when Cpl Bruce had told him to report to the platoon office the operation had been ready to run. The morning patrol would leave camp as usual with an officer, sergeant, corporal and ten men. The change in normal procedure would take place in the distant bush. The officer and the sergeant would climb the hill. The group from No. 2 hut would arrange to be nearest the stationary truck as they all waited for the officer and sergeant to come down from the summit. During this time—a period of some twenty minutes—Spragge would tell the corporal he'd noticed a loose bolt on the machine-gun on their way out. He and the corporal would get into the truck and make a check, while Rickman wandered up to see if they needed a hand. The gag and cords would be ready as arranged and Spragge was one of the biggest men in the camp. Tewson had allowed sixty seconds for the job; the others would see nothing.

Rickman would then go round to the cab, climb in and drive the truck in a U-turn past the rest of the patrol. For the first time in the whole operation they could now expect danger: the M.T. driver responsible for the truck would want to know why it was on the move. But it would be too late for him to do anything. As Rickman drove slowly past the men, Cleaver, Dobbs and Tewson himself would jump on board. Rickman would speed up for a hundred yards in case the M.T. driver gave chase; he would then stop the truck and wait while the corporal was lowered to the ground within sight of the five innocent men and the driver. At this point the corporal would be told that a relief transport was on its way to fetch the marooned party back to camp, in response to the message Tewson had left in safe hands for delivery to the guard room two hours after the 'morning patrol' had set out.

Within minutes the truck would be out of sight to the north of the hill. Nobody would have been hurt and no damage done.

After he had seen Lt Millburn the first time, Tewson had told the others that the operation was off. When he had reported back to the platoon office at 1400 hours, Millburn had simply said that he wanted to join them and take Sgt Proctor with them. Tewson, already unnerved by the continual on-off nature of his enterprise, was thrown completely now.

He had said: 'It's going to take a bit of reorganizing.' His laugh had been shaky.

'I realize that.'

'We hadn't reckoned on getting Proctor away.'

'I'll assume full responsibility for that part of it, if it can be managed at all.'

Tewson said: 'You can't assume *full* responsibility. We'll be obeying orders knowing them to be wrong—we can't use the famous Nazi excuse. But that doesn't matter to me. I'd say the others would have a go if I put it to them.' He thought for a moment. 'In fact I'm damned certain. It just needs working out, that's all. There's another thing: if we've got you as the patrol officer and Proctor as sergeant, I'd rather not leave a junior N.C.O. and five men out there alone at the hill. We've now got to change the roster again, cutting out the sergeant, corporal and the five men.'

Millburn said bleakly: 'I'm making things difficult for you. Just take Proctor and leave me here.'

Tewson lit a fresh cigarette from the butt of the last, his hands unsteady. 'No, we can use all the hands we can find. D'you mind if I speak frankly? We'll be glad to have you with us any-way, but if the lot of us get nabbed before we can leave camp it's going to count in our favour if there's an officer in it. Sorry, but you'll be partly—how do the Yanks put it so well?'

'I rather think it's "the fall guy". That suits me. It'll lessen my feeling that I've made the whole thing more difficult for you.'

'No,' Tewson said. 'You've made it possible.' He found it easy to talk to Millburn; they were both on the edge of their nerves and had to think very fast; it was like a ball bouncing between them. 'You couldn't let the rest of us go without you; if you did, Corporal Bruce would report that he'd warned you something was on, and you'd take the can back.'

'It would be worth it. As long as you freed Proctor.'

Tewson looked at him steadily. 'You've got strong feelings about him.'

'I have. And not long ago someone told me it could lead me into a lot of trouble.' Reflectively he said, 'I wish I had that kind of intuition.'

Tewson found his detachment unnerving. 'My God, I didn't think I was starting anything quite so big.'

'Big?' Millburn shook his head. 'Outside this dusty little reserve of gutlessness and bullshit there's a place called Africa and there are Europeans being murdered there, men, women and children, obscenely murdered. We're doing nothing big; all we can say is we've stopped doing nothing at all.'

The ashtray was full by the time Tewson left him. Millburn would initiate the new orders for the patrol roster through his own official channels. Tewson would try to work out how to free Proctor. There were two definite risks now: someone might recognize Proctor before they could get through the main gates, and it might be noticed that the patrol numbered only six men. The only way to deal with both risks was by putting on a good show and keeping a cool head.

Lieutenant Millburn had seen to one other thing before he went down to the armoury to draw weapons. He gave a sealed envelope to Sgt Getcliffe, saying that it contained secret orders for an exercise and that it was to be opened at precisely 0830 hours. He had told Tewson he felt this should be done and Tewson had agreed. The message in the envelope was brief and informal; it was to the effect that this morning's patrol intended to remain in the bush and lend help to isolated civilians; no anxiety should therefore be aroused, nor any search mounted.

Millburn had thought to add a final line: *We are encouraged to feel that most members of the unit will wish us luck.*

Sitting in the truck and sometimes glancing at the others' faces Tewson let himself relax for the first time and accept the new feeling that was coming into him. He could describe it to himself only as a sensation of wholeness. Inside the barbed wire nothing had meant much except the awareness of indignity: they had spent their days performing circus tricks and their nights being poked at with sticks through the bars, and in the way of caged animals they had snarled at each other and picked quarrels for no reason and to no purpose.

Now they'd come together, these few of them, eight men with a machine-gun and something to do, the land rolling under them and their dust flying out behind. They all felt it; it was in their faces. He saw Spragge watching him, his smile suddenly breaking and his big hand reaching out.

Tewson took it and said: 'Did a good thing, did we, Spraggey?'

A moment later Millburn, Proctor and Rickman in the driving-cab heard a cheer go up from behind them, and Proctor looked through the window to see what had happened.

Some thirty miles north of the hill the track became difficult, with loose shale covering the surface in patches. It was high ground and the land fell away on one side; thorn was thicker on the slope because in the rainy season water was trapped and spilled through natural channels. The tyres lost grip over the shale patches; here in the burning noon the conditions were similar to black ice on metalled roads. By the people of the village that had been here once the place was called Liko-hu Mala, the Place of More Trees, and it was here that the truck crashed.

CHAPTER SEVENTEEN

PROBABLY no one else would have chanced a chewing up but Capt Jones was feeling ashamed of himself. The sensation was so novel that he thought at first that it must be something he'd drunk, and it was some time before he had the courage to recognize the truth.

He should have done what Millburn had done.

Milly was a lop-eared intellectual with a bright career lined up for himself once he'd done his stint in the Army; he wasn't the type to go gunning up the bush in a stolen truck with a rebel crew; he hadn't the experience or even the physique. It should have been someone older anyway, someone with ingrained stubble and vintage corns and a liver creased up with gin, someone with nothing to lose but a misspent youth and the promise of a decadent old age. Someone like Jones.

Better still, of course, no one should have done it. The whole unit was bloody annoyed. The news had got round faster than a bush-fire: Proctor sprung from captivity and a platoon commander on his way to hell and glory with a bunch of the boys. They were glad about Proctor but it was the other thing that hurt. It had been bad enough sitting here on their arses and looking the other way whenever the wogs turned up to take the Mickey; now they'd been shown that they didn't have to go on doing it. Only two things, Jones thought, would stop a mass breakout after this. Nobody believed that Millburn's mob would be still alive by nightfall because there weren't hundreds of the Vendettu out there—there were thousands. And the C.O. was said to be in such a paddy that he'd shoot the first man whose cap wasn't straight.

So it was shame that pushed Jones into the Colonel's office. He was surprised the interview had been granted at all.

'Request permission to take out a search-party, sir.'

Gray didn't stand him at ease. He was sitting straight enough behind the desk but he looked ill. Jones thought that if the rest of the unit felt annoyed, the C.O. considered that he personally had been nailed to the cross.

'The object of your search, Captain Jones?'

'Millburn's party, sir.'

There was a clock ticking somewhere. Jones didn't remember having noticed it before. Wearily the C.O. said:

'You may have been too occupied, perhaps, to give much thought to what has happened. It has been my unhappy duty. So I shall explain something to you. Those men are not lost. They are deserters. They are deserters from my unit. From *my* unit.'

He went on looking at Jones but his eyes saw other and distant things. Nearly a minute went by, and Jones decided to chance it.

'They'll be up against it, sir, out there. All I want to do is take an armoured car and scout around a bit—you never know your luck. If we could find them by nightfall . . .'

The clock ticked. Jones actually found himself looking for it. The Colonel hadn't heard him.

'Worse, far worse than their wilful act of desertion, they have left this camp with the expressed intention of provoking the Vendettu tribe, of bringing to nothing the long endeavours we have made to see peace prevail in times when bloodshed abounds. How can I help you to understand that it was not folly that sent those men out there, but wickedness?'

Jones saw that the Colonel's whole body was now shaking. A paper-knife on the desk sent its reflection dancing feverishly across the wall.

There didn't seem anything useful to say. The C.O. was beyond anger and beyond argument. He'd wasted his time coming here. Maybe he could tackle the Adj and persuade him to lay on a special exercise, but there wasn't much hope; the Adj was an expert in avoiding trouble and in the last few weeks he'd practically gone to ground.

'And so your request is refused, Captain Jones.' The pale eyes were focused now and none too friendly. 'I would add that when you are discussing this tragic event with your fellow officers it is your duty to persuade them—as I hope I have persuaded you—that we should temper our natural admiration of the courage of these men with a cold appreciation of their treachery to this unit and to the Regiment. They did not march out of here with flags flying, engaged in a righteous cause; they absented themselves under false colours, knowing that what they did was wrongful.' His hands had come to rest on the desk, and now the fingers began beating a soft tattoo. 'There will be no more thoughts of "search-parties". We must see these men, however it may grieve us, as they truly are. Not lost sheep, but lone wolves.'

Sergeant Getcliffe murdered every squad in its tracks that afternoon; not that he had anything against the men. He drilled them so hard that even if they'd fainted in the heat they'd have done it by numbers. Tonight he'd get drunk but there was a long wait so he had their guts for garters to fill in the time and they didn't mind, the men didn't mind, that was the funny thing. They'd all got their blood up and wouldn't break, and when they banged their boots down they banged them down on him. It was the same kind of fever you saw in the wogs when they worked themselves up to a war-dance, though a bit better drilled, hope to Christ.

He'd soldiered since he was a snotty-nosed torn-arsed young

tearaway, Getcliffe had, and he meant to end up in the full-dress uniform of a Chelsea Pensioner, kick the bucket in his eightieth year on a surfeit of pickled cockles.

'*Get* them feet up—*Le*-ef'—*le*-ef'—*le*-ef'—get 'em *up* now, will you!' He drilled them and they drilled him, no quarter, nothing barred.

Because they should *all* have gone out there, not just them few upstarts, the whole bloody lot of them, M.G.s and armoured cars and all. And now it was too late. You'd never get near them gates with a penknife.

Soldiered since he was that young he'd not known what to do with a pussy but piss in it, two world wars and a lump of nickel in his left leg big as a paper-weight, obeyed a million orders and given a million more and here he was bashing the buggers about the square when he should have been out there where Millburn was and this lot with him.

Opportunity knocks but once. Give me that, 'ckin' give me that! '*Come on pick 'em up, pick 'em up—I want them feet on fire!*'

They murdered each other, all the long afternoon.

'Give it a long name, Sergeant, if you like, but it's only the dust and the sun. Conjunctivitis, that do you?'

Sergeant Giles worked all day in the signals hut, and five minutes in the open sun was enough to burn him up.

'So long as I know what it is, sir.'

They both glanced at the window as Sgt Getcliffe excelled himself in a shout fit to raze the walls of Jericho.

'That man's going to bust a blood-vessel,' the M.O. said.

'Not one of his own.'

The pen scratched. 'Most useful thing is to splash the eyes with cold water, morning and night. If you can find any.'

'*Herbooww—tun!*' The camp rang with their boots.

'All right, Sarn't, give this to Foster.' One of the drawers of the desk was open an inch and he gave it a prod with his thumb, delaying the moment. But it had to be asked. 'I suppose you're burning up the ether across there, are you?'

'Not so far, sir. Surprised me a bit.' He folded his prescription.

'Well,' said Major Ward, 'there's a chance they'll change their minds and turn about before the day's over. A bit early to go sending off signals.'

When the sergeant had gone he got up and paced the room, getting suddenly annoyed with Getcliffe and slamming the window, leaning with his back to it, arms folded and feet together, eyes looking at nothing. That was it, then. Something would have to be done and only he could do it. There were things he'd rather do—shove his head in a lion's mouth, dismantle a live bomb. But he couldn't choose. He had to do *this*.

'Sod it,' he said very softly. 'Sod it.'

CHAPTER EIGHTEEN

THE worst off was Rickman and he wasn't even hurt physically. While they were pulling Taffy out he stumbled over the slope alone and stood with his back to them; he might have been looking at the view.

All Dobbs could keep saying was, 'Christ, is he all right? Is he all right?' He meant Taffy, not Rickman. Some of the ammo-boxes had piled up as the truck went over. Three of them had managed to jump; the truck hadn't been going fast and there'd been time to think. Spragge, Dobbs and Cleaver were over the tailboard before it capsized. Tewson had thought someone should look after the machine-gun because Taff was on the other side of it, the wrong side. He'd dived out of its way as it rocked over and gashed the canvas—Tewson hadn't been strong enough to hold it—but the boxes went next and Taff was buried.

Sergeant Proctor was first round from the cab. They'd been all right in there because there was nothing to shift; they'd just been tumbled together.

'Quicker than that,' Proctor said. The fuel was still gurgling out of the split tank; it was safer than petrol but it wasn't fireproof.

'Christ,' Dobbs said, 'is he all right?' There was blood on Taffy's face.

'Oh shut up, Nob,' he said suddenly, and Dobbs walked away and was sick because he could spare the time now.

They got Taffy out and Lt Millburn looked him over. The blood was mostly from one arm; the shirt was ripped and the graze was a bad one. Millburn worked on him with stuff from one of the kits and Jamie Cleaver soaked some issue bandage with water from his bottle and wiped all the blood from his face. The others heaved the rest of the ammo out and Spragge dismantled the gun and brought it clear in sections; then Sgt Proctor walked over the slope to where Rickman was standing.

'It wasn't your fault, you bloody fool.'

Rickman swung round on him with his eyes bright.

'No? Then who was driving?'

'There was nothing wrong with your driving. We hit some loose stuff, that's all.'

'That all?' He could only just about speak. 'Enough though, wasn' it?'

He looked down at the wreckage of the truck. It was something Millburn had said earlier on that wouldn't give him any peace. 'This is the only home we've got.'

'Come on,' Proctor told him. 'We need you down there, give a hand.'

'Need *me*? I've done my bit, haven' I? Smashed up the fuckin' truck?' His laugh was ugly, toneless like his voice.

'All right, Rickman. Wipe your eyes like a good boy and forget it. Now let's have you, quick.'

Rickman's rage was against himself but he wasn't mean with it. '*Who the hell are you, Proctor?*'

The others were looking towards them, hearing Rickman's tone. The sergeant's hand came up and his fingers hooked themselves along the top edge of the chevrons on his sleeve and gave a jerk. He did the same with the other sleeve and looked at Rickman again.

'I'm nobody,' he said. 'But I'm still tellin' you. We need a hand—you strong enough?'

He turned away. He knew what Rickman felt like but a man of his type would sulk for hours if you didn't pull him out quick.

Millburn hadn't seen what had happened; he was still dressing Taff Williams's arm. 'What's wrong with Rickman?'

'He was just asking if there was a general store round here, where he could get some L-plates.'

'It wasn't his fault.'

'You tell him, sir. I've tried.'

But Rickman was out of his mood. He spoke to no one, working with them in silence until all their gear was out of the truck. Nobby Dobbs had rigged some torn canvas to give Taffy some shade, so Taffy stood up and wobbled a bit and began helping the others while they swore at him and tried to make him lie down again.

Each of them, as they worked, had been thinking his own thoughts on their situation. It was Tewson who said to Millburn at last: 'Well. You've got the maps. Tell us the worst.'

Rickman went to the cab and climbed over the side, squinting through the smashed glass. 'We've done ninety miles,' he said when he came back, 'close on.'

Millburn opened the maps and they took a look. There weren't any roads between here and the Mission; they were safari-maps showing natural features, game-trails and water-points. 'There are several advantages about our situation,' Millburn said. He was still shaking a little because of the way young Williams had looked. 'We don't have to keep to the major game-trails any more, so we can cut pretty well straight north across the scrub and save a third of the distance because we'll avoid this loop. Another thing is we shan't raise any more dust as an advertisement, and we shan't kick up so much noise.'

Spragge looked at the shimmering flatlands beyond the slope of thorn. The north horizon was lost in bloom-blue haze.

'Been better if we'd started out on foot, really.' Seventy-odd miles to go. 'Wonder we didn't think of it.' Seventy miles with the M.G. and the ammo and the sun up there. Getcliffe'd seem like their fairy-godmother at the end of three days.

Proctor was keeping a watch on Williams; the kid felt worse than he made out; it wasn't the arm so much as the shock. Rickman had taken a closer look at the truck, thinking they might do a trick with the tow-rope and some levers, rolling her back on the wheels. It was no good, though; the nearside stub-axle had sheared and that was that. Dobbs noticed Cleaver was limping and asked him:

'You get hurt anywhere, Jamie?'

'Ay. Trod on a thistle.'

Tewson helped Millburn fold the maps. He had to stop himself thinking about the distance. They could march it in three days over this kind of terrain, less. But not with the gun and the ammo, and without the gun and the ammo they were dead men before they began.

'We'd better make stretchers,' he said.

'Blimey, who's tired?'

'For the ammo-boxes.'

It took two hours and they finished up with slings rather than stretchers, using the floorboards and strips from the canvas, chopping the ends of the boards narrow for handles. The rounds were emptied from the boxes and the boxes thrown aside to keep the weight down; the ten Mark III grenades were wrapped and stowed under sheaves of dry grass because the sun was noon-high and they'd be too hot to hold even for a few seconds if they had to use them in a hurry. Every so often Cleaver climbed to the top of the slope with the field-glasses and they were all rather silent until he came down.

'There's enough game in this area to blow our navels out.'

'And we'd make enough smoke cookin' it to bring the lot of 'em on us.'

It was the first time anyone had mentioned the Vend'u and nobody liked it.

It took another hour to hack thorn and spread it over the truck; some of the metal, bared by the rocks as it had turned over, would heliograph its presence for miles. It was when Lt Millburn was foraging for more thorn that he came upon the sergeant's stripes lying on the ground.

That must, he thought, have taken some doing. Proctor had been a sergeant for twenty years and these arrow-head shapes were part of his identity; he'd been aware of them, without actually seeing them, every time he took off his tunic, every time he put it on, every day for twenty years. It was only what they'd do to him if he ever went back—strip him to a ranker—but it must have taken some doing of his own free will.

Millburn looked around him and when he saw that no one was watching he wrenched off his shoulder-tabs and dropped them beside the chevrons. There was no gesture to anything in this; it had meant something to Proctor but it meant nothing to him. They'd come away from the places where emblems of rank served a purpose; out here the leader among them would be the man who broke last, or the man who by sustaining the others ensured that no one broke at all. He didn't think that man would be himself.

They sorted their gear, throwing aside everything that wasn't essential to their reaching the Mission. The rest was stowed on the three slings: the machine-gun, the rifles, the grenades and ammunition. There wasn't much else. The boots on their feet.

Not long before they were ready, Rickman spoke to Proctor, as Proctor had known he would.

'You didn't have to do that.'

'I didn't need them.'

In a moment Rickman said: 'That's right. You didn't.'

Each meant a different thing, and both knew it.

The sun was half-way down from its noon heights when they marched out of the Place of More Trees, leaving behind them their last shelter and the cast-off symbols of their tribe.

They thought there could never have been men so alone.

In some of them it had started a kind of slow panic and they pitied themselves as they stumbled in silence over the stones. They hadn't known it would be like this in the bush; they hadn't known what the camp meant, what the truck meant. Home.

Millburn appealed to his own reasoning as he had done before when he'd been on the morning patrol: *You could never be lost, because wherever you were you were here, and the only place was you.* He knew now that there'd been no reason to talk himself out of his fears before; there had been the truck and if the truck had broken down there would have been a search-party sent to the hill as soon as they were an hour overdue; there had been the camp to go back to.

It lay over them all, this feeling of panic, and for a time each thought it was only himself who felt it, until a word or two brought out the truth. It was Dobbs who said when they halted for the first time:

'Let's have a shufti at the map.'

If he hadn't said it someone else would have. They leaned over the sheet of paper, their fears allayed for a few minutes because the vastness in which they were lost was now contained by it, the unknown becoming known. *Thompson Range. Pumice beds. Kuandouki Village (Sumi-hala Tribe). Dry-weather track to Verwoeld Farm. Intense Fly Area.* There it was, Africa, all down in black and white. Men had been here before or there wouldn't be any maps. Men would be here again. They didn't look at the distance-scale at the bottom; they didn't want to know that Verwoeld Farm was a hundred and ninety miles from here.

When they shouldered the slings and pushed on again through the withered scrub a memory nagged at Jamie Cleaver. It was something he'd seen in a geography book a long time ago, a thin flat book propped on his dried-scab knees, the comic tucked at the back where the teacher wouldn't find it. The book said that if you put the whole of Europe and America and India and New Zealand and Japan inside the map of Africa there would still be room for the Mediterranean Sea. You could forget things like that for years and suddenly it was all you could think about.

The slings chafed their shoulders. The sweat ran down their legs into their boots.

Spragge had to shorten his pace because Dobbs was on his sling. He kept thinking about the truck but he knew it didn't make any difference; if the bastards came for them here in the open they'd have had to get out of the truck anyway to set up the gun. If they'd been in the truck now they wouldn't have felt as lonely as they did but they'd only be kidding themselves; they'd be just as small in a truck, just as vulnerable. The heat was bothering his eyes but he couldn't break the habit of looking past Nobby at the horizon. It wasn't really a horizon; it was the limit of what you could see in the shifting blue haze. Often he thought he saw movement, a dark line nearing them with fresh dust above it. It'd be worse, somehow, to have to watch them coming from a long way off, hear their voices, faint at first and then louder, see the shine on their black skin and their ornaments bobbing as they ran, coming nearer, taking a long time but coming nearer. It'd give them a chance to set up the gun but somehow it'd be worse, the waiting.

The stones caught at their feet; they believed they were lifting their feet as high as they had when they'd started off; they weren't. Blue lizards flickered among the rocks; they saw them when they were there and they saw them when they weren't. Proctor had called them into step so that the rhythm of march would carry them on more easily, but they couldn't keep it up over the loose rock; you kept in step with the man on your sling and that was all you could do.

Gradually the panic was leaving their minds because panic is short-lived by its own terms, not being based on reason. They thought of their objective, the White Cross Mission; it was a place, it existed, and there was a certain distance between it and where they were now, and if they moved one foot and then the other and kept it up they'd reach there. Nothing could stop them.

'What price Carey's mob?' called Spragge.

'At least they've got bloody transport.' Jamie heard Bob Tewson give a hiss at him. 'Oh. Oh, ay.'

The horizon never moved. The sun had stopped. Time had stopped. Only their boots moved.

On the second night they camped near water and scooped some into their mess-tins to boil. Jamie said he was going to have a wash, not go in, just splash himself; but Proctor told him:

'You want to commit suicide, there's quicker ways than that.'

Jamie didn't touch the stream. He hadn't meant to have a wash; he'd just wanted to say he was going to, so he'd feel a mite cleaner, talking about it. They'd had enough lectures on bilharzia from the M.O. Trail your mitt in the water and the bug would get in through the pores of your skin. Internal bleeding, destruction of vital organs, eventual death.

Tewson had asked Dobbs to try getting the Mission on his transistor and after a while he managed it. The call was being repeated at half-hourly intervals and took much the same form as before: there had been no medical supplies brought in since the Vendettu had camped near Mukongo' go Village; rations were running out and they had very little ammunition for their few guns; there were seven young nurses on the staff and four hospitalized patients.

'It was five,' Dobbs said, 'the last time.'

Cleaver said: 'Maybe one of them's got better.'

Before sleeping they organized a guard-shift so that one man was always on the listen; he sat near the fully assembled gun. Whenever Taffy's turn came Dobbs stayed awake with him and sometimes heard him shivering and whispering things to himself. Taff had too much imagination, but it was almost as nerve-racking for the others. The moon was in its first quarter but the stars gave added light—enough to cast shadows and play tricks—and none of them could get through a two-hour guard without being certain that he saw and heard things that had nothing to do with any animal.

You'd sit with your arm against the tripod of the gun, your boots under your bum for comfort, and hear that awful dry giggling and its echo from the ridge. Hyena. And the rough sawing noise that Proctor said was leopard. And worse sounds, smaller and nearer, some of them crisp and scuttling and some slithering, so that you stared into the stones and shadows until you saw the scorpions and tarantulas and mambas that maybe weren't there. And the worst sounds of all, the ones you couldn't name, the ones that came from somewhere in front of you and then behind, until you sat with your fingers hooked round the stock of your rifle ready for the twentieth time, the fiftieth time, to heave it up and blast away at something you couldn't see, could only hear.

And always the subtler and more powerful fear in your mind that stopped you for the twentieth time, the fiftieth time, from waking the others: *If it's a false alarm they'll know I've just got the shits up.*

Tewson gave the first warning of real danger, but he'd forced himself to live with it until he was sure; it might have been minutes or half an hour before he woke them. It wasn't long before dawn and he was on the last guard-shift of the night.

Something heavy had come near, its feet scattering stones, something big, moving and then not moving, seen and then not seen, its shape covering and uncovering the stars low on the horizon. Its breathing was slow and deep, as if it had been moving fast through the bush and had now stopped, alerted by the scent of the men and the shape that sat by the gun. Tewson had known nightmares since he was a child, and he had to convince himself now that this wasn't just another one. It was difficult, because in a nightmare the dreamer doesn't question its reality; otherwise he wouldn't feel any fear. Sitting here wakeful among sleeping men and therefore alone in the wilderness of earth and sky, already prey to other and more abstract fears of punishment at the hands of his own countrymen or death at the hands of strangers, Tewson felt an instability of mind, a loss of focus; rational thought was just beyond his reach.

His scalp was drawing tight on his skull and he could feel the lifting of his hair; the stars grew unsteady in the sky; he became afraid that if he had to shout a warning to the others he wouldn't be able to, because his throat was full and even breathing was difficult.

The big shape moved again and its outline changed and the head became clearly defined against a moonlit rock, and his hands began lifting his rifle without conscious intention. A scent had come on the air, sharp and ammoniac. He couldn't remember ever having smelt anything, in nightmares.

The S.L. rifle was swinging by degrees in his hands and the moon's reflection poured in silence along the barrel; he looked nowhere but at the dark silhouette of the head against the rock. Then the barrel touched the tripod of the machine-gun and the big shape flattened and stones squeaked under the shifting weight of the beast as it swung to face the sound.

Tewson nearly fired. He couldn't tell how far away it was; it looked near because it looked big; it was near enough for him to smell the scent of it though there was no wind. It seemed to be crouched facing him; something small was moving just above it, flicking from side to side, and it was a minute or two before he realized it must be the tail. The beast was ready to spring.

It was one of the cats and he knew that most of them would have loped off by now; cheetah, puma, leopard didn't have this kind of courage. There was only one cat—only one beast in all Africa—that had this degree of arrogance, that would attack any other living thing in its path and kill it simply for its impudence in being there.

'Tewson?'
'Quiet.'

His heart knocked in his ribs. He pulled the rifle back, inching the barrel along the machine-gun tripod, feeling the rough vibration of metal on metal as he kept a slight pressure there so that he would know when the barrel was clear.

Millburn spoke again softly.

'What's on?'

The vibration of the two metals was tingling in his hands; he could visualize the microscopic scratches on the smooth-looking barrel and tripod. He leaned back inch by inch.

'Lion.'

When the tip of the barrel cleared the tripod leg the rifle swung suddenly because of the pressure he'd been keeping on it and his balance was sent askew so that one foot slid sideways instinctively to support him. A stone grated against another. His finger had closed on the trigger.

'Where?'

He knew that Millburn had only just wakened; his eyes wouldn't yet have adapted to the flat silver glow; if he could see the beast he would take it for a bush or rock.

'Close.'

He mustn't shoot before the rifle was bearing fully on the target. The noise alone wouldn't stop a charge. Nothing they had here would stop a charge once it was begun. A five-year-old lion in its prime would weigh a quarter of a ton and once it was launched on a twenty-foot leap even a machine-gun wouldn't stop it; a machine-gun would kill it but the dead weight would travel on and crush a man before he could get clear.

The light flowed back along the barrel and its tip grew dark as it swung to meet with the dark shape. Both were still.

Tewson said on a breath: 'Don't move. Or do anything.'

He watched the humped outline against the stars, waiting for the first sign of a charge.

'No.'

The silence was as big as the earth and the sky; it was a fourth dimension; the planet swung through the universe in accord with it and there was nothing to make noise. Here on the ground each mote of dust lay inert. The breathing of the beast was no longer audible; the breathing of the men was held in check, the air flowing to and from their lungs soundlessly.

Tewson could feel the strangeness again, the creeping away of his reason; the gun in his hands was beginning to mean nothing; his hands were clamped on the gun and his trigger-finger was hooked but it meant nothing; the nerves in his body, infinitely more sensitive than the gross spring of the gun, would change all this within a millisecond: movement from the humped shape would alter the pattern on his retina and the nerves would pull at his finger without his doing anything about it; but he felt nerveless. Even emotion had steeped away; he was a shape in the night, thinner and more fragile than the other shape; neither had any more significance; they were simply here, just as the stars were here, and the silence.

'Millburn.' He didn't know he'd been going to speak. Perhaps it was only a thought.

'Yes?'

So he must have spoken.

'I don't want to shoot.'

The light was losing its stillness along the edge of the shape over there; it meant nothing.

'Then don't.'

Light rippling on hide, dark melting into dark, a sound in the silence and the silence greater because of it. Time had lost meaning, too; it was only the difference between Millburn's not speaking, and speaking.

'I suppose that safety-catch is off?'

'What?'

'Safety-catch. If it's off, put it on, will you?'

Tewson felt the thing in his hands. The gun. He did it consciously, obeying Millburn; and it set off a kind of chain reaction through the whole of his body—his nerves went slack and the long strain was eased at once; the gun fell across his legs and he jerked it up again. 'Christ,' he said, waving the barrel about.

'It's all right,' Millburn told him, 'it's gone.'

'Has it?' He lowered the gun again. There was warmth flowing through him, as it had just after he'd flaked out in Millburn's office all that long time ago. 'I didn't see it go.'

'It's damned hard to see anything in this light.' Millburn was standing now, looking down at him, and he had a sudden frightening thought and said:

'Millburn . . . it *was* there, wasn't it?'

'Of course. You can still smell it.'

That made sense. You can hear things and see things that aren't there, but you never smell them.

'That's all right, then.'

He must have dropped into a dead sleep because it was light when he looked around him. Millburn was still standing there as if he'd never moved; he was using the field-glasses, sweeping them in a slow circle. There was nothing but yellow grass, a million acres of it, the sky and yellow grass. Then Millburn stopped turning, and in a minute gave the glasses to him.

'Over there. Near the thorn.'

He took them and the sea of yellow rushed through the circle of the lens, carrying a darker object, a blob of gold. He swung the glasses back and fixed on it. The lion was standing flank-on, its massive head turned in his direction.

He shivered, perhaps because of the size or because it looked no more real, gold against yellow and framed like a picture, than it had looked when it had been dark against the faint glow of stars. He brought the glasses down and looked again in the same place, and saw it still. It was more natural-seeming now and he felt better about it.

The others took turns with the field-glasses and Rickman said: 'If it comes any closer we'll have to fix it. Short burst with the M.G., be enough.'

'You can't do that,' Tewson said.

'Why not?'

Millburn saw Tewson's face pucker and knew that he was trying to think of a reason that would sound logical. He obviously didn't know what had made him say it, that they couldn't shoot the lion.

'For one thing,' Millburn said, 'the sound of gunfire could give us away.'

'That's what I meant,' said Tewson. 'We don't want to push our luck.'

They began shouldering the slings. Cleaver was on the rear-guard and Proctor told him: 'Keep that beast in sight. It's all we need do for the moment.'

Their shadows lurched beside them as they marched north through the morning, flickered across the black baked rock and rippled over the grass. At noon their shadows climbed by slow degrees on to the litters and swayed there exhausted. They marched with their heads down and watched the shade made by their own bodies; it was the only shade for a hundred miles but they couldn't crawl into it.

Spragge took over the rearguard, then Tewson. He said nothing to the others when he saw, well after midday, that the lion was still with them.

CHAPTER NINETEEN

MILLBURN had changed places again, giving the map and compass to someone else and shouldering the slings, adjusting his pace to the other man's until he realized after a time that he was out of step.

The litter shunted and swung and he couldn't seem to pick up the rhythm; it must be the other man trying to keep in step with *him*. He heard himself mutter: 'We'll never get anywhere *this* way.' The litter grew steady again and then the other man stumbled on a rock and the litter swung badly, hitting against his thighs. It was only when this happened that he jerked his head up and opened his eyes to see what was wrong; in the times between there had been no point in keeping his eyes open; there was nothing to see but his own shadow floating about on the litter and the sweat-dark shirt of the other man and the blue haze beyond. Even the withered grass was blue, the yellow grass blue.

His thoughts were no help. They made part of the scene out here and he was worried by it all. Heat, glare, pain, the blue wall of haze that took the place of the horizon, the sea-sickening movement of the litter—they were the physical aspects of the scene; the rest was furnished with fears, doubts, and his thoughts on Tewson. Why hadn't he wanted to shoot the lion? Tewson was odd, unstable, going off into a trance whenever his nerves were put under strain. The lion hadn't seemed ready to attack; the rifle had been brought into the aim; it was a sub-machine model and the range was close. Then why hadn't he fired? Was it *because* the lion hadn't seemed ready to attack?

'Party . . . halt!'

Proctor was using the correct parade-ground terms by way of irony; there was no bark in his tone.

Millburn eased off the slings. Flies were gathering on his thighs because the shunting of the heavy litter had broken the skin. The others flopped down prone on the half-dead grass, their hands clasped across their eyes. It was Proctor who sat down beside Millburn and for a time neither spoke; they'd sat together like this at the top of the hill, elbows on their knees; but that had been in another life.

'I've been told,' Proctor said off-handedly, 'that it was you that gave the orders to get me out.'

Millburn laughed, and it sounded horribly like the noise the hyenas made. 'Orders? There weren't any orders, man. We were playing the whole thing by ear.' He began trying to pull his boots off but they were stuck; it wasn't sweat after all, but blood from the blisters.

'What put you in mind to get me out?'

'Well, my God, it was no place for you, was it? Being fed from a tray and taken for walks like a dog. Was it?'

He wondered if Proctor was wishing they'd left him there, safe in the camp where life was simple and everyday demands on a man were slight, where even thoughts of reduction to the ranks and a term in the Glasshouse had a certain pattern that the simplest of men could understand. The sense of isolation out here was affecting them all; even the sense of purpose was wearing thin: they'd set out ready to take on the Vendettu and people had said the open bush was full of them, but all they were on now was a grinding route-march.

Proctor sat with the ends of his mouth turned up, squinting against the blue.

'Did you want to be left there?' Rickman asked. They didn't realize he'd been listening. 'Is it gettin' you down, then, this lot?'

Then Proctor laughed. It didn't sound like Millburn's laugh a minute ago; this was the real thing and they took good from it, remembering the easy days in camp, beds and a clean shave and a beer in the NAAFI.

'No,' Proctor said lazily, 'it's not gettin' me down. I'll march with you mudlarks till you drop, and when you drop I'll carry you on me back an' one underneath each arm an' Taff in me pocket. Boots an' all, guns an' all.' He stood up and gazed across the plains northwards. He'd always been tall but now they were lying down and he stood like a column holding up the sky. He said: 'You didn't get me out for nothing.'

He said no more. He'd only wanted them to know, because they needn't have done it—that was the thought that had carried him along as if his boots were bed-springs. They'd have had it easier for themselves breaking out of camp if they'd not remembered him, if they'd left him there to rot.

Before they started off again Rickman noticed Tewson using the field-glasses, and said: 'That chum of ours is in range, I'd say. Closer than he was. The M.G.'d knock him down from here, no trouble.'

Millburn was eyeing him, wondering if he'd said it just to get Tewson's back up.

Tewson lowered the glasses. 'We didn't hump this load of ammo all the way to waste it on game.'

Rickman picked up his slings.

'Say that again tonight when that thing's hungry.'

'All right,' said Proctor, 'on parade . . .'

They went through the afternoon; their shadows slid gradually off the litters and limped along beside them. Taffy was the first. It wasn't that he gave up; he fell asleep on his feet, cutting his head on one of the tripod spigots of the M.G. as he went down. His front man on the litter was Jamie Cleaver and he called out: 'Who's rockin' the boat back there?'

Ammunition had spilled from the canvas, flowing minnow-silver on to the ground. They helped Taffy up and he fought them off, angry with shame.

'I tripped over!'

'Rearguard,' Tewson told him and gave him the field-glasses.

'Can't I trip over, man?'

'You've done two shifts as it is,' Proctor said, 'didn't you know?' He got some bandage and wound it round Taffy's head to keep the flies from the cut. 'Now get on the rearguard.'

'Yes, Sarge.'

They started off again and Millburn was the next. He didn't fall. He just slowed up and stood swaying, the slings stopping him from going over, the last of his reserves keeping his knees locked.

Proctor was at the back end and called a break, and Spragge came down from the vanguard and took the weight of the slings from Millburn, who lifted his head and looked at him with bloodshot eyes.

'Changing shifts?' He had the tone of a drunk.

'Ten-minute break,' Proctor said.

'We ought to press on.'

'We will, in ten minutes.'

The others were looking at Millburn, wondering how long he was going to last. He was a thin stick of a man; what flesh was on him had peeled away with his skin; you'd take him for a skeleton. Spragge watched him sit down, trying not to make it look like a collapse, and Spragge wondered what had decided him to make this trip. Millburn hadn't known the truck would crash but Spragge thought that if he'd known he would still have left camp with them. It was something he'd had to do; it wasn't an impulse. He'd burned his boats that day, and when the guard had presented arms at the main gates he'd known it was going to be for the last time. He'd renounced his rights, privileges and obligations as an officer; but that was the lesser half of it; he'd taken on a job, as a man, that was liable to kill him.

So whatever was in him, Spragge thought, would drive him on and get him to where they were going. And if his body wouldn't have it, they'd carry him just as Proctor said, and the will inside the skin and bone would still be there for when he needed it.

It was a half-hour break, not ten minutes, but they were the better for it and made faster going until sundown. Cleaver was asleep as soon as they stopped, but Dobbs and Tewson got their boots off and fiddled with the transistor, trying to get the Mission wavelength. Radio Lisolaville kept coming in so they listened for a time.

Forces of the Tamalese Ranger Police were called into the East Province border district last evening but arrived too late to assist the staff of the Anglo-American Crop Experimentation Centre, who had been warned earlier of an approaching body of Vendettu terrorists. The building was fired and the immediate count of casualties is reported as fifteen dead and three injured.

No one looked at anyone else as they sat listening. It was always like that: more dead than injured. The Vend'u didn't make war; they carried out massacres.

There are reports from the safari networks of three main Vendettu groups still committed to organized terrorism near the coast, in the hill country south of Lisolaville, and in North Province. It is their expressed intention to wipe out all—

Dobbs span the dial. You'd think the more you listened the less it would mean, but it sounded worse, every time.

'Try again,' Tewson told him. He meant the Mission.

They tried for another hour but on that wavelength there was only silence.

Tewson took first guard. There was pain all over him and in him but he wouldn't have slept if he had lain down. He knew the lion was near but it didn't worry him.

It had been with them all day, sometimes moving in closer, perhaps losing its fear of the shapes they had with them: it had probably seen hunters' guns and what they could do. It had vanished for an hour during the afternoon and Rickman had said good riddance; Rickman hated the lion and was all for killing it. Soon after it had vanished the whole of the horizon started to move. Dust blew up into the windless air and hung in a mile-long cloud, and the ground here, where the men marched, was set drumming underfoot. They had stopped, awed by it and asking one another what was happening. Taffy had stood with wonder in his eyes and you could see he was awaiting big events, the coming of the Lord out of Heaven's Gate or the birth of a mountain from the womb of earth. The horizon flowed gold and birds fled from it; the dust floated like the smoke of apocalyptic fires; the ground trembled.

Proctor said it was a zebra herd; the lion had gone there to kill and eat and the herd had scented it and was running, mad for life, two or three thousand of them with no hope but in their hooves.

Taffy had stood unbelieving. 'One lion?'

'Sure it's not a hurricane?' Cleaver had said.

Proctor had shouldered the slings. 'They're much the same thing.'

Yet Tewson, propped by the machine-gun on guard, was not worried by the nearness of the lion. He was thinking about the Mission, because it had stopped signalling now. When they had switched off the transistor Spragge had opened his thoughts without meaning to, meaning only to comfort him, speaking quietly so that the others shouldn't hear, even though they wouldn't have believed it. 'I've been thinking, the last few miles, what a bloody long way you've brought us, just to see your girl.'

Tewson sat by the gun and remembered her. All through the march he'd found himself trying to remember everything he could, every detail, every word spoken, remembering things that had never happened but that he wished had happened, afraid that it might be lost if he didn't make the effort of remembering, afraid that it was lost anyway by now. He'd wanted to talk about it but it was a private thing and he'd believed the others hadn't known, until Spragge had said that.

He looked at the north star as he did every night. It seemed as bright.

Sometimes he thought he could hear the lion and for reason's sake lifted his rifle; there were other lives here as well as his. Once he saw it or believed so, massive against the milky line where earth met sky.

He slept when Millburn relieved him. His last waking thought had been: I mustn't imagine things that might not have happened, because in some way it could help them to happen. But he knew it was only the measure of his hopelessness.

The light woke them. There was no moisture here, no early mist across the arid land. The sun's rim sparked along a ridge of rock and the plain took fire. Proctor was first on his feet and asked:

'Where's Rickman?'

The others rolled over on to their hands and knees, swinging their heads up like punch-drunks, their feet starting to throb again before they put them on the ground, their skin starting to itch again before the ticks came at them. They looked at the litters with their heavy loads and knew they could never lift them again and would have to.

Then they heard Spragge say viciously: 'The stupid *bastard*.' Proctor lurched for the machine-gun and Millburn was trying to focus the field-glasses, though they weren't necessary: Rickman was less than a hundred paces from them. His rifle was up and the lion had turned for the charge.

CHAPTER TWENTY

THERE was nothing they could do. Proctor was at the gun but he couldn't get the lion alone in his sights. It was over quickly.

Beyond Rickman the lion grew very big. Afterwards Dobbs remembered thinking it was like watching a small boat going into a wave—the wave was suddenly higher and the boat was dwarfed by it. Rickman looked smaller, unnaturally shrunken, as the lion made its leap with the forelegs splayed out and the great pads extended to free the claws. Even the rapid series of shots sounded thin and inadequate; the bullets were going in but they made no difference; at this range they would have stopped a man dead, knocked him backwards; now they made no difference.

Some thought they saw blood springing on the tawny hide as the beast came through the air at the man. Others thought—because in a crisis people see different things—that the shots must be going wide despite the range because they were having no effect. Spragge later remembered thinking, *Oh Christ, they're blanks.*

Half-way through its charge the lion was still alive. The forelegs were coming slowly together until the spread pads were touching, the white claw-sheaths naked in the fur. When the fifth shot went into the brain nothing changed. Momentum was carrying the lion against the man. Whether Rickman realized this or not he threw down the rifle and tried to run, slipped on the shale and fell, sliding with one hand keeping his body at an angle until he could roll over on to both hands and push himself up, push himself outwards.

The lion's shadow covered his head and shoulders. He looked up at it; there was no longer any shape: the sky had gone and this was in its place. He could hear men shouting to him and they seemed a long way off. Then he swung on to his back and was kicking at the shale with his heels as hard as he could, not knowing that he did it. When the beast crashed to the ground it didn't even touch him. Stones broke and the splinters flew and a groan, the most terrible sound he had ever heard, was pushed from the huge throat as the lion's dead weight came down on the rib-cage, squeezing the air from the lungs.

Rickman passed out.

Proctor was first there, crouching over him looking for damage, and Rickman came to when he felt his hands on him.

'I'm all right.' He tried to knock Proctor away.

Proctor straightened up and left him. The others had reached the spot and saw Rickman getting up. They didn't go to help him. They saw Proctor's face was white and his eyes little slits of anger. He went back to where they'd been camped, and started dismounting the gun. The rest of them looked at the dead lion. Most of them had been awake only a matter of minutes and couldn't take it all in; there had been the sun, then Spragge saying something about a stupid bastard, then this. They felt it had happened without their being here and wondered why they had to be here now, part of it but not quite understanding.

Millburn went back to help Proctor, saying: 'It's no good blaming him.' Proctor didn't answer so he said no more.

The others began coming back. Tewson came first, not wanting to look any more at the lion. He wanted to remember it as he had seen it by night. It had come near them, meaning no harm, and now they had killed it. It had been stronger than they were and it still was; he felt belittled by its death.

Not unexpected. He'd seen the itch in the man to murder the beast: Rickman had said, 'If it comes any closer we'll have to fix it.' They'd all had their different reasons for coming here. Rickman had stood up to the kill-and-run attacks of the Vend'u less well than the others and when he'd left the camp it had been to get his own back in the same way, the kill—to kill anything he met because whatever he met would be Africa. A gun in his hands and still nothing to do with it, even out here where they were asking the Vend'u to come and get them. He'd been on the last guard of the night and must have seen the lion when the light had come into the sky and had gone out to meet it. To fix it.

Proctor and Millburn had the M.G. dismantled and stowed on the litter again. 'All right,' Proctor called. 'When you're ready.' His voice was harsh and he looked at none of them.

They got their boots on, lacing them gingerly over their swollen feet, and stood up, moving to the litters and waiting for Rickman. He came slowly, finding his rifle and looking once at the corpse of the lion, dismissing it.

'Lo, the conquering hero comes,' said Cleaver and saw Proctor jerk a look at him.

'*That's enough.*'

'What have I said?' Jamie looked at the others. He couldn't have cared less about the lion or who'd shot it; people shot beasties every day in Africa, made rugs of them for the parlour.

As Rickman neared them they took up their positions, taking no more notice of him than if he'd been off for a pee.

'*It was dangerous, wasn't it?*' The flat tone understated the heat in it. 'Could've fuckin' killed us, couldn' it?'

It would only get worse if no one answered so Millburn said: 'We were hoping to reach the Mission before anything happened. Sound carries a long way in this terrain.'

Spragge saw that Rick was still shaking. He wouldn't have minded what they thought of him for doing what he had; it was the way he'd done it. Gone out there alone to face a thing that size, trusting his rifle wouldn't jam, it took guts, that, and it wouldn't have looked so bad if he'd not finished up in a panic, scrambling on the ground like a dog in a funk. That beast, dying, had looked more dignified than he had, trying to live. And he knew it.

On top of that, Spragge knew, there was the shock. Rick hadn't passed out because he was afraid; it had happened when he heard the lion hit the ground and realized he was still alive and couldn't believe it.

'I'm lucky to be here—you know that?'

'We all are,' Dobbs said. 'Still half asleep and not a word of bloody warning—that thing would've carved up the lot of us once you'd got its blood up.'

'Get no more chance now, will it?'

Dobbs turned away and the silence went on until Proctor said quietly: 'Take first vanguard, Millburn. Spragge on the tail, Williams with me on this one. Come on, son.'

Taffy took the forward end and they lifted the load, moving

off behind Millburn. Rickman slung his rifle across the rest on the third litter and jerked up on the slings, and Jamie settled his step. They marched without speaking, as they mostly did. The day was no different now than it might have been.

Millburn moved to the side after a while, letting them go past while he swung the field-glasses full-circle to make sure they were still alone. They had crossed the unmarked frontier of North Province late yesterday and the Mission wasn't far. The Vendettu group reported by Radio Lisolaville in this region would be the same one that the Mission had said was camped astride the supply-route to the coast. Twelve miles from here, maybe more; the sound of the shots wouldn't carry that far but there were villages to the east, much closer. The Vendettu had no followers anywhere in Tamala; they were a warrior tribe, a rogue group turned into a terrorist machine in the name of the Tamalese Democratic Front. In the farmstead massacres they had killed off more of their own race than the whites, and every tribe lived in fear of them. Those in the bush villages, hearing the sound of shots at a time when all safaris were suspended, were likely to panic and pass the panic on. And the Vendettu knew the language of the drums.

Millburn dropped the glasses back into the case and caught up with the party, going ahead again with the compass open in his hand and his eyes covering the trail in front; yesterday they'd halted more than once to wait for a snake to slide into the bush before they could go on.

Sometimes Spragge, as they made their way through the mounting heat, fell to thinking of Rickman. He should have made it easier for him, said something to him, because a dead lion didn't add up to so much when you remembered they weren't a man short, that Rick was still here with them, hating their guts but still here.

They marched, some of them, in a kind of hypnotic sleep as the sun climbed and their feet lost feeling. There was nothing to see but the swaying loads and the ground going by, nothing to hear but the tramp of boots and the strain of their own breathing.

They marched till noon before they caught the new sound on the air. Cleaver was first.

'Listen.'

They didn't stop. They had reached the stage where it was as hard to stop marching as it was to start. Life had become simple for them; they were oxen. The loads were shunting again

and they stumbled, breaking step. Cleaver had worried them.
Listen, he'd said. They didn't want to listen. It would mean
problems.

Then Proctor called out and they took more notice, raising
their heads. They had no impression of halting, but now they
were standing with their feet still.

They heard what they always heard: the hum of flies. And
the new sound.

'Drums,' said Cleaver.

Proctor stood with his head turning by degrees, trying to fix
the direction. They began lowering the slings and he had to wait
until it was quiet again. Dobbs was sitting on the ground taking
his boots off. The drums had the far sound of thunder among
hills. Proctor said:

'East.'

'How far?' Millburn was trying to stand still; a lot depended
on keeping the knees locked; once they went you were down.

'You can't tell,' Proctor said. 'Five miles, ten. Bush telegraph.'

They stared across the floor of the dust-bowl. The nearest
umbrella-topped thorn were a mile or two distant, wads of
motionless green smoke, the ground dark below them because
of their shadows. Beyond them ran a low blue rift of quartz,
its crest gilded by the light; then there was haze, walling in the
horizon.

Proctor took the field-glasses. Between here and the rift he
could see a patch of land on the move, a herd of impala on its
way to water southwards. Three dark humps: rocks, ant-hills
or buffalo, he couldn't tell which. A drift of smoke wallowed,
drawn by an up-current near the rift.

'There's a village.'

Millburn got the map and spread it on the ground; they
kneeled to look at it. Dobbs had got his boots free and lay on
his back, listening to the drums.

'Ka'malo-moto,' said Millburn. 'We passed this water-point
yesterday.' Sweat ran into one of his eyes and he let it water,
pulling his glasses off.

'They can't have seen us,' Spragge said. He meant, *I hope to
Christ they haven't seen us,* and they knew he meant that. He
didn't want to see them coming from a long way off; he knew
he'd be all right when they were close and there was something
to do, but he didn't want to see them small at first and growing
bigger, with nothing to do but wait.

'They're village drums,' said Proctor.

Spragge said again: 'They can't have seen us.'

'They heard us,' said Cleaver. 'They heard the gun.' Nobody answered him. Rickman's face was wooden.

Proctor helped Millburn fold the map; it was torn half across and there were dead flies in the creases; they handled it reverently because it was the most valuable thing they owned; it didn't show the way too clearly but it made Africa small.

'There's always drums,' Proctor told them, 'in these villages. Chief's daughter got toothache or someone's lost a pig. That's the town crier.'

Millburn stood up. 'So now we know our position. If that's Ka'malo-moto we should reach our objective some time tomorrow.'

Tewson swung his head up. 'The Mission?'

'That's where we're going, isn't it?'

They began moving.

'Tomorrow,' said Jamie Cleaver. 'Well that's not so far.'

Proctor passed a glance over them. Their legs were in a state and there wasn't much left of their shirts—the thorn had been thick all yesterday when they'd lost the game-trails; their eyes were sunk into masks of dust-caked stubble and their noses were peeled raw. Cleaver had been limping the whole time since the truck had turned over, and he'd left the laces loose on one boot. Millburn was all-in, mostly because of the effort he had to make not to show it, and young Taff was asleep on his feet again. The other four were in better shape, if you could call it a shape at all.

Proctor stood with his feet apart and his hands behind him. Softly he intoned the ritual.

'All right, lads, let's have you. Heads up, now, chins in an' chests out.'

Their shadows straightened one by one.

'That's more like it. Dobbs, in the front with the compass, and keep a sharp look-out. Rest of you on the slings, now—come on, we've not got all day.'

The front one was the heaviest; it had the gun. He shared it with Spragge. He would have put Williams as leader but he'd walk with his eyes shut and there was no future in that.

His tone was like a mother's and he wondered what old Getcliffe would have done if he'd heard it.

'Company . . . forward—march. Le-eft, right—le-eft, right— pick up that step now, you can do better than that. . . . Le-eft —le-eft—le-eft. . . .'

They'd never keep the step but it had got them started; that was a marvel in itself.

They moved and their shadows moved, and the dust came up from their boots and settled slowly behind them on the scarred earth of the trail. They marched a yard, two yards, ten, and then a mile, and sometimes Proctor spoke to them and they remembered what he'd said, that they hadn't got him out for nothing.

They reckoned they made another nine miles that day. There were trees where they halted but it made no difference: the sun was down and it was the edge of the world that gave them shade.

There were drums in the night. They sounded a long way off but the trees to the north would muffle them. Every man, going on guard, listened to them with the same thought. If Rickman hadn't used his rifle it might have been quiet here tonight.

Proctor said they were village drums and maybe they were.

He had them on their feet before first light and they marched for half an hour through the cool of the morning. He changed shifts often with the man in front, using the field-glasses 'to make sure of their bearings', as he told them. He'd done a bit of thinking in the dark hours, trying to muster a semblance of generalship; the problem was simple: would they have more chance if they turned eastwards and took it easy—an hour's march and an hour's rest—and offered themselves in the open plain, or pushed on hard to the north and the Mission? East, they'd be running straight into the area where the Vend'u were camped, and the Vend'u already knew they were coming. They weren't village drums. If they went slow and saved their strength they'd fight better at the end. North, they'd reach the Mission first but endanger the women.

If they went at an angle towards the supply-road the Vend'u would see them coming. Eight men in the middle of open land— it'd be tempting bait.

He had to make the decision for them all. Millburn had a logical mind but he was far gone and the thought of having to stand up and fight in this condition could undermine him. Tewson would say they should make direct for the Mission but that was because it was all he could think about. This had been his plan from the start; it was an obsession with him, you only had to see his face when somebody mentioned the White Cross. Most likely he was a Catholic and faith was a wonderful thing and might save him, but it wouldn't save them all if they were caught in the wrong place at the wrong time.

It was best they should fight in the open and alone.

They halted this side of noon for one hour. Nobody asked why he let them lie there for so long. When they started off again Millburn took the lead and once came back to walk beside Proctor for a minute.

'If we follow this game-trail too far it'll bring us a bit east of the Mission.'

'So if they try a raid,' Proctor nodded, 'we'll be right in their way.'

'Yes, I see.' He tried to tell something from Proctor's face but he was looking ahead of him. 'Suppose they decide to come for us in the open? Before we get there?'

'I shouldn't think we'd get such luck, but you can always hope, can't you?'

'Yes.' Millburn walked ahead and took up the vanguard again.

Proctor halted them in another twenty minutes. He'd been watching the horizon and wanted to use the field-glasses. As they lowered the litters and lay beside them they noticed that the drums had stopped. There was only the fly-hum, and the clink of the ammo-belts as Proctor straightened them out on the canvas, Taffy helping him.

The sun was high. They were in open terrain; the game-trail had petered out and they'd marched across baked earth with fissures in it for the past hour. The rift of quartz was still just visible in the haze; it was all that rose above the flat yellow land, except the dark line to the north-east.

Tewson and Cleaver were propped back-to-back, knowing that if they lay down it would be hell getting up again. Dobbs was prone, the remains of a handkerchief across his face. Millburn and Spragge lay near him, Spragge on his front with his face buried in his hands, his bush-hat across his neck. None of them spoke. They lay without moving, their minds just this side of sleep because of the noise Proctor was making as he shifted the gear about to settle it better.

Taffy helped him, not asking him what they were doing. The sergeant liked things tidy.

'Fall over, lad. Get yourself a minute's kip.'

Taffy lay down where he was and listened to the musical sounds of the metal as Proctor busied himself. Then he slept.

Proctor took the field-glasses again and studied the north, watching the dark line and trying to see if there was any sign

of the Mission; there seemed to be trees to the west of it, to the
west of the moving line. Maybe the Mission was among the
trees. He put the glasses down and went on with his work, pulling
open the legs of the M.G. tripod and locking the spigots. There
was dust on the gun and when it was mounted he began wiping
it, sometimes looking up, his hand slowing, the cotton pad finding
its own way along the barrel and back until he looked down
again. The smell of machine-oil was in the air and he savoured
it; it was the sun's heat bringing it out.

He checked the mounting again, swinging the gun on its
pivot. It was marvellously balanced, floating like a feather on
water. He set the vector limits at 90 degrees and swung it again,
taking pleasure. Then he raised the field-glasses again and
refocused. The eye-pieces misted quickly as they always did out
here because of the evaporating sweat; he lowered the glasses
and slid them into the case, getting to his feet and looking down
at the men.

He'd given them as long as he could.

'All right, lads, rise an' shine.'

They began getting up, Spragge first, and Jamie Cleaver.

'Now we're all set,' Proctor told them, 'and it's going to be cosy,
a right carve-up.'

They saw the machine-gun mounted and cleaned and the
ammo-belts laid out beside it. Spragge turned and looked northwards, hearing a sound from there, a faint cry of voices. He saw
the dark line moving, a thin black wave rolling towards them
over the yellow plain. It was what he'd wanted never to see.
His breath was in his stomach now and he felt his scrotum
shrinking. He listened to Proctor.

'The sun's behind us, lads, an' we've no worries, so pick up
your rifles. Dobbs with me on the belt. Millburn, Rickman an'
Williams on my left behind the gun, oblique stations. Spragge,
Tewson, Cleaver on my right. You all know the drill, it's open-
bush defence, Section 39 in the book; done it enough times,
haven't we?'

They obeyed him, not hurrying, taking care with the magazines,
fanning out right and left of him and standing to face the north.
Dobbs dropped to one knee and clipped the first belt into the
socket of the gun, and Proctor got down behind it.

The cries were louder now, and the dark wave higher.

CHAPTER TWENTY-ONE

In the last five days the heat had come down on the camp worse than they had ever known. It was like the sky lying on the ground, soggy and shimmering. The comparative hygrometer in the orderly-room stood at 90 and the temperature was 110.

Somebody said those had been the figures for weeks, ever since they'd taken over the camp. All right, then it just seemed worse, what difference did it make? You couldn't breathe and you couldn't eat and you couldn't think straight and it made no bloody odds what the bloody figures said.

This morning the sick-parade reached as far as the signals hut and when Major Ward arrived he told Cpl Foster: 'Go out there and tell those men that anyone coming to me without something definitely wrong with him will go straight on a charge.'

He pushed the window open and tried to get the fan working. The bloody thing would turn for a while and then the cracked ball-bearing would catch up and bring it to a grinding stop and send down a shower of dead flies.

Halfway through the morning Captain Jones rang him.

'Can I come and see you, Doc?'

'Oh my God, not *you*.' Jones was never sick; like a sensible fellow he kept his blood full of alcohol.

'Nothing medical, just for a chat. Something urgent's come up.'

'Give me half an hour—will it wait that long?'

'Just about.'

The M.O. was through with the last six men in twenty minutes but Jones was there by then. He looked very on edge.

'I've just found out where they are,' he said.

'Wait a minute.' Ward went over and shut the door. He didn't ask who 'they' were; they were the only people anyone ever talked about.

He sat down again. 'Where?'

'That medical mission up north near the province frontier.'

'The White Cross?' Ward glanced at the map on the wall. 'What the hell are they doing there?'

'There'd been some signals from there asking for help——'

'You've picked up a call from our boys?'

'No. Corporal Bruce told me where they'd gone.'

Bruce had been odd about the whole thing; Jones had asked him: 'Why didn't you come to me before?'

'I didn't think there'd be much notice taken, sir.'

'Why the devil not? We're all anxious to know where they are!'

Bruce had stood in front of him looking even more swede-faced than normal. 'I'd overheard them talking about it, sir, about going up there. That's the on'y evidence I've got. Over-hearin' things doesn't make for much evidence, so I understand.'

Jones hadn't wasted time in any probing; the man had some chip on his shoulder and he'd have to go on wearing it; he was well in the fashion these days. 'Well I'm glad you finally managed to speak up, Corporal. I'll take what action is necessary.'

He sat watching the M.O. Ward's round face had shrunk recently and he'd become difficult to talk to in the mess.

'Bruce told you? Is he sure that's where they are?'

'He heard them say that's where they were going.'

Carefully the M.O. asked: 'Why come to me about it? Have you told Colonel Gray?'

'No.'

Gingerly now: 'Why not?'

'Because I want to go and bring them back.' He paused to reflect. 'Or at least see if they need a hand.'

'And you don't think the Colonel would let you.'

Jones gave a grunt. 'Do you?'

'Probably not. But why come to me?'

'There's no one else I can talk to, you know that. You've got to look under stones to find the Adj these days and anyway he couldn't authorize me without the C.O. knowing.'

'Nor can I.'

'Course not. I just wanted your advice. Nothing official, obviously.' And as he said it he realized he hadn't got the same guts as young Millburn. He had to come for a fellow-officer's advice before he could muster the spunk to break out of camp. He'd misjudged Millburn that day in the mess bar; he'd thought he was just a tin Galahad trying to share Sgt Proctor's martyrdom by yapping about it. He'd done more than yap; he was out there taking on the Vendettu, and Proctor with him.

'My advice?' Ward was saying. 'It depends what you've got in mind.'

'I suppose,' Jones told him thoughtfully, 'I don't really need anyone's advice. I shouldn't have involved you anyhow.'

Ward said with emphasis: 'I'm not involved. I've got enough on my plate already.'

Jones flicked him a glance. He suddenly had the feeling that they'd changed places. He'd come to see Ward because he needed a non-militant partisan, someone who would tell him that what he was going to do was right; but Ward had something else on his mind and was bursting to talk about it, and apparently couldn't.

'I mean,' Jones said, 'I shouldn't have bothered you with this.'

Ward dismissed it. 'What's your idea, exactly?'

'I'm taking the three "B" Company armoured cars with all we can carry—petrol, ammunition, combat-rations, water, the lot.'

'When?'

'As soon as I can set it up. Take an hour.'

'I see.'

Jones got up and said impatiently: 'What d'you mean, you "see"?'

The M.O. looked surprised. 'Well, the best of bloody luck, then.' He realized he hadn't been giving Jones much of his attention. 'I mean it, of course.' He pushed his chair back and went to the map on the wall. Jones, after all, was taking something on; the lives of five men would be his personal responsibility from the minute they left the camp: he had no authority to take them farther than the gates. 'It looks like a clear run except for this bit of mountain.' He turned and said: 'I really do wish you luck.'

'Thanks. That's all I wanted. Someone's blessing. Preferably yours.' He picked up his cap. 'The only other thing is, do I try persuading Millburn to bring his merry men back with us if they're still in one piece?'

'Why not?'

'Well, they're all for the chopper, you know.'

'Oh, I see.' Ward folded his arms and leaned on the wall, and a corner of the map came away from the drawing-pin. 'Yes, that's tricky.'

'There'll be no question of come home to mother, all is forgiven. The minute they show up here the C.O.'s going to slap them straight into irons. Actually I went to see him, you know, the day they buggered off—told him I wanted to take a search-party out. If I'd called it a firing-squad he'd have let me go.'

'Yes.' Ward had a vacant stare and Jones was certain he hadn't been listening; but when it came at last the answer seemed to fit in. 'Tell them to come back. They'll be all right.'

'Think so?'

'Yes.'

'I'm buggered if I do.'

'There are extenuating circumstances,' Ward said. 'The C.O. is mad.'

'Christ, we all know that. But—'

He broke off because Ward was looking directly at him and the vacancy had gone.

'He's what?' Jones asked.

'Colonel Gray is mad. Mentally deranged.'

The final signal was received at 1505 hours and the M.O. went with the Adjutant to see their commanding officer. The exchange of signals with the War Office had lasted three days because Ward had been asked for the fullest information and there were details the Adjutant had been requested to corroborate.

The last signal was to the effect that Lt-Col Gray was temporarily relieved of his command pending the arrival of two Inspectors and an Army psychiatrist appointed by the Fifth Military Member of the Army Council, Deputy Chief of the Imperial General Staff. They had already left London by air and the helicopter base on the Simbu-Tamalese frontier had been ordered to ensure their transport direct to the camp.

In his series of brief depositions by wireless Major Ward had stressed the difficulty of submitting a precise diagnosis in a branch of medicine outside his field, but maintained that he would be prepared to support his opinion that Lt-Col Gray was no longer mentally fit to command.

He was quite confident that his opinion would stand up later to any bombardment the official thinkers would lay on. The Colonel's stomach-pains had demanded increasingly frequent visits to his room, and his first clinical diagnosis—peptic ulcer—still held good. Peptic ulcers were claimed by even some of the most orthodox people to be psychologically induced, and the other symptoms of mental disturbance served as more than partial confirmation.

He had put it to Captain Jones as a general picture: 'It's one of those things where a lot of small pointers start cropping up and you ignore them for a bit because they're all different kinds and don't make any sense. Then suddenly you see—without even *looking*—that they're all pointing to the same thing. We thought it was bloody absurd when he trumped up a mutiny charge just because a few blokes were banging on their mess-tins, right? But that's *all* we thought. It was also perfectly obvious that his judgement was slipping: he understood the Vendettu but he didn't understand his own men. But you can't call a bad commander certifiably insane.'

Jones had sat down quietly on the corner of the desk, simply because he hadn't got the strength to stand up any more.

'When did you know?'

'I can't say. But I *began* knowing soon after Proctor let fly with that gun. The C.O. told me there was an unceasing exchange of signals going on with the War Office and that the Prime Minister was being kept informed—'

'He told me that, too—'

'He probably told everyone. The next day Sergeant Giles happened to report sick with a spot of eye-trouble, and of course I told him it was partly due to overwork. He laughed, obviously thinking it was meant for a joke, and I asked him what was funny. He said there hadn't been a signal sent or received for the last three days. So then I had to think out why Gray should tell everyone such a stupid lie, and of course it was the bit about the Prime Minister that stuck out a mile.'

Jones asked: 'You got a cigarette?'

The M.O. fished in a drawer. 'They're damp, of course. Have the shirt off your back.'

'Thanks. You mean it's some sort of megalomania?'

'What's in a name? Ideas of aggrandizement, illusions of power —they'll give it a name when they've put the poor sod under the microscope. I don't know whether he sees himself as a political strong man on a peace mission at the right hand of the Prime Minister, or the much more common false image: Christ at the right hand of God.' He tried to get his cigarette going again but it was no good and he slung it into the waste-paper basket. 'I'll tell you one thing. I'm pretty sure that the general orders for this unit at the present time are to keep the peace *unless provoked*.'

Very softly Jones said, 'Oh, blimey . . .'

'That's why he couldn't signal London saying one of his N.C.O.s had knocked off a score of terrorists. London would have said "So what?" That's why Giles had nothing to do at a time when there was meant to be an "unceasing exchange of signals" going on.' He put his head on one side and narrowed his eyes at Jones—'You know there's been no signal even about Millburn's little lark?'

'Christ. Are you sure?'

'I sounded Sergeant Giles, the day they left camp—said I supposed he was burning up the ether. He said no, and he seemed surprised about it, of course. What could he signal? That a patrol had gone out to take a poke at the Vendettu? Again—so what? That's what we're *meant* to be doing.'

'Oh, shit,' Jones said, looking away.

'Yes. We lost some good men, didn't we? I only hope Millburn's boys are still all right.'

'I'll go and find out.'

'Take care of yourself.'

Jones gave a sour grin. 'Don't worry. I'm no hero. That's why I'm taking a fleet of armoured cars.'

It was the first thing Colonel Gray asked the Adjutant when he went with Major Ward to show him the final signal.

'Have you been able to find out on whose authority Captain Jones believed himself to be acting when he took out his patrol?'

There was no anger in his voice, only immeasurable hurt.

'It was just a routine exercise, sir.'

A petulant smile appeared on the C.O.'s mouth. 'You still don't understand. There can be no such exercises mounted without my express authority.'

'No, sir.' The Adjutant unfolded the signal form and held it out. 'This has just been received.'

'But I am talking about Captain Jones.'

'The signal is urgent, sir.'

They watched him read it. The clock on the desk ticked busily beside the photograph in the silver frame. The dampness in the air was already soaking into the sheet of paper and Colonel Gray slowly raised his other hand to keep it straight.

When he spoke, the M.O. noticed the tone of terrible satisfaction in his voice.

'So here is my Calvary.'

CHAPTER TWENTY-TWO

THEY came in a single line across the plain, spread out perhaps instinctively to pretend they numbered more than they did, just as with some animals the fur becomes raised before battle to give them greater size and put fear in the adversary.

The dust, churned from the dry earth by their feet, rolled

above them, yellow and smoky; they looked like a bush-fire taking hold. Their cries were shrill and not human; there was nothing aggressive in the sound; they were expressing only excitement at the thought of an easy kill. A ripple of silver flowed against the dark of their bodies as the light touched the blades of their spears. Some carried pangas, bush-knives, and waved them above their heads; they were half dancing as they ran towards the eight men who were waiting.

Millburn said dully, 'It's going to be a massacre.'

Proctor turned his head. 'You never seen a machine-gun in action?'

'Yes.' He had been there in camp the night when a mad sergeant had run amok. 'That's what I mean. We're going to massacre them.'

Proctor didn't know if he was saying it to reassure the men. They didn't look as though they wanted stiffening. Spragge's face was chalky and his stare was fixed as he watched the Vend'u coming, but he was the sort to fight better at close quarters. Young Williams looked as if he was watching a heavenly visitation but he knew what to do with a gun once he'd got the orders. The rest seemed all right; the first to run out of ammo would be cocky Rickman.

It was Rickman who answered Millburn.

'Put down our guns, then, should we? They're on'y kids—the C.O. told us that.' He gave a sudden laugh and it froze them; it was no more human than the cries shrilling across the bush. 'You remember a mate of mine, Mackenzie? I do.' The knuckles of his left hand were white against the S.L. rifle. 'I do.'

Proctor said: 'All right, this is the drill.' The ripple of silver was altering, flowing higher; the spears were going up. 'I'm on a 90-degree vector an' I'm firing first. You'll need no orders. When you see them still comin' on at the flank, start pickin' them off.'

He didn't think it would ever come to that. The Vend'u knew what guns could do but they weren't scared till they heard the noise they made; once the noise started they'd take a lot more notice.

Spragge watched them coming, and braced his legs because there was a force mounting in him and he could feel it and knew what it was: he wanted to go forward, run, run to meet them, see them close, feel them under his hands; he'd got big hands and he trusted in them; he couldn't feel what he was doing, with a gun, couldn't feel anything break.

Dobbs was thinking of Taffy; nothing must happen to him;

he'd said he wasn't responsible for him any more but that wasn't true. He couldn't ever go home alive and Taffy dead.

Tewson could see their faces now and saw some of them were laughing in excitement and wondered if they'd been to the White Cross Mission yet, that one there with the painted rings on his arms and the bone ornaments clacking on his waist, the laughing one—had he been to the Mission the day before or the day before that or the night when the transmitter had gone off the air? A lightness was coming into his head and he felt suddenly impatient and wanted to lower his gun and shout to them, to that one, the laughing one—*Wait a minute, I want to ask you something, then we can go on and kill each other, but have you been to the Mission?*

'Steady up,' he heard Millburn say.

'Have they been to the Mission?'

'Of course not.' And after what seemed ages Millburn said: 'We've got to kill them just the same. You all right now?'

Then the machine-gun began firing and the line broke and the gap got bigger and the rest of the line went ragged and Dobbs began coughing in the cordite fumes as he fed the belt. Some of them had thrown their spears a second or two before the gun opened up but they'd thrown short, too soon, being excited. Proctor had judged it precisely, putting out the initial burst before they were in spear-range because a spear was deadly, worse than a bullet once it struck. The blades were rooting into the baked earth and the shafts leaned shivering.

Rickman was moving now and Proctor saw him from the tail of his eye as he brought the M.G. against the left vector-stop and began travelling back. He'd known Rickman would go off on his own as soon as they'd got warmed up but it would have been no good trying to give him prior orders and no good trying to stop him now. His S.L. was already jumping and he wasn't wasting his ammo. Spragge was backing him up, going well out to leave a clear field of fire as a group broke from the end of the line and came in with their knives, drunk or fanatical or just frightened into attacking.

It was difficult for Proctor now because the dust was getting thick, as bad as a smoke-screen. Most of them were running; the few still coming in at the flanks were berserk, and Cleaver was going out on the other side from Rickman and Spragge while Millburn tried to cover him. Tewson was firing at the same man, time and again, the one with a lot of bone ornaments round his waist. Proctor could see he was dead but he came pitching forward and wouldn't fall because the motor reflexes were still alive in his legs and Tewson kept on pumping the shots into him and wouldn't stop when Proctor yelled at him.

The dust was so thick now that he couldn't use the M.G. any more: Rickman was out there somewhere and he couldn't see Cleaver, so he hit Dobbs on the shoulder—'Get your rifle, boy—shoot on'y what you can see!' He went off to pick up an S.L. and try sorting things out. He'd been half right and half wrong: they'd come in at the flank but there wasn't much to it. The noise of the subs was easing up. He found the Welsh boy picking off a near-giant who was coming for Tewson while he was caught off his guard reloading. Rickman was lying in some blood and still putting out a burst at a running man till he lurched over.

Proctor saw two men standing together and went over to them. One was Spragge. His rifle was on the ground; maybe the magazine was empty or it had jammed. The man with him was a Vendettu, a big man with his face painted white and two short scarlet streaks going from nose to ears. His arms were puckered with ritual blisters and incisions; the skulls of small mammals rattled at his waist to the movement of his body. Proctor thought he was young, maybe sixteen or seventeen, but he had the strength of a mature chief and the fanaticism of the bewitched. Even against Spragge he was huge.

One of the broad-bladed pangas lay on the ground not far from the rifle. Spragge had probably shot it out of the man's hand. As Proctor moved round them, bringing the barrel up and choosing a close-range trajectory that would be safe for Spragge if the bullet passed right through, the Vend'u tried to duck out from under the hold Spragge was using, and Spragge had apparently been waiting for that, because his right arm whipped round for a throat lock so fast that Proctor hardly saw what had happened. He knew Spragge was having trouble because of the oil on the man's body; the throat lock was one of the few holds that were any use. The Vend'u was curving backwards, his long spine arched and one hand trying to knuckle into Spragge, and Proctor said:

'Keep him still, can't you?'

It was dangerous because even a kidney shot could ricochet on a bone and Spragge was part of the target.

'Don't shoot,' Spragge said. It wasn't anything like his usual voice; the words were squeezed out.

Proctor said: 'Well, hurry up.' He turned away, thinking he ought to go and look at Rickman, but Millburn and Dobbs were

over there and Rickman was still conscious. He turned back
impatiently. He didn't like this kind of thing; it wasn't soldierly.
He knew Spragge had to do this to get back his self-respect; he'd
stood here with the fear of Christ in him when they'd been
coming across the bush. But Proctor had been brought up in the
tradition that the enemy was a stranger and must remain one,
dead or alive; there mustn't be anything personal.

Then he saw Spragge's other hand come up, curve up and
catch his wrist, and as the pressure came on the Vend'u jerked
once and dropped like a felled tree as Spragge opened his arms
and turned away to pick up his rifle. When he straightened up
he looked at Proctor and asked:

'Any of our blokes hurt?'

'Only Rickman.' They walked together to where the others
were. 'He went out and asked for it, you know that.'

'P'r'aps he's satisfied now.'

'You're the most undisciplined bunch of buggers I've ever had
to look after in all my puff. I on'y wish old Getcliffe was here—
he'd fix you.'

Millburn was supervising the job of getting Rickman on to
one of the litters. There was a lot of blood about but someone
had slashed a strip of canvas and made a tourniquet round the
upper thigh. Millburn was still busy with the medical kit; a
panga had sliced through to the bone; it was a clean wound but
a big one.

'No, put him on his other side. This leg up.'

Proctor looked round him. The dust had settled and he saw
the main body of the Vend'u a long way off. They'd run like hell
for a mile and now they'd stopped; they were in a close group
now, not strung out any more.

'Williams, what's your trouble?'

'I feel sick, Sarge.'

'That'll pass. Come on, gimme a hand setting up this lot, we've
got to be pushin' on. Fetch them knives in, they're always useful.'

Taffy's face was lard-white and his eyes were still seeing things
that were over now. Proctor chivvied him up and got him working. For most of them this had been their first action; some had
never seen dead men before.

'Tewson, what the bloody hell are you doing?'

He went over to where Tewson was kneeling on the ground
beside one of the wounded Vend'u.

'D'you know their language, Proctor?'

'No.'

'He doesn't understand Swahili.'

'You won't get any sense out of him. What d'you want to tell him anyway?' Tewson looked very quiet and steady; maybe he wanted to give the man his last sacraments or whatever they called it.

'I don't want to tell him anything.' He stood up. 'I wanted to ask him something.'

'Go an' give the others a hand. We're shoving off soon as we can.' He waited until Tewson was clear and then moved round where the Vend'u couldn't see him and put a single shot into the brain and came away.

Millburn was satisfied with Rickman's position on the litter and when he'd checked the bandaging and tourniquet he tidied the medical kit and strapped the lid down. Proctor came up and said:

'You mind using your revolver?'

Millburn looked around the patch of churned earth. One of the wounded was moving, trying to crawl away. He looked back at Proctor.

'I can't.'

'Lend it to me, then. It's quieter.'

Before he went off he called to the others: 'All right, we're on our way, so get started. I'm bringin' up the rear to keep a look-out.'

He waited until they were moving and then made his way about, using a full magazine and reloading. The sky was already mottled, eastwards. There was only one time when he jibbed, and that was when he heard his own language being spoken; the man didn't wear a loin-cloth, but a pair of dyed shorts and safari boots.

'Say Christian thing, *bwana*.'

Proctor kept the revolver behind him. This was one of the urbanized; probably he'd spent a bit of time at a mission school before they'd roped him in as a soldier of the Tamalese Democratic Front and sent him into the farmsteads with a knife.

There was something wrong, Proctor thought, about having to do this thing for a man and then the other thing. Somewhere the politicians and generals and bishops and all the rest of the national bloody monuments had gone and got the whole auction well and truly cocked up and never had to admit it because they never had to stand out here on the earth under the sky and comfort a man and then kill him.

He was shaking with anger and had to wait till it passed.

'God will have mercy on your soul, lad, and you'll go to Heaven.'

He walked away and turned and shot from six paces and turned again and went on across the quiet land, alone now. After a while he caught up with the others and took over from Williams, putting him on rearguard.

'Watch those Vend'u. If they look like coming closer give me the word.'

They'd gone a mile before they heard the first of the flock cackling as they wheeled down from the sky. Millburn stared over his shoulder; there were hundreds; it looked like a storm of black paper blowing.

Later there was shade sometimes from trees and it was easier going until they had to choose between following a game-trail or the compass. The trail was an old one, going westwards and curving southerly after half a mile so they went back and hacked their way through scrub-jungle for three hours. It brought them to a dirt road that went south-west to north, a good road curving through taller trees. There were wheel-tracks, and they knew their choice had been right.

Towards evening they came upon buildings in an open space. There were three long huts making a disjointed U, and patches of fresh grass with paths running through them. The white-painted cross stood high at the end of the longest hut. It was very quiet here. The windows were open and none of the doors locked, so they were able to go through every room, but found nobody.

CHAPTER TWENTY-THREE

THE African stopped on the patch of lawn and stood looking up at the verandah. He was small and wore a pair of white trousers; there was nothing in his hands.

Dobbs's eyes had just opened and he grabbed for his rifle but Proctor said: 'It's all right.' He had watched this man walking across from the trees. There was a fine gold chain round his neck with a crucifix on it. He looked at them in turn and addressed Proctor, who was the only one standing up.

'Good afternoon. Do you need our help?'

Rickman, raising himself from the stretcher with one elbow, peered through the uprights of the verandah, thinking there was someone else with the African because the voice had spoken in perfectly clear American.

'I don't think so,' Proctor said. 'We thought you needed ours.'

The African looked again at the pile of guns and ammunition dumped on the path. 'I guess we might.' Then he saw Rickman on the verandah. 'Do you have a casualty there?'

'No,' Rickman said. 'I'm shagged out, that's all.' He had lost blood but his brain was still alert and he'd been frustrated on the way in from the plain because of having to be carried.

'You're what?' The African looked at Proctor again. 'We heard some firing, and the tribe in the village said some men had come up to the Mission. I'll go fetch Dr. Locke.'

As he turned away Tewson called: 'Are they all right? The Mission people?'

'So far we are.' He went back into the trees.

Proctor sat down again in the canvas chair. 'I thought they were in trouble.'

Tewson let out an easy breath. 'And they're not. Who's complaining?'

Dobbs said, 'Well, Jesus, it was a long way, wasn't it?'

Jamie Cleaver tilted his head. 'You mean to, or from?'

'What's that in English?'

'I was doin' a wee bit of thinking the past few days. I was wondering how much we were bustin' our guts to reach the Mission and how much we were bustin' our guts to get away from the camp.'

There was a silence while they thought about it; then Dobbs said: 'We're sure of one thing.'

Rickman nodded. 'We were bustin' our guts.'

They came through the trees, eleven of them, the last group carrying the stretchers. There were seven Africans and four whites, and among them was the man who had gone to fetch Dr Locke.

Millburn went down the steps from the verandah, suddenly conscious of his filthy state. He asked the nearest white girl: 'Is Dr Locke coming?'

'Yes.' She glanced back to the group bringing the stretchers. The eldest of the women straightened up from reassuring one of the patients and came across the lawn, retying the belt of her torn white smock. The small African in trousers followed her.

Millburn was standing in front of the group of men so she spoke to him. 'Well hello . . . I'm Dr Locke.' She held out her hand.

'My name's Millburn.'

'It's nice to have you here.' Her smile took in the others. 'Are you Captain Carey's people?'

Proctor felt the men pulling themselves straighter. Dobbs murmured a word to Spragge. They knew they looked like something the cat had sicked up but this was a bit much.

Millburn hadn't introduced himself correctly; it didn't seem logical to leave your badges of rank on the ground seventy miles away and then talk straight from the book when you reached civilization; but there was a risk of confusion now.

'No,' he said formally, 'we are the 4th Royals, British Army.' He threw in a salute for good measure.

'The British Army!' She was nice enough to make it sound as if Montgomery had called personally, but he knew what the white people in Tamala thought of the British Army.

'We haven't been able to shave for a day or two—water ran a bit short.'

'Did you get lost in the bush, Mr Millburn?'

Proctor was now standing correctly at ease. Only if you'd been twenty years as an N.C.O. could you have known without looking round that the men behind you had taken up the dressing.

'No,' said Millburn. 'We came straight here.'

'You mean you walked?'

'We marched.'

'With all those guns?'

He felt sudden impatience. It didn't matter how they'd got here. 'I wonder if you've any fresh drinking-water, Dr Locke? We've been a bit short.'

She went on studying him with her very steady eyes for a moment. 'I guess you have.' When she had told one of the girls to go for some water she asked: 'You met up with some Vendettu, didn't you?'

'Yes.'

'Were none of you wounded?'

He indicated the man on the stretcher and she looked round for the small African in trousers. 'Mr Millburn, this is Wilbur Tshimali, my chief assistant. Wilbur, there's a little work here for us. Trypan injections for all our guests, and this boy's arm, this one's ankle. A casualty on the verandah there. Can we fill one of the water-tanks again?'

'We can try, Doctor.'

As Wilbur left them she said: 'You told me you came straight here, Mr Millburn. How did you know we needed assistance?'

'We heard your wireless call.'

'But we stopped transmitting three days ago when we moved to the village.'

'We thought there might still be a chance.'

She nodded. 'I see. There wasn't, but there is now.'

The place was white-painted everywhere inside and everything was simple and clean. They walked about with their feet bare on the cool floors and didn't believe it; they'd been given towels to wear round their waists while their clothes were washed, and Spragge, the biggest man, had been given the biggest towel, and he'd draped it across one shoulder and was striding about demanding news from the Forum.

The stuff she was putting on Tewson's palms turned into froth on the opened blisters and he asked what it was, so that he could listen to her voice.

'Hydrogen peroxide. It's all we have now.'

'I'm lucky to get it.'

'Keep them palm-upwards for a while.' Then for the first time she looked directly at him. 'I didn't recognize you before.' There seemed a question in her eyes.

'I shouldn't think so, underneath all that muck.' The stuff went on frothing; she screwed the cap back on to the bottle.

'Did you recognize me?'

So that had been the question he'd seen.

'Yes,' he said.

'What's funny?'

'It was a funny question.'

'Why?'

'Well, I'd never forget you.'

Spragge was still drifting about the place in his bath-towel: 'Friends, Romans and poor bloody infantry, pin back your ears. . . .'

As she turned her head with a quick smile Tewson remembered the other time when they had stood under the tree on the pavement and one of the boys had given her a wolf-call. He wanted to go on talking to her but there was nothing he wanted particularly to say; this was enough, to be able to see her, because often on the way here he'd been sure he would never see her again.

She was looking up at him.

'I'll have to see to the others,' she said.

'To hell with the others. They'll survive.'

She didn't smile. 'How was it, Bob, that out of the whole of your camp—' She looked away, arranging the things on the surgery trolley and smiling quickly again at Spragge across the room; he was warming up on a new theme and telling Mark Antony to straighten his wreath and get fell in.

'It had to be someone,' Tewson said.

Lightly she said, 'But it was you.'

They shared a meal at one of the trestle tables under a hissing Coleman lamp that hung from the ceiling. In its glare the men from the unit saw the strain on the faces of the Mission people that they hadn't noticed when they had arrived.

Rickman was at the table with them. Dr Locke hadn't been able to keep him in the ward. 'The less frustrated I am, the quicker I'll heal,' he'd told her. His skin was bloodless and his eyes unnaturally bright.

They were offered nothing in the way of meat except dried biltong strips poked into balls of maize posho. The medical staff ate very little, and sat mostly in silence; the drums had started again at nightfall and the young African nurses looked often at the windows.

'I wonder,' Millburn asked Dr Locke, 'if you'd tell us what's been happening to you here? We need to know what the position is.'

'Briefly, Lieutenant, we were waiting for the Vendettu to come. I guess we still are. A lot of them survived your defence operation out there, and returned to their base. I doubt if their original plans have changed.'

'You seem well informed.'

'We read the drums.'

The scream was so sudden and so close that Rickman knocked over his posho bowl and Dobbs was on his feet.

'That's Sammy,' said Dr Locke, and turned to Edna. 'Honey, you'd better go give him his mango before he does it again.'

'What,' asked Dobbs as he sat down, 'is Sammy?'

'A tree-hyrax. He comes in around this time and hollers out for his victuals. He's cute but kind of pushing.'

The scream had been so unnerving that Millburn had to wait for the shock to pass before he spoke again. 'What makes you so sure the Vendettu will be coming here?'

Conversationally she said: 'It's their declared intention to clear the North Province of Makarik sympathizers, which automatically includes all white people, all Africans working for them and with them, and all foreigners even if they are Africans of neighbouring states. Since a week ago they've been moving from the coast through the settlement zone, and the White Cross is next along the line—it's as simple as that. Three days ago the headman of the village came to fetch us and we went.'

He thought that despite the gentleness in her face there was a hardness of mind that enabled her to make decisions like that; the Mission was her home.

'You've got friends in the village, then?'

She smiled and looked younger. 'I've been here fifteen years, which makes me midwife and godmother to half the population. That's not too many but it's a lot of friends. They would have done their best for us but we didn't have a chance—it was just that there was no place else to go. They're not a warrior tribe and there's a limit to where you can hide people in a village that small.' She lifted a feminine hand. 'Speaking personally I could use a hair-do but I'm still no stand-in for a grass hut.' More quietly she said: 'I think maybe it needs saying, gentlemen. We're glad you came.'

Millburn glanced across the table.

'You should thank Mr Tewson. It was his idea.'

'We all thought of it,' Tewson said quickly. 'The thing is, Millburn, what sort of campaign do we mount?'

He saw Edna looking at him and obviously thinking hard suddenly about the whole thing. He wished Millburn hadn't said that.

'Ask Proctor. He's the most experienced.'

They heard the drums again above the hissing of the lamp. It would be all right, thought Dobbs, so long as that bloody tree-animal didn't holler again.

Before Proctor could say anything Edna asked them: 'You "thought of" coming here? Wasn't it an official patrol?' She was looking at Bob, but he was studying the blisters on his hands.

Millburn said, 'Well, no. We're on our own. Sort of—freebooters.'

Jamie Cleaver tilted his chair back and Spragge was looking into the middle distance. Dr Locke said quickly:

'It's none of our concern, of course?'

'That's all right,' Millburn said. 'I expect you get the news from Radio Lisolaville, in which case you'll know that our unit hasn't been too active.'

'Obviously you had orders, Lieutenant, to keep the peace. That seems a very wise policy.'

'Probably.' Millburn used a finger to prod his glasses straight.
'It's just that we didn't think so.'

The silence drew out and got on their nerves and Rickman
said in his dull bulldozing tone: 'You might as well know that
we'd have stayed cooped up in camp till the crows came home if
we'd followed orders. It got to the point when we couldn't stick
it any more, listenin' to what the wireless said every day about
the massacres an' that.' He stared at Dr Locke with a shade of
defiance. 'So we scarpered, an' what you're looking at is eight
jolly deserters. It's a shame we didn't come up here with the flags
flyin' and the band playin' but we brought the guns an' that's
what's goin' to count when it comes to it.'

Edna had got up and was helping the girls clear the table. She
had been watching Bob but he wouldn't look at her.

In a moment Dr Locke said: 'I see.' She looked at them quickly
in turn as if she hadn't seen them properly before. 'That wasn't
easy for you.'

'It was like fallin' off a log.'

'For a soldier,' she said quietly as if he hadn't spoken, 'it must
be often easier to follow orders than the appeal of the heart.'

Millburn said crisply: 'The thing is, Dr Locke, we need a little
more information. Do we assume there's a strong force of
Vendettu still based on the east of the village? Across your
supply-route?'

'We do, Lieutenant.'

'How far is that from here?'

'Ten miles.'

Millburn turned to Proctor. 'Three hours' march?'

'Five, with the guns, providing the road's fair.' He asked Dr
Locke: 'You've got no kind of transport here, ma'am?'

'No, sir. The Mission truck had gone out for supplies when
the Vendettu moved in from the coast. Our driver didn't come
back.'

Proctor looked away and Millburn said: 'We'd have to make
it a daylight operation, yes?'

'Yes. Tomorrow, first light. Do a pincer job.'

The drums in the village had stopped again; there was only
the hiss of the lamp. Dr Locke was leaning forward over the table.

'You mean to go out there and attack them?'

'Yes,' Millburn said.

'But you can't do that.'

Proctor told her: 'There's no risk. They've got no real weapons,
or they'd have used them on us before.'

'Our machine-gun,' Millburn nodded, 'is an extremely effective weapon. In the absence of return fire—' but suddenly he knew what she meant and knew there wasn't much point in finishing— 'we can deal quite successfully with even a strong force . . . of virtually unarmed tribesmen. . . .'

She saw that he had understood; her hands, which had been tightly clasped on the table, relaxed.

'But you can't do it, Lieutenant. Can you?'

He felt the others watching him, and knew that in a way he was letting them down.

'No. We can't.'

He got up and carefully replaced his chair, leaning with his hands on its back. He was the only one standing and although there was nothing consciously symbolic in the gesture it was apt enough: he was the only abstainer. They went on watching him. The first of them to move was Tewson.

He gave a short frustrated laugh. 'Oh dear oh dear . . .' He left his chair where it was, going to the screened door, standing a moment, coming slowly back, poking his fingers through his hair. 'Just like old times again,' he said to Millburn, 'isn't it?'

'It is rather.' Then he added: 'The point is, do you agree?'

'Of course. Bit annoying, though.' He was looking down at Proctor.

'It's them,' Proctor said, obstinate-faced, 'or these women, isn't it?'

'No,' Tewson told him. 'Not while we're here.'

Rickman got up stiffly, knocking the chair over, clumsy and impatient with his bad leg.

'What's goin' on? Why can't we go an' attack those bastards? We've done it before, haven't we? This mornin', wasn't it?'

'No,' Spragge said. 'They attacked us.'

Jamie Cleaver sat with his head tilted back, squinting at him for enlightenment. 'I think I've missed something, mates. Just put it a wee bit more simply for me will you?'

Spragge left his chair, restless and worried. 'All right Jamie. We can't go out and kill off a hundred men in cold blood.'

'Why not?'

Rickman jerked his head. 'Thank Christ one of you can see sense!' He swung back to Millburn. 'Why not? They'd come here an' do it to us if they could, wouldn't they? Kill us off in cold blood? They've done it often enough before now haven't they? What's so special about those bastards that we can never go for 'em without they go for us first?' He was facing Tewson now, his skin blotchy-white under the sunburn and the tsetse-bites. 'What was the idea then, breakin' out of camp, creasin' up an M.P. to get Proctor out, layin' up so much trouble for ourselves we'll spend the next year on the run or in the Glasshouse?'

Some of the African girls had come as far as the kitchen doorway, frightened by his voice.

'I thought it was because that stupid git of a C.O. wouldn't let us take a crack at the Vend'u.' He was talking to Spragge now. 'I thought we'd been bustin' our guts through seventy mile of bush to get at the bastards.' He flung a hand at the guns and ammunition stacked at the end of the hut. 'What did we bring that lot for? Just to pick off a handful of 'em out there an' then say we're sorry an' we won't do it again?'

He turned his back on them all, limping across to the guns and staring down at them as if they were all he had, his only argument; then he was facing the others again, his squat body leaning forward as if he had to push the words against them physically. 'I think it's the heat got into you. I think you've gone rotten—soft—troppo. Can't attack those bastards in cold blood, can't we? Well, Cleaver's said it—*why not?*'

Dobbs sat with his face in his hands, trying to think.

Taffy had been staring at Rickman and Mr Millburn and the lady at the end of the table. Now he was watching Sgt Proctor. He wasn't sure what it was all about; Dr Locke seemed a nice sensible person, the kind who would always do what was right; but there was something in what Rickman had said: why had they come here if it wasn't to find the Vend'u? He looked at Proctor now because he was bigger than any of them. He'd do what the Sergeant told him. Whatever Sgt Proctor did, he would do too.

Tewson was looking at Spragge. He was the only one who could handle Rickman. Rickman held his own opinion, fair enough; the danger was that if the rest of them voted to stay here and wait till they were attacked, Rickman might take it into his head to go dodging out there with a gun when no one was looking, as he had with the lion. He wouldn't come back alive.

Spragge saw Tewson's appeal and said: 'Rick. What makes you call them bastards?'

Rickman came slowly away from the guns.

'Talk sense, will you?'

'All right—because they kill people out of hand, people without a hope in hell of defending themselves. That's plain murder in cold blood. So I'm with you there, Rick—they're bastards. But we're not.'

Rickman stopped and stood still, looking at all of them. In a minute he said contemptuously, 'I get it. A bunch of upright bloody Britishers. Got a touch of what Colonel Gray's gone rotten with—all think we're Jesus Christ.'

The silence went on and Millburn started to say something when he saw Dr Locke leaving the table. She pushed her chair back neatly and walked down the hut to Rickman, facing him with her arms hanging in front of her and her hands loosely clasped. Then she waited, not wanting to speak until he would look at her.

He turned his head at last. 'Things I shouldn't have said? Then I'm sorry.'

She smiled. 'I'm a medical missionary, Mr Rickman, not a school-marm. I guess I've seen things and heard things that would make even your hair curl. You had a right to say, and a need to say, everything that you did. Let me just correct one mistake, though. We don't think we're Jesus Christ; we think we're like he was once: human. Do you know very much about the Vendettu, Mr Rickman?'

'I don't seem to get much chance.'

'They're a tough people. Warriors. They were here among these trees a thousand years ago. They've killed their own kind, their own race, over the centuries—killed them without mercy. Tomorrow or the next day they may kill off the village tribe here —the people I think of as my friends and my godchildren because I've known them for so long. The Vendettu are the worst, but there have been others as bad—you remember Kenya, and the Congo? The place is feverish with new and bewildering ideas of independence and self-government. It is also, as it has always been, diseased, hungry and stricken. That's why, among others more capable, I came out here; and it's why you came too. To help them. It's a little inconvenient that they want to bite the hand that's trying to feed them, but we in the West feel we've grown up enough to understand that and have patience with it. If we lost that patience, think how easy it would be for us. We could do a very slick job on the Vendettu. Imagine it. One bomber squadron, a few tanks, and inside a week from now there wouldn't be a Vendettu left alive. It would require as much effort as it would need to snuff out a candle. And that is what we'd be doing.'

Spragge was watching Rickman's face; it was set like a bulldog's. Did he understand anything she was saying? It was doubtful. To get through Rick's case-hardened skin you'd want a battering-ram.

Taffy sat enthralled, his halo of gold hair aglow under the lamp, his blue eyes clouded with the magic of it. It wasn't so much what the lady said, it was her voice, like a bugle it was, very far away. She was some kind of angel, you could tell that now. She ought to marry Sgt Proctor, then they could go stamping out cholera plagues and building temples together; marvellous that would be.

Tewson thought: Rickman and Cleaver could handle that gun between them if they made up their minds. Just out of sheer pig-headedness.

Dr Locke hadn't moved. Rickman had been standing with his head down, listening; now he looked at her and said:

'They might wipe out that village, tomorrow?'

'If it occurs to them. It would only have to occur to them.'

'And you don't think that's wrong?'

'I think it's very wrong. We have to show them what we think don't we? So they might learn from us. And how can we show them it's wrong to wipe people out, by wiping them out?'

She waited but he didn't answer. Seeing the obstinacy on his face she turned away and went back to the others at the table. She had said all she could.

Millburn took his hands from the chair-back and looked at the men in turn. 'You all realize, I know, that when I left the camp I was burning my bridges. I renounced my rights, privileges and obligations as an officer. So I can't give you any orders. We've just got to work out the answer for ourselves. I've done that already, as you know. If anyone's marching out of here tomorrow at first light with the guns, I shan't be with them.'

Tewson nodded. 'Agreed. I stick.'

It looked like a vote so Spragge said: 'Me too.'

Proctor asked Dr Locke: 'If we don't go out there and get them, what do we do?'

'Wait till they come for us.'

'It's going to be more difficult, ma'am. The best defence is attack. They won't come up the garden path in a nice straight line; they'll come in from all sides, through the trees.'

'Yes, Mr Proctor. It's going to be more difficult.'

He glanced across to the doorway where some of the girls were, and back to her. She said: 'I considered everything; that was difficult too.'

He said: 'It must have been.' But they couldn't send the girls to the village; if the Vend'u went there first they'd be found soon enough; two of them were white and the others wouldn't have the same tribal features. They couldn't be sent anywhere else. They were safer where the guns were. 'All right,' he told Dr Locke, 'I'll be stayin' here.' He turned and looked at the others, pitching his voice up for Rickman's sake. 'When I left camp I did the same as Millburn and a bit more, chucked up a career. So I'm not givin' orders either but I'm tellin' you this. We stay together as an armed body of men. You listening, Rickman? You an' Spragge knocked up a tidy stretch in the Glasshouse for yourselves when you got me out, but I've told you before—you didn't do it for nothing. I'm here to look after you lot, an' if any man tries to go off alone on a bloody-minded crusade against the Vend'u I'll have his guts for garters so quick you'll see Getcliffe was an amateur.'

Towards midnight the lamps went out and the Mission was dark. The trees were silent. Sometimes in the later hours the starlight showed a man's face at a window, and glinted on the metal of his gun. It was the first night of the waiting.

CHAPTER TWENTY-FOUR

NOBODY in the camp had been killed since Lumsden had received twenty arrows into his body while on guard duty. Either on the orders of their leader in Lisolaville, or on their own initiative, the Vendettu had reverted to a war of nerves.

As a new trick they were trying witchcraft, coming out of the moonlit bush in a group of fifty or sixty and setting up what the men of the 4th Royals called 'Sambo's Circus'. The performance consisted of a tribal dance to the drums followed by a solo turn by a witch-doctor, who had a good sense of the dramatic and a verbal range that ran from a snake-like hissing to a fiendish wail as he stamped in the dust and pointed his bones at the gate guards. The only thing the M.O. didn't like about it was the frequent laughter of the personnel who came out of their huts to watch. It had the sound of a pantomime audience when the demon appeared and fond parents believed their children couldn't really be frightened, because they were laughing.

On this particular night Major Ward didn't watch the performance; he had turned in before they came, hoping to catch up on some sleep. The past few days had been harrowing and now that the awful business in Colonel Gray's office was over, reaction was setting in.

They came some time before midnight when the moon was still in the western sky; as usual they came creeping, their shadows merging with the shadows of the bush, so that the guards at the wire weren't sure whether anything was happening or whether they were imagining it, while their scalps began itching and their fingers moved uneasily over the safety-catches.

It finished in a sudden rush that alerted the machine-gun crews and brought the main searchlight on. Late this evening there had been new orders from the Adjutant to the effect that no chances were to be taken: if one spear or a single arrow were sighted coming across the wire the M.G. crews were to open fire and shoot to kill.

The preliminary dance was not unimpressive; by daylight its savagery would have been manifest enough; in the glare of the searchlight it took on an added aspect of ghostliness, the shadows of the dancers flitting larger than life-sized over the ground beyond and—as the dust drifted higher—against the sky itself, their heads monstrous, their hands fretting at the moon. Their oiled bodies writhed eel-like, silvered by the light, until the dust smothered them and they grew dark. Their very identity became in doubt as the dance intensified; the shape of man, beast, ghost was gradually lost; they assumed the shapelessness of nightmare.

Some of them were drunk, their bellies heavy with maize beer: they were the urbanized of the tribe, the less disciplined; these gave trouble when the others drew away to make a space for the witch-doctor, and he had to curse them before they would grow quiet.

He was an old man, shrivelled and unsteady on his feet, and his cloak of rabbits' fur dragged through the dust as he took a step towards the main gates of the camp; he moved like a sloth, unnaturally, and in the silence the bones in his bag of magic rattled together, remindful of death.

He was half-way to the gates when Colonel Gray brought the guards to attention; he had given them no order but they had recognized him and presented arms. He opened the gates himself and walked through them alone.

Seeing him, the witch-doctor stopped moving. The distance between them was some fifty yards. Gray walked steadily, his pace measured and his figure erect. The beam of light threw his shadow in front of him.

From the gates the two guards watched him.

One whispered: 'Bloody hell . . . Does he know what he's doing?'

'Rather 'im than me, mate.'

An N.C.O. made to go through the gates but the officer of the guard pulled him up.

'Stand fast, there!' More quietly he said: 'We don't want to start anything.'

Among those who had come out of the huts to watch the performance was the Padre; beside him was Maj. Shaw of 'A' Company.

The Padre said: 'This is very foolish.'

'It's not very intelligent.'

Somewhere a guard, in turning, caught the muzzle of his gun against the barbed wire and the wire quivered, hazy in the light.

The crew on the big lamp swung it a degree to keep the beam centred on the walking man. Beyond him the Vendettu were moving, seeming to sway, perhaps mesmerized by the light, perhaps uneasy that the white warrior should approach their sacred *mundumugu* like this.

Within a dozen yards of the witch-doctor Colonel Gray halted. The thing in its rabbit-fur expanded, spitting at him, then contracted, toad-like, shrinking back into the shapelessness; the bones clacked inside the bag of magic. Gray looked around him at the swaying tribesmen and slowly lifted his arms.

From inside the camp they heard him clearly, but only a few understood.

'*Uo hiba'nai rindui ti hiba'nai. . . .*'

Major Shaw said to the Padre: 'You know this lingo don't you?' It wasn't Swahili or coast-Tamalese.

The Padre nodded. '*My god is greater . . . than your god. . . .*'

The Colonel's voice was strong and his arms moved in slow rhythms. '*Fao uo hiba'nai? Gb'owan? Tomo-i? Moso. . . .*'

'*Who is your god? The sun? Where is he? He is gone. . . .*'

The Padre turned his head, hearing someone approaching.

It was the M.O. and he murmured: 'The Adj fetched me.'

Shaw said: 'There's nothing you can do, Doc.'

'*Gb'ali? Suo gb'ali? Woum-ei! Nak hiba'nai, . . .*'

Though few of them understood, they listened as if to low music, caught up by the sound alone. The Vendettu had stopped swaying; some looked upwards towards the western sky.

'Is he the moon?' murmured the Padre. *'Look at the moon. . . . It is broken! You have no god. . . .'*

Major Ward saw movement at the fringe of the tribesmen; one of them was striking another and a spear-blade flashed for a moment.

Major Shaw said: 'This is going to be a bit touch and go.' He was glad not to be commanding the guns tonight; they wouldn't know where the hell to shoot, or when.

'Yes,' Ward said. This was his fault. He should have put a discreet guard on Colonel Gray before turning in. If anything happened they'd censure him at the inquiry, hard up for a scapegoat. But as he listened to the voice out there, and to the murmuring of the Padre, he forgot his own involvement in this scene; he was watching an apocalypse.

'But I have my god within me . . . he is here. He speaks with me . . . and this is his voice. . . .'

Either the *mundumugu* was moving back from the Colonel, so slowly that it was no more than an oozing across the ground, or it was a trick of the light. The gun crews were sweating as they watched.

'And he speaks peace to you. . . . Peace!' The shadows of his arms flowed across the tribesmen, and some whimpered as if struck.

'I am the chief of all my warriors . . . and they obey my laws. Know you that I have but to speak to them . . . even now . . . and they would make the metal noise at you . . . the thunder that kills. They would kill all of you . . . all!'

Some of the men, hearing the Padre was translating, came near to listen.

'I suppose,' said Major Ward softly, 'there's nothing we can do?'

Shaw answered without taking his eyes from the man out there. 'It might be all right, if nobody rocks the boat.'

'Va wan'oi lahi-mo . . . Iku-i mas'wei guro. . . .'

'Yet we shall not kill you . . . even one of you '' ' because we are here to save you . . . the children of these dark lands . . . from your false gods . . . and your false beliefs against us. . . .'

There was a movement again among the Vendettu, and Maj. Ward drew in a breath slowly, looking up and behind him to where the barrels of the machine-guns poked out against the light. He looked back at the man who spoke.

What was in Gray's mind? Vainglory, a lot of it. Self-pity, self-sacrifice, inverted arrogance expressed in a need for martyrdom . . . not a healthy mind, though it was reasoning, perhaps:

denied by his own men, his power thrown aside, he might still prevail and find his niche in history as Lieutenant-Colonel Sir Philip Gray, the soldier and the man of peace who went forth alone into the midst of the enemy and in the name of God. Gray of Tamala.

'*Therefore I say to you, go in peace . . . and come not again with your hearts hardened against us. . . .*'

How much, Ward wondered, was the Padre affected by this little show? It had all the trimmings: the beam of light shining through the clouds, the lone figure speaking among the multitude . . . Forget the guns up there and the spears in the hands of those bloody savages, and you were watching the Sermon on the Mount.

'*Humo-b'gami nai! Humo-kwalei guruk'mbwanai. . . .*'

'*For we are your brothers . . . we are come to your lands peace-bringing. . . .*'

Major Ward remembered afterwards that at this moment the arms of Colonel Gray were raised from his sides at shoulder-level, so that his whole shadow, enormous against the ground and the massed Vendettu, was in the shape of a cross.

And it was at this moment that there came another sound from the fringe of the throng as one of them, perhaps one of those whose bellies were full of maize beer, broke clear and raised his spear-arm. He was the first and he missed, but within seconds the air flowed silver towards the figure of Colonel Gray and he was down before the camp guns began their fusillade.

CHAPTER TWENTY-FIVE

AT the Mission in the North the waiting was not easy. People jumped at ordinary sounds and took offence at a chance word; Rickman was still sunk in resentment and even Spragge couldn't pull him out; the others left him alone.

There'd been two false alarms the first night and Proctor had manned the machine-gun. The next day the clearing was quiet and the men lay on the grass and tugged at the short sweet blades and sucked at them, listening in their heads to the snick of the ball as the bat took it away, the call of the umpire. A few of them slept. At some time in the morning Cleaver heard what he thought was a helicopter, and called the others. They stared at the sky southwards but couldn't see anything against the glare.

Cleaver was sure it was a helicopter and wanted to make a bet. Millburn said that since the sound was already fading they'd never find out what it was anyway, and Dobbs told Jamie:

'Suppose you win, then. You can't take it with you.'

It was the first time anyone had looked at things like that. It wasn't the Vend'u that scared them, but the waiting.

Dr Locke spent most of her time with the patients. There was a sewing-machine in the main room and one of the girls was making Taffy a new shirt, because his was the worst. He talked to her all morning and fell in love and out again by evening; then Dr Locke came in from the sick-ward and they all sang hymns round the frail mildewed piano until the girls forgot to watch the windows and gave their hearts to the singing.

Edna talked to Tewson as much as she could, and asked him: 'Aren't you worried about going back?'

'I worried about that,' he said, 'before we left camp.'

If they lived they would all go back, they knew now. Taff was still taken with the scheme of jumping a ship in Bristol, but that was Taff. Millburn said that all they wanted was a good defence counsel at Aldershot and there was a chance of getting off lightly.

'I've been talking to Dr Locke,' Edna said. 'If there's a court martial she's going to England to give evidence. She'll have the whole Mission Board up in arms.'

Tewson didn't want her to talk about it. They were sitting on the narrow lawn in front of the ward and he wanted to look at her eyes sometimes and marvel again at the light in them, and then look away and believe it was Market Cross beyond those trees, and that when they heard feet running it would be the boys of the College on a paperchase.

'. . . myself by July,' he heard her saying. His eyes had closed against the sunshine.

'What did you say, Edna?'

Her smile went right through his body, flowing like light. He'd always thought he was immune and had lost sleep once because it could be that there was something wrong with him— perhaps he'd been born heartless. Now there was this and already he couldn't imagine a world without Edna.

'Were you dozing off?' she asked, still smiling.

'No. What was it you said?'

'I'll be over there myself, by July.'

'Where?'

'England.'

'England?' He sat up straight. 'You will?'

'Yes. Why?'

'Well I didn't know——'

'Didn't I tell you before?'

'No. I'd have remembered.'

She said as if having to make excuses: 'We only do a six-month overseas period, the lay-nurses, when it's the tropics. It's part of the training-programme.'

'Yes. I see.' It was difficult to sound casual. 'When you're back in England, will you drop me a line?'

'Of course. And I'll even post it.'

'I'm sorry?'

'I wrote a couple of letters to you when I got back from leave in Lisolaville.'

'What for?' He frowned and looked away from her, thinking he was behaving like a bloody child. It was just that he couldn't take it all in—they said it took you like this the first time it hit you: you became a drooling idiot. Maybe it was worse for him because this was the first and the thousandth in one go, the full treatment.

She said, sounding surprised, 'Because I felt like writing.'

'Then why the hell didn't you post them? Is that what you meant—you didn't post them?'

'Yes. There wasn't much point. We haven't been able to send urgent letters, leave alone the "wish-you-were-here" sort of thing.'

She was looking away from him, perhaps because she knew her eyes always told everyone what she was thinking.

'Edna,' he said, to make her look at him.

'Yes?'

'Did you wish I were here?'

'Yes.'

'Well I am.'

Proctor sat with the gun.

The tall eucalyptus trees had turned black against the sundown and now stood invisible in the night. The drums had started again from the village. Light from inside the ward touched the dull metal fittings of the gun as Proctor moved his hands over them, using cotton waste. Taff Williams crouched watching him.

'Would you call this a war, Sergeant?'

In camp, off parade, Taff had called him 'Sarge' like the others; but ever since Proctor had torn off his tapes he'd called him 'Sergeant' and was most particular about it.

'Eh?' He looked into the lad's eyes. They'd had them this age in Normandy and it was wrong, very wrong. 'No. Be a bit of target practice, a night exercise like.'

Sergeant Proctor's hand moved with a gentleness that made Taffy feel a grown man; he felt strength coming into him from the movement of the strong hand on the gun.

'We couldn't tell anyone, afterwards, we'd been in a war? Not even a small one?'

'No. An' you don't want to. I've been in a lot of wars, an' I'll tell you one thing, son. They're no bloody good to anybody.'

They sat in the low light listening to the drums. A shadow fell and Proctor turned and saw Dr Locke at the open window of the ward.

'I've been trying to make Mr Rickman rest his leg,' she said. 'Can you do anything about it?'

'No, ma'am. I could have, once. I can't now.' He looked into the black trees. 'What are they sayin', on those drums?'

'The same thing, over and over. *We have no young women in our village, nor pigs, nor goats, nor chickens, nothing of any value, nothing that anyone could want to take from us. We are poor and have nothing.*'

Taffy stared up at her. The light from behind her clung to her hair and he couldn't look anywhere else, because of the light and her voice.

'It sounds like a prayer,' he said.

'That's about what it is. They hope the Vendettu will hear.'

Proctor folded the cotton waste and tucked it into the canvas bag under the machine-gun. 'They beatin' those drums quicker now, the past few minutes, or is it my imagination?'

She listened for a while and said: 'They're beating quicker.'

She had left the window by the time Millburn came past on his rounds. 'Dobbs says he can hear something.'

Proctor nodded. 'There's voices.'

Millburn stood with them a moment and moved on. 'We're all at stations.'

Proctor didn't answer, but his hand cupped the stock and eased the barrel left and right. He had set up the stations the night before and done the rounds himself to make sure they'd got it right. From this corner of the main hut the machine-gun could sweep a 200-degree vector through the clearing; that left 160 for the six S.L. rifles, shooting into the thicker trees. He'd based his pattern of defence on the guess that the Vend'u would fear the guns most at the outset of the attack because until they fired they wouldn't know their positions; most likely, then, they'd come in a body for the clearing, where the trees were thin and gave more room. It wouldn't make much odds if he guessed wrong because the concerted fire-power of the six subs was about equal to his own, up to reloading; but if he were one per cent more right than wrong it might save a life and there were none to spare.

The voices were louder and he listened to them. There was a tremble starting in the ground. He said to Taffy:

'Feed her gently, boy, an' don't look at anything else. You're on the belt, an' that's an important job because she won't bark unless she's fed right.'

The metal lay heavy in Taff's hands.

'You'll give me the word, Sarge? Sergeant?'

'Oh, yes. Bit of an introduction, it's only decent.'

The ground was alive with trembling.

Dr Locke went to the Coleman lamp and turned it out. She had been here at the White Cross Mission for fifteen years and every day of all those years the people from the villages of the North Province had come here to be healed and comforted, sometimes as many as two hundred in a day when the rains brought sickness, and now she heard these other people coming, and turned out the lamp.

Their voices were sharp among the trees. They were calling to one another as they came, running fast now. Millburn, stationed to cover a neck of the clearing where some of them were bound to break in, wondered how many of these had been on the plain yesterday and how many were still unblooded and ignorant of what a bullet could do. Their screams were no longer those of excited children: this was the war-cry. He prodded his glasses higher, as if he were about to launch himself into debate instead of battle.

Tewson was closest to the ward where the machine-gun was set up; Proctor had wanted him at the edge of the giant eucalyptus on the far side but he'd asked him to put someone else there and Proctor hadn't insisted: he'd seen Tewson talking a lot to one of the girls, and all the girls were now together in the ward. Tewson's scalp tightened as he waited; being at last in adoration of a woman he could not have borne the thought of being anywhere but near her now that she was in danger; but he knew also the dark side of love: it would be unthinkable if, being near her, he failed to save her. It would depend on his wits, courage and bodily strength, but also on luck; and it was this thought that

chilled him and left him weak in the limbs. You could walk the
narrow top of a six-foot wall without a qualm; only if it were a
cliff-top would you be in danger of falling—and it would be the
mind that killed, not the drop. Edna would have more help
from him if she were a stranger to him, someone of whom he
could feel careless.

'You all right, Tewey?'

'She's a stranger. I don't know her.'

'What?' Spragge clicked off the safety-catch. 'You okay?'

'We just shoot to kill. All we can do.'

'That's it. Pick 'em off. It's a pushover.'

'I'm not scared, you bloody fool.'

'Of course you're not.'

Dobbs heard them talking and wished they'd shut up. His
arms were bare and the sweat was running down to the elbows.
He'd told Proctor: 'Take Taffy on the belt, for God's sake. Look
after him for me.' That was what sergeants were for: to take the
responsibility. So Dobbs knew now that if Taff saw morning it
wouldn't be thanks to him. It didn't have to matter. All he
wanted was for that golden-headed kid to stay alive and get a
chance to grow.

'Nobby?'

'Shuddup.'

It was Jamie Cleaver, farther along. He said: 'If you get into
trouble, I'm here.'

'I don't care where you are, so long as that little Bleeder's on
the belt.'

Spragge, at the far corner of the hut, began calling but they
didn't catch what he said because Millburn had lobbed the first
one. They had known that the worst danger was the darkness;
there mustn't be any light from inside the buildings to guide
the Vend'u but there had to be something to see by when the
guns opened up. Millburn was timing the grenades aloud,
pitching the first one high across the gap in the trees that he
knew was there.

The flash was orange and not too blinding and he looked to
the left of it and saw nothing moving and lobbed the next to
the right and saw the headlong cluster running full into the flash
and lobbed again as the machine-gun came in and there was a
scream of terror from the tree-hyrax somewhere on the roof and
then one of the subs joined in and raked the moving shapes as
the fourth grenade burst short and showed up the bright oiled
skin where the main group began falling under the fragmentation.

They were closer than anyone had thought and Rickman began going forward, limping steadily with the rifle at his hip, the series of percussions shaking him as he kept up his fire, reloading with the care of anger and waiting with his gun quiet until he heard a bunch of them breaking through the underbush clear of the M.G. vector; then he went forward again towards them, seeing their eyes in the flickering of his own shots and bringing his aim up to string the bullets along the tallest of them because those were the ones who were still on their feet. He shot without anger now, his movements precise; the death he was dealing came out of the gun and also out of himself and he could no longer feel angry with the dying.

There was another thing: the Vend'u had come here just as they'd come to the camp, but at the camp he'd not been allowed to do anything about them. Now he could walk towards them with the cordite stinking under his nose and the flash-flash-flash lighting them up as they broke and scattered, tripping on their own dead as they tried to run clear of the bullets. He followed them. They might as well try running from rain.

A different rhythm broke into the night. Dobbs, his back to the hut-wall, realized that the machine-gun had stopped. There was only the jerky bark of the S.L. rifles, and for a moment there was total silence as their need to reload became synchronized by chance. It was then that Proctor opened up again to cover them, bringing the M.G. hard round to the end of the vector, the best he could do. Dobbs could hear the wind-rush of the heavy-calibre shots as they passed close to him. The sweat was getting in his way: his palms slipped as he banged in another magazine and he tore skin from his thumb and cursed and brought the barrel up and pulled on the trigger again as a group of them drew together and began throwing their spears in a cone-pattern. The wall behind him was splintering and he dropped flat, crawling five yards and firing again.

It was shadow-shooting and it was all they could do because the Vend'u were night-sighted and the flash of the guns was giving them the target. Spragge had come lurching past him a minute ago, getting clear of a bright flicker he'd glimpsed in the air: someone, in firing, had lit the steel of the spearheads and he'd seen them coming. Close to where Spragge was now lying, firing a burst from the ground, Tewson listened for the enemy. They were grunting and chattering to each other and to themselves, naming their gods, more in fear of their gods than of the British warriors because if the death-bringer came he would be sent by their gods and the bullet had nothing to do with it.

As Tewson listened to them, firing at sounds and letting up to listen again and fire again, he had a sudden vision of leaves and the dark of men's bodies moving against them as if faint light coloured the trees, pinking the black of the night; there was the glint of metal and the white of eyes and for a time he believed it was the concerted flash of the guns. A grenade burst high and he fell flat with his left arm crooked about his head: Millburn had thrown wild and in the orange glow some of them could see the drift of dark leaves as the fragmentation tore them away. Spragge was yelling something against the rattle of Proctor's gun and Tewson raised himself, feeling the sticky ooze of blood between his hand and the rifle. He fired again, full into a running man.

The vision did not fade. He could see the thick trunks of the eucalyptus and the humped shape of Proctor at the M.G. with Taff beside him. Other voices came and he tried to hear what they were saying. Something that looked like a tracer-bullet was falling slowly, curving through the pinkish light, and he watched it go out on the ground. He was suddenly afraid of fainting, and drew a breath deeply, throwing his head back and staring at the sky and seeing that in the sky there was smoke drifting. Another spark came down and he sagged with relief. The vision was real. A fire had started, lighting the trees. He staggered to one side as a bush-knife whittled through the glow and buried into the timber behind him. Something tripped him and he went head-long, losing his hold on the S.L. and finding it again, furious, getting up and looking at the shape that had tripped him.

'Oh, Christ . . .' The trees leaned towards him and leaned away; the voices grew faint and were loud again. The shaft of the spear stood vertically from the shape on the ground.

He was lurching away, calling something, seeing a man coming for him at a run. He fired at close range and the big blade sparked across the barrel of his gun as the man tumbled, straightened, and dropped against the hut-wall.

'They've got Dobbs,' he was calling, and someone was close to him suddenly.

'Get him to the ward!'

Someone else was with them and he couldn't recognize him because blood was covering half his face. He said again, 'They've got Dobbs.' There was the crackling of timber going down, some-where towards the main building, and a flock of sparks sailed across the clearing.

Spragge pulled out the spear and got the body into his arms.
Someone said in a cold voice: 'It's too late, old boy.' It sounded
like Tewson.

A man called *'Watch it!'* and Cleaver fired three shots into
sudden movement, dropping to dodge a blade that came fluting
into the light of the fire. There was smoke in their throats and
the glow was bright now, shining on the smooth trunks of the
eucalyptus. Millburn fell and got up and went on, knowing that
the machine-gun had stopped and wanting to find out what had
happened to Proctor. The rifles had gone quiet and Millburn
waited for the M.G. to put out covering fire but nothing
happened.

'Rickman! Where's Sergeant Proctor?'

'Shiftin' the gun.'

Rickman was doubled against the wall of the hut but Millburn
ran on. Most of them were coming into the M.G.'s vector now
and Tewson asked: 'Is that the lot?'

Millburn didn't answer, simply because he didn't know. He
had to find Proctor and work out what was happening. He
stopped dead as the wall near him began leaning across the
pathway; he thought at first that it was an illusion due to nerves;
then he had to run clear as the whole side of the hut billowed
out and dropped flat with a shriek of wrenching nails as the
joists gave way; above it there rose a cloud of sparks that were
slowly lost in the smoke.

He started off again and found Proctor and Williams lugging
the gun clear of the heat. A lot of people were here and some
carried stretchers: the ward-hut was catching fire and the hospitalized patients had been brought out. Spragge was standing
near Dr Locke, perfectly still, with a body in his arms. Wilbur
Tshimali was opening a canvas stretcher, flicking the buckles
deftly, the gold crucifix catching the light as it swung on its
fine chain. When the stretcher was ready he tried to help Spragge
but he was already lowering his burden and for a moment
remained kneeling over it as if it were an offering he'd placed
on a sacrificial stone.

'Who's that?' asked Millburn.

'Dobbs.'

'Can anything be done?'

'No,' said Dr Locke. 'Not by us.' Her hair hung dankly in
rats'-tails; Wilbur had thrown water over them all before they
began fighting the fire. 'Do you know his church?'

Millburn stooped and turned the identity-tags. 'R.C.'

'Thank you.'

He went away, hearing how gentle her voice was. He found Proctor setting up the machine-gun, one of the girls trying to get a bandage round his forearm; blood dripped steadily on to her lap as she knelt beside him. Williams had run off and was staggering back with an ammunition-belt across his shoulder. Millburn said: 'How's it going, Proctor?'

'A bunch of 'em got away. They'll be back.'

The nurse looked up at Millburn. 'Who was it, please?'

'What?'

'The man on the stretcher.' She watched him steadily. Timber crashed and a wave of heat swept against them but she kept her eyes on Millburn.

'He's dead,' he told her.

'Yes. What was his name, please?'

'Dobbs.'

She looked down and finished the bandaging. Proctor saw Rickman and Cleaver taking a stretcher clear of the ward-hut and shouted to them. *'Don't leave your rifles!'* Millburn went across to them, the weight of the last two grenades in his pocket swinging against his thigh. A face watched him from the stretcher; it was one of the Mission patients, a child, its eyes questioning with a hunger that unnerved him because he didn't know the answer; he didn't know whether this small life would go out with the night or go on into the morning; all he knew was that it would survive him and the other men if only by minutes, because that was what they were here for.

'Rickman!' he called angrily. 'Go and get your wounds dressed while there's time. Cleaver, help him over there.' He went away to see if he could find Dobbs's rifle.

Dr Locke had set up her dressing-station clear of the blazing huts and Proctor was shouting again, telling the men to take up stations behind him on the other flank of the Mission staff. Tewson was already positioned and Cleaver moved up beside him; Rickman was prone on the burned grass but he was conscious and his rifle was up. One of the girls had followed him with her medical kit and was telling him not to move if he could help it.

The clearing was filled with the roar and the light of the flames as the end of the ward-hut caved in and the roof dropped, the trapped air pushing out a wave of heat. There seemed to be no wind but the smoke hung in a reddened pall to one side, blanking out the trees. Millburn was coming back with Dobbs's rifle and three magazines when the machine-gun began banging away and a scream of voices in unison rose and became louder than the gun, louder than the flames, until Tewson was running from his flank station and wheeling to put out a burst of low fanning shot in support of Proctor. The Vendettu broke black from the trees, many of them, the first going down with their weapons falling ahead of them.

'Keep stations!'

A grenade exploded and the fragments rang against blades. The main group of the attack broke up and flowed to the sides; the first of the Vend'u to get through the hail of shot was in Millburn's sector and he came for him with his bush-knife swinging high; there was blood spraying from an artery and he was dying but the momentum carried him on and the blade flew across Millburn's shoulders as he brought his rifle up and went for the head, spinning clear as the man pitched down.

Some of the Vend'u were regathering at the fringe of the smoke area and their spears caught the light and flew rose-red through the air. Someone was going forward from the flank stations, firing below the spears' trajectories, and Cleaver yelled to him— 'Rickman!'—but he went on and the smoke enveloped him; they could hear his rifle for a minute more but no one was certain when it stopped. Spragge's eyes were streaming because of the smoke and he reloaded through a blur of tears. Two of the Vend'u were coming straight for him and he took such care with his shots that he had time to see their faces: their mouths were open in a war-yell and their nostrils were spread; they were faces in agony—not pain or fright but the agony of blood-lust; they were animal faces and out of them screamed animal sound.

He put six shots into them, working up from the stomach and finishing at the head; their legs still drove them forward but their bodies were pushed back by the force of the bullets until slowly they toppled; then he went on, making for the area of silence where Rick had gone. It was when he entered the smoke and started looking for Rick that the machine-gun stopped firing.

In Proctor's sector a group of Vend'u had drawn together and Millburn threw his last grenade, covering his face until the whine of the fragments died away; then he went forward against the survivors with a fresh magazine in his gun. Somebody was shouting, not far from him; he thought it was Tewson.

'Ammo . . .'

Millburn ran on. His own ammunition was low and he fired only when he was certain of a killing hit. He could hear Dr

Locke calling to Tshimali for a stretcher. The machine-gun was still silent.

'*Ammo* . . .' No one answered. Tewson dropped his rifle and found a broad-bladed *panga* near one of the bodies, taking it and working round the edge of the smoke, keeping close to the dressing-station because that was where the Vend'u must never go. Movement showed and he went to meet it, holding the haft of the big knife Commando-fashion, blade-upwards. The man coming for him was half-naked, a young giant of his tribe, and his mouth was open in a yell. Tewson felt cold and his brain very clear; sounds seemed to have become faint, even the sound from the Vend'u. He came over the littered ground with a speed that would send him headlong if he tripped; and Tewson noted this. The right arm was swinging a bush-knife high and Tewson waited with a cold brain, unafraid because his emotions had gone dead as if a hypodermic had hit the nerve-centres.

When the savage was close and the knife-arm was swinging down he let himself drop and took the great legs against his shoulders; their force knocked him backwards and they were both on the ground and he could hear the hiss of the knife again and again, its blade cleaving in a wild series of jerks as he twisted away and hooked with his own, finding the intestines and driving it in as far as the hilt before he turned the blade and felt the resistance and then the lesion of the gut, pulling it out and trying to raise himself as the Vend'u found a purchase and dropped against him, crushing his legs. The dark arm, thick as a sapling and beautiful in the red light with its muscles sculpted in ebony, was lifting, the broad-bladed *panga* jutting from the bunched fingers. Tewson lay watching it, knowing the man had not even felt the stomach-wound that was pouring his blood from him while the brain ran on and ordered the nerves to aim the knife and the muscles to bring it down.

Tewson let his own knife fall so that his hands were free, and brought his arms upwards and locked them together to form a bridge of bone. The knife-blows were aimed for his throat and he parried them until they became weaker as the man's system was drained of its blood. It took Tewson less than a half-minute to pull his legs free of the weight but by that time the Vend'u was dead.

He got up and staggered across the crimson earth, trying to see where people were. '*Ammo* . . .' he called. His rifle was where he had dropped it and he picked it up. '*Ammo* . . .' There were shapes coming near him through the smoke and he swung to

face them, turning the gun and gripping the barrel so that he
could use it as a club; but they were only walking towards him.

'You okay, Tewey?'

The coldness was leaving his head and he could hear the
laboured sawing of his breath. Other sounds were growing louder
but there was no gunfire now.

'Tewey! You okay?'

By the size of the man it was Spragge. The others were wandering about.

'Yes. You got any ammo?' He saw Millburn stumbling along
with his hands to his eyes. It all looked different from when the
Vend'u had come at him. 'What's wrong with Millburn?'

'Smoke in his eyes.' Spragge was suddenly close to him, peering
at his face. 'What happened, then?'

'Christ, I'm clean out of ammo! D'you know if there's any to
spare?'

A light voice sounded. 'Is that Bob?'

'Yes.'

'Are you injured?'

'No.'

He saw her for a moment in the glow of the dying fire; then
Dr Locke called: 'Edna, I need you over here. Bring what
you can.'

Spragge looked at him and asked: 'Is that your own blood?'

'I don't think so.' Then he saw the machine-gun as Spragge
turned. Taff Williams was standing there. Everything seemed
very still and nobody moved quickly. Dr Locke and one of her
staff were coming away from the machine-gun.

'Spraggey, what's happened?'

'We did for 'em.'

'The lot?'

'A few ran off. We let them go. Rickman's dead.'

Tewson focused his eyes on the bloodied face and the reflective
tilt of the head. 'Poor old Spraggey.'

'I'm not dead.'

'But you got on well with him.'

'I was no help to that man.'

'He didn't ever want any.'

'No. That was Rick.'

Tewson let his rifle slide from his hand. It fell across the Vend'u
he had killed; he knew there were more, many more, lying like
this on the ground. He said to Spragge dully, 'What a way to
help them, the "emergent Africans". What a stupid bloody way.'

'They came for us,' Spragge said. 'We didn't go for them. That's progress, isn't it?'

Tewson looked up from the dead face. 'Oh sure. We live in very enlightened days.' He could see Taff Williams not far off in the lowering light of the flames, and something worried him about the way Taff was standing there. He went across to the machine-gun, Spragge with him. From the other side Tshimali was coming up with a rolled stretcher.

Sergeant Proctor lay with his head raised a little on something one of the nurses had put there for him, and his eyes had been closed. Above him Taffy stood straight and lonely, and in his voice there was the hush of disbelief.

'He said to me, "Dig one for me, mates. Dig one for me." That's what the Sergeant said.'

It was a fine morning, cooler than at this time yesterday. Dew slid from the eucalyptus leaves with a flash of diamond light; the tops of the trees were already lit by the sun.

Those who were left kept watch from dawn onwards, two mounting guard while the other three slept. Many of the village tribe had come to the Mission, fetched by Dr Locke to help bury the dead. They said that the road to the east was empty and that there were no more of the Vendettu there; but Millburn said there should be lookouts posted because a few had survived and might still try a surprise attack.

There was clear scrub to the south of the clearing, open land falling away to the watercourse and the blue plain; and in the late afternoon Jamie Cleaver saw dust rising and called the others.

Millburn took the field-glasses but it was some time before he could pick out the three vehicles.

'They're armoured cars,' he said.

'They flying pennants?' Tewson asked him.

After a long time Millburn nodded. 'Yes. 4th Royals.'

Spragge said: 'Someone must've called the Army out.' He turned away. 'Bit late, wasn't it?'

BROUGHT IN DEAD

Harry Patterson

'Brought in Dead' is published by
John Long Ltd.

MAB/61—G*

The Author

Harry Patterson was born in 1929 and spent his early years in Northern Ireland. After National Service in the Royal Horse Guards he has enjoyed a varied career ranging from circus tent-hand to insurance underwriter, and has travelled widely. He is now a lecturer in Liberal Studies in the north of England. He holds an Honours B.Sc. degree of London University, having specialized in psychology and criminology.

For Dorothy Limón—a real fan

CHAPTER ONE

THE girl was young and might have been pretty once, but not now. Her right eye was almost closed, the cheek mottled by livid bruises and her lips had been split by the same violent blow that had knocked out three teeth.

She hobbled painfully into the Line-Up room supported by a woman P.C., a pathetic, broken figure with a blanket over her shoulders to conceal the torn dress. Miller and Brady were sitting on a bench at the far end of the room and Brady saw her first. He tapped his companion on the shoulder and Miller stubbed out his cigarette and went to meet her.

He paused, noting her condition with a sort of clinical detachment, and the girl shrank back slightly from the strange young man with the white face and the eyes that seemed to stare right through her like dark glass.

Detective Sergeant Nicholas Miller was tired—more tired than he had been in a long, long time. In the ten hours he had already spent on duty, he had served as investigating officer at two burglaries, a factory break-in and a closing-hours brawl outside a pub near the market in which a youth had been slashed so badly across the face that it was more than likely that he would lose his right eye. This had been followed almost immediately by a particularly vile case of child cruelty which had involved forcible entry, in company with an N.S.P.C.C. inspector, of a house near the docks where they had found three children huddled together like animals, almost naked, showing all the signs of advanced malnutrition, squatting in their own dirt in a windowless boxroom that stank like a pigsty.

And now this. Compassion did not come easily at five o'clock on a dark February morning, but there was fear on this girl's face and she had suffered enough. He smiled and his whole personality seemed to change and the warmth reached out to envelop her so that sudden, involuntary tears sprang to her eyes.

'It's all right,' he said. 'Everything's going to be fine. Another couple of minutes and it'll be all over.' He turned to Detective Constable Brady. 'Let's have them, Jack.'

Brady nodded and pressed a red button on a small control panel on the wall. A hard white light illuminated a stage at the far end of the room and, a moment later, a door opened and half a dozen

204   BROUGHT IN DEAD

men filed in followed by two constables who marshalled them in line.

Miller took the girl gently by the arm, but before he could speak, she started to tremble violently. She managed to raise her right hand, pointing at the prisoner who stood number one in line, a great ox of a man, his right cheek disfigured by a jagged scar. She tried to speak, something rattled in her throat and she collapsed against Miller in a dead faint.

He held her close against his chest and looked up at the stage. 'Okay, Macek, let's be having you.'

A thick-set, fourteen-stone Irishman with fists like rocks, Detective Constable Jack Brady had been a policeman for twenty-five years. A quarter of a century of dealing with human wickedness in all its forms, of walking daily in squalor and filth and a gradual erosion of the spirit had left him harsh and embittered, a hard, cruel man who believed in nothing. And then a curious thing had happened. Certain villains now serving collectively some twenty-five years in one of Her Majesty's Prisons had thrown him down a flight of stairs, breaking his leg in two places and fracturing his skull, later leaving him for dead in a back street.

Most men would have died, but not Jack Brady. The priest was called, the last rites administered and then the surgeons took over and the nurses and physio-therapists, and in three months he was back on duty with a barely perceptible limp in his left leg.

The same, but not the same. For one thing he was noticed to smile more readily. He was still a good tough cop, but now he seemed gifted with a new understanding. It was as if through suffering himself, he had learned compassion for others.

The girl painfully signed her name at the bottom of the typed statement sheet and he helped her to her feet and nodded to the woman P.C.

'You'll be all right now, love. It's all over.'

The girl left, sobbing quietly and Miller came in holding a teletype flimsy. 'Don't waste too much sympathy on her, Jack. I've just heard from C.R.O. She's got a record. Four previous convictions including larceny, conspiracy to steal, breaking and entering and illegal possession of drugs. To cap that little lot, she's been on the trot from Peterhill Remand Home since November last year.' He dropped the flimsy on the table in disgust. 'We can certainly pick them.'

'That still doesn't excuse what Macek did to her,' Brady said. 'Underneath that surface toughness she's just a frightened little girl.'

'Sweetness and light,' Miller said. 'That's all I need.' He yawned, reaching for a cigarette. The packet was empty and he crumpled it with a sigh. 'It's been a long night.'

Brady nodded, applying a match to the bowl of his pipe. 'Soon be over.'

The door opened and Macek entered, escorted by a young probationer constable. The Pole slumped down on one of the hard wooden chairs at the table and Miller turned to the probationer.

'I could do with some tea and a packet of cigarettes. See what the canteen can offer, will you?'

The young constable went on his way briskly for Miller was a particular hero of his—Nick Miller, the man with the law degree who had made Detective Sergeant with only five years' service. All this and an interest, so it was rumoured, in his brother's business that enabled him to live in a style to which few police officers were accustomed.

As the door closed, Miller turned to Macek. 'Now then, you bastard, let's get down to it.'

'I've got nothing to say,' Macek said woodenly.

Brady laughed harshly and there was a heavy silence. Macek looked furtively at Miller who was examining his fingernails and said desperately, 'All right, so I knocked her around a little. Bloody little tart. She had it coming.'

'Why?' Brady demanded.

'I took her in,' Macek said. 'Gave her a place to stay. The best of everything. Then I find her sneaking out at two in the morning with my wallet, my watch and everything else of value she could lay her hands on. What would you have done?'

He sounded genuinely aggrieved and Miller picked up the girl's statement. 'She says here that you've been living together for five weeks.'

Macek nodded eagerly. 'I gave her the best—the best there was.'

'What about the men?'

'What men?'

'The men you brought round to the house every night. The men who called because they needed a woman.'

'Do me a favour,' Macek said. 'Do I look like a pimp?'

'Don't press me to answer that,' Miller told him.

'You've kept the girl under lock and key for the past two weeks. When she couldn't take any more, you beat her up and threw her out.'

'You try proving that.'

'I don't need to. You said you've been living together as man and wife.'

'So what? It's a free country.'

'She's just fifteen.'

Macek's face turned grey. 'She can't be.'

'Oh, yes she can. We've got her record card.'

Macek turned desperately to Brady. 'She didn't tell me.'

'It's a hard cruel world, isn't it, Macek?' Brady said.

The Pole seemed to pull himself together. 'I want a lawyer.'

'Are you going to make a statement?' Miller asked.

Macek glared across the table. 'You get stuffed,' he said.

Miller nodded. 'All right, Jack, take him down and book him. Make it abduction of a minor and rape. With any luck and his record, we might get him seven years.'

Macek sat there staring at him, horror in his eyes and Jack Brady's iron fist descended, jerking from the chair. 'On your way, soldier.'

Macek stumbled from the room and Miller turned to the window and pulled the curtain. Rain drifted across the glass in a fine spray and beyond, the first light of morning streaked the grey sky. The door opened behind him and the young probationer entered, the tea and cigarettes on a tray. 'That'll be six bob, sarge.'

Miller paid him and slipped the cigarettes into his pocket. 'I've changed my mind about tea. You have it. I'm going home. Tell Detective Constable Brady I'll 'phone him this afternoon.'

He walked along the quiet corridor, descended three flights of marble stairs and went out through the swing doors of the portico at the front of the Town Hall. His car was parked at the bottom of the steps with several others, a green Mini-Cooper, and he paused beside it to light a cigarette.

It was exactly five-thirty and the streets were strangely empty in the grey morning. The sensible thing to do was to go home to bed and yet he felt strangely restless. It was as if the city lay waiting for him and obeying a strange, irrational impulse he turned up the collar of his dark blue Swedish trenchcoat against the rain and started across the square.

For some people the early morning is the best part of the day and George Hammond was one of these. Lock-keeper in charge of the great gates that prevented the canal from emptying itself into the river basin below, he had reported for duty at five-forty-five, rain or snow for more than forty years. Walking through the quiet streets, he savoured the calm morning with a conscious pleasure that never varied.

He paused at the top of the steps at the end of the bridge over the river and looked down into the basin. They catered mainly for barge traffic this far upstream and they floated together beside the old Victorian docks like basking sharks.

He went down the steps and started along the bank. One section of the basin was crammed with coal barges offering a convenient short-cut to the other side and he started to work his way across.

He paused on the edge of the final barge, judging the gap between the thwart and the wharf. He started his jump, gave a shocked gasp and only just managed to regain his balance.

A woman stared up at him through the grey-green water. In a lifetime of working on the river George Hammond had found bodies in the basin before, but never one like this. The eyes stared past him, fixed on eternity and for some inexplicable reason he knew fear.

He turned, worked his way back across the river, scrambled up on the wharf and ran along the bank.

Nick Miller had just started to cross the bridge as Hammond emerged from the top of the steps and leaned against the parapet sobbing for breath.

Miller moved forward quickly. 'Anything wrong?'

'Police!' Hammond gasped. 'I need the police.'

'You've found them,' Miller said crisply. 'What's up?'

'Girl down there in the water,' Hammond said. 'Other side of the coal barges beneath the wharf.'

'Dead?' Miller demanded.

Hammond nodded. 'Gave me a hell of a turn, I can tell you.'

'There's an all-night café on the other side of the bridge. 'Phone for a patrol car and an ambulance from there. I'll go down and see what I can do.'

Hammond nodded, turned away and Miller went down the steps quickly and moved along the bank. It had stopped raining and a cool breeze lifted off the water so that he shivered slightly as he jumped for the deck of the first coal barge and started to work his way across. He couldn't find her at first and then a sudden eddy of the current swirled, clearing the flotsam from the surface and she stared up at him.

And she was beautiful—more beautiful than he had ever known a woman to be, that was the strangest thing of all. The body had drifted into the arched entrance of a vault under the wharf and hung suspended just beneath the surface. The dress floated around her in a cloud as did the long golden hair and there was a look of faint surprise in the eyes, the lips parted slightly as if in wonder at how easy it had been.

Up on the bridge, there was the jangle of a patrol car's bell and in the distance, the siren of the approaching ambulance sounded faintly. But he couldn't wait. In some strange way this had become personal. He took off his trenchcoat and jacket, slipped off his shoes and lowered himself over the side.

The water was bitterly cold and yet he was hardly conscious of the fact as he swam into the archway. At that moment, the first rays of the morning sun broke through the clouds, striking into the water so that she seemed to smile as he reached under the surface and took her.

A line of broad steps dropped into the basin twenty yards to the right and he swam towards them, standing up when his knees bumped a shelving bank of gravel, lifting her in his arms.

But now she looked different. Now she looked dead. He stood there knee-deep, staring down at her, a lump in his throat, aware of a feeling of personal loss.

'Why?' he said to himself softly. 'Why?'

But there was no answer, could never be and as the ambulance turned on the wharf above him he went up the steps slowly, the girl cradled in his arms so that she might have been a child sleeping.

CHAPTER TWO

Detective Superintendant Bruce Grant, head of the city's Central Division C.I.D. stood at the window of his office drinking a cup of tea and stared out morosely at the driving rain. He had a slight headache and his liver was acting up again. He was getting old, he decided—old and fat through lack of exercise and the stack of paperwork waiting on his desk didn't help. He lit a cigarette, his first of the day, sat down and started on the In-tray.

The first report was headed *Found Dead—Unidentified*. Grant read it through, a slight frown on his face and pressed the button on his intercom.

'Is Sergeant Miller in?'

'I believe he's in the canteen, sir,' a neutral voice replied.

'Get him for me, will you?'

Miller arrived five minutes later, immaculate in a dark-blue worsted suit and freshly laundered white shirt. Only the skin that was stretched a little too tightly over the high cheekbones gave any hint of fatigue.

'I thought you were supposed to be having a rest day?' Grant said.

'So did I, but I'm due in court at ten when Macek is formally charged. I'm asking for a ten day remand. That girl's going to be in hospital for at least a week.'

Grant tapped the form on his desk. 'I don't like the look of this one.'

'The girl I pulled out of the river?'

'That's right. Are you certain there was no identification?'

Miller took an envelope from his pocket and produced a small gold medallion on the end of a slender chain. 'This was around her neck.'

Grant picked it up. 'St. Christopher.'

'Have a look on the back.'

The engraving had been executed by an expert: *To Joanna from Daddy—1955*. Grant looked up, frowning. 'And this was all?'

Miller nodded. 'She was wearing stockings, the usual in under-clothes, and a reasonably expensive dress. One rather sinister point. Just beneath the maker's label there was obviously some sort of name tab. It's been torn out.'

Grant sighed heavily. 'Do you think she might have been put in?'

Miller shook his head. 'Not a chance. There isn't a mark on her.'

'Then it doesn't make sense,' Grant said. 'Suicide's an irrational act at the best of times. Are you asking me to accept that this girl was so cold-blooded about it that she took time off to try to conceal her identity?'

'It's the only thing that makes sense.'

'Then what about the chain? Why didn't she get rid of that, too?'

'When you habitually wear a thing like that you tend to forget about it,' Miller said. 'Or maybe it meant a lot to her — especially as she was a Catholic.'

'That's another thing—a Catholic committing suicide.'

'It's been known.'

'But not very often. There are times when such things as statistical returns and probability tables have their uses in this work—or didn't they teach you that at the staff college? What have Missing Persons got to offer?'

'Nothing yet,' Miller said. 'There's time of course. She looks old enough to have been out all night. Someone could conceivably wait for a day or two before reporting her missing.'

'But you don't think so?'

'Do you?'

Grant looked at the form again and shook his head. 'No, I'd say anything we're going to find out about this one, we'll have to dig up for ourselves.'

'Can I have it?'

Grant nodded. 'Autopsy isn't mandatory in these cases but I think I'll ask the County Coroner to authorize one. You never know what might turn up.'

He reached for the 'phone and Miller went back into the main C.I.D. room and sat down at his desk. There was an hour to fill before his brief court appearance—a good opportunity to get rid of some of the paperwork in his In-tray.

For some reason he found it impossible to concentrate. He leaned back in his chair, closing his eyes and her face rose out of the darkness to meet him, still that faint look of surprise in the eyes, the lips slightly parted. It was as if she was about to speak, to tell him something but that was impossible.

God, but he was tired. He settled back in his chair and cat-napped, awaking at exactly five minutes to ten feeling curiously refreshed, but when he went downstairs and crossed the square to the county court building, it wasn't the Macek case he was thinking about.

The City Mortuary was at the back of the Medical School, a large ugly building in Victorian Gothic with stained glass windows by the entrance. Inside, it was dark and cool with green tiled walls and a strange aseptic smell that was vaguely unpleasant.

Jack Palmer, the Senior Technician, was sitting at his desk in the small glass office at the end of the corridor. He turned and grinned as Miller paused in the doorway.

'Don't tell me—let me guess.'

'Anything for me?' Miller asked.

'Old Murray's handled it himself. Hasn't had time to make

out his report yet, but he'll be able to tell you what you need to know. He's cleaning up now.'

Miller peered through the glass wall into the white tiled hall outside the theatre and saw the tall, spare form of the University Professor of Pathology emerge from the theatre, the front of his white gown stained with blood.

'Can I go in?'

Palmer nodded. 'Help yourself.'

Professor Murray had removed his gown and was standing at the sluice, washing his hands and arms when Miller entered. He smiled, speaking with the faint Scots accent of his youth that he had never been able to lose.

'Hardly the time of the year to go swimming, especially in that open sewer we call a river. I trust you've been given suitable injections?'

'If I start feeling ill I'll call no one but you,' Miller said, 'that's a promise.'

Murray reached for a towel and started to dry his arms. 'They tell me you don't know who the girl is?'

'That's right. Of course she may be reported missing by someone within the next day or two.'

'But you don't think so? May I ask why?'

'It's not the usual kind of suicide. The pattern's all wrong. For one thing, the indications are that she did everything possible to conceal her identity before killing herself.' He hesitated. 'There's no chance that she was dumped, is there? Drugged beforehand or something like that?'

Murray shook his head. 'Impossible—the eyes were still open. It's funny you should mention drugs though.'

'Why?'

'I'll show you.'

It was cold in the theatre and the heavy antiseptic smell could not wholly smother the sickly-sweet stench of death.

Her body lay on the slab in the centre of the room covered with a rubber sheet. Murray raised the edge and lifted the left arm.

'Take a look.'

The marks of the needle were plainly visible and Miller frowned. 'She was a junkie?'

Murray nodded. 'My tests indicate that she had an injection consisting of two grains of heroin and one of cocaine approximately half an hour before she died.'

'And when would you say that was?'

'Let's see now. You pulled her out just before six, didn't you?'
I'd say she'd been in the water about five hours.'

'Which means she went in at one a.m.'

'Or thereabouts. One can't be exact. It was a cold night.'

'Anything else?'

'What can I tell you? She was about nineteen, well nurtured.
I'd say she'd been raised in more than comfortable surroundings.'

'Was she a virgin?'

'Anything but—two months pregnant.' He shook his head and
added dryly. 'A young woman very well acquainted with the
sexual act.'

'What about her clothes?'

'A chap was here from your Forensic Department. He took
them away along with the usual things. Scrapings from under the
fingernails, hair samples and so on.'

Miller moved to the other side of the slab, hesitated and then
pulled back the rubber sheet revealing the face. Murray had
closed the eyes and she looked calm and peaceful, the skin
smooth and colourless. Murray covered her again gently, his face
sombre. 'I think she was someone who had suffered a great deal.
Too much for one so young.'

Miller nodded, unable to speak. That strange aching dryness
clutched at his throat again and he turned away quickly. As he
reached the door, Murray called softly, 'Nick!' Miller turned.
'Keep me posted.'

'I'll do that,' Miller said and the rubber doors swung together
behind him.

As he went out into the pale morning sunshine, Jack Brady
crossed the car park to meet him.

'Grant thought you might need some help on this one. Have
they finished the autopsy?'

Miller nodded. 'Murray says she went into the river somewhere around one a.m. She was pregnant, by the way.'

Brady nodded calmly. 'Anything else?'

'She was a junkie. Heroin and cocaine.'

'That should give us a lead.' Brady took a buff envelope from
his overcoat pocket. 'I've checked with Forensic. They'll have
a report ready by noon. These are from Photography.'

Miller opened the envelope and examined the prints it contained. Those photography boys certainly knew their job. She
might almost have been alive, an illusion helped by the fact that
the photos had been taken before Murray had closed her eyes.

Brady took one and frowned. 'A damned shame. She looks like a nice kid.'

'Don't they always?' Miller slipped the other prints into his pocket. 'I think I'll go and see Dr. Das. He knows just about every junkie in town.'

'What about me?'

Miller took the gold St. Christopher from his breast pocket and handed it over. 'You're a good Catholic, aren't you, Jack.'

'I go to Mass now and then.'

'Maybe the girl did. There's an inscription on the other side. Work your way round the parish priests. Someone may recognize her photo or even the medal.'

'More shoe-leather,' Brady groaned.

'Good for your soul this one. I'll drop you off at the Cathedral if you like.'

They got into the car and Brady glanced at his copy of the girl's photograph again before putting it away in his wallet. He shook his head. 'It doesn't make sense, does it? Have you any idea what it's like down there on the docks at that time in the morning?'

'Just about the darkest and loneliest place in the world,' Miller said.

Brady nodded. 'One thing's certain. She must have been pretty desperate. I'd like to know what got her into that state.'

'So would I, Jack,' Miller said. 'So would I,' and he released the handbrake and drove rapidly away.

Drug addicts are possibly the most difficult of all patients to handle and yet Dr. Lal Das specialized in them. He was a tall cadaverous Indian, with an international reputation in the field, who persisted in running a general practice in one of the less salubrious parts of the city, a twilight area of tall, decaying Victorian houses.

He had just finished his morning calls and was having coffee in front of the surgery fire when Miller was shown in. Das smiled and waved him to a seat. 'A pleasant surprise. You will join me?'

'Thanks very much.'

Das went to the sideboard and returned with another cup. 'A social call?'

'I'm afraid not.' Miller produced one of the photos. 'Have you ever seen her before?'

Das shook his head. 'Who is she?'

'We don't know. I pulled her out of the river this morning.'

'Suicide?'

Miller nodded. 'Professor Murray did an autopsy. She'd had a fix about half an hour before she died.'

'What was the dosage?'

'Two grains of heroin—one of cocaine.'

'Then she can't have been an addict for long. Most of my regulars are on five, six or seven grains of heroin alone. There were the usual tracks in her arm?'

'Only a few.'

'Which would seem to confirm my theory.' Das sighed. 'What a tragedy. She looks such a pleasant child.' He handed the photo back. 'I'm sorry, I can't help. You have no idea as to her identity at all?'

'I was hoping she might be a registered addict.'

Das shook his head emphatically. 'Definitely not. We have a new scheme operating under which all registered addicts must attend my clinic at St. Gregory's Hospital on Saturday mornings.'

'Is this as well as their visits to their own doctor?'

Das nodded. 'Believe me, sergeant, if she was registered I would know her.'

Miller swallowed the rest of his coffee. 'I'd better get moving. Got a lot of ground to cover.'

'Why not have a chat with Chuck Lazer?' Das said. 'If anyone could help, he could.'

'That's an idea,' Miller said. 'How is he these days? Still dry?'

'For ten months now. A remarkable achievement, especially when one considers that his intake was of the order of seven grains of heroin and six of cocaine daily.'

'I hear he's running a small casino club now.'

'Yes, The Berkley in Cork Square. Very exclusive. Haven't you been?'

'I got an invitation to the opening, but I couldn't make it. Does he still play a good jazz piano?'

'Oscar Peterson at his best couldn't improve on him. I was there last Saturday. We were talking about you.'

'I'll drop in and see him,' Miller said. 'Where's he living now?'

'He has an apartment over the club. Very pleasant. He'll probably be in bed now, mind you.'

'I'll take that chance.'

They went out into the hall. Das opened the front door and shook hands formally. 'If I can help in any way . . .'

'I'll let you know,' Miller said and he ran down the steps to the Mini-Cooper and drove away.

Cork Square was a green lung in the heart of the city, a few sycamore trees scattered here and there, the whole surrounded by quiet, grey-stone Georgian houses, most of them occupied by consultant physicians and barristers.

The entrance to the Berkley Club was a cream painted door, its brass handle and plate shining in the sunlight. Even the neon sign was in perfect taste with the surroundings and had obviously been specially designed. Miller pulled into the kerb, got out and looked up at the front of the building.

'Hey, Nick, you old so-and-so! What gives?'

The cry echoed across the square and as he turned, Chuck Lazer moved out of the trees, a couple of Dalmatians straining ahead of him on twin leads.

Miller went to meet him, leaving the path and crossing the damp grass.

'Hello there, Chuck. What's all this?' He bent down to pat the eager dogs.

The American grinned. 'Part of my new image. The customers love it. Gives the place tone. But never mind that. How are you? It's been too long.'

He was bubbling over with genuine pleasure, the blue eyes sparkling. When Miller had first met him almost a year previously during a murder investigation, Lazer had been hopelessly hooked on heroin with the gaunt fleshless face of an emaciated saint. Now, there was meat on his bones and the neatly trimmed dark fringe beard combined with the expensive sports coat to give him a positively elegant appearance.

He slipped the dogs' leads and the Dalmatians moved into the flower beds as he and Miller sat down on a bench.

'I've just seen Das. He told me he'd been to the club. Gave me a glowing report.' Miller offered him a cigarette. 'On you too.'

Lazer grinned. 'No need to worry about me, Nick. I'd cut my throat before I'd take another shot.' He lit his cigarette and exhaled smoke in a blue cloud. 'What did you want with Das—business?'

Miller produced one of the photos and passed it across. 'Know her?'

Lazer shook his head. 'Can't say I do.' He frowned suddenly. 'Heh, isn't that a morgue photograph?'

Miller nodded. 'I pulled her out of the river this morning. Trouble is we can't identify her.'

'Suicide?'

'That's right. The autopsy showed she was an addict. I was hoping she might be registered, that Das might know her.'

'And she isn't? That makes it difficult.'

'What's the drug market like now, Chuck?' Miller said. 'Where would she get the stuff?'

'Difficult to say. I've been out of circulation for quite a while, remember. As far as I know, there isn't any really organized peddling if that's what you mean. Remember where you first met me?'

Miller grinned. 'Outside the all-night chemist's in City Square.'

'That's where it changes hands. Most registered addicts see their doctors at his evening surgery and usually get a prescription dated for the following day. Legally, they can have it filled from midnight onwards which is why you always find a bunch waiting in the all-night chemist's in any big city round about that time. The non-registered users hang around outside hoping to buy a few pills. They're usually in luck. Quite a few doctors tend to over-prescribe.'

'So all I have to do is go down to City Square at midnight and pass her photo around?'

'If she was an addict, someone will recognize her, that's for sure. The most exclusive club in the world.'

'Thanks very much,' Miller said. 'I didn't get any sleep last night either.'

'You shouldn't have joined.' Lazer chuckled and then his smile faded.

Miller glanced across to the club as a dark blue Rolls eased into the kerb. The first man to emerge was built like a pro wrestler, shoulders bulging massively under a dark blue overcoat. The driver came round to join him, a small, wiry man with jet black hair, and held open the rear door.

The man who got out was large and rather fleshy with hair so pale that it was almost white. He wore a single-breasted suit of dark grey flannel that was straight out of Savile Row, a white gardenia in the buttonhole, and carried himself with the habitual arrogance of a man who believes that he exists by a kind of divine right. The small man said something to him and they all turned and glanced at Lazer and Miller.

'Friends of yours?' Miller said as they moved across the grass.

Lazer shook his head. 'I wouldn't say that exactly. The fancy

boy is Max Vernon. Came up from London about four months
ago and bought out Harry Faulkner. Took over his betting shops,
the Flamingo Club—everything.'

'What about his minders?'

'The big boy's called Carver—Simon Carver. The little guy's
the one to watch. Stratton—I don't know his first name.'

'Have they been leaning on you?'

Lazer bared his teeth in a mirthless grin. 'Nothing quite so
obvious. Let's say I've got a very nice little business and Mr.
Vernon would like a piece of the action. For a consideration,
of course. All nice and legal. Unfortunately, I'm not interested
in selling.'

Vernon paused a couple of yards away. Carver and Stratton
on either side of him. 'Hello there, old man,' he said cheerfully.
'I was hoping to find you in. Time we had another little chat.'

'Not in my book it isn't,' Lazer replied.

Carver took a step forward, but before anything could develop,
Miller said quickly, 'That's an Old Etonian tie you're wearing,
did you know that?'

Vernon turned, his smile still hooked firmly into place. 'How
very gratifying. You're the first person to recognize it since I've
been here. Of course, we are a little far north.'

'Dangerous country,' Miller said. 'We've been known to roll
boulders down the hillside on unwary travellers—stone strangers.'

'How fascinating.' Vernon turned to Lazer. 'Introduce me to
your friend, Chuck.'

'A pleasure,' Lazer said. 'Nick Miller. Detective Sergeant,
Central C.I.D.'

Vernon hesitated momentarily and then extended his hand.
'Always a pleasure to meet the law.'

Miller stayed where he was on the bench, hands tucked
casually into his pockets. 'I can't say it's mutual.'

'You watch your mouth, copper,' Carver said harshly.

He started to move, Lazer whistled twice and the Dalmatians
arrived on the run. They stood beside him, pointing at Carver,
something rumbling deep down in their throats.

Carver hesitated, obviously uncertain and Miller laughed.
'Know why they call them carriage dogs, Carver? They were
specially bred during the eighteenth century as travelling companions to take care of highwaymen.'

Something glowed deep in Carver's eyes and Vernon chuckled.
'That's damned good. Damned good.' He grinned at Carver.
'See, you learn something new every day of the week.'

He turned away without another word and walked back to the Rolls, Carver and Stratton hurrying after him. Lazer leaned down to fondle the ears of the two dogs and Miller said softly, 'I think you could have trouble there, Chuck.'

'If it comes, I'll handle it.'

Miller shook his head. 'You mean I'll handle it and that's an order.' He got to his feet and grinned. 'I've got to get moving.'

Lazer stood up and produced a small gold-edged card from his breast pocket. 'I know it's illegal to do it this way, but there's a membership card. Why not drop in? It's been a long time since I heard you play the piano.'

'I might just do that,' Miller said and he turned and walked away across the grass.

As the Rolls-Royce moved out into the main traffic stream, Max Vernon leaned forward and slid back the glass panel of the partition.

'This chap Miller,' he said to Carver, 'know anything about him?'

'Not a thing.'

'Then start digging. I want to know everything—everything there is to know.'

'Any special reason?' Carver said.

'Well, let me put it this way. The only other copper I've ever met who made a practice of wearing sixty-guinea suits is doing a five stretch in the Ville for corruption.'

Carver's eyes widened and Vernon closed the glass panel, leaned back in his seat and lit a cigarette, a slight smile on his face.

CHAPTER THREE

HENRY WADE was fat and balding and his several chins and horn-rimmed spectacles gave him the deceptively benign air of a prosperous publican or back street bookie. He was neither. He was head of the department's Forensic section with the rank of Detective Inspector and the ready smile concealed a brain that in action had the cutting edge of a razor.

When Miller went into the small office at one end of the police lab. he found Wade at his desk filling in a report, covering the paper with the neat italic script that was his special pride.

He turned and smiled. 'Hello, Nick, I was wondering when you'd turn up.'

'Anything for me?'

'Not much, I'm afraid. Come on. I'll show you.'

Miller followed him into the lab., nodding to the bench technicians as he passed. The girl's clothing was laid out neatly on a table by the window.

Wade went through the items one by one. 'The stockings are a well-known brand sold everywhere and the underwear she bought at Marks & Spencer's along with just about every other girl in the country these days.'

'What about the dress?'

'Reasonably expensive, but once again, a well-known brand name available at dozens of shops and stores. One interesting point. Just below the maker's label, a name tab's been torn out.'

He picked up the dress pointing with a pair of tweezers and Miller nodded. 'I noticed.'

'I had a hunch about that. We matched up a piece of the tab that was still attached to the dress and my hunch paid off. It's a Cash label. You must have seen them. Little white tabs with the individual's name woven in red. People buy them for school-children or students going away to college.'

Miller nodded. 'Thousands of people, including my sister-in-law. Her two kids have them sewn into just about every damned thing they own. Is that all?'

'No—one other thing. When we checked the nail scrapings we discovered a minute quantity of oil paint. There were one or two spots on the dress, too.'

'An artist?' Miller said. 'That's something.'

'Don't be too certain. Lots of people do a little painting these days.' Henry Wade grinned and slapped him on the shoulder. 'You shouldn't have joined, Nick lad. You shouldn't have joined.'

Grant was still working away at his desk when Miller peered round the door. 'Got a minute?'

'Just about.' Grant sat back and lit a cigarette. 'How's it going?'

'So far, not so good, but it was something else I wanted to mention. What do you know about a man called Vernon?'

'Max Vernon, the bloke from London who took over Faulkner's casino and betting shops?' Grant shrugged. 'Not much. The Chief introduced him to me at the Conservative Ball. Obviously a gentleman. Public school and all that sort of thing.'

'Right down to his Old Etonian tie.' Miller suppressed a

strong desire to burst into laughter. 'He's leaning on Chuck Lazer.'

'He's what ?' Grant said incredulously.

'It's true enough,' Miller said. 'I was chatting to Lazer in the Square outside his place when Vernon turned up with a couple of heavies named Carver and Stratton. No comic Vaudeville act those two, believe me. Vernon wants a piece of the Berkley Club. He'll pay for it of course, all nice and legal, but Chuck Lazer better play ball or else . . .'

Grant was a different man as he flicked one of the switches on his intercom. 'Records? Get on to C.R.O. in London at once. I want everything they've got on Max Vernon and two men now working for him called Carver and Stratton. Top priority.'

He turned back to Miller. 'What happened?'

'Nothing much. Vernon didn't say anything in the slightest way incriminating. On the face of it, he's making a perfectly legitimate business offer.'

'Did he know who you were?'

'Not until Lazer introduced us.'

Grant got up and walked to the window. 'I don't like the sound of this at all.'

'It certainly raises interesting possibilities,' Miller said. 'Those houses Faulkner was running in Gascoigne Square. His call-girl racket. Has Vernon taken those over too?'

'An intriguing thought.' Grant sighed heavily. 'It never rains but it pours. Try and look in this afternoon at about three. I should have heard from C.R.O. by then.'

When Miller went back into the main C.I.D. room a young P.C. was hovering beside his desk. 'I took a message for you while you were in with the super, sergeant.'

'Who from?'

'Jack Brady. He said he was ringing from St. Gemma's Roman Catholic Church in Walthamgate. He'd like you to join him there as soon as you can.'

'Anything else?'

'Yes—he said to tell you that he thinks he's traced the girl.'

The lights in the little church were very dim and down by the altar the candles flickered and the figure of the Virgin in the chapel to one side seemed to float there in the darkness.

For Miller, this was unfamiliar territory and he paused waiting as Jack Brady dipped a knee, crossing himself reverently. The man they had come to see knelt in prayer at the altar and when he got to his feet and came towards them, Miller saw that he was very old, the hair silvery in the subdued light.

Brady made the introductions. 'Father Ryan, this is Detective Sergeant Nick Miller.'

The old man smiled and took Miller's hand in a grip that was surprisingly firm. 'Jack and I are old friends, sergeant. For fifteen years or more he ran the boxing team for me at the Dockside Mission boys' club. Shall we sit in the porch? A pity to miss the sunshine. It's been a hard winter.'

Brady opened the door and Father Ryan preceded them. He sat on the polished wooden bench that overlooked the quiet graveyard with the row of cypress trees lining the road beyond the high wall.

'I understand you might be able to help us with our enquiry, Father,' Miller said.

The old man nodded. 'Could I see the photo again?'

Miller passed it across and for a moment there was silence as Father Ryan examined it. He sighed heavily. 'Poor girl. Poor wee girl.'

'You know her?'

'She called herself Joanna Martin.'

'Called herself . . . ?'

'That's right. I don't think it was her real name.'

'Might I ask why?'

Father Ryan smiled faintly. 'Like you, I deal with people, sergeant. Human beings in the raw. Let's say one develops an instinct.'

Miller nodded. 'I know what you mean.'

'She first came to my church about three months ago. I noticed something different about her at once. This is a twilight area, most of the houses in multiple occupation, the tenants constantly coming and going. Joanna was obviously the product of a safer more ordered world. She was out of her element.'

'Can you tell us where she lived?'

'She had a room with a Mrs. Kilroy, a parishioner of mine. It's not far from here. I've given Detective Constable Brady the address.'

Somehow, the fact that he had used Brady's official title seemed to underline a new formality in the interchange. It was as if he were preparing himself for the question that he knew must come.

'I know this must be a difficult situation for you, Father,' Miller said gently. 'But this girl had problems and they must have been pretty desperate to make her take the way out that she did. Can you throw any light on them?'

Brady cleared his throat awkwardly and shuffled his feet. The old man shook his head. 'For me, the secrecy of the confessional must be absolute. Surely you must be aware of that, sergeant.'

Miller nodded. 'Of course, Father. I won't press you any further. You've already helped us a great deal.'

Father Ryan stood up and held out his hand. 'If I can help in any other way, don't hesitate to get in touch.'

Brady was already moving away. Miller started to follow and hesitated. 'One more thing, Father. I understand there could be some difficulty regarding burial because of the manner of death.'

'Not in this case,' Father Ryan said firmly. 'There are several mitigating circumstances. I intend raising the matter with the Bishop personally. I may say with some certainty that I foresee little difficulty.'

Miller smiled. 'I'm glad.'

'Forgive me for saying so, but you appear to have some personal interest here? May I ask why?'

'I pulled her out of the river myself,' Miller told him. 'Something I'm not likely to forget in a hurry. I know one thing—I'd like to get my hands on whoever was responsible.'

Father Ryan sighed. 'It's a strange thing, but in spite of the fact that most people believe priests to be somehow cut off from the real world, I come face to face with more human wickedness in a week than the average man does in a lifetime.' He smiled gently. 'And I still believe that at heart, most human beings are good.'

'I wish I could agree, Father,' Miller said sombrely. 'I wish I could agree.' He turned and walked away quickly to where Jack Brady waited at the gate.

Mrs. Kilroy was a large, unlovely widow with flaming red hair that had come straight out of a bottle and a thin mouth enlarged by orange lipstick into an obscene gash.

'I keep a respectable place here, I've never had any trouble before,' she said as she led the way upstairs.

'No trouble, Mrs. Kilroy,' Brady said persuasivly. 'We just want to see the room, that's all and ask a few questions.'

The landing was long and dark, its polished lino covered by a strip of worn carpeting. The door at the far end was locked. She produced a bunch of keys, opened it and led the way in.

The room was surprisingly large and furnished in Victorian

mahogany. The curtains at the only window were partially closed, the traffic sounds outside muted and unreal as if from another world and a thin bar of sunlight fell across the floor adding a new richness to the faded colours of the old Indian carpet.

It was the neatness that was so surprising and the cleanliness. The bed had been stripped, the blankets folded into squares and stacked at one end of the mattress and the top of the dressing table had quite obviously been dusted. Miller opened one or two of the empty drawers, closed them again and turned.

'And this is exactly how you found the room this morning?'

Mrs. Kilroy nodded. 'She came and knocked on my door last night at about ten o'clock.'

'Had she been out?'

'I wouldn't know. She told me she'd be moving today.'

'Did she say why?'

Mrs. Kilroy shook her head. 'I didn't ask. I was more interested in getting a week's rent in lieu of notice which was the agreement.'

'And she paid?'

'Without a murmur. Mind you there was never any trouble over her rent, I'll say that. Not like some.'

Brady had busied himself during the conversation in moving around the room, checking all drawers and cupboards. Now he turned and shook his head. 'Clean as a whistle.'

'Which means that when she left, she must have taken everything with her.' Miller turned to Mrs. Kilroy. 'Did you see her go?'

'Last time I saw her was about half ten. She knocked on the door and told me she'd some rubbish to burn. Asked if she could put it in the central heating furnace in the cellar.'

'Have you been down there since?'

'No need. It has an automatic stoking system. Only needs checking every two days.'

'I see.' Miller walked across to the window and pulled back the curtains. 'Let's go back to when you last saw her. Did she seem worried or agitated?'

Mrs. Kilroy shook her head quickly. 'She was just the same as she always was.'

'And yet she killed herself less than three hours later.'

'God have mercy on her.' There was genuine horror in Mrs. Kilroy's voice and she crossed herself quickly.

'What else can you tell me about her? I understand she'd been a tenant of yours for about three months.'

'That's right. She arrived on the doorstep one afternoon with a couple of suitcases. As it happened, I had a vacancy and she offered a month's rent in advance in lieu of references.'

'What did you think of her?'

Mrs. Kilroy shrugged. 'She didn't really fit in. Too much of the lady for a district like this. I never asked questions, I always mind my own business, but if anyone had a story to tell it was her.'

'Father Ryan doesn't seem to think Joanna Martin was her real name.'

'I shouldn't be surprised.'

'What did she do for a living?'

'She paid her rent on time and never caused any trouble. Whatever she did was her own business. One thing—she had an easel set up in here. Used to paint in oils. I once asked her if she was a student, but she said it was only a hobby.'

'Did she go out much—at night, for instance?'

'She could have been out all night and every night as far as I was concerned. All my lodgers have their own keys.' She shrugged. 'More often than not I'm out myself.'

'Did anyone ever call for her?'

'Not that I noticed. She kept herself to herself. The only outstanding thing I do remember is that sometimes she looked really ill. I had to help her up the stairs one day. I wanted to call the doctor, but she said it was just her monthly. I saw her later that afternoon and she looked fine.'

Which was how one would expect her to look after a shot of heroin and Miller sighed. 'Anything else?'

'I don't think so,' Mrs. Kilroy hesitated. 'If she had a friend at all, it was the girl in number four—Monica Grey.'

'Why do you say that?'

'I've seen them going out together, mainly in the afternoons.'

'Is she in now?'

'Should be. As far as I know, she works nights in one of these gaming clubs.'

Miller turned to Brady. 'I'll have a word with her. You get Mrs. Kilroy to show you where the furnace is. See what you can find.'

The door closed behind them and Miller stood there in the quiet, listening. But there was nothing here—this room had no personality. It was as if she had never been here at all and after all, what did he really know about her? At the moment she existed only as a series of apparently contradictory facts. A well-bred girl, she had come down to living in a place like this. A sincere Catholic, she had committed suicide. Educated and intelligent, but also a drug addict.

None of it made any sense at all and he went along the corridor and knocked at number four. There was an immediate reply and he opened the door and entered.

She was standing in front of the dressing table, her back to the door and dressed, as far as he could judge in that first moment, in stockings and a pair of dark briefs. In the mirror, he was aware of her breasts, high and firm, and then her eyes widened.

'I thought it was Mrs. Kilroy.'

Miller stepped back into the corridor smartly, closing the door. A moment later it opened again and she stood there laughing at him, an old nylon housecoat belted around her waist.

'Shall we try again?'

Her voice was hoarse but not unattractive with a slight Liverpool accent and she had a turned-up nose that gave her a rather gamin charm.

'Miss Grey?' Miller produced his warrant card. 'Detective Sergeant Miller—Central C.I.D. I wonder if I might have a word with you?'

Her smile slipped fractionally and a shadow seemed to cross her eyes as she stepped back and motioned him in. 'What have I done now? Over-parked or something?'

There were times when the direct approach produced the best results and Miller tried it now. 'I'm making enquiries into the death of Joanna Martin. I understand you might be able to help me.'

It had the effect of a physical blow. She seemed to stagger slightly, then turned, groped for the end of the bed and sank down.

'I believe you were pretty good friends,' Miller continued.

She stared up at him blindly then suddenly got to her feet, pushed him out of the way and ran for the bathroom. He stood there, a slight frown on his face and there was a knock on the outside door. He opened it to find Jack Brady waiting.

'Any luck?' Miller asked.

Brady held up an old canvas bag. 'I found all sorts in the ashpan. What about this for instance?'

He produced a triangular piece of metal, blackened and twisted by the fire and Miller frowned. 'This is a corner piece off a suitcase.'

'That's right,' Brady shook the bag in his right hand. 'If the bits and pieces in here are anything to go by, I'd say she must have put every damned thing she owned into that furnace.'

'Including her suitcase? She certainly wasn't leaving any-thing to chance.' Miller sighed. 'All right, Jack. Take that little lot down to the car and put in a call to H.Q. See if they've any-thing for us. I shan't be long.'

He lit a cigarette, moved to the window and looked out into the back garden. Behind him the bathroom door opened and Monica Grey emerged.

She looked a lot brighter as she came forward and sat on the edge of the bed. 'Sorry about that. It was rather a shock. Joanna was a nice kid.' She hesitated and then continued. 'How—how did it happen?'

'She jumped in the river.' Miller gave her a cigarette and lit it for her. 'Mrs. Kilroy tells me you were good friends.'

Monica Grey took the smoke deep into her lungs and exhaled with a sigh of pleasure. 'I wouldn't say that exactly. I went to the cinema with her sometimes in the afternoons or she came in for coffee mainly because she happened to live next door.'

'You never went out with her at any other time?'

'I couldn't—I work nights. I'm a croupier at a gaming club in Gascoigne Square—the Flamingo.'

'Max Vernon's place?'

She nodded. 'Have you been there?'

'A long time ago. Tell me about Joanna? Where did she come from?'

Monica Grey shook her head. 'She never discussed her past. She always seemed to live entirely in the present.'

'What did she do for a living?'

'Nothing as far as I could tell. She spent a lot of time paint-ing, but only as a hobby. I know one thing—she was never short of money.'

'What about boy friends?'

'As far as I know, she didn't have any.'

'Didn't that seem strange to you?' She was an attractive girl?'

'That's true, but she had her problems.' She appeared to hesitate and then went on. 'If you've seen her body you must know what I'm getting at. She was a junkie.'

'How did you know that?'

'I went into her room to borrow a pair of stockings one day and found her giving herself a shot. She asked me to keep quiet about it.'

'Which you did?'

Monica Grey shrugged. 'None of my affair how she got her kicks. It was one hell of a shame, but there was nothing I could do about it.'

'She was a Catholic,' Miller said, 'Did you know that?'

She nodded. 'She went to church nearly every day.'

'And yet she killed herself after burning everything she owned in the central heating furnace downstairs and ripping the name tab out of the dress she was wearing when she died. It's only by chance that we've managed to trace her this far and when we do, nobody seems to know anything about her. Wouldn't you say that was peculiar?'

'She was a strange kid. You could never tell what was going on beneath the surface.'

'Father Ryan doesn't seem to think that Joanna Martin was her real name.'

'If that's true, she certainly never gave me any clue.'

Miller nodded, turned and paced across the room. He paused suddenly. The table against the wall was littered with sketches, mainly fashion drawings, some in pen and ink, others colour-washed. All showed indications of real talent.

'Yours?' he said.

Monica Grey stood up and walked across. 'That's right. Like them?'

'Very much. Did you go to the College of Art?'

'For two years. That's what brought me here in the first place.'

'What made you give it up?'

She grinned. 'Forty quid a week at the Flamingo plus a dress allowance.'

'Attractive alternative.' Miller dropped the sketch he was holding. 'Well, I don't think I need bother you any more.' He walked to the door, paused and turned. 'Just one thing. You do understand that if I can't trace her family, I may have to ask you to make the formal identification?'

She stood there staring at him, her face very white, and he closed the door and went downstairs. There was a pay 'phone fixed to the wall by the door and Brady leaned beside it filling his pipe.

He glanced up quickly, 'Any joy?'

'Not really, but I've a feeling we'll be seeing her again.'

'I got through to H.Q. There was a message for you from Chuck Lazer. Apparently he's been passing round the copy of the photo you gave him. He's come up with a registered addict

who sold her a couple of pills outside the all-night chemist's in
City Square just after midnight. If you guarantee no charge, he's
agreed to make a statement.'

'That's all right by me,' Miller said. 'You handle it, will you?
I'll drop you off at Cork Square and you can go and see Chuck
right away. I've a 'phone call to make first.'

'Anything special?'

'Just a hunch. The girl liked to paint, we've established that.
Another thing—that name tab she ripped out of her dress was
a type commonly bought by students. I'm wondering if there
might be a connection.'

He found the number he wanted and dialled quickly. The
receiver was picked up almost at once at the other end and a
woman's voice said, 'College of Art.'

'Put me through to the registrar's office please.'

There was a momentary delay and then a pleasant Scottish
voice cut in, 'Henderson here.'

'Central C.I.D. Detective Sergeant Miller. I'm making
enquiries concerning a girl named Joanna Martin and I've good
reason to believe she might have been a student at your college
during the last couple of years. Would it take you long to check?'

'No more than thirty seconds, sergeant,' Henderson said
crisply. 'We've a very comprehensive filing system.' A moment
later he was back. 'Sorry, no student of that name. I could go
back further if you like.'

'No point,' Miller said. 'She wasn't old enough.'

He replaced the receiver and turned to Brady. 'Another
possibility we can cross off.'

'What now?' Brady demanded.

'I still think there's a lot in this idea of Father Ryan's that
Martin wasn't her real name. If that's true, it's just possible she's
been listed as a missing person by someone or other. You go and
see Chuck Lazer and I'll drop round to the Salvation Army and
see if a chat with Martha Broadribb produces anything.'

Brady grinned. 'Don't end up beating a drum for her on
Sundays.'

But Miller had to force a smile in reply and as he went down
the steps to the car, his face was grim and serious. At the best
of times a good copper was guided as much by instinct as solid
fact and there was something very wrong here, something much
more serious than appeared on the surface of things and all his
training, all his experience told him as much.

CHAPTER FOUR

The small office of the Stone Street Citadel was badly over-crowded, half a dozen young men and women working busily surrounded by filing cabinets, double banked to save space.

'I'll see if the Major's in her office,' said Miller's escort, a thin, earnest young man in blazer and flannels and he disappeared in search of Martha Broadribb.

Miller leaned against a filing cabinet and waited, impressed as always at the industry and efficiency so obviously the order of the day. A sheet of writing paper had fallen to the floor and he picked it up and read the printed heading quickly. *Missing Relatives Sought in any part of the World: Investigations and Enquiries carried out in Strictest Confidence: Reconciliation Bureau: Advice willingly Given.*

The biggest drawback to tracing a missing person from the official point of view was that there was nothing illegal about disappearing. Unless there was a suspicion of foul play, the police could do nothing, which produced the ironical situation that the greatest experts in the field were the Salvation Army who handled something like ten thousand British and foreign enquiries a year from their Headquarters in Bishopsgate, London, and who were constantly in touch with centres throughout the country such as the Stone Street Citadel.

The young man emerged from the inner office, his arm around the shoulders of a middle aged woman in a shabby coat who had obviously been weeping. He nodded briefly without speaking and Miller brushed past them and went in.

Major Martha Broadribb was exactly five feet tall, her trim uniformed figure bristling with a vitality that belied her sixty years. Her blue eyes were enormous behind steel rimmed spectacles and she had the smooth, unused face of an innocent child. And yet this was a woman who had laboured for most of her life in a China Mission, who had spent three terrible years in solitary confinement in a Communist prison camp.

She came forward quickly, a smile of genuine affection on her face. 'Nicholas, this *is* nice. Will you have a cup of tea?'

'I wouldn't say no,' Miller said. 'Who was that who just left?'

'Poor soul. Her husband died a year ago.' She took a clean cup and saucer from a cupboard and moved to the tea-tray that stood on her desk. 'She married one of her lodgers last month.

He persuaded her to sell the house and give him the money she received to buy a business.'

'Don't tell me, let me guess,' Miller said. 'He's cleared off?'

'That's about the size of it.'

'She's been to the police?'

'Who told her that as he hadn't committed a criminal offence they were powerless to act.' She stirred his tea briskly. 'Four lumps and much good may it do you.'

'Do you think you'll find him?'

'Certain to,' she said, 'and he'll face up to his responsibilities and do right by the poor woman after I've had a chance of talking to him. I'm certain of that.'

Another one who thought most people were good at heart. Miller smiled wryly, remembering their first meeting. On his way home one night he had answered an emergency call simply because he happened to be in the vicinity and had arrived at a slum house near the river in time to find a graceless, mindless lout doing his level best to beat his wife to death after knocking Martha Broadribb senseless for trying to stop him, breaking her right arm in the process. And the very next day she had visited him in the Bridewell, plaster-cast and all.

She lit a cigarette, her one vice, and leaned back in her chair. 'You look tired, Nicholas.'

'I feel tired,' he said. 'A perpetual state these days, but don't let's go into that.' He passed one of the photos across. 'Ever seen her?'

Martha examined it with a slight frown. 'This is a mortuary photo, isn't it?'

'That's right. I pulled her out of the river this morning.'

'Suicide?' There was an expression of real grief on her face. 'Poor child. Poor, poor child.'

'No ordinary suicide,' Miller said. 'This girl did everything she could to destroy her identity before she died.'

He sketched in the main facts and she nodded sombrely. 'So Father Ryan thinks that Joanna Martin wasn't her real name?'

'He got that impression which the other two people I've spoken to who knew her confirm. Coming to see you was just a hunch really. I was hoping that somebody might have put out a search for her—that you might recognize her photo.'

Martha nodded and held up the medal. 'She still hung on to Joanna. Interesting that—they nearly always do hang on to their Christian name. It's as if they're afraid of losing themselves entirely.'

She gave him back the medal and made a few notes on her pad. 'Let's see what we've got. About nineteen, fair hair, blue eyes. Well spoken, educated, obviously from a superior background and an artist. We'll look under the name of Martin first, just in case, and we'll check the Christian name.'

'I didn't know you could do that?'

'As I said, so many of them hang on to their Christian names that it's worth cross-indexing and Joanna isn't very common these days. We'll see what we've got here and I'll also put through a call to London. Should take about fifteen minutes.'

Before he could reply, the 'phone on her desk rang. She took the call and then held out the receiver. 'For you—Detective Constable Brady.'

Martha went into the outer office and Miller sat on the edge of the desk. 'What have you got?'

'Plenty,' Brady said. 'I've just had a session with a character named Jack Fenner. He's been a registered addict for just over a year now. He makes a living as a dance band drummer.'

'I think I've seen him around,' Miller said. 'Small, fair-haired.'

'That's him. He says he had a prescription for heroin and cocaine filled at the all night chemist's in City Square at midnight on the dot. Joanna Martin stopped him on his way out and offered him a couple of quid for enough pills for a shot. His story is that he felt sorry for her. Said she had the shakes.'

'No chance of a mistake?'

'Definitely not.' Brady laughed harshly. 'In fact this is where it gets interesting. Fenner says he's seen her before.'

'Where?'

'At Max Vernon's place, the Flamingo, about six weeks ago. The regular drummer was ill that night and Fenner stood in for him. Apparently it was Vernon's birthday and he threw a big private binge. Fenner remembers the girl because Vernon kept her with him for most of the evening which Fenner says is highly unusual. Apparently our Max prefers variety.'

'Now that *is* interesting,' Miller said. 'Fenner's certain he's never seen her at any other time?'

'Dead certain—is it important that he should have?'

'Could be. Look at it this way. The girl wasn't a registered addict, we know that so where did she get the stuff from? If she'd been working the prescription racket outside the all-night chemist's regularly, Fenner would have seen her many times. An addict needs at least one fix a day remember. Usually more.'

'Which means that someone must be peddling the stuff?'

'Could be.' Behind Miller, the door opened as Martha Broad-ribb returned and he added hastily, 'I've got to go now, Jack. I'll see you back at the office in half an hour.'

He turned, eyebrows raised enquiringly and Martha shook her head. 'I'm sorry, Nicholas. Not a thing. There was one Joanna on file, that's all—a West Indian nurse.'

Miller sighed and stood up. 'Never mind, Martha, it was just a hunch. Thanks for the tea anyway. I'll leave you a copy of the photo just in case.'

He dropped it on the desk and as he turned, she placed a hand on his arm, concern on her face. 'You're worried about this one, aren't you? There's no need to be. Something will turn up. It always does.'

He grinned and kissed her briefly on the forehead. 'Don't work too hard, Martha. I'll be seeing you.'

The door closed behind him. She stood there staring blankly at it for a moment, then took a deep breath, squaring her shoulders, sat down at her typewriter and started to work.

Brady was sitting on the other side of Grant's desk when Miller looked round the door of the superintendent's office. Grant waved him in at once.

'Jack's been filling me in on your progress so far. You don't seem to be doing too badly. At least you've got a name for her now.'

'Which doesn't seem to mean a great deal,' Miller said. 'I'm afraid Martha Broadribb couldn't help at all.'

'Never mind,' Grant said. 'Something will turn up.'

Miller smiled. 'The second time I've been told that today. Anything through from C.R.O. on Max Vernon and company yet?'

Grant nodded, his face grim. 'And it doesn't make pleasant reading.' Brady started to get up and the superintendent waved him down. 'You might as well hear this, Jack. I'll be circularizing the information anyway.'

He put on his reading glasses and picked up the white flimsy that had been delivered from Records ten minutes earlier. 'Let's start with his two bully boys and a nice pair they are. Benjamin Carver, 35. Last known profession, salesman. Four previous con-victions including five years for robbery with violence; con-spiracy to steal; larceny; grievous bodily harm. He's been pulled in for questioning on twenty-three other occasions.'

'And Stratton?'

'Even worse. Mad as a March Hare and twisted with it. William, "Billy" Stratton. 34. Three previous convictions including a five stretch for robbery with violence. Remember the Knavesmire Airport bullion robbery?'

'He was in on that?'

Grant nodded. 'The psychiatrists did what they could for him during his last stretch, but it wasn't much. Psychopathic tendencies and too damned handy with a chiv. The next time he stands in the dock it'll be for murder, mark my words.'

'And Vernon?'

'Nothing.'

'You mean he's clean?' Miller said in astonishment.

'As a whistle.' Grant dropped the flimsy on the table. 'Six years ago he was invited to help Scotland Yard with their enquiries concerning the Knavesmire Airport bullion robbery. The interview lasted exactly ten minutes, thanks to the best lawyer in London.'

'And that's all?'

'All that's official.' Grant picked up another flimsy. 'Now let's look at what they have to say about him unofficially. Believe me, it'll make your hair stand on end.'

'Maxwell Alexander Constable Vernon, 36. Younger son of Sir Henry Vernon, managing director of the Red Funnel shipping line. From Eton he went to Sandhurst and was commissioned in the Guards.'

'Only the best, eh?'

Grant nodded. 'The rot set in when he was seconded for duty with a Malayan infantry regiment during the emergency. Vernon proved so successful at rooting out the Communists in his area that he was awarded the D.S.O. Then they discovered he'd been indulging in an orgy of sadism and torture. No one could afford a public scandal at the time so he was simply persuaded to resign his commission. His family disowned him.'

'He took to crime?'

'That's what it looks like. Organized prostitution—he started with a call-girl racket—illegal clubs, protection, dope peddling —anything that pays, that's our Maxwell. And he's a bright boy —don't make any mistake about that. The Knavesmire Airport hoist was only one of half a dozen big jobs he's probably been behind during the past five or six years.'

'Why move up here though?' Brady put in. 'It doesn't make sense.'

'I'm not so sure,' Grant said. 'Since the middle of last year there's been open warfare in London between the four most powerful gangs, mainly over the protection racket. These things always run to a pattern. The villains carve each other up—in this case they're even using shooters—and the police stand by to pick up the pieces when it's all over. Nobody wins that kind of fight and Vernon was clever enough to realize that. As soon as he heard the first rumblings, he sold out to one of his rivals and dropped out of sight.'

'To reappear here?' Brady said.

Grant got to his feet and paced to the window. 'I've always thought this might happen one day. That the London mobs would start looking for fresh fields. I'll have to have a word with the old man about it.' He shook his head. 'I'd love to know what Vernon's been up to since he's been here.'

'Maybe Chuck Lazer could give me a few pointers,' Miller said.

Grant swung round, his face brightening. 'That's a thought. See what you can get out of him.'

'I'll do my best,' Miller said, 'but don't expect too much. To a certain extent Lazer's on the other side of the fence, remember. I'll keep you posted.'

He returned to the main C.I.D. room and Brady followed him. 'What now?'

'About the girl?' Miller shrugged. 'I'm still considering. There are one or two interesting possibilities.' He pulled a packet of cigarettes out of his pocket and the gold medal and chain fell to the floor. Brady picked it up and examined the inscription again. 'At least we know one thing for certain—her Christian name.'

Miller paused in the act of lighting his cigarette. 'My God, I must be losing my touch.'

'What do you mean?' Brady asked.

'I'm remembering something Martha Broadribb told me. How most people who go missing hang on to their Christian name— there's a pretty obvious psychological explanation for that. It's such a common behaviour pattern that they cross-index missing persons under their Christian names as well.'

'And where does that get us?' Brady demanded looking puzzled. 'She still couldn't help, could she?'

'No, but I'm wondering whether we might have just a little bit more luck at the College of Art,' Miller said simply.

'This must be her,' Henderson said suddenly, turning from the file and handing Miller a white index card.

He was a small, greying Scot with a pleasant, lined face, obviously fascinated by the present situation which had turned what would otherwise have been a day of dull routine into a memorable one.

Miller read the details on the card aloud and Brady made notes. 'Joanna Maria Craig, address, Rosedene, Grange Avenue, St. Martin's Wood.'

Brady pursed his lips in a soundless whistle. 'Pretty exclusive. We were certainly on the ball there.'

'Apparently she dropped out of the course just over three months ago,' Miller said. 'It says here see personal file.'

'That's what I'm looking for. Henderson had opened another filing cabinet and was flicking rapidly through the green folders it contained. He nodded suddenly, took one out and opened it as he turned.

After a while he looked up and nodded. 'I remember this case now, mainly because of her father.'

'Her father?'

'That's right. A hell of a nice chap. I felt sorry for him at the time. He's managing director of that new firm out on the York Road. Gulf Electronics.'

'Why do you say you felt sorry for him?'

'As I recall, she was giving him a hard time. When she first started here everything was fine and then about four months ago she seemed to go to pieces. Cutting lectures, not turning in her work on time, that sort of thing. We called him in to discuss the position.' He frowned suddenly. 'Now I remember. He brought his other daughter with him. Charming girl. A school-teacher I believe. It emerged during the interview that he was a widower.'

'What happened?'

'He promised to try and straighten the girl out, but I'm afraid he had no luck in that direction. There was a nasty incident about a week later with one of the women lecturers. Harsh words and then the girl slapped her in the face. Naturally she had to go after that.'

Miller sat there in silence for a moment, thinking about it, and then got to his feet. He held out his hand. 'You've helped us a great deal, Mr. Henderson.'

'Anything else I can do don't hesitate to get in touch,' Henderson said.

Outside, the pale afternoon sun picked out the vivid colours of the mosaic in the concrete face of the new shopping precinct

on the other side of the road and Miller paused at the top of the
steps to light a cigarette.

Jack Brady looked up at him, eyebrows raised and Miller
sighed. 'And now comes the unpleasant bit.'

St. Martin's Wood was on the edge of the city, an exclusive
residential area not far from Miller's own home. The houses ran
very much to a pattern, turn of the century mansions in grey
stone, each one standing in an acre or two of garden. The house
they were seeking stood at one end of a quiet cul-de-sac behind a
high stone wall. Miller turned the Cooper in through the gates
and drove along a wide gravel drive, braking to a halt at the
bottom of a flight of shallow steps which led to the front door.

The bell push was obviously electronic, the sound echoing
melodiously inside, and after a while the door was opened by
a pleasant faced young maid in a nylon working overall.

'Yes, sir?' she said to Miller.

'Is Mr. Craig at home by any chance?'

'Colonel Craig,' she said in a tone of mild reproof, 'is in London at the moment, but we're expecting him home tonight.'

'Who is it, Jenny?' a voice called and then a young woman
appeared from a door to the right.

'The gentlemen wanted to see the colonel, but I've told them
he isn't at home,' the maid said.

'All right, Jenny, I'll handle it.' She came forward, an open
book in one hand. 'I'm Harriet Craig. Is there anything I can
do?'

She was perhaps twenty-two or three and nothing like her
sister. The black shoulder-length hair framed a face that was
too angular for beauty, the mouth so wide that it was almost ugly.
And then, for no accountable reason, she smiled and the trans-
formation was so complete that she might have been a different
person. Miller produced his warrant card. 'I wonder if we could
have a word with you, Miss Craig?'

She looked at the card and frowned. 'Is anything wrong?'

'If we could go inside, miss,' Brady said gently.

The drawing room into which she led them was beautifully
furnished in excellent taste and purple and white hyacinths made
a brave splash of colour in a pewter bowl that stood on the grand
piano. She turned, a hand on the mantelshelf.

'Won't you sit down?'

Miller shook his head. 'I think it might be a good idea if you
did.'

She stiffened slightly. 'You've got bad news for me, is that it?' And then as if by intuition, 'Is it my sister? Is it Joanna?'

Miller produced one of the photos from his inside pocket. 'Is this her?'

She took the photo from him almost mechanically and her eyes widened in horror. When she spoke, it was in a whisper. 'She's dead, isn't she?'

'I'm afraid so,' Miller said gently. 'She was taken out of the river at dawn today. To the best of our knowledge, she committed suicide.'

'Suicide? Oh, my God!'

And then she seemed to crack, to break into a thousand fragments and as Miller's arms opened to her, she lurched into them, burying her face against his chest like some small child seeking comfort and strength in a world she could no longer understand.

Jack Palmer lifted the sheet and for a brief moment Harriet Craig looked down on the dead face of her sister. She swayed slightly and Miller's grip tightened on her elbow.

'All right to use your office for ten minutes, Jack?'

'Help yourself.'

It was warm in the tiny glass office after the cold outside. Miller sat her in the only chair and perched on the edge of the desk. Jack Brady leaned against the door, notebook and pencil ready.

'I'm afraid I'm going to have to ask you some questions,' Miller said.

She nodded, gripping her handbag so tightly that her knuckles gleamed white. 'That's all right.'

'Were you aware that for the past three months your sister was living at a house in Grosvenor Road under the name of Joanna Martin?'

She shook her head. 'No—in fact it doesn't make sense. We understood she was in London. We've had three letters from her and they were all postmarked Chelsea.'

'I understand there was some trouble at the College of Art?' Miller said. 'That she had to leave? Could you tell me about that?'

'It's rather difficult to explain. Joanna was always a sweet kid. Very talented, but a little naïve, that's why my father thought it would be better to let her attend the local college and live at home instead of going away.'

She took a deep shuddering breath and when she continued, her voice was much stronger. 'And then, about four months or so ago she seemed to change overnight. It was as if she'd become a different person.'

'In what way exactly?'

'Her whole temperament altered. She became violently angry on the slightest excuse. It became almost impossible to handle her. She came home drunk a couple of times and then she started staying out all night. Naturally my father didn't like that, but he's often away on business and in any case, she was hardly a child.'

'How old was she?'

'Twenty last month. After a while, there was trouble at the college. She behaved so badly that she was asked to leave.'

'What happened then?'

'She had a furious row with my father and ended by packing her bags and leaving. She said she intended to continue her studies at one of the London colleges.'

'What about money? Did your father agree to support her?'

'There was no need. She had some of her own. Just over a thousand pounds. A legacy from an old aunt a year or two ago.'

'What about boy friends? At the college, for instance?'

'In the two years she was there, she never brought a single one home. As I've said, until that sudden dreadful change in her she was a shy, rather introverted girl, very much bound up in her work.'

'Did she ever mention a man named Max Vernon at all?'

Harriet Craig frowned slightly. 'Not that I recall. Who is he?'

'Just someone who apparently knew her, but it's of no consequence.' Miller hesitated and went on, 'Your sister was a drug addict, Miss Craig. Were you aware of that fact?'

His answer was plain in the incredulous horror in her eyes as she looked up at him sharply. Her head moved slightly from side to side, her mouth opened as if to speak, but no sound was uttered.

Miller stood up as she buried her face in her hands and broke into a storm of weeping. He patted her gently on the shoulder and turned to Brady. 'Take her home, Jack. You can use my car.'

'What about you?'

'I think I'll have another little chat with Monica Grey and this time I'll have some straight answers. You can catch up with me there.'

He went out quickly, fastening the belt of his trench-coat as he moved along the corridor and the expression on his face was like the wrath of God.

CHAPTER FIVE

THE door of her room was unlocked and when he opened it gently and went in, she was sitting on the edge of the bed buffing her nails. She glanced up sharply and Miller closed the door.

'Sergeant Miller,' she said then her voice faltered.

Miller produced one of the photos and held it up. 'Joanna Maria Craig.' He slipped the photo back into his pocket. 'Why did you lie to me?'

'I don't know what you mean.'

'Joanna Craig was a student at the College of Art for the best part of two years. So were you. And don't try to tell me you never came across her. You were in the same year group. I've just checked.'

She stared up at him, her face white and he took his time over lighting a cigarette. 'Another thing. Mrs. Kilroy told me that Joanna had just arrived on the doorstep one day complete with baggage; that there just happened to be a vacancy. Now that isn't true, is it? She knew there was a vacancy because you told her.'

She shook her head vigorously. 'It isn't true.'

'Isn't it? Then try this for size. You work for Max Vernon, don't you?'

And this time he had her. Her eyes widened in horror, and he went on relentlessly, 'Joanna was his girl friend—I've got proof. Are you going to try to tell me you didn't know that as well?'

She tried to get to her feet and he flung her back across the bed fiercely. 'Come on, damn you! What about the truth for a change?'

She turned her face into the pillow and burst into a flood of tears, her whole body shaking. Miller stood looking down at her, something close to pity in his eyes and then he moved across the room quickly and went into the small kitchen. He found half a bottle of gin in one of the cupboards, poured a generous measure into a tumbler and went back.

He sat on the edge of the bed and she turned her tear-stained face towards him. 'He'll kill me. I know he will.'

'No one's going to kill you.' Miller held out the glass. 'Drink this. You'll feel better.'

She struggled up against the pillows. 'You don't know what he can be like.'

'Max Vernon?'

She nodded and sipped some of her gin. 'He's a devil—a walking devil. Cruel, arrogant—anything he wants, he takes.'

'And that included Joanna Craig?'

Her eyes widened in amazement. 'How did you know that?'

'Just a hunch. But tell me about it—everything that happened.'

'All right.' She swung her legs to the floor, stood up and paced restlessly about the room as she talked. 'You were right about the College of Art. I knew Joanna for nearly two years. Not that we were close friends or anything like that. I liked to live it up. Joanna was more interested in her work.'

'What about boy friends?'

'She hardly ever bothered. This may sound crazy to you, but she had something about her. She was sort of untouched by life if you know what I mean.'

'I think I do,' Miller said.

'Not that there was anything weird about her. Everybody liked her. She was the sweetest person I've ever known, but they treated her with respect, particularly the men. That's something for art students, believe me.'

'And yet she changed,' Miller said. 'So utterly and completely that she might have been a different person. Why?'

'She met Max Vernon.'

'I wouldn't have thought he was her type.'

'He wasn't—that was the whole trouble.' She swallowed the rest of her gin and sat on the edge of the bed. 'I answered an advertisement for female croupiers at the Flamingo. As I told you earlier, the money was so good that I dropped out of the college course and started working there. Max was always throwing big parties and he was pretty free and easy about us bringing our friends along.'

'You took Joanna to one?'

'That's right. About four months ago. I bumped into her one afternoon quite by chance. There was a party that evening and I asked her to come on impulse. I never expected her to say yes, but she did.'

'What happened?'

'Max took a fancy to her. I don't know what it was—maybe it was just her innocence. She was certainly different from every other girl there.'

'Did she respond?'

'Anything but and he tried everything, believe me. Then she passed out. I thought that maybe she'd had one gin too many or something. Max took charge. He said she could sleep it off there.'

'And you left her?'

'There was nothing I could do.' She got to her feet and crossed to the window. 'She 'phoned me here next day and asked me to meet her in town. Poor kid, she was in a hell of a state.'

'I'm not surprised.'

She swung round to face him. 'Oh, no, it was worse than that. Much worse. You see someone had given her a fix while she was unconscious.'

The bile rose in Miller's throat threatening to choke him. He got to his feet and walked towards the door, fists clenched and when he turned, she recoiled from the terrible anger on his face.

'Max Vernon?'

'I don't know—I haven't any proof.'

Miller crossed the room in three quick strides and grabbed her savagely by the shoulders. 'Was it Max Vernon?'

'Well who the hell else could it have been?' she cried.

For a long moment he held her and when he turned away, she dropped down on to the bed. 'She didn't know what had happened to her. All she knew was that her body needed something.'

'And only one person was able to supply it,' Miller said bitterly. 'She wasn't only hooked on heroin and cocaine. She was hooked on Max Vernon.'

When Monica Grey continued, her voice was dry and lifeless. 'She had a lot of trouble at home and then they asked her to leave the college. Her whole personality changed. That's how it affects them. I've seen it before.'

'So she came to live here with you?'

'Max thought it was a good idea. It's a funny thing, but for a while there I thought he was really gone on her. He had her at the club all the time and if any other man even went near her . . .' She shuddered. 'He keeps a couple of heavies around called Carver and Stratton. One night at a party some bloke made a pass at Joanna and they took him into the alley and half killed him. I heard he lost his right eye. That's the kind they are.'

'When did the rot set in?'

She looked up at him quickly. 'You don't miss much do you?'

'In my job I can't afford to.'

'I don't know what happened, but Max changed towards her just like that about two or three weeks ago.'

'She was pregnant, did you know that?'

She shook her head quickly. 'No—no I didn't. Maybe that would explain it.'

'Did he drop her completely?'

She nodded. 'Told her to stay away from the club. She did, too, until last night.'

'What happened then?'

'Max was throwing a private party—just a small affair. Mainly personal friends.'

'You were there?'

'I'm always there,' she said. 'All part of the job. Something else he didn't tell me at the interview. Anyway, it must have been about nine o'clock. Things had just started to swing when the door opened and Joanna walked in.'

'Just like that?'

'Apparently she still had a key to the private door in the alley. Max was furious. He dragged her into a corner and started telling her where to get off. I couldn't hear what she was saying, but you'd only to see her face to know that she was pleading with him.'

'What happened?'

'As I say, I couldn't hear what she said, but he laughed right in her face and said, 'There's always the river, isn't there?' I wasn't the only one who heard that.'

There was a long silence and then Miller said calmly, 'It would seem she took him at his word.' Monica Grey didn't reply and he got to his feet. 'Does he know she's dead?'

'Not as far as I'm aware.'

'You haven't been in touch with him since I was last here?'

She shook her head and he nodded, moved to the door and opened it. 'You do and I'll crucify you.'

As he went downstairs, Brady opened the front door. He paused, waiting for Miller to join him. 'Any luck?'

'You could say that. How about Harriet Craig?'

'She'll be fine once she gets over the initial shock. She's got a lot about her that one. Where to now?'

'The Flamingo Club,' Miller said, 'to have a few words with Mr. Maxwell Vernon. I'll explain on the way.'

He went down the steps quickly and when he slipped behind the wheel of the Cooper, his hands were shaking.

Max Vernon's office was a showpiece in cream and gold and furnished in perfect taste, the walls lined with expensive military

prints, a fire flickering brightly in the Adam grate. He made a
handsome figure sitting there at his desk, the last rays of the
afternoon sun lighting up the fair hair, picking out the colours
of the green velvet smoking jacket, the Guards Brigade scarf
at his throat.

There was a knock on the door, it opened and Stratton came
in. 'I've got those figures you wanted.'

Vernon put down his pen and sat back. 'Good show, Billy.
Just leave 'em on the desk. Anything else?'

'Yes, this copper you were asking about.'

'Miller?'

'That's right. You're on a bum steer there. He's anything but
bent. It seems his brother owns a chain of television shops.
Miller's a sleeping partner, that's where all his gelt comes from.'

'But that's illegal,' Vernon said. 'Coppers aren't encouraged to
have business interests on the side.'

Stratton nodded. 'Apparently they all know about it on the
force, but they simply look the other way. It seems Miller's a
blue-eyed boy. He's been to University, got a law degree and that
sort of thing.'

'Has he now?' Vernon said. 'Now that *is* interesting.'

There was a sudden disturbance in the corridor outside and
then the door was thrown open and Miller walked in. Behind
him, Jack Brady and Carver glowered at each other, chest to
chest. Stratton took one quick, fluid step forward like a ballet
dancer, his right hand sliding into his pocket and Miller raised a
finger warningly.

'You do and I'll break your arm.'

Vernon sat there, apparently unmoved, a slight smile hooked
firmly into place. 'Do come in,' he said ironically.

'I intend to,' Miller told him. 'Get rid of these two. We've
got business.'

'Now look here, you bastard,' Carver began and Vernon's
voice rang across the room like cold steel.

'I'll call if I need you.'

Carver and Stratton obeyed without another murmur and
as the door closed behind them, Vernon grinned. 'Good discipline—that's what I like to see.'

'Once a Guardsman, always a Guardsman, is that it?' Miller
said.

'The most exclusive private club in the world.' Vernon fitted
a cigarette into a green jade holder and gave a mock sigh. 'You've
been checking up on me, sergeant.'

'And how,' Miller said. 'The Yard was more interested to hear you'd turned up again.'

'Let's get one thing clear,' Vernon said. 'I run a perfectly legitimate business here and that applies to everything else I own. If you've anything else to say I suggest you discuss it with my lawyers.'

He reached for the telephone and Miller said calmly, 'We pulled Joanna Craig out of the river this morning, Vernon.'

For a brief moment only Vernon's hand tightened on the 'phone and then an expression of shock appeared on his face.

'Joanna—in the river? But this doesn't make sense. You're quite sure it is her?'

'Why shouldn't we be?'

'The fact is, I understood she'd been living under an assumed name. Nothing sinister—just to stop her family from running her down. She'd had trouble at home.' He shook his head. 'This is terrible—terrible.'

It was all there, beautifully detailed by a steeltrap mind which had assessed the situation in a matter of seconds and had come up with the only possible counter with the speed of a computer.

'When did you first meet her?'

The answer came without the slightest hesitation. 'About four months ago. Someone brought her along to one of my parties. I discovered she was a very talented artist. I wanted some murals for the club and she agreed to accept the commission. It was as simple as that.'

'And that was all—just a business arrangement?'

'The murals are on the wall of the main casino, you can see them for yourself,' Vernon said. 'Anything else that was between us is no damned business of yours. She wasn't a child. She had a good body and she liked the pleasures of the flesh as much as the rest of us.'

'So you did have an affair with her?'

'If you mean by that did she ever sleep with me, the answer is yes. If you're really interested so do lots of other women, though I can't see what in the hell it has to do with you.'

'Did you know she was a junkie—that she was main-lining on heroin?'

'Good heavens, no.'

'Not good enough. You didn't even bother to look surprised.' Miller shook his head. 'You're a liar.'

Something glowed deep in Vernon's eyes. 'Am I?'

Miller gripped the edge of the desk to keep his hands from

shaking. 'I know this girl, Vernon. The first time I clapped eyes on her, she was floating off the central quay two feet under the surface and yet I know more about her now than I do about my own sister. She was a sweet, shy girl, a little bit introverted, interested only in her work. To use an old-fashioned word for these times, she was a lady—a term that wouldn't mean a damned thing to you in spite of Eton, Sandhurst and the Guards.'

'Is that a fact now,' Vernon said softly.'

'You're from under a stone, Vernon, did you know that?' Miller said. 'Now let me tell you what really happened between you and Joanna Craig. She was brought to one of your parties by an old student friend and she must have looked as fresh as the flowers in spring compared to the usual rubbish you keep around. You wanted her, but she didn't want you and that wasn't good enough for the great Maxwell Vernon because what he wants he takes. You got her boozed up and gave her a fix and from then on she was hooked because she had to have one every day of the week and that meant coming to you—accepting your terms. That's the terrible thing about addiction to heroin. There's no degradation to which the victim won't stoop to get the stuff and you must have been just about as low as she could get.'

Vernon's face was white, the eyes burning. 'Have you quite finished?'

'I'll let you know when I have. When you'd had enough, you threw her out and then last night she forced her way into your party to beg you to help her because she was going to have a baby. You laughed in her face, Vernon. You told her there was always the river and she took you at your word.' Miller straightened up and took a deep breath. 'I'm going to get you for that.'

'Are you now?' Vernon said calmly. 'Well let me tell you something, Mr. Bloody Miller. I knew a girl called Joanna Craig just like I know a hell of a lot of other girls. She painted some murals in the main casino downstairs. You or anyone else can see them whenever you like. Anything else is pure fantasy. You try bringing it out in an open court and I'll knock you down so hard you'll never get up again. Now I'm giving you one minute to get out of here or I'm calling my lawyer and you know what that means.'

'Perfectly,' Miller said. 'It means you're frightened to death.' He smiled coldly. 'See you in court, Vernon.'

He turned and nodded to Brady who opened the door and they went out. For a while Vernon sat there staring into space and then he lifted the 'phone and pushed a button.

'Is that you, Ben?' he said. 'Send Stratton up right away. I've got a little job for him.'

Monica Grey came out of the bathroom listlessly. She'd hoped a good hot tub would make her feel better. Instead, she felt depressed, drained of all energy. How she was going to get through the long night at the Flamingo, she didn't know.

The knock, when it came, was so faint that at first she thought she'd imagined it. She hesitated, fastening the belt of her robe quickly and it sounded again.

When she opened the door, she had a vague impression of someone standing there, of an arm sweeping up and then liquid splashed across her face. She staggered back, a scream rising in her throat, her hands covering her eyes as they began to burn. She was aware of the door closing and then a hand slammed against her shoulder, spinning her round so that she fell across the bed. Someone laughed coldly and fingers fastened in her hair, jerking her head back painfully. 'Come on now, dearie, open up for Uncle Billy.'

She opened her eyes, aware that the smarting had somehow eased and looked into Billy Stratton's white, bloodless face. Only his lips had any colour and he smiled showing a row of sharp, even teeth.

'Water, dearie, mixed with a little disinfectant to make your eyes sting. Just imagine what it could have been—vitriol, for instance.' He chuckled mirthlessly. 'You'd have been blind now.'

She was absolutely terrified and lay there staring up at him in horror as he patted her on the cheek. 'You've been a naughty girl, haven't you? You've been talking to the wrong people. Mr. Vernon doesn't like that—he doesn't like that at all. Now get your clothes on. You're coming with me.'

It was almost dusk when Miller turned the Cooper in through the gates of the house in Grange Avenue and braked to a halt at the bottom of the steps leading up to the front door. It had been a long day and he was so tired that he sat at the wheel for a moment before getting out.

When he rang the bell, the door was opened by Jenny, the young maid and her eyes were red and swollen from weeping. 'Sergeant Miller,' she said. 'You'd better come in.'

'There was a message for me at Headquarters,' Miller said. 'Apparently Colonel Craig called at the Mortuary to view his daughter's body. I understand he'd like to see me.'

'The Colonel and Miss Harriet are out walking in the garden,' Jenny said. 'I'll get him for you.'

'That's all right,' Miller told her. 'I'll find him for myself.'

It was cold in the garden and rooks cawed uneasily in the bare branches of the beech trees as he crossed the lawn already damp with the evening dew. Somewhere there was a low murmur of voices above the rattle of a small stream over stones and then a familiar voice called to him on the quiet air. 'Over here, Sergeant Miller.'

Harriet Craig leaned against the rail of a tiny rustic bridge. The man who stood with her was perhaps a shade under six feet in height with iron grey hair cut close to his skull.

The eyes were very calm above high cheekbones. For a moment they considered Miller and then he held out his hand. 'It was good of you to come so quickly.'

There was an extraordinary impression of vitality about him, of controlled force that Miller found strangely disturbing. He must have been at least forty-eight or nine and yet he carried himself with the easy confidence of a man half his age.

'Your message said that you'd like to talk things over with me,' Miller said. 'I'll be happy to help in any way I can.'

'I've seen your Superintendent Grant,' Colonel Craig said. 'He gave me as comprehensive a report as he could, but felt that the full details would be better coming from you.' He hesitated and then went on, 'I believe Harriet gave you some indication of the trouble we were having with Joanna.'

'That's right.'

'I've been given to understand that she'd become addicted to the drug heroin.'

'Which explains what otherwise would have been her completely inexplicable change in character,' Miller told him. 'You must understand that heroin produces a feeling of well-being and buoyancy, but in between fixes an addict is sick, unwell and has only one thought in mind—to get another fix. They become paranoid, irritable, subject to extremes of emotion.'

'And that's what happened to Joanna?'

'The girl who gave you all that trouble wasn't your daughter, colonel,' Miller said gently. 'She only looked like her.'

For a long, long moment there was silence and then Colonel Craig said, 'Thank you for that, sergeant. And now, if you don't mind, I'd like you to tell me everything—everything there is to know about this whole sorry affair.'

It didn't take long, that was the strange thing and when he had finished, Harriet Craig leaned against the rail crying quietly, her father's arm about her shoulders.

'This man Vernon,' Craig said. 'He'll be called as a witness at the inquest?'

'That's right.'

'Is there any possibility of a criminal charge being preferred against him?'

Miller sighed heavily and shook his head. 'I might as well be honest with you. I don't hold out much hope.'

'But he murdered Joanna,' Harriet Craig cried passionately. 'Murdered her as surely as if he'd used a gun or a knife.'

'I know that,' Miller said. 'Morally he's as guilty as any man could be, but the facts are all that matters and this is how it will look in court. Your sister committed suicide. She was pregnant and she was also a drug addict. One witness, Monica Grey, has indicated that someone gave your daughter an injection of heroin at a party at Max Vernon's after she'd passed out, but even she can't swear definitely that it was Vernon. She wouldn't last five minutes on the stand with the kind of counsel he'd bring in. Another thing, this isn't a criminal matter at the moment. All she's done is give me a general verbal statement that she might change completely once she's on the stand.'

'But Vernon was responsible,' Harriet said. 'He was responsible for everything. You believe that yourself.'

'Proving it is something else again.'

There was another long silence and then Craig said, 'There's just one thing I don't understand. Joanna did everything she could to conceal her identity before she killed herself. Why would she do that?'

'Do you really want me to answer that, colonel?'

'More than anything else in the world.'

'All right. I'd say she did it for you.'

The expression on Craig's face didn't alter. 'Please go on.'

'In those final moments, I think she must have been thinking more clearly than she had for a long time. She'd let you down enough. She didn't want to shame you any more. I think she wanted the river to swallow her up as if she'd never been.'

When Craig replied, only the slightest of tremor disturbed the even tenor of his voice. 'Thank you, sergeant. Somehow I thought it might be something like that.'

CHAPTER SIX

WHEN Brady opened the door of the Coroner's Court and peered inside, proceedings had already started. In spite of the fact that there were no more than half a dozen members of the public present, the court seemed overcrowded with the jury taking up almost one side of the room and the coroner high above them on the bench, the court officers below.

Miller was just leaving the stand. He noticed Brady at once and they went outside quietly and closed the door.

'Sorry I'm late,' Brady said. 'I had a remand. How's it going?'

'I've just done my little act. Craig's down front with Harriet. Vernon's got Henry Baxter with him.'

'That old shark?' Brady whistled. 'He'll charge him plenty.'

'Any word from Grant?'

Brady nodded. 'Not good I'm afraid. He's just heard from the office of the Director of Public Prosecutions. They've considered the matter and as far as they're concerned, there isn't even the beginnings of a case against Vernon.'

'Never mind. It was worth a try and there's still the hearing. You can never be sure what's going to happen at a coroner's inquest.'

They went back inside and sat down in time to hear Monica Grey take the oath.

'You are Monica Alice Grey and you reside at 15, Argyle Road?'

'That's right.'

'When did you first meet the deceased?'

'About two years ago. We were both students at the College of Art.'

'We have heard from Detective Sergeant Miller that she came to reside at the same address as yourself under the name of Joanna Martin. Why was that?'

'She was having trouble at home. She decided to leave, but she didn't want her father to know where she was living.'

Miller leaned forward slightly, intent on the proceedings. In his own case he had been compelled to stick strictly to the facts and what Monica Grey said from now on was going to be of crucial importance.

'You were on close terms with the deceased?'

'We were good friends—yes.'

'She confided in you—discussed her troubles. For example, were you aware that she was a drug addict?'

'I was, but only found out by accident. I happened to go into her room one day and found her giving herself a fix.'

The coroner glanced over the top of his spectacles sharply. 'I beg your pardon?'

'An injection of heroin.'

'And did she tell you what had started her on the habit?'

'Yes, she said she'd passed out after having too much to drink at some party or other. Someone had given her an injection while she was unconscious.'

'Why would anyone do that?'

'I don't know. For a giggle, maybe.'

'Indeed.' The coroner examined the papers in front of him, his face impassive. 'Did she ever suggest to you that the party in question was at a gaming club called the Flamingo owned by Mr. Maxwell Vernon?'

'Definitely not.'

The coroner looked at her steadily for a moment and then nodded. 'You were aware that she was pregnant?'

'Yes, she told me a couple of weeks ago.'

'In what circumstances?'

'She was very upset. She asked me if I knew anyone who could help her.'

'To get rid of the child?'

'That's right.'

The coroner made another note. 'One final question. As regards the state of mind of the deceased. Would you say she was a balanced individual?'

Monica Grey shook her head. 'Not during the time she lived with me. She sometimes had terrible bouts of depression, but I think that was the drugs.'

'Thank you, that will be all.'

The fat, well-dressed man who was sitting at the front beside Vernon half rose and the coroner stayed Monica Grey with his hand. 'Yes, Mr. Baxter.'

'I appear on behalf of Mr. Maxwell Vernon, called as a witness in this matter. Certain rumours seem to be circulating which connect my client and the deceased. I think we might be able to clarify the situation if I could put a question or two to Miss Grey.'

'By all means.'

'I shan't keep you long, Miss Grey,' Baxter said. 'I'd like to return to this question of the deceased's pregnancy. Did she ever tell you who the father was?'

'I asked her, but she wouldn't disclose his name.'

'It has been alleged in certain quarters that my client was responsible.'

'He couldn't have been.'

'You seem very positive. Might I ask why?'

Monica Grey hesitated, glanced across at Vernon and said with obvious reluctance, 'To tell you the truth, I knew Joanna had been out with Mr. Vernon a few times and I thought it might be him. When I put it to her she said definitely not. That it was someone else entirely.'

'A last question, Miss Grey. I understand you were present at a private party given by Mr. Vernon at his flat at the Flamingo Club on the night the deceased died.'

'That's right.'

'Please tell us what happened.'

'It was about nine o'clock. The party had just got started when Joanna walked in. She was in a bit of a state so Mr. Vernon took her into the corner to calm her down.'

'Could you hear their conversation?'

'Not really. She was obviously very upset and Mr. Vernon seemed to be trying to take her out of herself. After a while she just turned and walked out.'

'What did Mr. Vernon do?'

'He took me on one side and said he hadn't liked the way she was talking. He asked me to keep an eye on her, to let him know if there was anything he could do.'

'Thank you, Miss Grey.'

Monica Grey returned to her seat as Baxter sat down and Vernon was called. He made an impressive figure in the dock, erect and manly in a well-cut suit, the Guards tie standing out against a snow white shirt. His occupation, given as company director, made the impression on the jury that Miller had expected.

'Mr. Vernon, how long had you known the deceased?'

'About four months,' Vernon said. 'Miss Monica Grey, an employee of mine, brought her to a party at my place one night. I understood they'd been students together.'

'And you became close friends?'

'I think it would be fair to say that.' Vernon shrugged. 'As an artist, she had real talent and I admired her work. I commissioned her to paint a series of murals at my club.'

'I see.' The coroner's voice was dry, remote. 'Was the relationship ever anything more than a business one?'

'I took her to dinner now and then or to the theatre. We got on very well together. I liked her immensely.'

'And on occasion you were intimate with her?'

Vernon managed to inject just the right amount of outrage into his voice when he replied. 'The girl's dead, damn you! Can't she be left in peace!'

There was a flurry of movement amongst the jury, an outburst of whispering. One man even nodded approvingly and the coroner had to call for silence.

He removed his spectacles and leaned back in his chair.

'Mr. Vernon, I can respect your feelings in this matter, but I must insist on a reply—and you are still under oath, sir.'

Vernon's shoulders sagged. 'Yes, we were intimate.' He drew himself up suddenly and glared fiercely at the coroner. 'And why not? She wasn't a child. It was our own affair.'

The coroner replaced his spectacles and examined the papers before him again. 'Were you aware that she had become a drug addict?'

'Certainly not. Do you think I could have stood by and done nothing if I'd known?'

'We've already heard that on the night she died, she appeared at a private party you were giving at your club.'

'That's right.'

'What happened on that occasion?'

'There really isn't much to tell. She was depressed and unhappy. She told me that she'd lost the urge to paint, that life didn't seem worth living any longer. I realize, in retrospect, that it was the drugs which had reduced her to that state. I advised her to go home. She'd told me previously that she and her father hadn't been seeing eye to eye, but it seemed to me that didn't matter any longer. That home was the best place for her.'

'How did she react to that advice?'

'She didn't, I'm afraid. I went to get her a drink. When I returned, she'd gone.'

'Thank you, Mr. Vernon. You may stand down.'

As Vernon went back to his seat, Baxter rose again. 'If I might insert a word at this time on my client's behalf?'

The coroner nodded and Baxter continued, 'Certain allegations do seem to have been made in connection with this unfortunate young woman's death, allegations which would suggest that my client was in some way responsible. I would suggest his complete honesty in answering the question put to him, and his bearing on the stand, added to the statement of Miss Monica Grey, an independent witness, make nonsense of these allegations which are completely without foundation. My client is Managing Director of a company which controls several important enterprises. I might also add, although he has attempted to dissuade me from so doing, that he was at one time a regular officer in the Brigade of Guards and in 1951 was awarded the Distinguished Service Order for gallantry and outstanding leadership during the Malayan Emergency.'

Vernon looked suitably embarrassed as Baxter sat down. 'Thank you, Mr. Baxter,' the coroner said. 'Call Colonel Craig, please.'

All eyes turned on Craig as he got to his feet and moved to the stand. He stood there, hands resting lightly on the rail, the eternal soldier in spite of his dark suit and tie.

'You are Colonel Duncan Stuart Craig and you reside at Rosedene, Grange Avenue, St. Martin's Wood?'

'That is correct.'

'Did you see the body of a woman at the City Mortuary on Tuesday of this week?'

'I did.'

'Who was she?'

'My daughter—Joanna Maria Craig.'

'I will issue you with a burial order.' There was a pause as the coroner made a note and he continued, 'I know this must be most distressing for you, Colonel Craig, so I shan't keep you long. Until four months ago or thereabouts, your daughter was a perfectly normal young woman for her age in every way?'

'That is so. The change, when it came, was inexplicable to us. Temper tantrums, extremely emotional behaviour, that sort of thing. She became a completely different person. I realize now that her general deterioration was a direct consequence of her addiction to heroin.'

'From the time your daughter left home until her death did she ever communicate with you?'

'There were three letters, all postmarked Chelsea. They are before the court.'

The coroner nodded. 'I have read them. They would seem to imply that she was residing in London and studying at a College of Art there. Presumably some acquaintance posted them for her.' He hesitated and then went on, 'Colonel Craig, you have heard the evidence before the court. Have you anything to add?'

Miller felt Brady stir beside him and held his breath, waiting for Craig's answer. 'I have nothing to add, sir. The evidence in this matter seems clear enough.'

'And you can make of that what you like,' Brady whispered to Miller.

And then, with a rush, it was all over. The jury didn't even bother to retire and the foreman, a small, greying bank clerk, rose self-consciously. 'We find that the deceased took her own life while the balance of her mind was disturbed.'

'And that is the verdict of you all.' The foreman nodded and sat down. 'Let it so be entered.'

There was a sudden hush as people sat up expectantly, waiting for the coroner's closing words. 'It is not within my province to make moral judgements. It is sufficient for me to say that on the evidence presented I must agree completely with the verdict of the jury. There is one disturbing feature of this case and it is this, Joanna Craig was not a registered drug addict and yet somehow or other she managed to obtain a daily supply. I trust that the representatives of the police present in court will see that this aspect of the affair is most thoroughly investigated.'

'The court will rise for Her Majesty's Coroner.'

There was a general move towards the exit and Brady turned towards Miller, his face grim. 'And that's that. The swine's got away with it.'

'What else did you expect?' Miller said.

Colonel Craig and Harriet were still sitting down at the front and Vernon and Baxter had to pass them. For a moment, Vernon hesitated as if about to speak and then obviously thought better of it. He nodded to Miller and Brady as he passed them, face grave, and went out.

'I wonder what Craig would have done if the bastard had tried to speak to him?' Brady said.

Craig came towards them, Harriet hanging on to his arm. He smiled tightly. 'Have you gentlemen time for a drink?'

Brady shook his head reluctantly. 'Not me, I'm afraid. I'm in court again in ten minutes.' He nodded to Miller. 'I'll catch up with you later.'

For the moment, they had the court to themselves and Harriet Craig said bitterly, 'Justice—is that what they call it?'

'I'm sorry,' Miller said. 'More sorry than I can say. We tried the Director of Public Prosecutions but he told us we hadn't got even the shadow of a case. I was hoping something might come out at the hearing. As you probably noticed, things are pretty informal in a coroner's court. No one gets worked up over procedure and so on which usually means that things have a chance to break through to the surface.'

'But not in this case, it would appear.'

Craig put an arm around her shoulders and gave her a quick squeeze. 'Let's have that drink, shall we? Do us all good.'

They sat in the saloon bar of the George across the square and Craig ordered brandy all round and offered Miller a cigarette while they waited. Behind them, the bar was lined with solicitors and their clerks and counsel in wig and gown, most of them snatching a beer and a sandwich between cases and talking shop.

Harriet leaned across and covered one of Miller's hands with her own. 'I'm sorry I sounded off back there in court. I wasn't getting at you. You believe that, don't you?'

'That's all right.'

'You know Vernon's a very clever man,' Craig said. 'He handled himself superbly. Made an excellent impression on the jury.'

'And the girl helped, don't forget that,' Miller said.

'Yes, she lied, didn't she?'

'Too true she did, probably under extreme coercion.' Miller hesitated and then went on. 'It wasn't her fault, you know. She's just as much a victim of circumstances as Joanna was. Actually, she's quite a nice girl.'

Craig swirled the brandy around in his glass and drank some. 'You know I've been finding out a few things about our Mr. Vernon. He's quite a character.'

'Is that so?' Miller said carefully.

'Come off it, sergeant, you know what I mean.' Craig swallowed the rest of his brandy and waved to the waiter for another. 'You've heard of Pedlar Palmer, I suppose?'

'Detective Superintendent Palmer of the Special Branch at Scotland Yard?'

'That's right. We did some soldiering together in the Middle East back in '43. I gave him a ring yesterday, just to ask him what he could tell me about Vernon. He owes me a favour or two. That's in confidence, mind you.'

'Naturally.'

'Quite a boy, Max Vernon. Do you think he's getting up to the same sort of capers in these parts as he did in London?'

'Leopards don't change their spots.'

'That's what I thought.' Craig nodded, a slight abstracted smile on his face. 'What is it they say about justice, sergeant? It must not only be done, it must be seen to be done? But what happens when society falls down on the job? What happens when the law isn't adequate? Wouldn't you say the individual was entitled to take matters into his own hands?'

'I know one thing,' Miller said. 'It wouldn't be the law he was taking.'

'You've got a good point there.' Craig glanced at his watch. 'Good heavens, is that the time? I must go. Can you get a taxi, Harriet?'

Miller cut in quickly before she could reply. 'I'll see she gets home all right. I have my own car.'

'Thanks a lot. I'll see you later then, my dear.' He squeezed Harriet's shoulder briefly and was gone.

'Another drink, Miss Craig?'

'No, I don't think so. I'd like to go if you don't mind. I'm feeling rather tired. These past few days have been something of a strain.'

The Mini-Cooper was in for servicing and he was using his brother's E-type Jaguar that day. She was suitably impressed. 'I didn't know police pay had improved quite this much.'

'It hasn't,' he said as he handed her in and closed the door. 'This belongs to my brother. He has more money than he knows what to do with and he worries about me.'

He took the car out into the main traffic stream expertly. 'You're a teacher, aren't you?'

She nodded. 'That's right. Dock Street Secondary Modern. I took the day off.'

'A pretty rough neighbourhood.'

'Good experience. They're pulling the school down soon. There'll be a new Comprehensive opening about half a mile away.'

They drove in silence for a while and then he said, 'You don't think your father will try to do anything silly, do you?'

She frowned. 'What on earth do you mean?'

'I wasn't too happy about that conversation we had back at the pub. All that stuff about taking the law into one's own hands when society falls down on the job.'

'It's worth a thought, isn't it?'

Miller shook his head. 'Not if he wants to stay alive. Max Vernon's a powerful, ruthless criminal without the slightest scruples about who he hurts or how he does it. He'd crush your father like an ant under his foot.'

She turned on him, her mouth slack with amazement. 'Crush Duncan Craig—that worm?' She laughed wildly. 'Don't you know who my father is? If he's made the decision I think he has, then Maxwell Vernon is a dead man walking.'

CHAPTER SEVEN

WHEN Monica Grey opened her door and found Duncan Craig standing there, she tried to close it quickly, but he was inside before she could stop him.

She backed away, her throat going dry, and he shook his head slowly. 'I'm not going to hurt you, I'm not going to harm you in any way. Just sit down like a good girl and listen to me.'

Suddenly she was no longer afraid. In fact for some strange reason she felt like crying and she did as she was told and slumped down on the bed.

'You lied at the inquest, didn't you?'

'I had to. God knows what would have happened to me if I hadn't done as I was told.'

'Then your original statement to Sergeant Miller was true? It was Max Vernon who first gave my daughter heroin?'

'It had to be him,' she said. 'It couldn't have been anyone else.'

'And Vernon who continued to supply her.'

She nodded. 'One of his little sidelines.'

'You know a great deal about him, don't you?'

'Plenty,' she said, 'but you needn't think I'm going to sing out in open court for you or anyone else.'

'You won't have to. Have you got a passport?'

She nodded. 'Somewhere around the place. Why?'

He took a large buff envelope from his inside breast pocket. 'You'll find traveller's cheques in here for one thousand pounds plus a ticket on the four-thirty flight to London Airport.'

'And just how long do you think it would take Max Vernon to catch up with me?'

'At least a couple of days. Long enough for you to complete any formalities, have any necessary inoculations and so on. You'll find another plane ticket in the envelope—a first-class single to Sydney. You could be on your way by Wednesday.'

'You mean Sydney, Australia?'

'That's right. You'll also find a letter to a business friend of mine out there. He'll fix you up with a job and help you get started. You'll be all right. He owes me a favour.'

Her eyes were shining and the lines had been wiped clean from her forehead. Colonel Craig laid the envelope down on the bed beside her.

'In return I want you to tell me everything there is to know about Max Vernon.'

She didn't hesitate. 'It's a deal. You talk and I'll pack.'

'They tell me he was the brains behind one or two big jobs in the London area. The Knavesmire Airport bullion robbery for instance. Has he pulled anything like that up here?'

'Not as far as I know, but I think there's something in the wind. There's been some funny customers in and out of the place lately.'

'What about the Flamingo? Is the game honest?'

'It has to be.' She pulled a suitcase down from the top of the wardrobe. 'It caters for the most exclusive clientele in town.'

'You wouldn't have a key to the place by any chance?'

'Sure—to the back door.' She opened her handbag, produced a Yale key and threw it across. 'My pleasure.'

'What other little enterprises does Vernon operate?'

'There's the betting shops.'

'I'm looking for something rather more illegal.'

'That's easy. He runs a cut liquor still up the York Road. Gibson's Furniture Factory it says outside, but it's a front. Supplies clubs all over the north.'

'Where does the liquor come from in the first place?'

'Your guess is as good as mine. Some from long distance lorries that took the wrong turning. Some they make on the premises. He's got money tied up in that place.'

'But more still in the Flamingo?'

She fastened the lid on one suitcase and took down another. 'Better than a hundred thousand. Without the Flamingo he's nothing. He had to take what he could get when he sold up in London. They say he dropped a bundle.'

'And what about the betting shops?'

'He operates them on a day-to-day basis using the cash from the previous night's take at the Flamingo. He still hasn't got on his feet up here yet.'

'So everything revolves around the Flamingo.'

'I suppose you could say that.' She frowned suddenly. 'What are you getting at?'

'Never you mind, you've got other things to think about now.' He glanced at his watch. 'We'll have to get moving. We've got exactly half an hour to get you to the airport.'

The Bull & Bell Yard was not far from the market, a dirty and sunless cobbled alley named after the public house which had

stood there for more than two hundred years. Beside the
entrance to the snug stood several over-flowing dustbins and
cardboard boxes and packing cases were thrown together in an
untidy heap.

It was raining slightly and an old man squatted against the
wall, a bottle of beer in one hand, a sandwich in the other. He
wore an ancient army greatcoat and his hair and beard were
long and matted.

The door opened and a barman appeared in the entrance,
a bucket in one hand. He was a large, hefty young man in a
white apron with long dark sideboards and a cold, rather
dangerous face. He emptied the bucket of slops across the cobbles
and looked down at the old man in disgust.

'You still here, Sailor? Christ Jesus, I don't know how you can
stand it.'

'Go on, Harry,' the old man said hoarsely. 'Ain't doing any
'arm, am I?'

The barman went back inside and Sailor raised the bottle of
beer to his lips. He lowered it slowly, his mouth gaping in
amazement. The man who stood facing him had the most extraordinary eyes the Sailor had ever seen, quite dark and completely
expressionless. He wore a three-quarter length British warm, a
bowler hat and carried a tightly rolled umbrella.

His hand disappeared into a pocket and came out holding a
pound note. 'Do you know Mr. Vernon?' He said. 'Mr. Max
Vernon?' Sailor nodded. 'Is he inside?'

'In the snug, governor.'

The man in the bowler hat dropped the pound note into his
lap. 'I'm very much obliged to you,' he said and went inside.

Sailor waited for no more than a moment and then he
scrambled to his feet, pushed open the door an inch or two and
peered in.

The Bull & Bell did ninety-five per cent of its trade in the
evenings which was why Max Vernon preferred to patronize it in
the afternoon. For one thing it meant that he could have the
snug to himself which was handy for business of a certain kind.

He sat on a stool at the bar finishing a roast beef sandwich,
a pint of bitter at his elbow, and Carver and Stratton lounged
on the window seat chatting idly.

It was Carver who first noticed Craig standing in the doorway.
'Christ Almighty,' he said and then there was a long silence.

Craig moved into the snug and paused against the bar three

or four feet away from Vernon. 'There you are, Vernon. You know you're a damned difficult fellow to run down. I've been looking everywhere for you.'

'I'm in the telephone book, colonel,' Vernon said calmly.

'Ah, but that wouldn't have suited my purpose at all, I'm afraid,' Craig said. 'What I was hoping for was a private chat —just the two of us.'

He glanced at Carver and Stratton and Vernon shrugged. 'There's nothing you can say to me that these two can't hear.'

'Suit yourself.' Craig took a cigarette from a pigskin case and lit it carefully. 'I expect you'll be wondering why Monica Grey didn't turn up for work last night. She gave me a message for you.'

'Did she now?'

'I'm afraid you'll have to manage without her in future.' Craig blew smoke up towards the ceiling in a long streamer. 'Actually I had a very informative chat with her after which I put her on a plane with a first-class ticket to somewhere so far away that she can forget she ever knew a man called Max Vernon.'

'What is this?' Vernon said. 'A declaration of war?'

'To the knife,' Craig said pleasantly. 'First of all I'm going to destroy the things that are important to you, Vernon. After that, and only when I'm ready, I'm going to destroy you.'

Stratton took a sudden step forward and Vernon raised his hand quickly. 'Stay where you are!' He looked Craig up and down and shook his head slowly. 'It's been tried, colonel. It's been tried by the best in the business and they all ended up flat on their faces.'

'But you did have to get out of London in rather a hurry.'

'So what—I'll be up there on top again. I'm on my way now. I'll run this town before I'm finished.'

'The great Max Vernon,' Craig said. 'He always gets what he wants.'

'That's it.'

'Including my daughter.'

'Including your daughter. She saw things my way by the time I was through with her.'

For the first time, Craig's iron composure cracked and his hand tightened around the handle of his umbrella. He half raised it as if to strike, but quickly regained control.

'Thank you for saying that, Vernon. You've made it a lot easier for me.'

Vernon's easy smile vanished in an instant. 'You know something, you remind me of my old colonel. I couldn't stand him either. Harry?' he called. 'Get in here!'

Harry came in from the other bar drying a pewter tankard. 'Yes, Mr. Vernon?'

Vernon nodded towards Craig and picked up his newspaper. 'Get rid of him.'

'Certainly, Mr. Vernon.' Harry lifted the bar flap and moved out. 'Right, on your way, mate.'

'I'll go when I'm ready,' Craig said pleasantly.

Harry's right hand fastened on Craig's collar and they went through the door with a rush to a chorus of laughter from Stratton and Carver. As the door to the alley burst open, Sailor ducked behind a packing case and waited.

Harry was grinning widely, an arm around Craig's throat. 'We don't like fancy sods like you coming around here annoying the customers.' He didn't get the chance to say anything else. Craig's right elbow swung back sharply connecting just beneath the ribs and, as Harry swung back gasping, he pivoted on one foot.

'You should never let anyone get that close. They haven't been teaching you properly.'

Harry gave a cry of rage and sprang forward, his right fist swinging in a tremendous punch. Craig grabbed for the wrist with both hands and twisted it round and up so that he held him in a Japanese shoulder lock. Harry cried out in agony and still keeping that terrible hold in position, Craig ran him head-first into the stack of packing cases. As he bent down to retrieve his umbrella, Vernon appeared in the doorway, Carver and Stratton crowding behind him.

Craig nodded briefly. 'I'll be in touch, Vernon,' he said and walked briskly away.

It was perhaps ten minutes later that the 'phone rang on Nick Miller's desk in the main C.I.D. room. He picked up the receiver at once and a familiar voice roughened by years of drink and disease sounded in his ear.

'That you, Sergeant Miller? This is Sailor—Sailor Hagen. I'm ringing from a call box in City Square. I've got something good for you. What's it worth?'

'Depends what it's about,' Miller said.

'The bloke who took over Harry Faulkner's place, the Flamingo. Max Vernon.'

Miller was already on his feet. 'I'll meet you by the fountain in five minutes,' he said and hung up.

When Miller was shown in, Vernon was in the main casino looking over arrangements for the evening opening. 'You're getting to be a permanent fixture around here,' he said.

'You can cut out the funny stuff,' Miller told him. 'What happened at the Bull & Bell?'

'I haven't the slightest idea what you're talking about.'

'Duncan Craig visited you there no more than an hour ago. As I understand it, he threatened to kill you.'

Vernon leaned against the edge of the roulette table and laughed gently. 'Someone's been pulling your leg, old man.'

'This is serious, Vernon,' Miller said. 'I don't give a damn what happens to you, but I do care what happens to Duncan Craig.'

Vernon shrugged. 'As far as I'm concerned the whole thing's over and done with.' He glanced at his watch. 'They're burying his daughter at St. Gemma's Church at four o'clock. I sent a wreath. Could I do more than that?

'You did what?' Miller said incredulously.

Vernon smiled blandly. 'One does have to do the right thing on these occasions.'

When Miller's hands came out of their pockets, they were both tightly clenched. For a long, long moment he stood there fighting the impulse to knock Vernon's teeth down his throat and then he swung on his heel and walked rapidly towards the exit. Behind him, Vernon started to laugh gently.

It was raining quite hard when Miller drove up to St. Gemma's. He parked the Cooper in the main road and went in through the side gate and along a narrow path lined with poplars leading to the cemetery.

He could hear Father Ryan's voice as he went forward and then he saw them. There were no more than half a dozen people grouped around the open grave and the old priest's voice sounded brave and strong as the rain fell on his bare head.

Miller moved off the path and stood behind a large marble tomb and after a while, Father Ryan finished and the group broke up. Harriet Craig was crying steadily and moved away in company with Jenny the young maid, and Father Ryan followed them. Craig was left standing on his own beside the grave and Miller went forward slowly.

'It wouldn't work,' he said softly. 'It wouldn't bring Joanna back.'

Craig turned to face him. 'What are you, a mind reader or something?'

'I know what happened at the Bull & Bell this afternoon.'

'I haven't the slightest idea what you're talking about.'

'That's what Vernon said when I called on him. But someone dislocated Harry Parson's shoulder and broke his nose. Who the hell was that? Mr. Nobody?'

Craig looked down into the open grave. 'She was a nice kid, sergeant. A lot of dreams gone up in smoke there.'

'I'm sorry about the wreath,' Miller said.

Craig turned, frowning. 'What wreath?'

'The wreath Vernon sent. God knows where he gets his gall from.'

'I'm happy to say you've been misinformed,' Duncan Craig said. 'We've certainly received no wreath from Max Vernon.' As the rain increased into a solid downpour he turned up his collar. 'You must excuse me now, but Harriet's taken this afternoon rather hard. I'd like to get her home as soon as possible.'

'Of course. If there's anything I can do . . .'

'I don't think so.' Craig smiled briefly, shook hands and walked briskly away.

Miller watched him until he had disappeared round the side of the church and then he turned and went back to his car.

It was just after ten on the following morning and Max Vernon was having a late breakfast at a small table in front of the fire when there was a knock on the door and Carver came in.

'Now what?' Vernon demanded irritably.

Carver held up a large and very beautiful wreath of white lilies without a word.

'What is it, for God's sake?'

'It's the wreath you told me to get for the Craig girl's funeral. The one I had delivered yesterday. The porter's just found it pinned to the private door in the alley.'

'Has he now?' Vernon said softly.

'But that's not all, Max,' Carver said. 'This came with it.'

Vernon took the small pasteboard card that Carver offered and held it up to the light. It was edged in black and the inscription was simple and to the point. *In memory of Maxwell Vernon. 1929—1967. R.I.P.*

CHAPTER EIGHT

MILLER came awake slowly and stared up at the ceiling through the early morning gloom. He checked his watch. It was just coming up to six and then he remembered that he was on a rest day. He gave a sigh of pleasure and turned over.

The outside door opened suddenly and as he struggled up on one elbow, there was laughter and the pounding of feet across the floor of the lounge. A moment later, the bedroom door was flung open and his nephews erupted into the room, a large and very eager Airedale leading the way.

The dog scrambled on to the bed and Miller shoved it away with a curse. 'Get down, you brute.'

Tommy was eight and Roger ten and they moved in on him from both sides gurgling with laughter. 'Come on, Uncle Nick, we're taking Fritz to the park for a run.'

'Not with me you aren't,' Miller said, hitching the blankets over his shoulders.

'Uncle Nick, you promised.'

'When?'

'Oh, ages ago.'

Fritz leapt clear across the bed and circled the room briskly and Miller sighed. 'All right, I know when I'm beaten. But get that brute out of here. You can wait for me in the yard.'

After they had gone, he went into the bathroom, splashed cold water on his face and dressed quickly in cord slacks, polo necked sweater and suède boots. He lit a cigarette and went outside.

His brother's house stood in two acres of garden, a large Victorian villa in grey Yorkshire stone and Miller's flat was above the garage block at the rear. As he went down the fire escape, an engine roared into life inside the garage and the Mini-Cooper reversed into the yard.

Tommy and Fritz were in the rear, Roger at the wheel and Miller opened the door quickly and pushed him into the passenger seat. 'Don't you ever let your mother catch you doing that,' he said. 'You'll get me shot.'

When they reached the park, they left the car near the main gates, but instead of going inside, walked down the road to the public playing fields where Miller released Fritz. The Airedale bounded away and the boys ran after him, shouting and laughing.

Miller followed at his own pace, hands in pockets. The morning was cold and grey and yet the wind was bracing and he felt alive again for the first time in weeks.

The boys had reached the line of iron railings that marked the boundary of the park. Suddenly Roger gave a cry that was echoed by Tommy and they disappeared over the skyline.

Miller hurried after them and when he squeezed through a gap in the fence and looked down into the sports arena, a man in a black track suit was running round the grass track, Fritz in hot pursuit. Roger and Tommy were hopping about in the centre calling ineffectually.

By the time Miller reached the bottom of the hill the runner had secured a grip on Fritz's collar and was leading him to the boys. They stood together in a little group and Miller heard a burst of laughter.

'Sorry about that,' he said as he approached.

The man in the track suit turned and grinned. 'Surprise, surprise.' It was Duncan Craig.

'You're right, it is,' Miller said. 'You're up early.'

'The best part of the day. Besides I like to keep fit.' He ruffled Roger's hair. 'These two imps yours?'

'My nephews,' Miller said. 'For my sins. Roger and Tommy. Boys, this is Colonel Craig.'

They were enormously impressed. 'Were you in the war?' Roger demanded.

Craig grinned. 'I'm afraid so.'

'Commandos?'

'Nothing so romantic.'

They looked disappointed and Miller snapped the lead to Fritz's collar. 'Don't you believe him. Colonel Craig was something a whole lot more romantic than any commando.'

Craig glanced sharply at him. 'Been doing a little research, sergeant?'

'You could say that.' Miller brought Fritz to heel and nodded to the boys. 'We'd better be getting back.'

They turned and ran across the arena and Miller nodded to Craig. 'I'll be seeing you.'

'I'm sure you will.'

When he reached the top of the hill, the boys were waiting for him and Miller paused to catch his breath. Below, Craig was already half-way round the track.

'I say, Uncle Nick,' Roger said, 'he certainly likes running, doesn't he?'

'I suppose he does,' Miller said, a slight frown on his face, and then he smiled. 'I don't know about you two, but I'm starving. Come on, I'll race you to the car.'

Their excited laughter mingled with the dog's barking died into the distance and below in the silent arena, Duncan Craig started on his second circuit, running strongly.

There was a time when Nick Miller had aspired to a black belt in *karate* or *judo*, but the pressure of work had interfered with that pursuit as it had with so many things. When he entered the premises of the Kardon Judo Centre on the following morning, it was his first visit in a month.

Bert King, the senior instructor, was dressed for the mat, but sat at his desk reading the morning paper, a cup of coffee in his hand. He was a small, shrunken man whose head seemed too big for his body and yet in the *dojo*, he was poetry in motion, a third dan in both *judo* and *aikido*.

'Hello, Mr. Miller, long time no see,' he said cheerfully.

'I don't seem to have time to turn round these days,' Miller said, 'but I've got an hour to spare this morning. Any chance of a private lesson?'

Bert shook his head. 'Sorry, I've got a client in the *dojo* now warming up. I was just going to go in.'

'Anyone I know?'

'I don't think so, he isn't one of the regulars. A chap called Craig.'

Miller paused in the act of lighting a cigarette. 'Colonel Duncan Craig?'

'That's right. Do you know him?'

'We've met. Is he any good?'

'You're telling me he is,' Bert King said emphatically. 'His *aikido* is murder—brown belt standard at least. Maybe even first dan and the strange thing is, he isn't even graded. He's been coming in two hours each day for a fortnight now and it's taking me all my time to hold him, I can tell you.'

'Mind if I watch?'

'Help yourself.' He moved out of the office, opened the door to the *dojo* and went inside. Miller hesitated for a moment and then followed him.

Craig and King faced each other in the centre of the mat. The Colonel was wearing and old *judogi* and looked fit and active, vibrant with energy like an unexploded time bomb.

'Free practice?' Bert King said.

Craig nodded. 'All right by me.'

The contest which followed lasted just under fifteen minutes and was one of the finest Miller had seen. When it finished, both men were damp with sweat and Bert King looked shaken for the first time since Miller had known him.

'I must be getting old,' he said. 'Ten minutes' rest and then we'll brush up on some of the finer points.'

'Thats fine by me. Craig picked up his towel from the bench to wipe the sweat from his face and noticed Miller in the door-way. 'Hello, sergeant, we seem to be running into each other all over the place.'

'We'll have to get Sergeant Miller on the mat with you one of these days,' Bert said.

'Miller shook his head. 'No thanks. He's too rich for my blood.'

'Don't you believe it,' Bert told Craig. 'He'll give you a run for your money.'

'I'm sure he will.' Craig dropped his towel on the bench. 'I'll go through a few routines till you're ready, Bert.'

There was a full length mirror on the wall and he stood in front of it and started to practise *karate* kicks, knee raised, flicking each foot forward in turn with lightning speed.

'He's good, isn't he?' Bert King observed.

'Too damned good for comfort,' Miller said and he turned and went out quickly, his face grim.

'So he likes to take early morning runs in the park and he's keen on *judo*,' Grant said. 'So what? Plenty of men of his age like to keep fit. Wish I had the time myself.'

'But Duncan Craig is no ordinary man,' Miller said. 'I've been doing a little research on him. He took a B.Sc. in Electrical Engineering at Leeds University in 1939, joined a tank regiment at the outbreak of war and was captured at Arras when the Panzers broke through in 1940. His grandmother was French and he speaks the language fluently which helped when he escaped from prison camp and walked to Spain. Special Operations Executive recruited him when he got home and dropped him into France on four separate occasions to organize the *maquis*. On his last job, he was betrayed, but managed to slip through the net again. They posted him to the Middle East after that and he spent the rest of the war working for the Special Air Service organizing guerrillas in the Cretan Mountains.'

'He must have been a pretty hard apple,' Grant observed.

'You're telling me. When the war ended he was twenty-seven

and a Lieutenant-Colonel. D.S.O. and bar, M.C., Legion of Honour—you name it, he's got it.'

The early March wind drove hail like bullets against the window of Grant's office and he sighed. 'Look here, Nick, don't you think you're getting this thing completely out of proportion?'

'Do I hell,' Miller said. 'Can you imagine a man like that sitting back while his daughter's murderer walks the streets a free man?'

'Now you're being melodramatic.' Grant shook his head. 'I don't buy this one, Nick. I don't buy it at all. Not that I don't want you to stop keeping a fatherly eye on Max Vernon. He'll make his move sooner or later and when he does, I want us to be ready for him. As for Craig—just forget about him.'

Miller crumpled the sheet of paper he was holding into a ball of paper and Grant lost his temper. 'Just let me put you straight on one or two things before you go. In this town alone crime has quadrupled over the past seven years. We've a clear-up rate for housebreaking of sixteen per cent, the average week in the C.I.D. is seventy hours and you want to waste your time on a thing like this? Go on, get out of here and get on with some work.'

Miller went back into the outer office and sat down at his desk. Jack Brady came across, a sympathetic grin on his face, and leaned against the wall as he filled his pipe.

'You did ask for it, you know.'

Miller sighed and ran his hands over his face. 'I'm right, Jack —I know I am.'

'Perhaps you are, but I fail to see what you can do about it until something happens. Did you see that note I left for you?'

'This one?' Miller picked a sheet of paper from his in-tray.

'That's right. It came in half an hour ago. You did say you wanted to know of anything concerning Chuck Lazer's place, didn't you?'

Miller read the report quickly and then picked up the telephone. 'Get me the District Inspector for the R.S.P.C.A.' He looked up at Brady. 'This could mean trouble.'

'That's what I thought.'

A voice clicked in on the other end of the wire. 'Forbes here.'

'Good morning, inspector. Detective Sergeant Miller, Central C.I.D. You've sent us a routine report on two poisoned dogs —Dalmatians. I wonder if you'd mind telling me what happened?'

'We got a call from a Mr. Lazer of the Berkley Club in Cork Square at nine o'clock this morning. He found his dogs dead in the alley at the side of the club. Arsenical poisoning which was why I reported it.'

'Did he have any idea who was responsible?'

'He said very little. He was obviously quite distressed—and I don't blame him. They were beautiful animals.'

Miller thanked him and replaced the receiver.

'What do you think,' Brady said. 'A declaration of war?'

'I should imagine so.' Miller stood up and took down his trenchcoat from the stand. 'We'd better go round and see if we can damp down this little affair before it bursts into flame.'

Chuck Lazer was sitting at the piano in the empty casino, a glass at his elbow. He gave a tired grin when Miller and Brady entered and kept right on playing.

'Bad news travels fast.'

'It certainly does,' Miller said. 'Why didn't you let me know?'

'My affair.'

'Not in my book.' Miller pulled a chair forward and sat astride it, arms resting on the back. 'He's going to squeeze you out, Chuck. This is only the first step.'

Lazer shrugged and moved into a pushing, intricate arrangement of *Blue Moon*. 'I can look after myself.'

'What with—a gun?'

Lazer cracked suddenly and completely. 'What in the hell do you expect me to do? Bow out gracefully and let him take over? I've put a lot of sweat into this place, Nick. I run an honest game for a nice class of people which suits me and suits them. I'm damned if I'm going to let Max Vernon walk all over me.'

Miller got to his feet, walked across to one of the green baize tables and picked up a pair of dice. He rattled them in his hand and turned, a frown on his face.

'When do you think they'll start, Jack.'

'Probably tonight if what happened to the dogs is anything to go by,' Brady said. 'Half a dozen heavies mingling with the regular members, complaining about the service, starting a punch-up or two. The usual pattern. Before you know where you are this place will be as dead as the Empire music hall.'

Lazer's face had gone grey and his shoulders sagged as he stopped playing. 'Okay—you win. What do I do?'

'You do nothing,' Miller said. 'Just leave everything to us. What time do you open?'

'Eight o'clock, but things don't really get moving till nine-thirty or ten.'

Miller turned to Brady enquiringly. 'Feel like a night on the town, Jack?'

'Suits me,' Brady grinned. 'Naturally I'll expect my chips to be on the house.'

Lazer managed a faint smile. 'I might as well get ruined that way as the other.'

Miller clapped him on the shoulder. 'Don't worry, Chuck, we'll have the heavy brigade standing by. Anyone who starts anything tonight is in for the shock of their lives.'

On returning to Headquarters, Miller went in to see Grant to report on this latest development and then sat down at his desk and started to work his way through some of the paper that had accumulated in his in-tray. It was just before one and he was thinking about going down to the canteen for a sandwich when the 'phone rang.

It was a woman's voice, cool, assured and faintly familiar. 'Detective Sergeant Miller?'

'Speaking.'

'Harriet Craig here.'

'What can I do for you, Miss Craig?'

'I was wondering if we could have a chat.'

'I don't see why not. Are you free this afternoon?'

'No, I'm afraid not, and this evening I'm going to the symphony concert at the George Hall with friends.' She hesitated as if slightly uncertain. 'It finishes at ten. I could meet you then or would that be too late?'

'Not at all,' Miller said. 'Shall I pick you up outside?'

'No, I'd rather not if you don't mind. There's a bar in Gascoigne Square—the Romney. Do you know it?'

'I certainly do.'

'I'll meet you in the lounge at ten fifteen.'

Miller replaced the receiver and stared into space, thinking about Gascoigne Square by night and the lounge bar of the Romney, the neon lights of the Flamingo Club flashing across from the other side.

'And now what's she up to?' he asked himself softly.

CHAPTER NINE

THE evening started slowly at the Berkley as it did at most gaming clubs, but from eight o'clock on, Miller and Brady waited, sitting in comfort in Chuck Lazer's office, watching the activities in the main casino through a two-way mirror.

Lazer was at the piano as always, working his way through one standard after another, stopping occasionally to chat with a favoured customer. He looked cool and immaculate in a mohair evening suit and showed no sign of strain.

Gradually the numbers built up until most of the tables were surrounded by those who came only to watch and all seats were taken. It was just after nine-thirty when Brady gave a sudden exclamation and touched Miller's sleeve.

'Coming through the door now. The three at the back.'

Miller nodded. 'I've got them.'

'The man at the front is Manchester Charlie Ford, followed by Frank Butcher. I sent him down for G.B.H. once. Three years. The little bloke with hair like patent leather is Sid Tordoff—a right villain.'

'They aren't local lads?'

'Are they hell—Manchester. They've been imported specially —probably via a middle man. You know how it goes. A pound to a penny they don't even know who they're working for.'

They waited and a few moments later he nodded again. 'I thought so. Arthur Hart and Martin Dereham—he's the good looking one with the buttonhole and the moustache. Tries to come the public school touch, but the highest he ever got up the educational ladder was class four at Dock Street Elementary.'

'Okay,' Miller said, getting to his feet. 'I'm going in. Better put a call through to H.Q. We'll have the heavy brigade standing by just in case.'

It was a quiet, well-behaved crowd, mostly moneyed people, the kind who'd run for cover and never come back at the slightest hint of violence or trouble of any sort. Miller scanned the faces quickly, noting that the gang had dispersed themselves which probably indicated outbursts of trouble in several different places at once.

And then he saw Manchester Charlie Ford on the other side of the roulette wheel. Ford was of medium height with powerful sloping shoulders, the scar tissue beneath his eyes indicating that he had once been a prize fighter. He was wearing a surpris-

ingly well-cut suit and pushed his way through the crowd with
an arrogance that was obviously beginning to alarm several
people.

He paused behind a rather attractive woman. It was impossible to see what actually happened, but she turned sharply and
her escort, a dark-haired young man, rounded on Ford. 'What's
the game?'

So this was how it was to start? Miller slipped through the
crowd, arriving from the rear, and secured a grip on Ford's left
wrist before he knew what had hit him.

'Get moving!' he said softly into Ford's ear. 'Try anything
funny and I'll break your arm.'

Before the young couple could say a word, Miller and Ford
had been swallowed up by the crowd. They came to rest behind a
pillar, Miller still retaining his grip. Ford's right hand dived
into his pocket. As it came out again, Jack Brady arrived on
the scene and relieved him of a wicked looking spiked knuckle-
duster.

'Well, well, if it isn't my old friend Manchester Charlie Ford.'

Ford looked ready to commit murder and when Miller turned
and glanced over the crowd, he saw the others making rapidly for
the exit.

'Are they leaving you then, Charlie?' Brady said. 'Isn't that a
shame?'

They hustled him into Lazer's office between them and Miller
shoved him down into a chair. 'Who's paying the piper on this
little caper?'

'Why don't you get knotted?' Ford said.

Brady dangled the knuckle-duster in front of him between
thumb and forefinger. 'Carrying an offensive weapon, Charlie,
and with your record? Good for six months that.'

'I can do that standing on my head.' Ford turned as Lazer
entered the room, a worried look on his face. 'Are you Lazer?'
He laughed harshly. 'Had to bring in the bloody scuffers, eh?'
That's your lot, boyo. I hope you realize that. You're dead meat.'

'Why don't you shut up?' Miller said and glanced at his
watch. 'I'll have to go, Jack. I've got a date. Will you book him
for me?'

'My pleasure.'

Brady yanked Ford to his feet and took him out through the
side door and Miller turned to Lazer. 'Don't take any notice of
that goon, Chuck. We've made a good start. They'll think twice
the next time.'

'Oh, sure—sure they will,' Lazer said, but his eyes were unhappy and Miller knew that he didn't believe him for a moment.

The lounge bar of the Romney was only half full when Miller entered shortly after ten, but there was no sign of Harriet Craig. He sat on a stool at the end of the bar, ordered a brandy and ginger ale and lit a cigarette. When he glanced up, he could see her in the mirror standing in the doorway behind him.

She was wearing an evening coat in green grosgraine which hung open at the front to reveal a simple black cocktail dress and when she smiled on catching sight of him, she looked quite enchanting.

'Am I late?' she asked as she sat on the stool beside him.

'No, I was early. How about a drink?'

'Please. A dry martini.'

'How was the concert?'

'Fine—Mendelssohn's *Ruy Blas* and a Mozart piano concerto. Do you like classical music?'

'Some—I'm a jazz man myself. How's your father?'

'Fine—just fine.' She stared down into her glass and sighed. 'Look, I'm afraid I've rather got you here under false pretences.'

'You mean you don't want to chat after all?'

She nodded. 'As a matter of fact I was hoping you might take me out.'

'Now there's an attractive idea,' he said. 'Where would you like to go?'

'I'd like to go to the Flamingo.'

'May I ask why?'

'Those murals Joanna painted for Vernon—I'd like to see them. The only other way would be to ask his permission and I'd hate that.' She opened her bag and took out a gold edged card. 'I've got a membership card—one of Daddy's business friends arranged it for me and members are allowed to take guests in with them.'

Miller sat there looking down at the card for a long moment, a slight frown on his face and she put a hand on his arm. 'Please, Nick? I'd feel safe with you.'

'You make a very appealing liar,' Miller said, 'but I'll still take you. In fact I wouldn't miss it for the world. I'm sure it will prove more than interesting.'

The Flamingo had altered a lot since Miller's last visit, but that had been in the old days when Harry Faulkner had owned it and it had been more a night club than anything else with

gambling relegated to a strictly illegal small back room. The
Gaming Act had changed all that and now there was money to
burn.

The small, thickly carpeted foyer had been decorated in
excellent taste and the man who moved forward to check Harriet's
membership card was greying and distinguished and wore
hunting pink. They went through a door at the end of a short
passage and found themselves at the top of a flight of steps which
dropped into the main casino.

'Oh, look, Nick! Look!' Harriet clutched at his arm.

The murals were astonishingly good. There were four of them
in enormous panels, two on either side of the long room. They
were all battle scenes, the Foot Guards figuring largely in each
one and had been executed in a rather stylistic seventeenth-
century manner and yet had a life and originality that was all
their own.

Miller shook his head slowly. 'I just didn't realize she was that
good.'

'She could have been a great painter, Nick,' Harriet said.
'Something special.' She took a deep breath and smiled as though
determined to be cheerful. 'Well, as long as we're here we might
as well have a look round.'

There were the usual games—Chemmy, Roulette, Blackjack
and, in a small side room, Poker was on offer. But it was the
clientele which Miller found most interesting. There was little
doubt that Vernon was catering for the top people with a
vengeance. The kind of money being wagered would have been
sufficient to indicate that, but in any case, Miller recognized
faces here and there. Wool barons, industrialists, the managing
director of one of the world's largest ready-made clothing
factories. There were at least four millionaires present to his
personal knowledge.

The whole place had the atmosphere of a West-End club,
only a low buzz of conversation disturbed the silence and grave-
faced waiters in hunting pink moved from table to table
dispensing free drinks.

Manchester Charlie Ford and his boys would never have got
past the door, but if they had, they would have closed the place
down by just one visit. With the kind of clientele it catered for,
a club like the Flamingo depended on its reputation. Take that
away from it and it was finished.

They stood by the roulette wheel watching the play and she
turned suddenly. 'I'd like to have a go. What do I do?'

'Decide how much you can afford to lose, that's lesson number one.'

She opened her handbag and produced two five-pound notes. 'Will this be all right?'

He grinned. 'It won't go far in a place like this, but never mind. Who knows? You may even break the bank. Wait here, I'll get you some chips.'

Max Vernon sat at his desk, magnificent in a midnight blue dinner jacket, a white gardenia in his buttonhole. For supper, the chef had presented him with a mixed grill done to perfection and a glass of champagne was at his elbow.

The man who stood on the other side of the desk, an open ledger in his hand, was Claudio Carelli, the casino manager, and he looked worried.

'But it isn't good, Mr. Vernon. We put a lot of money into this place. The new décor and refurnishing came to twenty-two thousand and then there are the running expenses. At the moment, we're virtually living from day-to-day.'

'You worry too much, Claudio,' Vernon said. 'It takes time to build up a prestige club like this. But they're coming now—all the right people. Another three months and we'll be in the clear.'

'I certainly hope so.'

As Carelli opened the door to leave, Stratton came in, his face pale with excitement. 'Miller's downstairs in the casino.'

'How did he get in?'

'He's with the Craig girl. Ben saw them come in. He checked with Bruno on the door. She's a member all right, everything square and above board. She brought Miller in as her guest.'

'Who put her up?'

'Bruno says it was Sir Frank Wooley. Shall we get rid of them?'

'You bloody fool.' Vernon reached across the desk and grabbed him by the tie. 'How many times have I got to tell you? No trouble in the club. What do you want to do—bankrupt me?' He shoved Stratton away from him and poured another glass of champagne. 'Keep an eye on them. I'll be down myself in ten minutes.'

Harriet had a small, but exciting run of luck at Roulette that took her up to seventy pounds.

'I think I'd better try something else while I'm ahead,' she said. 'What are they playing over there?'

'One of the oldest games of chance in the world,' Miller told her. 'You simply throw the dice and pray that the right number comes up.'

'Any skill required?'

'Not to my knowledge.'

'Then that's the game for me.'

The table was a popular one and not only were all the seats taken, but a fair sized crowd stood around watching. Harriet had to wait for five minutes before her chance came. The first time she threw, she didn't cast the dice far enough and the croupier handed them back to her with a whispered instruction. There were one or two good humoured remarks and then she made two straight passes and doubled her money.

There were encouraging smiles from the crowd and she laughed excitedly. 'These dice can't possibly have any more luck in them. Can I have a new pair?'

'Certainly, madame.'

The croupier passed them across and removed the others. Harriet rattled the dice in one hand threw a pair of ones. 'Snakes' eyes,' said a military looking gentleman with a curving moustache who was standing next to her. 'Bad luck.'

She tried again with no better luck and the third throw cleaned her out. 'How strange,' she said with a little laugh. 'I just keep getting a pair of ones, don't I?'

'The luck of the game, my dear,' the military looking man said.

She picked up the dice and rolled them gently no more than a foot or so. 'Look, there they are again. It just isn't my night.'

The croupier's rake reached out, but the military man beat him to it, a frown on his face. 'Not so fast there.'

'I hope monsieur is not suggesting that there could be anything wrong with the dice?'

'We'll see, shall we?'

He rattled the dice together and threw them the length of the table. *Snakes' eyes*. The croupier's rake moved out, but the military man beat him to it again. 'Oh, no you don't, my friend. These dice are loaded.' There was a sudden hubbub amongst the crowd and he turned to an elderly, white-haired man at his side. 'See for yourself.'

The elderly man tossed the dice across the table and the result was plain for all to see. Voices were raised suddenly, people got up from other tables and came across as the news spread like wildfire.

Harriet Craig moved through the crowd to Miller's side. 'They *are* getting excited, aren't they?'

Before he could reply, Vernon appeared on the scene, pushing his way through the crowd, his face angry. 'What's going on here?'

'I was just going to ask you the same question, Vernon,' the white haired man said. 'To start with you'll oblige me by throwing these dice.'

Vernon stood there, holding them in his hand, a bewildered frown on his face and then he threw. There was a roar from the crowd and the white haired man gathered them up quickly.

'That settles it. Somebody better get the police.' He turned and addressed the crowd. 'I don't know about the rest of you, but I've dropped four hundred pounds here during the past couple of weeks and I'm not leaving till I get it back.'

'Ladies and gentlemen—please.' Vernon raised his arms in an attempt to placate them, but it was no use.

The voices rose angrily on either side and Miller pushed his way forward and tapped the white haired man on the shoulder. 'I think I'd better have those, sir.'

'And who the devil might you be?'

'Detective Sergeant Miller, Central C.I.D.' Miller produced his warrant and the dice were passed over without a murmur.

Miller looked across at Vernon. 'Are these your dice, sir?'

'Of course not.'

'I notice that in accordance with a specific regulation of the Gaming Act, they carry this club's registered mark as placed there by the makers. What you are saying is that you have a full set without this pair? That these are forgeries?'

'But that's rubbish,' the white haired man put in. 'What on earth would be the point of a player substituting for the real dice a pair that would make him lose every time he threw.'

Vernon's shoulders sagged and his knuckles gleamed whitely as he gripped the edge of the table. He glared across at Miller who returned his stare calmly.

'Right—I think that's it for tonight, Mr. Vernon.'

'What in hell do you mean?' Vernon demanded furiously.

'I mean that I'm closing you up.'

'Yes, closing you up for good, you damned crook,' the white haired man said, leaning across the table.

For a moment, Vernon gazed wildly about him and then he turned, pushed his way through the crowd and disappeared upstairs.

It was just after eleven when Miller went down the Town Hall steps to the Cooper. The radio was playing faintly and when he opened the door, Harriet Craig sat in the passenger seat, humming softly to herself.

'All finished?' she said brightly.

Her handbag was at her feet and he picked it up without answering and searched it quickly.

'What on earth are you looking for?'

'The other pair of dice—the ones you palmed. Where are they?'

'I haven't the slightest idea what you're talking about.'

Miller tossed the handbag into her lap, switched on the engine and drove away. 'I don't like being used.'

'Not even in a good cause?'

'For God's sake, Harriet, don't you realize what you've done? You've finished the Flamingo. An exclusive gaming house lives on its reputation. All it takes is one tiny scandal—just one and the clientele disappear like the snow in the springtime.'

'Poor Mr. Vernon. What rotten luck.'

'If you imagine for one moment he's going to take it lying down, you've got another thought coming.'

'We'll see, shall we?' She settled back in her seat, arms folded and sighed. 'Those murals were wonderful—really wonderful. Who knows? Maybe he'll be willing to sell them now.'

'You'll come in for a drink?' she said when they reached the house.

'Are you sure it isn't too late?'

'Of course not. We'll have something to eat if you like. I'm starving.'

She unlocked the front door and led the way into the hall and Miller was at once aware of the low persistent hum of a dynamo. 'Daddy must still be working,' she said. 'Come on. I'll take you through to the workshop. You two can chat while I make some supper.'

When she opened the door at the end of the corridor Miller paused in astonishment. The room had been expertly equipped and fitted, of that there could be no doubt. The walls were lined with shelves which seemed to carry just about every kind of spare imaginable in the electrical field. There was an automatic lathe, a cutter and several other machines whose purpose was a complete mystery to him.

Duncan Craig leaned over a bench, spot-welding a length of steel rod to what looked like the insides of a computer. He glanced up as the door opened, killed the flame on the blow torch and pushed up his goggles.

'Hello there,' he said. 'And what have you two been up to?'

'Nick took me to the Flamingo,' Harriet said. 'Quite an experience, but I'll tell you all about it later. Keep him occupied while I get the supper.'

The door closed behind her and Craig offered Miller a cigarette. 'She seems to have enjoyed herself.'

'How could she fail to? Seeing Max Vernon fall flat on his face must have quite made her day.'

Craig's expression didn't alter. 'Oh, yes, what happened then?'

'Apparently the casino was using crooked dice. There was quite a fuss when it was discovered.'

'My God, I bet there was.' Craig contrived to look shocked. 'This won't do Vernon much good, will it?'

'He might as well close up shop. There'll be a prosecution of course, but even if it doesn't get anywhere, the damage is done.'

'How did he react?'

'Oh, he said he'd been framed. That the loaded dice must have been passed by one of the players.'

'But that's ridiculous,' Craig said. 'I could imagine a player trying to substitute dice that would win for him, but not a pair that would lose. Anyway, a club's dice have to be specially manufactured and accounted for. It's a regulation of the Gaming Act expressly aimed at stamping out this sort of thing.'

Miller moved along the bench and picked up a small stick of lead. 'Easy enough for a man with some technical know-how to inject a little lead into a pair of plastic dice.'

'But what would be the point of the exercise?'

'I think that's been achieved, don't you?'

'Well, I'm hardly likely to shed tears over Max Vernon, am I?'

'I suppose not.'

Miller wandered round the bench and paused beside a curious contrivance—a long, chromium tube mounted on a tripod. It had a pistol grip at one end and what appeared to be a pair of small headphones clipped to a hook.

'What's this—a secret weapon?'

Craig chuckled. 'Hardly—it's a directional microphone.'

Miller was immediately interested. 'I've heard of those. How do they work?'

'It's a simple electronic principle. The tube is lined with carbon to exclude side noises, traffic for instance. You aim it by ear through the headphones. It can pick up a conversation three hundred yards away.'

'Is that so?'

'Of course these are even handier.' He picked up a small metal disk that was perhaps half an inch thick and little larger than a wrist watch. 'Not only a microphone but also a radio transmitter. Works well up to a range of a hundred yards or so if you use a fountain pen receiver. Wire that up to a pocket tape recorder and you're in business.'

'What as?' Miller asked.

'That depends on the individual, doesn't it?'

'I suppose you're aware that all these gadgets are illegal?'

'Not for the Managing Director of Gulf Electronics.'

Miller shook his head. 'You're a fool, colonel. Carry on like this and you'll be in trouble up to your neck.'

'I don't know what you're talking about.' Craig smiled blandly. 'By the way, harking back to what you said earlier about doctoring the dice. One would have to get hold of them first.'

'Easy enough to get into a place like the Flamingo, especially in the small hours just after they've closed.'

'I should have thought that might have presented some difficulty.'

'Not for the kind of man who broke into a Vichy prison in 1942 and spirited away four resistance workers who were due to be executed next morning.'

Craig laughed. 'Now you're flattering me.'

'Warning you,' Miller said grimly. 'It's got to stop. Carry on like this and you'll go too far and no one will be able to help you—just remember that.'

'Oh, I will,' Craig said, his smile still hooked firmly into place.

'Good.' Miller opened the door. 'Tell Harriet I'm sorry, but I've suddenly lost my appetite.'

The door closed behind him. Craig's smile disappeared instantly. He stood there staring into space for a while, then pulled down his goggles, re-lit the blow torch and started to work again.

Max Vernon walked to the fireplace and back to his desk again, restless as a caged tiger and Carver and Stratton watched him anxiously.

'This is serious,' he said. 'Don't you stupid bastards realize that? One single scandal—that's all you need in a prestige club like this and you're finished. My God, did you see their faces? They'll never come back.'

'Maybe things aren't as bad as you think, Mr. Vernon,' Carver ventured and Vernon turned on him.

'You bloody fool, we've been living from day-to-day, waiting
for things to build up. I've been using the take from the Flamingo
to keep the betting shops running. Now what happens?'

He sat down behind his desk and poured himself a brandy.
'Who's done this to me—who?'

'Maybe it was Chuck Lazer,' Stratton suggested.

'Do me a favour?' Vernon drained his glass. 'I know one thing.
Whoever it is will wish he'd never been born before I'm through
with him.'

He slammed his fist down hard on the desk and something
dropped to the floor and rolled across the carpet. Vernon leaned
over and frowned. 'What was that?'

Stratton picked up the small steel disk and passed it over.
'Search me, Mr. Vernon. It fell off the desk when you hit it.
Must have been underneath.'

Vernon stared down incredulously and then grabbed a paper
knife and forced off the top. 'I've seen one of these before,' he
said. 'It's an electronic gadget—a microphone and transmitter.'
His face was suddenly distorted with fury and he dropped the
disk on the floor and ground his heel into it. 'We've been wired
for sound. Some bastard's been listening in.'

He reached for the brandy bottle and paused, eyes narrowing.
'Just a minute—Craig's Managing Director of an electronics firm,
isn't he?'

Stratton nodded eagerly. 'That's right and his daughter was
here tonight remember.'

'So she was,' Vernon said softly. 'Plus that nosy copper, Miller.
Come to think of it, that's twice he's stuck his nose into my
business in one night. That won't do—that won't do at all.'

'Do you want Ben and me to handle it?' Stratton said.

Vernon shook his head and poured himself another glass of
brandy. 'Not on your life. Contract it out, Billy. A couple of
real pros should be enough. One of the south London mobs
might be interested. Just make sure they don't know who they're
working for, that's all.'

'How much can I offer?' Stratton asked.

'Five hundred.'

'For Craig?' Stratton's eyes widened. 'That's a good price, Mr.
Vernon.'

'For both of them, you fool. Miller and Craig.' Vernon raised
his glass of brandy in an ironic salute. 'Down the hatch,' he said
and smiled grimly.

CHAPTER TEN

IT was dark in the office except for the pool of light falling across the drawing board from the anglepoise lamp. Duncan Craig put down his slide-rule and stretched with a sigh. It was almost eight o'clock and for the past two hours he had worked on alone after the rest of his staff had left.

There were footsteps in the corridor and as he turned, the door opened and the night guard entered, a black and tan Alsatian on a lead at his side. He put a thermos flask on the desk and grinned.

'Just checking, colonel. I've brought you a cup of tea.'

'Thanks very much, George.' Craig ruffled the dog's ears. 'What time's your next round—nine o'clock isn't it?'

'That's right, sir. Will you still be here?'

'The way this thing is going I'll probably be here all night.'

The door closed behind George and Craig stood there listening to his footsteps move along the corridor outside. When they had finally faded away, he went into the washroom quickly and closed the door.

When he reappeared five minutes later he presented a strange and sinister picture in dark pants and sweater, and wearing an old balaclava helmet, his face darkened by a brown make-up stick. In his left hand he carried a canvas hold-all. He dropped it on the floor beside his desk, picked up the telephone and dialled a number.

The receiver was lifted instantly at the other end. 'Yes?'

'I'm leaving. I'll ring you again in thirty-five minutes.'

'I'll be waiting.'

He replaced the receiver, picked up the hold-all and opened the door, listening for a moment before moving into the corridor.

He took the service lift down to the basement, walked through the work's garage helping himself to a jerry can full of petrol on the way and left through a small judas gate. It was raining slightly and he crossed the yard, keeping to the shadows, scrambled over the low wall and dropped down on to the grass bank that sloped into the canal.

He crouched at the water's edge, opened the hold-all and pulled out the collapsible dinghy it contained. When he activated the compression cylinder, the boat inflated with a soft hiss and he dropped it into the water and pushed off into the darkness.

He'd kept Gibson's Furniture Factory under careful observation for three days now from the top floor of his own factory, even going to the lengths of obtaining a ground-floor plan of the place from the City Engineer's Department for most of the area was scheduled for demolition and municipal development.

It was no more than four hundred yards up the York Road from Gulf Electronics and an approach from the rear via the canal had seemed obvious. He grinned as he paddled out into mid-stream to pass the barge and moved back into the shadows again. Just like the old days—other times, other places when to live a life like this had seemed as natural as breathing.

He passed the coaling wharf of the steel plant, dark and lonely in the light of a solitary yellow lamp. The furniture factory was the second building along from there and he paddled in quickly, scrambled out on to a narrow strip of mud and pulled the dinghy clear.

The brick wall above his head was about nine feet high, but old and crumbling and in spite of being encumbered with the jerry can he found no difficulty in scaling it. For a moment he sat there peering into the darkness and then dropped into the yard below.

A light glowed dimly through the dirty windows and he moved round to the front of the building keeping to the shadows. The whole area was enclosed by a crumbling brick wall. The main gates were of wood, ten feet high and secured by a massive iron bar which dropped into sockets on either side.

In one corner of the yard was a jumbled mass of packing cases and rubbish which had obviously accumulated over the years and it was for this that he had brought the petrol. He emptied the jerry can quickly, scattering its contents as widely as possible and then returned to the gates and removed the holding bar.

He checked his watch. It was exactly fifteen minutes since he had left his office. From now on, speed was essential.

He hit his first snag when he reached the main door of the factory. It was locked. He hesitated only for a moment and then tried his alternative route up an old fire escape to the second floor. The door at the top was also locked, but several panes of glass in the window beside it were broken and it opened with little difficulty.

He stood in the darkness listening, aware of voices somewhere in the distance, and moved along a short corridor. There was a door at the end with a broken panel through which light streamed. He opened it cautiously and was at once aware of a strong smell of whisky.

He was on a steel landing. The hall below was crowded with crates, and a large six-wheeler truck, that certainly didn't look as if it belonged, was parked a yard or two away from the main doors.

The voices came from his left and he went along the landing, passing a small glass-walled office which stood in darkness. There was a light in a room at the very end of the landing and he peered round the edge of the glass partition and found three men playing poker.

He withdrew quietly, went back along the landing and descended the iron stairs to the hall below. The truck was loaded with crates of whisky consigned to London Docks and when he looked inside the cab, the ignition key was in the dashboard.

The main doors were the real snag. They were chained together and secured by a large padlock. He examined it carefully, turned and went back upstairs.

He crouched in the darkness of the little office, the 'phone on the floor beside him, and dialled the number he wanted carefully.

The reply was instant. 'Police Headquarters. Can I help you?'

'Central C.I.D.—Detective Sergeant Miller,' Craig said in a hoarse voice. 'I think you'll find he's on duty tonight.'

Miller was sitting behind his desk listening to a well-known housebreaker indignantly deny the offence with which he was charged when the 'phone rang.

'All right, Arnold, you can take a breather,' he said and nodded to Brady who leaned against the wall cleaning his fingernails with a penknife. 'Give him a cigarette, Jack, while I see what we've got here.'

He picked up the telephone. 'Detective Sergeant Miller.'

The voice at the other end was strangely hoarse and completely unfamiliar to him. 'Gibson's Furniture Factory on the York Road—interesting place—they even make their own booze. You'd better get round here quick and bring the Fire Brigade with you.' He chuckled harshly. 'I do hope Vernon's insured.'

Craig replaced the receiver and looked at the luminous dial of his watch. He was running late, but there was nothing he could do about that now. He waited exactly four minutes, went back downstairs and climbed into the cab of the truck.

He pulled out the choke, pressed the starter and the engine burst into life with a shattering roar. There was a cry of alarm from the landing above his head and he rammed the stick into first gear, let in the clutch sharply and accelerated. The doors burst open and the truck rolled out into the yard. Craig swerved sharply, braking to a halt near the outside gates, switched off and jumped to the ground taking the ignition key with him.

He struck a match quickly and tossed it on to the stacked crates, picked up his jerry can, turned and ran into the shadows. Somewhere in the night, the jangle of a police car's bell sounded ominously.

When he drifted into the side of the canal below the wall of his own factory yard five minutes later, there was already a considerable disturbance in the vicinity of the furniture factory and a red glow stained the darkness, flames leaping into the night from the stack of burning crates.

He took a knife from his pocket and slashed the dinghy in several places, forcing out all air so that he was able to stuff it into the hold-all again, then he tossed it over the wall with the jerry can and followed them.

He left the can with a stack of similar ones on his way through the garage and returned to the tenth floor in the service lift. The moment he was safely inside his office, he reached for the 'phone and dialled his home. As before the receiver was lifted instantly at the other end.

'You're late,' Harriet said.

'Sorry about that. I must be getting old.'

She chuckled. 'That'll be the day. Everything go off okay?'

'Couldn't be better. I won't be home just yet, by the way. I want to finish the details on the vibrator modification in time for the staff conference tomorrow.'

'How long will you be?'

'Another couple of hours should do it.'

'I'll have some supper waiting.'

He replaced the receiver, went into the washroom, scrubbed the filth from his body and changed quickly. He had hardly returned to the other room when there was a knock on the door and George came in.

'Hell of a fuss going on up the road, sir. Don't know what it's all about, but everybody seems to be there. Fire, police—the lot.'

'Go and have a look if you like,' Craig said.

'Sure you don't mind, sir?'

'Not at all. I'd be interested to know what's happening myself.'

He sat down at the drawing board and picked up his slide-rule and George went out quickly.

Miller and Grant stood by the ashes of the fire and surveyed the scene. The Fire Brigade had left, but the big black van that was known throughout the Department as the Studio was parked just inside the gates and the boys from Forensic were already getting to work on the truck.

'So no one was around when the first car got here?' Grant asked for he had only just arrived on the scene and was seeking information.

'That's right, sir. Whoever was here must have cleared off pretty sharpish. Of course the fire was bound to attract attention.'

'What about the truck?'

'Hi-jacked two days ago on the A1 near Wetherby. Carrying a consignment of export Scotch to the London Docks. Valued at £30,000.'

Grant whistled softly. 'That's going to bring the county's crime figures down a bit. And you say you didn't recognize the informer's voice?' he added incredulously.

'I'm afraid not.'

'Well, all I can say is you've got a good snout there, by God.'

Jack Brady emerged from the factory and came towards them, an open document in one hand. 'We've found the lease on this place in a filing cabinet in the office, sir,' he said. 'It's made out in the name of Frank O'Connor. The property's been made the subject of a demolition order so it's owned by the city. O'Connor's a citizen of Eire by the way.'

'And probably on his way back there as fast as he can run at this very moment,' Grant observed and turned to Miller. 'You're sure the snout mentioned Vernon's name?'

'Absolutely.'

'Doesn't make sense then, does it?'

'It does if O'Connor was just a front man.'

'I suppose so. Just try proving that and see where it gets you. I know one thing—if it is Vernon's place then someone certainly has it in for him.' He glanced at his watch. 'My God, it's almost eleven. Too late for me. See you two in the morning.'

He moved away and Brady turned to Miller. 'Ready to go, Nick? Not much more we can do here.'

'You know, Grant's right,' Miller said. 'Whoever set this little lot up for us must really have it in for Vernon. Hang on a minute. I want to make a 'phone call.'

'Checking on someone?'

'That's right—Duncan Craig.'

'Not that again, Nick,' Brady groaned. 'Why don't you leave it alone?'

Miller ignored him and went to the 'phone box on the corner. Harriet Craig sounded cool and impersonal. 'Harriet Craig speaking.'

'Nick Miller.'

'Hello, Nick.' There was a new warmth in her voice. 'When are you coming round to finish your supper?'

'Almost any day now. I'm just waiting for the crime figures to fall. Is your father in? I'd like a word with him.'

'I'm sorry, he isn't. He's working late tonight. Was it important?'

'Not really. I've got a rest day Saturday and I thought he might be interested in a game of golf.'

'I'm sure he would. Shall I tell him to give you a call?'

'Yes, you do that. I'll have to go now, Harriet, we're having a hard night.'

'Poor Nick.' She laughed. 'Don't forget to keep in touch.'

'How could I?'

He replaced the receiver and went back to Brady. 'Now there's a thing—guess where Craig is at this very moment? Working late at the factory.'

'Gulf Electronics is only just down the road,' Brady said. 'The big new block. You can see it from here. There's a light in one of the top-floor offices.'

As Miller turned, the light went out. 'Let's take a look.'

'Suit yourself,' Brady said as they moved to the car. 'But I think you're making a big mistake.'

As they drove away there was a low rumble of thunder in the distance and quite suddenly, the light rain which had been falling steadily for the past hour turned into a solid driving downpour. The main gates of Gulf Electronics stood open and Miller pulled into the side of the road and switched off.

At the same moment, the glass entrance doors opened and Duncan Craig appeared, the night guard at his side with the Alsatian.

'That's old George Brown,' Brady said. 'Sergeant in "B" Division for years. Got himself a nice touch there.'

Brown went back inside, locking the doors and Craig stood at the top of the steps, belting his raincoat and pulling on his gloves. He turned up his collar, went down the steps and hurried into the darkness of the car park. A second later, two men moved out of the shadows at the side of the door and went after him.

'I don't like the look of that one little bit,' Miller said wrenching open the door. 'Come on!'

He turned in through the gates, running hard, and from somewhere in the darkness of the car park there came a scream.

Duncan Craig had almost reached his car when he heard the rush of feet through the darkness behind and swung round. A fist lifted into his face as he ducked and he staggered back against the car, flinging himself to one side. One of his assailants raised an iron bar two-handed above his head and brought it down with such force that he dented the roof of the Jaguar.

A razor gleamed in the diffused light from the street lamps on the other side of the railings and he warded off the descending blow with a left block, and kicked the man sharply in the stomach so that he screamed in agony.

There was another rush of feet through the darkness and Miller and Brady arrived. The man with the iron bar started to turn and Brady delivered a beautiful right to the jaw that had all his sixteen stone behind it.

There was a sudden silence and Craig laughed. 'Right on time. I don't know what I'd have done without you.'

Miller snapped the cuffs on the man who was lying on the ground and hauled him to his feet. 'Anyone you know, Jack?'

Brady held the other one against Craig's car. 'They're not off our patch, that's certain. Specially imported I shouldn't wonder.'

Miller turned on Craig savagely. 'Maybe you'll listen to reason from now on.' He sent his prisoner staggering into the darkness in front of him. 'Come on, Jack, let's take them in.'

Craig stood there in the darkness without moving until the Cooper had driven away and then he unlocked the door of the Jaguar and climbed behind the driving wheel. He knew something was wrong the moment she refused to start. He tried several times ineffectually, then took a flashlight from the glove compartment, got out and raised the bonnet. The rotor arm had been removed, an obvious precaution in case he'd beaten them into the car. He sighed heavily, dropped the bonnet and moved across to the main gates.

It was only twenty past eleven and there were plenty of late buses about, but in any case, he would be able to get a taxi in City Square. He crossed the road quickly, head down against the driving rain.

Someone moved out of a doorway behind him, he was aware of that and then the pain as a sharp point sliced through his raincoat and jacket to touch bare flesh.

'Keep walking,' Billy Stratton said calmly. 'Just keep walking or I'll shove this right through your kidneys.'

They turned into a narrow alley a few yards further along, Craig walking at the same even pace, hands thrust deep into his pockets. A lamp was bracketed to the wall at the far end and beyond, the river roared over a weir, drowning every other sound.

'A good thing I came along, wasn't it?' Stratton said. 'But then I have an instinct for these things. I knew something would go wrong just as I knew you were trouble from the first moment I clapped eyes on you. But not any more, you bastard. Not any more.'

Craig took to his heels and ran and Stratton cried out in fury and went after him. The cobbles at the end of the alley were black and shiny in the light of the old gas lamp and beyond the low wall that blocked the end, the river rushed through the darkness.

As Craig turned, Stratton paused, the knife held ready, a terrible grin splitting the white face and then he moved with incredible speed, the blade streaking up. To Duncan Craig, it might have been a branch swaying in the breeze. He pivoted cleanly to one side, secured the wrist in a terrible *aikido* grip and twisted the hand back in the one way nature had never intended it should go, snapping the wrist instantly.

Stratton screamed soundlessly, his agony drowned by the roaring of the river. He staggered back clutching his broken wrist, mouthing obscenities, and as Craig picked up the knife and moved towards him, turned and stumbled away.

Craig went after him, but Stratton thundered along the alley as if all the devils in hell were at his heels, emerged into the main road and ran headlong into the path of a late-night bus.

There was a squeal of brakes as the bus skidded, a sudden cry and then silence. A moment later voices were raised and when Craig reached the end of the alley, passengers were already beginning to dismount, men crouching down to peer under the wheels.

'Oh, my God, look at him!' A woman sobbed suddenly and Craig turned up his collar and walked away quickly through the heavy rain.

CHAPTER ELEVEN

THE disk shot high into the air, poised for one split second at the high point of its trajectory and disintegrated, the sound of the gunshot reverberating through the quiet morning.

The rooks lifted into the air from their nests in the beech

trees at the end of the garden, crying in alarm, and Duncan Craig laughed and lowered the automatic shotgun.

'I'm not too popular, it would seem. Let's have another.'

As Harriet leaned over the firer to insert another disk, Jenny came out through the french windows. 'There's a gentleman to see you, Colonel Craig. A Mr. Vernon.'

Craig paused in the act of reloading the Gower and turned to Harriet who straightened slowly. 'Is there now?' he said softly. 'All right, Jenny, show him out here.'

Harriet came to him quickly, anxiety on her face, and he slipped an arm about her shoulders. 'Don't get alarmed. There's nothing to worry about. Not a damned thing. Let's have another one.'

The disk soared into the air and this time he caught it on the way down, a difficult feat at the best of times, snap-shooting from the shoulder, scattering the fragments across the lawn.

'Am I supposed to be impressed?' Vernon said and Craig turned to find him standing in the french windows, Ben Carver at his shoulder.

'Well, well, if it isn't Mr. Vernon,' Craig said. 'And to what do we owe the honour?'

Vernon nodded towards Harriet. 'What about her?'

Craig smiled faintly. 'Anything you say to me, you say to Harriet. She's my right arm.'

Vernon took a cigarette from a platinum case and Carver gave him a light. 'All right, colonel, I'll put my cards on the table. I made a mistake about you, that I freely admit, but I know when I'm beaten.'

'I wish I knew what you were talking about,' Craig said.

Vernon obviously had difficulty in restraining himself. 'Let's stop beating about the bush. I've lost the Flamingo and my place up the York Road and then Billy Stratton meets with a nasty accident. You aren't going to tell me I'm just experiencing a run of bad luck?'

'It can happen to the best of us.'

'All right—I'll lay it on the line. You've had your fun—you've broken me, so I'm getting out just as soon as I can find a buyer for whats left. I'm asking you to leave it alone from now on— all right?'

'Oh, no, Mr. Vernon,' Craig said softly. 'Not in a thousand years. I'll see you in hell first and that's a very definite promise.'

'That's all I wanted to know.' Far from being angry Vernon now smiled amiably. 'You're being very silly, old man. I mean it isn't as if you've only got yourself to consider, is it? There's Harriet here . . .'

He got no further. There was an ominous click and the barrel of the shotgun swung round to touch his chest. Craig's eyes seemed to look right through him and the voice was cold and hard.

'If you even try, Vernon, I'll shoot you down like a dog. In your own home, in the street—you'll never know when it's coming —never feel safe again.'

For a long moment Vernon held his gaze and then quite suddenly he nodded to Carver. 'Let's go.'

They walked across the lawn and disappeared round the side of the house. Harriet moved to her father's side. 'Why did he come?'

'For another look at the opposition I think. Nothing like knowing the enemy—a cardinal rule of war and Vernon was a good officer, make no mistake about that.'

'But what was the point of all that business about selling out and asking you to lay off?'

'Who knows? It might have worked—perhaps that's what he was hoping. He may even be up to something.' Duncan Craig smiled. 'We'll have to find out, won't we?'

'What now, Mr. Vernon?' Ben Carver said as he turned the Rolls into the main road.

'We'll go back to the club,' Vernon told him. 'After lunch I want you to drive down to Doncaster to pick up Joe Morgan. I told him to leave the London train there just in case.'

'Do I bring him back to the Flamingo?'

Vernon shook his head. 'No more indoor meetings—too risky. I'll be waiting on one of those benches next to the fountain in Park Place.'

'Thinking of Craig?'

Vernon nodded. 'There's always the odd chance that he has more of those gadgets of his planted around the place.'

'When are we going to do something about him?'

'Thursday morning,' Vernon said. 'Right after the job and just before we leave.' He leaned forward and his voice was cold. 'And you can forget about the *we* part right now. I settle with Craig personally—understand?'

It was cold in the mortuary and when Jack Brady lifted the sheet to reveal Billy Stratton's face it was pale and bloodless.

'But there isn't a mark on him,' Grant said.

'I wouldn't look any lower if I were you,' Miller told him.

'What a way to go. You're satisfied with the circumstances?'

'Oh, yes, the driver of that bus didn't stand a chance. It was raining heavily at the time and Stratton simply plunged across the road, head-down. He'd been drinking, by the way.'

'Much?'

'Five or six whiskies according to the blood sample.'

Grant nodded to Brady who replaced the sheet. 'Who did the formal identification?'

'Ben Carver—reluctantly, I might add.'

Brady chuckled. 'I had to twist his arm a little. He wasn't too pleased.'

'Oh, well, I'm not going to weep crocodile tears over the likes of Billy Stratton,' Grant said. 'We're well rid of him.' He shivered. 'I don't know why, but this place always makes me thirsty. They must be open by now. Let's go and have one.'

The saloon bar of the George had just opened and they had the place to themselves. They stood at the bar and Grant ordered brandies all round.

'What about these two villains who had a go at Craig last night?' he asked Miller. 'Have you got anywhere with them?'

'Hurst and Blakely?' Miller shook his head. 'A couple of real hard knocks. We've had a sheet on each of them from C.R.O. a yard long.'

'Which means they were specially imported,' Brady said.

Grant nodded. 'I don't like the sound of that at all.' He swallowed some of his brandy and gazed down into the glass reflectively. 'You know I'm beginning to think I may have been wrong about this whole thing, Nick. It's just that it seemed such an incredible idea.'

'Duncan Craig's a pretty incredible person,' Miller said. 'I tried to make that clear at the very beginning.'

'Have you seen him since last night?'

Miller shook his head. 'I tried this morning, but he wasn't available. Gone to Manchester on business I was told. Of course he'll have to come in to swear a formal complaint.'

'When he does, let me know. I think I'd better have a word with him myself.'

'You'll be wasting your time, sir,' Miller said. 'He'll insist that the whole thing was quite simply a common assault and we can't prove otherwise.'

'But Hurst and Blakely won't get more than six months apiece for that'

'Exactly.'

Grant frowned. 'There's no chance at all that they might crack and admit who hired them?'

'If I know Max Vernon, they won't even know his name,' Miller said.

Grant sighed and emptied his glass. 'All in a day's work I suppose. Let's have another one.'

'On me,' Miller said.

'Oh no you don't,' a cheerful voice interrupted. 'My round. The same again, Maggie, and make them big ones.'

Chuck Lazer grinned hugely as he climbed on to a stool next to Brady.

'What's all this?' Miller demanded. 'Last time I saw you, you were on your knees.'

'With the world falling in on me, but not now, boy. Not with the pressure off.'

'What are you talking about?'

'Max Vernon.' Lazer shrugged. 'I mean he's on the run, isn't he? Everyone knows his betting shops have taken a hammering since the Flamingo closed and now last night's little affair.'

'And what little affair would that be?' Brady put in.

'Come off it,' Chuck said. 'You know what I'm talking about. That place he was running up the York Road. The cut liquor racket.' He chuckled. 'He was making a packet there, too.'

'You mean Max Vernon was behind that place?'

'Sure—everyone knows that.' Lazer looked surprised. 'Didn't you?'

Miller looked at Grant. 'See what I mean, sir?'

Grant sighed. 'All right. So I was wrong, but just try proving it, that's all. Just try proving it.'

Park Place was a green oasis on the fringe of the city centre surrounded by old Victorian terrace houses already scheduled for demolition to make way for an inner Ring Road.

It was much favoured by office workers during their lunch-break, but at three-thirty when Max Vernon arrived it was quite deserted except for the cars parked round the edges and the small, greying man in the camel-hair coat who sat on a bench near the fountain.

He was reading a newspaper and didn't even bother to look up when Vernon sat beside him. 'I hope you aren't wasting my time?'

'Did I ever, Joe?'

'What about that Cable Diamonds job? I got nicked—five hard years while you sat laughing your head off in some fancy club or other.'

'Luck of the draw.'

'You never get involved personally, do you, Vernon? You never dirty your hands.'

'Two hundred to two hundred and ten thousand quid, Joe. Are you in or out?'

Morgan's jaw dropped. 'Two hundred grand? You must be joking.'

'I never joke. You should know that by now.'

'What's in it for me?'

'Half—you provide your own team and pay them out of your cut.'

'And what in the hell do you do?'

'I've done my share.' Vernon patted his briefcase. 'It's all here, Joe. Everything you could possibly need and it'll go like clockwork—you know me. I never miss a trick.'

'Not where you're concerned you don't.' Morgan shook his head. 'I don't know. Fifty per cent. That's a big slice to one man.'

'You'll only need three men in the team. Give them ten thousand each—contract it beforehand. That still leaves you with seventy—maybe more. Morgan sat there, a frown on his face and Vernon shrugged. 'Please yourself. I'll get somebody else.'

He started to his feet and Morgan pulled him back. 'All right —no need to get shirty. I'm in.'

'On my terms?'

'Whatever you say. When do we make the touch?'

'Wednesday night.'

'You must be joking. That only gives us two days.'

'No, it's got to be then—you'll see why in a moment. There's an express to London in an hour. You'll catch it easily. That'll give you plenty of time to recruit your team, gather your gear together and be back here by tomorrow night.'

'What will I need?'

'That depends. You'll do the vault yourself?'

'Naturally. What is it?'

'Bodine-Martin 53—the latest model. Burglar proof naturally.'

'They always are.' Morgan chuckled. 'A snip.'

'What will you use—nitro?'

'Not on your life.' Morgan shook his head. 'There's some new stuff the Army's been experimenting with going the rounds.

Handles like nitro, but three times as powerful. It'll open that vault up like a sardine can.'

'How long will you need?'

'On the vault itself?' He shrugged. 'I'll have to cut a hole into the lock. Let's say forty-five minutes.'

'And twenty to get you inside.' Vernon nodded. 'Just over an hour. Let's say an hour and a half from going in to coming out.'

'Sounds too good to be true.'

'You'll need a good wheelman to stand by with the car.'

'Frankie Harris is available. He's just out of the Ville. Could do with some gelt.'

'What about a labourer?'

'That's settled to start with—Johnny Martin. He knows how I like things done.'

'And a good heavy and I don't mean some punch-drunk old has-been. You'll need someone who can really handle himself, just in case of trouble, though I don't think he'll even have to flex his muscles.'

'I know just the man,' Morgan said. 'Jack Fallon. He used to run with Bert Keegan and the Poplar boys, but they had a row.'

Vernon nodded approvingly. 'That's a good choice. I remember Fallon. He's got brains, too.'

'Okay—now that's settled let's get down to brass tacks. What's the pitch?'

'Chatsworth Iron & Steel down by the river. Only five minutes from where we are now as a matter of fact. Nine thousand workers and the management are still daft enough to pay them in cash. It takes the staff two days to make the wages up which means there's never less than two hundred thousand, sometimes as much as two hundred and twenty in the vault Wednesday and Thursday depending on earnings of course.'

'Isn't there a night shift?'

'Only for the workers. The admin. side closes down at five-thirty on the dot. It's housed in a brand new ten-storey office block between the factory and the river and they've installed just about every kind of alarm known to man.'

'Bound to with loot like that lying around. How do we get in?'

'About a hundred yards from the factory there's a side street called Brag Alley. I've marked it on the map I'm giving you. Lift the manhole at the far end and you'll find yourself in a tunnel about three feet in diameter that carries the Electricity Board main cables. You'll know when you've reached Chatsworth Steel because they've been obliging enough to paint it on the wall.

There's a single-course brick wall between you and the cellars of the office block. If it takes you longer than ten minutes to get through that I'll eat my hat.'

'What about the alarm system?'

'I'm coming to that. When you get into the cellar you'll find a battery of fuse boxes on the far wall and they're all numbered. I've numbered the ones you'll have to switch off in your instructions, but the most important thing to remember is to cut the green cable you'll find running along the skirting board. It looks innocent enough, but it controls an alarm feeder system in case the others fail.'

'Are the vaults on the same level?'

'That's right—at the far end of the corridor.'

'What about night guards?'

'They only have one.' Morgan raised his eyebrows incredulously and Vernon grinned. 'I told you they'd installed every gadget known to man. The whole place is rigged for closed-circuit television which is operated by one man from a control room off the main entrance hall. The moment you leave that cellar and walk down the passage you'll be giving a command performance. All he does is lift the 'phone and the coppers are all over you before you know it.'

'Okay,' Morgan said. 'The suspense is killing me. How do we sort that one out?'

'They run a three shift system and our man takes over at eight. He always stops in at a little café near the main gates for sandwiches and a flask of coffee. On Wednesday night he'll get more than he bargained for.'

'Something in his coffee?'

Vernon grinned. 'Simple when you know how.'

Morgan looked dubious. 'What if he hasn't had a drink by the time we arrive. We'd be in dead lumber.'

'I've thought of that. You won't break in till midnight. That gives him four hours. If he hasn't had a drink by then, he never will.'

There was a long silence as Morgan sat staring into the distance, a slight frown on his face. After a while he sighed and shook his head.

'I've got to give it to you, Max. It's good—it's bloody good.'

'See you tomorrow night then,' Vernon said calmly and passed him the briefcase. 'Everything you need is in there. Your train leaves at five o'clock. You've got twenty minutes.'

He watched Morgan disappear into the side street in the far

corner of the square and nodded. So far, so good. The sun burst
through the clouds, touching the fine spray of the fountain with
colour and he smiled. There were times when life could really
be very satisfying. He lit a cigarette, got to his feet and strolled
away.

Duncan Craig watched him leave from the rear window of the
old Commer van which was parked on the far side of the square.
He, too, was smiling, but for a completely different reason. He
turned and patted the chromium barrel of the directional microphone mounted on its tripod and started to dismantle it.

CHAPTER TWELVE

IT was raining hard when the van turned into Brag Alley and
braked to a halt, the light from the headlamps picking out the
faded lettering of the sign on the wooden doors that blocked the
far end. *Gower & Co—Monumental Masons.*

'This is it,' Morgan said. 'Right—let's have you, Jack.'

Fallon, a large, heavily built Irishman, jumped out, a pair of
two-foot cutters in his hands that sliced through the padlock that
secured the gates like a knife through butter. The gates swung
open and Harris, the wheelman, took the van into the yard and
cut the engine.

Fallon was already levering up the manhole in the alley and
Morgan and Martin unloaded the van quickly and joined him.
He dropped into the tunnel and they passed down the heavy
cylinders for the oxy-acetylene cutter and the other equipment
and followed him.

Harris dropped to one knee and Morgan whispered, 'Replace
the manhole, shut yourself into the yard and sit tight. An hour
and a quarter at the most.'

The manhole clanged into place above his head as he dropped
down to join the others. He switched on the powerful battery
lantern he carried and its beam cut into the darkness. In spite of
the thick cables, there was room to crawl and he moved off without a word, Fallon and Martin following, each dragging a canvas hold-all containing the equipment.

It was bitterly cold, the insulating jackets of the heavy cables
damp with condensation, and at one point there was a sudden
whispering like dead leaves rustling through a forest in the
evening and a pair of eyes gleamed through the darkness.

'Jesus Christ, rats,' Jack Fallon said. 'I can't stand them.'

'At these prices you can afford to,' Morgan said and paused as his torch picked out the name Chatsworth Steel painted in white letters on the wall. 'Here we are.'

'Not much room to swing,' Martin commented.

'Never mind that. Get the bloody gear out and let's have a go.'

Martin was a small, undersized man with prematurely white hair, but his arms and shoulders were over-developed from a spell of working in the rock quarry at Dartmoor and he lay on his side and swung vigorously with a seven pound hammer at the cold chisel which Fallon held in position.

When the wall gave, it was not one, but a dozen bricks which collapsed suddenly into the cellar on the other side. Martin grinned, his teeth gleaming in the light of the lamp.

'There's present-day British workmanship for you. I don't know what the country's coming to.'

Morgan shone his lantern into the darkness on the other side and picked out the control panel at once. 'Come on, let's get in there,' he said. 'We're right on time. Let's keep it that way.'

It was the work of a couple of minutes to enlarge the hole sufficiently to allow him to pass through and he left the others to manage the equipment and made straight for the control panel.

There were thirty-seven boxes on the board, each one numbered, and he had to pull the switch on nine of them. He had memorized the numbers, but checked them from the list Vernon had given him just to make sure.

'Everything okay?' Martin said at his shoulder.

'Couldn't be sweeter.' Morgan dropped to one knee, located the green cable running along the edge of the skirting board and severed it neatly with a pair of pocket cutters. 'That's it unless Vernon's made a mistake somewhere, which I doubt.'

When he opened the door, the outside corridor was brilliantly lit by neon light. 'What in the hell is the idea of that?' Martin demanded.

'For the television cameras, you fool. They wouldn't see much in the dark, would they?' Morgan led the way out into the corridor and grinned tightly. 'Keep your fingers crossed. If that bloke upstairs is still awake, he's seen us already.'

'I can't see any cameras,' Martin said in bewilderment.

'No, but they can see you.' Morgan paused at the foot of the service stairs. 'You stay here. Jack and I will go and take a look.'

He went up the stairs quickly. The door at the top had a Yale lock and therefore opened from the inside with no difficulty. The hall was tiled in black and white and brilliantly illuminated, its great glass doors protected by a bronze security grill. Morgan knew exactly where he was making for. He crossed the hall quickly, found the third door on the right with *Control Room* painted on it in black letters and turned the handle gently.

The guard had obviously tumbled from the black leather swivel chair in front of the control panel and sprawled on his face. The thermos flask stood open on a small table at one side and Morgan poured a little into the empty cup and tested it.

'Cold—he's been out for ages.'

'Would you look at this now?' Fallon said in wonder.

There were at least thirty separate screens on the control panel. Not only was every entrance to the building covered, but cameras had obviously been positioned at strategic sites in all the main corridors.

'There's Johnny,' Fallon said, pointing.

They could see Martin clearly as he stood in the basement corridor, the two canvas hold-alls at his feet.

'Looks nervous, doesn't he?' Morgan said and leaned forward. 'There's the entrance to the strongroom and that's a picture of the vault door. Look, they've even got a shot of the interior. Would you credit it.'

'It's fantastic,' Fallon said. 'You can see everything from up here.'

Morgan nodded. 'Come to think of it, it might be a good idea if you stayed up here, Jack. You've got every entrance to the building covered. If anyone did turn up, you'd know in a flash. Johnny and I can manage below.'

'And how will I know when to join you?' Fallon said.

'You'll see on the screen, won't you?'

Fallon grinned delightedly. 'And so I will. Off you go then, Joe, and God bless the good work.'

Morgan went down the service stairs quickly and rejoined Martin. 'Let's get moving,' he said and picked up one of the canvas hold-alls.

The entrance to the strongroom was at the end of the passage, a steel door with a double padlock that took him exactly three minutes to pick.

He crossed the room quickly and examined the face of the vault door, testing the handles. Behind him, Martin had already got the first cylinder out of his hold-all. He screwed home one end of the flexible hose that connected it to the blow torch and ignited the flame.

Morgan pulled on a pair of protective goggles and held out his hand. 'Okay, let's get to work,' he said.

A few moments later he was cutting into the steel face of the vault, six inches to the right of the locking mechanism, with the precision of an expert.

For something like forty-five minutes, Jack Fallon had a seat at the show that couldn't have been bettered if he'd been sitting in the front circle at his local cinema. He leaned back in the swivel chair, smoking one cigarette after the other, intent on the drama that was being enacted below.

He was at Morgan's side when he finished cutting the hole and waited, biting his fingernails, while the explosive was gently poured inside the lock, sealed with a plastic compound and fused.

He heard no noise, but the visual effect of the explosion was dramatic enough. The door seemed to tremble, then a portion of it around the lock seemed to disintegrate before his eyes and smoke rose in a cloud.

He saw Morgan and Martin rush forward, heaving on the door together, swinging it open and switched his gaze to the next screen in time to see them enter the interior of the vault itself.

He jumped to his feet, excitement racing through him, started to turn away and paused, a cold chill spreading through his body.

He was looking at another screen—the one that gave a view of the passageway linking the cellar by which they had entered the building with the strongroom. A man was moving along the passage cautiously, tall and dark in sweater and pants, gloves on his hands and a nylon stocking pulled over his face.

Fallon cursed savagely, turned and ran to the door, knocking over the chair in his haste.

Beyond the van a monumental cross reared into the night and here and there, marble tombstones gleamed palely. The mason's yard was dark and lonely, a place of shadows that was too much like a cemetery for comfort and Frankie Harris huddled into the driver's seat miserably, hands thrust deep into the pockets of his overcoat.

He was getting old, that was the trouble—too old for this sort of action by night. He seemed to have been waiting there for hours and yet it was no more than forty-five minutes since his three companions had entered the manhole.

His feet were so cold that he could no longer feel them and after a while he opened the door and stepped into the rain. He walked up and down for a minute or two, stamping his feet to restore the circulation, and then paused to light a cigarette, his hands cupped around the flaring match.

He gave a sudden, terrible start as the light picked a face out of the night—a dark, formless face lacking eyes and mouth that could belong to nothing human.

He staggered back in horror, the match dropping from his nerveless fingers and his throat was seized in a grip of iron.

'Frank Harris?' The thing had a voice. 'You're just out of the Ville, aren't you?'

The pressure was released and Harris nodded violently. 'That's right.'

'How long?'

'Ten days.'

'You bloody fool.' Suddenly he found himself being jerked round and propelled towards the gate. 'Now start running,' the voice said harshly, 'and don't stop. Anything that happens to you after this, you deserve.'

Harris ran along the alley as he hadn't run since he was a boy and when he reached the end, paused, leaning against the wall.

'Christ Jesus,' he sobbed. 'Oh, Christ Jesus.'

After a while he pulled himself together, turned into the main road and started walking briskly in the direction of the Central Station.

Duncan Craig moved rapidly along the tunnel towards the patch of light that streamed in through the broken wall from the cellar. When he reached the opening he paused to examine his watch, wondering if he had timed things right and a sudden, muffled explosion reverberating throughout the basement told him that he had.

He dropped into the cellar and moved out into the passage, a strange and sinister figure in his dark clothing, a nylon stocking pulled down over his face.

A cloud of dust and smoke filtered out through the half open door of the strongroom at the far end of the passage and he moved towards it cautiously and peered inside.

The room was full of dust and smoke and beyond through the half open vault door, he was aware of a vague movement. He stepped back into the passageway and slammed the strongroom door shut, jerking down the handle, the locking bolts clanging into their sockets with a grim finality. Without the key he was unable actually to lock the door, but the important thing was that it would be impossible for it to be opened from the inside. He turned and moved back along the passage.

As he passed the entrance to the service stairs, Fallon jumped on him from five steps up, fourteen stone of bone and muscle driving Craig into the floor.

For the moment, he was winded and as he struggled for air, the Irishman's massive forearm wrapped itself around his throat. As the pressure increased, Craig rammed the point of his right elbow back hard, catching Fallon in the stomach just under the rib cage. Fallon gasped and again Craig drove his elbow home with all his force. As the Irishman's grip slackened, Craig twisted round and slammed him backwards with the heel of his hand.

Fallon rolled against the wall, the instinct derived from a hundred street fights bringing him to his feet in a reflex action, but Craig was already up and waiting for him. As Fallon moved in, Craig's right foot flicked out in a perfectly executed *karate* front kick that caught the Irishman in the stomach. He started to keel over, and Craig's knee lifted into his face like a battering ram, sending him into darkness.

Ruth Miller waved the last of her guests goodbye and closed the door. She looked at her watch and smothered a yawn. One o'clock. A good party and the clearing up could wait till morning. She started across the hall and the 'phone rang.

Nick Miller and his brother were having a final drink in front of the fire when she looked in. 'It's for you, Nick. He wouldn't say who he was. I do hope you don't have to go out.'

'On a night like this? Not on your life.' He went out into the hall and picked up the 'phone.

'That you, Miller?'

'Yes, who is it?'

'Never mind that. Chatsworth Iron & Steel—they usually keep a couple of hundred thousand in their vault on a Wednesday night, don't they? You'd better get down there quick. They almost lost it.' There was a hoarse chuckle. 'Poor old Maxie. Talk about the best laid schemes . . .'

But Miller had already cut him off and was dialling the best known telephone number in England furiously.

The main C.I.D. office was a hive of industry when Grant entered at two a.m. and Miller got up from his desk and went to meet him.

'Well, this is a turn up for the book and no mistake,' Grant said.

'You've had a look at Chatsworth's, sir?'

'Never seen anything like it. Any chance of a cup of tea?'

Miller nodded to a young D.C. who disappeared at once and they went into Grant's office.

'What about the guard?'

'I've just had a 'phone call from the man I sent with him to the Infirmary. Apparently his coffee was laced with enough chloral hydrate to put him asleep for twelve hours so he still hasn't come round.'

'Who have we got in the bag?'

'Joe Morgan for one.'

'Have we, by George?' Grant's eyebrows went up. 'We certainly don't need a scratch sheet on him. One of the best petermen in the game. Was Johnny Martin with him?'

Miller nodded. 'That's right.'

'I thought so—they usually work together. Who else?'

'We found a nasty looking piece of work lying in the basement passageway. He'd taken quite a beating.'

'Is he okay now?'

'Alive and kicking, but making things awkward for us. Jack Brady's running his fingerprints through C.R.O. now. We found their transport, by the way, parked in a monumental mason's yard in Brag Alley at the other end of the tunnel which they used to gain access. No sign of a wheelman.'

'Maybe they didn't use one.'

'Could be—I've put out a general call anyway, just in case.'

The tea arrived and Grant drank some gratefully, warming his hands around the cup. 'Fantastic, Nick—that's the only word for it. This thing was planned to the last inch, you realize that don't you? They'd have been in London by morning. God knows where after that.'

'Except for an elusive someone who shut the strongroom door on Morgan and Martin and left this other bloke lying unconscious in the passageway.'

'Your informer, presumably. And he mentioned Vernon?'

'As far as I'm concerned he did. Vernon's the only Maxie I know and planning a job like this would be right up his street.'

Grant emptied his cup and sighed. 'I suppose you think it's Craig?'

'I can't see who else it could be.'

'No, I suppose not.'

'Do I pull him in for questioning?'

'On what charge?' Grant spread his hands. 'We'd have to think up a brand new one just for him.'

'What about accessary before the fact? He knew the caper was coming off—he should have passed on the information to us.'

'I can't imagine a judge giving him more than a stern wigging for that. Anyway, how could Craig have obtained such detailed information?'

'Simple,' Miller said. 'He's an electronics expert. Directional microphones, transistor transmitters the size of matchboxes, fountain pen receivers. You name it, he's got it.'

'Nothing illegal in that considering the nature of his business.' Grant shook his head. 'Proof, Nick—real proof. That's what you need. You haven't got it and you never will have unless I miss my guess.'

'All right,' Miller said. 'You win. What about Vernon? Do we bring him in?'

Grant hesitated. 'No, let him stew for a while. He's always covered his tracks perfectly in the past so there's no reason to think things will be any easier for us this time. If we're going to get him, it must be through Morgan and his boys. Put two men on watch at his club and leave it at that for the moment.'

Brady knocked on the door and entered, a sheaf of teletype flimsies in his hand. 'I thought I'd get the facts on all of them while I was at it. Our awkward friend is a bloke called Jack Fallon—a real tearaway. He's even done time for manslaughter.'

'He certainly met his match this time,' Grant said.

Miller was reading the reports quickly and he suddenly frowned. 'Cable Diamonds—that has a familiar sound.'

'It should have,' Brady said. 'It was mentioned in that confidential file on Vernon that we got from C.R.O. in London. Another of the jobs he was supposed to be behind.'

Miller grinned. 'You're going to love this, sir,' he said to Grant and passed one of the flimsies across. 'Joe Morgan was nicked for that job after getting clean away. He did five years, but the diamonds were never recovered.'

'He doesn't seem to be having much luck with Max Vernon, does he?' Brady said.

Grant nodded and got to his feet. 'Let's go and remind him of that fact, shall we?'

CHAPTER THIRTEEN

FROM one-thirty onwards Max Vernon knew in his heart that
something had gone badly wrong. By two-fifteen he was sure of
it. He poured himself a large brandy, went to his desk and flicked
one of the switches on the intercom.

'Get in here, Ben.'

The door opened a few moments later and Carver entered.
'Yes, Mr. Vernon?'

'Something's up—they're way over time. Take the car and go
for a drive past Chatsworths. See if you can see any action.'

Carver nodded obediently and left and Vernon lit a cigarette
and moved across to the fire. He stared down into the flames, a
frown on his face. What could have possibly gone wrong? It
didn't make any kind of sense. The thing was foolproof.

The door swung open behind him and Carver came in looking
pale and excited. 'A couple of coppers out front, Mr. Vernon.'

'Are you sure?'

'Certain—I can smell 'em a mile away. I'll show you.'

Vernon followed him out into the corridor and Carver turned
into the cloakroom and paused by the window. 'I came in for
my overcoat. Lucky I didn't turn on the light.' He pointed across
to the sycamore on the other side of the fence beyond the first
street lamp. 'There, in the shadows.'

'Yes, I've got them.'

'What do you think?'

'I think it stinks to high heaven,' Vernon said, and the telephone started to ring in the other room.

He moved back quickly, Carver at his heels, and stood by the
desk looking down at the 'phone.

'It's Morgan,' Carver said. 'It has to be. Who else would be
ringing in at this time in the morning?'

'We'll see shall we? You take it on the extension.' Vernon
lifted the receiver. 'Max Vernon here.'

'That you, old man?' Craig's voice rang mockingly in his ear.
'I'm afraid Joe Morgan and his boys won't be able to join you
after all. They ran into a little trouble.'

Vernon sank down in his chair. 'I'll kill you for this, Craig.'

'You've had it,' Craig said cheerfully. 'Joe Morgan and his boys
are being squeezed dry at this very moment. How long do you

think it will be before one of them spills his guts? You're on borrowed time, Vernon.'

'As long as I've enough left for you that's all I ask,' Vernon said.

'Sorry, old man. I've decided to take myself off into the country for a couple of day's shooting. Nothing like a change of pace. If you want me, you'll have to come looking.'

He was still chuckling as Vernon slammed down the receiver. Carver replaced the extension 'phone, a bewildered look on his face. 'But how could he have known?'

'How the hell do I know? Another of his damned gadgets probably.'

'What do we do now?'

'Get out while the going's good—on foot the back way. I've got an old Ford brake parked in a lock-up garage on the other side of the river. I always did believe in covering every eventuality.'

'Where are we going, Mr. Vernon—Ireland?'

'You can if you like. I can manage a couple of hundred. That should see you through.'

'What about you?'

Vernon unlocked a drawer in his desk and took out a Luger pistol. 'I've got an account to settle.'

'With Craig? You don't even know where he's going.'

'I shouldn't imagine I'll have any difficulty in finding out.'

Carver frowned in bewilderment. 'I don't get it.'

'A challenge, Benny. A challenge—something you wouldn't understand.'

'You mean Craig wants you to follow him?'

Vernon opened the wall safe and took out a black cash box. 'That's the general idea.' He returned to his desk with the cash box and unlocked it. 'This is what he's been aiming at from the beginning—him and me in a final showdown, but he's made a big mistake.' When Vernon smiled he looked like the Devil incarnate. 'I was a good man in the jungle, Ben—the best there was. Craig's still got to find that out.'

He opened the cash box, tossed two packets of fivers across and started to fill his pockets with the rest. 'There's two hundred there and good luck to you.'

Carver shook his head slowly and threw the money back. 'We've been together a long time, Mr. Vernon. I'm not dropping out now.'

Vernon stared at him incredulously. 'Loyalty at this stage,

Ben?' And then he laughed harshly and clapped him on the shoulder. 'All right then. Let's see if we can't show the bastard a thing or two.'

'But who turned you in, Morgan, that's what I can't understand?' Miller said.

It was just after four a.m. and the pale green walls of the Interrogation Room seemed to float out of the shadows, unreal and transitory as if they might disappear at any moment.

Joe Morgan sat at the plain wooden table under a strong central light that made him look old and sunken. Brady leaned against the wall near the window and a young constable stood stolidly in the corner.

'Nobody turned us in. The whole thing went sour, that's all.'

'Then who closed the strongroom door on you and Martin?'

'I don't know—maybe it just slammed shut.'

'All right, miracles sometimes happen. That still doesn't explain how we found Jack Fallon lying beaten and unconscious in the passageway.'

Morgan didn't reply and Brady said helpfully, 'Maybe Fallon just doesn't like you any more. Maybe he decided to lock you and Martin in the strongroom just for kicks and took off. Unfortunately he tripped and fell in the passage, knocking himself unconscious.'

Morgan turned away contemptuously. 'You ought to see a psychiatrist.'

'We'll provide you with one for free,' Miller said. 'You're going to need him badly, Morgan. You're going to sit for the next ten years staring at the wall, asking yourself the same question over and over again until it drives you out of your mind.'

Morgan snapped, suddenly and completely. 'But I don't know what went wrong. I don't know.' He hammered on the table with a clenched fist. 'Can't you get that through your thick skull?'

In the silence which followed Grant peered round the door, eyebrows raised. Miller shook his head, nodded to Brady and they joined the superintendent in the corridor.

'Anything?' Grant said.

Miller shook his head. 'No more success than we've had with the others.'

'He seems genuinely bewildered to me,' Brady put in. 'I get the impression he'd like to know what happened as much as anybody.'

'Right,' Grant said briskly. 'This is where keeping them separate might have paid off. Put them together in cell 15 and let's see what happens.'

When the constable pushed Joe Morgan into the cell, Martin was sitting despondently on a bench against the wall. Morgan frowned in bewilderment as the door closed behind him.

'What is this?'

Martin shrugged. 'Search me.'

'Maybe the place is wired for sound?'

Morgan looked the walls over carefully and behind him, the door opened again and Jack Fallon was pushed into the cell. He looked a mess. His lips were swollen and gashed, several teeth missing and the front of his shirt was soaked in blood.

He staggered forward, a wild look in his eyes and grabbed Morgan by the lapels. 'What happened for Christ's sake? Who was he?'

Morgan tore himself free with some difficulty. 'Who was who?'

'The bloke who came in through the tunnel and locked you and Johnny in the strongroom.'

'What are you talking about?' Morgan demanded.

'I'm trying to tell you. I saw him on the bloody television screen. Big bloke all in black with a stocking over his face. He locked you and Johnny in the strongroom and I jumped him from the stairs.'

'You had a barney?'

'Not for long. Henry Cooper couldn't have hit me any harder than he did.'

'Maybe it was Harris?' Martin said.

'Do me a favour.' Fallon laughed harshly. 'I could break him in two with one hand tied behind my back. It wouldn't make sense anyway. What would he stand to gain?'

'Then why haven't they put him in with the rest of us?'

'Search me.'

Morgan turned away, his hands gripped tightly together. 'Only one man knew we were pulling this caper,' he said. 'The man who organized it.'

'Vernon?' Martin's eyes widened. 'It don't make sense, Joe.'

'I've just got one prayer,' Morgan said. 'That one day they put him in the same nick as me. That's all I ask.'

In the next cell, Grant reached up to switch off the tannoy and nodded to Miller and Brady. 'That'll do me. In we go.'

They went out into the passage and the constable who was

standing at the door of cell 15 unlocked it quickly and stood back.

'Did I hear somebody mention Max Vernon's name?' Grant said as he led the way in.

'Why don't you take a running jump at yourself,' Morgan told him bitterly.

'Oh, to hell with it.' Jack Fallon cursed savagely. 'If you think I'm going to rot while that bastard goes free you can think again. If you don't tell him, I will.'

'You don't have much luck with Vernon, do you?' Grant said to Morgan. 'Remember that Cable Diamond affair? I suppose he saw you all right when you came out.'

'Five hundred,' Morgan said. 'Five hundred quid for five bloody years in the nick.' The anger came pouring out of him in an uncontrollable flood. 'All right—Vernon's your man and much good it'll do you. We were supposed to be back at his place no later than one-thirty. If he's still there when you call then I'm Santa Claus.'

It was almost five-thirty when Miller went into Grant's office. The superintendent was reading through the statements made by Morgan and his cronies and looked up sharply.

'Any luck?'

'Not a sign. Must have cleared out the back way on foot. I've put out a general call. We've alerted the County and the Regional Crime Squad as well.'

'He'll probably try for the Irish boat at Liverpool.' Grant said. 'He won't get far.'

'I'm not so sure, sir. What if he's still in town?'

'Why should he be?'

'There's always Craig. He has a score to settle there.

'I shouldn't think he'd be foolish enough to hang around while he still had time to get out.'

'All the same, sir, I'd like your permission to give Craig a ring. I'd feel happier.'

Grant leaned back in his chair and looked at him reflectively. 'You like him, don't you?'

'I suppose the simple answer to that is yes—a hell of a lot.'

Grant indicated the 'phone on his desk with a sweep of his hand. 'Be my guest.'

The 'phone rang for a long time at the other end before it was lifted and Harriet Craig said sleepily, 'Yes, who is it?'

'Harriet—is that you? Nick Miller here.'

'Nick?' There was a pause and he had a mental picture of

her struggling up on to one elbow, a bewildered frown on her face. 'Nick, what time is it?'

'Twenty to six. I was hoping to speak to your father.'

'I'm afraid he's gone away for a few days.' Suddenly, her voice changed and she came wide awake. 'What is it, Nick? Is something wrong?'

There was genuine alarm in her voice and he hastened to reassure her. 'Everything's all right, I promise you. Are you on your own?'

'No, Jenny's here.'

'Tell you what. How would you like to give me breakfast? I'll tell you all about it then.'

'That's fine by me. What time?'

'Seven-thirty too early?'

'Not at all. If you think I could go to sleep again after this you're mistaken.'

Miller replaced the receiver and turned to Grant. 'She's on her own—her father's out of town. Mind if I put a car on watch up there? Just in case.'

'Just in case?' Grant said and smiled. 'Young love—it's marvellous. Go on—get out of here.'

It was raining heavily when Miller drove up to the house and the patrol car was parked by the entrance to the drive. He got out of the Cooper and walked across and the driver wound down his window.

'Anything?' Miller asked.

'Not a thing, sarge. Some bird came out of the door about five minutes ago and took a walk in the garden, that's all. She must be nuts in this weather.'

'Okay,' Miller said. 'I'll take over. You can shove off now.'

The patrol car moved away and he got back into the Cooper and drove up to the house. As he got out, a voice hailed him and he turned to find Harriet crossing the lawn. She was wearing an old trenchcoat of her father's and a scarf was bound around her head peasant-fashion.

'I saw the police car at the gate when I came downstairs,' she said, her face grave. 'What is it, Nick?'

'Maybe we'd better go inside.'

'No, I'd rather not. Jenny's in the kitchen . . .'

'And she doesn't know what you and your father have been up to, is that it?'

She turned away, an angry flush staining her cheeks and he

pulled her round to face him. 'You said your father had gone away for a few days. Is that the truth?'

'Of course it is.'

'And you didn't know what he was up to last night?'

She shook her head, her eyes anxious. 'Please, Nick—I don't know what you're talking about.'

He looked at her searchingly for a moment and then nodded. 'All right—I believe you.'

He sketched in the events of the night briefly and when he finished, she looked pale and drawn. 'I can't believe it.'

'But you knew about the other things.'

She gazed up at him searchingly. 'Are you here as a friend, Nick, or as a policeman?'

'As a friend, damn you.' He took her hands and held them fast. 'You must believe that.'

She nodded. 'Yes, I knew about the other things. It seemed wrong somehow that Max Vernon should get away with what he did.' She looked up at him fiercely. 'I'm not sorry.'

'You will be if he gets his hands on your father.'

'You think that's possible?'

'Not really, he's too many other problems facing him at the moment, but you never can tell what a man like Vernon might pull. We'd better give your father a ring just in case.'

'But there isn't a 'phone,' she said. 'He's staying in our house-boat on the river at Grimsdyke.'

'In the marshes?'

'That's right, he goes for the shooting.'

'That's about twenty miles, isn't it?'

'Eighteen on the clock.'

'Good—we'll drive down and see him. It's early yet and the roads will be quiet. Shouldn't take more than half an hour.'

She nodded briefly. 'I'd better tell Jenny. I'll only be a moment.' She turned and ran across the lawn to the terrace and Miller walked back to the car.

It was no more than ten minutes after they had left when the 'phone rang and Jenny answered it on the kitchen extension.

'Colonel Craig's residence.'

The voice was smooth and charming. 'Good morning—my name's Fullerton. Gregory Fullerton. I'm a colleague of Colonel Craig's. He told me he was going away for a few days and gave me his address so that I could get in touch with him if anything came up. Damned stupid of me, but I've mislaid it.'

'It's the houseboat you'll be wanting, sir,' Jenny said. 'That's on the river at Grimsdyke in the marshes about a mile south of Culler's Bend.'

'So kind of you.'

'Not at all.' She replaced the receiver and went back to her work.

When Max Vernon emerged from the telephone box at the end of the small country lane he was grinning wolfishly. He opened the door of the brake and climbed into the passenger seat next to Carver.

'Right, Benny boy, we're in business,' he said. 'Let's have a look at that map.'

CHAPTER FOURTEEN

THE marsh at Grimsdyke on the river estuary was a wild lonely place of sea-creeks and mud flats and great pale barriers of reeds higher than a man's head. Since the beginning of time men had come here for one purpose or another—Roman, Saxon, Dane, Norman, but in the twentieth century it was a place of ghosts, an alien world inhabited mainly by the birds, curlew and red-shank and the brent geese coming south from Siberia to winter on the flats.

Miller turned the Cooper off the main road at Culler's Bend and followed a track no wider than a farm cart that was little more than a raised causeway of grass. On either side, miles of rough marsh grass and reeds marched into the heavy rain and a thin sea mist was drifting in before the wind.

Harriet lowered the window and took a deep breath of the salt-laden air. 'Marvellous—I love coming here. It's like nowhere else on earth—a different world.'

'I must say I'm impressed,' he said. 'I've never been here before.'

'Lost in a marsh punt in a sea mist it can be terrifying,' she said. 'In some places there are quicksands and mudholes deep enough to swallow a cart.'

The closer they got to the estuary, the more the mist closed in on them until visibility was reduced to no more than twenty yards. Finally the track emerged into a wide clearing of rough grass surrounded by thorn trees. Craig's Jaguar was parked under one of them and Miller braked to a halt.

'We have to walk from here,' Harriet said. 'It isn't very far.'

They followed a narrow path through the reeds. Wildfowl lifted out of the mist in alarm and somewhere a curlew called eerily. The marsh was stirring now, water swirling through it with an angry sucking noise, gurgling in crab holes, baring shining expanses of black mud.

'If we don't hurry we might miss him,' Harriet said. 'The tide's on the ebb. The best time for duck.'

She half-ran along the track and Miller followed her and suddenly, the wind was cold on his face and she called through the rain, waving her hand.

The mist had cleared a little so that one could see the river, the houseboat moored to the bank forty or fifty yards away. Duncan Craig was about to step into a flat-bottomed marsh punt and straightened, looking towards them.

He was wearing an old paratrooper's beret and combat jacket and carried a shotgun under one arm. He stood there staring at them, one hand shielding his eyes from the rain and then ran forward suddenly.

His face was white and set when he grabbed Harriet by the arm, the first time Miller had known him to show real emotion. 'What the hell are you doing here?'

Harriet was bewildered by the anger in his voice. 'What is it, Daddy? What's wrong?'

'We tried to arrest Max Vernon early this morning, but he gave us the slip,' Miller told him. 'I thought you ought to know he was on the loose.'

Craig gave Harriet a quick push forward. 'Get her out of here, Miller! Get her out now before it's too late!'

Harriet swung round, her face white and Miller said softly, 'My God, you're actually expecting him, aren't you? You've arranged the whole damned thing?'

'Every step of the way.' Craig patted the shotgun. 'Vernon shall have his chance—all part of the game.'

'It isn't a game any longer, you bloody fool,' Miller said. 'Can't you get that through your head? If Max Vernon comes looking for you he'll have only one thought on his mind.'

'Which suits me just fine.' Suddenly there was iron in his voice. 'No more arguments. Just get Harriet out of here.'

Miller shrugged and said evenly, 'All right, if that's the way you want it. I might point out that the first thing I shall do is contact the County Police.'

'Good luck to you. There's a village bobby at Culler's Bend

two miles up the road—Jack Berkley. He's fifty years of age
and it takes him all his time to get on his bicycle.'

'They do have such things as patrol cars.'

'Fair enough—it'll be interesting to see just how efficient they
are.'

'He isn't worth it, Craig,' Miller said desperately. 'He isn't
worth what it would do to you.'

'He murdered my daughter,' Craig said calmly. 'He wasn't
even fit to tie her shoes, but I'm still giving him his chance, Nick.
God help me, but I can't play the game any other way.'

'Which means only one thing in the final analysis. That you
won't be able to kill him,' Miller said, 'Can't you see that? It's
the essential difference between you and Vernon.'

Craig didn't reply and Harriet simply stood there, white and
terrified. Miller sighed and took her arm. 'All right. Let's get
going.'

When they reached the clearing, he helped Harriet into the
passenger seat of the Cooper, climbed behind the wheel quickly
and started the engine. He slid back the window and leaned
out.

'For the last time, Duncan—please.'

Craig smiled strangely and leaned down. 'Thanks, Nick—for
everything. Now get her out of it, there's a good chap.'

Miller moved into gear and took the Cooper back along the
track and beside him Harriet started to sob bitterly.

'Oh, Nick, I'm so afraid,' she said. 'He isn't like Vernon—not
when it comes down to it. He's going to die. I know he is.'

'Not if I can help it.' Miller said and braked violently as a
Ford station wagon appeared from the mist.

The two cars were not more than twenty feet apart. For one
horrified moment they stared at Max Vernon and Carver and
then Miller slammed the stick into reverse and took the Cooper
back along the track.

Vernon jumped out of the Ford, the Luger in his hand, and
fired twice, his second shot punching a hole in the Cooper's
windscreen. It slewed wildly and went half over the edge of the
track.

As Miller got the door open Duncan Craig appeared on the
run. He dropped to one knee and fired once in the direction of
the Ford.

'You two all right?'

Harriet nodded shakily. 'I think so.'

'Get her down into the reeds,' he told Miller briskly. 'I'll lead them off. As soon as they pass, get her out of here.'

He scrambled to his feet before Miller could argue and ran through the mist towards the Ford.

Vernon waited, the Luger ready and Carver crouched on the other side of the Ford, a Smith & Wesson revolver in his hand.

'Do you think it was Craig who fired that shot, Mr. Vernon?'

Craig answered for himself, his voice drifting mockingly out of the mist. 'So you got here, Vernon? All right, then. Let's see how good you really are.'

For a brief moment he appeared from the mist and turned and ran and Vernon went after him, cold with excitement.

They reached the Cooper half-blocking the track and Craig called, 'This way, Vernon! This way!'

As they disappeared into the mist, Miller emerged from the reeds pulling Harriet behind him. They ran back along the track and paused beside the Ford. The key was missing from the dashboard, but he reached underneath, wrenched out the ignition wires and looped them together quickly. A moment later the engine roared into life.

He turned to Harriet. 'Can you get this thing out of here?'

'I think so.'

'Good—I noticed a telephone box about a mile up the road on the way in. Ring through to Grant—he'll know what to do. The County boys would probably wonder what in the hell you were talking about.'

'What about you?'

'You don't think I'm going to let him cut his own throat at this stage do you?' He shoved her into the car. 'Go on—get out of it!'

As the Ford reversed away, a pistol shot echoed across the marshes that was answered by the blast of a shotgun. Miller turned and ran along the track in the direction of the sound.

Duncan Craig turned off the path to the left, ran across an expanse of coarse marsh grass into the shelter of the mist and doubled back on his tracks. He paused and listened intently. The only sound was the lapping of water and further along, geese lifted into the sky, voicing their annoyance at being disturbed.

By all the rules he should now be behind Vernon and Carver and he moved out of the shelter of the mist and approached the path cautiously. Somewhere to the right, there was the sound of running footsteps and as he crouched, shotgun ready, Nick Miller ran out of the mist.

'Over here!' Craig called softly and Miller paused on the edge of the raised path and looked down at him chest heaving.

'Thank God—I didn't think it would be this easy.'

There was a sudden cold laugh and Max Vernon scrambled on to the path from the other side about twenty yards to the left. 'It never is,' he called harshly and his hand swung up.

The bullet caught Miller in the upper arm, knocking him back off the path into the soft earth as Craig fired his shotgun in reply. Max Vernon had already slipped back into cover and Craig reached down and dragged Miller to his feet.

'Can you still run?'

Miller nodded, his face white with shock. 'I think so.'

'Then let's get out of here.'

They stumbled across the rough ground into the mist, two more bullets chasing them on their way, and suddenly the water was knee-deep and the reeds lifted to meet them.

Another bullet echoed wildly through the mist and Miller crouched instinctively, stumbling to one knee. Craig pulled him to his feet and they moved on through a thick glutinous slime covered by water, which in places was thigh deep.

Miller was conscious of the pain in his arm as the first shock wore off, of the coldness of the water as it ate into his flesh like acid, and struggled for breath.

Suddenly Craig disappeared with a startled cry, the water closing over his head. Miller lurched forward, reaching out, and followed him in. It was a terrible sensation as the filthy, stinking water forced its way into his mouth and nostrils. His feet could find no bottom as he struggled frantically and then an iron hand had him by the collar. A moment later, he was on his hands and knees amongst the reeds and breathing again.

Craig crouched beside him. He had lost his red beret and his face was streaked with black mud and slime. 'All right?'

Miller coughed and brought up a little marsh water.

'What about you?'

'Lost the shotgun, I'm afraid. If you think you can keep on the move, we've a chance of circling round to the houseboat. There are a couple of sporting rifles and an extra shotgun there.'

Miller nodded, getting to his feet and they moved forward again. A couple of minutes later the reeds started to thin and a dyke lifted out of the mist. They scrambled up out of the water and Craig started to run at a jog-trot, Miller stumbling after him.

The pain in his arm was much worse now and there was a stitch in his side. He stumbled into a thorn tree at the top of a grassy knoll above a small, scum covered pool and managed to cry out.

'No use, Duncan. I can't go on.'

Craig didn't even attempt to argue.

'Get out of sight and wait,' he said crisply. 'I'll be back in ten minutes.'

There was a clump of bushes just below the path and Miller rolled underneath. He pillowed his cheek against the wet earth, struggling for breath, and was suddenly aware of footsteps approaching from the direction in which they had come. A moment later, Ben Carver came into view.

He paused, his feet no more than a yard away from Miller's head, the Smith & Wesson held in his left hand, and Miller didn't hesitate. He grabbed for the ankles with all his force. Carver fell on top of him, the Smith & Wesson flying out of his hand into the pool below.

Miller cried out in agony as the pain in his arm seemed to spread throughout his entire body and he reached for Carver's throat with his right hand. Together, they burst out of the bushes and rolled down the slope.

For the briefest of moments Miller was on top as they reached the bottom and he used it well. His right hand rose and fell, the edge catching Carver full across the throat. He screamed and turned over, tearing at his collar.

Miller tried to get to his feet and Max Vernon said, 'Hold it right there—where's Craig?'

He was standing half-way down the slope, the Luger ready, his face pale. 'Right here, Vernon!' Craig called.

He came down the slope like a rugby forward, head down, catching Vernon round the waist. The Luger exploded once and then they were locked together and falling backwards.

The waters of the pool closed over them and they rose separately. Vernon seemed bewildered, his face black with mud and Craig surged forward and hit him again and again, solid heavy punches that drove him into the centre of the pool.

Vernon lost his balance and went under the surface. As he got to his feet, he screamed suddenly. 'My legs—I can't move my legs! I'm sinking!'

Craig floundered back towards the edge of the pool, the mud releasing him reluctantly with great sucking noises. When he reached firm ground he turned, a slightly dazed expression on his face and wiped the back of a hand wearily across his eyes.

Vernon was going fast, the quagmire under the surface of the water drawing him down. 'For God's sake, help me, Craig! Help me!'

Miller pushed himself to his feet and staggered forward clutching his arm, blood oozing between his fingers. Vernon was already chest-deep and he went to pieces completely, babbling hysterically, arms thrashing the water.

Miller started forward and Craig pulled him back. 'And I thought it was going to be so easy,' he said bitterly.

He unzipped his combat jacket, taking it off as he waded into the pool. He held it by the end of one sleeve and reached out to Vernon.

'Hold on tight if you want to live.'

Vernon grabbed for the other sleeve with both hands like a drowning man and Craig started backwards. He was already beginning to sink himself and for a moment, nothing seemed to be happening. Miller moved to help him, extending his one good arm and Craig grabbed at his hand. A moment later, Vernon came out of the slime with a rush.

He crawled from the water and lay face down at the side of the pool, his whole body racked by sobbing. Miller and Craig moved back to the bottom of the slope and slumped down.

'So you were right and I was wrong?' Craig sighed wearily. 'I should have known I couldn't go through with it.'

'All part of the service,' Miller said.

Craig turned with a wry grin. 'It's been fun, hasn't it? We must do it again some time.'

As they started to laugh, a police whistle sounded somewhere in the distance and scores of brent geese rose in a protesting cloud and flew out to sea.

A DEADLY SHADE OF GOLD

John D. MacDonald

*'A Deadly Shade of Gold' is published
by Robert Hale Ltd.*

The Author

John D. MacDonald was born in western
Pennsylvania. A graduate of Syracuse University
and Harvard Graduate School of Business
Administration, he began his writing career
when he was serving overseas with the United
States Army during World War II. Instead of
the usual letter home, he wrote a story to his
wife which she successfully sold to a magazine.
It was the forerunner of more than 333 short
stories and forty novels. Mr. MacDonald is
interested in chess, golf and duelling pistols.
His home is in Florida.

CHAPTER ONE

A SMEAR of fresh blood has a metallic smell. It smells like freshly sheared copper. It is a clean and impersonal smell, quite astonishing the first time you smell it. It changes quickly, to a fetid, fudgier smell, as the cells die and thicken.

When it is the blood of a stranger, there is an atavistic withdrawal, a toughening of response, a wary reluctance for any involvement. When it is your own, you want to know how bad it is. You turn into a big inward ear, listening to yourself, waiting for faintness, wondering if this is going to be the time when the faintess comes and turns into a hollow roaring, and sucks you down. Please not yet. Those are the three eternal words. Please not yet.

When it is the blood of a friend. . . .

When maybe he said, Please not yet. . . . But it took him and he went on down. . . .

It was a superb season for girls on the Lauderdale beaches. In a cool February wind, on a bright and cloudless afternoon, Meyer and I had something over a half dozen of them drowsing in pretty display, basted with sun oil, behind the protection of laced canvas on the sun deck atop my barge type houseboat, *The Busted Flush*, moored on a semi-permanent basis at Slip F-18, Bahia Mar, Fort Lauderdale. Meyer and I were playing aceydeucy. I heard my phone ring, went on down to my lounge and answered it with one very cautious depersonalized grunt.

'McGee?' the voice said. 'Hey McGee? Is this Travis McGee?'

I stuck a thumb in my cheek and said, 'I'm lookin' affa things while he's away.'

The voice was vaguely familiar.

'McGee, buddy, are you stoned?'

Then I knew the voice. From way back. Sam Taggart.

'Where the hell are you,' I said, 'and how soon can you get here?'

The voice faded and came back. '. . . too far to show up in the next nine minutes. Wait'll I see what it says on the front of this phone book. Waycross, Georgia. Look, I've been driving straight on through, and I'm dead on my feet. And I started thinking suppose he isn't there, then what the hell do you do?'

'So I'm here. So hole up and get some sleep before you kill somebody.'

'Trav, I got to have some help.'

'Doesn't everybody?'

'Listen. Seriously. You still . . . operating like you used to?'

'Only when I need the money. Right now I'm taking a nice long piece of my retirement, Sam. Hurry on down. The little broads are beautiful this year.'

'There's a lot of money in this.'

'It will be a lot more pleasant to say no to you in person. And by the way, Sam?'

'Yes?'

'Is there anybody in particular you would like me to get in touch with? Just to say you're on your way?'

It was a loaded question, about as subtle as being cracked across the mouth with a dead mackerel. I expected a long pause and got one.

'Don't make those real funny jokes,' he said in a huskier voice.

'What if maybe it isn't a joke, Sam?'

'It has to be. If she had a gun, she should kill me. You know that. She knows that. I know that. For God's sake, you know no woman, especially a woman like Nora, can take that from anybody. I dealt myself out, forever. Look, I know what I lost there, Trav. Besides, a gal like that wouldn't still be around. Not after three years. Don't make jokes, boy.'

'She's still around. Sam, did you ever give her a chance to forgive you?'

'She never would. Believe me, she never would.'

'Are you sewed up with somebody else?'

'Don't be a damn fool.'

'Why not, Sam?'

'That's another funny joke too.'

'She's not sewed up. At least she wasn't two weeks ago. Why shouldn't her reasons be the same as yours?'

'Cut it out. I can't think. I'm dead on my feet.'

'You don't have to think. All you have to do is feel, Sam. She'll want to see you.'

'How do you know?'

'Because I was the shoulder she cried on you silly bastard!'

'God, how I want to see her!'

'Sam, it will tear her up too much if you walk in cold. Let me get her set for it. Okay?'

'Do you really know what the hell you're doing, McGee?'

'Sam, sweetie, I've been trying to locate you for three years.'

He was silent again, and then I heard him sigh. 'I got to sack out. Listen. I'll be there tomorrow late. What's tomorrow? Friday. What I'll do, I'll find a room someplace. . . .'

'Come right to the boat.'

'No. That won't be so smart, for reasons I'll tell you when I see you. And I've got to talk to you before I do anything about seeing Nora. What you better do, Trav, tell her I'm coming in Saturday. Don't ask questions now. Just set it up that way. I . . . I've got to have some help. Do it my way, Trav. I'll phone you after I locate a place.'

After I hung up, I looked up the number of Nora Gardino's shop. Some girl with a Gabor accent answered, and turned me over to Miss Gardino.

'The McGee!' she said with irony and pleasure. 'Let me guess. Something in a size eight or ten, lacy, expensive and, of course, gift wrapped.'

'Nope. This time I want the boss lady. Gift wrapped. Instead of package delivery, I'll pick it up in person. About seven? Gin, steak, wine, dancing and provocative conversation.'

'Seven o'clock then. But why? I'm pleased and so on, but why?'

'Because a McGee never gives up.'

'Wow, you're after me every minute, huh? Tireless McGee. Once a year, with bewildering frequency, turning a poor girl's head, never giving her a chance to catch her breath. But make it seven-thirty. Okay?'

I went back topside and lost my game, and the next, and the next. Meyer turned and gave me a sombre hairy look. 'After that phone call, you played even worse, if that is possible.'

'An old friend.'

'With a problem, of course. McGee, that expression is rapidly becoming obsolete too. In our brave new world there will be nothing but new friends.'

He lumbered down my ladderway, refused an ultimate brew, and went trudging off toward his ugly little cruiser tied up to a neighbouring dock. On its transom, in elaborate gold was the name *The John Maynard Keynes*.

At the appropriate time I drove over to the mainland, across the 17th Street Causeway, and from there north to the back street where Nora Gardino lives in what was once a gardener's cottage for a large estate. I drive a Rolls, vintage 1936, one of the big ones. Some previous owner apparently crushed the rear end, and seeking utility, turned her into a pick-up truck. Another painted her that horrid blue that matches the hair of a grade school teacher I once had, and I have named her, with an attack of the quaints, after that teacher, Miss Agnes. She is ponderously slow to get up to cruising speed, but once she has attained it, she can float along all day long in the medium eighties in a rather ghastly silence—a faint whisper of wind, a slight rumble of rubber. Miss Agnes was born into a depression, and suffered therefrom.

My lights made highlights on Nora's little black Sunbeam parked deep in the curve of the driveway. I went up onto the shallow porch, and a girl answered the door. She was big and slender. She had a broad face, hair the colour of wood ashes. She wore a pale grey corduroy jump suit, with a big red heart embroidered where a heart should be. I did not catch her name exactly, not with that Gaborish accent, but it sounded like Shaja Dobrak. She invited me in, after I had identified myself, and said that Nora would soon be ready. She made me a drink and brought it to me, and sat with her own in a chair facing me, long legs tucked under her, and told me she had worked for Nora seven months, and had been living at the cottage for four months. She was a grown-up, composed, watchful and gracious, and extraordinarily attractive in her own distinctive way.

In a little while Nora came hurrying out, and I got up for the quick small old-friends hug, the kiss on the cheek. She is a lean, dark, vital woman, with vivid dark eyes, too much nose, not enough forehead. Her voice is almost, but not quite, baritone. Her figure is superb and her legs are extraordinary. In spite of the strength of her features, her rather brusque and impersonal mannerisms, she is an intensely provocative woman, full of the challenging promise of great feminine warmth.

She was in a deep shade of wool, not exactly a wine shade, perhaps a cream sherry shade, a fur wrap, her blue-black hair glossy, her heels tall, purse in hand, mouth shaped red, her eyes sparkling with holiday. Her face looked thinner than I remembered, her cheeks more hollowed.

We said good night to the smiling Shaja, and as we went out Nora said, 'I haven't had a date in so long, I feel practically girlish.'

'Good. My car or yours?'

'Trav, you should remember that I would *never* slight Miss Agnes that way. She'd sit here and sulk.' Then after I closed

her in, got in beside her, started up and turned out of the drive,
I said, 'I thought you were a loner.'

'Oh, Shaja? She is a jewel. I'm in the process of setting the
shop up so that she can buy in, a little at a time. She's married to
a man years older than she is. She gets two letters a year from
him. He's in a Hungarian prison. Four years to go, I think, and
then the problem of trying to get him out of the country somehow, and get him over here, but she has a wonderful confidence
that it is all going to work out. We're doing just fine.'

I said, 'How about the Mile O'Beach?'

'Hmmm. Not the Bahama Room?'

'Later, if we feel like it. But food and drink in the Captain's
Room.'

'Fine!'

It was a conversational place, a small dark lounge far from
the commercial merriment, all black woods, dark leather, flattering lighting. We took armchairs at the countersunk bar, and
I told Charles to bring us menus in about forty minutes, and
told him what sort of table we would like. We talked very
busily and merrily, right through the drinks and right into
dinner.

I do not know if she ever actually realized, while things were
going on, how it all was with me. Sam and Nora were so inevitably, totally, glowingly right for each other, that the reflected
aura deluded Nicki and me into thinking we had something
just as special. A habitual foursome can work that kind of uneasy magic sometimes. When Sam Taggart and Nora broke up
in that dreadful and violent and self-destructive way, Nicki and
I tried to keep going. But there wasn't enough left. Too much
of what we thought we were to each other depended on that
group aura, the fun, the good talk, the trusting closeness.

I waited until she had finished dinner and had argued herself into the infrequent debauch of Irish coffee.

Not knowing any good way to do it, I waited until one line
of talk had died into a not entirely comfortable silence, and then
I said, 'Sam is on his way back here. He wants to see you.'

Her eyes went wide and deep lines appeared between her
dark brows. She put her hand to her throat. 'Sam?' she
whispered. 'He wants. . . .' The colour drained out of her face
abruptly. She wrenched her chair sideways and bent forward
to put her head between her knees. Charles came rushing over. I
told him what I needed. He returned with it in about twelve
seconds. I knelt beside her chair and held the smelling salts to

her nostrils. Charles hovered. In a few moments she sat up, her colour still ghastly.

She tried to smile and said, 'Walk me, Trav. Get me out of here. Please.'

CHAPTER TWO

WE walked on the dark grounds of the big hotel, among the walks and landscaping. In exposed places the wind was biting.

'Feel better?'

'Terribly maidenly, wasn't it? What did they used to call it? The vapours.'

'I didn't do it very well. I sort of slugged you with it.'

'How did he sound?'

'Exhausted. He'd been driving a long way.'

'From where?'

'He didn't say.'

'How did he sound . . . about me?'

'As if he's convinced you can never forgive him.'

'Oh God! The fool! The damned fool! All this waste. . . .' She turned and faced me in the night. 'Why should he think I couldn't ever understand? After all, a man like that is always terrified of . . . any total commitment. It was cruel and brutal, the way he did it, but I could have. . . .'

She whirled away and made a forlorn sound, staggered to a slender punk tree, caught it with her left hand, bent forward from the waist and began to vomit. I went to her, put my right hand on her waist to hold her braced and steadied, her hip pulled against the side of my thigh, my left hand clasping her left shoulder. As her slim body leapt and spasmed with the retching, as she made little intermittent demands that I leave her alone, I was remembering just how brutal it was, so all involved with that dreary old business of killing the thing you love the best. Because you are afraid of love, I guess.

Sam was a random guy, a big restless, reckless lantern-jawed ex-marine, a brawler, a wencher, a two-fisted drinker. He loved the sea and knew it well. He crewed on some deep water racers. He worked in boat yards. He went into hock for a charter boat, did all right, then had a run of bad luck and lost it. He worked on other charter fishermen, and did some commercial fishing. A boat bum. An ocean bum. For a time he captained a big Wheeler for an adoring widow. He was a type you find around every resort port. Unfocused. A random, rambling man. After you knew him a long time, if he trusted you, you would find out that there was another man underneath, and a lot of the surface was a part he played. He was sensitive, perceptive. He had a liberal arts degree from one of the fine small colleges. He had a lot of ability and no motivation.

Then he met Nora Gardino, and she was the marvellous catalyst that brought all the energy of Sam Taggart into focus, into some sense of purpose.

At that time I picked up with Nicki and the four of us ran in a small friendly pack. Nicki and I got in on the planning phase. Her shop was doing well. Sam scouted a good piece of waterfront land. He wanted to start a marina from scratch, and he had sound ideas about it, and good local contacts. Once he got it started, they would be married. She would continue with the shop until too pregnant, and then she would sell out and put the money into the marina project. They designed the big airy apartment they would live in, right on the marina property.

Maybe he felt the walls closing in. Maybe he felt unworthy of all the total trust and loyalty she was so obviously giving him. Maybe he was afraid that, in spite of all his confidence, he would fail her in some way. By then he was earning pretty good money in a boat yard, and saving every dime of it. She had a dull little girl working for her at the time, plump and pretty, with an empty face. Her name was Sandra. Maybe, subconsciously, he wanted it to happen just the way it happened. Maybe, after he got drunk, it was just accidental. But it was cruel, and it was brutal, to have Nora, after a day and a night of searching for him, find him at last, see his blurred self-destructive grin as he stared at her from the tangled bed, with all the naked fattiness of Sandra snoring placidly beside him.

She turned on her heel quickly, closed the door with barely a sound, and went away from there.

By the next day he was packed and gone. I helped her try to find him. She put a thousand dollars into agency fees without their finding any trace of him.

After a while you give up. Or maybe you never give up.

Nora straightened up at last, weak and dizzy, and held the slim tree with both hands and stood with her forehead resting against the soft silvery bark.

'I must be a very atractive date,' she said in a half whisper.

'It's been three years.'

'Not knowing if he was sick or dead or in trouble.' She shivered visibly.

I patted her shoulder. 'Come on. Go freshen up and we'll get away from here.'

'When will he be here?'

'Saturday.'

'What time?'

'I don't know.'

'Will he . . . come to the shop?'

'Or phone you. I don't know.'

'Does he know you've told me about him?'

'Yes.'

'He hasn't found anybody else?'

'Neither of you have. For the same reason.'

'I'm glad to have some warning, Trav. But I will be a complete wreck by Saturday.'

I waited in the lobby for her. When she was ready, I drove to Bahia Mar. We could talk aboard *The Busted Flush.* Obviously she wanted to talk.

I turned the heat up. I made her a tall mild drink. She took her shoes off and sat on the far curve of my yellow couch in the lounge, her legs tucked up, her colour better, her frown thoughtful.

'Damn it all, Trav, I just don't know how to handle it. Rush into his arms? I want to. But does he want me to? Or does he want to be punished? She was a dreadful little bit of nothing, you know.'

'I don't know how he wants you to act.'

'Boy, it was a real belt to the pride.'

'He was drinking.'

'What started the drinking?'

'Fright, maybe.'

'Of what?'

'A real live complete entire woman can be a scary thing.'

'Did I come on too strong or something?'

'You have to be what you are, Nora. The complete package.'

'Now I'm twenty-nine. Three lousy stinking wasted years. What did he *say*? Tell me some of his words.'

'Quote God how I want to see her unquote.'

She jumped up and went back and forth with panther stride. 'What the hell did he think I was? A white plaster saint? I don't know how to handle it, meeting him.'

'Don't plan anything. Play it by ear, Nora. Don't try to force any kind of reaction. It's the only thing you can do.'

'Why did he call you?'

'To find out if you were still around,' I lied. 'To find out if there were any chances left. To find out if it was too late to come home.'

'It isn't too late. Believe me, it isn't too late.'

CHAPTER THREE

SOUTH of Lauderdale on U.S. 1 there are junk strips dating back to the desperate trashiness of the thirties. They are, as a governor of the state of Florida once said at a Press conference, a sore eye.

Sam Taggart was in one of six cabins out behind a dispirited gas station that sold some kind of off-brand called Haste.

A bed creaked as Sam got off it and came to the door. He let me in and hit me solidly in the chest and said, 'You're an uglier man than I remembered.'

'I compensate with boyish charm, Taggart.' We shook hands. He motioned to the only chair in the room and sat on the bed. I had never seen him so dark. He was the deep stained bronze of a Seminole. His hand was hard and leathery. He wore faded khaki pants and a white T shirt with a ripped shoulder seam. He looked leaned down, all bones and wire. He had a crescent scar on his chin that hadn't been there before. He was missing some important teeth on the upper right. His black hair was cropped close to his skull.

'How are things, Trav?'

'You mean with Nora?'

'Okay. With Nora. How did she take it?'

'First she got faint and then she threw up, and then she decided she loves you and wants you back.'

'Boy, I come back like a hero, don't I? I come back in great shape.'

'But you came back.'

'She's a sucker for punishment, eh?'

'Why did you do her that way, Sam?'

He braced his arms on his knees and stared at the floor. 'I don't know. I just don't know, Trav. I swear.' He looked up at me. 'How has she been? How does she look? How's she been making out?'

'She looks a little thinner in the face. And she's a little bit quieter than she used to be. She's made a good thing of the shop. It's in a new place now. More expensive stuff. She's still got the best legs in town.'

'Coming back is doing her no favour.'

'Leave that up to her, Sam. Unless you plan to do it the same way all over again.'

'No. Believe me. Never. Trav, have there been any guys?'

'When you two get back together, you can decide whether you want to trade reminiscences.'

'You know, I wondered about you and her. I wondered a lot.'

'Forget it. It was a mild idea at one time, but it didn't work out. Where have you been all this time, Sam?'

'Most of the time in a little Mexican town below Guaymas. Puerto Altamura. Fishing village. I became a *residente*. Helped a guy build up a sports fishing layout, catering to a rich trade.'

'You don't look so rich.'

'I left real quick, Trav. Jesus, you've never seen fishing like we had there. Any day, you quit because your wrist is so sprained you can't hold a rod.'

'How nice for you, Sam.'

He peered at me. 'Sure. Sure, you son of a bitch. When you don't think much of yourself, you can't think much of anything else.'

'You said you're in trouble.'

'You're still doing the same kind of hustling, McGee?'

'I am still the last resort, Sam, for victims of perfectly legal theft, or theft so clever the law can't do a thing. Try everything else and then come to me. If I can get it back, I keep half. Half is a lot better than nothing at all. But I am temporarily retired. Sorry.'

'I've done some thinking since I talked to you. When I decided to come and see you, was I thinking about getting help, or an excuse to see Nora? I don't know. Everbody kids themselves. How can you tell. I knew I'd find out she's married, two kids by now. I could see the guy, even. One of those development guys, very flashy, speeches to the service clubs, low golf handicap, flies his own plane. A nice guy with thirty forty sports jackets.'

'She's twenty-nine. She's not married. She should be.'

'To me? To me, Trav? Take a good look.'

His eyes moved away. He made a knotted fist and stared at it. I said, 'Maybe you've gotten all the rest of it out of your system now. Maybe you're ready.'

He sighed. 'I could be. God knows I could be. I did some thinking. If there's a chance of her. If there's a good chance, then the thing that seemed so important to get your help on

. . . maybe it isn't all that important. Oh boy, they gave it to me good, friend. The stuff was mine, and they took it. You see, without Nora, it was a lot more important to get it back, or get half of it back, half to you. If you could do anything about it. Maybe not, even if you wanted to. This is not minor league.'

'I don't have very much idea of what you're talking about.'

'I suppose it's pride,' Sam Taggart said. 'Getting pushed around like a stupid kid. But it is better, I guess, to just get out of it with what I have.' He stood up. 'Stay right there. I want to show you something.' He went out to the rusty car with the California plates. In a few moments he came back in. He sat on the bed and untied coarse twine, unrolled a piece of soiled chamois, reached and handed me a squat little figurine about five and a half inches tall. The weight of it was so unexpected I nearly dropped it.

It was a crude little figure, dumpy, a male representation like a child would make out of clay. It was startlingly emphatically male. It was of solid metal, dull yellow, and orange, blackness caught into the creases of it, shinier where it had been handled.

'Gold?' I asked.

'Solid. Not very pure. But that doesn't make the value of it. It's Pre-Columbian. I don't know whether this one is Aztec. It could be. It's worth a hell of a lot more than the gold, but nobody can say exactly what it is worth. It's worth what you can get a museum or a collector to pay for it. I imagine this one was some kind of a potency symbol. I had twenty-eight of them, some bigger, some smaller. Not all the same source or same period. Two were East Indian from way way back. Three were, I think, Inca. When they took the others, they missed this one because that night by luck or coincidence, this one wasn't with the others.'

'They were yours?' I couldn't read his eyes.

'Let's just say there was nobody else they could have belonged to, the way things had worked out. Somebody might develop an argument on that, but when I had them, they were mine. A rough, a very rough estimate of the value of the whole collection would be three to four hundred thousand. Take the gold alone, it was two thousand, two hundred and forty-one point six ounces, discount that for impurities, it's still a nice bundle.' He slowly rewrapped the figurine, knotted the twine. 'Finding the right buyer for the whole works would be touchy.'

'A question of legal ownership?'

'Who owns things like these anyway?'

'I'm not looking for a project, Sam.'

'So you keep saying. And this one is too rough for one man. Some people have been hurt on this thing already. I thought it all over and I decided, what the hell.' He bounced the wrapped lump of gold on the palm of his tough hand. 'It scalds them they missed this one, not so much from the value of it, but because I could use it as a lever and give them a lot of agitation. If I wanted to give up any chance at any of it, and give this little fellow up too, I could raise political hell with them. So, earlier today, I made the decision to pull out with what I could salvage. I used most of the pennies I had left to stop along the road and make a couple of phone calls. They'd like to have this little fellow, and close the books. So I said fifteen, and then said ten, and it looks as if it will be twelve thousand five. They're sending a guy to close.' He grinned widely enough to expose all the gap where the teeth were gone. 'At least I come back with a trousseau. Twelve-five plus Nora is better than three hundred without her. Lesson number one.'

'It takes you a while. But you learn.'

'Can I tap you for some walk-around money?'

I looked into my wallet. 'Forty do it?'

'Forty is fine, Trav. Just fine.'

'When are you going to see Nora?'

He looked uneasy. 'After I get this thing closed out. God, I don't know how to handle it. I don't know how to act toward her. I ought to drop onto my knees and smack my head on the floor. Tomorrow is the day. Three years of thinking about her, and remembering every little thing about her, and tomorrow is the day. I've got stage fright, Trav. How should I set it up?'

'What you do, you hire fifty female trumpet players and dress them in white robes and then you. . . .'

'Okay. It's my problem. Trav, how's Nicki?'

'I wouldn't know. She isn't around any more.'

'Oh.'

'When she left, we shook hands. What she really wanted was a barbecue pit in the back yard, tricycles in the car port, guest towels, daddy home from the office at five-fifteen. She tried to be somebody else, but she couldn't make it. She lusted to join the PTA.'

He gave me a strange look. 'So do I.'

'You'll make it, Taggart.'

'We'll have you to dinner every once in a while.'

'I'll use your guest towels.'

'We'll feed the kids first.'

So I left him there and went on back to the boat, depressed in a vague way. I must do anything, but stop remembering the way Sam Taggart looks with all the wandering burned out of him. Stop remembering the sly shy way Nicki would walk toward you, across a room. Stop remembering the way Lois died. Get in there and have fun, fella. While there's fun to have. While there's some left. Before they deal you out.

CHAPTER FOUR

THE insistent bong of the bell awakened me. I stared at the clock dial. Quarter after midnight. I hadn't gone out at all. I had read my book, gotten slightly tight, broiled myself a small steak, and baked myself a large potato, watched the late news and weather and gone to bed.

I put a robe on and went out through the lounge and put the afterdeck lights on. I looked out and saw Nora Gardino re-hooking my gangplank chain. She came aboard and swept by me and into the lounge and turned on me, one fist on her hip, her eyes narrow. 'Where is he?'

I yawned and rubbed my eyes. 'For God's sake!'

'You know Beanie, over at the Mart.'

'Yes, I know Beanie.'

'She called me, over an hour ago. Maybe an hour and a half. She said she saw Sam about eight o'clock over at the Howard Johnson's. She was sure it was him.'

'Can I fix you a drink, Nora?'

'Don't change the subject. Where is he? You said he wouldn't get here until tomorrow.'

'So I lied.'

'Why? Why?'

'Settle down, honey. He had a little matter to take care of first.'

'I called you and called you, and then I decided you'd turned the phone off again, so I came on over. I want to see him, Travis.'

'He wants to see you. Tomorrow.'

She shook her head. 'No. Now. Where is he?'

She stood there staring at me, tapping her foot. She wore flannel slacks, a yellow turtleneck sweater, a pale leather hip-length coat over the sweater, swinging open. She looked fervently, hotly, indignantly alive.

'Let him set it up his own way, Nora.'

'I am not going to wait through this night, believe me. It's ridiculous. The time to have it out is right now. Where is he?'

'I don't know.'

'Travis!'

I yawned again. 'Okay, okay, honey. Let me get dressed. I'll take you there.'

'Just tell me where.'

I was tempted, but then I thought that Sam Taggart would be sore as hell if I let her go to that fusty little cabin without warning, bust in on him in the midst of that kind of squalor without warning. The best way I could retrieve it would be to have her wait out in the car and go get him and warn him and send him on out to her.

I dressed quickly, woke myself up by honking into double handfuls of cold water, locked up, went out with her and woke up Miss Agnes.

Nora sat very perky and alert beside me.

'What was it he had to take care of?'

'I'll let him tell you that.'

'When did he arrive?'

'This afternoon, late.'

'How does he look?'

'Fine. Just fine. He's in great shape.'

I drove over to Route 1 and turned left. She was as rigid as a toy with the spring wound too tightly. When I glanced at her, she gave me a big nervous white-toothed grin in the reflection of the passing street lights. The gas station was dark. I parked on the asphalt beside the pumps and got out.

'In one of those crummy little cabins?'

'He isn't broke.'

'I don't care if he's broke. I'll come with you.'

'Nora, damn it, you stay right here. I'll send him out. Okay?'

'All right, Trav,' she said meekly.

I walked around to the back. Cupid McGee. His car was beside his cabin. There was a pickup truck parked beside the end cabin on the left. The others looked empty. I rapped on his door. Night traffic growled by on Route 1. 'Sam?' I called. I rapped again. 'Hey, Sam!'

I tried the latch. The door swung open. I smelled musty linoleum, ancient plumbing. And a sharp metallic smell, like freshly sheared copper. I fumbled my hand along the inside wall beside the door. The switch turned an unshaded light on. The light bulb lay against the floor, on the maple base of a table lamp, the shade a few feet away. The eye records. The eye takes vivid, unforgettable pictures. Sam Taggart was on his side, eyes half open in the grey-bronze of the emptied face, one chopped hand outflung, all of him shrunken and dwindled by the bulk loss of the lake of blood in which he lay. A flap of his face lay open, exposing pink teeth, and I thought, idiotically, the missing teeth are on the other side.

They're sending a guy to close the account.

I heard the brisk steps approaching across cinders, and it took me too long to realize who was coming. 'Sam?' she called in a voice like springtime. 'Darling?'

I turned too late and tried to stop her. My arms were wooden, and she tore loose and took a step in and stared at what they'd left her of him. There are bodies you can run to. But not one like that. She made a strange little wheezing sound. She could have stood there forever. Lot's wife.

I had enough sense to find the switch and drop him into a merciful blackness. I took her and turned her slowly and brought her out. She was like a board.

In the darkness, with faint lights of traffic touching her face, she said in a perfectly conversational tone, 'Oh, no. I can't permit that. I can't stand that. He was coming back to me. I can't have anything like that. I can't endure that. There's only so much, you know. They can't ask more than that, can they?'

And suddenly she began to hurl herself about, random thrusts and flappings like a person in vast convulsions. Maybe she was trying to tear herself free of her soul. She made a tiny continuous whining sound, and she was astonishingly strong. I wrested her toward brighter light and her eyes were mad, and there was blood in the corner of her mouth. She clawed at me. I caught her by the nape of the neck, got my thumb under the angle of her jaw, pressed hard against the carotid artery. She made a few aimless struggling motions and then sagged. I caught her around the waist and walked her to the car, holding most of her weight. I bundled her in on the driver's side, got in and shoved her over, and drove out of there.

By the time I walked her into her cottage, she was crying with such a despairing, hollow, terrible intensity that each sob threatened to drive her to her knees. Shaja wore a slate blue robe, her ashy hair tousled, her broad face marked with concern.

'I took her to Sam,' I said. 'When we got there he was dead. Somebody killed him. With a knife.'

She said an awed something in a foreign tongue. She put her arms around the grief-racked figure of the smaller woman.

'Do what you can,' I said. 'Sleeping pills, if you've got any.'

'We haff,' she said.

'I've got to use the phone.'

She led Nora back to the bedrooms. I sat on a grey and gold couch and phoned the country sheriff's department. 'A man has been murdered at the X-Cell Cottages, in number three, half a mile below the city line on the left. My name is McGee. I found the body a few minutes ago. I'm going back there right now.'

I hung up in the middle of his first question. I went back to Nora's bedroom. Shaja was supporting Nora, an arm around her shoulders, holding a glass of water to her lips. A coughing sob exploded a spray of water.

'I'll be back later,' I said. She gave me a grave nod.

When I parked at the gas station, a department sedan was already in front of the cottage. The cottage lights were on. Two deputies were standing outside the open door. A middle-aged one and a young one.

'Hold it right there!' one of them said.

I stopped and said, 'I phoned it in. My name is McGee.'

'Okay. Don't touch anything. We got to wait for the C.I. people,' the middle-aged one said. 'My name is Hawks. This here is Deputy DeWall.' He coughed and spat. 'Friend of yours in there?'

'Yes.'

'When'd you find him?'

'A little after quarter of one. A few minutes after.'

Cops do not have to be particularly acute. The average citizen has very few encounters with the law during his lifetime. Consequently he reacts in one of the standard ways of the average citizen, too earnest, too jocular, too talkative. When someone does not react in one of those standard ways, there are only two choices, either he has been in the business himself, or he has had too many past contacts with the law. I could sense that they were beginning to be a little bit too curious about me. So I fixed it.

'God, this is a terrible thing,' I said. 'I suppose you fellows see a lot of this kind of thing, but I don't think I could ever get used to it. Jesus, as long as I live I'll never forget seeing Sam there on the floor like that with the light shining on his face. I can't really believe it.'

Hawks yawned. 'Somebody chopped him pretty good, Mr.

McGee. The registration on the steering post says Samuel Taggart.'

'That's right. Sam Taggart. He used to live here. He went away three years ago, just got back today.'

The doctor arrived next. He stared in at the body, rocked from heel to toe, hummed a little tune and relit the stub of his cigar. Next came another patrol vehicle followed by a lab truck and by a Volkswagen with two reporters in it. A young square-shouldered, balding man in khaki pants, in a plaid wool shirt, and a baggy tweed jacket seemed to be in charge. Hawks and DeWall muttered to him as he stared in at the body. They motioned toward me. Everything was casual. No fuss, no strain. When a man with a hundred dollar car gets killed in a four dollar cabin, the pros are not going to get particularly agitated. The official pictures were taken. A reporter took a few shots. They weren't anything he could get into the paper. Tweed Jacket waved the doctor in. The ambulance arrived, and the two attendants stood their woven metal basket against the outside wall of the cabin and stood smoking, chatting, waiting for the doctor to finish his preliminary examination.

The doctor came out, spoke briefly to Tweed Jacket and drove away. The ambulance boys went in and wrapped Sam, after Tweed Jacket checked his pockets, put him in the basket, strapped him in and toted him out and drove away with him— no siren, no red lights. Tweed Jacket waved the lab crew into the cabin and I heard him tell them to check the car out too.

He came wandering over to me, the two reporters drifting along in his wake. He turned to them and said patiently, 'Now I'll tell you if there's anything worth your knowing. You just go set and be comfortable, if you can spare the time.'

He put his hand out and said, 'Mr. McGee, I'm Ken Branks. We appreciate it when people report an ugly thing like this rather than letting it set for somebody else to find, like when they come in the morning to tidy up. You come on over to the car where we can talk comfortable.'

We got into the front seat of his car. He uncased a little tape recorder and hooked the mike onto the dash and plugged it into the cigarette lighter. 'Hope you don't mind this. I've got a terrible memory.'

'I don't mind.'

'Now tell me your full name and address.'

'Travis D. McGee, Slip F-18, Bahia Mar, aboard *The Busted Flush*.'

'Own it or run it?'

'I own it.'

'Now you tell me in your own words how you come to find this body.'

'Sam Taggart used to live here. He went away three years ago. He got back today and called me up this afternoon, aboard the boat. I came right over and we talked for about an hour, about old friends and so on. I loaned him forty dollars. He said he was back to stay. I went on back to the boat. I spent the evening alone. I had my phone turned off. I went to bed and went to sleep. At quarter after twelve a woman came to the boat, a friend of mine. She used to know Sam. She said a mutual friend had phoned her and told her Sam was back in town. She thought I might know where he was. She thought it would be a good idea if we both paid him a visit. I got dressed and drove her over here. She left her car back at Bahia Mar. His car was here. I knocked and there wasn't any answer. I tried the door and it opened. I found the light switch. She came to the door and looked in at him too, and she went all to pieces. She used to be pretty fond of him. I took her back to her place, phoned in from there, and then came right back here. There's somebody to take care of her at her place. When I got back here, the two deputies were already here. So I waited around.'

'Who is this woman?'

'She's a local businesswoman. It wouldn't help her any if it was in the newspapers that she was with me when I found the body.'

'I can understand that, Mr. McGee. Who is she?'

'Nora Gardino. She has a shop at Citrus Gate Plaza.'

'I know the place. Expensive. She knew this type fella?'

'I guess he didn't have much luck during the three years he was away.'

'Where did he work and where did he live when he lived here?'

I remembered some of the places he had worked, and a couple of the addresses.

'Would the law around here have any kind of file on him?'

'It wouldn't be anything serious. Brawling, maybe.'

'Who phoned Nora Gardino about seeing this man in town?'

'A girl called Beanie who works in the Mart, across from Pier 66. I don't know her last name.'

'Do you know where she saw Taggart?'

'In that Howard Johnson's opposite the Causeway, about eight o'clock.'

'Anybody with him?'

'I don't know.'

'How long did you know Taggart before he moved away?'

'About two years.'

'How did you meet him?'

'Through friends. A mutual interest in boats and the water and fishing.'

'Where has he been living?'

'In California. And he spent some time in Mexico.'

'And he came back broke?'

'He borrowed forty dollars from me.'

'What do you do for a living?'

'I get into little ventures every now and then. Investments. Land deals. That kind of thing.'

'It was sort of a gag, going to call on Taggart so late?'

'I guess you could call it that. She wanted to see him again, I guess.'

'You didn't see anybody driving away from here or walking away from here when you drove up?'

'No.'

'Was he the kind of fella goes into a bar and gets in trouble?'

'Sometimes.'

'I'll have to check this out with Mrs. Gardino.'

'Miss. She might be pretty dopey by now. Sleeping pills. It was a terrible shock for her to see anything like that.'

'A knife is messy. There's no big rush about talking to her. How about Taggart's folks?'

'I wouldn't know. I think he has some cousins somewhere.'

A man appeared at the window on Branks's side. Branks turned the tape machine off. 'All clear, Ken. We got more prints than anybody needs, most of them smudged.'

'How about that end cabin?'

'A farmer from South Carolina and a half wit kid. They didn't see anything or hear anything. No other cabins occupied.'

'How about the owner?'

'He should be here any minute. He lives way the hell and gone out.'

'Runs the gas station?'

'Yes.'

'Check him on anybody coming to see Taggart. How about Taggart's gear?'

'I'd give you about twenty-eight cents for everything he owns, Ken.'

'Have Sandy tag it and take it in and store it, and arrange to have that heap driven in to the pound.'

The man went away. Ken Branks stretched and yawned. 'He had a little over twenty left out of the forty, Mr. McGee. These things have a pattern. The way I see it, Taggart went out to do some cruising on your money. So he hit a few bars, and got somebody agitated, and that somebody followed him on back here and went in after him with a knife. In the dark, probably. Taggart did pretty good. The place is pretty well busted up. From the wounds, the guy was hacking at him, and got him a dozen times on the hands and face and arms before he finally got him one in the throat. So somebody left here banged up and spattered all to hell with blood. It won't be hard, I don't think. Leg work. Hitting all the likely saloons and finding where the trouble was, and who was in it. We'll pretty Taggart up for a picture we can use to show around here and there. Don't expect to see your name in the paper. Or Miss Gardino's. It won't get big coverage. The season is on, you know. Can't upset the sun-loving merrymakers.' We got out of the car. He shook his head and said, 'Some poor son of a bitch is out there tonight burying his clothes, throwing the knife off a bridge, trying to scrub the blood off his car seat, and it won't do him a damn bit of good. By God, nobody can get away with making a pass at *his* girl. She can drive up to Raiford once a month and pay him a nice visit. You can take off, Mr. McGee. If I remember something I should ask you, I'll be in touch.'

He would check me out with care and precision, and Nora too, and when his estimate of the situation did not pay off, he would go over us again.

A single lamp was lighted in Nora's living room. I saw Shaja, still in her blue robe, get up from the chair and come to unlock the door. I followed her into the living-room. 'How is she doing?'

'She fell to sleep, not so long ago.' I noticed that she had brushed her hair, put on her makeup. 'Such a wicked think,' she said. 'My hoosband, yes. One could expect, from a prison sickness. Some kind. Her Sam, no. Please to sit. You drink somesink, maybe?'

'If you've got a beer.'

'Amstel? From Curaçao?'

'Fine.'

She went to the kitchen and brought back one for each of us, in very tall tapered glasses, on a small pewter tray.

'About him returning, she was so excite. So 'appy. It breaks my heart in two.'

'Shaj, I had to tell the police she went there with me.'

'Of course!'

'The way I told it, I made Sam a lot less important to her. I'll tell you exactly what I told them, and you remember it and tell her as soon as she wakes up. A man named Branks will come to see her. She should tell him exactly the same thing. It shouldn't be hard, because most of it is the truth.'

She agreed. I repeated what I had said to Branks. She gave little nods of understanding.

When I had finished she frowned and said, 'Excuse. But what is wrong to tellink this man she was in love with her Sam, all the three years he was gone? Is no crime.'

'There is a reason for it. You see, there is something else too.'

I saw a little flicker of comprehension in her eyes, product of a mind nicely geared to intrigue. 'Somesink she does not know yet?'

'That's right.'

'But you will tell her?'

'When she feels better.'

She was thoughful for long moments. She looked over at me. 'You do not see her often, but you are a good friend, no?'

'I hope so.'

'I am her friend too. She is good to me for a long time now.'

'You're a nice person, Shaj.'

She smiled, perhaps blushed slightly. 'Thank you.'

I leaned back into heavier shadow and sipped the beer. The light came down over her shoulder, backlighting the odd pale hair, shining on the curve of her broad cheek. This one had the same thing Nora had, such a total awareness of herself as a woman. She lifted the glass to her lips, and I saw the silken strength of the pale throat work as she swallowed.

'What did your husband do for a living, Shaja?'

She shrugged. 'A teacher of history. A man not quite as tall as me. A mild man, getting bald on his head in the middle. Just one year married. It was necessary, what he did. But then all of the world turned its back on our land. As you know. That is the shame of the world. Not his shame. Not mine. I came out because I was no use there. Not to help him there.' She put her hand out. 'Good night,' she said. 'Thank you.'

It was the abrupt continental handshake, accompanied by a small bow, an immediate release of the clasp. As I walked to my car I looked back and saw her still standing there in the open door silhouetted against the hallway lights, hips canted in the way a model stands. We both knew of the hidden smouldering awareness. But there would be no breaking of vows, not with that one.

As I drove back to Bahia Mar I wanted to hold fast to all the small speculations about her, the forlorn erotic fancies, because I knew that as she slipped out of my mind, Sam Taggart would take her place.

And he did, before I was home. I found a slot and then I shoved my hands into my pockets and walked across to the public beach. I walked slowly where the outgoing tide had left the sand damp and hard.

Lofty McGee, shoulders hunched against the cold of the small hours, trying to diminish the impact of the death of a friend.

But Sam was still there, in a ghastly dying sprawl on the floor of my mind.

So I had to have a little word or two with the account closers.

That was what I had been trying not to admit to myself.

It wasn't dramatics. It wasn't a juvenile taste for vengeance. It was just a cold, searching, speculative curiosity.

What makes you people think it's that easy?

That was the question I wanted to ask them. I would ask the question even though I already had the answer.

It isn't.

CHAPTER FIVE

AT fifteen-minute intervals I went into the bedroom to look at Nora Gardino.

At ten thirty I heard a sound in there. I went in. She stood by the dressing-table, belting a navy blue robe. I startled her. She stared at me, shaped my name with silent lips, then came on the run for holding and hugging, shuddering and snorting against me, her breath sour.

'It was a dirty dream,' she whispered, and made a gagging sound. 'Just a dirty wretched dream.'

I stroked her back and said, 'He never came back. That's all.'

She pushed herself away. 'You think you can make it that easy?'

'Not really.'

'Don't try then,' she said, and ran into the bathroom and slammed the door. I went back to the kitchen and poured my-

self some more coffee. Nora came in, taking small steps. I got
the orange juice from the refrigerator and handed it to her.

She sat at the table and took several small sips and said,
'I'm pretty flippy today, Trav. Don't listen too hard to anything
I say.'

'Shaj took off at quarter to nine. She said the shop is under
control.'

'Bless her. And you too, my friend.'

She had not put on makeup. Her face had a new dry papery
texture, as though it would crackle to the touch.

I told her about Branks. I gave her the same detailed report
I'd given Shaj.

'Can you handle it?' I asked.

'I guess so. You mean, on the level that he was nothing more
than a friend who's been away. Yes. I can manage. But why?'

'Maybe I don't want him to know that we have a very intense
personal interest in finding out who. . . .'

'Who killed him. Don't hunt for easier words. Use the brutal
ones. Let them sting. Why shouldn't he know we have that
personal interest, Trav?'

'Because we don't want him interfering with any looking
we may want to do. If it is personal. If it is intense, we want a
part of it, don't we?'

She put the empty juice glass down. 'Do you know something
about it?'

'I think so.'

'Did you tell that man?'

'No.'

I cannot describe the look on her face then, a hunting look,
a merciless look, a look of dreadful anticipation. 'I want to keep
it very very personal,' she whispered.

'Then don't give Branks the slightest clue. He's a sharp man.'

'If I thought there was no point to it, if it was just some
murderous animal trying to rob cabins. . . .'

'More than that.'

She locked icy fingers on my wrist. 'Then what? The thing he
had to take care of. What?'

'Later, Nora. It will keep.'

I saw her accept that promise.

I had at least given her a simplification she could live with and,
if the need should arise, die for.

Branks phoned at eleven-fifteen and came by at quarter to
twelve.

She had dressed by then. Her heart said black, but she dressed in pink, a pleated skirt, an angora sweater, a mouth red for polite smiling.

Just a friend, she said. And it seemed like a kick to go visit him at such a crazy hour. But it was the sort of thing he would do. And Beanie had phoned her because she knew Nora used to run around with the guy sometimes. And McGee was an old friend too. It was just for kicks. Welcome home. You know. But, God, who ever thought we'd walk in on any thing like that! Oh, yes, I went all to pieces completely. I never saw anything so horrible in my whole life, never. Maybe I should have stayed there, but I couldn't, really.

Branks thanked her and thanked me again. He said that Beanie had said Taggart was alone when she had seen him, eating at the counter. The owner of the cabins, who ran the gas station also, had seen Taggart drive out about seven and when he had closed at nine, Taggart had not returned.

'We'll find him,' Branks said with absolute confidence. 'You'll see it in the paper one of these days.'

As he drove out, Nora's casual smile crumpled.

'F-Find out about services for him, Trav. All that.'

'Courtesy of the county.'

'No!'

'Honey, just what difference does it make to Sam now?'

She lit a cigarette, her hand shaking. 'I've been tucking money away, for the time when he'd come back. He came back. What do I do with the money? It doesn't mean anything.'

'What do you want to do? Buy a plot? And bronze handles. Hire a hall? For two mourners?'

'I just . . . want it to be nice.'

'All right. We'll do what we can, in a quiet way, like a hundred dollar way. On top of the country procedure, so that if Branks should ever wonder or ask, we took up a collection. Flowers, and a lengthier reading at the graveside, and a small marker.'

I stalled her on the other until after the small ceremony. Six of us there, under the beards of Spanish moss blowing wildly in a crisp wind on a day of cloudless blue. Shaja, Nora and me, a pastor and two shovellers. The wind tore the old words out of his mouth and flung them away, inaudible. The single floral offering bothered me, a huge spray of white roses, virginal, as a bride might carry. We took her home, bleached with grief, moving like an arthritic. She was pounds lighter than on the night we had gone to see him.

Shaj hastened back to the shop. I set out a gigantic slug of brandy for Nora Gardino. Then I told her everything I knew.

Her numbness turned slowly to anger. 'That is all you know? What does that mean? What can we do about that, for God's sake?'

'He wanted me to help him, and then because of you he changed his mind and decided to make a deal with them.'

'But you've let me think it was . . . somebody we could find right here, right now!'

'There's something to go on.'

'But how far?'

'I can tell you one thing. From what we know right now, if we handle ourselves well, if you follow orders, we can get close.'

Her right hand turned into a claw. 'I would like that.'

'Close is all I can promise. Remember this, Nora. Sam was tough and quick and smart. You saw what he got out of it.'

'Don't. But . . . where is the starting point?'

'Finding out just what it was that he thought was his. That's my job. While I'm doing that, you get Shaj set up so she can run the store on her own.'

Professor Warner B. Gifford was a fat, sloppy, untidy young man.

It had taken two hours to thread my way through the labyrinth of exotic specialties and find my way to him.

'A what?' he said. 'A what?'

I found myself raising my voice, enunciating clearly, as through he were deaf. I described the little golden figurine with greatest care, and he looked pained at my layman's language. He brought a big book back, sat down, riffled the pages, turned it to face me and laid a dirty finger against a photographic plate. 'Like this, possibly?'

'Very much like that, Professor.'

He went into a discourse, pitched in a penetrating monotone, and it took me a long awed time to realize that he was still speaking English.

I stopped him and said, 'I don't understand any of that.'

He looked pained and decided he had to speak to me in Pidgin English. We both needed a course in Communications. With each other.

'Eight hundred years old. Um? Fired clay. National Museum

in Mexico City. Gold is rare. Um? Spaniards cleaned it out, melted it into ingots, shipped it to Spain. Indian cultures moving, changing. Some used gold. Ceremonial. Open veins in mountains. Um? Low melting point. Easily worked. No damn good for tools. Pretty colour. Masks, et cetera. Then conflict of cultures. Changed the meaning of gold. Cleaned them out, hunted it down. Torture, et cetera. Gold and silver. Um?'

'Then there isn't much left?'

'Museums. Late finds. Overlooked. Uh . . . less archæological significance than one would think. Have the forms in clay, carvings, bone, et cetera. Duplication. Um?'

'But a museum would be interested in the thing I described?'

'Of course. Highly. Not scholarship. Museum traffic. Publicity.'

'What about a collection of twenty-eight little statuettes like that, some bigger and some smaller, all gold, and from different places? Aztec, Inca, some East Indian.'

He shrugged. 'Ancient man made little ceremonial figures. Handy materials. Ivory, bone, wood, stone, clay, gold, silver, iron, lead. Gods, spirits, demons, fetishes, from very crude to very elegant. Merely being of gold, it would not be a museum collection. A museum could assemble perhaps such a showing from other specific collections. Egypt. China. Not very professional.'

'Then such a collection would be a private collection?'

'Possibly. They should will collections to museums. Let the professionals sort them out.'

'But such a collection would be valuable?'

'In money? Um? Oh yes.'

'Who would know if such a collection exists, Professor?'

Again he went searching among the chaotic debris. He dug into a low cupboard. He took out correspondence files, put them back. Finally he extracted a letter from a folder, tore the letterhead from it and put it back. He brought me the letterhead. Borlika Galleries, 511 Madison Avenue, New York.

'They might know,' he said. 'Supply collectors. Hunt all over the world. They might know. Business on an international scale.'

He was bent to his lonely work again before I had reached the door of his office.

Miss Agnes seemed glad to take me away from there, and we were soon whispering toward home, through a hundred miles of cold February night.

CHAPTER SIX

GRIEF is a strange tempest. Nora Gardino, her strong and handsome face becoming mask-like, bobbed about in her own storm tides, supporting herself with whatever came to hand.

Shaja and I were partners in the cooperative venture of keeping her calm.

On the morning I was to fly up to New York, she drove me down to Miami International in her little black Sunbeam. We had time to spare, so we went to the restaurant atop the Airport Hotel.

'I shouldn't be so impatient,' she said. 'But it just. . . .'

'This will keep, Nora. It's a case of whether you want an emotional release, or whether you really want to accomplish something.'

'I want to. . . .'

'Okay. We do this my way. I had to learn the hard way. I had to learn patience and care.'

They announced my flight. She went down with me. At the gate she gave me a sister's kiss, her dark eyes huge in her narrow face, eroded by loss. 'As long as you're not just kidding me along, as long as we really will do something, okay then, Trav. We'll do it your way.'

New York, on the first day of March, was afflicted by a condition a girl I once knew called Smodge. This is a combination of rain, snow, soot, dirt, and wind.

At two forty-five I ducked out of the sleety wind into the narrow entrance to the Borlika Galleries.

I pushed the door open and went in, wondering if I was dressed for the impression I wanted to make.

A cluster of bells jangled as I pushed the door open.

A young man came toward me up the aisle from the back, with bone-pale face and funeral suit. It was a hushed place and he spoke in a hushed voice.

'May I help you?' He had taken me in at a glance, and he spoke with precisely the intonation which fitted my appearance, a slight overtone of patronizing impatience.

'I don't know. I guess you sell all kinds of old stuff.'

'We have many types of items, sir.' He said the sir as though it hurt his dear little mouth. 'We specialize in items of anthropological and archæological significance.'

'How about old gold?'

He frowned. He was pained. 'Do you refer to old coins, sir?'

'No. What I'm interested in is old statues made of gold. Real old. Like so high. You know. Old gods and devils and stuff like that.'

It stopped him for a long moment. Finally he gave a little shrug. It was a long slow afternoon. 'This way, please.'

He had me wait at a display counter in the rear while he went back into the private rooms behind the store. It took him five minutes. I guessed he had to open a safe or have someone open it. He turned on a pair of bright little lamps, spread a piece of blue velvet, tenderly unwrapped an object and placed it on the blue velvet. It was a golden toad, a nasty looking thing the size of my fist. It had ruby eyes, a rhino horn on its head, and a body worked of overlapping scales like a fish.

'This is the only object we have on hand at the moment, sir. It is completely documented and authenticated. Javanese Empire, close to two thousand years old.'

It had a look of ancient, sardonic evil. Man dies and gold endures, and the reptiles will inherit the earth.

'What do you get for a thing like this?'

He put it back in its wrappings and as he began to fold the cloth around it, he said, 'Nine thousand dollars, sir.'

'Did you hear me say I didn't want it, Charlie?'

He gave me a baleful glance, a murmured apology, and uncovered it again. 'Lovely craftsmanship,' he said. 'Perfectly lovely.'

'How did you people get it?'

'I couldn't really say, sir. We get things from a wide variety of sources. The eyes are rubies. Badly cut and quite flawed, of course.'

'What would you people pay for a frog like this?'

'That wouldn't bear any relationship to its value, sir.'

'Well, put it this way, Charlie. Supposed I walked in off the street with this frog. Would I be one of those sources you said you use?'

It put the right little flicker of interest and reappraisal in his indoor eyes. 'I don't quite understand, sir.'

'Try it this way, then. It's gold. Right? Suppose somebody didn't want to get involved in a lot of crap, Charlie. Like bills of sale and so on. If he wants to make a cash deal, the easiest thing is to melt old frog down.'

'Heavens!' he said, registering shock.

'But maybe that way he cheats himself a little.'

'A great deal! This is an historical object, sir. An art object!'

'But if the guy doesn't want any fuss, Charlie?'

His eyes shifted uneasily. 'I suppose that if . . . this is just hypothetical, you understand . . . if someone wished to quietly dispose of something on a cash basis . . . and it wasn't a well-known piece . . . from a museum collection, for example, something might be worked out. But I. . . .'

'But you just work here, Charlie. Right?'

He touched the toad. 'Do you care to purchase this?'

'Not today.'

'Would you wait here, please?'

He wrapped it up and took it away. I had a five minute wait. I wondered what they did for customers. A little old man came shuffling out. He had white hair, a nicotined moustache, a tough little face. I don't think he weighed a hundred pounds. In a deep bass voice he said his name was Borlika.

He peered up at me, his head tilted to the side, and said, 'We are not receivers of stolen goods, mister.'

'Unless you're damn well sure they'll never be traced, old man.'

'Get out!' he bellowed, pointing toward the front door. We both knew it was an act.

I put my hand on my heart. 'Old man, I'm an art lover. It'll hurt me here to melt all the beautiful old crap down.'

He motioned me closer, leaned on the counter and said, 'All?'

'Twenty-eight pieces, old man.'

He leaned on the counter with both arms and kept his eyes closed for so long I began to wonder if he'd fallen asleep. At last he looked at me and blinked as the gold toad would blink if it could and said, 'My granddaughter is in Philadelphia today, doing an appraisal. In this area, you will talk to her. Can she see the pieces?'

'That can be arranged later. After we talk.'

'Can you describe one piece to me?'

I gave him a crude but accurate description of the sensual little man. His eyes glittered like the toad's.

'Where can she find you this evening, mister?'

'I can phone her and arrange that.'

'You are a very careful man.'

'When I have something worth being careful about, old man.'

He wrote the phone number on a scrap of paper, told me her name was Mrs. Anton Borlika, and told me to phone after eight o'clock. When I got back to the hotel I checked the book. The listing was under her name, an address on East 68th which would place it close to Third Avenue. With time to kill, I got a cab and kept it while I made a tour of inspection of the neighbourhood. It was a poodle-walking area. At about five o'clock I found a suitable place about two blocks from her apartment.

Her voice on the phone, flat as only Boston can make it, had not prepared me for the woman. She was in her late twenties, black Irish, with blue eyes and milky skin, slightly overweight, dressed in a conservative suit, a big grey corduroy rain cape, droplets of the night moisture caught in her blue-black hair. As she walked along the alcove toward the booth I stood up and said, 'Mrs. Borlika?'

'That's right,' she said, slipping the cape off. I hung it up. 'You made yourself easy to find, Mister. . . .'

'Taggart. Sam Taggart.' I watched for reaction and saw none.

She smiled and smoothed her suit skirt with the backs of her hands and slid into the booth. 'Betty Borlika,' she said. 'Have you eaten? I had a nasty sandwich on the train.'

'Drink first?'

'Of course.' The waiter appeared, took our drink order and hastened away.

With all her friendly casualness, I knew I was getting a thorough inspection. I returned the favour. No rings on the ring finger. Plump hands. Nails bitten down. Plump little double chin. Small mouth, slightly petulant.

'Your husband do the same kind of work?'

'He used to. Before he died.'

'Recently?'

'Three years ago. His father and his uncle are active in the business. And his grandfather, of course. His father and his uncle are abroad at this time.'

'Or I'd be talking to them?'

'Probably.'

'I like it this way better.'

'You won't get a better deal from me than you would from them.'

'If we deal.'

'Is there any question of that, Sam?'

'There's a lot of questions, Betty. Right now there's two real good gold markets. Argentina and India. And safer for me that way.'

'Safer than what?'

'Than making any kind of deal with something . . . not melted down.'

She scowled. 'God, don't even *say* that.'

'This stuff isn't hot in the ordinary sense. But, there could be some questions. Not from the law. Do you understand?'

'Possibly.'

'Another drink?'

'Please.'

When the waiter was gone, she said, 'Please believe me when I say we are used to negotiating on a very confidential basis. Sometimes, when it's necessary, we can invent a more plausible basis of acquisition than . . . the way something came into our hands.' She smiled broadly, and it was a wicked and intimate smile. 'After all, I'm not going to make you tell me where you got them, Sam.'

'Don't expect to buy them cheap, Betty.'

'I would expect to pay a bonus over the actual gold value, of course. But you must consider this, too. We're one of the few houses in a position to take the whole thing off your hands. It simplifies things for you.'

'The whole thing?'

'The . . . group of art objects. Did you say twenty-eight?'

'I said twenty-eight. Twenty-eight times the price of that frog would be. . . .'

'Absurd.'

'Not when you sell them.'

'Only when you sell them to us, Sam.'

In spite of all the feminine flavour, this was a very darned cool broad.

'If I sell them to you.'

She laughed. 'If we want to buy what you have, dear. After all, we can't buy things unless we have some reasonable chance of selling them, can we?'

'These things look all right to me.'

'And you are an expert, of course.' She opened her big purse and took out a thick brown envelope. She held it in her lap where I could not see it. She frowned down as she sorted and adjusted whatever she took out of the envelope.

Finally she smiled across at me. 'Now we will play a little game, Sam. We take a photograph for a record of everything of significant value which goes through our hands. These photographs are from our files. There are fifty-one of them. So that we will know what we are talking about, I want you to go through these and select any that are among the twenty-eight you have.'

'I haven't looked at them too close, Betty.'

She handed the thick stack across to me. 'Just do your best.' They were five by seven photographs in black and white and double weight paper, with a semi-gloss finish, splendidly sharp and clear, perfectly lighted. In each picture there was a ruler included to show scale, and, on the other side of the figurine, a little card which gave a complex series of code or stock or value numbers, or some combination thereof. I made my face absolutely blank, knowing she was watching me, and went through them one at a time. I felt trapped. I needed some kind of opening. Somewhere in the middle I came across the same little man I had seen, squatting on his crude lumpy haunches, staring out of the blank eye holes. I did not hesitate at him. I began to pay less attention to the figures, and more to the little cards. I noticed then that, written in ink, on most of them, were tiny initials in the bottom right hand corner of the little code card. I leafed back to my little man and saw that the initials in the corner were CMC. I started through the stack again, looking for the same initials, and saw that they appeared on five of the photographs. The figurines were strange—some beautiful, some twisted and evil, some crude and innocent, some earthily, shockingly explicit.

I looked at her and said, 'I just don't know. I just can't be sure.'

'Try. Please.'

I went through the stack and began putting some of them on the table top, face down. You have to gamble. I put nine photographs face down. I laid the stack aside. I looked at the nine again, sighed and returned one of them to the stack.

I handed her the eight of them and said, 'I'm pretty sure of some of these. And not so sure of others.'

I tried to read her face as she looked at them. The small mouth was curved in a small secretive smile. She had to show off. She handed me back three photographs. 'These are the ones you're not so sure of, Sam?'

I registered astonishment. 'Yes! How could you know that?'

'Never mind,' she said, and slid all the photographs back into the envelope and returned it to her purse. 'One more drink and let's order, shall we?'

'Good idea.'

'Mr. Taggart, your credentials are in order. But I didn't know he would have so many.'

'Who would have so many?'

'Oh, *come* now!' she said. 'Couldn't we stop playing games

now? He bought from us. Of course, he would have other sources, in the position he was in.'

'Put it this way, Betty. There was another party in the middle.'

'You aren't acting as his agent, are you?'

'Why do you ask a thing like that?'

'I don't think you are completely the rude type you pretend to be, Sam. I can understand how, in the present circumstances, he might want to sell out through a clever agent. If you could prove you're his agent, we might see our way to being a little more liberal. After all, he was a good customer, long ago.'

'If I knew his name, I'd try to convince you I was working for him.'

'Politics creates a lot of confusion, doesn't it?'

'I don't even know what you mean by that.'

'Then you are quite an innocent in this whole thing, and I shan't try to confuse you, Sam. Let me just say that I am personally convinced that the twenty-eight items are legitimate, and we would like to purchase them.'

'For how much?'

'One hundred thousand dollars, Sam.'

'So I melt them, Betty. Maybe I can get that for the gold alone. Maybe more. I'm talking about a hundred and forty pounds of gold.'

'A lot of trouble, isn't it, finding a safe place to melt them down, then smuggling the gold out, finding a buyer, trying to get your money without getting hit on the head?'

'I've had little problems like that before.'

'This would be cash, Sam. In small bills, if you'd like. No records of the transaction. We'll cover it on our books with a fake transaction with a foreign dealer. It would just be a case of meeting on neutral ground to trade money for the Mente . . . the collection, with a chance for both parties to examine what they are getting.'

'What did you start to say?'

'Nothing of importance. You're very quick, aren't you?'

'Money quickens me, Betty.'

'I too have a certain fondness for it. That's why I don't part with it readily.'

'You won't have to part with a single dime of that hundred thousand.'

'What would I have to part with?'

'Let's say twice that.'

'Oh, my God! You *are* dreaming.'

'So are you, lady.'

'I'll tell you what. If the other pieces are as good as the five we know, I will go up to one twenty-five, absolute tops.'

'The other pieces are better, and one seventy-five is absolute bottom. Take it or leave it.'

We ordered. We haggled all the way through the late dinner. She was good at the game. Over plain coffee for me, coffee and gooey dessert for Betty Borlika, we worked our way down to a five thousand dollar difference, and then split that down the middle, for an agreed price of a hundred and thirty-seven thousand, five hundred dollars. We shook hands.

'Even if you were his agent, I couldn't give you a penny more.'

'You'll get a quarter of a million when you sell them.'

'We might. Over a period of years. There isn't an active market in this sort of thing, Sam. You saw the jewelled toad. We've had that for over four months. We have considerable overheads you know. Rent, salaries, money tied up in inventory.'

'You'll have me crying any moment.'

'Don't cry. You drove a very good bargain. How would you like the money?'

'Used money. Fifties and smaller.'

'It will take several days to accumulate it, Sam.'

'I haven't exactly got the little golden people stashed in a coin locker.'

'Of course not. From my estimate of you, they are probably in a very safe place. How long will it take you to bring them here?'

'You just get the cash and hang onto it and I'll phone you when I get back to town. How will we make the transfer?'

'Do you trust me, Sam?' I could not get used to being called that. I kept seeing those pink teeth.

I returned her smile. 'I don't trust anybody. It's sort of a religion.'

'We're members of the same sect, dear. And that gives us a problem, doesn't it? Any suggestions?'

'A very public place. How about a bank? Borrow a private room. They have them. Then nobody can get rough or tricky.'

'You are a very clever man, Mr. Taggart. Now we can forget it all until I hear from you again. And could you order us a brandy? The deal is made. From now on it's social.'

'Social,' I agreed. Her eyes were softer, and her smile a little wider.

'You are a very competent ruffian, Sam. You give me problems. Did you know that?'

For the first time I could see that the drinks were working on her. 'Not intentionally.'

I had seen the same thing happen with businessmen. The deal in process would sustain them, keep them alert and organized and watchful, and when it was settled, they would turn into softer more vulnerable mechanisms.

I paid the check and helped her into her cape. The place was nearly empty.

We went out. It was well below freezing, and the sky had cleared, the high stars weak against the city glow. The sidewalks were dry. We walked to her place, her tall heels tocking, her arm hooked firmly around mine.

'You don't say anything about yourself, Sam.'

'Nothing much to say. I keep moving. I hustle a little of this and a little of that. I avoid agitation.'

'When this is over, what will you do?'

'Bahamas, maybe. Lease a little ketch, ram around, fish, play with the play people. Drink black Haitian rum. Snorkel around the coral heads and watch the pretty fish.'

'God! Can I sign on?'

'As cabin boy. Sure.'

We arrived at her place. Three stone steps up to the street door. 'Nightcap time?' she said as she got her key out.

'If it doesn't have to be brandy.'

'Right. The hell with brandy.'

Her apartment was big. She bustled about, turning on strategic lighting, tossing her cape aside. She opened a small lacquered bar and made us two tall highballs.

Then she said, 'I do have one little collection of eighteenth century art. Come along.' With a brassy and forlorn confidence she marched me into her bedroom.

'Very nice,' I said.

'Look at them closely, dear,' she said, with a mocking smile.

I did so, and suddenly realized that they were not what they appeared to be, not innocent little scenes of life in the king's court. They were not pornographic. They were merely exquisitely, decadently sensual.

'I'll be damned!' I said, and she gave a husky laugh of delight. She moved closer and pointed to one. 'This is my favourite. Will you just look at the fatuous expression on that sly devil's face.'

'And she looks so completely innocent.'

'Of course,' she said. Her smile faded as she looked at me. She turned and with exaggerated care placed her empty glass on a small ornate table with a white marble top. It made a small audible click as she set it down. She turned back with her eyes almost closed and groped her way into my arms, whispering, in a private argument with herself, 'I'm not *like* this. I'm really not *like* this.'

The physical act, when undertaken for any motive other than love and need, is a fragmenting experience. The spirit wanders. There is a mild feeling of distaste for one's self. She was certainly sufficiently attractive, mature, totally eager, but we were still strangers. She wanted to use me as a weapon against her own lonely demons. I wanted information from her. We were more adversaries than lovers.

'This is the last thing I expected to happen,' she said, with a luxurious stretching. 'You're very sweet.'

'Sure.'

She took my wrist, guided my cigarette to her lips. When she exhaled she said, 'Did you expect it to happen?'

'Let's put it this way. I hoped it would. Life is full of coincidences, Betty. Some of them are nasty. Some of them are fine. I guess they're supposed to balance out sometime. I suppose, in a sense, that guy brought us together.'

'Who, darling?'

'The guy who collected the little gold people.'

'Oh,' she said in a sleepy voice. 'Carlos Menterez y Cruzada.'

'Who's he?'

I made it a bored question, as indifferent as her response had been.

'Sort of a bastard, dear. A Cuban bastard. Very close to Batista. A collector. Those five you picked out, he bought them from us. She yawned, snuggled more comfortably against me and gave a little snorting sound of derision and said, 'He collected me, too. In a sort of offhand way. I guess women were a lot more abundant than gold for Senor Menterez. I hated him a while. I don't any more.'

'How did it happen?'

'Because I was a stupid young girl and he was a very knowing man.'

'How old was he then?'

'Mmm. Eight years ago. Early forties. Twenty years older than I was.'

'Nice looking man?'

'No. Not very tall. Sort of portly, even. Thin little moustache and going bald. Very nice eyes. Long lashes. Beautiful suits and shirts, and beautiful grooming. Manicures and facials and cologne and massages. A car and driver picked me up after work the next day too. He was in New York on business with several other Cuban businessmen, but he had the suite to himself.

'What kind of business was he in in Cuba?'

She yawned. 'I don't know. Lots of things. After the roof fell in on all those people down there, I used to wonder what happened to the Menterez collection. I suppose he got out with it. And whatever else he could carry. I wondered if we would ever hear. Or if he would show up to peddle it all back to us. But somebody got it away from him, and you got it away from somebody else?'

'Something like that.'

'It doesn't matter does it, darling? Whether he's alive or dead. I'm so deliciously sleepy, dear. Let's sleep for a little while.'

Something awakened me, perhaps the little tilt of the bed as she left it. I turned over, feigning sleep, and through slitted lids saw her, nude-white in the small amber of the night light, staring back at me, her body slightly crouched, the dark hair tangled across her pale forehead. After I took several deep breaths, she went plodding silently over to the chair where I had tossed my clothing. Though I could not see her clearly, I knew she was going through the pockets. She would find cigarettes, lighter, change and a thin packet of bills. All identification was back in the bureau drawer of my locked room in the Wharton. When she was through, she came stealthily back to bed, lay silently beside me for perhaps ten minutes, and then set about gently awakening me. When she dropped off into sleep again, I could sense that it was a very deep sleep. I tested it by shaking her, speaking her name. She made querulous little sounds that faded into a small buzzing snore. Ten minutes later I flagged down a hurrying cab on Third Avenue, in the first grey of a tomcat dawn. At the Wharton, I got my key at the desk and went up and took a shower.

After the shower, I sat on the bed and went through the envelope of photographs I had taken from her purse as I left her apartment. I took out the five pictures of the statues which had definitely belonged to Carlos Menterez y Cruzada and stowed them in my suitcase. I printed her name and address on the outside of the envelope in square block letters. It is an old caution, and the only way any person can completely disguise their own handwriting. Merely hold the pencil as straight up and down as possible, use all capitals, and base them all on a square format, so that the O for example, becomes a square, and an A is a square with the base line missing and a line bisecting it horizontally. No handwriting expert can ever make a positive identification of printing done in that manner, because it bears no relation to your normal handwriting. After I awoke, I would get it sealed downstairs, buy the stamps and mail it.

I slid between the hotel sheets and turned out the bed lamp. There was a brighter morning grey at the windows. I tried to sort out the facts I had learned. Facts kept getting entangled with textural memories of the woman, so gaspingly ardent. The facts and the woman followed me down into sleep, where the little gold figures came alive and one of them, an East Indian one, a woman with six graceful arms, made tiny little cries and fastened herself to my leg like a huge spider, bared little golden teeth and sank them into the vein while I tried to kick her away.

CHAPTER SEVEN

I CAUGHT an early afternoon flight out of Kennedy, after phoning Nora from the terminal. She was waiting at the gate.

'You look better,' I told her.

'It was a lovely afternoon, and I spent it in the side garden, soaking up the sun. You didn't find out anything, did you?'

'A little bit.'

'Really? What?' The sudden intensity gave her that hawk look, the dark eyes very fierce, the lips thinner, the nose predatory.

I drove out of the lot. When I was clear of the airport area, I said, 'A rich Cuban, a buddy of Batista's, collected the figurines. He bought five of them from the Borlika Galleries. By the best luck you can imagine, one of the five he bought was the one Sam showed me. That gave me the break, and I did a little gambling, and it opened up very nicely. Carlos Menterez y Cruzada. Businessman, age about fifty now if still living.'

'They told you all that? Why?'

'They got the impression I have the collection. Twenty-eight pieces. They don't care how I got them. We agreed on a price. A hundred and thirty-seven thousand, five hundred. Cash. A very quiet deal.'

'Sam thought they were worth more.'

'They are, if you can sell them in the open. They're worth less on a back street. Anything is. I don't think Sam's title was exactly airtight.'

'Did Sam steal them from Carlos Whosis?'

'That wasn't quite Sam's style.'

'I wouldn't think so. Then how?'

'However he got them, Nora, it attracted the wrong kind of attention.'

'All right. So you know who used to own them, you think. Does that really mean very much?'

'When we get to the boat I'll show you something.'

I fixed her a drink and left her in the lounge. I took my bag into the master stateroom, changed quickly to slacks and a sports shirt, and took the pictures out and handed them to her. 'The one on top is the one Sam showed me. The other four are from the Menterez collection.'

She looked at them very carefully, lips compressed, frown lines between her heavy dark brows. She looked up at me. 'They're strange and terrible little things, aren't they?'

'I keep wondering how many people have got killed over them. I saw a golden toad with ruby eyes in New York, two thousand years old. He looked as if he couldn't count the men he'd watched die.'

She rapped the sheaf of cards against her knuckles. 'This is something definite. This is real, Trav. I . . . don't know much about all the conjecture and analysis and so on. But something I can hold and touch. . . .'

I took them away from her and took them forward and put them in my safe. Any fifty-four foot boat has innumerable hiding places, and a houseboat has more than a cruiser. Once I turned a very accomplished thief loose aboard *The Busted Flush*. I gave him four hours to find my safe. He was a friend. I watched him work. He was very very good. When his time was up, he hadn't even come close.

'What will you do with the pictures?' Nora asked when I returned to the lounge.

'I don't know. They're bluff cards. And they'll come as a great shock to somebody.'

'What do we do next?'

'Find out a little bit more about Menterez.'

That evening, in Miami, it took me well over an hour to

locate my friend, Raoul Tenero. He is nearly thirty and looks forty. He was just beginning his career as an architect in Havana when Castro took over. I met him at some parties in Havana pre-Castro. When he got out of Cuba, he looked me up. I introduced him to some people. He worked for a time, and then went back in and was captured at the Bay of Pigs. He was finally exchanged with the others. His pretty wife, Nita, had a vague idea of his schedule. I finally caught up with him in a youth centre building, part of the park system.

I spotted him on the far side of the room in a small group of about nine men, chairs pulled into a circle. Raoul has the true Spanish look, the long chalky face, deep-set eyes, hollow cheeks, and elegant way of handling his body when he moves. He saw me and held his hand up, thumb and first finger a half inch apart in the universal Latin gesture of indicating just a little bit more time. Six or seven groups were in discussion. Some of them were very loud. I moved out into the night and leaned against the building and smoked a cigarette and watched the asphalt hiss of night traffic. In about ten minutes he came out.

'You all sewed up?' I asked him.

'No, I'm through in there.'

'I need some information and a drink.'

'I'll watch you drink, Senor. While I have milk.'

'Still messed up?'

He gave a mirthless laugh. 'I gave my stomach for my country. How'd you find me? You see Nita?'

'She looks wonderful.'

'How about her English? She's working hard.'

'It's flawless.'

'Oh boy. Hey, you follow me, okay?'

I followed his decrepit old Chev to a side street bar. The clientele was a hundred per cent Cuban. He was known there. I went to a table in a far corner. He had to stop and talk to half a dozen people. Finally he came to the table, a glass of milk in one hand, dark rum on the rocks in the other.'

'How's the work going, Raoul?'

He shrugged. 'They trust me more now. What's on your mind?'

'I want to know something about a man. Carlos Menterez y Cruzada.'

Raoul stared at me. '*Hijo de. . . .* A long time since I heard that name. A son of a bitch, Travis. A murderous crafty son of a bitch. He is remembered. How long would he last in Miami? With luck, twelve minutes. Where is he?'

'I don't know. If I can find out more about him, maybe I can find him.'

He leaned back. 'I will tell you about that one. You have to understand how it was under Batista. You people here have never understood. He was, for my father, for other successful men in Cuba, a fact of life. They all knew him. They walked on eggs. Very important, Menterez. Import, export, warehousing, shipping. Big home, big grounds. His speciality, my friend, was catching some man in a political indiscretion. Then he would say that only Carlos Menterez could give protection. Sell me just fifteen per cent of your business for so many thousand pesos. Cheap. Then somehow would come litigation in corrupt courts, and finally Menterez and his cronies would own the entire business, with a suitable dummy ownership to cover the men in the government who had to have their share, of course. If a protest was too strenuous, the man might disappear. He was a barracuda, Travis. One little whiff of blood, and he would find a big meal. All honest men were afraid of him. He broke hearts and lives. No, he would not live long in this city. He got out in time, of course. But where did he go? I heard one rumour he is in Switzerland, another that he is in Portugal.'

'What about his personal life?'

He had a wife, no children. A small silent woman, cowed by him I think. He was a womanizer. Always several mistresses in Havana. Many times they were foolish American girls he would keep there for a time. Big cars. A personal bodyguard. Another house at Varadero. A big cruiser. Also, a personal taste for gold. Gold fittings in cars and home and boats, gold accessories for himself and his women, art objects of gold. A vulgar man, my friend. A dangerous and vulgar man, a kind we breed too often in Latin America.'

'Not just there. Everywhere.'

'But old Cuba was a place where such an animal can thrive. If you find him, Travis, promise you will tell me where he is. It would not be the same name, of course.'

'If I find him alive, I'll get word to you Raoul. But my hunch is that he is dead.'

'Why do you think that?'

'Some day when there is some kind of an end to the story, *amigo*, some day when your stomach can take the booze, we will sit around and get stoned and I will tell you all of it.'

He nodded, accepting that.

'Excuse me then. Come to our house soon, Travis. Nita will

use the long words. She is in a strange limbo now, where neither Cubans nor Yankees can understand her. But she has become quite a good cook.'

By the time I reached the door, I looked back and saw Raoul hunched in fierce argument with men who all seemed to be speaking at once, in fierce low tones.

I drove north at a sedate pace, measuring the new reality of Carlos Menterez y Cruzada, collector of gold, of women, and of many kinds of pills. I went back to Bahia Mar.

Ken Branks, in yellow knit shirt, shapeless felt hat and race-track tweeds, sat in my lounge and took cautious sips from the steaming mug of coffee and made small talk and watched me with clever eyes in a supremely ordinary face. Finally he said, 'You've been questioned a few times, McGee. Here and in Miami.'

'I haven't been charged with anything.'

'I know. But you seem to get a piece of the action on little things here and there. It interests me.'

'Why?'

'Sam Taggart's death interests me too. It didn't check out the way I thought it would. We worked all the bars and came up with nothing. You know, I thought it was an amateur hacking, some guy working blind in the dark, drunk maybe chopping at him, finally getting him.'

'Wasn't it like that?'

'I thought maybe the murder weapon could have been ditched behind those cabins, somewhere in all those junked automobiles, so I had a couple people check it over. They found it. A brand new dollar-nineteen carving knife. Fifty supermarkets in the area carry that brand. There was some other stuff with it. One brand new cheap plastic raincoat, extra large. One brand new pair of rubber gloves. One set of those pliofilm things that fit over shoes. The stuff was bundled up, shoved into a car trunk, one with a sprung lid. Except for the blood, which is a match for Taggart's, the lab can't get a thing off that stuff. What does that all mean to you?'

'Somebody expected to get bloody.'

'Somebody didn't like Taggart. They wanted it to last. They were good with a knife and they made it last. They wanted him to know he was getting it. Look at it that way, and study the wounds, and it was a professional job. Somebody played with him, and then finished him off. We traced Taggart's car. It was bought for cash off a San Diego lot nearly two weeks ago.'

'What do you want to ask me?'

'Who could take that much of a dislike to him?'

'He's been gone three years. He never wrote.'

Branks scowled at his coffee. 'You saw him that afternoon. You'd take an extra large size. Maybe he came back to find out if you were still sore at him. Maybe you got back to your boat minutes before Nora Gardino arrived there.'

'If you could sell yourself that idea, you wouldn't be trying it on me.'

His smile was wry. 'You're so right. We're understaffed, McGee. We haven't got time to futz around with something that gets too cute.'

'A man would get an extra large size to cover more of himself.'

'Sure. I don't want pressure. I don't want newspapers howling about a mystery slaying. So I'm trying to keep it on the basis of a brawl, a vagrant, a dirty little unimportant killing. No release on the blood-proof clothing. I've asked California if they've got anything at all. I've checked him out three years ago here, and I don't find anything special. He had a job. He worked at it. He took off. What did the two of you talk about that day?'

'People we'd both known, where are they, how are they. Do you remember this and that. He said he was back for good, and he borrowed forty dollars.'

'He was right about that. He's back for good. A man doesn't get burned that black in any kind of job except on boats.'

'I got the idea that's what he'd been doing.'

'Out of California?'

'Or Mexico. I told you before he said he'd spent some time in Mexico.'

'You take a man on boats, and an international border, and you can come up with reasons for somebody getting killed. Smuggling. Maybe he was a courier, and he kept the merchandise and ran with it.'

'He had to borrow forty dollars.'

'Maybe he had something he could change into money. And somebody came after him and took it back. Maybe he tried to make a deal.'

'Aren't you reaching pretty far?'

'Sure. Maybe there were two of them, and he didn't say anything to you about the other party. Maybe they couldn't agree on how to split it up. Maybe it was woman trouble, and the husband followed him. I can reach in a lot of directions, McGee. It doesn't cost anything. It's just that something like that, a man carefully dressing up to do bloody work, it bothers me. If he took that much care, he took a lot of other kinds of care too. I don't think my chances of unravelling it from here are very good. I can't believe anybody was waiting here three years to do that to him. They came with him or followed him, or agreed to meet him here. That's what my instinct says.'

'I'd have to agree.'

He was noodling. Good cops have that trait, and talent. The best solution is to give them a little bit, particularly when you suspect they might already have it.

'I may have misled you about one thing, but I don't think it's too pertinent,' I said.

'Did you now?'

'Maybe I understated the relationship between Nora Gardino and Taggart. I told you she was fond of him. I guess it was a little more than that. And I guess Sam had some business he wanted to take care of before he saw her again, because he told me to tell her he wasn't going to be in town until the next day, Saturday. I guess you could say they were in love with each other.'

'And he went away for three years? Were they in touch?'

'No. It was a misunderstanding.'

'So if this was a lover's reunion, what the hell were you doing there, McGee?'

'She didn't know where he was staying.'

'So what made her think you'd know?'

'Well . . . I'd told her he was due back in town.'

'Now how would you have known that?'

'He phoned me Thursday from Waycross, Georgia, to ask me if she was so sore at him she never wanted to see him again. I said no.'

'Couldn't he wait to get here to find out?'

'Maybe he wasn't even going to come here if I told him she was too angry, or married, or moved away.'

'Okay, so why didn't you just tell her where she could find him?'

'Sam wasn't in very good shape, and that was a crummy place he was staying. And I didn't want him to think I'd tipped her off that he'd come in Friday instead of Saturday. I thought it would give him a chance to pull himself together, and go out to the car. It wasn't much of a setting for a reunion, you see."

'I can buy that. It ties up a few loose ends, McGee. Like the way she damned near passed out on Thursday night out at the Mile O'Beach.'

'That's when I told her he was coming back. Did you think that's when I told her somebody was going to kill him?'

'The thought passed through my mind. I even wondered if last night in Miami you were trying to find the Cuban who did it.'

'You're pretty good.'

'I wondered if you went to New York to find out which Cuban to look for.'

'You make me very happy I levelled with you.'

'Did you?'

'And I intend to keep right on levelling with you. Nora is still pretty shaky about this whole thing. We're old friends. She has a gal who can run the store. I think it would do her good to get her away from here for a while.'

He thought that over. 'Mexico?'

'It might be a nice change at that.'

'You are a brassy bastard, McGee. Don't push it too hard.'

'Listen to me. I did not kill him. Nora did not kill him. Neither she nor I have any idea who did kill him. We would both like to know. You have a limited budget and you have a limited jurisdiction. And a lot of curiosity. And some anger about the way it was done. We're angry too. What do you know that could be any help to us? I trade that for my confidential report to you about how it all comes out. If you don't want to play, you won't get a chance to listen.'

'My God, you *are* a brassy bastard! If there's anything that turns my stomach, friend, it is the amateur avenger sticking his civilian nose into a rough situation, muddying everything up.'

'I've seen it rough here and there, around and about.'

He thought it over. He leaned back and looked at the lounge, tilted his balding head and gave me an oblique glance. 'Just what is it you do?'

'I do favours for friends.'

'Did Taggart want you to do him a favour?'

That damned instinct of his. 'I don't know. Either he didn't get around to bringing it up, or he changed his mind.'

'Nobody gives me the same story on you, McGee.'

'I never exert myself unless I have to. A genuinely lazy man is always misunderstood.'

'I even heard that you won this barge in a crap game.'

'A poker game.'

He waited, and then gave a long sigh. 'All right. Except for this little morsel, I would have taken you in, just for luck. I don't think it's going to do me much good to sit on it. A bartender made him from the picture. A highway bar a half mile south of here. He came in about quarter of nine. He made a call from the pay booth. He sat at the bar and nursed beers. At maybe quarter after he got a call on that phone. He seemed jittery. A half hour later a well dressed man arrived, carrying a briefcase. Dark, medium height, maybe about thirty. They seemed to know each other. They went back to a booth. They had a long discussion. They left together, somewhere around eleven. This was a handy bartender. Observant. The well-dressed type did not drink. He kept his hat on. Dark suit, white shirt, dark tie. The bartender said they seemed to be dickering over something, making some kind of a deal, and they didn't seem very friendly about it.'

'It isn't very much.'

'It's something, but not very much. It's enough to take pressure off you. He called somewhere and left a number. Briefcase phoned him back and he told him where to come. When Taggart thought he had the deal made, he took Briefcase back to the cabin. Assume Taggart was selling something. Two cars. Briefcase followed him. They make the deal. Briefcase leaves. He goes down the side road, parks by the car dump, puts on his blood suit, takes the knife and comes back, having cased the cabin. Maybe his orders were to make the deal, but rescind it good if Taggart gave him half a chance. Five dirty minutes used up in killing Taggart. Recover the money. Stash his costume in a junk car, drive away.'

'In a rental car? Back to the Miami airport?'

He looked at me approvingly. 'Maybe you're not a clown after all.'

'But you couldn't check it out?'

'How many phone messages come in? How many cars are checked out? How many medium-sized, darkhaired guys, thirty years old fly in and out every day? Maybe it's an organization thing, and Briefcase is a local operator. It fades out into nothing, McGee. When it's professional, it always fades out into nothing, unless we get one hell of a break.'

'What's so professional about hacking him up like that?'

'A professional with a personal interest, maybe. Or maybe that's the way he goes for kicks, when he has the time.' He grinned. 'I'm a pro too. That's why you're going to come along and sit in my car while I talk to Miss Gardino. It's the only way I can be sure you don't get on the phone.'

He couldn't trick her or trap her. All he could do was break her down to the tears and the truth. And he left me there at the shop with her, back in the office, steadying her down. The big sobs were less frequent. Shaj stared in at us and gave a little nod and went away.

Nora launched herself back into self dependence, giving a little push at me to turn herself away, delving for tissue, honking into it and then trying to smile. 'He hits the nerve, doesn't he?'

'He opens you up like a guide book. It's his trade.'

'Trav, I didn't . . . let him make me say anything about . . . the gold.'

'I didn't think you would.'

'But he got the rest of it. The loving.' That narrow, vital, ugly-lovely face twisted into a grimace that pulled the flesh against the bone, showing the skull shape, the tooth-look of death.

'So we can leave any time,' I said. 'As soon as you're ready.'

She looked flustered. The eagerness was still there, but the actual fact of departure made her uncertain. 'I . . . I have a lot to do.'

'As soon as you're ready.'

CHAPTER EIGHT

THE travel agent in Los Angeles was a darling fellow, in tight green pants, yellow shirt, green ascot, desert boots. I had made it clear to him that it was Miss Gardino and Mr. McGee.

He looked pained and said, 'If that is *really* the sort of thing you have in mind, I think you would be *terribly* pleased with Mazatlan or Guaymas, or perhaps as far down as Manzanillo. Puerto Altamura is so *difficult.*'

'In what way?'

'Transportationwise, sir.' He went over to a large map of Mexico on the side wall. Really I can *truly* recommend a lovely place in . . .'

'Puerto Altamura sounds pretty good to me,' I said. 'We'd like something . . . a little off the beaten track.'

His eyes moved sidelong toward Nora, a reptilian flicker of understanding. He gave up. 'I'll see what I can do, sir. It may take some time to arrange. How long would you want to stay there, sir?'

'A month. Six weeks.'

'My word!' he said, aghast. 'Uh . . . two rooms, sir?'

'Please.'

He looked at his watch. 'I suggest you phone me in, say, an hour and I may be able to report some progress.'

We went out into the milky overcast sunlight of the March morning. She looked up at me with a crooked smile and said, 'Isn't he a dear?'

'He seems to know what he's doing.'

'Could we just walk for a while? I feel very tense and restless.'

'Sure, Nora.'

I phoned him at noon. He said, 'I'm doing *much* better than I expected, sir. I have you reserved there, beginning tomorrow night. The manager, a Mr. Arista, assures me the accommodations are most pleasant. He suggested a way of getting there, and I have ticketed you through to Durango, leaving at nine-twenty tomorrow morning. I am working on the link from Durango to Culiacan, where a hotel vehicle will meet you. Suppose you stop by at three this afternoon, and I shall have everything all ready for you.'

The Aviones de Mexico prop jet made one stop at Chihuahua, and then flew on to Durango. About thirteen hundred miles all told. It was one-thirty when we got there. It was a mile in the air, wind-washed, dazzlingly clear, very cool in the shade. The men in the customs shack were efficient in an offhand way, armed uniformed, officially pleasant. The one who spoke English phoned Tres Estrellas Airline for us, and ten minutes later an ancient station wagon appeared and took us and our luggage on a fast and lumpy journey to a far corner of the field. We waited a half hour for the third passenger to arrive, a young priest. The plane was a venerable Beechcraft. The pilot looked far too young. He wore pointed yellow shoes, a baseball hat, and a mad smile. Between us and the sea were peaks of up to ten thousand feet, all jungled green with occasional outcroppings of stone. It was over two hundred miles to Culiacan and nearly four o'clock when we arrived. There was a round and smiling little man there in a bright blue uniform. It said Casa Encantada on his hat, and it said Casa Encantada on the side of the bright blue Volkswagen bus.

We whined north on Route 15 to Pericos, and there he made a violent left onto an unpaved road. We had twenty miles of it, part sand, part shell, part crushed stone, part mud. The tropic growth was dense and moist on both sides.

At five-thirty we came bouncing out of the jungle, climbed a small ridge, and went dashing down into the town of Puerto Altamura, a grievous disappointment in spite of the blue bay and the low green of the tropic islands shielding it. The village was a semi-circle on a curve of the bay, and between the water-front building we could see rotting docks, a scrabbly beach, nets drying, crude dark boats.

'Paradise,' Nora murmured.

We saw the Casa Encantada, low and white and clean-looking, with many white out-buildings, all roofed with orange-red tile.

The driver beamed, nodded at us, pointed and said, 'Hello!'

'Paradise?' I said to Nora.

'It is absolutely unbelievably fantastic.'

A bald brown moustached man in a white suit came down the few broad steps and said, 'Miss Gardino? Mr. McGee? My name is Arista. I am the manager here. I hope your stay with us will be most pleasant.'

'It's lovely here,' Nora said.

'Was your trip enjoyable, Senorita?'

'Yes. Thank you.'

We went in and registered. The lobby was small, with a centre fountain, tiled floor, massive dark beams, bright mosaics set into the walls.

He said, 'We are almost half full at the moment. Dinner is served from eight until eleven-thirty. We are happy you are staying with us. Will you follow me, please?'

He snapped his fingers and the boys picked up the luggage. He took us down a long passageway, with room doors on one side and, on the other, open arches overlooking the sea. We were two-thirds of the way down that wing, in rooms 39 and 40. The interconnecting door was open, thus saving him the minor awkwardness of unlocking it for us.

'These rooms are satisfactory? Good.' A shy brown broad-faced young girl in a blue uniform dress appeared in the door-way. Arista said, 'This is Amparo. She will be your room maid while you are here. She has some English.' The girl smiled and bobbed her head. She had coarse black braids tied with scraps of blue yarn. A wiry little man in blue with a face like braided leather appeared behind her, with gold-toothed smile. 'And Jose is your room waiter,' Arista explained. 'You push the top button here for Amparo and the other for Jose. She will do laundry, pressing, sewing, that sort of thing. Please tip them at the time you leave us. I have given you table ten, and you will have the same waiter each day, so arrange the tip with him in the same fashion, please.' He gave a little bow to each of us in turn. 'Welcome to La Casa Encantada,' he said, and left.

Nora selected number 39, Jose moved her luggage into that room. Amparo went in to help her unpack and Nora closed the interconnecting door. Jose unpacked my two bags. I took out the two items I did not want him to handle, the zipper case which contained the statuette pictures, and my slightly oversized toilet kit. When he was through, and had asked if I wanted anything else, and had bowed himself out, with golden smile, I checked the room for a suitable hiding place for the five pictures. I did not hope to find anything that would defeat a professional search. I just wanted to thwart amateur curiosity. One table lamp had a squat pottery base. I dismantled the fixture. The base was half full of sand for stability. There was ample room for the pictures, slightly curled, shoved down partway into the sand. I put it back together again. Now the leather folder contained misleading information, a sheaf of typed sheets of computations, per centage returns on real estate and investments, detailed recommendation for purchase of things I would never by.

I took the toilet kit into the bathroom. It has a shallow false bottom, so inconspicuous as to be quite effective. I had debated bringing a weapon, and had at last decided on a flat little automatic pistol I had filched from an unstable woman's purse, a Parisian woman. It is a ridiculous little thing made in Milano, silver-plated, with an ivory grip, one inch of barrel, without safety or trigger guard. The six clip has a sturdy spring however, unusual in these junk weapons. It is 25 calibre. I'd brought a full clip and a dozen extra shells. At eight feet I could be reasonably certain of hitting a man-sized target every time. At fifteen feet I would be half sure. At twenty-five feet it would be better to throw stones. It is a bedroom gun, with a brash bark like an axious puppy. Its great advantage is its size. It is very thin. The grip fits the first two fingers of my hand. I can and have carried it in my wallet, tucked in with the money. It makes an uncomfortably bulky wallet. I lumped the toilet gear out, pried up the false bottom and felt a little ridiculous as I looked at the toy gun. I had more faith in the other two items concealed there, the little vial of chloral hydrate, and the tin of capsules of a tasteless and powerful barbiturate, labelled respectively as nose drops and cold medicine. I checked the clip on the little gun and transferred it to the side pocket of my trousers. It was safe. It could not fire until I had jacketed a shell into the chamber. I left my medicines and extra shells concealed.

After I had showered and changed, Nora rapped on the inter-connecting door. I opened it and she came in, in an ivory linen dress that darkened her skin. 'Amparo is a jewel,' she said.

'Nice rooms.'

'Maybe the food will be good too.'

'I hope so.'

'Shall we walk around? Explore?'

'If you'd like.'

'Why are we almost whispering?' she asked, and smiled nervously, her dark brown eyes glinting in the diminishing light of dusk.

'Before we go out, is there anything in your room, anything that ties you to him in any way?'

'You told me to be sure of that. I was. There's nothing at all, Trav. But . . . he could have talked to someone about Gardino and McGee. Old friends.'

'There has to be a scrap of bait left out, a hint of bait, nothing definite.'

'I have the feeling someone is listening to us.'

'Not from this room. You'll feel that way all the time we're here. Until we know. Until we're sure.'

'It isn't anything like I thought it would be.'

We walked to the far end of our exterior corridor, away from the lobby and found a sun deck at the end, large, with an iron railing, with a short curved staircase leading down to a path that led to the apron of the pool. The sunbathers were gone.

We took a flagstone path through the flowers toward the main entrance.

'Were almost opposite La Paz,' I said. 'I guess it's just a little south of us.'

'You've been there?'

'Once upon a time.'

'Trav, tell me why I feel so strange and uncertain and . . . unreal?'

'After we find the bar.'

'Okay. After we find the bar.'

It was on the level below the lobby, an upholstered little room hoked up with candles, nets, tridents, glass floats, but dim and pleasant enough. We got our drinks at the bar, took them to a banquette corner. Several tables had been pulled together to seat ten people, five couples—the men big and brown and beefy, and their women smallish, tough, leathery. I needed one glance for the whole story.

'Those are the big game fish buffs,' I told Nora.

'How about the four dark suit types in the corner?'

'Mexican businessmen. Maybe looking for another place to stick up a hotel.'

'And those kids at the end of the bar?'

Three towering and powerful young men, and two slim sun-browned girls, and a huge black dog. 'That's tougher. I'd say scuba types, if this was a better area for it. I'll say it anyway. From the way they're dressed, they've got a boat here. Probably came down the coast of Baja California and around to La Paz and cut across to here and will end up in Acapulco. How about the gal clothes?'

'That simple little beach shirt on the blonde is a forty-dollar item.'

'It would have to be a good hunk of boat. So it's that big motor sailor at the far dock out there. Fifty-something feet.'

'And the couple just coming in?'

'Ah, the firm tread and the steady eye of shutter-bug tourists. Kodachrome and exposure meters, and hundreds of slides of the real Mexico.'

She lowered her voice. 'And the couple at this end of the bar?'

The woman was dark, hefty and handsome, glinting with gem stones. The man was squat and powerful, with an Aztec face and a gleaming white jacket.

'Just a guess. They're from one of the houses over there beyond the boat basin. Drinks and dinner at the hotel tonight, for a change.'

'You're good at that, Trav.'

'And often wrong,' I said, and went to the bar and brought fresh drinks back.

She sat closer to me and said, 'Why do I feel so strange?'

'Because on the other side of the continent it looked easy, Nora. Now all you can see is closed doors, and no way of knowing if any of them will open. Baby, nothing is easy. Life comes in a thousand shades of grey, and everyone except madmen think what they do is reasonable, and maybe even the madmen do too. They give us an unlimited number of strikes, so you swing until your arms get too tired, and hope you don't get hit in the head.'

She leaned closed and said, 'What kind of a lousy defeatist attitude is that?'

'It's the attitude that keeps me from getting anxious and careless. And dead.'

Her eyes looked sick and I knew the vision of Sam dead had flashed in her mind.

'You're in charge,' she said.

Table ten overlooked a sunken flood-lighted garden behind the hotel.

After a little while she said, 'Maybe he would have brought me here some day.'

'Cut it out, Nora.'

'I'm sorry.'

A few minutes later she stood up and said, 'Good night, Trav. I'll try to . . . keep things under better control.'

'Want me to walk you back?'

'No thanks. Really.'

'Sleep well, Nora.'

I watched her, slim and slow, her dress pale in the warm night, climb the stairs to the sun deck and disappear along the corridor.

After a little while I went back to the bar for a cold Carta Blanca. One thing was obvious to me. From what Sam Taggart said, he had spent an appreciable amount of time here. He had become a *residente*. He would be known. It was inescapable that he would be known, and known well. He said there had been trouble. So people would not want to talk. I had to find some way of unwinding it, of following the single strands to the marks he had left on this place and these people.

I signed my chit and went to my room. Amparo had turned the bed down. Nora slept beyond the closed door. Or lay restless and heard me come in, and wondered what would happen to us here, among the flowers and fishermen.

CHAPTER NINE

I slept heavily, and longer than is my habit. Nora was not in her room.

I dressed quickly, but as I left the room, I saw her coming along the corridor in swim suit, pool coat and clogs, towel and swim cap in her hand, the ends of her dark hair damp. Her weight loss had not changed the impact of these excessively lovely legs, so beautifully curved, so totally elegant.

'I've been up forever,' she said. 'And I'm absolutely starving. Are you going to breakfast now? Tell Eduardo I'm practically on my way. It's a lovely pool. A lot of boats went out early. You were right about those kids on the motor sailer. They're checking tanks and things. Isn't it a gorgeous morning? I won't be long. What will I put on? What are we going to do?'

'Walk to the village. Skirt instead of shorts, I'd say. Flat heels.'

By the time we reached the public square, we had adjusted to the rich odours of the town.

We wandered, looked at the stalls, then sat on a bench in the square, where the inevitable pigeons pecked at the walks and the scrub grass. I thought of using the post office as a possible approach. Looking for an old friend. Yes indeed. Good old Sam Taggart. He still around here? But it seemed clumsy.

A young priest walked by us and glanced over and said, 'Good morning!'

'Good morning, Father,' Nora said meekly. I recognized him as the same one who had been on the Tres Estrellas flight. I watched him head towards the church on the other side of the square and disappear into the dark interior. And I had a little idea worth developing.

'Are you Catholic?' I asked Nora.

'If I'm anything. Yes, I don't work at it. But it sort of builds up . . . and then I go to Mass.'

'Check me on the routine. Any talk you have with a priest is privileged information, isn't it?'

'Up to a point. I mean if a person confessed a murder, the priest would have to tell the police. What are you getting at?'

'That priest might know some things that would help us.'

She looked startled, and then she comprehended. 'But . . . how could I go about. . . .'

'Ask for his help in a confidential matter. Wouldn't that keep him quiet?'

'I suppose it would.'

'Tell him you were in love with the man, that you lived in sin with him and he left you and you have been searching for him for three years. I have the idea these village priests know everything that goes on. And he speaks English.'

'It would feel so strange . . . to lie to a priest.'

'I hear it's done frequently.'

'But not this way.' She looked in her purse. 'I have nothing to cover my head.'

We went to one of the sidewalk stalls. She picked a cotton

scarf. It was ten pesos, then five, then four, and finally three pesos fifty centavos, sold with smiles, with pleasure at the bargaining.

She gave me a tight-lipped and nervous look, and went off toward the church. I went back to the bench.

Nora was gone a long time. A very long time. Though I was watching the church, I did not see her until she was about twenty feet from me. Her colour looked bad, her mouth pinched.

'Let's walk,' she said.

I got up and went with her. 'Bad?'

'He's a good man. It got to me a little. Let me just . . . unwind a little bit.' She gave me a wry glance. 'Mother Church. You think you've torn loose, but . . . I don't know. I lit candles for him, Trav. I prayed for his soul. What would he think of that?'

'Probably he would like it.'

We headed back out of town, toward La Casa Encantada.

'He didn't speak very much English, Trav. Enough, I guess. When he realized who I was asking about, he became very upset. He said perhaps some people hoped Sam would come back here, but he hoped the man would never return. He said he had prayed that Sam would never return. Prayer answered, I guess. He kept getting excited and losing his English. He came here four years ago, as just about the time the hotel was finished. Sam showed up, he thought, over a year later. He arrived on a private yacht from California. He was the hired captain. There was some kind of difficulty, and Sam was fired. He stayed. The yacht went on. The hotel needed somebody to run one of the fishing boats for guests. They helped Sam get his workpapers straightened out, a *residente* permit. Then he . . . he lived with a girl who worked at the hotel, a girl from the village. Felicia Novaro. Then there was some trouble at the hotel, and he left and went to work for one of the families in one of those big houses beyond the hotel. Their name is Garcia. He abandoned Felicia for someone in the Garcia household. And there was trouble there. He left suddenly. I didn't get all of it, Trav. Federal police came after he left, and asked questions. It's possible that he killed someone. The priest was very cautious about that part. Trav . . . it didn't sound as if he was talking about Sam. He was talking about some stranger, some cruel, dangerous, violent man.'

'What did he do for the Garcias?'

'Ran their cruiser, apparently, and perhaps something more. Several times he seemed on the verge of trying to tell me something, and then he would stop. Felicia Novaro doesn't work at the hotel any more. She works in town. She does not go to church, but if she comes back to God, He will forgive her.'

'Will he talk to anyone about this?'

'I'm sure he won't.'

I touched her shoulder. 'We've got the starting place, Nora.'

'Maybe I don't want to find out all these things.'

'We can stop right here.'

'No. I do want to find out. But I'm scared.'

In my room, I rang for Jose, and he said it was perfectly possible to have 'ahmboorgers' served at poolside, with cold Mexican beer, and he would do it at once. I told him fifteen minutes would be better than at once.

After lunch the pool boy got us two sun mattresses and I had him put them over on the far edge of the big apron, near the flowers and away from the other people. We stretched out under a high hot sun, with just enough sea breeze to make it endurable.

'So?' she said at last in a sun-dazed voice.

'So we don't rush things. We don't charge around. We give the folks a chance to label us.'

'As what, Trav?'

'Furtive romance, woman. You had to show identity for the tourist card. Connecting rooms. We couldn't be Mr. and Mrs. Jones.'

'I realize that! But I just. . . .'

'Excuse me,' a girl voice said. I sat up. It was one of the two scuba girls from the motor sailer, the blonde who had been in the bar in the expensive shirt. She was mildly, comfortably stoned.

'What it is,' she said, 'it's a bet. How about two years ago, three years ago? You were offensive end with the Rams. Right?'

'Wrong.'

'Oh shit,' she said. 'You play pro with anybody?'

'Just pro ball for a college.'

'End?'

'Defensive line backer. Corner man.'

She looked at me like a stock yard inspector. 'You're big enough for pro.'

'It wasn't such a big thing when I got out. And I had knee trouble off and on the last two years of it.'

'Excuse me too,' Nora said and got up and headed for the pool.

The sun bunny peered after her. 'My asking you gave her a strain?'

'She just wants to cool off I guess.'

'She's built darling for an older woman. I guess I got to get back and say I was wrong.'

'Are you people moving on soon?'

'I guess so. Maybe tomorrow. Chip hasn't said. What we figured, we'd stay longer. It used to be there was always a brawl going on they say, one of the houses over there. None of us were here before, but Chip had a note to the people, a friend of a friend, you know, so we'd get in on the action, but he couldn't even get past the gate, and Arista says no parties this year up there, so that's it and it's pretty dead here. I want to go where there's good reefs. I just want to go down and cruise the reefs. It's the only thing I can't ever seem to get sick of. All the colours. Like dreaming it. Like I'm somebody else.'

'What house was it, where the parties were?'

'Oh, the pink one furthest up the hill there. People name of Garcia. Real rich and crazy, Chip's friend said. Fun people, house guests and so on. Well, see you around.' She stood up and trudged back to her friends, giving me a parting smile over a muscular brown shoulder.

Nora came back and towelled herself, saying, 'Just think how many of them would flock around if you were alone, dear.'

'She said you're built darling for an older woman.'

'God, I couldn't be more flattered.'

'She came up with something.'

'I beg your pardon?'

I told her about the fine parties, now over. And then I said, 'What we're both thinking becomes pretty obvious after a while.'

'Garcia. That's like calling yourself John Smith, isn't it?'

'Instead of Carlos Menterez y Cruzada.'

'But wouldn't that be terribly difficult for him to arrange?'

'Expensive, maybe. But not too difficult. He had to scoot out of Havana nearly five years ago. He would be afraid of people wanting to settle old scores. A remote place like this would be perfect. Big house, wall and gate, guards. Enough money to last forever. But he'd want a chance to live it up. Raoul told me about his taste for celebrities when he lived in Havana. And for American girls. He could make cautious contact with friends in California. He'd be afraid to go where the parties are, so he'd have to bring them here. Big cruiser at the dock over there on the other side. Goodies shipped in. It probably would have been impossible for him to get into any kind of business venture in Mexico. Is he dead? Is he sick? Has somebody gotten so close to him he's had to slam the gates and stop the fiesta? Maybe the people who sold him the immunity have kept on bleeding him. Sam worked for Garcia. Sam got hold of the Menterez collection. And somebody knew he had it and took it away from him. We find that somebody by finding out what went on here.'

'How?'

'We nudge around until we find somebody who would like to talk about it.'

'Felicia Novaro?'

'Maybe. I'll try her, alone. Tomorrow night.'

'Why not tonight?'

'I saw that cantina. It's just off the square. I want to do a little window trimming tomorrow afternoon. With your help.'

'Like what?'

'I'll tell you as we go along. It'll be more convincing.'

An hour later Nora got sleepy and went yawning back to her room to take a nap. With a vague idea I went down the steps to the boat basin. It was the siesta lull. I padded slowly around, looking at the boats. The dockmaster had a shed office and supply store at the end of the basin.

A man with red-grey hair and a perpetual sunburn sat sweating at a work table, copying figures from dock chits into a record book. He turned pale blue eyes at me and said, 'Ya?'

'You the dockmaster?'

'Ya.'

'Pretty nice layout you've got here.'

'Something you want?' he asked. He had a German accent.

'Just looking around, if you don't mind. I live aboard a boat. In Florida. I wish I could get it over here, but there's no way, unless I want to deck-load it on a freighter.'

'Big boat?'

'Barge type houseboat. Custom, fifty-two feet, two little Hercules diesels. Twenty-one foot beam. I've got a four hundred mile range at nine knots, but she won't take much sea.'

'Not good for these waters. Better where you are.'

'I guess so.' I wandered over to the side wall and began to look at the pictures. They were black and white polaroid prints, scores of them, neatly taped to the composition wall. Boats and fish and people. Mostly people, standing by fish hanging from hooks from a sign saying La Casa Encantada, smiling, sundark, happy people, and limp fish. And I saw Sam Taggart. In at least a dozen of them, off to one side, grinning, always with a different group of customers.

The dockmaster had gone back to his records. He kept the office very tidy. I saw the books on a shelf, four of them, each labelled by year, each titled Marina Log.

'Mind if I see if I know any of the boats that stopped here?'

'Go ahead.'

I took the one for three years back, and sat on a crate by the window and slowly turned the pages. The sign-in columns were for boat name, length, type, port of registry, owner, captain. I found it for July 11th, over two months after Sam had left Lauderdale. *Quest IV*, 62 ft, custom diesel, Coronado, California, G. T. Kepplert, S. Taggart, Capt. All in Sam's casual scrawl. It jumped out of the page at me. Business wasn't tremendous. Page after page was blank. I put it back and took down the more recent book and went through that and put it back.

'You get some big ones in here,' I said.

'Anything over eighty feet, they anchor out, but it's a protected harbour.'

I went back to the wall where the pictures were. He finished the accounts and closed his book and stood up. 'Lock up here now for an hour,' he said.

I had found the picture I wanted. 'This man looks familiar to me. I'm trying to remember his boat.'

He came over and looked at the picture. 'Him? He had no boat. Look, he is in this picture, that one, that one, lots of them. No, he worked for me.'

'That's funny. I could have sworn. Haggerty? Taggerty?'

'So! Maybe you did know him. Taggart. Sam Taggart.

'That must be it.'

He put his hand out. 'My name is Heintz. You want some nice fishing, it's a good time for it now, and I reserve you a good boat, eh?'

'I'll think it over. McGee is my name.'

'Five hundred pesos all day. The hotel packs lunch, Mr. McGee. A big man like you can catch a big fish, eh?'

'I can't imagine how Taggart happened to come work here. Is he still around?'

'No. He hasn't worked for me a long time. He took over a private boat. He's gone now.'

I sensed that one more question was going to be one question too many. I went out with him and he locked the office door. He gave me an abrupt nod and marched away, and I climbed the steps back to the pool level.

That night, at dinner and in the bar afterwards, Nora was strange. She wore a slate blue dress so beautifully fitted it made her figure seem almost opulent. She was very gay and funny and quick, and then she would get tears in her eyes and try to hide them with hard little coughs of laughter. At last, in the bar, the tears went too far, and when she saw she could not stop them, she said a strangled good night and fled. I did not stay long. I took a walk in the night. I thought of ways things could be done, ways that seemed right and ways that felt wrong. Slyness has no special logic. Sam had done something wrong. Knowing the shape of his mistake could help me. I took the problems to bed, and they followed me down into sleep.

But sleep did not take hold.

I got up, barefoot on cool tile, and made a soundless circuit of the room and stopped at the interconnecting door and, holding my breath, heard the faint sound that was disturbing me, a tiny little smothered keening, the small frail noise of the agony of the heart.

I put my robe on and tried the door. It opened soundlessly into the other darkness of her room.

'Nora?' I said in a half whisper, so as not to alarm her. The answer was a hiccuping sob. I felt my way to her bed, touched a shoulder, thin and heated and shivering under silk. I sat with her. I stroked the lean firm back. She was down there in a swamp of tears and despair, where I could not reach her. Much of lust is a process of self delusion. If I stretched out with her, could I hold her more securely, could I make her feel less alone? If I gathered all this straining misery into my arms, tucked the hot fierce salty face into my throat, gave her someone to cling to in the night? These caresses were merely for comfort, were they not? They had absolutely nothing to do with the spectacular legs, and the clover-grass scent of her hair, and her lovely proud walk. This was just my friend Nora. And if all this began to turn into anything else, I had the character to walk away from it, didn't I? And certainly she could sense that seduction was the furthest thing from my mind, wasn't it?

But there was one place to stop, and then the gamble of waiting just a little longer, and just a little longer. She had long since stopped crying. Then another stopping place passed, and beyond that there was a slope too steep for stopping, a slope that tilted it all into a headlong run. After the peak of it for her, she said something blurred and murmurous, something I could not catch, and fell almost at once into a heavy, boneless, purring sleep.

At nine-thirty, showered and dressed, I wondered if I should knock at her door. I decided against it and went to the dining-room. Eduardo said she had not yet arrived. Just as I finished the papaya, I glanced up and saw her approaching the table, walking with a slightly constricted demureness, her head a little on the side, her smile crooked. She wore dark green bermudas and a green and white striped blouse. I stood up for her, and Eduardo hurried to hold the chair for her. A flush darkened her face as she looked at me with eyes vast, dark and quizzical and said, 'Good morning, darling.'

'Good morning.' Eduardo took her order. She ordered a huge breakfast. When he went away, I leaned toward her and lowered my voice and said, 'Nora, all I want to say. . . .'

She leaned and reached across the small table very quickly and put two fingers against my lips, stopping what I had rehearsed saying to her. 'You don't want to say anything, Trav. There isn't anything you have to say.'

'Are you sure of that?'

'I know things. I know we are very fond of each other. And I know that words don't do any good. It was a lovely and beautiful accident, and I cherish it. Is that enough?'

'Yes,' I said. 'But I just wanted you to know that. . . .'

'Hush now.'

There is no man so assured that he cannot be made to feel slightly oafish if a subtle and complex woman puts her mind to it.

During our sun time and swim after breakfast, no sensitive observer could have been left in doubt about our relationship. And when we went back to the rooms, she came to me sun-hot, eyes heavy and blurred, lips swollen and barely moving as she murmured, 'No accident this time.'

Later, when once again I succumbed to the dreadful compulsion to try to explain us to each other, she stopped me with fingertips on my lips. Hers was the better wisdom. Merely accept what had come to us. I wanted Nora for the sake of Nora, and her response was affectionate, joyous, and weighted with a sturdy practicality. She was saying, in effect, 'Let's not talk about what it means until we know what it means. But it means something, or it wouldn't be like this.'

While she was dressing for lunch, I told her I would see her in the lobby. I had noticed that Senor Arista was usually at his desk in the small area behind the registration desk during the hour before lunch.

I leaned on the registration desk and said, 'This is a fine place, Mr. Arista.'

He smiled carefully. 'So glad you like it, sir.'

'No complaints. Say, I was wondering about land around here. Like on the knoll over there where those houses are. Is it expensive?'

He got up and came over to the counter. 'The land itself, by the square meter, is not too dear. But you see, the big expense is in construction. Skilled labour has to be brought in, as well as all the materials. And, of course, it is very awkward for a tourist to purchase land. One must have a change of status, to resident or immigrant. Are you really interested, sir?'

'Well . . . enough to want to talk to somebody about it.'

'All that land to the south of the hotel, approximately two miles and a half a mile deep, is owned by the same syndicate which established the hotel, sir.' He got a card out of his desk and brought it to me. 'This man, Senor Altavera, handles these matters for the group. This is his Mexico City office. The way it is handled here, there is the one road that winds up the hill, and the present houses, six of them only, are on that road, and they are connected with the hotel water and electricity. It would be a case of extending the road and the utilities, and there would be added charges for that, of course. But if you are genuinely interested. . . .'

'Maybe you could give me some kind of an estimate of what the average house and land and so on would cost in dollars, total.'

'I would estimate . . . let us say a three bedroom house, with appropriate servant quarters, walled garden, a small swimming pool, all modern fixtures and conveniences, I would say that for everything, it would be about one hundred thousand American dollars. One must use the architect the syndicate recommends, and build to certain standards of quality and size. I suspect that the same kind of land in the United States, and an equivalent house, would be perhaps as much as half again that cost.'

'With use of the boat basin?'

'Of course, sir. And if one were to close the house for a time, an arrangement can be made with the hotel for care of the grounds, an airing of the house from time to time.'

'There are five houses now?'

'Six.'

'What kind of neighbours would I have?'

Arista looked slightly pained. 'There is one United States citizen, a gentleman from the television industry. He is not in residence at this time, sir. And one Swiss citizen, quite an elderly man. The others are Mexican. It is not . . . a neighbourhood in the social sense, sir. They are here for purposes of total privacy. You understand, of course.'

'Of course. I wonder if any of the existing houses are for sale.'

He hesitated, bit his lip. 'Perhaps one that would be far more than the figure I . . . Excuse me. It is not at all definite. Really, that is all not a part of my duties. You should contact Senor Altavera on these matters. I am, of course, anxious that the property should be developed. It eases certain overhead expenses for the hotel operation, and it improves the hotel business.'

'How about the local supply of people to work for you? Cook, gardeners, maids and so on?'

'Oh, these people are most difficult, sir. They are a constant trial. They learn well, and they have energy, but they have a fierce independence.'

Out of the corner of my eye I saw Nora approaching and I thanked him for all the information.

I followed Nora into the dining room, smugly and comfortably aware of the sleek flexing of elegant calves, taut swing of round hips under the linen skirt, the valuable slenderness of her waist. The long days of strain, compression, despair had been eased for her. She had reached her breaking point and had endured through it and beyond it. Now her mouth was softened, personal, intimate—but still spiced with a small wryness, an awareness of the irony of our relationship to each other.

CHAPTER TEN

THE village of Puerto Altamura lay steaming in siesta.

The Cantina Tres Panchos was down the side street toward the sea, a few doors from the square. The hot still air was flavoured with stale spilled beer, perfume, sweat and spiced cooking. I put Nora at a table near the doorway and went over to the bar. The bartender had a flat, broad, brown, impassive face, tiny hooded eyes, and a huge sweep of curved black moustache. In too loud and too contentious a voice I ordered a beer, a Carta Blanca, for Nora, and a tequila añejo for myself. The imitation of drunk is nearly always overdone. To be persuasive, merely let the lower half of your face go slack, and when you want to look at anything, move your whole head instead of just your eyes. Walk slowly and carefully, and speak loudly, slowly and distinctly.

I went back to the table. In a little while the bartender brought the order over, bringing a salt shaker and wedge of lemon with my shot glass of tequila. In slow motion I took a wad of pesos out of my shirt pocket, separated a bill and put it on the table. He made change out of his pocket and picked it up. He went away. I left the change there. I had told Nora how to act, told her to sit unsmiling and look everywhere except at me.

I heard the clatter of heels. A girl came down the stairs in back and came out of the left doorway, a narrow, big-eyed girl with her dark hair bleached a strange shade of dull red. She wore an orange blouse and a blue skirt and carried a big red purse. She stared at us and went to the bar and had a brief and inaudible conversation with the bartender, and then went out into the sunlight, with one more glance at us, walking with a great deal of rolling and twitching. I hoped it wasn't Felicia. The girl had a look of brash impenetrable stupidity.

I signalled the bartender and pointed to my empty glass. Nora's beer was half gone. He brought me a shot and another wedge of lemons, took some money from the change on the table.

On cue, Nora said in a voice of dreadful clarity, 'Do you really need that?'

'Shut up,' I said. I sprinkled the salt on the back of my hand, the one in which I held the wedge of lemon. I picked up the shot glass in the other hand. One, two, three. Salt, tequila, lemon.

'Did you really need that?'

'Shut up.'

She got up and hurried out. I sat there stupidly, and then I got up and lumbered after her. I left my change on the table.

'Hey!' I yelled. 'Hey.'

She kept walking swiftly. I broke into a heavy run and caught up with her as she was walking through the square. I took her arm and she yanked it away and kept walking, toward the hotel, her chin high. I stood and watched her, and then caught up with her again.

When we were well beyond the village she looked behind us

and then looked at me with a little nervous grin and said, 'Did I do it right?'

'Perfectly.'

'I still don't get the point.'

'Credentials. I'm the big drunken Americano who's having trouble with his woman. I went away and left my money. When I go into town tonight, they'll have me all cased. I'll be the kind of a pigeon they can understand. Ready for plucking. I'll have a lot of friends when I go in there tonight.'

I arrived at the cantina at about eight-thirty. The tables were full, the bar was crowded, the juke box was blasting. The room was lighted by two gasoline lanterns. The bartender came at once and placed the forgotten change in front of me. He stared at me without expression. I carefully divided it into two equal amounts and pushed half of it across to him. He gave me a big white smile, and, with suitable ceremony, gave me a free tequila. We were closely watched. He made explanation to all, of which I did not understand a word, and the room slowly came back to the full decibel level I had heard as I walked in. I looked no more and no less drunk than before. My only change was a constant happy uncomprehending smile.

It took them about ten minutes to rig the first gambit. She edged in beside me, shoving the others to make room for herself, a chubby, bosomy little girl with a merry face, a white streak dyed in her curly black hair, a careless and abundant use of lipstick. 'Allo,' she said. 'Allo.'

I pointed at my glass and pointed at her and she bobbed her head and gave the bartender her order. When it came I pointed to myself and said, 'Trav.'

'Ah, Trrav. Si.'

I stabbed her in the wishbone with a heavy finger and looked inquisitive.

'Rosita,' she said, and laughed as if we had made wonderful jokes.

'Speak English, Rosita.'

'*Aí, no puedo, Trrav. Lo siento mucho, pero. . . .*'

I smiled at her, took her by the shoulders and turned her away and gave her a little pat, then filled up the space at the bar, my back to her. When I glanced back at her, she was giving me a thoughtful look. I watched her make her slow way through the crowded room and finally edge in near the wall and bend over and whisper to a girl who sat with three men. I could not see her very distinctly in the odd light, but I saw her look toward me, shake her head and look away. Rosita made her way back to the other end of the bar. She beckoned to the bartender. He leaned over and she spoke to him. He gave her a brief nod. A few minutes later he made his way to the girl at the table and bent over her and whispered to her. She shook her head. He said some more. She shrugged and got up. A man at the table yanked her back down into the chair. She sprang up at once. The man lunged at her and the bartender gave him a solid thump on the side of the head. There was a moment of silence, and then all the talk started again, over the persistent sound of the rrrrock and rrrroll. I saw the girl making her way in my direction, and I saw that she was what they call *muy guapa*. She wore an orange shift, barely knee length slit at both sides. She was quite dark, and she was big. Her dark hair was braided, pulled tight, coiled into a little shining turret on top of her head. Her jaw was squared off, her neck long, her mouth broad and heavy, her eyes tilted, full of an Indigo glitter. Her bare arms were smooth and brown, slightly heavy. The shift made alternate diagonal wrinkles as she walked, from thrust of breast to round heavy hip. She came toward me with a challenging arrogance, the easy slowness of a lioness. She was not pretty. She was merely strong, savage, confident . . . and *muy guapa*.

Just as she reached me, there was a disturbance behind her, shouts of warning, a shift and tumble of chairs. The bar customers scattered, leaving the two of us alone in the emptiness. She turned her back to the bar, standing beside me. The man who had been thumped in the head crouched six or eight feet from us. He was young, and his face was tense and sweaty, his eyes so narrowed they looked closed. He held the knife about ten inches from the floor, blade parallel to the floor, winking orange in the light. He swung it slowly back and forth, the muscles of his thin arm writhing.

The bartender gave a sharp command. The young man bared his teeth and, looking at my belt buckle, told me exactly what he was going to do to me. I didn't understand the language, but I knew what he said.

The girl made a lazy sound at him, a brief husky message, like a sleepy spit. She stood with an elbow hooked on the bar behind her, her rich body indolently curved. Whatever she said, in that silence between records, was like a blow in the face to him. He seemed to soften. He sobbed, and forgetting all skill, lunged forward, clumsily hooking the knife up toward her belly. I snapped my right hand down on his wrist, brought my left hand up hard, under his elbow, twisting his arm down and under, giving an extra leverage to his lunge that sent him by her in a long running fall into the tables and people as the knife clattered at her feet. I swear that she did not make the slightest move until she bent and picked the knife up. The next record started. The man thrashed around. People shouted. His friends got him, one by each arm, and frog-marched him out. He bucked and struggled, crying, the tears running down his face.

As they reached the doorway, the girl swung the knife back and yelled *'Cuidado, hombres!'* They gave her a startled look and dived into the night. She hurled the knife and it stuck deep into the wooden door frame. The populace whistled and cheered and stomped. A cautious hand reached in out of the night and wrenched the knife out of the wood and took it away.

She leaned on the bar again and turned toward me, a deep, dark, terrible amusement in her eyes, and in a clumsy accent, but a total clarity, said, 'So what else is new?'

Then we were both laughing helplessly, and they applauded that too. She staggered and caught my arm for support, the tears squeezing out of her eyes. I bought her a drink. When we had stopped gasping, I said, 'He would have killed you.'

'He? No! He would stop. So close, maybe.' She held up thumb and finger, a quarter inch apart. 'Or cut a little small bit.'

'You are sure?'

She shrugged big shoulders. 'Maybe.'

'You didn't move.'

'It is . . .' she frowned, 'how you say it. Proud. I am not proud to run and fright from such a one. Ai, you are quick for so big a one. You can think he cuts me, no? How could you tell? Maybe this time he does. I say him a bad word. Very bad. Everybody hear it. Proud for him too. You unnerstan?'

'Yes.'

She spread that big mouth in a warm approving grin. 'Thank you for so brave, mister. Rosita say one man here wants a girl speaking English, but I say no. Then I say yes. Now I am glad. Okay?'

'Okay. So am I. What's your name?'

'Felicia.'

'I am Trav.'

She tilted her head slightly, a small memory nudging her perhaps. 'So, Trrav?'

'No, dear. Trav. Trav.'

'Trav? I say it right?'

'Just right, dear. Another drink?'

'Yes, please. You like some dancing maybe? Tweest?'

'No thanks.'

'Okay here? Or a table is better?'

'Okay here, Felicia.'

'Good!' Over the rim of her glass she looked at me with approving speculation. This was no wan foolish heartbroken village girl. She had a coarse, indomitable vitality, a challenging sexual impact. 'You like the hotel?'

'It's a nice place.'

'I was there. Kitchen work. Not any more.'

'Hard work?'

'Not so much. But every day the same. You unnerstan?'

'Sure.'

She leaned closer, breath heating my chin. 'I like you, Trrav. You unnerstan that too?'

I looked down into the dark face, the soft-coarse pore texture, the unreadable darkness of her eyes. False jewels twinkled in her pierced ears. 'I understand.'

With a twisting and eloquent lift of her head she managed to convey the idea of a place of refuge for us on the floor above. 'You want to make some love with Felicia, Trrav? Two hundred pesos. Especial for you, uh? Much better than your skinny woman at the hotel, uh? I do this sometimes, only. When I like.'

'Okay, dear.'

She nodded, biting her lip. 'What we do, you stay here ten minutes, okay?' She was leaning close to me, leaning against me to be heard over the uproar. 'Go out, go to the left, that way. Go beside this place to the back. To stairs. Up stairs is a door, unlock. Go in. Count three doors inside. One, two, three. Okay? It is number three door, mine.' She dragged her fingernails down the back of my hand, squeezed her eyes at me, and then went away in that lazy, swaying, hip-rolling walk. She stopped at tables, talked to people, kept moving, and disappeared into the left hand doorway. I knew her departure had not gone unobserved. I hunched over the bar. I had the feeling that eight out of every ten people in that room knew how soon I would leave and where I was going. After a while I settled up, left a generous tip for the moustache and departed.

The alley beside the building was so narrow, my shoulders nearly brushed the side walls. There was a fetid smell in the narrow space. I stepped in something wet. After about twenty feet, it opened out into a small courtyard. I waited and listened. The noise from inside the place muffled the sound of anybody who might want to try something cute. The courtyard was littered with papers and trash. The stairway was open, with no guard rail. It creaked and sagged alarmingly as I went up it, brushing the side of the building with my fingertips. Mist had come with the night, haloing the few faint lights I could see.

I was careful about the door. Always be careful about doors. They can be the handiest surprise packages around. Do not carry your head inside just where it is expected to be, or at a predictable velocity. There was a clackety latch, the kind you push down with your thumb. It opened inward. I stayed against it as it opened, then moved swiftly sideways to flatten against the corridor wall. There was no sound close by that I could detect over the louder din from the room underfoot. No movement in the narrowing light as the door creaked slowly shut. When it was shut I had only a faint memory of the corridor. The blackness was total, except for a faint line of light ten feet or so away, close to the floor. I used my lighter, shading it with my other hand to keep from dazzling myself. One, two, three, with the thread of light under hers. It was the same kind of latch. I thrust it open abruptly and went in swiftly, and at an angle, giving her a dreadful start. She spun from her mirror, eyes and mouth wide.

I closed the door, saw a bolt lock and thumbed it over.

She stood up from the stool and tossed the hairbrush aside. The orange shift had been draped over the footboard of the iron bed. She had undone the braids and combed her hair out. It came below her shoulders. She was naked. She stood there for me, obviously and properly pleased with herself. Her body, a half shade lighter than her face, was broad and rich, rounded, firm and abundant, the slender waist flowing and widening into the smoothly powerful hips. *Muy guapa* and *muy* aware of it. She made me think of one of P. Gauguin's women, framed against the Macronesian jungle. She came smiling toward me, two steps to reach me, arms lifting. She looked puzzled when I caught her wrists, turned her gently, pushed her to sit on the edge of the bed, near the footboard.

God, they were noisy downstairs, thumping and yelping. I turned away from her, took a fifty dollar bill from my wallet, turned back with it and held it out to her. Her eyes widened, and a look of sullen Indio suspicion came over her face. This much money might mean that something highly unpleasant was required.

'What for?' she asked, glowering.

'All I want to do is talk about Sam Taggart.'

She sat motionless for perhaps two seconds, then came at my face with such a blinding, savage speed that she nearly took both my eyes with those hooked talons, actually brushing the eyelashes of my right eye as I yanked my head back. She followed it up, groaning with her desire to destroy me with her hands. I have never tried to handle a more powerful woman, and the heat in the room made her sweaty and hard to hold. I twisted in time to take a hard smash of round knee against my thigh instead of in the groin. I got her wrists, but she wrenched one free and tore a line across my throat with her nails. She butted me solidly in the jaw with the top of her head, and then sank her teeth into the meat of my forearm, grinding away like a bulldog. That destroyed any vestige of chivalry. I chopped the side of her throat to loosen her bite, shoved her erect and hit her squarely on the chin with a short, chopping overhand right. She fell into my arms and I heaved her back onto the bed. I found a pile of nylon stockings on the lower shelf of the sash stand. I knotted her wrists together with one, her ankles with another, then bent her slack knees and tied the wrists to the ankles with a third, leaving about ten inches of play. Then I looked at the lacerated arms which had made the whole procedure slightly messy. I wondered if girl bite was as dangerous as dog bite. There was a half-bottle of local gin on the floor by the comic books. Oso Negro it was called. Black bear. I poured it over the tooth holes, and clenched my teeth, and said a few fervent words. I looked at my throat in her mirror, and rubbed some gin into that too. I tore away a piece of white sheeting and bound my arm and poured a little more gin on the bandage. Then I tried the gin. Battery acid, flavoured with juniper. I picked my fifty dollars off the floor and put it in my shirt pocket with the pesos. She began to moan and stir. She was on her right side. I sat on the bed near her, keeping a pillow handy. Her eyes fluttered and opened, and remained dazed for about one second. Then they narrowed to an anthracite glitter, and her lips lifted away from her teeth. She had good leverage to use against the nylon, all the power of her legs thrusting down, all the power of arms and back pulling. She tried it. I do not know the breaking strength of a nylon stocking. Perhaps it is a thousand pounds. She closed her eyes, her face contorted with effort. Muscles and tendons bulged the smooth toffee hide. Her face bulged and darkened, and sweat made her body shine. She subsided, breathing hard, and then without warning, snapped at my hand like a dog. I yanked it away, and the white teeth clacked uncomfortably close to it. I saw her gather herself, and I picked the pillow up, and at the first note of the scream, I plopped it across her face and lay on it. She bucked and writhed and made muffled bleating noises. Slowly she quieted down. The instant I lifted the pillow, the scream started and I mashed it back down again, and held it until she was really still. When I lifted it she was unconscious, but I could see that she was breathing. In about three minutes her eyes opened again.

'What the hell is the matter with you, Felicia?'

'Sohn of a beech!'

'Just listen to me for God's sake! I wasn't trying to insult you.'

'You wanna find Sam, uh?'

'No! I'm his friend, damn it. When I said my name, you had a look as though you heard it before. Travis McGee. From Florida. Maybe he said my name to you.'

'His friend?' she said uncertainly.

'Yes.'

'I remember he say the name one time,' she said in a forlorn voice. Surprisingly the dark eyes filled, tears rolled. 'I remember. So sorry, Trrav. Please tie me loose. Okay now.'

'No tricks?'

'I swear by Jesus.'

She had pulled the knots fantastically tight. I had to slice them with my pocket knife. She worked feeling back into her hands. As I started to get up, she caught my arm and pointed to her foot. She turned it so that the lamps shone more squarely on the broad brown instep. 'See?' she said.

There were about a dozen little pale puckered scars on the top of her foot, roughly circular, smaller than dimes.

'What's that?'

'From the other ones who say questions about Sam.' She pronounced it Sahm. 'Where is he? Where he go? Where he hide. Sohns a beech!' She looked at me and firmed her jaw and thumped her chest with her knuckles. 'Pain like hell, Trrav. Not a cry from me. *Nunca palabra*. Fainting, yes. You know . . . proud.'

'Who were they?'

She peered at my throat and made a hissing sound of concern. She slid off the bed and tugged me over to sit on the stool. She wiped my throat with something that stung, though not as badly as the gin, and put a Band Aid on the worst part of the gouge. When she unwrapped my arm, she said, '*Ai, como perra, verdad. Que feo!*' She had iodine. That too was less than the gin. She wrapped it neatly, taped the bandage in place.

'So sorry,' she said.

'Put something on, Felicia.'

'Eh?'

'I want to talk. Put on a robe or something.'

'Some love maybe? Then talk? No pesos.'

'No love, Felicia. But thank you.'

'The skinny woman, eh? But who can know?' She stared at me, then shrugged and went to one of the cardboard wardrobes and pulled out a very sheer pale blue hip-length wrap. Before she slipped into it, she dried her body with a towel, and slapped powder liberally on herself, using a big powder mitten, white streaks and patches against bronze-brown hide. She knotted the waist string, flung her long hair back with a toss of her head and sat in the upholstered chair.

'So?'

'Who were the men who hurt you?'

'Two of them, burning, burning with cigarette, Trrav. *Cubanos* I think. One with the good English. Then they want love. Hah!' She slapped her bare knee. 'With this I finish love forever for one of them I think. Screaming, screaming. He say to other one, cut the bitch throat. But the one, the one with the English, say no. Help his friend into car. Go away. Leave me there, seven *kilometros* from here. I walk on this bad foot back to here.'

'When did this happen, Felicia?'

'Perhaps five-six weeks. Sam gone then. Gone . . . three days I think. One night in this room. My friend is Rodriguez, with the fish truck going to Los Mochis. Sam walked before the day was light. Rodriguez, stop for him at a place on the road. I fix that. Every man think's he is gone by boat. He. . . .' She stopped and frowned. 'Sam said come here?'

'In a way.'

'How is that—in a way?'

'Sam is dead.'

She sat bolt upright and stared at me. 'No,' she whispered.

'Somebody followed him to Florida and killed him.'

She made a gargoyle mask, the stage mask of tragedy, and it would have been laughable had it not been so obviously a dry agony. She thrust herself from the chair, bending, hugging herself, passed me in a stumbling run to throw herself face down on the iron bed, gasping and grinding into the bunched pillow. The rear of the little blue wrap was up around her waist, exposing the smooth brown slope of buttocks. She writhed and strangled and kicked like a child in tantrum. I went and sat on the bed near her. At my first tentative pat of comfort on her shoulder, she made a twisting convulsive leap at me, pulling me down in the strong warm circle of her arms, making a great WhooHaw, WhooHaw of her sobbings into my neck. I wondered how many women were going to hold me and cry for Sam. I endured that close and humid anguish, perfume and hot flesh and the scent of healthy girl. The storm was too intense to last, and as it began to dwindle I realized that in her little shiftings, changing, holdings, she was beginning to involve herself in seduction, possibly deliberately, but more likely out of that strange and primitive instinct which causes people to couple in bomb shelters while air raids are in process. I firmly and quietly untangled myself, tossed a towel over to her and went and sat in the chair near the window. I looked down and saw that the comic book on top of one of the stacks was an educational epic in the Spanish language. I guessed that she would call it Oliver Tweest.

Finally she sat up in weariness, put a pillow against the bars of the headboard, hunched herself back and leaned there, ankles crossed. She swabbed her face and eyes and blew her nose, she sighed several times, her breath catching.

'He was a man,' she said in a soft nostalgic voice. I sensed that she had wept for him, and would not have to weep again.

'How did you meet him?'

'I worked in the kitchen there. I have seventeen years, no English, just a dumb kid. He is a boat captain, like Mario and Pedro. A little room he has there, not in the hotel. Near. Men and boys are after me, you know, like the dogs walking fast, tongue hanging out, so, follow the she? Sam chase them away, move me into his room. Ai, such trouble. The padre, my family, everyone. But to hell with them. We have love. I work in the kitchen all that time. A year I guess. More. Then he works for Senor Garcia. Big boat. Lives there in the big house. No so much time for love, eh? Time for the *rubia* . . . how you say . . . blonde. Yes. Blonde bitch in the big house. I work a little time more in the kitchen. They make laughs at me. Screw them all, eh? I am waiting like a mouse for when he wants love? Hell, no. I come here. Sam find me out. He beats me. Four-five times. Change nothing. He wants the *rubia*, I do what I like. Okay? More trouble from the padre, my brothers, everybody. Bad words.

Puta. I have twenty years. By God I do what I want. Pretty good room, eh? Not so hard work. Dancing, *copitas,* making love. Sam come here sometimes. Give me pesos. I rip them in front of the face. I hear things about the big house. Trouble. Danger. Then he come in the night to hide. Marks from fighting. He is here all day. I fix with Rodriguez. Sam say he will send much money to me one time, so I am here no more. Such a fool! This is good place I think. Many friends. Then two men give a ride in a pretty car. Out the road and then into the woods, burning, burning the foot. Where is Sam? Then you are here. Sam is dead. In Florida.' She made one stifled sobbing sound.

'Who is that blonde? Is she still around?'

'She is a friend with Senor Garcia. It is a hard name for me. Heechin. A thing like that, I think.'

'Hitchins?'

'I think so. Many fiestas in that house. Very rich man. Very sick now, I think.'

'Is the blonde still there?'

'They say yes. I have not seen.'

'Felicia, what was going on at Garcia's house?'

'Going on? Parties, drunk, bitch blondes. Who knows?'

'Did Sam say anything?'

'He say he keep what he earn. Some big thing he had, locked. He was sleeping. I try to look. Very very heavy. Big like so.' She indicated an object about the size of a large suitcase. 'Black metal,' she said. 'With a strap he fix to carry. Only a strong man like Sam can carry far.'

'He got to Los Mochis?'

'Rodriguez say yes.'

'You were willing to help him, to hide him here?'

She looked astonished. 'How not? He is a man. No thing changes that, eh? I am wife for a time. This stupid girl pleased him good, eh? He . . . we have a strong love. It can not be for all my life, with such a one.'

'He never told you anything about what went on at Garcia's house?'

'Oh yes. Talk, talk, talk. Persons coming and going in big cars and boats. *Mucho tumulto.* What is a word? Confusion. I do not listen so much to him, I think. When he is close I do not want all the talking. I say yes, yes, yes. He talks. Then soon I make him stop talking. I think *misterioso y peligroso* that house and those persons. No man from here ever works at that house. Just Sam.'

She got up from the bed and padded over and got a nail file and took it back to the bed and began working on her nails, giving me a hooded glance from time to time. The downstairs hubbub was vastly diminished.

'Is now late, I think, Trrav,' she said. 'You can stay, you can go. I think those two man find Sam, eh?'

'Perhaps.'

'Shoot him?'

'A knife.'

She made the Mexican gesture, shaking her right hand as though shaking water from her fingertips. 'Ai, a knife is a bad dying. Pobre Sam. You look for them?'

'Yes.'

'Because you are a friend? Maybe you are a clever man, eh? Maybe what you want is in that heavy box.'

'The box is why he was killed.'

'Maybe you send me some money instead of Sam, eh?'

'Maybe.'

'Down stairs you make me think of Sam. So big. Dark almost like me, but white, white, white, like milk where the sun is not touching.'

'Felicia, please don't tell anyone what we've talked about. Don't tell anyone he's dead.'

'Maybe only Rosita.'

'No one. Please.'

'Very hard for me,' she said, and smiled a small smile. I took the fifty, folded it into a small wad, laid it on my thumbnail and snapped it over onto the bed.

'Not even Rosita,' I said.

'Okay, Trrav.'

I stood up. 'I may want to come back and ask more questions.'

'Every night I am down there. I am not there, you wait a little time, eh?'

'Sure.'

She yawned wide, unsmothered, white teeth gleaming in membranous red, pointed tongue upcurled, stretched her elbows high, fists close to her throat.

'Love me now,' she said. 'We sleep better, eh?'

'No thanks.'

She pouted. 'Felicia is ugly?'

'Felicia is very beautiful.'

'Maybe you are not a man, eh?'

'Maybe not.'

She shrugged. 'I am sorry about the biting. Good night, Trrav. I like you very much.'

I let myself out into the blackness of the corridor. Downstairs a single male voice was raised in drunken song, the words slurred. I hesitated when I reached the mouth of the narrow alley. The street was empty. There were no lights at night in the village. But I had the feeling I was observed from the darkness. The American spent a long time with Felicia. I walked in the middle of the dusty road. A warm damp wind blew in from the sea. When I reached the outskirts of the village I could see the hotel lights far ahead of me.

As I crossed the small empty lobby, Arista appeared out of the shadows, suave and immaculate. 'Mister McGee?'

'Yes?'

'There was some trouble in the village tonight?'

'What do you mean?'

'Over a village girl?'

'Oh. Yes, a young fellow started waving a knife around and I knocked it out of his hand.'

'And you were drinking?'

'You are beginning to puzzle me, Arista.'

'Forgive me. I do not want you to be hurt, sir. It would be bad for our reputation here. Perhaps you were fortunate tonight. Those men are very deadly with knives. Forgive me, but it is not wise to . . . to approach the girls in the Tres Panchos. There has been much violence there. People tell me things, and the story worried me. I believe a girl named Felicia Novaro was involved.'

'People tell you very complete things, I guess.'

'Sir, she is a wild reckless girl. There is always trouble around her. She worked for me here. Her . . . behaviour was not good. She cannot be controlled. And . . . that is a squalid place, is it not, sir?'

'It seemed very cheerful to me.'

'Cheerful?' he said in a strained voice.

I clapped him on the shoulder. 'Sure. Local colour. Song and dance. Friendly natives. Salt of the earth. Pretty girls. Man, you couldn't keep me away from there. Good night, Senor Arista.'

He stared at my arm. 'You have been hurt?'

'Just chawed a little.'

'B-Bitten? My God, by a dog?'

I gave him a nudge in the ribs, a dirty grin and an evil wink, and said, 'Now you know better than that, pal.' I went humming off to my room.

CHAPTER ELEVEN

As soon as I turned my room lights on, Nora came out of the darkness of her room, through the open doorway, wearing a foamy yellow robe with a stiff white collar.

'You were gone so long I was getting. . . . What's wrong with your arm?'

'Nothing serious. It's a long story.'

I held her in my arms. After a little while she pushed me away and looked up at me. 'Darling, you are a veritable symphony of smells. You are truly nasty.'

'It is, in some ways, a nasty story.'

'I am *particularly* curious about the perfume, dear.'

'First I need a shower.'

She sat on the foot of my bed and said, primly, 'I shall wait.'

When I came out of the bathroom, the lights were out, and she was in my bed. When I got in, she moved into my arms and said, 'Mmmm. Now you smell like sunshine and soap.'

'This is quite a long story.'

'Mmmmhmmm.'

'When I got there, that bartender with the moustache presented me with the change I left on the table when. . . . Are you listening? Nora?'

'What? Oh sure. Go ahead.'

'So I split it with him. That was a popular gesture. He bought me a free drink. . . . I'm not sure you're paying attention.'

'What? Well . . . I guess I'm not. Not at the moment. Excuse me. My mind wanders. Let me know when you get to the part about the perfume.'

'Well, the hell with it.'

'Yes, dear. Yes, of course,' she said comfortably.

After breakfast, Nora and I walked up the winding road past the houses on the knoll beyond the boat basin. There were entrance pillars at the private driveways. There were small name plates on the entrance pillars. I made mental note of the names. Martinez, Guerrero, Escutia, in that order, and then Huvermann—who had to be the Swiss by process of elimination. Arista had said the Californian was not in residence, and I could see, in a gravelled area, a man carefully polishing a black Mercedes, and a swimming pool glinting a little further away.

The next one was Boody. There was a chain across the drive.
The last one was Garcia, the big pink one at the crest of the knoll.
The grounds were walled. I made Nora walk more slowly. The
wall, better than ten feet high, curved outward in a graceful
concavity near the top. At the top, glinting in wicket festive
colours in the sun, I could see the shards and spears of broken
glass set into cement. A man moved into view and stared morosely
at us through the bars of the spiked gate. He wore wrinkled
khaki, a gun belt, an incongruous straw hat—one of those jaunty
little narrow-brim cocoa straw things with a band of bright batik
fabric.

In a low voice I told Nora what to call out to him. She turned
to him and in a clear, smiling voice, called out *'Buenos dias!'*

He touched the brim of the hat and said, *'Buenuh dia.'*

Beyond the far corner of the wall, at a wide turnaround area,
the road ended. 'He's a Cuban,' I said to Nora. 'I didn't think he
would answer me if I tried it.'

'How can you tell?'

'They speak just about the ugliest Spanish in the hemisphere.'

We were around a curve and out of sight of the Garcia place
when we came to the Boody house. I stepped over the chain and
said. 'Let's take a look.'

She looked a little alarmed, but came with me. It was a pale
blue house, with areas of brick painted white. It was shuttered.
Within the next year it was going to need some more paint. The
pool area behind the house was, despite an unkempt air, a
nymphet's dream of Hollywood. A huge area was screened. The
pool apron was on several levels, separated by planting areas.
There was a bar area, a barbecue area, heavy chaises with the
cushions stored way, a diving platform, a men's bathhouse and
women's bathhouse with terribly cute symbols on the door,
weatherproof speakers fastened to palm boles, dozens of outdoor
spots and floods, a couple of thatched tea houses, storage bins, big
shade devices made of pipe, with fading canvas still lashed in
place. The pool was empty, the screening torn in a few places, the
bright paint peeling and fading. It all had a look of plaintive
gaiety, like an abandoned amusement park.

I took a closer look at the rear of the main house. An inside
hook on a pair of shutters lifted readily when I slid the knife
blade in.

'Are you out of your damned mind?' Nora asked nervously.

'I'm just a delinquent at heart,' I said. The windows behind
the open shutters were aluminium awning windows, horizontal,

with the screen on the inside. I closed the shutters and wedged them shut with a piece of twig, and continued my prowl.

'Do you want to get in there? Why?'

'Because it's next door to Garcia.'

'Ask a stupid question,' she said.

It finally turned out that the front door was the vulnerable place. The immediate procedure was to set up rapid access. She watched me rig the door at the side, a solid door opening onto the pool area from the bedroom wing. It was locked by an inside latch, and the aluminium screen door beyond it was latched. I unlocked them both. I found a piece of cord in the kitchen and tied the screen door shut. Anyone checking the house would find it firm. But if I wanted to come in in a hurry, all I had to do was yank hard enough to break the cord, then latch both doors behind me.

I used my lighter to look at the cans in the storage pantry. 'See, dear? Plenty of canned fruit juices. And stuff that doesn't taste too bad cold—beans, beef stew, chilli. This is an advance base, next to unfriendly territory. Maybe we never use it.'

She followed me to the library, staying very close to me, saying, 'It just make me so damned nervous, Trav.' When I sat at the desk and began to look through the papers in the middle drawer, she sat on the edge of a straight chair, turning her head sharply from side to side as she heard imaginary noises.

'Claude and Eloise Boody,' I said finally, 'of Beverly Hills. Claude is Amity Productions. He is also Trans-Pacific Television Associates, and Clabo Studios, unless these are all obsolete letterheads.'

'Can we leave now? Please?'

We went back out the front door. It locked behind us. She was a dozen feet in the lead all the way to the driveway chain, and she kept that lead until we were a hundred feet down the road. She slowed down then, and gave a huge lifting sigh of relief.

'I don't understand you, Trav.'

'Carlos Menterez y Cruzada has or had a taste for the Yankee celebrity, show biz variety. He partied it up here. Boody would be a pretty good procurement agent. He lived next door. I wanted the California address. If things peter out here, it's another starting point.'

'But still. . . .'

'The houses seem to have been done by the same architects. I wanted the feel of one of the houses, what to expect about the interior planning—materials, surfaces, lighting, changes of floor level. Garcia's is bigger and it will sure as hell be furnished differently, but I know a lot more about it now.'

'But why should you. . . .'

'Tonight I'm going to pay an informal call.'

She stopped and stared at me. 'You can't!'

'It's the next step, honey. Over the wall, like Robin Hood.'

'No, Trav. Please. You've been so careful about everything and. . . .'

'Care and preparation can take you just so far, Nora. And then you have to make a move. Then you have to joggle the wasp nest. I'll be very very careful.'

Her eyes filled. 'I couldn't stand losing you too.'

'Not a chance of it. Never fear.'

After an after-dinner drink, Nora and I left the bar and went back to the rooms. She paced back and forth, complaining, while I improvised a grapnel. I had bought three monstrous shark hooks, some heavy wire and some cheap pliers. I bound the shanks of the hooks together to form a huge gange hook, using plenty of wire to make it firm and also give it a little extra weight. I had also purchased fifty feet of nylon cord that looked as if it would test out at about five hundred pounds breaking strength.

'If you insist on being an idiot, why go so early in the evening?'

'When people are moving around, a little extra noise doesn't mean too much.'

'When people are moving around, where are you?'

'Watching them, dear. If everybody is asleep and all the lights are out, I can't find out anything, can I?'

'Do you expect to be invisible?'

'Practically, dear.'

'How long will it take?'

'I haven't any idea.'

'Honest to God, Trav. I don't see why. . . .'

I put the pencil flashlight in my pocket and took her by the shoulders and shook her. 'How did Sam look?'

The colour seeped out from under her tan. 'You cruel bastard,' she whispered.

'How did he look?'

'My God, Trav! How can you. . . .'

I shook her again. 'Just say the word, honey. I'll put away my toys and we'll get into the sack. And then we'll go back home anytime you say, and you can refund my split of all the expenses, and we'll forget the whole thing. Call it an interesting vacation.

Call it anything you want. Or you can let me go ahead my way. It's your choice, Nora.'

She moved away from me. She walked slowly to the other side of the room and turned and looked at me. Barely moving her lips she said, 'Good luck tonight, darling.'

'Thank you.'

I had on dark slacks, a long sleeved dark blue shirt, dark canvas shoes. I had no identification on me. I had the silly bedroom gun in one trouser pocket, the pencil light and pocket knife in the other, the grapnel coiled around my waist. We turned the lights out. I opened the draperies and cautiously unhooked the screen, turned it and brought it into the room and stood it against the wall beside the window. I looked out, it was all clear. I turned back to her and held her and kissed her hungry nervous mouth. She felt exceptionally good in my arms, good enough so that I wished for a moment she had said the hell with it. Then I straddled the sill, turned, hung by my fingertips, kicked myself away from the side of the building and dropped. It was about nine feet down to soft earth. I had the right window marked by its relationship to a crooked tree. On my return, I would flip pebbles against the window to signal her. I would toss the line in and she would make it fast. If for any reason we could not anticipate, anyone had to come into the rooms, she would turn my shower on and close the bathroom door before answering the hall door.

She had the waiting. Maybe that was the hardest part.

CHAPTER TWELVE

IT was almost over before it began.

When I got to the Boody place, I stepped over the chain and went around to the side of the house opposite the swimming pool, and made my way to the Garcia wall through the Boody grounds. I stood by the wall a long time, listening, and heard nothing but the normal noises of the night, and the whining of mosquitoes looking for the meat of my neck.

After debating a moment, I decided to try a place where the top of the wall wasn't shadowed by the trees inside. I might be more visible, but I had that damned glass to fool with. I wanted the hooks to catch the inside edge of the wall. If they'd rounded it off, I'd have to try flying it into a tree. That made retrieving it more of a problem. I straightened the loops out and tossed the hooks over the wall. I heard them clink against the inside of the wall. I pulled them slowly, worrying about sawing the nylon against sharp glass. They caught, but when I put on a little pressure there was a tink of breaking glass, and a piece of glass and the hooks came back to me. After a third try, and more glass each time, I knew the wall was rounded off on the inside, another little touch of professionalism. I moved back away from the wall and moved along parallel to it, moving further away from the road, until I came to a tree I liked, growing on the inside. I held the very end of the line in my left hand, the loops between thumb and finger, and swung the grapnel around my head a few times with my right hand and let it fly. It arched into the leaves with too much noise. I listened, then slowly pulled it tight. It was fast, and apparently on a good solid branch, because when I put my weight on it, there was only about a six-inch give. The angle of the line took it across my edge of the wall. At least it was out of the glass. I put my rubber soles against the white wall and walked up it, at an acute and unpleasant angle. The damned nylon was so thin it dug painfully into my hands. The concavity near the top was tricky, but I took a giant step and got one foot on the edge, and then the other, and pulled myself erect, wriggling my toes into areas between the shards of glass. Holding the line lightly for balance, I looked into the grounds. Off to my right I could see a faint light which I guessed was the gate light. I could see the lights of the main house almost dead ahead, between the leaves. I broke a few shards off, snubbing at them with the toe of my right shoe, and got myself a more balanced place to stand, then tried to yank the damned hooks free. They would not come free. All I did was make a horrid rustling in the leaves. I certainly could not go up such a thin line hand over hand to free it. As I decided it was hopeless, I gave a last despairing yank and it came free so unexpectedly that I did a comedy routine on top of the wall, my back arched, waving my arms wildly to keep from falling back outside.

When I had balance, I brought the grapnel up and fixed it firmly on to the outside corner of the wall at a place where the line lay between the sharpness of glass as it crossed the top of the wall. I lowered myself on the inside, and let myself down in the same way as I had climbed up. I knew I might want to find the line in one hell of a hurry. There were too many trees, and the wall was too featureless, the white of the line too invisible against it. Then I had an idea, and I fumbled around and found some soft moist earth and took it in both hands and made a big visible smear on the white wall. I knew I could find that in a hurry.

I started toward the house. I had not gone ten feet from the wall when I heard it. Something coming at me fast, with a little guttural sound of effort, a scrabble of nails skidding on the ground. It came into the silver of moonlight a dozen feet away, and made one more bound and launched itself up at me, a big black silent murderous Doberman. I was pivoting and falling as I felt my fingers of both hands dig into the corded forearm of the dog, with no memory of how I had managed to grasp it, an index finger hooked around the knob of the elbow. Unless I could impart enough centrifugal force to keep his head away from my hands, I was going to lose meat in a painful and ugly way, so I heaved as hard as I could, combining his leap, my backward fall, the pivot, into a single flight. I felt something give as I let go, heard a small whistling whine, a meaty thud as he struck the wall combined with a clopping sound as it snapped his jaws shut, a softer thud as he fell to the ground. I bounded up, feeling as cold as if I'd handled snakes. From the instant he bounded at me until he fell to the ground at the base of the wall, the total elapsed time was perhaps less than two full seconds. I wiped my hands on my thighs and waited for him.

I moved to him carefully, screened the small pencil beam with my body and took a two second look. He was about eighty pounds of sinew, black hair and fangs—and he was quite dead.

It put an unknown limit on the time I could spend there. I had no way of knowing when they would call him. Perhaps they pulled in the human guard at nightfall and let the dog roam the grounds all night. He was too near my escape line. I waited until my eyes had readjusted to the night, then with a squeamish hesitation, took him by the hind paw and dragged him a dozen yards into a thickness of shrubbery covered with fragrant white blooms. Some variety of jasmine. Suddenly I wondered if they had a pair of dogs, and the thought nearly sent me hustling toward my escape line. I couldn't expect that much luck twice. Few men have ever given me as much instant fright as that dog gave me. And it was an unpleasant clue to the Garcia attitude about visitors. Uninvited visitors. Watchdogs trained to bark are a lot more common, and more civilized.

As I moved carefully toward the house, avoiding open patches of moonlight, listening for the slightest sound of a charging dog, I took note of direction and landmarks. I wanted to be able to leave at a headlong run, if need be, with a certainty of hitting the wall at the right place. When I had an unimpeded view of the big pink house, I stopped in the shadows and moved to one side and leaned against the trunk of a tree and hooked my thumbs in my belt and stared at it. By assuming one of the postures of relaxation you can trick your body into thinking things are perfectly under control. I was still shaky from the extra adrenalin the black dog had stimulated. I looked at the roof shape against the sky. There weren't many windows lighted. It was a big house, at least double the size of the Boody place. The complex of smaller buildings behind it was more elaborate, and there were lights showing there, too, and a faint sound of music from there.

I selected the next spot. There was a shallow patio with a low broad stone wall, the patio next to a wing of the house, parallel to it and up against it. Two sets of glass doors and two windows were encircled by the patio wall. The doors and window to the right were lighted. The light seemed to come through opaque white draperies. The doors and window to the left were dark. Once you decide, it is a strategic error to wait too long. Then it becomes like jumping off a roof. The longer you wait, the higher it looks. I had to cross a moonlit area. I bent double and moved swiftly, angling toward the dark end of the shallow patio. I went over the wall, moved close to the side of the house and lay on rough flagstones close against a low line of plantings. I listened. Now the fact of the dog was in my favour. Nobody was going to stay terribly alert, not with a monster like that cruising the grounds. When they've killed you, they stand and bay until somebody comes to congratulate them.

I wormed on over to the lighted doors, and found a place at the bottom corner I could look through. I was looking into a big bedroom with a sitting-room area at one end of it, the end nearest the doors. A wall mirror showed me the reflection of the end of an elaborately canopied bed. A man sat on a grey chaise, turned away from me, so that all I could see of his face was a shelf of brow, curve of cheek. He wore shorts. One leg was outstretched, one propped up. They were pale legs, thick and powerful, fuzzed with a pelt of springy black hair. He was reading a book. His left side was toward me. Gold wrist watch and gold strap were half submerged in the curl of black hair on forearm and wrist.

I saw a movement in the mirror and then a girl came into view. She was walking slowly, barefoot, fastening the side of

a green knit skirt, her head angled down so that a heavy sheaf
of shining blonde hair obscured her face. She wore a white bra
covering small breasts. Her upper torso was golden tan, with
the narrow and supple look of youth. She fixed the skirt as she
reached the foot of the chaise. She threw her hair back with a
toss of her head, and stood and looked at the man with a cool,
unpleasant expression. It was a very lovely face. I could guess
that her earliest memories were of being told how pretty she was.
It was a cool and sensuous face. The springing blonde hair, with
a few tousled strands across her forehead, fell in a glossy heaviness
in two wings which framed the sensitive and bad tempered face.
I had seen her before, and I groped for the memory, and finally
had it. She had stared very earnestly at me many times, looked
deeply into my eyes, held up a little squeeze bottle and told me
it would keep me dainty all day long. Despite all rumours to the
contrary, these huckster blondes are not interchangeable. I knew
this one because her eyes were set strangely, one more tilted
than the other.

   She said something to the man. The curl of her mouth looked
unpleasant. He lowered the book, said something, lifted it again.
She shrugged and turned away and walked out of my field of
vision. I lay in controlled schizophrenia, split between my interest
in the lighted room, and my alertness for any sound behind me
in the night. When she appeared again she was fastening the top
half of the green knit two piece suit and she wore shoes. She had
that contrived walk of the model, like Nora's walk but more so—
the business of putting each foot down in direct line with the
previous step, toeing outward slightly, to impart a graceful sway
to the body from the waist down. She was not tall. Perhaps
five-four. She made herself look tall.

   She stopped at the right side of the chaise and perched one
hip on it, facing the man. She spoke to him. I could hear the
very faint cadence of her voice. She was intent, persuasive, half-
smiling. It was like a commercial with the volume turned down.
As she talked, he put two cigarettes between his lips, lit them,
handed one to her. She stopped talking and looked expectantly
at him. He reached and caught her wrist. She sprang up and
wrenched her wrist away, her face ugly with sudden fury. She
called him a ten letter word, loud enough for me to hear it
through the doors. She was no lady. She strode out of range in
the opposite direction, and I heard a door slam.

   She left with the look of somebody who was not coming back
immediately. There was no profit in watching a hairy man read

a book. I eased back and crouched in the moon shadows and stood up slowly. From what I had seen of the Boody house and what I could observe of this one, the dark doors and window would open on to another bedroom unit. They were sliding doors, in an aluminium track. I tried the outside handle. Locked. It would turn down about an inch, and then it stopped. I stood close to it, got a good grip on it, then began to exert an ever-increasing pressure. Just as my muscles began to creak and protest, some part of the inner mechanism snapped with a sharp metallic sound. I waited and listened. I tried the door. It slid open with a muted rumble. I crouched, tensed up, ready to go. Burglar alarms seemed like a logical accessory to a killer dog. It didn't have to be a clanging. It could be a muted buzz at a guard station, inaudible to me. So I counted off six hundred seconds before I slipped through the eighteen-inch opening, brushing the draperies aside. I stood in the darkness in total concentration. We are given certain atavistic faculties which can be trained through use. You can stand in a dark room and after a time be absolutely certain there is no other person there. When I was quite certain, I used the pencil light, pinching the beam smaller between thumb and finger. It was a big bedroom-sitting room, less luxurious than the one I had looked into. There were no coverings on the two three-quarter beds. I went back and closed the door I had broken, and checked the three other doors. One opened into a roomy dressing-room. One opened into a tiled bath, where an astonished cockroach sped into the darkness. The third opened on to a broad and dimly lighted hallway. There was a window at the blind end. The other end opened out into a big room as weakly lighted as the hallway. I could see the dark shapes of heavy furniture. Four doors opened on to the hallway. Two on each side. Four guest bedroom units, I assumed. The resident quarters would be in the other wing. I could hear no sound. I debated trying my luck with a quick and silent run into the living room at the end of the corridor, taking a chance on finding a dark pocket behind some of that heavy furniture. But there was too much chance of being cut off. I locked the bedroom door on the inside, and went back out through the glass doors, listened for a time, then left the patio and moved along the side of the house and around to the back, feeling more confident.

That is the familiar trap of course, the one that catches the cat burglars. They begin to feel invulnerable, and they push it a little further and a little further, until one day in their carelessness they wake up the wrong person—and then kill or are killed.

I sped through an area of moonlight, and crouched beyond the swimming pool, a layout identical to the Boody construction, near the building where the servants would be housed. Mexican radio was loud. Windows were lighted. The rooms were small and plain. I wanted a reasonable head count. The smell of cooking was strong. I saw a heavy woman walking to and fro in a small room, carrying a whining child, while a man sat alone at a table playing with a set of greasy cards. A screen door slapped. Somebody hawked and spat. I saw three men in a room, playing dominoes, placing them with large scowls and gestures, loud clacks of defiance. One of them was my wistful gate guard. A woman sat near them, stirring something in a large pottery bowl. A kitten mewed. The radio advertized Aye-low Shahm-boo. I looked through a gap in a sleazy curtain and saw, on a cot, under the bright glare of an unshaded bulb, in the direct blast of the music of the plastic radio, a muscular man and a very skinny woman making love, both of them shiny with sweat.

A quiet evening in the servant's quarters. I drifted away, and made my way back across to the big house, and came up to it at the rear, on the other side. I looked into a big bright white kitchen. A square-bodied, square-faced, dark skinned woman in a black and white uniform sat on a high red stool at a counter, polishing silver. A man leaned against the counter near her. A guard type, in khaki, armed, eating a chicken leg.

I passed dark windows. I came to a lighted one. I looked in. It was a small bedroom. A thin drab-looking, middle-aged woman sat there in a rocking chair without arms. She wore a very elaborate white dress, all lace and embroidery, strangely like a wedding dress. It did not look clean. Her hair was unkempt, strands of grey long and tangled. She had her arms folded across her chest. She was rocking violently, seeming to come close to tipping the chair over backwards each time. Her underlip sagged and her face was absolutely empty. There is only one human condition which can cause that total terrible emptiness. She rocked and rocked, looking at nothing.

As I moved along the side of the house I heard a woman's voice. I passed more dark windows and came to three lighted ones in a row. They were open. As I crept closer I heard that she was speaking Spanish. And as it went on and on, I realized from the cadence of her voice that she was reading aloud. The accent seemed expert, as far as I could tell, the voice young and clear, nicely modulated. But she stumbled over words from time to time.

She seemed too close to the first window for me to take a chance, so I wormed on along to the last of the three lighted windows. I straightened up beyond it, and took a careful look. I saw a fat brown woman in a white uniform sitting on a couch sewing, her fingers swift and her face impassive. And off to the right, near the first window, I could see the blonde girl in the green knit suit, sitting on a straight chair beside a bed, her back to me, bending over the book she held in her lap. I could not see who was in the bed.

I waited there. She read on and on. Mosquitoes found my neck and I rubbed them off. I settled into the stupor of waiting. She could not read forever. Something had to change. And then I might learn something. At last she closed the book with an audible thump, and in a lazy, loving tone she said, 'That's really all I can manage tonight, darling. My eyes are beginning to give out. I hope you don't mind too much.'

There was no answer. She put the book aside and stood up and bent over whoever was in the bed. All I could see of her was the rounded girl-rump under the stretch of knitted green. The fat woman had stopped sewing and she was watching the girl, her eyes narrowed.

The girl made the murmurous sound of a woman giving her affection and then straightened. 'Carlos, darling,' she said, 'I'm going to ask you to try to write your name again. Do you understand, dear? One blink for yes. Good.'

She went out of my range and came back with a pad and pencil. She apparently sat beside him on the bed. I could see her slim ankles. 'Here, darling. That's it. Hold it as tightly as you can. Now write your name, dear.'

There was a silence. Suddenly the girl sprang up, and made a violent motion and there was the sound of an open palm against flesh. 'You filth!' she shouted. 'You dirty bastard!' The pad and pencil fell to the floor. The fat woman started up off the couch, hesitated, settled back and picked up her sewing.

The girl stood back from the bed, her body rigid, her fists on her hips. 'I suppose that's your idea of a joke, writing a dirty word like that. God damn you, you understand me. I *know* you do. Try to get this through your head, Carlos. The pesos in the household account are down to damned near nothing. If you expect me to stay here and care for you and protect you, you are going to have to write your name clearly and legibly on a power of attorney so I can go to the bank in Mexico City and get more money. You have to trust me. It's the only chance you have, brother. And you better realize it. When the money stops, these people of yours are going to melt away like the morning dew, and you'll die and rot right here. Oh brother, I know how your mind works. You think I'm going to grab it all and run. If I did, you wouldn't be any worse off, would you? And what the hell good is money going to do you from now on? Listen, because I probably owe you something, Carlos, I swear I'll go and get the money and come back here and take care of you. I'll keep them from killing you. Don't you realize those men must have told somebody else before they came here to fix you? You think it over, my friend. You're not going to get too many more chances. I'm getting sick of this whole situation. Gabe and I may leave at any time. Who have you got left who could go for the money? Your wife, maybe? Your kook wife? We'll put wheels on her rocking chair. Jesus Christ, you make me sore, Carlos. Do me a personal favour. Have lousy dreams tonight. Okay.'

She whirled and went out. She was a door banger.

I went back to the first window and took a look. The bed was directly under the window. Carlos Menterez was propped up on a mound of pillows. They'd dressed him in a heavy silk robe. With his bald head and his shrunken face, he looked like the skeleton of a monkey. The left eye was dropped almost shut, and the left side of his mouth and face fell slack, in grey folds. The look of severe stroke. But the right eye was round and dark and alert. In my interest, I had gotten a little too close to the screen. The good eye turned toward me, and suddenly became wider. His mouth opened on the good side, pulling the slack side open. He made a horrid cawing, gobbling sound, and lifted his right hand, a claw hand, as though to ward off a blow. I ducked down and heard the fat woman hurry to him. She made comforting sounds, patting and adjusting, fixing his pillows. Carlos made plaintive gobblings, wet sounds of despair. She worked over him for quite a while, and then she turned several lights out.

I went around the front of the house, completing the circuit. There was a light over the gate, but no guard. I could see that a heavy chain was looped through the bars of the gate. I wanted to get around and see what the blonde and Gabe were doing. I wondered how I could make myself a chance to hear what they were saying. It would be too much to expect that he might

have opened the window. He hadn't. But as I lowered myself
to look through the same place as before, I heard him bellow,
'For Chrissake, Alma!' She was sitting huddled on the foot of
the chaise. He was pacing back and forth, making gestures. He
had a hard handsome face, glossy black hair worn too long.

Then behind me I heard a shrill whistle. A man yelled,
'Brujo! Eh, *perro*! Brujo!' He whistled again. But Brujo had
retired from the dog business. I went from the patio into the moon
shade of the trees. I heard two men talking loudly, arguing. I
saw lights moving beyond the leaves.

They both called the dog. And I made a wide furtive circle
behind them as they moved, angling toward my escape line. I
could sense that they were getting too close to where I'd left
the dead dog.

There was a sudden silence, and then excited yelling. Then
a shocking and sudden bam-bam of two shots rupturing the
night. I was flat on my face before I could comprehend that they
had not been aimed at me, that they were warning shots, fired
into the air. More lights went on. There were more voices, raised
in loud query. Suddenly at least fifty decorative floodlights went
on, all over the pool area, all over the grounds. I guess I had
seen some of the lights. They hadn't registered. I was in the cone
of radiance of one of them. I swiftly pulled myself into darkness,
momentarily blinded. Somebody ran by me, a few feet away,
shoes drumming against the earth. All I had to do was wait for
them to spot the smear on the wall, investigate, find the thin
nylon rope, then hunt me down. Already they were beginning
to fan out, five or six of them, shining flashlights into the dark
places. And one was moving slowly toward me. He would have
a gun in one hand and the light in the other. There was an
unpleasant eagerness about them, as if they were after a special
bonus.

I could not circle behind him. I would have had to cut through
the revealing lights. I moved back, came up against a tree,
wormed around it, stood on the far side of it and went up it
almost as fast as I can run up a flight of stairs. It had sharp
stubby thorns sticking out of the trunk, and I did not pay them
much attention at the time. I stood a dozen feet up, balanced
in the crotch of a fat branch, holding the main trunk for support.
Below me, the diligent fellow came through the lights and
swept the light back and forth where I had been. I looked around.
The others were just about far enough away. When he moved into
the relative darkness under my tree, I stepped into space and

dropped on to him, feet first, landing on the backs of his shoulders, driving him down to the ground. I rolled to my knees and snatched his flashlight. It had rolled away from him. I swept the beam over, saw his hand gun and picked it up. He stirred and I hammered him down again, laying the side of the revolver against the back of his skull. I stood, sweeping the light back and forth, as though searching.

A man thirty feet away rattled a question at me.

'No see,' I grumbled. Avoiding the lights, I worked my way away from him. A few moments later, I reached the stain on the wall. I found the line. It was firm. In that instant all the lights flickered and went out, and I knew it was midnight. The big generator had been turned off. They called to each other, swinging their lights around dangerously. Somebody yelled, 'Chucho? Chucho?' I guessed I had his gun and light. I turned the light off, then threw it toward the house as hard as I could, arching it up over the trees. There was a satisfying crash and chime of glass. As the shouts came, as they all began moving toward the house, I went up the line, stood on the wall, freed the hooks and jumped into the darkness. I landed on uneven ground, hit my chin on my knee and jarred my teeth, rolled over on to my side. I yanked the rest of the line over the wall, and hastened across the Boody grounds, coiling it as I went, the gun a hard lump between belt and belly. I could hear more shouts, and I wondered if they'd found Chucho. I wondered if he was the wistful one, the chicken eater, the lovemaker or one of the others.

When I rattled the first pebble into the room through the open window, she whispered, 'Trav? Darling?'

'Get away from the window.'

I tossed the hooks in. They clanked on the tile. She dug the hooks into the overlap of the wooden sill. I walked up the side of the building, caught at the edge, slid over the sill belly down, and spilled into the room. As I rolled over, she nestled down upon me, sobbing and laughing, smothering the sounds against my chest. 'I heard shots,' she said. 'Far away, and I thought. . . .'

'There was some excitement while I was leaving.'

She let me up. I pulled the line in. We went into the bathroom to inspect damage. The only room lights on the night circuit were weak bulbs in the bathrooms. Twenty-five watts. Those thorns had torn me up pretty good, puncturing and tearing the flesh on the insides of my arms and legs. Fear had been a marvellous anaesthetic. I put the gun on the shelf above the sink and stripped down. It was a respectable weapon, a Smith and Wesson .38, a standard police firearm with walnut grips. It hadn't received tender loving care, but it looked deadly enough. And the damn fool had been carrying it hammer down, on the empty chamber, instead of hammer back with a fresh one in position.

Nora made little bleatings of concern when she saw how torn up I was. She hurried off and came back with antiseptic, cotton and tape. I took a cold shower first, bloodied a towel drying myself, then stretched out in the restricted area of the bathroom on my back so she could do a patch job. She bit down on her lip as she worked. She had trouble getting out of her own shadow. I could feel the exhaustion seeping through me. I told her there was a bad dog and I had killed it. I said I had been in the house. I had seen a few things, heard a few things, and I would tell her about them later. I had had to hit a man on the head to get out of there. It had been a little closer than I cared for things to be. The closeness of it made her weep, and then I had to make jokes to prove it had not been really that close.

Then we went to bed. She was dubious about my obvious intentions, but she was very very glad to have me back. And we had grown to know each other. It was no longer the mysterious business of strangers being too curious about the reaction to this or that, holding themselves in a kind of tentative reserve. Now I knew the arrangements of her, the strictures and the willingnesses, the fashioning of her for her needs and takings, so that I could lose myself in all that and become one striving thing with her, both of us all of one familiar flesh.

CHAPTER THIRTEEN

AFTER breakfast I sat in umbrellaed shade while Nora swam, shirt and slacks covering the thorn wounds, my curled hand concealing the random stigmata, the girl-bite bandage also hidden under the long sleeves of the white shirt. I had some sore and creaking muscles, and a couple of bruises which felt as if they went all the way down into the bone marrow.

The revolver, sealed by a rubber band fastening into a plastic shoe bag, rested in the bottom of her toilet tank. The improvised grapnel was buried in the soft black dirt under a bush. I had rinsed the smeared stains of blood from my hands off the thin nylon rope, coiled it and stowed it in a bureau drawer. The ruined slacks and shirt were a minor problem. Nora had them stowed in her beach bag, tightly rolled. We could bury them at the beach.

She came out of the pool and returned to our table. She towelled her face and shoulders, fluffed her dark hair, moved her chair into the sun and frowned at me. 'What's the matter?' I asked.

'There was something between Sam and the blonde.'

'If Alma's last name is Hitchins, and if Felicia is right, yes.'

'Then she's been there a long time.'

'Maybe. Back and forth is a better guess, I'd say. The intermittent house guest. For a nice long stay every time.'

'Who is Gabe?'

'God knows. The relationship with Alma had a flavour of intimacy. But she seems to be in charge.'

'Do you think she wants to get the money and run?'

'What else? Maybe Menterez was a lot of laughs before something gave way in his head. But what's there for her now? You know, she has it locked up pretty good. If anybody comes around who really wants to help him, she can keep them from getting past the gate. He is incapable of communicating with anybody. Speech is gone, but he can understand and he can write. I don't think that fat nurse understands English. I have the idea nobody gets into that room except Alma and the fat nurse. I don't think anybody else will get in there until he's ready to sign a power of attorney. I would bet the bulk of his fortune is in Switzerland, but he's likely to have a nice chunk of cash in a lock box in Mexico City. I don't think it would be on deposit. I'd lay odds it's in dollars or pounds. And he damn well knows she wants to clean him out. If she does, who can touch her? How far can he get by complaining to the Mexican authorities? I think I know what's eating her. She's afraid he'll have another one before she can soften him up. I think he's suffering the fate of all vultures. When they get sick, the others eat him.'

'Don't be so damned vivid, Trav.'

'I'd like to unravel that remark she made about some men having told somebody else where he was before they came here to fix him. They tried and they didn't make it, and evidently they didn't survive the experience. That was the inference. But if any kind of big dramatic violence went on around here, I think Felicia would have known about it and told me about it. How did Sam earn those gold figures? Who got all but one of them away from him? Honey, we're up to here in questions.'

'What are you going to do about it?'

'Pry Alma open.'

'You can't go back there!'

'Nora dear, I wouldn't go over that wall again for a thirty dollar bill. So we got to get sweetie pie out of there somehow.'

'Is she another one of those . . . what did you call them? . . . sun bunnies?'

'Not this one. This one is bright and cold and hard and beautiful.'

She gave a mirthless laugh. 'Sam kept pretty busy.'

'I think this one would have gone after Sam if she thought he could do her some good. And I think if she went after him, he wouldn't stand much of a chance. And I think her nerves are good enough to carry on another intrigue right in Menterez' house. This one has that cool sexually-speculative look.'

'She and that Gabe are a team?'

'I don't know. He's a little too pretty. She'll cross him up when it comes his turn. I think he's just a stud she imported to liven the dull days of waiting. But I have the idea he knows what she's trying to do.'

'I keep thinking of that black dog.'

'Please I keep trying not to think about him. How do we get her out of there?'

'Darling, the mail comes to the village by bus, and they bring the mail for those houses out here to the hotel. I . . . I might put a little note in there for her. My handwriting is obviously feminine. So is my note paper.'

'Nora, you are a fine bright girl.'

'I don't know what to say. But it should be something that. . . . She shouldn't be able to rest until she finds out the rest of it. Maybe I should phone her.'

'There is one phone in this whole hotel, in Arista's office. I think there are two in the village. There are none on the hill.'

'Oh.'

'But the idea is superb. Let's give it a lot of thought.'

'Shouldn't we make sure of her name? Wouldn't that help?'

'It would help indeed.'

It seemed a difficult project, but like many such problems, it turned out to be extraordinarily simple. I found one of the hotel porters at a small table near the lobby door sorting mail, the mail he would carry up the hill and leave at the tenanted house. He was checking the addresses against a tattered, dog-eared sheet. The principal names had been typed. Other names in the household had been written under them in pencil. There was a long list under Garcia, well over a dozen names. Among them was the girl's name. She had phonied up the first name, as girls are inclined to do these days. Almah. Miss Almah Hichin. The porter was trying to tell me I would not find my mail in that batch. I misunderstood him. By the time Arista came over to straighten me out, I had what I needed.

Nora and I spent a long time composing a draft of a very short note.

'My dear Miss Hichin, I have heard so many things about you, I feel that I know you. ST told me many things, including one thing I must pass along to you in person. He said it would *deeply* concern you, and might change your future plans. It does not mean much to me, but from the sound of it I would judge it important. I am at La Casa Encantada, but for obvious reasons, that would not be a good place for us to meet.'

'What obvious reasons?' Nora asked, scowling.

'If you don't have any, she will. Or she'll wonder what the hell your reasons are.'

'Where should we meet?'

'I saw three cars up there. One is a dark red convertible Ghia. Say this: Drive the little red car down to the village tomorrow at one in the afternoon. Stop in front of the largest church. Please be alone. I shall be.'

Her initials, NDG, were embossed in the top corner of the blue note paper. There was no address. I had her sign it with merely an N.

'What if she should know Sam is . . . dead?'

'She'll wonder what he said before he died.'

'Do you think she'll come?'

'She'll have to.'

'Tomorrow will mean the day after tomorrow. We can't get it to her until. . . .'

'I know. You'll give it to that old porter, with a lovely smile, and a five peso note.'

'Then what do we do with her if she does come?'

'I'm going to take a long walk to find out, dear.'

'Can I come?'

I did some mental arithmetic. A kilometer is six-tenths of a mile. 'Can you manage ten miles in the heat?'

She could do better than that. She proved it. She became
very mysterious, made me wait for her, came back full of suppressed amusement, then led me out to the back of the hotel,
to the out buildings there, the supply sheds, generator building,
staff barracks, back to a place where Jose, our room waiter, stood
proudly beside a fantastic piece of transportation. It was an
Italian motor-scooter with fat doughnut tyres, all bright coral,
poisonous yellow-green and sparkling chrome. It was incongruous
transportation for that severe, polite little man. He would not
consent to rent it until he had checked me out on it.

When the deal was struck, Nora straddled the rear compartment, her dark hair tied in a scarf, and we took off for the
village. I ruptured siesta by making three circuits of the public
square.

When we stopped Nora was amused and indignant.

'Really, Trav! My God, what were you trying to prove?'

'That we're nutty harmless Americans. Smoke screen, honey.
Anybody who went over that wall couldn't possibly clown
around on this gaudy machine the very next day. And I think
the village damn well knows they had trouble up there last
night. And what point is there in looking as if we had any
special destination? When we come back, we'll bomb them
again.'

We leaped onto the machine and took off again.

We met a bus coming to the village. After a while, I found
the place Felicia had probably been talking about. A smaller
road, just a trace of a road, turned off to the left. It ended after
about a hundred feet, in a little clearing which the jungle was
reclaiming. I silenced our vehicle and we got off. The silence was
intense.

There was an eeriness about the place that made it more suitable to speak in a half whisper.

'This is where they brought that girl?'

'Yes. Three days after Sam took off.'

'Who were they?'

'Nobody from the house. Three days, it would be time to
come in from somewhere else.'

'And you want me to bring that girl here?'

'Yes.'

'What are you going to do?'

'I'll be here when you get here with her. I'll have to walk
it. I think her nerves are very good. I think she's tricky and
subtle. So we have to plan it carefully, Nora. We have to make

it look very good to her. So I'm going to give you some lines to say, and we're going to go over them, and then you're going to walk away from it, because I don't want to give her a chance to read you.'

'Will she read you, dear?'

'I don't know. At least I know enough not to try to over-act.'

'What do you mean?'

'Sympathy and reluctance are a hell of a lot more impressive than imitation villainy, Nora.'

I arrived at the clearing a little before one in the afternoon. I had cut across country rather than going through the village. I had had to take cover from only one vehicle, a burdened fish truck labouring out towards the markets. I had sweated the layer of repellent off, and I rubbed on more. I paced and worried about Nora. If Almah Hichin showed up, if Nora did exactly as I had told her, as I had demonstrated to her, if she had tried no improvisation, and had kept her mouth shut, maybe it would work.

I paced back and forth in the clearing. I cut a reedy-looking thing and tried to make a whistle. The bark wouldn't slip. I kept stopping, tilting my head, listening. When I heard it, it seemed to merge with the bug whine and die away, and then it came back, stronger than before. Then it was recognizable as the doughty whirr of a VW engine. It turned into the overgrown trace. I saw at last the glints of dark red through the foliage. It came into the clearing and stopped, ten feet from me. Almah Hichin was at the wheel. She stared at me, frowning slightly as I walked over to the car. I reached in and turned the key off. The top was down. Almah wore a dark blue kerchief, a pale blue sleeveless silk blouse, a white skirt, flat white sandals. She looked up at me with respectable composure and said in a reasonable tone, 'May I ask who you are, and what this is all about?'

'No trouble?' I asked Nora.

'None at all.' She sat half turned toward Almah, holding my little bedroom gun six inches from Almah's waist. I reached over her, picked up Almah's purse, took the bills out, tossed the money into Nora's lap and slung the purse deep into the brush. I looked at the girl. Her eyes had widened momentarily. They were an unusually lovely colour, a deep lavender blue, and their asymmetry made them more interesting.

'Won't somebody find that?' Nora asked on cue.

'It isn't likely.' I knew how the inevitable formula worked in the girl's mind. Nobody expected her to be able to go look for it. I saw a slight twitch at the corner of the controlled mouth.

I took the coil of nylon line off my shoulder, separated an end and dropped the rest of it. 'Clasp your hands and hold them out,' I told her.

'I will not!'

'Miss Hichin, you can't change anything. All you can do is make a lot of tiresome trouble. Just hold your hands out.'

She hesitated and then did so. Her wrists looked frail, her forearms childish. I lashed them together, swiftly and firmly. I opened the car door, gave a firm and meaningful tug at the line and she got out, saying, 'This is altogether ridiculous, you know.'

Nora slid over into the driver's seat and pulled the door shut. 'Enough gas to make Culiacan?' I asked.

She turned the key on and checked. 'More than enough.'

I reached and plucked the dark blue kerchief from Almah's blonde head and handed it to Nora. 'This might confuse things a little.'

She nodded. She glanced at Almah. 'How about her blouse too?'

'I'll bring it along,' I said. 'You don't want any part of this do you?'

Her little shudder was very effective. 'No, dear.'

'Neither do I. Park it up there in the shade, just short of that last bend. Okay?'

'Yes, dear. Miss Hichin? Please don't be stupid about this. You see, we have a lot of time. The plane doesn't come until eight to pick us up. You're such a pretty thing. It will be very difficult for him if you . . . let it get messy.'

'Are you people out of your minds?' Almah demanded.

'I'll handle this. You get out of here,' I ordered Nora.

She spun the little red car around deftly and headed back out again. The motor sound faded, and then it stopped.

I picked up the rest of the line and led the girl over to the spot I had picked, near the ruin of the shack. I flipped the line over a low limb, caught the end, took it over to another tree, laced it around the tree and then carefully pulled until she had her arms stretched high over her head, but both feet were firmly on the ground. I made it fast. I went to her and reached and checked the tension of the line above her lashed wrists. I wandered away from her and lit a cigarette and stood with my back to her, staring off into the brush.

'You're making some kind of fantastic mistake,' she said.

'Sure,' I said and went back to her. She looked sweaty but composed. Small insects were beginning to gather around her face, arms and legs.

'No need for you to be eaten alive,' I said. I took out the 6-12 and poured some into the palm of my hand. 'Close your eyes.' She obeyed. I greased her face, throat, arms and legs with the repellent. I made it utterly objective, with no slightest hint of caress. She stared at me and moistened her lips. I knew that the small courtesy had shaken her more than anything which had gone before.

I walked away from her again. I wanted to sag against a tree and give a great bray of laughter. I had properly anticipated most of it, but not the comedy of it. The most wretched melodrama becomes high comedy. This was a little darling, a little lavender-eyed blonde darling, trussed up like a comic book sequence, and I could not harm a hair of her dear little head. And, of course, she could not believe it either. Nobody hurts the darlings. So our spavined act was balanced on that point, which was just beyond our comprehension or belief. She was right. It was some kind of a fantastic mistake. Nora had bought it more readily than blondie or I could. Her Mediterranean acceptance of the violence just under the surface of life, perhaps.

I turned and looked at her. She stood sweaty and indignant and uncomfortable, reaching high, ankles neatly together. She was, of course, weighing me most carefully, estimating my capacity for violence, even though she could not believe this was real. It was a ponderous, embarrassing joke. She was angry and wary. She was trying to guess if I could hurt her. I saw myself through her eyes—a great big brown rangy man, wiry hair, pale grey eyes, broad features slightly and permanently disarranged by past incidents. I went close to her, and looked through the hypnotic impact of so much prettiness, and got a better look at the details of her. Caked lipstick bitten away, fingers narrow and crooked and not pretty, nail-polish chipped and cracked, the thumbnails bitten deep, a furzy little coppery stubble in her armpits, little dandruff flakes in the forehead roots of the blonde hair, slender ankles slightly soiled, pores enlarged in her cheeks and a blackhead near the base of the delicate nose, a tiny hole burned in the front of the pale blue blouse, a spot on the hip of the white skirt. She was lovely, but not very fastidious. It made her seem a little sexier, and more manageable. The signs of soil were slightly plaintive.

'You and that woman are going to get into terrible trouble about this,' she said. 'I'm an actress. A lot of people know me. Apparently you don't know who I am.'

'I think you got mixed up in a lot of things, Almah, without knowing how serious they were. I guess it works sort of like the law. Ignorance is no excuse.'

'You don't make any sense. I am a house guest.'

'That's what Carlos Menterez y Cruzada called a lot of his shack jobs, I guess. House guests. But you'd be a little young for the Havana scene. Actually I guess you aren't any different than any of the rest of them. But you are the last one he had. And when he had no more use for you, in that sense, you should have gone back where you belonged. The big mistake was hanging around, Almah.'

She stared at me as though she was peering at me through gloom, trying to identify me. She started to say something and stopped and licked her lips again.

'Who are you?' she asked.

'I'm just somebody who's been ordered to confirm a few things. Double check the details. They'll think you left when the going got rough. We sent some people in there last night to look around. It's all falling apart now. It's over for him, Almah. And it's over for you.'

'But it isn't the way you think!'

'How do you know what we think?'

'You sound . . . you make it sound as if I'm there with Carlos out of some kind of loyalty or something. My God, it isn't like that! Honestly, I don't know anything about the political side of it. Listen, I came down here a lot, when there were parties and all. By boat a couple of times and private airplanes. For over two years, and I'd stay on for a couple of weeks or a couple of months. Okay, so I belonged to Carlos when I was here, and that was understood. Is that some kind of a crime all of a sudden? His wife is crazy. Ever since he built that house, she'd been out of her head. He liked me. He wanted me to stay there all the time, but I went back and forth. I mean I have a life of my own too.'

'You should have left for good when you had the chance, Almah.'

'You have to understand something. I lost some good opportunities on account of him. I mean they would have called me for more things, if I'd been handy all the time. A good series I could have been in. But they couldn't get hold of me for the pilot because I was here. So he owes me something. Right?'

'What are you driving at?'

'Look. There's a boy there with me. Gabe. Gabriel Day. You could check it out. He's a lawyer. He can't practise in Mexico, but he knows the right forms and everything they have to use down here. He's been down here for three weeks. I sent for him. You can check that out. Carlos is going to sign something for me, and people are going to witness his signature, and then Gabe and I can go get the money. It's in Mexico City. He's got over six hundred thousand dollars there. That's why I'm staying. It isn't political or anything like that. This is all some kind of a mistake.'

'Sweetie, that's what they used to say in Batista's prisons and what they say now in Fidel's prisons. This is some kind of a mistake.'

'I didn't have anything to do with the political part.'

'No more than Sam Taggart did? He had enough to do with the political part so that it got him killed.'

She stared. 'Sam is dead?'

'Thoroughly.'

'Gee, it's hard to believe. He. . . . He told me it was time to get out, when Carlos got the stroke and Sam couldn't get the money Carlos promised him. I guess they could have guessed it was Sam who . . . got rid of those people.'

I sat on my heels, my back against the tree. I said, 'I don't want to play pyschological games with you, Almah. We know some of it, and there's some of it we don't know. But you have no way of knowing the parts we know and the parts we don't. I can't promise you anything, because there's nothing to promise. Suppose you just tell me the whole thing.'

'And you'll let me go?'

'I want to see if you put in any mistakes.'

'The way it started? All of it?'

'Yes.'

'I guess you could say it started when Cal Tomberlin came down on his boat, with a lot of kids. That was about five months ago. Cal is sort of spooky. Maybe from having everything he ever wanted, and getting it right now. His mother was Laura Shane, from the old movies. And she put all the money she made into land. No taxes then. She got fabulously rich and Cal was the only child. He'd met Carlos one time in Havana, and they didn't get along, and he didn't know that Carlos was here calling himself Garcia. It made Carlos sort of nervous when Cal showed up. Carlos had three collections in the study, in glass cases. The gold statues and the jade and the coins. But Cal Tomberlin saw the

gold statues and wanted to buy them. He couldn't imagine anybody saying no. When he wants something, he has to have it.
And sooner or later he gets it. It can be a boat or a special kind
of car or a piece of land or somebody's wife or those horrid little
gold statues. They were here about five days and he kept after
Carlos all the time, and it got pretty ugly. Toward the end, Cal
Tomberlin started making little hints, talking about what a nice
hideaway Carlos had found for himself. But that just made Carlos
more stubborn. Finally they left. Some of the kids stayed on for
a while.

'About a month later, Cal Tomberlin came back on the boat
again. What I think he was doing, he was just trying to put some
pressure on Carlos to make a deal with him. Maybe he knew
how much trouble he was causing. Maybe he was just trying to
get even with Carlos for turning him down. But he brought a
Cuban man with him, and the Cuban man stayed sort of hidden
on the boat until there was a big party and Cal Tomberlin
went down and got the man and smuggled him into the party. I
was there when Carlos saw him. I thought he was going to have
a heart attack. I didn't know anything could terrify Carlos so
much. He never talked to me about such things, but that night
in bed he had to talk to somebody, I guess. He said that he had
been in a business deal in Havana with that man's brother. It
had gone wrong somehow, and the brother had killed his wife
and himself, and then their son had tried to kill Carlos and had
been arrested and had died of sickness in prison. He kept saying
he would have to leave Mexico and go somewhere else. But after
a few days he quieted down. He stopped going outside the walls
for anything. I guess he couldn't think of a place where he would
be safer.

'About two weeks later, that boat came down, that *Columbine
IV* out of Oceanside. It anchored out. That same man was on
it, and two other men. They looked Cuban. I saw them in the
village. They called me a filthy name. Carlos had Sam find out
everything he could about them. The boat was chartered, and
they were running it themselves. It was small enough so they
could have tied up at the docks, but they anchored out. They
didn't do anything. It made Carlos very nervous. He'd watch it
with binoculars. The other two men were younger. I guess they
could have been friends of the one who died in prison. They just
seemed to be waiting for something. Then one night they tried
to kill Carlos. When they ran, they left the ladder against the
wall. They'd fired at him, he thought with a rifle, from the top

of the wall, from a place where you could see into his bedroom.
It ripped through his smoking jacket and made a little red line
across his belly, and just barely broke the skin. Instead of going
all to pieces about it, he got very calm and thoughtful. I said he
should get the police, but he said there were political reasons
why he couldn't ask for that kind of protection. He had to make
do with the people he had brought from Cuba.

'I think it was two nights later he came to my room as I was
going to bed and told me he knew all about me and Sam. He
knew I'd been cheating on him with Sam from just about the
second time I'd come down to visit. He said it had amused him.
I made some smart remark and he gave me a hell of a slap across
the face and knocked me down. He wanted me to work on Sam
to get Sam to do what Carlos wanted him to do. He told me the
lie he had told Sam. He had told Sam that the men on the boat
were Castro agents, and that for several years Carlos had been
financing underground activities against Castro, and those men
were assigned to kill him so it would stop. I guessed Sam never
thought much about that sort of thing. I guess it would sound
reasonable to him. He offered Sam a hundred thousand dollars
in cash to get rid of those men on the boat. Carlos had it all
worked out how it could be done. But Sam didn't want to kill
anybody. It made me feel funny to think of Sam killing anybody.
With Carlos not going out in his own boat any more, not since
Cal had brought that Cuban man around, Sam didn't have
much to do. The man who helped him on Carlos' boat is named
Miguel. He's still at the house.

'When I was with Sam, it was usually on Carlos' boat, and
sometimes in Sam's room. It wasn't anything important with us.
It was just something to do. And I enjoy it. Unless there were
parties, it was quiet around there. Sort of sleepy. Siestas in the
afternoon. I don't like to sleep in the day. Maybe I'd be by the
pool and Sam would give me a look and go away and I'd stay
there and think about him, and then I'd have to go find him.
I thought the servants probably knew. I didn't know Carlos
knew. Anyway, I made Sam tell me about it, not letting on I
knew, and then I worked on him to do it. I told him if he didn't
have any guts, I wasn't interested any more. And besides, it was
sort of patriotic. I said if he did it, I'd arrange to go away with
him for a while. He was always a little more eager than I was.
I guess guys always are. I didn't tell him Carlos had promised
me a little money for talking him into it. And I wouldn't do
anything with him until he said yes. I told him when he said

yes, it would be the most special thing that ever happened to him. It did get me pretty excited, thinking of him killing those men in the way Carlos had it all figured out.

'They did it. Sam and Miguel. On the first calm dark night. They went out in the dinghy from Carlos' boat, I guess about three in the morning, making no sound at all. They went aboard barefoot. Sam told me all about it. He held on to me, shivering like a little kid. He was too sick to make love. Twice he got up and he went and he was sick. It wasn't like he thought it was going to be. One of the men was sleeping on deck. Miguel sneaked over to him and cut his throat. Sam said the man flopped and thumped around while he was dying. But it didn't wake the others. They went below. One of the men was easy. The other one put up a terrible fight. He knocked some of Sam's teeth out, hitting him with something. Sam strangled him. Then there was the woman. Nobody had known anything about the woman. She'd stayed below the whole time. There was some kind of little light on below. She came out of the front of the boat somewhere, and flew at Sam. He got her by the wrists. He said she was dark and pretty. He said that holding her, he could feel Miguel putting the knife into her back, and he could see her face changing as she knew she was dead. That was what made him so sick. He cried in my arms like a little kid.

'The dinghy was tied astern. They cut the anchor lines. Sam started the boat up and they went out the main pass, dead slow, without lights, heading south west. Once they were pretty well out, Sam put the boat on automatic pilot. Miguel had taken the other body below. Sam disconnected the automatic bilge pumps and opened a sea cock. He said Miguel had been scrambling around with a sack, getting money and watches and rings and cameras and things like that. He made Miguel quit and got into the dinghy. Sam closed it up below. He went to the controls then and yelled to Miguel to cast off, and he put it up to cruising speed, and ran and dived over the rail and swam back to the dinghy. They sat in the dinghy. He said they could see the boat for just a little while, and then they could hear it for a lot longer. When they couldn't hear it any more, they started the little outboard on the dinghy and came on back. They were about five or six miles out. They stopped the motor and rowed the last mile in.

'Sam said he estimated that the cruiser would run for maybe an hour before the bilge got full enough to stop the engines. Then it would go down pretty fast, and it would be nearly twenty miles out by then. About two or three days later we heard they were hunting for a boat. There were some search planes. Some men came and asked questions at the hotel. But all they could say was that the boat had left one night. That was about two months ago. After he did it, Sam wanted the money right away so he could leave. But Carlos stalled him. He said he had to make a trip to Mexico City to get it. He said he would go soon. I guess I was going to go with him. I don't know. Maybe I was partly to blame. He wanted to shove some of the blame off on me, so he could feel a little better about it.

'Then one morning Carlos was sitting by the pool and I was swimming. I heard a woman scream. I climbed out and I asked Carlos if he heard it. I was looking around. He didn't answer me. I looked at him again, and I realized he had made that sound. The doctor came up from Mazatlan by float plane. At first he thought Carlos would die. He was unconscious for four days. Then he was conscious, with his whole left side paralysed and he couldn't talk. The doctor said there might be some future improvement, but probably not much. Dead brain cells don't come back. Sam was drunk for days. Then I found him in the study. He'd opened the glass case and he was putting those gold statues in the case Carlos had had made for them when he left Cuba. They go in little fitted places. He said he was going to get his money one way or another, and the whole thing made no sense at all unless he got his money. He said he was going to take them away and sell them to Cal Tomberlin. He said he'd earned them. I said they were worth more than what Carlos had promised him, that Cal had offered Carlos a lot more. He said then it would have to be a bonus, and the way he felt about it, the bonus could be for the woman. But maybe Cal wouldn't want to pay him as much as he had offered Carlos anyway. He told me I should leave with him. But he was acting sort of wild and unreliable. I didn't see how he could get those things across the border. He looked as if he was going to get into terrible trouble. And by then—I didn't tell him—I'd gotten into Carlos' wall safe, in his bedroom. He'd watch me with that one eye whenever I was in there. I looked everywhere and found the combination in his wallet, written on the edge of a card. I thought there would be a lot of money in there, but there was just some pesos, a little over twenty thousand pesos. And some bank books for accounts in Zurich, and the keys and records of the bank drawer in Mexico City. The money there is in American dollars.

'Sam left. That case was terribly heavy. He fixed it so he could sort of sling it on his shoulder. He wanted to take one of the cars. I didn't want any trouble to be traced back to Carlos. I told the men not to let him take a car, to let him take the heavy case, but no car. But before he could leave, two men came. They had been at the house before. Friends of Carlos, from the old days in Havana. When they would visit him, they would have long private conferences about money and politics. They didn't know Carlos had had a stroke. It made them very nervous. I took them to him and showed them how to talk to Carlos. He can blink his good eye for yes and no, and if you hold his wrist steady he can scrawl simple words on a pad. I wanted to stay there, but they shoved me out of the room and locked the door. At dusk—they were still in there—Sam decided that they were going to take over, and if they knew what he was going to take, they would stop him. So he left, and he told me to tell those men, if they asked, that he'd left by boat. He thought they would get around to looking for him.

'Those men spent a long time with Carlos. They talked to me about what the doctor had said. They spent most of the next day with him. I guess it was slow work, finding out things from him. Maybe he didn't want to tell them. That would make it slower. Once I listened at the door and heard Carlos make that terrible sound he makes when he gets frightened or angry. At last they knew all they wanted to know, from him. They found out I could open the safe. They made me open it. I'd hidden the keys and records for the Mexico City box. They didn't seem to know or care about that. They took the Swiss bank book. They said fast things to Carlos and laughed, and the tears ran out of his good eye. They took the jade and the coin collection too. They asked me about Sam. One's English was good, as good as Carlos'. They said Carlos had done a very stupid thing, and that Sam had been very stupid to obey Carlos' orders. They said that the friends of the people who had been on that boat would be told what had happened, so that nobody would start blaming the wrong people. And they said it would be very nice if they could turn Sam over to those friends, because that would satisfy them, and then the security of a lot of people living quietly in Mexico would not be endangered through political pressures. They said it would be nice if I told them every helpful thing I could think of about Sam, because if the authorities caught him with all that gold, and if Sam talked too much about where he got it, a lot of private and semi-official arrangements might collapse, and the newspaper publicity might make certain officials take steps they had already been bribed not to take.

'I made a sort of arrangement with them. I said I would stay on and sort of take charge of the household. They gave me some money. They said they would send me drafts on the bank in Culiacan to cover household expenses, plus a salary for me. Then when Carlos dies, they'll send people to arrange about disposing of the house, getting the staff resettled, getting Mrs. Menterez into an institution. And they said I'll get a bonus at that time. But I was to live quietly. No big parties and lots of house guests like before. They gave me an address in Mexico City to write to if anything happens. So . . . I told them all I knew about Sam, about how he planned to sell the statues to Cal Tomberlin. And I told him his village slut, Felicia, might know something. They went away in their car. After a few weeks I . . . thought of Gabe and sent for him. He's been here three weeks. Then yesterday I got that note . . . and I wanted to know what the message was. From Sam.'

Her voice had gotten increasingly husky. Her head lolled. 'Please,' she said in a faint voice. 'I'm getting awful uncomfortable.' Perspiration darkened the blue blouse, pasting it to her midriff. I got up and stretched the stiffness out of my legs and went over and gave her three feet of slack and made the line fast in that position. She brought her arms down, moved in a small circle, rolling her shoulders.

'I've levelled with you,' she said. 'Completely. I've told you everything. Maybe it doesn't make me look so good. I can't help that. I know one thing in this world. If you don't take care of yourself, nobody else is going to.'

'Have they sent you money?'

'Once. I guess it's going to come once a month. It wasn't as much as they said it would be.'

'What are the names of those two men?'

'They never said. One was Luis and the other was Tomas. They had a white Pontiac convertible, great big sunglasses, resort clothes, a very sharp pair. The other times they were here, they were very respectful to Carlos.'

'Do you know the names of the people on the boat?'

'Just the one that Cal brought to the house, the older one. Senor Mineros. I don't know his first name.'

'Where does Tomberlin live?'

'He has a lot of places. The only one I was at was a sort of lodge, way up near Cobblestone Mountain. I don't mind fun and games. But that got a little too rich for me, believe me. He had a lot of kids up there that weekend. I knew most of them. It got crazy up there. You couldn't walk without stepping on a jumbled up pile of kids and getting pulled down into a lot of messy fooling around. I got out of there.'

She looked at me with delicate indignation, a righteous little snippet, asking my moral approval.

'How old are you, Almah?'

'Twenty-four.'

Nora was having a long wait, I looked at the lovely and slightly soiled little blondie. I wondered what I would do with her if I really had the power to judge her and sentence her.

She had explained something I had felt about Sam Taggart. There had been a strangeness about him. During the short time I'd been with him, I'd felt that we could never again be as close as we had once been. He'd travelled too far. That little boat ride had taken him a long long way. At the time he died, he was trying to come back, but he probably knew he could never make it all the way back. He could pretend for a time. But the act of murder was still with him. Nora would have immediately sensed that strangeness, that apartness. And she would not have rested until she learned the cause of it.

Little Almah Hichin, with her lavender eyes, and her slender girlish figure, and her greedy and available and random little loins, was going to go her way, making out, aiming for the money, spicing it with her kicks.

'Why don't you say something?' she asked.

Suddenly it didn't seem suitable to merely untie her.

'I guess I'm stalling. This isn't something I'm going to enjoy.'

'What do you mean?'

I shrugged. 'Chivalry or something, I guess. And when . . . a girl is as pretty as you are, Almah, it seems like such a hell of a waste. And, to tell the truth, I'm sort of an amateur at this. I've never killed a woman before.'

Her mouth sagged and her eyes bulged. 'Kill!'

'Sweetie, I told you I couldn't promise a thing.'

'But I've told you everything! My God! You can't be serious! Look, I'll do anything you say. You could get in terrible trouble. People will look for me.'

I pointed a thumb over my shoulder. 'They won't look back in that jungle. I guess I'm not doing you any favour by stalling. I know I have to do it. But I feel squeamish about it.'

She tried to smile. 'This is some kind of a nasty joke, isn't it?'

'I wish it was. I'll make it easy on you. I won't hurt you.'

'But I haven't done anything!'

'I have to do as I'm told.'

I stared sombrely at her. Her colour had become quite ghastly. 'Now wait a minute!' she said, her voice high and thin. 'I'm going to get that money. Listen, you could come back with me and I could get you into the house. You could be with me every minute. You could come with me when we go to get the money. You can have half of it. You can have *all* of it.'

'You can scream now if you want to. It might help a little. It won't make any difference, but it might help.'

She had begun to babble, her voice high and thin and fast and almost out of control. 'But you don't even know me. You've got no reason! Please! I can hide here. You can say you did it. Then I'll go wherever you want me to go. I can wait for you. Please. I'll belong to you. I'll do anything for you. Please don't do that to me!' She began to dash back and forth, yanking at the rope, making little yelping sounds of panic.

I went to the line and hauled it tighter than before, bringing her up on to tiptoe. Again I felt that urge to howl with sour laughter. Melodrama made me self-conscious. But I thought of what she had talked Sam into doing, and I wanted to make a lasting impression on her. I wanted her to feel death so close she could smell the shroud and the dank earth.

I took the pocket knife out and opened the ridiculously small blade. I walked up to her. Her eyes showed white all the way around the lavender irises. She had bitten into her underlip. There was a smear of blood at the corner of her mouth. She made a maddened humming sound, and her body spasmed and snapped and contorted in the animal effort to run. She looked at the knife, and the ultimate terror of it loosened her control over her bodily functions. Now she was beyond all pretence, perhaps for the first time since childhood. Sam's last duchess. Menterez's last blonde slut. As I raised the blade, she opened her jaws wide in a final yawning caw of despair, and I lifted it above her hands and cut the line.

She fell in a sprawling soiled heap, sobbing and shuddering, rolling her face against the earth. I looked down at her for a moment, pocketed the knife and walked out to the car. Nora started to say something, and looked at my face and stopped abruptly. She slid over and I got behind the wheel. I drove in silence to the hotel. Nora got out there. She said, 'Are we going to leave?'

'Tomorrow.'

'All right, dear.'

'I think I'll go back and pick her up.'

'Yes, dear.'

CHAPTER FOURTEEN

ALMAH HICHIN had taken a long time to free her hands and pull herself together enough to start walking west, toward the village. Felicia had walked it.

She was only about a hundred yards from the obscure entrance to the isolated clearing. She stopped when she saw the car coming. She looked small, lost, displaced in time and space. I went on by her, turned around in the road and came back, through my own drift of dust. I stopped beside her. She leaned on the closed door and gave a gagging cough. Then she looked at me with a hideous remnant of flirtatiousness, like the grin on a cholera victim, and said in a trembling voice, 'Did you . . . want to give me a ride?' Her glance met mine and slid away, utterly humble.

'Get in.'

She slid in, wary and apologetic and self-effacing. As I started up I told myself that something would have broken her sooner or later. Something died in that clearing. And she would never fit together as well again.

I pulled over and stopped abruptly, short of the ridge where the village would be in view. She had ridden with her head bowed, her small fists and marked wrists cradled in her lap. I got out and said, 'You can take it from here.'

She raised her head slowly and looked at me through the sheaf of spilled blonde hair, her face crinkled and puzzled, like a child wondering whether to cry.

'Why?' she said. Her lip was badly swollen where she had gnawed it in her terror.

'Because you have to play these games with real blood and real people.'

'Who are you?'

'Sam was my friend a long time ago,' I said. 'The woman on the boat was real. The knife was real. The blood was real. Sam died on that boat too. It was just your turn to die a little.'

'I'm just sick now. I'm just terribly terribly sick.'

'So is Carlos.'

She coughed into her fist. 'I don't meant to hurt anybody.'

There was no answer I could give her. I began walking toward the village. The red car went by me, slowly, as far over on the other side as she could get it. She gave me a single empty look and went on, clutching the wheel at ten after ten, the blonde hair blowing in the dusty wind.

I went right to the Tres Panchos. It was a little after five. There were a half dozen fishermen in there, smelling of their trade. The juke was playing the brass *pasadoble* of the bull ring. I leaned into a corner of the bar, and made Moustache understand with bad Spanish and gestures that I wanted a glass of ice and a bottle of tequila añejo. '*Botella?*' he asked. '*La Botella?*' I reached and took it out of his hand. Twenty *pesos*. He shrugged and watched me pour the glasses and shrugged again and walked away.

I know that for a long time there was a respectful area of emptiness around me, even when the place had filled up. I know there was a purchase of another bottle.

I awoke into suffocating heat, to barbed needles of light which went through my eyes and into my brain. Tequila hangover, in a gagging density of perfume, under a tin roof, on the sweat-damp sheets of a village whore. She stood naked beside the bed, bending over me, looking at me with melting concern, the heat in the room making her look as if she had been greased.

'Leedle seek?' she said.

'Oh God. Oh God.'

She nodded and shouldered into something pink and went out the door. When she came back she had a tin pitcher of ice water, a jelly glass, and some ice wrapped in a towel. I drank water until my belly felt tight as a drum. Then I lay back and chewed ice, with the chilly towel across my forehead and eyes, wondering where she had gone. She came back and took the towel off my face and handed me a half glass of reddish brown liquid.

'Drink fast,' she said, making the gesture of tossing it off.

I did so. I think one could achieve the same result by drinking four ounces of boiling tabasco sauce. I sprang up. I roared and paced and wept. I sweated and gasped and wept and held my throat. I ran back to the bed and opened the towel and stuffed my mouth with ice and chomped it up like Christmas candy. When the worst of it was over, I subsided weakly on the bed. Felicia had watched the whole performance calmly, standing leaning against the door frame, her arms folded. As I became aware of my headache again, I realized it was not quite as bad. I mopped my face with the cool towel.

She went over to her dressing-table, opened a box, and came back with my watch and wallet. It was five of eleven by my watch. She said, 'Every goddam *peso* is there, Trrav.'

She went over and filled the wash basin, laid out soap and towel and comb. She tossed her pink wrapper aside, searched one of the cardboard wardrobes and pulled out that orange shift I had seen her in before and pulled it on. She gave a couple of casual swipes at her hair with a brush, painted her mouth, yawned and said, 'I am downstairs, okay?'

'Okay. I guess I was a damn fool.'

She shrugged. 'Pretty dronk, Trrav.' She gave me a broad merry smile. 'Almost too dronk for the love.' She went out and closed the door.

Getting dressed was sad and enormous labour. When I found the inside staircase and went down, I was glad to see that only Moustache and Felicia were there. As I trudged toward the bar, Moustache uncapped a bottle of beer and set it on the bar with a flourish. He knew a glass would be superfluous. I held the bar with one hand and tilted the bottle up with the other, and set it down when it was empty. I stopped him from opening another one.

Felicia took me by the wrist and tugged me over to a table. I told her I had to get back to the hotel. She said we had to talk first.

She sat opposite me and looked at me with a certain sombre speculation. 'One man from Garcia loves a hotel girl. I hear a thing. I wonder something. You go in there? Kill a dog? Almost kill some man too?'

'Me? No.'

'Yesterday your skinny woman is in the red car with the Heechin *rubia*. Then you are alone in the red car. And one time you are in the car with your skinny one. And one time Heechin is alone, eh?'

'So?'

She slitted the anthracite eyes. 'Felicia is not stupid. It is about Sam, eh? These things?'

'Felicia, those men who hurt you, they had a white car?'

'Ah, such a beautiful car, *si*.'

'How was Sam going to get to the States from Los Mochis?'

'He gets to Ensenada by little airplane, it is easy from there, Trrav. Many ways.'

'Where no one will look in that heavy case he had?'

'Many ways. For a man who has some Spanish and some money.'
She closed her strong coppery fingers around my waist. 'The hotel
girl says one thing. There is one bad man at Garcia. One killer,
eh? Miguel, I think. You are trouble to Garcia, maybe they send
him. *Cuidado, hombre.*'

'Why would they think I'm trouble?'

'The *rubia* could think so, eh? Too many questions, maybe?
One thing. You have trouble, Trrav, you have friends here.
Okay?'

'Okay.'

'Miguel is most sad of the dog. His dog, Brujo.'

'What does Miguel look like?'

'Tiny small skinny man with a sad face. Maybe forty years.
Very quick.'

'And he worked with Sam on the Garcia boat?'

'Ah, you know it too! On that boat, *La Chispa*. Very pretty.
But not using it now a long time. Months, maybe. Garcia use it
every day almost, long ago, many people, fishing, drinking, music.
Nobody to run it now, unless Miguel.' She patted my hand. 'Have
care, *amador*. Come back to Felicia.'

'I think we are leaving soon.'

She concealed a sharp look of disappointment with an almost
immediate impassivity. She nodded. 'Maybe this is not a good
place for you.'

I trudged the seven hundred miles to the Casa in my dirty
shirt, feeling unwell. When I went to the desk for my key, I had
the impression everybody knew exactly where I had been all
night. Arista seemed blandly contemptuous.

He said, 'At the lady's request, sir, I made flight arrangements
for you. But you would have had to leave here at ten-thirty by
bus. It is now too late. Please let me know if you want this
arranged again for tomorrow. It is a considerable inconvenience
to me when such plans are changed.'

'Aren't you being paid to be inconvenienced, Arista?'

'In the case of valued guests, I would say yes.'

For a moment I debated pulling him over the counter by the
front of his spotless jacket, and running him down his front steps.
But the effort would joggle my head.

'What kind of guest am I, Arista?'

He smiled. 'We have discovered a small difficulty in the reservations. We shall require that your rooms be vacated by tomorrow,
sir. I trust you will be able to settle your account in cash?'

'Or you will call the village cop?'

'I would not imagine you are entirely unacquainted with the police, sir.'

I had difficulty in thinking clearly. I could not imagine what had so abruptly changed his attitude. Could Almah Hichin have made some kind of complaint? Had I been seen going in or out of my room window? Could he really be so prim about a night on the town?

'That's a dangerous smile, Arista. It tempts me to see if I can knock it off.'

He took a hasty step back. 'If you and . . . the lady leave quietly tomorrow, sir, I will not cause you any trouble. As you leave I shall turn over to you an object I now have in my office safe. It is not customary for tourists to bring such things into Mexico. The room maid reported that a toilet was not flushing properly. The maintenance man discovered . . . the hidden weapon and turned it over to me. I will give it back to you when you leave. I wish to operate . . . a quiet and respectable resort, sir.'

I stood for a few minutes in thought. 'I suppose your whole staff knows about this by now.'

'It is the sort of thing that would entertain them.'

'When was it found?'

'Yesterday, in the early afternoon. I expected you to deny any knowledge of it, sir.'

'Why?'

'Possession of a weapon can be an awkwardness for a tourist, I would think.'

I smiled at him. 'Arista, it just grieves me that I can't ever tell you how stupid you're being. I might be able to tell the owners, but I can't ever tell you.'

It was a childish counterattack, but it knifed him neatly. I saw his face go blank as he began to think of certain legitimate reasons why I might have a gun in the room. 'But, sir, I can only go by what. . . .'

'Forget it, Arista.'

'But . . . it could be possible that reservations might be rearranged so that. . . .'

'Forget that too. Set us up to get out of here tomorrow morning.'

'Operating a place such as this is often a very. . . .'

'You have lots of problems,' I said and walked away.

It was after twelve. The interconnecting door was closed. It was locked on her side. There was no answer to my knock. I took a tub, hot as I could stand it, and topped it off with a cold

shower. I pared the sandpaper stubble from my jaws. All the
thorn gashes were cleanly scabbed, and I got rid of the last of
the little bandages. The gnawed place on my arm was healing
well too, and did not look too much like toothmarks, so I left the
bandage off also. I dressed in fresh clothing, and looked at my
face in the mirror. Eyes sunken and slightly bloodshot. Slight
tendency toward cold sweat. A faint beginning of hunger. Small
motor tremor of the hands. Just as I was about to leave the room,
I heard Nora stirring around on the other side of the door. I
knocked and heard her call, 'Just a minute!'

In a little while she unlocked the door and opened it and said,
'Yes?' She wore a robe and a small and rather formal smile.

'I thought you might have wondered about me.'

'Not particularly, Trav.'

'Oh.'

'I wandered out to the road and I saw Miss Hichin go by,
alone, heading up toward the house, driving quite slowly. I
thought you would come back and tell me what she had told you.
I thought you might realize I was quite anxious to know. When
it got to be dark, I sent Jose down to the village to find you, on
his scooter. He said you were singing and dancing. I hope you
had a jolly time. I made reservations, but. . . .'

'I know. I talked to Arista. He's making them again for
tomorrow.'

'I've been at the pool. I'll be going down to lunch in a little
while.'

'I don't think that would be a good place to talk to you.'

'Why not?'

'It's public. You might be upset.'

'I don't imagine anything can get me that upset.'

'It upset me, Nora. I got pretty drunk.'

'Evidently. You look it.'

'I stayed there.'

'More research, no doubt.'

'You can't do much research after you pass out.'

'Let me explain something to you. You don't have to justify
yourself to me. I haven't put any strings on anything. You're a
free agent, Trav. I expected a little more consideration. Not on
the basis of anything between us, but just because . . . you know
I was anxious to know what you found out.'

'When you get dressed come in here and I'll tell you.'

She came in when she was ready. I told her. Long after she
kept denying that Sam could have done that, tears running down

her face, I knew that she had begun to accept it. Then I told her
about Arista and the gun. She understood then why Arista had
been rude and impertinent to her.

'There's something else about the gun,' I said. 'All the hotel
servants know about it. They lost a gun up there the other night.
It makes a pretty easy two plus two. But I don't think anybody
will make a move. Menterez is helpless. The girl is demoralized.
I don't think any of them want any police problems. Some girl
that works in the hotel sees one of those Cubans. Word would
get back that way, probably last night. Probably water swirling
out of the tank moved the gun and it got in the way of the
mechanism. One of those things.'

'If those guards decide it was you, Trav, what would they
think you were trying to do?'

'Friend of Mineros, maybe, coming to take another crack at
Menterez. If they know about the gun, let's assume they know
we're leaving. There's nothing more here, Nora. We go and try
it from the other direction. Tomberlin and Mineros, the friends
of Mineros.'

'Why haven't those friends come after Carlos Menterez before
now?'

'Maybe they have been around. Killing a man in that shape
would be doing him a favour. And it would have to be a personal
thing. Mineros could blame Carlos for the death of his brother,
his brother's wife, his nephew. Maybe the people who knew what
Mineros was trying to do, maybe they don't have strong reasons.
This is remote. It's hard to get at him. And it's obviously
dangerous. Maybe the two younger men who were killed along
with Mineros are the only ones who would have had the push to
make another try. Hell, maybe somebody is setting it up more
carefully for the next attempt. We're in the dark, Nora.'

'And the girl and that lawyer will get the money?'

'If she can get him to sign. If the bank accepts it. If somebody
isn't waiting for her to walk out with it. If the cash isn't found
at the border and impounded. Carlos Menterez must know
exactly what she is. And he knows that's all he has left. Money
he can't get to, and a girl who doesn't give a damn about him.
A big house and a crazy wife and not much more time left. And
a stranger's face at his window. Nora?'

'Yes?'

'Does it do any good to tell you I'm sorry?'

'It was probably a good thing, Trav. Maybe I was getting
emotionally dependent. Maybe . . . things were getting too

important.' She tried to smile. 'I guess it's a little bit like waking up.'

I checked my watch. It was two-thirty. 'Do you want lunch?'

'I guess not. Not now.'

'What do you want to do?'

'Lie down for a little while, I guess.' She went into her room. In a few moments she rapped and came back in and handed me the garish little bedroom gun.

'By the way, you handled that well,' I told her.

She made a sour mouth. 'I imagined her with Sam. I guess it made me pretty convincing. That plus a natural antagonism toward pretty blondes.' The door closed.

I was able to get a sandwich at the hotel bar. Afterwards I wandered down to the boat basin and walked around to the other side reserved for resident boats. There were four tied up there. I would have expected *La Chispa* to have been one of the two bigger ones. But it was a flush deck cruiser, about 42 feet, twin screw, doubtless gas fueled.

I went back past the sign which said Owners and Guests Only, and hunted for Heintz and found him in the shed behind the dock office putting a new diaphragm in a complex looking fuel pump. I made some small talk, and when I thought I could do it casually enough, I said, 'It looks like one of those over there is going to sink at the dock one of these days.'

'Oh, *La Chispa*? The owner is sick.'

'Doesn't he have anyone to look after it?'

'The man left when he got sick.'

'I hate to see that happen to a boat.'

'I know. One of these days, maybe, I'll see if I can get permission to fix it up.'

'Pretty small to go anywhere from here, isn't it?'

'Just a local boat. He had it freighted to Mazatlan and brought up here. A long run for that boat, Mazatlan to here. You have to wait for good weather. If he wanted, he could run it over to La Paz, but nowhere from there except back. Not enough range. A damn fool maybe could get it up to Guaymas, or maybe even down to Manzanillo, but that's the end of the line. The big motor sailers are what you have to have on this coast.'

'I understand some pretty good-sized yachts get lost in these waters. I read about one a couple of months ago.'

He tightened up the last bolts on the housing of the fuel pump before answering. 'The *Columbine*. She was in here. She anchored off. A good sea boat.'

He put the tools away and walked to his office. I walked
along with him. He stopped suddenly and stared across the
small boat basin. 'Maybe we can both stop worrying about *La
Chispa*,' he said. I looked over and saw a swarthy little man in
khakis trot out along the finger pier and leap nimbly aboard the
boat, a cardboard carton under one arm, and a bulging burlap
sack over the other shoulder. 'That one worked as mate aboard,'
he said. '*Hola!* Miguel!' he called.

The man looked around the side of the trunk cabin. I could
not see him distinctly at a hundred and fifty feet, but I saw the
white streak of grin.

'*Buena tarde,* Senor Heintz!' he called back.

Heintz said about two hundred words at high speed, ending in
an interrogating lift of his voice.

Miguel answered at length. Heintz laughed, Miguel disappeared.

'I told him he should be ashamed of the condition of the
boat, and he said that if one works twenty hours a day, there is
no time for playing with toys. Now he is ordered to put it in
condition to sell it, very quickly and cheaply, and perhaps he
will buy it himself and compete with the hotel for fishing charters.
That was a joke. He's not that good with a boat, and you couldn't
run that thing at a profit. I've been relieved not to have him
around for a couple of months. He's a violent little man. He
hurt two of my men badly. They were making loud remarks
about Cubans, for his benefit. If Taggart hadn't broken it up,
he might have killed them both. He looked as if he wanted to.
Taggart grabbed him and threw him off the dock.'

'Was he taking supplies aboard?'

'Maybe. There'd be a better market for it in La Paz or Mazatlan. The owner will never use it again. But I wouldn't want to
trust Miguel to get it there. I've seen him at the wheel. He tried
to handle it like Taggart did. That is like letting a child drive
a sports car.'

After I had left Heintz, I went up to the pool level and sat at
a shady table overlooking the boat basin and had a bottle of beer.
I watched Miguel working around the boat and I felt curious
and oddly uneasy about it.

I saw him squatting and fooling with the dockside power
outlet, trotting back and forth. Finally dirty water began to
squirt off the bilge. Then, one at a time, I saw him lug four big
batteries over to the office shed, where Heintz probably had a
quick charger. Miguel went back and stood and studied the

lines. It was well moored, with four lines and two spring lines. He took three lines off and coiled them, leaving the bow line, the stern line and the bow spring line on.

Then he went up the steps on the far side, and up the path and disappeared, moving very spryly. A few minutes later I saw a car going up the road, one of the three I had spotted while scaring hell out of myself. It was one of those Datsun things, the Nipponese version of a Land Rover. Carlos was fine for cars—the Datsun, the Ghia, and a big black Imperial. In addition to the steps and walk, there was a steep curve of narrow road which came down to the boat area. And I wondered why Miguel hadn't used that. He had the car for it. The Boody jeep would make it easily. And I wondered if Miguel hadn't been just a little too jolly in his long range conversation with Heintz. Also, he was doing nothing about dressing the boat up. Maybe she wanted to sell it in a hurry. That much of a hurry?

Nursing another bottle of beer, I waited and watched. A half hour later the Datsun came back and parked along the road at a place I could not see. Miguel came down the path, heavily laden, and pounced aboard. He had comported himself in that super-casual manner of someone who wishes to avoid attention by seeming to perform perfectly ordinary acts. He went and got the batteries, one at a time, and brought them back and spent enough time aboard so I was certain he had strapped them in and hooked them up. The cruiser rode higher. The bilge outlet was spitting dirty spray. He took his power line off the dockside connection and it stopped. He coiled the power line, knelt and tied it, and took it aboard. Again he hurried back up to the truck and went back up to the last house at the crest of the knoll.

What if Carlos' condition had suddenly worsened? Miguel would know it would make sense for him to take off the moment Menterez died. I could not imagine him being very close to the other Cubans in the compound. Those little deadly ones are loners, just as his dog had been.

I went to the desk and made arrangements about the bill. The fun-loving, sun-loving tourists were milling around. Arista was looking for an opening, perhaps to cover himself in the absurb eventuality that I had some sort of official status. I told him we would pay cash for breakfast, so he could have the account ready. The luggage would be ready to bring out at ten-fifteen. Yes, the bus would leave at ten-thirty, and make the air connection in Culiacan in plenty of time.

'I shall turn your property over to you upon departure, sir.'

'What property?'

'Uh . . . the weapon, sir.'

'I don't know anything about any weapon, Arista.'

'But, sir, you admitted that. . . .'

'I don't know what you're talking about. You don't have anything of mine. If you think you have something of mine why you just keep it.'

'But it was found. . . .'

'I'm not responsible for what other guests leave in the rooms.'

When I looked back at him he was dry-washing his hands, and I think his underlip was trembling. The rooms were empty. I went looking for Nora. I found her coming out of the bar. She was looking for me. She had changed. She wore a very simple sleeveless white dress with a sun back. She had flattened her hair, fastened it into severity. The white dress deepened her tan. She looked very composed. I steered her back into the bar, back to the far table where we had first sat. She wanted bourbon on ice, and I got two of them.

'Get some sleep?'

'No. I just . . . did a lot of thinking, Travis.'

'Any conclusions?'

'A few. I felt very savage about Sam. It all seemed so black and white. Maybe that's my flaw, to see everything as totally right or totally wrong. But it isn't like that, is it?'

'You mean the bad guys and the good guys? No, it isn't like that, not when you know enough about it.'

'I can't be some sort of abstract and objective instrument of justice, Trav, when I don't even know what justice is any more. I don't think I ever really knew Sam. I know that you brought me along as . . . as a disguise.'

'And because you had to get it out of your system one way or another.'

'One way or another,' she said. She nodded. 'Did you know that all that thirst for vengeanace was going to sort of . . . fade away?'

'No. But I knew it was possible.'

She took the last swallow, and the ice clicked against her teeth. She shook her head. 'It's such a . . . such a lot of bloody confusion. And here I am, wandering around in it with my dime store morality. I feel like such an ass.'

'It got to me yesterday. It shouldn't have. God knows I've been dry behind the ears for a long long time. But the little mental image of Sam holding the arms of the woman they didn't know was there, and that bloody little monster sliding up behind her with. . . .'

'Don't!' she whispered. 'Please.'

'I'd be better off without a little taint of idealism, Nora. Then I could accept the fact that man is usually a pretty wretched piece of work.'

'You asked for conclusions. Okay. I'm dropping the dime store morality bit, darling. Yesterday you had it up to here. I don't care what you did. I don't even care if you slept with that Felicia. Maybe it would have been a kind of brutal therapy. I don't have any special privileges. I haven't asked for any or granted any. If you left me in kind of . . . and agony of suspense, I should have had the sense to know that whatever you had to tell me would keep. So I am still in your bed, if I please you.'

'You do.'

'Everybody is so damned lonely, you have to take what there is. And if there are any good guys at all, you're one of them.'

'You'll turn my head.'

'Further conclusions. When we leave here, I would be perfectly content to head all the way back. I'll reimburse you for everything, and I want no argument on that. But if you want to take it further, in California, and you think I'd be of any use to you, I'll go with you and do as I'm told. I can let it all drop right here. But I can understand that you . . . might feel as if you'd left something unfinished.'

I went over and brought back two more bourbons. I thought it over and said, 'I don't know. Tomberlin interests me. Maybe I better try the California thing alone. In one sense, he started the whole mess. In another sense, Menterez spent profitable years building it up to the ultimate mess, and it had to happen sooner or later. Let me think about it. The first thing we have to do is survive that airplane ride to Durango.'

'If you hold my hand, we'll make it.'

'You sank those nails in pretty good the last time.'

'And we made it.'

'Did you get any lunch at all?'

'No. Look. It's after five. I can last. I may get kind of glassy if you force another drink on me, but I can last. If you forced another drink on me, you could lead me off to the room and have your way with me, sir.'

'Even without another drink?'

'One never knows unless one tries, does one.'

CHAPTER FIFTEEN

SHE wanted to put on something else, but I asked her to put on the white dress back on. I told her I had to walk up the road and see if I could get a word with Almah. I had a few questions about Tomberlin which might be helpful.

When I started up the road, I looked back. I saw her going down the steps toward the pool, a slender distant figure in white. I stretched my legs and made pretty good time up the curves of the road. I was better than halfway to the pink house when I heard the pounding of running footsteps. An instant later the young lawyer appeared around the next curve. He wore pink shorts, a knit shirt, white sweat socks and tennis shoes. Those heavy white muscular hairy legs were not built for running. He was making a tremendous effort, but not covering much ground. The handsome face was mostly gasping mouth.

'Hay-yulp! Hay-yulp!' he bawled, and tried to point behind him and run at the same time. He ground to a stop in front of me, gasping hard, and said, 'My God! He. . . . My God, the blood! Almah! My God . . . with a knife. . . .'

With a sudden rising roar, the Datsun came rocketing and sliding around the curve, and got a good grip and charged at us. I got the lawyer around the chunky waist and churned hard for the side of the road, with the tan vehicle aiming at us in a long slant. I scrabbled at the side hill beyond the ditch and almost pulled him clear, but the vehicle swerved into the ditch, bouncing hard, and one wheel caught his thick ankle against the stones in the ditch bottom and crushed it like pottery. He yelled and fainted. I left him there and took off after the vehicle. I came around a bend in time to see him pass the top of the path and brake hard and swing down the little steep side road to the boat basin. I swerved into the path. I was going too fast, slipped on loose stones, fell on one hip and skidded off into the brush. I got up and went on, running more slowly, and with a slight limp. When I got to the top of the steps, I could see the vehicle below me and see Miguel out on the finger pier, snatching the lines off and tossing them aboard. I raced down the steps and around the truck. I thought I might have a pretty good chance of running out and leaping aboard before he could get it started. He was aboard and scrambling toward the controls. Off to my right I suddenly saw Nora out of the corner of my eye, just past the sign saying boat owners and guests only, her hands clasped together, her eyes wide with alarm.

I didn't know how good an idea it might be to leap aboard with that desperate murderous little man, but I thought that if there was a handy boat hook, I might do some good.

The problem did not arise. A white blooming flower of heat picked me up and slammed me back against the side of the Datsun. I rebounded from it onto my face in the dust, too dazed to comprehend what had happened. Once upon a time I had been a hundred yards from a damn fool in a Miami marina when he had stepped aboard his jazzy little Owens and, without checking the bilge or turning the blowers on, had turned the key to start the engines. The accumulated gas fumes in the bilge had made a monstrous Whooompf. His fat wife was on the deck, and it had blown the sunsuit off her without leaving a mark on her. The owner had landed twenty feet away, in the water, with second degree burns and two broken legs. His crumpled beer cooler had landed on top of a car in the nearby parking lot. And what was left of the little cruiser had sunk seconds later.

This was no whooompf. This was a hard, full-throated, solid bam. It silenced that immediate portion of the world, and sent a thousand water birds wheeling and squalling. I picked myself up and fell. I saw Nora fifty feet away, trying to sit up. I started crawling to her. I stood up and took a dozen lurching steps and fell again and crawled the last few feet. She could not sit up. The white dress was not soiled. Her hair was not mussed. The only new thing about her was a crisp, splintery shard of mahogany. It looked as if it had been blown out of a portion of the rail. The rounded part of it was varnished. It was about twenty inches long. It was heaviest in the middle, tapering toward both ends. The middle of it was about as big around as her wrist. It was socketed into the soft tan hollow of her throat, at a slight angle so that the sharp splintered end stuck out of the side of her throat, near the back. She was braced up on one elbow, and with the fingertips of the other hand she touched the thing where it entered her throat.

She looked at me with an expression of shy, rueful apology, as though she wanted me to forgive her for being such a fool. Her lips moved, and then she frowned and coughed. She put her hand to her lips and coughed a bulging, spilling pint of red blood. She settled back. On hands and knees, I looked down into her eyes. She gave a little frown, as though exasperated at being so terribly messy, and coughed once again, and the dark eyes looked at me and then suddenly they looked through me and beyond me, and through the sky itself, glazing into that stare into infinity. She spasmed once, twitched those stupendous legs, and flattened slowly, slowly against the ground, shrinking inside that white dress until it looked too big for her, until she could have been a thin child in a woman's dress.

They said that things fell into the water for a long time, speckling the bay. They said that a broken piece of bronze cleat landed in the swimming pool. It blew the windows out of the office. They said that even flash-burned, with broken ribs and a sprained wrist, I kept four men busy getting me away from the body of Nora Gardino. They found some bits of Miguel. Enough for graveyard purposes.

The doctor who flew up from Mazatlan sprayed my burns, taped wrist and ribs. He treated the woman who had been so startled she fell down a short flight of stone steps. He did what he could with Gabriel Day's ruined ankle. I lay in bed and fought against the shot the doctor had given me. Then the first of the out of town police arrived, and after the first couple of questions, I stopped fighting the shot and let it take me under. It was easier down there.

We had special police from the state of Sinaloa. We had federal police and federal officials. And we had an influx of earnest young Mexicans in neat dark suits, carrying dispatch cases. They spoke fluent colloquial American.

I decided that I had better stay dazed for a while. I soon realized that they weren't looking for all the answers. They merely wanted something that sounded plausible. Something they could hand over to Press Association people as soon as they unlocked the gates and let them in.

As I saw the official version taking shape, I helped them along with it, and they seemed very pleased with me. I was just a tourist. Nora Gardino had been a friend of mine from Fort Lauderdale. I wouldn't want anybody to think, just because we had come down here together, that it was anything more than friendship. I had just taken an evening walk up the hill and ran into that fellow coming down, with some kind of a truck after him. I had done what I could, of course. What was he running from?

It made the men in the dark suits uneasy. But they had an official version for me. Mr. Day and Miss Hichin had been house guests of Carlos Garcia. Garcia had been seriously ill for many weeks, and Miss Hichin had stayed on to help care for him, as a gesture of friendship. She had asked Mr. Day to come and visit, with Garcia's permission. Now, to the consternation of everyone, they had discovered that Carlos Garcia was, in fact, Carlos Menterez, living in Mexico with falsified papers. He was a Cuban exile. Obviously, neither Miss Hichin nor Mr. Day had known this. Apparently one Miguel Alconedo, also Cuban, a servant in the household, evidently emotionally unbalanced, had become infatuated with Miss Hichin. Perhaps he had made advances to her and she had rebuffed him. At any rate, poor Mr. Day had been walking toward the swimming pool to ask Miss Hichin if he could bring her a drink when he had seen the aforesaid Miguel Alconedo go up behind the chair where Miss Hichin was sitting, grasp her by her blonde hair, pull her head sharply back and slash her throat with such a ferocity the head was almost severed from the trunk. Mr. Day had hidden in the brush. He had seen Miguel run to the gates, speak to the guard there, and swing the gates open. In terror, Mr. Day had run through the open gates and down the hill. The demented murderer, after trying to run him down, and succeeding only in injuring him badly, had sought to escape on the boat which he had made ready for flight. But, as everyone now knew, there had probably been an accumulation of gasoline fumes in the bilge, a highly explosive situation. It was a tragic thing that Miss Gardino should have been killed by the bit of flying debris. It was fortunate that more people were not injured. In the reports it would be clearly indicated that the murderer of the lovely young actress was also in Mexico without proper and complete documentation. Now the authorities had stepped in, of course, and would see what could be done officially about the invalid and the rest of the household and staff.

I knew and they knew that Menterez had greased some palms, probably with the understanding that his cover would remain intact so long as he had no trouble. And they knew and I knew that it had been more than gas fumes. But the fun-lovers will not patronize a resort area where people go around wiring bombs into boats.

It had to be the *Columbine IV*, of course. Perhaps they had worked their dinghy ashore in the dark of night. It had acted like a six stick blast, plus the added push of all that gasoline. Based on the habits of the pre-stroke Menterez, such a device had a good chance of getting him. And hate can be so strong you cease caring whether you get some other people too. You can tell yourself the other people would be either his friends or his employers, and the hell with them.

It wouldn't have been hooked up after the stroke. No point. And the boat hadn't been used since the *Columbine* had been there.

The rest of the staff knew absolutely nothing, of course.

And there wasn't much danger of Nora getting much publicity. Not with an Almah Hichin and a young pretty lawyer to write about. The hotel had no legal responsibility in the matter, of course. After all, the lady was in an area clearly marked as private.

The wrist was a minor sprain. It throbbed when I let it hang. It was more comfortable if I walked with my thumb hooked over my belt. I had lost eyelashes, singed hair and eyebrows, lost the white sun-baked hair on hands and arms. I wanted to get to Mr. Day. Because his ankle was like a bag of marble chips, they were making complex arrangements about flying him to the nearest hospital with special facilities for that of work, in Torreon. They had him in room twenty. I got to him at ten in the morning. They were due to tote him down to the dock and slide him aboard an amphib at noon. He had a couple of the black-suited ones with him.

He looked at me as I came in and said in a mild drug-blurred voice, 'You are the man who saved my life.'

I asked if I could have a little time alone with him. They bowed and smiled their way out, like oriental diplomats. They liked us. We were being good boys. We had taken our indirect briefing like little soldiers.

I took the straight chair beside the bed. Staring out of all that hair and hard white meat and handsomeness were two ineffectual blue eyes.

'I lost my head,' he said. 'I would have kept running right down the middle of the road. They said your name is McGee.' He put his hand out. 'I'm very grateful to you.' The handshake jiggled the bed, making him wince.

'What kind of law do you practise, Gabe?'

'Oh, theatrical mostly. Contract setups for independent producers. Special services contracts.'

'Are you honest?'

'Of course!'

'Then how did you happen to team up with Almah Hichin in a conspiracy, boy?'

The pain-killer had slowed him. He blinked at me. 'What are you talking about?'

'Almah's scheme to loot Menterez' lock box in Mexico City, boy.'

'Whose?'

'Come off it!'

'Who are you anyhow?'

'I'm a tourist. Didn't they tell you that?'

He put the back of his hand across his eyes. 'Jesus, I can't think. You . . . you have no idea how it was, seeing a thing like that. The way he jumped back, and all that blood. . . .'

'Was the money the big thing to you, Gabe? Over six hundred thousand in U.S. dollars. And Menterez in no shape to lodge a complaint. You had the papers all set up, didn't you?'

'He nodded. 'Power of attorney. Doctor's affidavit.'

'Was it the money?'

He took his hand away, but kept his eyes closed. 'No. If she'd asked me to crawl through fire, I'd have done that too. She knew I was hooked. She knew I'd been hooked for a long time. When she could use me, she sent for me.'

'It seems strange. You're good looking, and in a show biz area, and I'd think you could round up forty duplicates of her in one month.'

He turned his head and looked at me. 'Don't ask me to explain it, McGee. Infatuation. Sex. Put any word on it you want to. She was selfish and cruel and greedy. I know all that. She had a ring in my nose. And even when . . . it was the best for her, I had the idea it just happened to be me, and it could have been anybody. You know a funny thing? The closest I ever felt to her was the day before yesterday. She was out almost all afternoon. I don't know where she went. She didn't usually go out much at all. I didn't hear her come in. I didn't see her until she came out of the shower. She had a white robe on. She came to me and just wanted to be held. That's all. Just held close. She cried for a long time. She wouldn't tell me what was wrong. It was the only time . . . it was ever tender. He did it so quickly. He just yanked her head way back and. . . . Jesus, I am never going to be able to forget it. How could a man do a thing like that to so much loveliness?'

'How did you meet her?'

'Down here a year ago. I was at Claude and Ellie Boody's house, and the two house parties sort of got combined.'

I wondered if I should tell him that his little cruel darling had been a big help in getting four people murdered, and that was why Miguel had finished her off before leaving. A last minute errand.

But Mr. Day had all he could manage. And I decided I might as well leave her one mourner.

Suddenly he realized what he had been saying. 'There was no conspiracy involved, Mr. McGee. Almah was going to get that money out and bring it back to Mr. Garcia. That was the basis on which I agreed to help her.'

'Sure Gabe. They'll get a court order and open the box. A couple of bonded officials will discover about ten thousand dollars there, just enough to cover Menterez' hospital bills from now until he dies. But, of course, you didn't know his name was Menterez and his residency here wasn't entirely legal.'

There was one knowing glimmer in the mild blue eyes. 'I thought his name was Carlos Garcia.'

'If we don't know our lines, they can make an investigation down here drag on forever.'

'I . . . I'm sorry about that friend of yours, Mr. McGee.'

I gave him a big empty glassy smile and got out of there. I went back into the lobby just in time to be told my call had come through. It was my first chance to get through the heavy traffic on the single phone line. Shaja's voice was very faint. Apparently she could hear me all too well. It was the first inkling of disaster she'd had. Nora had been accidentally killed when a boat had blown up. Her people would probably want the body sent to New Jersey. There was a lot of red tape. No need for her to come down. I was all right. I would try to handle everything. I heard that faraway voice break into drab little heartsick fragments. I told her to inform Nora's local attorney.

I completed the necessary arrangements, with plenty of official help. To the couple of wire service stringers who filtered in, I was a very dull party. I was the fellow who answered the first question with a half hour lecture on boating safety.

But after all the white-washers had moved along, back to other pressing PR problems, a little man moved in on me who was considerably more impressive. He was bald and wide and brown, and had a face like the fake Aztec carvings gullible tourists buy. He had an eye patch, and carried himself as if he were in uniform. His name was Marquez. I had been vaguely aware of him in the background, coming and going, keeping to himself. He came to me at the bar and suggested we go over to a table.

He smiled all the time. He had a tiny gold and blue badge, and something that said he was Colonel Marquez, and something else that said he was in Investigationes Especiales for some kind of national bureau.

'That boat went up with one hell of a bang,' he said.

I gave him my water safety lecture. He listened to it with total attention, and when I ran down, he said, 'That boat went up with one hell of a bang, eh?'

'Yes it did indeed, Colonel.'

'Down in Puerto Altamura, in the village, you're a pretty popular tourist, McGee.'

'Every tourist should be an ambassador of good will.'

'That Garcia house, it's like a fortress, eh?'

'Maybe they have sneak thieves around here.'

'A man handles himself pretty well, and then he hides a gun in a john tank, for God's sake.'

'Colonel, you skip around so much, you confuse me.'

'This was the last place the *Columbine IV* was definitely seen.'

'Was it?'

'How many women do you need for one little vacation, McGee?'

'Now look, Colonel.'

'You pretend to be mad, then I'll pretend to be mad, and then we'll quiet down and play some more riddles, eh?'

He looked perfectly happy. I said, 'Can I play a game?'

'Go ahead. But watch yourself. You're semi-pro. This is a pro-league. Even if you're a pro in your own country, you're semi-pro here. We play hard ball.'

'Let's just imagine that a rich man hides himself away here because it's a place where he's hard to get at, and he expects sharpshooters. He would expect some because they plain hate him, and some because they think he might be in a situation where they can pick some of the loot off him. I guess they've picked him pretty clean. There's one thing left, maybe, like a lock box in a Mexico City bank, with better than six hundred thousand U.S. dollars in it.'

The smile remained the same size, but suddenly looked hemstitched. He got up and patted my shoulder and said, 'Wait right here, please.'

I had a twenty-minute wait. He came back. He signalled for a drink, and said, 'I suddenly thought of a phone call which could prevent a little error in bookkeeping. I am enjoying your game.'

'Thanks. We'll imagine a man comes down here after there's some trouble and tries to figure out who's been trying to do what to whom. The dust is settling, and he isn't too anxious to kick it up into the air again. How do we classify the little lady with the sliced throat? She brought along legal aid, so let's say she was after the loot. Maybe, along the way, she earned an assist on the *Columbine* thing, because she was anxious not to have anything drastic happen before she could get the loot.'

'And what have you been after?' he asked.

'Just a little fun in the sun, Colonel.'

'Like looking at the pictures on Heintz's wall? Heintz wants to be a company man, but he thinks it was a hell of a bang too. What if Taggart thought he would sleep better if Miguel for sure, and maybe the Hichin girl along with him, had one of those boating accidents you give the big talk about?' The man had a very flexible and interesting mind. I checked his concept for about twenty seconds. Sam did have the opportunity. And it would be a horrid irony if the package he had prepared had waited right there until Nora was in range.

'No. It wasn't his style.'

He shook his head sadly. 'You spoil the fun. You tell me too much too fast, McGee. See what you told me? That you knew him that well and that he's dead.'

'I've lowered my guard because I trust you, Colonel.'

'My God, that is so unique, I don't know how to handle it. I seldom trust myself, even.'

I was fascinated by the computer mechanism behind that Aztec face, so I put another little piece of data into the machine. 'Of course, Miss Gardino knew him better than I ever did.'

'So! An emotional pilgrimage. I'm disappointed in you, McGee. Or did I speak too fast, eh? Emotional for her? Loot for you?'

'Something like that.'

'One little area of speculation is left. It will never be proved one way or another. I think these things entertain you too. Taggart and Alconedo do some very dirty work for Don Carlos. Certain people are getting too close to Don Carlos. Perhaps he has promised them much money for special work they have done. So he makes a sly scheme, eh? He will leave the house with Miguel and Taggart to go to the boat. His pockets are full of bank books, eh? Perhaps an old and trusted friend is at the hotel with a car. There is a hell of a bang, and the car drives away, with Don Carlos hiding under a blanket maybe.' His smile broadened. 'But it is so difficult to arrange, so intricate, so full of suspense, eh? With the strain, a little blood vessel goes pop in Don Carlos' head. How many times can a man successfully disappear?'

'Son of a gun!'

'It entertains me too. Taggart left with loot. What if he had left, or planned to, on that boat. Perhaps with Miss Hichin. The possible combinations are interesting. Ah, well. You are scheduled to leave tomorrow. You can leave.'

'Thanks.'

'You are discreet with those drab little news people. There is no need to kick up dust now. Let it all settle. The dead women are in transit. Don Carlos and his wife will be in institutions. We have the problem of those other Cubans. The land syndicate will find a buyer for the house. May I say a few things to you, McGee? On a personal level?'

'Si, mi Coronel.'

'My God, what a horrible accent! I think you are a reckless man. I think you are a mischievous man. But you have good intuitions. You have a sour view of yourself, eh? You are . . . I would say a talented amateur in these matters. But an adult, I think. One finds so few American adults these days. To you, the village Mexicans are people. Not quaint dirty actors we supply to make the home movies look better. I have some problems I work on. Tampico, Acapulco, Mexicali. Three kinds of nastiness. If you're bored, we could have some fun. I can give you no official protection. I would use you, and pay you very little out of some special funds they give me. I would throw you into those situations, and see what happens.'

'I'm flattered, but no thanks.'

'No temptation at all?'

'Not very much. I guess I get into things, Colonel, because I get personally and emotionally involved.'

'The stamp of the amateur, of course. But why set up an order of which has to come first, my friend? Because you have the soul of an amateur, you will find that personal emotional involvement after you get into these things. You will always bleed for the victims. And always have the capacity for terrible righteous anger. This recruiting is very irregular, McGee. But when you are in the business of using people, it is hard to let a special person slip away.'

'Give me a great big medal for what I accomplished here, Marquez.'

'Don't be bitter about the woman. If she wasn't willing to accept risk she wouldn't have come here. She could stand there unharmed while a thousand boats blew up. This was the thousand and first.'

'You are over-valuing me, Colonel.'

'Maybe you mean this thing is not over for you yet.'

'Possibly.'

He put his hand out. 'When it is over . . . if you survive it . . . if you have some curiosity, write me at this address. Just say you are going to visit Mexico and would like to have a drink with me. By then I will know much more about you than I know now. But I don't over-value you, McGee. The affair of the knife at the Tres Panchos was very swift and competent. One day I would like to know just how you managed the dog. And before leaving, do not forget the interesting photographs in the base of the lamp.'

'Colonel, you are showing off.'

He made a sad face. 'That is the flaw in my personality. Vanity. And your flaw is sentimentality. They are the flaws which will inevitably kill us both. But let us enjoy them before the time runs out, eh? *Buena suerte, amigo.* And good hunting. And God grant we meet again.'

CHAPTER SIXTEEN

As I holed up in the City of the Angels, I was also aware of a comforting feeling of anonymity. I got in at six in the evening. By seven I was prowling the area where I hoped to work something out, the trash end of Sunset Boulevard. By ten I had a promising group in a crowded corner of a place called The Pipe and Bowl. I was Mack, a boat chauffeur by trade. They shuffled me around to one of the two free lassies and amalagamated me into the group. Her name, unfortunately, seemed to be Junebug. She had a round merry face, a lot of gestures, cropped brown hair. Her figure, as revealed by a little beige stretch dress, was quite pretty, except for a potentially dangerous case of secretarial spread. She was careful to tell me her boy friend was an engineer working on some kind of rugged project up in Canada.

'Junebug, I've been living a little too much tonight. This check will take me down to cigarette money.'

'Gee, Mack, I've got a few bucks in my purse if. . . .'

'It isn't only that, honey. What happened, this isn't home base for the boat I was running. And I got fired today. It's no real sweat. The owner got a wrong idea of me and his wife. I've got money coming. And no problem about a job. The man said get off my boat, and I got my gear and got off. But now I am definitely hung up for a place to stay. My gear is in a bus locker.'

She moved as far away from me as she could get, which was about six inches, and stuck her underlip out and said, 'If you think you're going to shack with me, buddy boy, if this is one of those cute ideas, I haven't had that much to drink. No sir. Oh-you-tee. Out.'

'Honey, believe me, you are a very exciting woman, but that wasn't my play. I want a place where I can hole up until the money comes through. That's all. Not your place. I thought you might know of a place. As soon as the money comes through, I'll pay you a going rent.'

'So how long is that supposed to be?' she asked with great scepticism.

I unstrapped my watch and handed it to her. 'This is a solid gold case. You can check it anywhere.'

'No. I don't want it. Look, I just thought you were trying to make it cute. Okay? Maybe one of the guys has an open couch.'

'As a last resort. But maybe if somebody is away. How about your engineer?'

'No. He lives with his folks in Santa Barbara. Let me think.'

She sat and pulled at that protruding underlip and scowled into her drink. Then she glowed with inspiration and went off to phone. She came back and wedged herself in again and in a conspiratorial tone said, 'Bingo. And we're neighbours yet. The girlfriend I phoned was sore as hell at being waked up at all hours. But she's the one Francine left her key with. And she'll go over and put it in my mailbox, she said.'

'Who is Francine?'

'Oh, she's away on this thing. What it is, the executives where she works, they take this trip and go to a whole mess of regional offices and have sales meetings. She's gone every year for a month about this time. It's pretty nice, going in a company plane and all, and they ball it up pretty good. She sacks out for days when she gets back, believe me. She shouldn't be back for another couple of weeks anyway.'

When the group decided to hit one more place, we broke away. Junebug had a little grey English Ford. She drove it with slap-dash efficiency. When I came out of the bus station with my bags and put them in the back seat, she said, 'You know, Mack, I damn near drove off. I was thinking, this is pretty stupid, not knowing you or anything.'

'I wondered if you would drive off.'

'What would you have done, baby?'

'Had some naps in the bus station.'

'Am I doing something real stupid?'

'I think you're smart enough to have a pretty good idea of whom you can trust.'

'Well . . . I guess that's the way it has to be.'

The place was off Beverly Boulevard, not too far from City College, Buena Villas.

She parked in front of her little villa. Number 11. While I got my gear out of her car, she went onto her porch and got the key from her mailbox. Then we went diagonally across the court to number 28.

After she put the key into the front door lock, she turned and whispered, 'Honey, honest to God, you got to promise me you won't make me regret this. I mean no big phone bills, or messing the place up, or breaking stuff or stealing stuff. I told Honey it was a girl friend I wanted it for. Even so, she dragged her heels.'

'You have no cause for alarm, Junebug.'

We went in. She found the light. Living-room, bedroom, kitchen and bath. Quick tour of inspection. No side windows. It would be depressingly dark by daylight. And Francine was a miserable housekeeper. Junebug found beer in the small noisy refrigerator. I agreed to replace anything I used up. We sat on the couch in the living-room. She was mildly, apprehensively flirtatious. She expected the pass, and I knew she could react in only three possible ways—rebuff, limited access, or totally— and I had not the slightest curiosity about finding out.

I poked around my new domain. Francine had left dirty sheets on the double bed. I found fresh ones in a narrow cupboard in the bathroom. She had left long blonde hair in all the expected places. I got rid of those, and the ring in the tub, and the hardened fragments of cheese sandwich on the kitchen table. I am a confirmed snoop. I went through the living-room desk and found out she was Mrs. Francine Broadmaster. Divorced. Age 27. I found some treasured little packets of love letters from several males. They were semi-literate, and so shockingly clinical they awed me.

After I had gathered up her stray garments and shoved them onto a closet shelf, I did the minimum of unpacking for myself and went to bed. I had become a city rabbit and found a burrow.

In the darkness, stretched out in Mrs. Broadmaster's play pen, aware of the late mumbles of the city, I took a tentative rub at the place that hurt. 'Forgive me,' her dying eyes said. 'Forgive me for being such a bloody mess.'

And the black anger came rolling up, turning my fists to stones, bunching the muscles of arm and shoulder. Don't go away, Mr. Tomberlin.

At eight in the morning the people of Buena Villas started going to work. The court made for considerable resonance. Apparently standard procedure was to bang every car door at least three time, rev up to 6,000 rpm, then squeak the tyres and groan out in low gear. I could have sworn half of them drove back in and did it all over again. By nine it had quieted down, and I got another hour of sleep before the phone started ringing. I began counting the rings, waiting for it to quit. It was beside the bed. It was a white phone. It had lipstick on the mouthpiece. After twenty-seven rings I knew who it had to be, so I reached and picked it up.

'Boy, you sleep pretty good,' Junebug said.

'I wanted to make sure it wasn't for her.'

'I was beginning to think you cleaned out the place and took off.'

'What would I steal, honey? Dirty underwear? Eddie Fisher records? That beautiful refrigerator?'

'Look, is everything okay? Honey didn't come over to check on who I borrowed it for before she went to work?'

'No callers.'

'Baby, you want to get in touch with me, you ask for Miss Proctor. You got something there to write down the number. I'll give you both numbers, my place and here. You got plans for after I get off today?'

'I'm not sure yet.'

'What I'll do to keep from waiting so long next time, I want to phone you, I let it ring once and hang up and dial you right back. Okay?'

'Fine.'

After I got dressed I checked the emergency reserve in my money belt. I had eight hundred there, in fifties. I moved half of it into my wallet. I had a Launderdale account I could tap at long range, but I still didn't want to have my name on anything. I imagined the car in front of the bungalow belonged to Francine. It was a sand-coloured Falcon. It took a ten minute search to turn up the keys. They were in a bowl on the table by the front door, under some old bills and circulars.

It was one of the only four cars left in the court. The battery sounded jaded, but it started in time. After I was out of the neighbourhood, I filled the tank and had a soft tyre pumped up. I found a breakfast place, and then looked in a phone book and found no listing for Calvin Tomberlin. I reviewed what I knew about him. Loads of money from his mother's real estate investments. Several residences, including a lodge up near Cobblestone Mountain. A boat big enough to go down the coast with. A persistent buyer of art objects, perhaps. And unlisted phones.

I started phoning the expensive retail establishments. I hit a vein on the third one, Vesters on Wilshire. I got a Mrs. Knight in the credit department and said, 'This is Mr. Sweeney of Sweeney and Dawson, Mrs. Knight. We're doing an audit on Mr. Calvin Tomberlin's personal accounts. Could you please tell me his present credit balance with you?'

'Just a moment, sir.'

I waited. If she thought to look in the yellow pages, she would find the accounting firm of Sweeney and Dawson listed therein. If she was bright, she would have suggested she call me back.

'It's just under eight hundred dollars, Mr. Sweeney. I imagine you want the exact figure. Seven hundred and eighty-eight twenty.'

'Thank you. Could you give me your billing address on that, please?'

'Yes sir. Care of the trust department, First Pacific National Bank.'

I thanked her for her cooperation, not heartily, but with the little touch of ice she might expect from diligent auditors.

I got First Pacific and asked for the trust department, and asked for the person handling the Tomberlin retail accounts. After some delay a very cool and cautious young voice said that she was Miss Myron.

'Miss Myron, I hate to bother you with this sort of a problem. This is Mr. Harmer in the credit department at Vesters. We show a balance in Mr. Calvin Tomberlin's account of seven hundred and eighty-eighty twenty. Would it be too much trouble for you to check that for me, please?'

'One moment, Mr. Harmer.'

Sooner than I expected, she was back on the line, saying, 'That's the figure I have here. These accounts are set up to be paid on the fifth working day of each. . . .'

'Good heavens, Miss Myron! I am certainly not pressing for payment on Mr. *Tomberlin's* account. We have a confusion on another item. I wanted to make certain you had not yet been billed for it. It was a phone order from Mr. Tomberlin late last month, and we had to special order it. You see, I thought that if you *had* been billed, your copy of our bill form would show delivery instructions. The sales person who took the order cannot remember which address to send it to. I thought of sending it along to the Cobblestone Mountain lodge . . . but you understand, we want to give Mr. Tomberlin the best possible service. It just came in and I *do* so want to send it to the right place. It took longer than we promised.'

'He's at the Stone Canyon Drive house, Mr. Harmer.'

'Let me see. I believe we have that number. Our records are in horrible shape. We're changing systems here.'

'Number forty, Mr. Harmer.'

'Thank you so much for helping us.'

'No trouble at all.'

Her girlish caution had evaporated when the figure I gave her checked with hers. We had become companions then. We shared the same arithmetic. And we were both eager to be of maximum service to Mr. Calvin Tomberlin. He used that handy tool of the very rich, special services from the trust department of a bank. All his bills would go there and they would pay them all, neatly and promptly. At the end of the year they would make up a detailed statement, take a percentage of the total as a service charge, send the statement to the tax attorney handling Tomberlin's affairs.

I had to buy a city map to locate Stone Canyon Drive. It angled west off Beverly Glen Boulevard, a winding road like a shelf pasted against the wall of a dry canyon. The houses were very far apart, and so were the numbers. Ten, twenty, thirty, forty. Everybody had a nice round number. I came to 40 after the canyon had gradually turned north. But the house was invisible. A smooth curve of asphalt flowed down around the rocks. Where it entered the main road, a small sign on one side said '40' and the sign on the other side said 'Private'. There was a rubber cable across the asphalt. I could assume that the weight of a car set off a signal somewhere.

I had to keep going. There was no place to pull off. After I passed a house—or rather a driveway—with the number 100 on it. I came to a turnaround, and there was no place to go but back. It was three and a half miles back to the boulevard. Ten houses in three and a half miles is reasonable privacy. I went back to Sunset and over to Sepulveda, and wiggled my way around through some semi-pretentious little areas, trying to work back toward Stone Canyon Drive. At last I found what I thought was a pretty good view of the ridge that formed the west wall of the canyon.

All I had learned was that if I was going to get any closer to C. Tomberlin, I was going to have to walk in. Or get him out of there.

At three o'clock, guessing I could catch Raoul Tenero at home in Miami, I loaded up with quarters and made a station to station call from a booth. Nita answered. I asked for Raoul. She carefully worked out the tense and construction and said, 'I am calling him now soon to be here with the phone, thank you.'

Raoul came on, chuckling. 'Yes?'

'No names. This is the hero of Rancho Luna, boy.'

'You have something to tell me? Maybe I heard it.'

'Maybe you did. The man we talked about is alive, but if he had the choice maybe he wouldn't want to be.'

'There have been some discussions about that. We wondered if it was the sort of story he could arrange to circulate, to take the pressure off.'

'I saw him.'

'Then I'll tell the others. We'll have a drink to that tonight. We'll drink to a long life for him.'

'Now for a name. Mineros.'

'Yes?'

'Can you fill me in a little? Background?'

'Of all the men in the world, perhaps he had the best reason to want to find the first man we were talking about. He disappeared, aboard a chartered boat.'

'I know. Who was with him? I could check old newspapers, but this is quicker.'

'Rafael Mineros. Enrique Mineros, his eldest son. Maria Talavera, who was at one time engaged to Rafael's nephew, who died in a Cuban prison. Manuel Talavera, her brother.'

'They are dead.'

'Presumed dead?'

The operator came on and told me to buy another three minutes. I fed the quarters in, and then said, 'Definitely dead. The man you are going to drink to—he gave the orders.'

'God in heaven, what a disaster that man has been to the Mineros family!'

'You can tell from the money how far away I am.'

'I have a pretty good guess.'

'Raoul, I need one contact here. Somebody I can trust. Trust as much as I trust you. Is there any kind of organized group here?'

'My friend, when two Cubans meet, the first thing they do is organize a committee. But I don't have to think a long time to think of a man out there. Paul Dominguez. I have it here in the book. Just a moment. 2832 Winter Haven Drive. Long Beach.'

'Thanks. How do I let him know I have your blessing?'

'Hmmm. Tell him he still owes me a pair of boots. If that isn't enough, he can phone me.'

'He is sensible?'

'More so than you or I, amigo. And as much man as the two of us.'

I found Dominguez in the book. A woman with a young and pleasant voice said he would be home about six. There wasn't enough time left to go down to Oceanside and find out who had chartered the *Columbine* to Rafael Mineros. I looked the name up in the book and found a Rafael Mineros in Beverly Hills and an Esteban Mineros in the Bel Air section.

I got back to Buena Villas at four thirty. About ten cars had come home. I parked in front of 28. As I got out of the Falcon, a woman came striding toward me. She looked like the young George Washington, except that her hair was the colour of mahogany varnish. 'Who are you and what the hell is going on?' she demanded at ten paces. She wore a Chinese smock and pale blue denim pants.

I let her march up to me and stop and wait for the answer. 'Are you Honey?'

'Yes. What the hell is Junebug trying to pull around here?'

'Maybe you can solve my problem, Honey.'

'I'm the one with the problem. I'm responsible. Turn over the house key and her car key and clear the hell out of here.'

I extricated one fifty-dollar bill and said, 'My problem is do I give this to Junebug? Do I leave it on the desk in there for Francine? Or do I turn it over to you?'

Her eyes wavered and her belligerence diminished. 'What do you think you're buying?'

'A quiet place. No fuss, no muss, nothing to upset Mrs. Broadmaster.'

'You know her?'

'I've seen quite a bit of her. Should I give this to Junebug?'

'I've got a responsibility.'

'In a few days you get the key back. And Junebug gets another of these.'

Her hand, faster than light, snapped the bill away and shoved it into the pocket of the oriental coat. 'I look after the place for Fran. I can see she gets this. But you shouldn't use the car. It's not right you should use the car. It should be more if you use the car. Did Junebug say it would be so much, like making a deal with her?'

'I don't think she realizes I intended to pay for it. I'll tell her the kind of deal I've made with you.'

'Why bother? It's my responsibility isn't it? Fran left the key with me. Maybe I'll have to go in and clean up when you leave. Junebug wouldn't do that, and you know it. So it can be between us. What Fran said, if I want to put somebody up, okay. A favour for a favour. But it should be more for the car.'

'How much more, Honey?'

'Well . . . the same again?'

'You know, if it was that much, I'd have to ask Junebug if she thought I was being taken.'

'You know, I don't have to dicker with you. You can get out.'

'Give me back the money and I'll give you the keys.'

'If you need a place, you need a place. How about twenty?'

'Twenty is fine.'

'Suppose you do this for my protection. You get a key made and give me hers back. Then . . . if somebody is looking for you and they find you. . . .'

'That's fair enough.'

She looked around, checking to see if anybody was looking at us. 'After dark, you put the regular key in my mailbox tomorrow. With that twenty dollars like we agreed. You won't bust the place up or anything?'

'I want to live quietly.'

'You tell Junebug I came over and we got along, and I said any friends of hers. Okay?'

'Fine.'

'Fran is back May tenth.'

'Oh, I'll be long gone. Don't you worry.'

'I worry about everything all day long and half the night. I worry about things you never heard of,' she said. She went scuttling away, up the line, and went into a bungalow four doors from mine.

Junebug rapped at my door at twenty after five. I got up and let her in. She hadn't been in her place yet. She wore her office outfit, a tight dark skirt and a white nylon blouse. She grinned a significant grin with her little comedy face, and squinched her jackolantern eyes, and hugged up for a big kiss of hello. Then she went stilting around on her office heels in a proprietary manner, and exclaimed at how I had neatened it up, saying I'd probably make a good husband even if I didn't look it. I told her Honey had been to call.

She looked stricken. 'Oh dear Jesus,' she said.

'What's the trouble? We got along fine. She said any friend of yours is a friend of hers. She gave me Francine's car keys and told me to drive carefully.'

'You're kidding!'

I showed her the car keys.

'I will be damned,' she said. 'Who would have thought? Well, it just goes to show you never know, do you? Mack, dear, I'm just sick about not thinking of something. I got paid today and when I cashed my cheque I thought of it. You poor dear, what have you done about food? Gee, I could have left you a few bucks, you know. Did you get your money yet?'

'I looked a guy up and got a small loan. I'm okay.'

'Well, thank goodness for that. Can I loan you some more?'

'No. I'm fine thanks.'

'What do you want to do tonight, honey? I like to swing a little on Friday because I can sleep in.'

'I have to go see a man.'

'About a job?'

'Yes.'

She gave me a sultry glance, with some contrived eyelash effects. 'Well, *that* won't take all night will it?' The glance matched the unanticipated kiss of hello at the door. Obviously she had been thinking about the situation, and had come to specific conclusions. The engineer was in Canada. I had to make the pass or we would never get to the corny dialogue. So I did not make it, thus saving herself from herself, or me from her, or something, and managed to leave such a tiny scratch on the surface of her pride any Miracle Cleanser would make it invisible in a moment.

I drove to a pay phone and called Paul Dominguez. His accent was very slight. I didn't tell him my name. I merely said that I needed help, and Raoul Tenero had said to remind him that he still owed Raoul a pair of boots.

After a thoughtful silence, he asked me where I was, then told me to meet him at eight o'clock at the bar at Brannigan's Alibi, a place near the Long Beach Municipal Airport. He said to look for a man with two packs of cigarettes on the bar in front of him, stacked one on the other. He named the brand. It was a very tidy little identification device, and I knew I would remember it and perhaps use it myself one day.

I got lost and arrived at ten past eight. It was one of those sawdusty places with joke signs on the wall, doing a good neighbourhood trade. I went to the bar and looked around and saw the two packs in front of a man who stood alone at the far end of the bar. He was tall and quite slender, with a tanned and almost bald head, a youthful face, big, powerful-looking hands. He wore slacks, a white sport shirt and a pale blue jacket. I moved in beside him and said, 'Hi, Paul.'

He gave me a quick look of inventory, smiled and greeted me, and then looked beyond me and gave a little nod. I turned and saw two men get up from a booth near the door. One finished the dregs of his beer, put the glass down and followed the other one out.

I got myself a beer and we carried them over to a booth.

'Precautions?' I asked.

He shrugged. 'I phoned Raoul. I got the description. McGee. Maybe somebody had you place that call to him. If somebody else had showed up, it would have turned out to be a different thing. Old habits, I guess. If there is anything I can help you with, let me know.'

I started it. It took a long time. When I got to the end of Nora, it uncorked a little more emotional involvement than I had intended to show, hoarsening my voice.

When I had finished, he got up without a word and brought two more bottles of beer back to the table. 'My youngest kid,' he said, 'the other day he fell off a chair. He jumped up and gave that chair such a hell of a kick, he nearly broke his toes.'

I saw what he meant. 'It isn't like that, Paul. Tomberlin had something to do with it. He took Mineros down there. He lit the fuse.'

'It was already an unstable situation. Carlos Menterez was too sociable. Sooner or later somebody who wanted him dead was going to find him. Once he had to leave Cuba, Menterez was an embarrassment to everybody, even to the little wolf pack of crypto-fascist exiles in Mexico City who think they can rebuild a Batista-type regime in Cuba when a power vacuum occurs after a successful invasion. God knows they funnelled enough money out to finance it, but they don't realize how fast the world is changing. Those boys you talked about in the white car, Luis and Tomas. They would be with that group. And those people know that their crazy dream would need the good will of families like the Mineros. So they would have to get the word back that what happened was all Menterez' doing. They would have to disavow Menterez, and explain how it happened. If they could have found your friend Taggart and killed him, it would have been a good will gesture.'

'To whom? Who is left, for God's sake?'

'Senora Mineros, the matriarch. In Cuba she lost a son, a daughter-in-law and a grandson to Menterez. In Mexico she loses the other son and another grandson. There are left, I think, two more grandsons, the younger sons of Rafael. They are about fifteen and sixteen. And the other daughter-in-law, Rafael's widow. Remnants, and tradition, and a hell of a lot of money. The family still exists. There would be property claims in Havana, a basis for cooperation. Oh yes, and there is another one too. Her brother. Esteban Mineros. An old man.'

'So you can assume word got back to the family about Taggart.'

'Yes, word that he would get in touch with Tomberlin to sell him what he had taken from Menterez, the statuettes Tomberlin wanted. Then it would be necessary to make some arrangement with Tomberlin so they could get their hands on Taggart. From what you say they got the gold, all but one piece of it, and missed the man.'

'When I talked to Sam, he at first wanted me to help him get the gold back. Then he decided to sell the one piece he had left. He seemed to think he was in a good bargaining position. He said something about being able to raise political hell.'

'All kinds of hell, man. Figure it out. The Mineros mystery. The Menterez collection in Tomberlin's possession. An anonymous letter to any good reporter out here could create an international incident. The Castro propaganda machine could have a lot of fun with it.'

'So who killed Sam?'

'Rhetorical question? If he'd died easy, I could make up a list of names. But it sounds like a very personal execution. There were three young Talaveras. Two died on that boat. Maria and her brother, Manuel. There is a third brother, a little older. Ramon. Not only Maria's brother, but a very good friend of Enrique Mineros. It surprises me he was not with them.'

'He would use a knife?'

'He is a very intense man. And he would consider it an obligation.'

'You know all these people?'

'I used to know them well. Just as Raoul used to know them well. Upper class in Havana was a small community, McGee. But now there is . . . a considerable financial difference between us, Raoul and I came out later. It is the Castro equation, my friend. The later you left, the cleaner you were plucked. So we no longer travel in the same circles.'

'What does Ramon Talavera look like?'

'Slender. Dark hair. Medium height. Pale. A quiet man. Unmarried. Do you think he should be punished—if he is the one? Do you see these things in such a cloudy way, my friend?'

'No. But if he did, he was pretty damned cold-blooded about it.'

'Somebody, for hire, kills his brother, his sister and his best friend with a knife. Man, you can expect a certain amount of indignation.'

'It all comes down to Tomberlin.'

'The way my kid kicked the chair.'

'But he does have the gold.'

'It isn't his. Okay. Is it yours?'

'I'll ask you a question. Maybe it was Ramon Talavera who decided it wasn't just that Sam should keep on living. Is it just that Tomberlin should be the only one who winds up ahead?'

'Greed or justice?'

'A little of both. Plus curiosity.'

He smiled. 'That's an answer I like.'

'Do you know the man?'

'I met him once. At a banquet at a big hotel. One of the rare times when the latino guest list is so big, it includes Pablo Dominguez. He is a grotesque. He likes the Spanish-Americans. I think it is a taste for our women. Apparently he can be depended upon to give money to certain causes. I think he is tolerated. I think he is a man who would have to buy his way into any kind of group.'

'How do I get close to him?'

Dominguez leaned back and ran his hand over his bald brown pate. 'It's an interesting problem. He is suspicious of strangers, I understand. I heard some gossip about him. His personal habits are not very nice. He buys his way out of trouble from time to time. He has a look of corruption. A rancid man, I think. And a very acquisitive man. A collector. Let me think about this, McGee. I must ask a few careful questions. I think if you try to make contact carelessly, you'll spoil any future chance. Can you meet me here tomorrow night at the same time?'

'Of course.'

CHAPTER SEVENTEEN

AGAIN I managed to get lost and again I was a little late. Paul Dominguez was sitting in the same booth, dressed much as before. He stood up and introduced the woman. She was attractive in a flamboyant way. She was big. Big shoulders, big hands, a big and expressive wealth of mouth and eyes. She was swarthy, with heavy black brows. Her hair was expertly bleached to a cap of soft silver curls. Her eyes were a pale yellow-green, feline, mocking and aware. Her voice was a baritone drawl, with an edge of Spanish accent. He introduced her as Connie Melgar. And he gave my name as John Smith.

Her hand was warm, dry and strong. Dominguez hesitated, then slid in beside her and pulled his drink over. I sat facing them.

'Constancia is Venezuelan,' he said. 'Very rich and very difficult.'

Her laugh was vital and explosive. 'Difficult! For whom? For you, Pablo, with all that machismo?' She winked at me. 'I throw myself at his head, and he calls me difficult.'

Dominguez smiled. 'I told her the problem,' he said.

'Your problem, Mr. Smith—certainly that cannot be your name—is to find a way to approach Calvin Tomberlin. I can arrange that, of course. Certain groups always have access to that gentleman. But I think it would be very pleasant if I could be assured that you will not waste the opportunity, Mr. Smith.'

'In what way?'

'If you can do him some great harm, I will be delighted.'

'If things work out, I hope to make him reasonably unhappy, Mrs. Melgar.'

She looked at me for five long seconds, her head tilting, then exhaled and patted Paul on the hand and said, 'Thank you, dear. Mr. Smith and I can get along very nicely.'

Paul looked at me in interrogation. I nodded. He stood up and said, 'When you see our friends, give them my best wishes.'

'Thank you for the help.'

He nodded and bowed to Connie Melgar.

After he had left, she said, 'He is such a very cautious man. But a very good man. Do you know that?'

'I met him through a friend. I like him.'

'He has asked me this favour, Mr. Smith. I owe him several favours. He told me not to ask you questions. That is a terrible burden for me, not to ask questions. And this is not a *simpatico* place to talk in any case. There is an animal at the bar who leers. You have a car here? Why don't you follow me?'

She drove a Mercedes 300 SL, battleship grey, with great dash and competence. I had to keep Francine's little car at a full gallop to keep her tail-lights in view. She stopped on a dark street and I pulled in behind her and parked. She had me get into her car, and we went another half block and down into the parking garage under a new high rise apartment house. She left it for the attendant to put away, and led me back to a passenger elevator, punched the button for ten. In her high heels she stood a vivid and husky six feet. She smiled and said, 'You are damn well a big fellow, Mr. John Smith. You make me feel almost girlish and dainty. That is a rare thing for me. But not so rare in California as other places.'

Her apartment was 10 B. It was huge, with dark panelling, massive dark carved furniture, ponderous tables, low ornate lamps with opaque shades. As she opened the door, a little maid came on the run to take her wrap. Constancia rattled off a long spate of Spanish which seemed to be half query and half instruction. The maid bobbed and nodded and gave small answers and went away. An older, heavier woman, also in uniform, made an appearance, and stood stolidly while more orders were given.

Connie Melgar led me to the far end of the room, on a higher level, to a grouping of giant chairs and couches. She said, 'The way it was here, it was like trying to live in a doll house. I had it all torn out and panelled in honest wood, and had the furniture shipped up from my house in Caracas, then I had to have walls changed to make two apartments into one. But still I feel cramped here. I like the ranch much better. I have a nice ranch in Arizona.'

'This is very nice here, Mrs. Melgar.'

She fitted a cigarette into a holder. 'I own the building,' she said. 'As Pablo said, I'm filthy rich. I've been riding the winds of change by slowly liquidating at home and reinvesting here. I don't like what's going on at home. It scares me. Could you fix us some drinks, please? That thing there is a bar when you open the door. Dark rum on ice for me, please.'

As I fixed drinks I said, 'Apparently you don't feel friendly toward Tomberlin.'

'I don't like the man. I have no idea why I keep seeing him. Perhaps it's some manner of challenge to me. I have one horse at the ranch I should get rid of. His name is Lagarto. Lizard. Hammer-headed thing with a mean eye. He is very docile, right up to the point where he sees a good chance to run me into a low limb or toss me into an arroyo. He may kill me one day.'

I took her the drink, and as she started to raise it to her lips, I said, 'Maybe I want you to get me close enough to Tomberlin so I can kill him.'

The drink stopped an inch short of her lips. The yellow eyes watched me, and then the drink moved the rest of the way. She sipped and lowered it. 'Was I supposed to scream?'

'I don't know you well enough to make any guesses.'

She studied me. 'If that's what you want, I would assume you have a reason. If you want to do it, you will do it in some way which will not implicate me. But he is not that kind of a nuisance.'

'How do you mean?'

'He's just a rich, sick, silly man. He might be killed by some other silly man. But a serious man would know he is not worth so much risk. He is an insect.'

I sat at the other end of the gigantic couch, facing her. 'What sort of insect?'

'You don't know him at all? He is a political dilettante. He supports strange causes. Each one is going to save the world, of course. He gives money to ugly little fringe groups and makes them important, and then he loses interest. He collects exotic things, and many of them are quite nasty. Antique torture instruments. Dirty books and films and pictures. Sickening books. Shocking bits of sculpture. He's impotent, apparently, and he is a voyeur. Bugged bedrooms, and two-way mirrors and group orgy, that sort of boyish amusement. A sad and tiresome case, really. He loves to make dark hints about all kinds of conspiracy going on, all kinds of nastiness. His latest cause is that Doctor Face.'

'Who?'

'Doctor Girdon Face, and his American Crusade. Oh, it's very big lately. Lectures and tent shows and local television and so on. And special phone numbers to call any time of day or night. If he ever was turned loose in the west wing of Cal's house up there at Stone Canyon, he would have a stroke. Cal keeps his various fields of interest quite well compartmented. It is a little frightening though, to think how quickly his little Dr. Face has established a huge eager following.'

'I heard Tomberlin gives money to Latin American projects too.'

'They tap him every chance they get. But he is most generous with the militant right, the savage little groups who want to buy arms and smash the peons right back to where they belong. He's not a moderate, my friend. What should I call you? I want you to call me Connie.'

'John Smith is a little too much, I guess. Mack Smith?"

'You want to play it close, don't you?'

'The name might mean something to Tomberlin.'

'How about the face?'

'It won't mean a thing. When can you set it up?'

'Tomorrow evening. We'll go to his house. He seldom goes out. There'll be the usual group of sycophants hanging around him. I'll invent some excuse for dropping in. You'll have to play a part, Mack Smith.'

'Who will I be?'

She stretched her long and opulent body and said, 'I think the proper designation is Connie's Latest, if you don't mind too much. Where did I find you?'

'I was running a boat for some friends of yours.'

'Perfect. I was up at Monterey last week. Their name is Simmins. Gordon and Louise. I hired you away from them because I am thinking of buying a boat. But Cal won't be particularly curious.' She held her glass out and I made her a fresh drink. She brushed my hand with her fingertips and said, as she took it, 'Are you going to suggest that we might as well have the game as well as the name?'

I sat closer to her and said, 'It would be normal to think about it, Connie. You are pretty spectacular, and you know it. But I don't think it is a very good idea.'

'That is what I was going to tell you. If you suggested it.'

'What are your reasons?'

'My dear, my young men think they are so bold and wild and free. But they are so easily tamed. You and I would be another thing, my friend. It would take us too long to find out who is winning, and in the process I might lose. No, I don't play games I can't win, Mr. Smith, Mister Mysterious Smith. But what were your reasons?'

I smiled at her.

'It would feel a little too much as if I had been standing in line, Connie.'

Her eyes changed to narrow slits of gold and her lips lifted away from her teeth. Then suddenly she gave that huge laugh and gave me a punch on the shoulder that made my hand go numb. 'See? You would beat me with that sort of talk. One day I would find myself weeping and begging your forgiveness. Like a woman. My God, we might be good enough together to take the risk. But no. Maybe five years ago. Maybe. Not now. I am too old to be physically beaten, and that is one of the things you would find it necessary to do. Because I am insufferable. I know it. Come with me.'

She took me into a study which was also a trophy room. African game. Some very good heads. Leopard, lion, buffalo. There was a case of fine weapons behind glass. There were framed photographs of her, younger, slimmer, just as vital, standing by the dead elephant, rhino, great ape. 'My guns,' she said. 'My dear dead animals. I took my sainted husband on safari five years running, thinking it would turn him into enough man for me. He killed like an accountant signing a ledger. He bent over a bush to pick a flower for me and a snake struck him in the throat. He was dead before he could fall to the ground. If it was permitted, I would have his head in here, mounted like the others. And the heads of all the young men. Now you know me better, Mack Smith. You might be enough man for me. I think I will always wonder about that. It's bad luck we're past the years of finding out. Be here at six tomorrow. We will use my car. Good night.'

I found my way out. I heard that laugh as I was leaving. I wondered if she had laughed the same way after downing old jumbo, the tusker, shown in the framed glossy, recumbent beside Mrs. Melgar in her safari pants, her smile, her big bore weapon at port arms.

A hard rain came smashing down as I ran for Mrs. Broadmaster's tiny front porch. It was a little after ten. Ten minutes later Junebug knocked at my door. She said she'd come for a cozy nightcap. But it was not my night for Junebugs. I played dense, evaded small traps, and finally managed to send her off home with just a few small scratches on her pride.

I had a drink in Connie's apartment while she finished dressing. She came out with the happy walk of a woman who knows she will be approved. She wore a dark sheath dress of some kind of knitted material. She was almost but not quite too big for knitted fabrics. Her shoulders were bare and honey-brown, smoothly muscled and magnificent.

'You're very elegant, Connie.'

'Thank you. Wear that same look all evening, dear, and you'll fit the category.'

'Drink?'

'The same as before. Please.'

She went to the phone and called the basement and told them to bring her car around front. She came back and took her glass, touched it to mine. 'To whatever you're after, Mack Smith. Mysterious Mack Smith. Your eyes intrigue me, Mr. Smith. Are pale-eyed people cruel? Your eyes are the colour of rain on a window in the early morning. At first glance last night, I thought you looked quite wholesome. That's a deception, isn't it?'

'I have wholesome impulses.'

'Kindly keep them to yourself. You know, I think you are just as violent as I am. But your control is better. What are you after?'

'A close look at Mr. Tomberlin.'

'That's all?'

'I might bend him a little.'

'What did he do to you, dear?'

'Let's say he set something in motion and it didn't work out very well for anybody except him.'

'Who did you last work for?'

'Gordon and Louise Simmins of Monterey. Why?'

'Am I a better employer?'

'The relationship is a little more personal.'

'My dear, the people at Tomberlin's will be a mixed bag. Fragmented groups spread about the place, serviced by his Hawaiian army. Circulate at will. I phoned him today. He is leaving in two or three days. He likes to go down to Montevideo this time of year.'

She put her empty glass down and said, 'Are we ready?'

I draped the pale fur over her shoulders, a broad stole about ten feet long, big enough for a big woman. She wore cat's eye studs in pierced ears, and a single ring, a narrow oblong emerald that reached from knuckle to knuckle. She brought no purse. She loaded me with her cigarettes, lighter, compact and lipstick —typical burden for the captive male. She led me like a small parade. Down in front the doorman handed her into the car with humble, tender ceremony. He gave me one glance of knowing appraisal. I got behind the wheel, identified the right gadgets, and stomped the car off into the bright evening.

CHAPTER EIGHTEEN

THE tilted rocky area immediately surrounding the Tomberlin place was enclosed by a high wire fence. The gate was open. A broad little uniformed man with a merry Chinese face intercepted us, peered in at Connie Melgar, then backed, grinning, touching his cap.

There were at least twenty cars in the parking area, ranging from a glossy Bentley to a scabrous beach buggy. The big house was spilled down the rock slope. It was a bleached grey wood, pale stone, glass, aluminium and slate. It was like three sizeable houses, each on stilts, each on a different level down the rock slope, all butted against each other. Our staircase crossed the pool and continued on, I saw, ending at a huge deck in front of the lowest portion of the house, a deck overlooking a steep drop and a broad and lovely view. But Connie turned off down a narrow branching staircase that brought us down to poolside under the middle segment of the house. Some sleek young things were enjoying the pool, swimming back and forth from sunlight to shadow. We climbed a curve of staircase into the middle portion of the house, into a vast room vaguely reminiscent of a Miami Beach hotel lobby, but in better taste. People stood in chatting groups. Eyes slanted toward us in swift appraisal, and I adjusted my mild and fatuous smile.

Calvin Tomberlin was in a small group. He was a grotesque. He was of middle size, fairly plump, and stood very erect. He was completely hairless, without brows or lashes. He wore a toupee so obviously fraudulent it was like a sardonic comment on all such devices. It was dusty black, carefully waved, and he wore it like a hairy beret. His eyes were blue and bulged. His face was pale pink, like roast beef. His lips were very heavy and pale, and they did not move very much when he spoke. His voice was a resonant buzz, like a bee in a tin can. He wore a pewter grey silk suit, with a boxy jacket, cut like a Norfolk jacket but without lapels. He wore a yellow ascot with it.

He greeted Connie with what I guessed was supposed to be warmth, gave her a little hug, and placed two firm pats on her ample knitted stern. But it was done in a curiously mechanical fashion, as though he was a machine programmed to make these social gestures.

Connie introduced us. His hand was cold and soft and dry. He looked at me as a butcher looks at a questionable side of meat, and turned away. I sensed the same recognition and dismissal in the others. They weighed me with their eyes, so much captive meat, and turned away. I did some drifting. Groups formed, broke, reformed, changed. I saw the pool people. I paced the big suspended deck. The lowest level was bedrooms. The upper level was lounge area, dining areas, a library. The day was gone, and the lights came on as they were needed.

I found Connie and, after a patient time, cut her out of the pack.

'What was that about a west wing or something?'

'Cal's little museum. Up the stairs and to the left. Locked tight.'

'Any way to get to see it?'

She frowned. 'I don't know. I can try. Hang around this area, dear. If it works, I'll be back to get you.'

While she was gone a wobbly type came up to me, a big blond kid with a recruiting poster face. He looked ready to cry.

'You have some good laughs when she pointed me out, pal?'

'You're wrong. She didn't.'

He shook his head. 'You're so smart, aren't you? You know every damn thing. She's worth millions, and she's the best piece you ever ran into, and you're set forever. That's the way it is, huh? Living high, boy. Well, brace yourself, because she's going to. . . .'

'Chuck!' she said sharply. He swung around and stared at her. She shook her head sadly. 'You're turning into the most terrible bore, dear. Run along, dear.'

'I want to talk to you, Connie. By God, I want to talk to you.'

'You heard the lady,' I said.

He pivoted and swung at me. I caught the fist in my own hand, slid my fingers onto his wrist. He swung the other fist, off balance, and I caught the other wrist. He bulged with the effort to free himself, then broke and started to cry. I let him go and he went stumbling away, rubbing his nose with the back of his hand.

'Nicely done,' she said. 'Come along. Cal is waiting. I told him I wanted to see how you'd react.'

'How should I react?'

'Suit yourself. It gives me a funny feeling.'

He was waiting for us, mild as a licensed guide. He unlocked a very solid-looking door, closed it and locked it again when the three of us were inside. Lines of fluorescent tubes flickered and went on. There were little museum spotlights. The room was about twenty by forty. There were paintings and drawings. There were pieces of statuary on pedestals and on bases, and set into glassed-in niches in the walls. There were display cases. It was all very tidy and professional and well-organized. The windows, two small ones, were covered with thick steel mesh.

'I have here, and in the next room,' he said in that buzzing voice, 'what is probably the most definitive collection of erotica in the world today.'

He showed us the cases of ancient instruments of torture and ecstasy. He turned a ground glass easel on, took large Ektachrome transparencies from a safe file and showed us a few of them, saying, 'These are studies of the Indian temple carvings at Konarak and Khajuarho, showing the erotic procedures which were always a part of the Hindu religion.'

He put them away and said, 'Beyond here we have the special library of books and films, a small projection room and a small photo lab. A recent project has been to duplicate the Konarak carvings, using amateur actors and period costuming. Stills, of course.'

'A project?' Connie said. 'Really, Cal! You make your own diseases sound so terribly earnest.'

He looked at her blandly. 'Connie, my dear, any time you wish to lend your considerable talent to any of these little projects. . . .'

'I would look a bit out of place among your poor hopped-up little actors and actresses, darling.'

'You are wonderfully well preserved, Connie.'

I wandered over to the side wall. The individual niches were lighted. I had counted one area of thirty-four of them. The gold statues were behind glass.

'Are these real gold, Mr. Tomberlin?'

He came up behind me. 'Yes. I recently had more space made for these. Most of these were a recent acquisition. As you can see, many of them do not fit in with . . . with the general theme of the entire collection. But I decided not to break the collection up. Strange and handsome, aren't they?'

'Where would you go to buy stuff like this?' I asked.

'I purchased a collection, Mr. Smith. I haven't had them properly identified and catalogued as yet.' He was bored. He had no interest in my reaction. He turned to Connie and said, 'Would you like to see a new film, dear? It's Swedish, and quite extraordinary.'

She shivered. 'Thank you, no. Once was enough for all time. Show it to Rhoda, darling. She adores that sort of thing. Thank you for the guided tour. Let's all get back to the people, shall we?'

After we were alone again, she shivered again and said, 'That's pretty snaky in there, isn't it?'

'He's a strange man.'

She pulled me into a corner and put her hands on my shoulders. 'Is it those gold things, dear?'

'Was I that obvious?'

'Not really. But it would be nice if it were those gold statues. He was so delighted to get them. He's had them only a few months. He must have made a very good deal. He kept chuckling and beaming. But, darling, it would be quite a project. That room is like a big safe. This place is alive with people at all hours. And I think he has burglar alarms.'

'It presents a few little problems.'

'Including the police.'

'No. They wouldn't come into it.'

'I beg your pardon?'

'They're not his. Twenty-eight of them aren't.'

She looked amused and astonished. 'Now don't tell me he stole them!'

'He sort of intercepted them after they'd been stolen.'

'It's very confusing, my dear. And you are . . . employed by someone?'

'Paul told you about asking questions.'

'I remember something about that. Don't you trust me, my dear?'

'Implicitly, totally, without reservation, Constancia. But if you don't have any answers, you can't answer any questions.'

'Will people ask me questions?'

'Probably not.'

'Darling, do as you wish. I. . . . What's the matter?'

'I just wondered if I know that man.'

She turned and looked. 'Oh, that's one of Cal's show business connections. A dreary little chap. Claude Boody.'

There was no hint of the imperiousness the artists had put into the oil painting in Puerto Altamura. The jowls were the same. The eyes were sad, wet, brown and bagged, like a tired spaniel, and he walked with the care of a heart case.

'I guess he just looks like someone I knew once.'

'He has some dreary little syndicated television things, and he buys old foreign movies and dubs the English and resells them to independent stations.'

'You sound knowledgeable, Mrs. Melgar.'

'I have some money in that, too. But not with him.'

'Does Tomberlin have some business association with him?'

'Heavens no! Calvin cultivates a few people like Boody because they can always round up some reckless youngsters for fun and games.'

We went back to the upper lounge where Tomberlin's hard-working staff had laid out a generous buffet. It was delicious, and we took loaded plates down to the big deck and ate like a pair of tigers. She licked her fingers, patted her tummy, stifled a belch and moaned with satisfaction. There is a direct relation between the physical approaches to all hungers. This great hearty woman would ease all appetites with the same wolfish intensity, the same deep satisfaction. She would live hard, play hard, sleep like the dead. Her strong rich body had that magnetic attraction based on total health and total use. She did not relate in any way to the sick subtleties, the delicate corruptions in Tomberlin's private museum. And I got the hell away from her before I had more awareness than I could comfortably handle.

I wandered again.

I mapped the place in my mind. Then I rechecked my dimensions. I wandered outside and identified the windows and the relationship between them. I charted in the power sources. I wondered how many Hawaiians the damned man had. I wondered what kind of nippers would bite that wire, and how I would get up to the window, and how I would get back up to it from the inside bearing a hundred and a half of ancient gold, if I could get it out from behind those glass ports.

I went out into the darker end of the garden beyond the lights of the now empty pool, and sat on a pedestal, sharing it with a welded woman perched upon one steel toe. I smoked a cigarette and felt a monstrous rejection. Too much had faded away, and the only target left was a grotesque pornographer with a voice like a trapped bee.

I got up and went back to the party. A new batch of faces had arrived and some had fallen off. A dusty little man in his middle years, with fierce eyes and a froggy bassoon of a voice was standing orating in the big room, surrounded by a mixed group of admirers and dissidents. He wore a beret and a shiny serge suit and he had a great air of authority. I drifted into the edge of the group and heard an earnest woman say, 'But, Doctor Face, isn't part of our heritage for anyone to be entitled to say what they think, right or wrong?'

'My dear woman, that is one of the luxuries of liberty, not one of the definitions thereof. And it is traditional and necessary in war that we forego the luxuries and concentrate on the necessities. My posture is that. . . .'

I moved away, to a different level of the house where I found that one of the strategic little bars had a fair brand of domestic brandy. So I got three fingers and one lump of ice and sat on a corner couch and looked across to where a group of young were sprawled up the side of some wide stairs.

Suddenly one of the little blonde cupcakes on the stairway jumped into focus as though I was using a zoom lens. It was the nameless sun bunny from the pool at La Casa Encantada, the one who had come over tipsy, wanting to know if I'd been an end with the Rams. She wore a little white linen dress and had her hair piled high and wore considerable eye makeup, but it was the same one. I felt as if I could not take a very deep breath. I looked at the others. There had been five of them on that motor sailer, three young men and two girls. I found one of the men, a big dark hairy one, the one who had seemed to be in charge of the scuba outing. What had she called him? Chip.

I could accept the presence of Claude Boody. A mild coincidence. But I could not accept the presence of the sun bunny. It was a little too much. And so nothing had been as I had imagined. I had to let the structure fall down and then try again. I had to find a new logic.

I knew the awareness was mutual. The bland, sensual little pug-face made automatic smiles and grimaces at the things people said to her. But she would angle her eyes at me now and again. Never a direct look, but only when her head was turned. It was unconsciously furtive. I could not read her big hairy friend. He was farther up the stairs and seemed totally involved with a little brunette who squirmed and giggled and squirmed.

I moved casually away, but not entirely out of range. I was considerably more alert. I had an uncomfortable feeling. Like a herd animal, shuffling along with the group, and gradually beginning to wonder what that faint thudding and screaming means way up at the head of the line. I was growing points on my ears and walking softly on my toes. I found Connie talking to a big broad balding fellow with tiny eyes and a large damp mouth and considerable affability. She introduced him as George Wolcott, introduced him in a way that told me she did not know him and found him boring.

'What kind of a boat are you going to help this lovely lady find?' he asked me, chuckling though no joke had been made.

'Just a comfortable day cruiser of some kind. Displacement hull. A good sea beam. Nothing fast or flashy.'

'I suppose you got all the licences to run one. Heh, heh, heh.'

'To run a charter boat for hire, with Coast Guard blessings, Mr. Wolcott.'

'Good. Heh, heh, heh. What kind of a boat do the Simmins have?'

'It is a great big gaudy vulgar Chris Craft,' Connie said. 'It's called the *Not Again!* Excuse us please, Mr. Wolcott.'

He chuckled his permission. His loose smilings did not alter the dead bullet look of his eyes. I was getting hyper-sensitive. When we were far enough away from him, I asked her who he was.

'Oh, he's part of that Doctor Face deal. Chairman of arrangements or rifle drill or some goddam thing.'

'He asks a lot of questions.'

'I think it's just Dale Carnegie. Show an interest. Keep smiling. Remember names. Darling, how much of this can you take? My God, this music is hurting my teeth. I'd much rather take you home to bed.'

'Give me another half hour here.'

I turned her over to Rhoda Dwight for some more infighting, and wandered on. The sun bunny appeared at my elbow, showing teeth that looked brushed after every meal. But she seemed uneasy.

'I never was with the Rams,' I said.

'I know. Look, I have to tell you something. Not here. Okay? Go down to the deck and over to the end, to the right as you go out on to the deck.'

Without waiting for my answer, she walked away. Suspicion confirmed. There can only be so much coincidence in the world. So I went where requested. I had that end of the deck to myself.

I looked at the night view. She hissed at me. I turned and saw her looking out of a dark doorway. I went to her. 'This way,' she said. It was a wide corridor in the bedroom area, a night-light panel gleaming.

She opened a corridor door and said in a low voice, 'I didn't want to be seen talking to you. We can talk in here.'

She walked in first, into darkness. I hesitated at the doorway, and went in. But I went in at a swift sidelong angle, and something smashed down on the point of my right shoulder, numbing my arm. I went down and rolled to where I thought the girl would be. The room door slammed. I rolled against her legs and brought her thrashing down, got an arm around her throat and one hand levered up behind her and stood up with her just as lights came on. Claude Boody stood with an ugly gun aimed toward us, and I turned the sun bunny quickly into the line of fire. But there was the faintest whisper of sound behind me, and before I could move again, a segment of my skull went off like a bomb and I fell slowly, slowly, like a dynamited tower, with the girl underneath. I was vaguely aware of landing on her, and of her strangled yawp as my weight drove the air out of her, and of tumbling loosely away.

I was not out. I retained ten percent of consciousness, but I could not move. The room was at the far end of a tunnel, and the voices seemed to echo through the tunnel.

'Oh, God,' a girl whined. 'I'm all busted up inside. Oh, God.'

'Shut up, Dru.'

'Both of you shut up,' an older male voice said, enormously weary. 'You let him get a look at me. It's a brand new problem.'

'I'm hurt bad,' the girl moaned.

Hands fumbled at my pockets, shifting and hauling. Down in my trauma drowse, I had the comfy awareness they would find nothing. I was entirely clean, just in case. My cheek was against a softness of rug. They hitched and tugged at my clothing.

'Nothing,' the tired voice said. 'This stuff must belong to the Melgar woman.'

'It's a Miami label in the suit. That mean anything?'

'Chip, I could be dying! Don't you care?'

'Lie down on the bed, Dru. And shut up, please.'

Chip, Claude and Dru. Three voices from far away. I heard the click of a lighter. A moment later, I felt a little hot area near the back of my hand.

'What are you doing?' Chip asked.

'Let's see how good you got him. Let's see if he's faking.'

Heat turned into a white stabbing light that shoved itself deep into my brain. Pain was like a siren caught on a high note. Pain cleared away the mists, but I would not move. I caught a little drifting stink of my own burned flesh.

'He's out,' Chip said. 'Maybe I got him good enough so there's no problem.'

'Or a worse one, you silly bastard,' Claude said. 'Depending on who he is.'

'Isn't *anybody* going to do *anything*?' Dru wailed.

They were kneeling or squatting, one on each side of me, talking across my back. The girl was farther away.

'You slipped up on this one,' Claude said. 'I don't mean here and now. I mean down there.'

'I told you, I wondered about him down there. So I had Dru check him out. She's no dummy. She has a feeling for anything out of line. You should know that. She threw the Garcia name at him and didn't get a thing back. He was with a woman down there. Gardino. And that was what it looked like, to be there to be with the woman and she looked worth it. And that was the same woman who had the bad luck. Honest to God, it was a one in a million chance, but she caught it. I'm still sick about that. It seemed like a hell of a big charge to me when I wired it in, but your expert was supposed to know what he was doing when he put it together. We were long gone by then, but still that woman didn't have any part of. . . .'

'Shut up! The problem is finding out who this bastard is and what he wants.'

'Honest to God, Claude, when Dru spotted him and pointed him out to me about forty minutes ago, you could have knocked me over with a pin.'

'Shut up and let me think. This is beginning to go sour. I don't like it. He's no fool. Coming here with the Melgar woman was almost perfect cover. And he made some good moves in this room. He nearly got out of hand. And he had good cover down there too, good enough to fool you and Dru, boy. So who is he working for? How did he trace it back to here? I thought we closed the door on that whole operation. I thought everybody who could make any connection was gone—Almah, Miguel, Taggart. But now this son of a bitch comes out of nowhere. I don't like it.'

'And you know who else isn't going to like it.'

'Shut up, Chip, for God's sake!'

'Why don't you drop it in his lap?'

'Because he doesn't like things fouled up. Let's come up with some kind of answer before I tell him.'

'One answer,' Chip said, 'is to make this character talk about it. The name he used down there was McGee. Tonight it's Smith. God knows what it really is.'

The girl made a groan of effort, as though struggling to sit up. 'Jesus, he ruined me, Chipper, you get him tied up and let me get at him with that little electric needle thing, and I'll make him talk about things he never heard of.'

'Shut her up,' Claude said.

There was a sudden movement, a solid and meaty slapping sound, and then the girl's muffled and hopeless sobbing. 'Goddam you, Chip,' she sobbed.

'Hasn't he been trying to work out something with the Melgar woman?' Chip asked.

'Just to get some shots of her in action. Send them down to Venezuela for mass distribution.'

'Why?'

'Use your head, you silly bastard. They know her face down there. Two brothers-in-law in the government. Notorious heiress having fun in the United States. But he hasn't been able to trap her.'

'Did he give up?'

'Chipper, baby, he *never* gives up. Some day he'll juice up a couple of her drinks, and she'll go wobbling in there like a lamb, with spit on her chin, and give a hell of a performance.'

'So if she brought this guy here, why not now? Two birds with one stone. Like the time with that state senator and that ambassador's wife.'

After a silence, Claude Boody said, 'We certainly got mileage out of that little session. You know, sometimes you show vague signs of intelligence. What he'll want done is keep this character and the Melgar woman stashed until the last drunk leaves. If he approves.'

'I don't see how he has too much choice.'

'I should get to a doctor,' Dru said plaintively. 'Every breath is like knives.'

'What I'll do,' Claude said, 'you sit tight here and I'll go lay it on for him, which I think we should have done in the first place.'

'He makes mistakes too.'

'How often? How big?'

'Look, he can punish me. He can give me the Melgar broad.'

'You're very, very funny.'

I gave a weak, heartbreaking groan and moved very feebly. I needed to manage a sudden change in the odds. And I couldn't do it face down.

'He's coming out of it,' Chip said.

I writhed over on to my back, then started up suddenly. They stood up and moved back. I got halfway to a sitting position, eyes staring, then fell back with a long gargling sound, held my breath, let my mouth sag open, left my eyes half closed.

'Jesus H. Christ!' Chip whispered.

'You hit him too goddam hard with that thing!'

I wondered how long they would take. I hadn't oxygenated, but I thought I could manage two minutes of it. They moved in again, squatting close. I felt fingers on my wrist. 'He isn't breathing, but his heart's still going good," Claude said. He released my wrist.

I snatched Claude by the windsor knot, and I hooked a hand on the back of Chip's neck, and slammed their heads together as hard as I could. I had fear and anger and a desperate hate working for me. It was like using a simultaneous overhand right and a wide left hook. Bone met bone with quite a horrid sound, much like smacking two large stones together underwater. Bone met bone hard enough to give a rebound that sent them both spilling over backward, settling slowly into the floor, both heads split and bleeding. I glanced at the girl, slapped at Claude, pulled the weapon out from between belt and soft belly. It was oddly light for such a large and ugly calibre. She had pushed herself halfway up, and she stared at me, eyes and mouth wide open. We were in a sizeable and elegant bedroom. I let her look down the barrel and she said, 'Wha-wha-what are you going to do?'

I moved back to the door, stepping over new acquaintances. There was an inside bolt and chain. I fastened them. There was a vent, a continuous whisper of washed air. The windows were closed and looked sealed. I had the idea sound would not travel far from that room. My conversational acquaintances hadn't seemed concerned about it. If any did get out of the room, it would have to fight that ubiquitous Hawaiian cotton candy music.

There was an object in the side pocket of Chip's green blazer. I took it out. I imagine our limey cousins would term it a home-made cosh. It was an eight-inch section of stubby pipe wrapped with a thick padding of black friction tape. I put Boody's hand gun in my jacket pocket and went over to the bed and sat on the edge of it, facing the sun bunny. Her eyes were puffed and apprehensive, her bland little face tear-stained.

'What do you want anyhow?' she demanded with false bravado.

I gave her a light touch across the ribs with the piece of pipe. She gave a thin whistling scream, the noise a shot rabbit will sometimes make. She lay back and said, 'Oh, don't. Oh, golly, there's something all broke. I can feel it kind of grind. You fell with your whole weight on me.'

'I have a headache, Dru, and a nasty burn on the back of my hand, and you were very anxious to play around with some sort of an electric needle. I lost a very marvellous woman in that clambake down there, and I am going to ask questions. Whenever I don't like the answer, I'm going to give you another little rap; with this.'

'What if you ask something I don't know?'

'You get a little rap for luck. Chip wired the explosive into Menterez' boat. Why?'

'To kill Alconedo. Miguel Alconedo. He'd goofed somehow. I don't know how. You see, we took down his orders for him. He was supposed to kill Almah, then take the boat up to Boca del Rio, ten miles offshore, where he thought we'd be waiting for him. He thought it was all set so we could take him someplace where he could go from there back to Cuba and be safe. But there wasn't any intention of that. The other three kids aboard, they didn't know anything about anything. Chip sneaked off the night before we left, after midnight when a lot of the lights went out, and fixed the boat.'

'Who did you think I might be? Why did you try to check me?'

'Chip wondered about you. You sort of didn't look like a tourist. You see, Almah couldn't be trusted any more. She told Taggart too much about things. And she got too anxious about getting that money. She was okay up until the time of the Mineros thing, and then she started cracking up. They thought that if she told Taggart too much, maybe she told somebody else too, maybe the wrong people, and maybe some C.I.A. was down there. Chip thought that's what you might be. Who are you anyhow?' She attempted a small shy friendly smile.

'Who got Taggart?'

'Gee, I don't know. I mean I'm not sure. I heard them making a joke about it. About the monkey's paw. It could have been a man named Ramon Talavera. They laughed a lot about Taggart. I know they picked him up before he had made any contact. They knew where he was. So when they made a date with him, to make arrangements about selling those statues to them, nobody showed up at the meeting place and when he went back all the others were gone, and all he had left was the one he'd taken along to prove he really had them. Then they got the last one back too, after somebody killed him."

'Tomberlin gave the orders about Almah and about the explosive?'

'I guess he told Claude what to do and who to pick to do it. Nobody meant for that woman with you to be. . . .'

'Why do you do what they tell you to do, Dru?'

'Me?' She looked astonished. 'Golly, I guess it's about the same with me as it was with Almah and a lot of other people. Those pictures of me, if they ever sent a print of even one of the cleanest ones to my daddy, I swear it would kill him. You don't know about the first pictures they take, and then they use those to make you do things for more pictures. Rather than have my daddy ever see me doing anything like that, his own daughter, I'd cut my wrists first. I'd do anything they ask. I think where Almah got out from under, her mother died while she was down there.'

I remembered the untidiness of Almah Hichin, the look of soil and wear and carelessness. It was easy to see now why she had ceased to value herself. And it was an ancient gambit, using the threat of the most horrid scandal imaginable to tame people to your will and use. And the son of a bitch had so casually mentioned his photo lab.

'You know what Tomberlin is? And Claude Boody?'

'I can't help that. I don't think about that.'

'Baby, you are going to have to think about it. You are an accessory to murder. And your dear daddy is going to have to know the whole filthy mess, and you are going to have to talk and talk and talk to save your sweet skin, sun bunny. Even so, you may spend ten years in a Mexican rest camp, living on tortillas and frijoles.'

'Leave me alone, you son of a bitch! I think I'm bleeding inside. You can't do anything to me. I bet you can't even get back through the gate out there.'

I turned and looked at the two slumberers. Chip was still bleeding. Boody had stopped, though his gash looked bigger. I had a sudden idea about him. I went over and put my ear against his chest. When I was still a foot away from him, I realized there wasn't much point in it. I was aware of the girl moving from the bed to go and bend over Chip. I listened to utter silence. All I could hear was my own blood roaring in my ear, like listening to a sea shell. Boody didn't live in there any more.

As I slowly got to my feet, there was a sharp brisk sound, like somebody breaking a big dry stick. The sun bunny had backed over toward a dressing table. She had a little automatic in her hand, a little more weapon than my shiny bedroom gun. She held it at arm's length, aiming it at me. She was biting her lip. She had one eye closed. The small muzzle made a wavering circle. It cracked again and I felt a little warm wind against my ear lobe.

'Cut it out!' I yelled, fumbling for Claude's gun, tugging it out of my pocket. She fired again, and I knew she was going to keep right on, and I knew she couldn't keep on missing at that range, particularly if it occurred to her to stop trying to hit me in the face. The third shot tingled the hair directly on top of my head, and Claude's pistol was double action, and I tried to get her in the shoulder. It made a ringing deafening blam, and the slug took her just below the hairline on the right side of her head, and the recoil of that light frame jumped the gun up so that it was aiming at the ceiling.

The slug slammed a third of the top of her skull away, snapped her neck, catapulted her back into the dressing-table, smashing the mirror, soiling the wall, leaving her in a limp, grotesque, motionless backbend across the dressing-table bench. The silent room was full of the stink of smokeless powder. I made a sound that was half retching and half hysterical giggle. Hero McGee wins the shootout. He's death on sun bunnies. I stood tense, half on tiptoe, trying not to breathe, listening, listening. I moved to the door, listening. I could not risk opening it. Not yet.

The little gun was under the dressing-table bench. I managed not to look at her as I retrieved it. I had assembled a rude script for my own survival, and I went through the motions like a wooden man, with everything but the necessities of the situation blocked out of my mind. I took the little gun over and stood over Claude and fired one slug down into his dead heart. I took the gun back and put it into Chip's hand and curled his fingers around it. I knelt beside him and gave him a solid blow on the side of the head with the length of pipe, to keep him sleeping. And, in the event he woke up too soon and wanted to rearrange the scene to fit some other pattern, I used the pipe to give him a knee that would keep him still and bother him as long as he lived. I folded the bigger gun into Claude's slack hand. I saw where the three times she had missed had put raggedy little holes into the panel meat of the door. I stood and looked at the scene. I knew I was going to wear it for a long, long time, right in there on one of my back walls, with studio lighting. I tasted blood and realized I had nibbled a small piece out of the inside of my under lip.

I was still so rattled that I came dangerously close to wiping the door hardware clean. That is like leaving a signal flag. I recovered and smeared it, using the heel of my thumb, bases of my fingers. I had to leave the room light on. I opened the door an inch. The corridor was silent. I heard steel guitars. I slipped out and pulled the door shut and went to the end of the corridor. The deck was empty. I went out there and closed the corridor door. Somebody had left half a drink on the rail. I picked it up. My right arm ached. There was a very tender area behind my right ear and slightly above it, but the skin was not broken. I fixed my tie and took deep breaths of the night air. I had the length of pipe in a trouser pocket. I ambled back to join the party.

I had the eerie expectation of finding everyone gone, chairs overturned, drinks spilled, signs of hasty exit. But the groups were still there, unsteadier now. Some of the kids were on the stairs, and others were dancing. Dr. Face still brayed disaster at his captive circle. I looked at my watch. It had all happened in about twenty-five minutes. I saw mine host in pewter silk standing in a group, his dull black wig sitting trimly on his naked skull, iced tea in his right hand, his left hand mechanically honking the buttock of a slender woman who stood beside him, like a child playing with an ancient auto horn. No one paid me any attention. I searched for Connie without haste, and found her down by the sheltered part of the pool, sitting on a bench, talking real estate tax laws with a slight young man with a mild face and fierce moustache. The young man, after the introduction, excused himself to go off and find his wife.

Connie stood up and said, '*Now* can we go back to my place? My God, darling, this is turning into one of the dullest evenings of my life.'

I hauled her back down on to the bench and she was a little off balance and came down too solidly.

'Hey? Are you tight?'

'Listen one damned minute, Mrs. Melgar. Listen to a suppose. Suppose you got a little foolish and reckless one night, and you got a little drunk, and you went back into that studio or whatever he has beyond that jolly museum of his, and somebody took some very unwholesome pictures of you. . . .'

'That may be his little hobby, dear, and he may have scads of friends who are sick enough to play, but it leaves me absolutely cold. He has made his oily little hints. For God's sake, you heard him. I may be lusty, dear, but I'm not decadent, not in any exhibitionistic sense.'

'So suppose he sets you up sometime, with something in your drinks, and he picks a couple of choice negatives and sends them to somebody in Caracas who will make a couple of thousand prints and distribute them. What would happen then?'

Her big hand clamped my wrist strongly. 'Dear God!'

'Two of your sisters are married to men in the government. What would happen?'

'My grandfather and my dead husband's grandfather were terrific men. They're sort of folk heroes now. It didn't help very much, having me leave for good. A thing like that would. . . . It could be put to terrible frightening use. What are you trying to tell me? That Cal would do a thing like that? But, my dear, it doesn't make sense! Everybody knows that Cal helps a lot of people fight the sort of people who would put pictures like that to political use. He gives loads of money to people who are fighting Communist influence in Latin America.'

'What if he strengthens the groups who are going about it in the wrong ways, in ways that merely help rather than hinder.'

'But that would mean he. . . .'

'He is a grotesque. He loves intrigue. Maybe he hates his own class, and particularly himself. Maybe he hides behind this façade of . . . political gullibility and this collection of erotica. Maybe he is not quite sane.'

'For goodness sake, he is just Calvin Tomberlin, a dull, self-important, rich, silly, sick little man.'

'I don't like wasting time with these questions, but I have to ask them. Was Rafael Mineros doing anything effective about the Cuban situation?'

In the shadowy reflections of the pool lights, she looked startled. 'He asked me to come in with them. Maybe I was too selfish. Maybe I didn't have his dedication. He had organized a group of wealthy people, about half of them from Cuba and the others from sensitive areas, Guatemala, Venezuela, Panama. His son Enrique and Manuel Talavera were his aides, and Maria Talavera did a lot of the office work. Now they are all gone.'

I took her by the upper arms and shook her. 'Now listen to me. Listen to two things. Make it three things. One. Tomberlin had that group killed. And then he had the people killed who had killed them. He used his collector's mania as window dressing. Two. I told you precisely the plan Tomberlin has in mind for you. Three. In one of the bedrooms of this house there are two very dead people right now, dead by violence, and this whole situation may blow up in our face at any moment. But there is too damned good a chance that Tomberlin can cover the whole thing up. He has too many personal pictures of too many people in his films. His big levers are money and blackmail. I didn't want to get you too involved. But now there isn't much choice. You can still say the hell with it. Or you can help. It depends on how much any of this means to you.'

She huddled her big shoulders. 'I . . . I've never been what you would call a p-patriot. But the way they think about my family . . . that's a precious thing. And . . . Rafael was a good man. What do you want of me?'

'Let's get him back into that museum.'

'How?'

'Be a little drunk. Tell him you want your picture taken. Tell him it has to be with me, and it has to be now, before you change your mind.'

'What are you going to do?'

'You said that layout is built like a safe. Nobody is going to get in and upset anything. Let's see what happens.'

CHAPTER NINETEEN

It took her about fifteen minutes to set it up. The party was now visibly dwindling. Tiresome drunks were in the majority of the diehards still left. I noted with approval that when we went in, Tomberlin locked the heavy door. Connie was doing a good job of simulating a constant high foolish giggle. I was unsteady on my feet, and wore a vacant, lecherous, fisheating grin. Tomberlin was very soothing, and kept turning a quick broad smile off and on as though he were hooked up to a repeating circuit.

He took us back through a library to a small studio. There was a shiny jungle of lighting equipment. A technician was fiddling around with cameras. I had not anticipated his presence. He was a little old fellow, a mixture of oriental blood lines, part Japanese.

'As I explained, my dear, you will have absolute privacy,' Tomberlin said. 'I wouldn't want you to feel too restrained. Charlie will get the cameras set up and then we'll leave you alone.' 'The film will last about fifty minutes, dears,' he added, wiping his pale lips on the back of his hand. 'Do try not to be too dull and ordinary.'

'What are you going to do with these pictures, Cal?'

'Darling, it's just a fun game, that's all. We can go over the contact sheets together and see what we have worth enlarging. I'll give you all the negatives. You'll have some very interesting souvenirs, Connie dear. The lady in her prime. Don't be too quick, dears, and waste all that film.'

'Is anybody likely to walk in?' she asked.

'There's not the slightest chance.'

'Where will you be?'

'I might rejoin the party and come back in an hour.'

I rambled over to the timer box and turned the switch on. The little old fellow hissed at me and slapped my hand away and turned it off. I'd wasted one exposure.

'Please don't touch the equipment,' Tomberlin said.

I went grinning over to where he stood. Bashful guy. I studied my fingernails, head bent, and said, 'There's one thing about all this, Mister Tomberlin.'

'Yes?'

I pivoted a half turn. I had screwed my legs down into the floor, and I pivoted with thighs, back, shoulder and arm, to see if I could drive my fist all the way through softness above his belt, right back to the backbone. The wind yawffed out of him and he skidded backward, bowing low, spilling tripod and camera, hitting the couch with the back of his knees, rolling up into a kind of curled headstand on the couch before toppling over onto his side.

Even though I started moving the instant I hit him, I still almost missed the old man. He had the speed of a lizard. I got him by the back of the collar just as he went through the doorway and hauled him back. He began to jump up and down and whoop and bat at me with his hands. He was too hysterical to listen to anything. I held him at arm's length, got the length of pipe, timed his leaps, and with due regard for the long fragile look of his skull, bumped him solidly right on top of the head. His eyes rolled out of sight and I lowered him to the floor. I don't think he weighed a hundred and ten. Within moments he was snoring heartily. They do that quite often.

Connie stepped out of my way as I went over to the couch. Tomberlin was on his side, his colour dreadful, knees against his chest, semi-conscious, moaning softly with each breath. I shook him and said, 'Greetings from Almah. And Sam. And Miguel,

Rafael, Enrique, Maria, Manuel. Greetings from the whole group. Dru is dead too. And so is Boody.'

'Boody!' Connie gasped. 'Claude Boody?'

'World traveller.'

I shook Tomberlin but I couldn't get through to him. I'd given him too much. He was going to be out of touch for a long time. I tore one of the cables loose and wrapped him up. I wondered if I should stuff his mouth. The black toupee peeled off with a sticky sound and I wedged it into his jaws. It muffled his moans. Connie stared at me with a wide and horrified grin, wringing her big hands.

'N-Now what?'

I took her out and we found his photo files. It was an extensive and complex system, with thousands of negatives cross indexed to proof sheets and print files. There was another complete filing system for colour, and a third for movies both black and white. It wasn't a collection you could burn in a wastebasket. Connie was fascinated by the files of finished prints. She kept dipping into them, looking for familiar faces, gasping with a mixture of horror and delight when she found them. I set her to work emptying all the files, dumping everything into a pile in the middle of that small room which adjoined the photo lab. I went back out into the museum part. The glass covering the gold statue niches was set permanently in place. I could see no clue that the niches were hooked up to any alarm system. It took three solid blows with the pipe to open up each niche, one to shatter the glass, two more to hammer shards out of the way so I could pull the heavy images out. I remembered the two big cushions on the couch and went back to the little studio. I ripped the covers off, and had two sizeable sacks. I divided the statues evenly between the two sacks. I took the whole thirty-four. The Menterez collection had grown. The sacks weighed close to a hundred pounds each, though the contents were not bulky. They were all jumbled in there, like jacks in a child's game. I bound them with twine. Little Santy Claus packs for good children. I lifted them carefully, one in each hand. The stitches held. I put them back down again.

I went back to the file office. Connie had finished her work. It was spilled wall to wall in the middle of the room, about three feet high at the peak. She was pawing through it, still looking at things.

'You have no *idea*!' she said. 'My God, some of these people are so proper! How in the world did he ever. . . .'

'Listen to me. I've got Tomberlin's keys here. Take them. I think this one unlocks the museum door. I've got things to carry. Now get the sequence. We take Tomberlin and the little guy out into the museum. I unwrap Tomberlin. I come back and get this stuff burning. We'll have to wait a few minutes to be certain it is going real good. Then we unlock the door and go out, yelling fire. Because there is going to be a nice fire, there is going to be considerable confusion. You head for the car as fast as you can. I'll be right behind you. We go to your place and split up. My car is there. You are going to pack quickly and get out quickly and take a little vacation.'

I saw fifty questions in her eyes, and then she straightened her shoulders and said, 'Yes dear.'

It nearly worked. It came within inches and seconds of working. She was trotting ahead of me, the ends of the big stole flying out behind her, a rather hippy and bovine trot but she was making good time. We were almost at the car when the voice of authority called 'Halt!' I risked a glance. It was George Wolcott, of the little leaden eyes and the large damp mouth.

'Keep going!' I ordered Connie.

'Halt in the name of the law!' he yelled with stentorian dignity and precision, fired once in the air as the book says, and fired the second one into my back, without a suitable pause. I was fire-hot-wet in back, and fire-hot-wet in front, without pain but suddenly weakened. I wavered and stumbled and got the gold into the car with a vast effort, ordering her to take the wheel and get us out of there. I clawed my way in. She had it in motion the instant the engine caught, and she slewed it between and among the few cars left, then straightened and headed for the gate. The man there jumped out and then back, like a matador changing his mind about a bull. We went over a hump, screeched down the long curve of drive and onto Stone Canyon Drive, accelerating all the time. She slammed into curves, down-shifting, shifting back, keeping the rpm well up toward the red, showing off, laughing aloud.

'Okay,' I said. 'Ease off. You're great.'

She slowed it down. 'My God, it's too much!' she said. 'What a change in a dull evening! My God, that couch for a frolic, and those cameras clucking like a circle of hens, and those dirty pictures curling and steaming in that lovely fire. And the great Tomberlin with his mouth full of wig. And a lovely lovely madman smashing glass and stealing gold. And shots in the night.

For God's sweet sake, I haven't felt so alive in a year. Darling, wasn't that that dull fellow, actually shooting?'

'That was that dull fellow.'

'But why?'

'It didn't seem a very good time to ask. I'm glad it was a fun evening for you. There's a pretty little girl back there with the top of her pretty head blown off. And Claude Boody is dead. He's always good for laughs.'

The edge of delight was gone from her voice. 'So there is going to be a big and classic stink about all this?'

'Yes.'

'But then I don't think it would be so very smart for me to go away, do you? I don't know very much. The little I do know, I can lie about. I think you had a little gun in my back. You forced me to do things. I don't know who you are or where you went.'

'That's fine, if it's police questions. But Tomberlin will have some questions. He won't ask them himself. He might send some people who wouldn't be polite.'

She thought that over as we waited for a light. 'But if I am just . . . absent, there'll be a stink about that, officially. I think the best thing is to . . . report this myself. As an injured party. I can make a statement, whatever they want, and tell them I am going away, and be very careful and go quickly.'

'That probably makes more sense.'

'How will I ever find you again?'

'Maybe you won't.'

'But isn't that a horrible waste? Don't you feel that way about it?'

'I can't guarantee the same kind of evening every time, Connie.'

'Are you sleepy? You sound sleepy. It's a reaction, I guess.'

'I parked around in that back street, the same as before.'

She spotted the little English Ford and pulled up behind it. I was assembling myself to get out. No pain yet. Just numb-hot on the right side, from armpit to hip. I had the feeling I was carrying myself in a frail basket. As with my care with the stitching on the pillow covers. I felt I had to stand up very slowly and carefully. I opened the car door. She put her hand on my knee. 'Will you be all right now?' she asked. 'You have everything all planned?'

'Nearly everything.'

I got out, feeling as if I moved in separate parts and pieces.

I felt as if the left side would work better than the right. I got one sack in my left hand and took the strain of it as I swung it out. Nothing seemed to tear, in the sack or in me. The sack weighed a mere thousand pounds. I marched slowly to the rear of the little car, put the sack down, found the keys, opened the boot. I was cleverly constructed of corn flakes and library paste. Her car lights were bright on the boot of the little car. I got the sack in and floated back to her car and got the other sack. I had dry teeth and a fixed grin. I put the second sack in and when I closed the back lid I folded against it for a moment, then pushed myself up to my dangerous height. Her car lights went off and suddenly she was with me, a strong arm around me.

'You're hit!' she said.

'There's probably some blood in your car. Wipe it off. Go home. Make your statement. Get the hell out of this, Connie.'

'I'll get you to a hospital.'

'Thanks a lot. That's a great idea.'

'What else?'

'Anything else. Because they'll nail me with some of the trouble back there. And make it stick. And I'd rather be dead than caged. So would you, woman.'

I expected the moral issue then and there. Did you kill anybody? But she was the kind who set their own standards.

'Do you have a place to go?' she asked. 'A safe place?'

'Yes.'

She helped me to the passenger side of the little car, and helped me lower myself in. She wrested the car keys out of my hand. I made protest.

'Shut up, darling. I won't be long. Try to hold on. In case you can't, tell me the address now.'

After hesitation, I told her. She hurried off. She didn't start her car for a few moments, and I suspected she was swabbing my valuable blood off her leather upholstery. She swung out and went up the street and turned into the underground garage. I undid my jacket, pulled my shirt out of my pants and looked at the damage in front, by the flame of my lighter. It was on the right side, in the softness of my waist. Exit holes are always the worst, unless it is a jacketed slug. This seemed about half dollar size, so the slug hadn't hit anything solid enough to make the slug mushroom very much. My posture kept the lips closed, and it was not bleeding badly. I tucked the soaked shirt tail back in and hugged myself. I wished I knew more anatomy. I wondered what irreplacable goodies were within that line of fire. From the absence of pain I knew I was still in shock. There was just a feel of wetness and looseness and sliding, and a feel of heat. But there was another symptom I did not like. There was a metallic humming in my ears, and the world seemed to bloat and dwindle in a regular cycle. I hugged and waited, wondering if on the next cycle the world would dwindle and keep dwindling and be gone. If she was a very smart woman, if she came back and found me too far gone, she would do well to take me to the address I gave her, and walk away from it.

That son of a bitch had been too eager. The look of people hurrying away with a burden had gotten him terribly excited. The business shot had come about a second and a half after the warning shot. He sounded official. Maybe he was after a citation.

I hung on. I felt suspended in a big membrane, like a hammock, and if anything jounced, it would split and I would fall through.

Suddenly she opened the car door and bounced in. The bounce stirred the first tiny little teeth of pain.

'How are you?' she asked. She threw a small bag into the back seat. She had changed her clothes. She was breathing hard.

'I'm just nifty peachy dandy, Mrs. Melgar.'

She got the little car into motion very swiftly, giving the little teeth a better chance to gnaw. She said, 'Just as I was leaving, the phone rang. Men down at the desk. Police. I told the night man to send them right up. I went down the stairs.'

'Fun and games. The romantic vision. Have fun, Connie.'

'My friend, once you decide you want the animal to charge, and once he begins the charge, you cannot change your mind. You stand there and you wait until he is close enough so you can be absolutely sure of him.'

'Grace under pressure. Kindly spare me the Hemingway bits.'

'Are you always so surly when you're wounded?'

'I hate to see people being so stupid for no reason. Get out of this while you have the chance.'

'Darling, I will take every chance to feel alive, believe me.'

The little man inside me decided that teeth weren't enough. He threw them aside and got a great big brace and bit, dipped it in acid, coated it with ground glass and went to work, timing each revolution to the beat of my heart. She parked in front of 28. I leaned against the side of the bungalow while she unlocked the door. She took me in. My legs were too light. They wanted to float it. It was hard to force them down to the floor to take steps.

She managed the lights and the heavy gaudy draperies. She had changed to a dark pleated skirt and a dark sweater. I kept my jaws clamped on the sounds I wanted to make, and settled for the occasional snort and whuff. We got the ruined jacket and shirt off. I sat on a low stool in the bathroom, forearms braced on my knees, head sagging.

She said, 'It's off to the right, in back, just under the last rib. You've got to have a doctor.'

'I've lasted pretty good so far.'

'You look ghastly,' she said. 'I think we can stop the bleeding, though.'

She went scouting around and I heard her tearing something into strips. She found a sanitary napkin and fashioned two pads and bound them in place by winding the strips around my middle and knotting them. Now I felt as if I had a heavy bar of lead through me, from back to front, red hot. She found the bourbon and poured me a heavy shot. I asked her to leave the bathroom. I urinated, but it was not bloody. I could take a deep breath without any inner rattling or gargling. But something essential had to be messed up.

As I headed for the bed, I went down. Very slowly, protecting myself, bracing myself, rolling onto my good side. She helped me up and onto the bed. I stretched out on my back, but it felt better to keep my knees hiked up.

She looked down at me and said, 'I'm going to use the phone.'

'What are you thinking of?'

'Pablo Dominguez. He might have an idea. At three in the morning, he might have an idea, you know. But is that all right with you?'

'That's very much all right.'

'Is it hurting a lot?'

'It didn't help it very much, falling down. This is a borrowed place.'

'It looks it.'

'And a borrowed car. I was planning on getting out of here without leaving a trace, without leaving people around with a lot of questions. Tell Paul that if he can manage it, if he can manage anything, getting out of here should be part of it.'

'I don't think you should be moved any more.'

'Tell him I have some interesting things to tell him.'

I heard her on the phone, close beside me, but I couldn't keep track of what she was saying. Her voice turned into three simultaneous voices in echo chambers, overlapping into a

resonant gibberish. I raised my hand to look at it. It came into
sight after a long time, hung there, and then fell back into darkness.

I was jolted awake. Somebody was saying in a husky whisper,
'Careful. Easy now!' They were trying to get my legs up over a
rear bumper. It was a panel delivery truck. I had clothes on.
There was a faint grey of dawn over Buena Villas. My gear was
in the truck. There was a mattress in there.

I helped them. I crawled toward the mattress. I had been
sawed in half and glued back together, but both ends worked. I
saw Dominguez and Connie staring in at me. 'There's one thing,'
I said.

'Don't try to talk, baby,' Connie said.

I made her understand about the promise and the money, and
she agreed that she would immediately put the key and the
seventy dollars in Honey's mailbox, don't worry about it, the
house is in good shape, everything's fine, don't worry. In the
middle of trying to form the next question, my arms got tired
of chinning myself on this bottom rung of consciousness, so
I just let it all go.

When I awoke again it was hot. Light came into the truck,
dusty sunlight. I was being jiggled and bounced. Connie sat on a
tool box. It was a bad road. She looked tired. Her smile was wan.
She said something I couldn't hear and felt my forehead. I saw
my gear and her small bag and the two sacks of golden idols.
I wanted to say something vastly significant, about a woman
and gold and a wound, like those things you say in dreams, those
answers to everything. But when I unlocked my jaw, all that
came out was a bellow of pain.

She knelt and held me and said. 'Just a little bit more, dear.
Just a little bit more now.'

I was on my face, in a rough softness, in a smell of wool and
a sharper smell of medicine. They'd let something loose at me
and it was eating its way into my back. I tried to roll over, but
a hand came down on my bare shoulder and forced me back. I
heard Connie in an excited clatter of Spanish, and a man's voice
answering. Suddenly a huge pain towered shining white and
smashed down on me and rolled me under.

I awoke slowly. I was in bed, I accumulated the little bits of
evidence one at a time, with a great slow drifting care. I was

naked. I was well-covered. I felt a stricture around my middle. I felt a wide, taut, professional bandage. It was dark where I was. There was a yellow light on the other side of the room. I turned my head slowly. Connie Melgar was over there, sitting, reading a book by a kerosene lamp, near the small open fire in a big fireplace. She seemed to be wearing pyjamas, and a man's khaki hunting jacket. There was a huge night stillness around us. I could hear the small phutterings of the fire.

'Connie?' I said, with somebody else's voice. A little old man's voice.

She jumped up and came over and put her hand on my forehead. 'I was going to have to try to wake you up,' she said. 'You have pills to take.'

'Where are we?'

'Pills first,' she said. She went out of sight. I heard the busy ka-chunking of a hand pump.

She came back with two big capsules and a glass of chill water. Nothing had ever tasted better. I asked for more, in my little old voice, and she brought me another glass. She brought the lamp over and put it on a small table, and moved a straight chair near. I saw that I was in a deep wide bunk, with another above me, and a rough board wall at my left.

She lit two cigarettes and gave me one.

'Are you tracking, Travis? Do you think you can understand what I tell you?'

After a slow count of ten, I said, 'Travis. My wallet?'

'That's the way a snoopy woman amuses herself, Mr. McGee. It is now midnight, my dear. You were shot about twenty-two hours ago. I am sorry we had to bring you such a terrible distance. I wouldn't have taken the risk. But Paul gave the orders and did the driving. You are in a cabin which belongs to one of Paul's friends. It is near the San Bernadino National Forest, and not far from Toro Peak, and it is five thousand feet in the air. You've been winking off and on like a weak light. You've had a doctor. He's a good doctor, but he doesn't have a licence in this country. He also is a friend of Paul's. He works for a vet in Indio. He did a lot of prodding and disinfecting and stitching, and he put in some drains. He doesn't ask questions and he doesn't report gunshot wounds. He says you are fantastically tough, and you took the bullet in a very good place. If he had you in a hospital, he would open you up. And it may still come to that. We'll wait and see. He'll be back tomorrow. We have provisions, firewood, water and an old jeep. There isn't a living soul within six miles of us.

You are not to move, for any reason. He gave you some shots. Paul went back. When you want the improvised bedpan, shout. It seems you might live. In the meantime, you are a big nuisance to everybody.'

I closed my eyes to think it over. I drifted away and came back.

'Are you still there?' she asked.

'I think so.'

'You can have some hot broth, if you think you can keep it down, and if I can make that damned wood stove work.'

'I could keep it down.'

She had to wake me up for the broth. She wanted to feed it to me, but after she got my head braced up. I was able to handle it.

'What about . . . have they said anything? Have you heard any *news*?'

'Strange news, Travis. Television executive slain in gun battle over beach girl, at millionaire's canyon home. Beauty contest winner slain by stray shot in bedroom gun battle. Charles 'Chip' Fertacci, skin-diving instructor, held in connection with the dual slaying, found unconscious in bloody bedroom. All very sexy and rancid, dear.'

'No mystery guest sought?'

'And no Venezuelan heiress either, according to the news. But they could be looking.'

'You can be damn well certain they are. What about Tombelin?'

'Oh, he's in the hospital. Smoke inhalation and nervous collapse after successfully fighting a fire that broke out mysteriously in his photo lab. It seems he is a hobby photographer. The official diagnosis is that it was some sort of spontaneous combustion of chemicals. Minor fire damage. No report of anything missing.'

'They don't tie it up with the other story at all?'

'Just that it was a coincidence it happened the same night at the same house, and that Tomberlin's collapse might be partially due to shock and learning of the murders.'

'When is Paul going to come back?'

'He didn't say. But he'll be back.'

I started to take the last sip of the broth, and without warning my teeth tried to chatter a piece out of the rim of the mug. My arm started twitching and leaping, and she reached and grabbed the mug. I slid down and curled up, wracked with uncontrollable chills. She tucked more blankets around me. Nothing helped. She went over and put logs on the fire, came back and took off the khaki jacket and came into the bunk with me. With tender and loving care, she wrapped me up in her arms, after unbuttoning the front of her pyjama coat to give more access to her body warmth. I got my arms around her, under the pyjama jacket, and held her close, my face in her sweet hot neck, shuddering and huffing and chattering. I was not a little old man. I had slipped back to about ten years old. I felt cold and scared and dwindled. This was the mama warmth, sweet deep musk of hearty breasts and belly, of big warm arms enclosing, and soft sounds of soothing, down in the nest of wool. At last the shuddering came less frequently. I was waiting for the next one when I toppled off into sleep.

I awoke alone in stillness, red coals on the hearth, a white of moonlight patterning the rough floor. I listened until I found the slow heavy breathing mingled with that silence, and traced it, and found it came from above me. At the foot of the bunk I could make out the rungs of the ladder fastened there. I swung my legs up and sat up. At the count of three I made it to a standing position. I held onto the edge of the upper bunk. She had her back to me, pale curls on pale pillow. The khaki jacket was on the straight chair. I was nine feet tall, and I had been put together by a model airplane nut. I got the jacket on, realizing it was not a case of gaining strength, but merely using what I had for what I had to do, before the strength ran out.

I made the door, opposite the fireplace. I leaned on the frame and slid the bolt over. It creaked as I let myself out. Porch boards creaked under my feet. There were no steps, just a drop of a few inches to stony ground. It was a pale landscape on the far side of the moon, sugar stones and a tall twist of pines and silence. Something far off made a sad sad cry. I braced my back against one of the four by fours that held up the porch roof. Huge and virile project for a hero. Relief in the night, a stream to arch and spatter, a small boy's first token of virility. As I finished the porch creaked again and she said, 'You fool! You absolute and utter idiot!'

'How high are we?'

'Five thousand feet. Come back inside.'

'What makes that mournful sound, Connie?'

'Coyotes. Come back inside, you burro.'

'I can make it.'

But I probably wouldn't have. I put a lot of weight onto those big shoulders. She sat me down, took the jacket, swung my legs in, tucked me in.

'If you want anything, wake me! Understand?' She laid the back of her hand on my head. She made a snort of exasperation and climbed back up her ladder. She flounced around up there, settling herself down.

'McGee?'

'Yes dear.'

'You are *muy macho*. You have to be the he-mule. Too much damned pride. That pride can kill you, the way you are now. Let me help you.'

'I'm not going to die.'

'How do you know?'

'I keep remembering how you cured my chill. If I was going to die, I wouldn't have that on my mind.'

'God help us all. Go to sleep.'

The little doctor came in an old Ford in the late afternoon, roaring up the final grade in low. He had a leathery frog-face, and it was part of the deal that he did not give his name. He asked questions about fever, appetite, elimination. He inspected the wounds. He made clucking sounds of satisfaction. He bandaged again. He left more pills. He said he would be back. He would skip one day and then come back.

On the following afternoon I was stretched out on a blanket in the side yard in my underwear shorts when I heard another car come up that last pitch. It sounded like more car than the little doctor had. Connie brought Dominguez and another man around the corner of the cabin and out to my blanket.

'See him?' she said. 'Disgusting. He said weak men have to have meat. I drove that foul jeep to Indio. I bought four steaks. He ate two for lunch.'

'How do you feel, *amigo*?' Paul asked.

'Perforated.'

'Permit me to introduce Senor Ramon Talavera.'

Talavera was a slim dark-haired man, with a Spanish pallor, a dark and clerical suit. I hesitated and then held my hand out to him. His hesitation was longer than mine, and then he bent and took it.

Paul turned to Connie. 'If you don't mind, *chica*.'

She plumped herself down on the corner of the blanket, affixed her stretch-pants legs Budda style and said defiantly, 'I sure as hell do mind. What do you think I am? The *criada* around here?'

Paul looked inquiringly at Talavera. The pale man gave a little nod of agreement. Paul got two fat unsplit chunks from the woodpile, and they used them like stools. Connie handed cigarettes around.

Paul said, 'It could be a mistake, but from what Connie said to me, I though it would be wise to bring Ramon here to talk to you.'

I looked at the pale man and said, 'You have my sympathy in the loss of your sister and your friends.'

'Thank you very much, sir.'

'I think I know what you want to know, Mr. Talavera. Tombelin wanted to stop Mineros' activities. He knew that, because of past history, he could make Mineros lose his head if he could bring him face to face with Carlos Menterez. If Mineros killed Carlos and was caught, it solved the problem. If Carlos killed Mineros, it solved the problem. Tomberlin had two people planted down there. Miguel Alconedo, on Menterez's staff, and Almah Hichin, his mistress. I imagine he got word to them to try to take care of Mineros. Tomberlin used the collection of gold figures as a smoke screen. He is a very devious man. Almah Hichin talked Taggart into helping Miguel kill those four people. Then Tomberlin began to worry, I think, about the reliability of Almah and Miguel. He sent people down—Fercatti and the beach girl—to deliver an order to Miguel to kill the Hichin woman and escape in the boat. They booby-trapped the boat. Tomberlin's orders were given through Claude Boody.'

'Who is dead,' Talavera said gently. 'We got word that one of the men who killed them was on the way up from Mexico to sell things to Tomberlin. We approached Tomberlin. He did not know anything about anything, but he promised to cooperate. When he was contacted, he let us know at once. We tricked the man out of the gold, but we missed him. When he made contact to sell the last piece, I had the honour of being selected to go and deal with him.' He looked into my eyes. 'I understand he was your friend?'

'He was. He didn't know there would be a woman aboard. He had been sold an entirely false story about the whole thing. Almah Hitchin was a sly woman. She made me believe she was telling me the whole truth by only telling me a part of it, in great detail.'

'Your friend, Taggart, tried to tell me these things, but it was too late by then. A sister can be the most special person one can have, Senor McGee.'

'He tried a bad gamble and it went wrong. There's been too much blood since then. It happened a long time ago, Talavera, and I have lost interest in it.'

'Thank you. These other things you say, are they guesses?'

I held my hand out. 'Boody burned my hand to be certain I was unconscious. But I wasn't. I listened to Boody talk to Fertacci about these things. I was able to fill in the blanks. I took a chance and knocked their heads together. I think Boody's heart gave out. The girl got a gun and started shooting at me. She missed with three shots from close range. I tried to knock her down with Boody's gun without killing her. But it threw high and to the right. So I disabled Fertacci and set the scene and let myself out. Neither Fertacci nor Boody nor the girl had the slightest idea who I could be. The girl remembered seeing me at Puerto Altamura. It made them very nervous. And I think that having Chip Fertacci in custody is going to make Tomberlin very nervous.'

'Bail was set at fifty thousand,' Paul said, 'and he was released today. I have a strong feeling that young man is going to disappear.'

Talavera got up quickly and walked away. He went about fifty feet and stood with his hands locked behind him, staring at Toro Peak.

'The poor twisted son of a bitch,' Paul said softly. 'He thought you would want to try to kill him. If it's any consolation to you, McGee, you took a perfectly legal authorized official bullet in the back. I have my little sources. The gentleman who plugged you broke his cover by doing so. He was assigned to infiltrate Doctor Girdon Face's organization. He had the idea that Face was using Tomberlin's dirty pictures to extract contributions for the cause. When he found there was a fire aboard, and saw you running with sacks, he thought the first was a coverup and you were taking off with the files and records. It upset him because he was on the verge of getting a search warrant. Even though I . . . do a little work on the side for the same organization, I am glad that stuff got burned. It shouldn't sit in government file cabinets.'

'Pablo,' I said, 'now that we know where Tomberlin stands, I get confused by this relationship with Dr. Face.'

He gave a latin shrug. 'Why should you be confused? Reasonable conservation is a healthy thing. But that kind of poisonous divisionist hate-mongering Face has been preaching is one of the standard Communist techniques. Now Tomberlin's other activities begin to seem most curious too. Suppose there are three groups of Cuban exiles eager to hurt the Castro regime. Two are plausible, sane and orderly. One is reckless and wild and dangerous. Tomberlin strengthens the dangerous element, thus dividing the cause. Perhaps he is under orders. Perhaps he is merely a dilettante. The effect is the same.'

Ramon Talvarera came back to the group.

He sat down and studied his knuckles and said, 'I can promise one thing. I can make them understand that Rafael's programme was so effective, it had to be stopped by them, one way or another. When they understood that, they will take heart. It will be organized again, stronger than before. I promise that.'

'Count me in,' Connie said. 'Count me in this time.'

Talavera smiled at her. 'Of course. I will squeeze money out of you, Senora.' The smile was gone abruptly. 'And there is that one small thing left unfinished, Mr. McGee. I would have thought, when you had the chance. . . .'

'I had no taste for it. Not after that girl.'

'Of course. But I have made a personal vow. I shall not please myself by doing it myself. It was no pleasure, actually . . . that other time.'

'It never is,' Paul said gently.

'That man did not beg. I wanted him to beg. He merely fought. I think this might be a good time. While that man is still in the hospital. There is some sort of rupture of the diaphragm which they wish to mend. He has special nurses, of course. If one became busy on other matters, I believe a replacement could be arranged.'

Connie shivered, though the sun was hot. 'Shall we drop it right there?'

'Of course, Senora. Forgive me. I was merely saying that it is not remarkable when persons die in a hospital.' He turned to Paul. 'I will need help to continue Rafael's project. There can be money for staff salaries.'

'Let's talk about that while we're driving back.'

Connie walked off with Talavera. Pablo grinned at me. 'So the adventurer has the woman and the gold and the healing wound, eh?'

'Thanks for the help. The place and the doctor. And the nurse.'

'A little money was needed. I found it in your wallet and in your belt.'

'Let's not say it's all roses, Paul.'

'I did not imagine that it was. Is it ever? You add things in

your mind and wonder where you are, and where you have
been, and why. But you have much woman for a nurse, my
friend. Sometimes a woman is a better solution than too much
thinking. No one has yet tamed this one. But it is amusing to
try, eh?'

'Are they looking for her?'

'Not seriously. What will you do now?'

'Mend. Send her home. Go back where I came from.'

He shook my hand. 'Good-bye. I think you have done some
good around here. I do not think you meant to do it. I think
it was incidental to the gold. But some people will think of
you with gratitude. Kiss Nita for me. And tell Raoul his is an
ugly fellow.'

I heard their car leave. Connie came back. She sat on the
blanket again, cocked her head, stared at me and sighed. 'Your
eyes look sad, *querido.*'

'I was doing some forlorn mathematics. Sam, Nora, Almah,
Miguel, Dru, Boody, Rafael, Enrique, Maria, Manuel. Ten.
And three to go.'

'Three?'

'Carlos Menterez. Chip Fertacci. Calvin Tomberlin. Thirteen,
Constancia.'

'And almost you, darling. Two inches to the left, and it would
be you too.'

'But who are the good guys and who are the bad guys?'

'Darling, death does not make those distinctions. With your
pale pale grey eyes, perhaps you are an angel of death. Perhaps
you are the branch that breaks, the tyre that skids, the stone
that falls. Perhaps it is not wise to be near you.'

'You can leave.'

We glowered at each other, her eyes golden slits, her big mouth
ugly, the cords of her neck tautened. She broke first, saying, 'Ah,
you are incredible. I have four and a half million of your dollars,
and here I am cooking and sweeping, carrying wood, pumping
water, making beds. Doesn't anything impress you?'

'Gentle, courteous, humble women always impress me favour-
ably.'

She stalked off, but as she went around the corner of the cabin
I heard her laugh.

The veterinary's assistant came just at dusk the next day. He
expressed delight, and I felt like a sad sick dog. I wanted no
part of anyone's care and attention.

Connie went out with the little doctor and talked for a long time in the night before he went rattling down the slope in his old car. When she came in she was thoughtful, absent-minded. I put a jacket on and sat in the old rocker on the porch while she cooked. She called me and we ate in front of the fire. A silent meal.

While she was cleaning up, I went back to bed as was the custom, after using the back lot privy and brushing my teeth in the out of doors.

I lay with my back to the room and heard her getting ready for bed. She flipped my blankets up and slid in with me, fitting herself to my back, naked as a partridge egg.

'I didn't realize my teeth were chattering,' I said.

'Perhaps mine are.'

'What the hell is this, Connie?'

'I had a long talk with that nice little man. He couldn't help noticing how morose you are. I told him that some very bad things had happened, and you thought they were your fault, and you were brooding about them. He said there is a certain depression which one can expect as an after effect of shock and weakness. I proposed a certain antidote for his consideration. He was dubious. But he is a very practical little man, and I am a very practical woman. There is one thing, Senor McGee, that is the exact opposite of death. Now turn over here, darling.'

That big husky vital woman was incredibly gentle. I don't believe that at any moment I bore more than five pounds of her enfolding weight. I do not think she expected anything for herself, but at the final time, she gave a prolonged shudder and sighed small love words in her own tongue and, after a little space of time, rested herself sweet beside me. '*Angel de vida*,' she murmured, '*de mi vida*.'

I held her close, stroked that silver head, her curls crisp to the touch, damp at the roots with her exertions, her breath a sighing heat against my jaw and ear.

'Happier?' she whispered.

'Bemused.'

'Sleep now, and we will awake singing. You will see.'

'You'll stay here?'

'From now on, *querido*. For whenever and however you want me. I was not designed by the gods for an empty bed.'

CHAPTER TWENTY

THE temptation was to stay there too long. I pushed myself to the limit each day. At first it was shockingly limited. A mile of walking, a few simple exercises, and I would get weak and sweaty and dizzy. When I had begun to improve, she left me alone for two days, went back to the city, and came back in the gunmetal Mercedes, bringing more clothes for herself, many gifts for me, games and exercise equipment and clothes and wine and target weapons. And she brought news. Chip Fertacci was being sought for jumping bail. After a minor hernia operation, Calvin Tomberlin had died in hospital of an embolism. The day after she returned, I went with her in the grey car to Palm Springs and brought back the jeep she had left there at the airport.

We had no visitors. We spread blankets and took the hot sun. She said it was foolish for her to do it, as she was already as dark as she cared to be. The hole in my back was healed first. I looked at it with an arrangement of mirrors, a shiny pink button, the size of a dime.

As I became fit again, able to split mountains of wood, jog my five miles up hill and down, do the forty pushups, and heartily service the lady, our relationship became ever more violent and disruptive. I was sometimes fool enough to imagine I could sate her, and even managed to, a very few times. But we were tearing each other apart in the constant clawing for advantage.

The symbol of the end of it was the sizeable wooden packing case I brought back from the town, along with a dime store stencil kit and excelsior. I got a big enough case so the size to weight ratio would not be unusual. I packed the thirty-four gold images, fastened the top on with wood screws, labelled it as marine engine parts and addressed it to myself in Lauderdale. I had about a hundred and seventy-five pounds of gold and twenty pounds of crate, and I took a childish pride in making the effort look easy when I swung it into the back of the jeep.

I took it down alone and shipped it out and got back in the first cool of dusk. It was a quiet and thoughtful evening. We finished the wine. In the night I missed her. I got up and put something on and went looking for her. I found her beyond the road, throwing the gifts and games and toys one by one down into the rocky gully, hurling them with great force, crying as she did so. It was foolish and petulant and very touching.

I held her and, in the rack of sobs, she kept saying, 'Why? Why?'

She was asking, I suppose, why she had to be the person she was, and why I had to be the person I was, and why it was impossible for us to find any way to be at peace with each other. She knew it was time to end it, and she wanted to end it, but resented the necessity of ending it. I led her back in and made love to her for the last time. I guess it should have been symbolic, or a special closeness or sweetness. But we had already lost each other. Our identities had been packed in separate crates, with the lids securely fastened. So it was merely competent and familiar, while our minds wandered. It had all been reduced down to an amiable service.

She was bright and cheerful in the morning. We tidied the place, buried the perishables and left the rest, stacked wood high and scrubbed the board floor. On the way down in the grey car, we did not look back. At Los Angeles International I found a flight that would leave for Miami in ninety minutes. I checked my luggage aboard and then walked her back out to her car. There was no point in her hanging around, and she showed no desire to do so.

After she got behind the wheel, I leaned in and kissed that indomitable mouth.

'Come around for the next incarnation,' she said. 'I'll be a better one next time.'

'I'd planned on being a porpoise.'

'I'll settle for that. Look for me.'

'How will I know you?'

'I'll keep the yellow cat eyes, darling. But I'll throw the devils out. I will be the sweet, humble, adoring girl porpoise.'

'I'll be the show-off. Big leaps. A great fishcatcher.'

She blinked rapidly and said, 'Until then, darling. Take care.' And she started up so fast she gave me a good rap on the elbow with the edge of the window frame.

There was no reason why I should not use the same name and the same hotel in New York. I came up with the golden goodies packed into two sturdy suitcases. I put them into a coin locker in the East Side Terminal. By three o'clock on that hot and sticky afternoon, I was settled into the Wharton as Sam Taggart. I used a pay phone to call Borlika Galleries. They said they expected Mrs. Anton Borlika back in about twenty minutes.

I had difficulty visualizing her until I heard that flat Boston accent, then I saw all of her, the Irish shine of the black hair, the whiteness and plumpness and softness of all the rest of her.

'It's Sam Taggart, Betty,' I said.

There was a long silence. 'I never expected to hear from you again.'

'What gave you that idea?'

'Let's say because you left so abruptly.'

'It couldn't be helped.'

'It's been months. What did you expect me to think?'

'Do you need those pictures back?'

'The negatives were on file. Keep them as souvenirs. What do you want?'

'I thought we had a deal lined up.'

'That was a long time ago.'

'Maybe they're more valuable now, Betty.'

After a silence she said, 'Maybe there's more risk.'

'How?'

'You bastard, I'm not that stupid. You took the pictures. You lined up the outlet first, and then you went after the merchandise. And it took you this long to get it. How do I know the whole thing won't backfire?'

'Betty, I had them all along. I was just busy on other things.'

'I can imagine.'

'But I did manage to pick up a few more.'

'Of the same sort of thing?'

'To the layman's eye, yes. Six more. Thirty-four total. So it will come to more money. And I'm ready to deal. I told you I'd be in touch. There's only one small change. I've lined up another outlet, just in case. But because we had an agreement, it's only fair to give you the chance first. If you're nervous, all you have to do is say no.'

It was one of those big pale banks on Fifth, in the lower forties, one of those which manage to elevate money to the status of religious symbolism. I arrived by cab at eleven, and toted my bloody spoils inside.

She got up from a chair in the lounge area and came over to me. She looked thinner than I remembered. There were smudges under her eyes. She wore a hot-weather suit, severely tailored and slightly wrinkled. 'Back this way, please,' she said.

We went through a gate and down a broad corridor. An armed guard stood outside a panelled door. When he saw her coming, he turned and unlocked the door, swung it open, tipped his cap and bowed us in. It was a twelve by twelve room with-out windows. When the door closed she smiled in an uncertain way and said, 'Hello, Sam.'

'How are you, Betty?'

'All right, I guess. I feel a little strange about . . . the last time I saw you. It wasn't . . . standard practice for me.'

'I didn't think it was.'

She lifted her chin. 'I'm engaged to be married.'

'Best wishes.'

'I'm going to marry the old man.'

'Best wishes.'

'He's really very fond of me, Sam. And he is a very kind man.'

'I hope you will be very happy.'

She stared at me for a long moment and then said, 'Well, shall we get at it?'

There was a long steel table in the room with a linoleum top. There were four chairs around the table. There was a blue canvas flight bag in one of the chairs. I put a suitcase on the table, opened it and began taking out the pieces. She hefted and inspected each one and set it aside. She did not make a sound. Her lips were compressed, her nostrils dilated, her blue eyes narrow. Finally all thirty-four were on the table. A little army of ancient spooks.

'Which six were not in the Menterez collection?'

'I have no idea.'

'Where did you get the extra ones?'

'From a cave at the bottom of the sea.'

'Damn you, I can't take the chance of. . . .'

'You will have to take a chance on my word that nobody misses them, nobody wants them back.'

She said she would take the whole works for her original offer. I immediately started packing them away again. She asked what I wanted. I said two hundred. She laughed at me. She made a phone call. She offered one fifty. I came down a little. After two long hours of dispute, we settled at a hundred and sixty-two five. She had a hundred and forty in the canvas bag, fifties and hundreds, bank wrapped. She went out into the bank and drew another twenty-two five, while I packed the heavy little figures of ancient evil back into the suitcases.

There was room for the extra money in the canvas bag, after I had completed my count. She put her hand out and when I took it she laughed aloud, that exultant little chortle of some-one who is happy with the deal just made.

'I'll use a porter and a guard to take these away,' she said. 'Perhaps you would like to leave first. I could arrange a guard if you like.'

'No thanks.'

'I didn't think so. Sam? Once you have this in a safe place, perhaps we could . . . celebrate the deal tonight?'

'And celebrate your pending marriage, Betty?'

'Don't be such a bastard, please.'

I smiled at her. 'Honey, I'm sorry. You just don't look to me like the kind to forgive and forget. I think you are itching to set me up somehow.'

There was just enough flicker in the blue eyes for me to know it had been a good guess. 'That's a silly idea,' she said. 'Really!'

'If I'm going to be free, I'll give you a ring at the apartment.'

'Do that. Please.'

A side door of the bank opened into the lobby of the office building overhead. I had marked it on my way in, so I went through in a hurry, got into an elevator and rode up with a back-from-lunch herd of perfumed office girls and narrow-faced boys. I rode up to twelve, found a locked men's room and loitered until somebody came out. I caught the door before it closed, and shut myself into a cubicle. The blue canvas bag was just a little too blue and conspicuous. I had the string and the big folded sheet of wrapping paper in an inside pocket. The blocks of money stacked nicely and made a neat package. I left the blue bag right there, walked down the stairs to ten, took an elevator back down.

A trim little gal with chestnut hair, wide eyes, a pocked face and not enough chin was just ahead of me. I caught up with her and took her arm and said quickly, as she gave a leap of fright, 'Please help me for thirty seconds. Just out the door and head uptown talking like old friends.'

I felt some of the tension go out of her slender arm.

'What do old friends talk about?' she said.

'Well, they talk about a man who'll leave me the hell alone if he sees me come out with a date.'

'Big date. Thirty seconds. This must be my lucky day.'

We smiled at each other. I did not look around trying to spot anybody. She came along almost in a trot to keep up with long strides. At Forty-fifth we had the light, and there was a cab right there waiting, so I patted her shoulder and said, 'You're a good kid. Thanks.'

As I got into the cab, she called, 'I'm a good kid, tenth floor,

Yates Brothers, name of Betty Rasmussen, anytime for thirty-second dates, you're welcome.'

At nine o'clock on an evening in late July, Shaja Dobrak invited me into the cottage she had shared with Nora Gardino. Her grey-blue eyes were the same, her straight hair that wood-ash colour, her manner quiet and polite. She was a big girl, and slender. She had been working at a gold and grey desk in the living-room. The two cats gave me the same searching stare of appraisal.

'Please to sit,' she said. 'You drink somesink maybe?' She smiled. 'There is still the Amstel, you liked last time.'

'Fine.'

She went to get it. She wore coral cotton pants, calf length, gold sandals, a checked beach coat. When she brought it to me, she stared frankly at me. 'In the eyes I think you are older. Terrible thinks?'

'Yes.'

She went to the couch, pulled her legs under her, grave and waiting. 'You wish to say them?'

'I don't think so. You went up to the funeral?'

'Yes. So sad. Less than one year I am knowing her, Travis, but I loved her.'

'I loved her too.'

An eyebrow arched in question.

'Yes. It started sort of by accident. It was very good. It surprised both of us. It pleased us both. It could have lasted.'

'Then I am so glad of her having that, to be happy that way a little time. Was it hard dying for her?'

'No. It was over in an instant, Shaja.'

'She was thinking she would die down there I think. There is this think of the will she made out. I have this fine house from her. Her family was given the store. But the way it is, I am in charge. The shares, they are in escrow. The bank, it is helping me run the store, and as I make money I pay it to her family and each time a little of the store is more mine, until finally all, if I have the luck and work very hard. By the time my hoosband can come, everything will be safe and nice here for us two.'

I had improvized my lie. 'Shaj, she was so happy that she was certain something might go wrong. We talked about you. She was very fond of you. As you know, we had a chance to come out of this with a profit. She said that if anything happened to her, you should have her share for a special purpose. I have it in a safe place for you.'

'A special purpose?'

'Something to do with a mild little man, getting bald on his head in the middle, a teacher of history.'

She leaned toward me, eyes staring, 'What you say?' she whispered. 'What you say to me?'

'These things can be arranged for money, can't they?'

'Ah, yes. Political things. Yes. A case of being very careful, of going to the right persons. I think it is done nicely with English pounds or Swiss francs or American dollars. About needing the exchange, I think. But it has to be *much much* money, and time to work so carefully.'

'How much?'

She made a mouth of distaste. 'They are greedy. An impossible amount. A hoondred thousand of dollars, maybe.'

'Then that will leave you an extra twenty-five thousand for expenses, Shaja.'

She did not move. Tears filled, spilled, rolled, fell. She turned and flung herself face down on the couch, sobbing. I went over and knelt beside her, patted her shoulder awkwardly.

When at last she raised her tear-stained face, I have never seen such a look in all my life, such a glow, such a lambent joy. 'We will not be too late for children,' she cried. 'Ah, we will not be too late for them.'

She pulled herself together. She tried to ask polite questions about Nora, but her heart was not in it. I knew I should leave her with her happiness. She went to the door with me. Her last question had an Old Testament ring about it. 'The guilty have all been punished, Travis?'

'Yes. Along with the innocent.'

She put her hands on my shoulders and kissed me on the mouth. 'Do not have sick eyes, my good friend. My hoosband is once telling me this strange thing. We are all guilty. Also, we are all innocent, every one. God bless you.'

I went back to *The Busted Flush*. I wanted to get very very drunk. I wanted to hallucinate, and bring back the women, one at a time, where I could see them, and tell each one of them how things had gone wrong, and how sorry I was.

But instead I got hold of Meyer and he came over with the backgammon board and we played until three in the morning. I took forty-four dollars away from him. He said, upon leaving, that he didn't know where I'd been or what I'd been doing, but it had certainly given me a nice rest and improved my concentration.

As I was going to sleep I decided I would look up Branks and tell him that Sam Taggart had been killed by Miguel Alconedo, now deceased. And, indeed, he had been, just as surely as if he'd driven the knife into Sam instead of into the woman whose arms Sam had held as it was done.

And I wondered if Shaja would want help on her mission. It would be nice to see one splendid thing come out of this, without accident. Good old Cal Tomberlin and good old Carlos Menterez had each chipped in, to bring back the history teacher. And there was some money to send down to Felicia . . . as Sam had promised her. . . .